SelectEditions

SELECTED AND EDITED

SelectEditions

BY READER'S DIGEST

THE READER'S DIGEST ASSOCIATION, INC.
MONTREAL • PLEASANTVILLE, NEW YORK

READER'S DIGEST

Vice-President, Books & Home Entertainment: Deirdre Gilbert

The condensations in this volume have been created by The Reader's Digest Association, Inc., by special arrangement with the publishers, authors, or holders of copyrights.

213-250-9803

CONTENTS

Pretend You Don't See Her

Mary Higgins Clark

Lacey Farrell
knows something
that could cost her
her life.
It's already cost her
her identity.

ATER *Lacey tried to find comfort in the thought that even if she had arrived seconds earlier, she would not have been in time to help. She would have died with Isabelle.*

But it didn't happen that way. Using the key she had been given as real estate agent, she had entered the duplex apartment on East Seventieth Street and called Isabelle's name in the exact instant that Isabelle screamed "Don't!" and a gunshot rang out.

Faced with a split-second decision to run or to hide, Lacey slammed the apartment door and slipped quickly into the hall closet. She had not even had time to fully close that door before a sandy-haired man came running down the stairs. Through the narrow opening she could see his face clearly, and it became imprinted on her mind. In fact, she had seen it before, only hours ago. The expression was now viciously cold, but this was the same man to whom she had shown the apartment earlier in the day: affable Curtis Caldwell from Texas.

She watched as he ran past her, holding a pistol in his right hand and a leather binder under his left arm. He flung open the front door and ran out of the apartment.

Lacey knew that Caldwell would realize immediately that whoever had come into the apartment was still there. A primal instinct made her rush out of the closet in order to shove the front door closed behind him. He wheeled around, and for a terrible moment their eyes locked, his pale blue irises like steely ice, staring at her. He threw himself against the door but not fast enough. It slammed shut, and Lacey snapped the bolt just as a key clicked in the lock.

Her pulse racing, she leaned against the door, trembling as the knob twisted, hoping there was no way Caldwell could get back in now.

Isabelle! Lacey thought. Fearing what she would find, she raced up the thickly carpeted stairs, through the sitting room, and into the bedroom. Isabelle lay crumpled across the bed, her bloodied hand frantically pulling at a sheaf of papers that had been under a pillow beside her.

Lacey dropped to her knees. "Isabelle," she said. She wanted to say that she would call an ambulance, that it would be all right—but the words refused to pass her lips. It was too late. Lacey could see that Isabelle was dying.

CHAPTER 1

 T WAS the week after Labor Day, and from the steady ringing of the phones in the offices of Parker and Parker, it was clear that the summer doldrums were over in the Manhattan co-op market. Now things would start moving again.

"It's about time," Lacey told Rick Parker. "I haven't had a decent sale since June." She reached for the coffee he offered. "Thanks. It's nice to have the son and heir wait on me."

"No problem. You look great, Lacey."

Lacey always felt as though Rick were undressing her with his eyes. Spoiled, handsome, and the possessor of a phony charm that he turned on at will, he made her distinctly uncomfortable. She wished his father hadn't moved him from the West Side office.

Her phone rang, and she grabbed for it with relief. "Lacey Farrell," she said.

"Miss Farrell, this is Isabelle Waring. I met you when you sold a co-op in my building last spring."

Lacey's mind went into its search-and-retrieve mode. She'd sold two apartments in May on East Seventieth—one an estate sale where she hadn't spoken to anyone except the building mana-ger, the other the Norstrum apartment just off Fifth. She vaguely remembered chatting with an attractive fiftyish redhead in the elevator, who had asked for her business card.

Crossing her fingers, she said, "The Norstrum duplex?"

Mrs. Waring sounded pleased. "Exactly! I'm putting my daugh-ter's apartment on the market, and I'd like you to handle it."

Lacey made an appointment with Mrs. Waring for the following morning, hung up, and turned to Rick. "What luck," she said. "Three East Seventieth. That's a great building."

"Three East Seventieth. What apartment?" he asked quickly.

"Ten B. Do you know that one by any chance?"

"Why would I know it?" he snapped. "Especially since my father, in his wisdom, kept me working the West Side for five years."

Rick left for his own office, which overlooked East Sixty-second Street. Lacey's windows faced Madison Avenue. She reveled in the constant traffic, the hordes of tourists, the well-heeled Madison Avenue types drifting in and out of the designer boutiques.

Lacey had inherited her love of New York City from her father, Jack Farrell. From the time she was little, they had explored the city together. She had inherited Jack's Irish coloring as well—fair skin, blue-green eyes, and dark brown hair.

A musician, Jack Farrell had worked in the theater, usually in the orchestra pit, although he sometimes played in clubs and the occasional concert. Growing up, there wasn't a Broadway musical whose songs Lacey couldn't sing along with her dad. His sudden death just as she finished college had been a shock.

After his death her mother, a pediatric nurse, bought a condo in New Jersey. She wanted to be near Lacey's sister, Kit, and her family. Once there, she'd taken a job with a local hospital.

Fresh out of college, Lacey had found a small apartment on East End Avenue and a job at Parker and Parker Realtors, one of the biggest real estate/building management companies in Manhattan. Now, eight years later, she was one of their top agents.

Humming, she pulled out the file on the Norstrum duplex she'd sold at Three East Seventieth. Nice-sized rooms. High ceilings. Now to find out something about Mrs. Waring's place.

Lacey liked to do her homework on a prospective listing. To that end, she'd learned that it helped to become familiar with the people who worked in the buildings her firm handled. It was fortunate now that she was friends with Tim Powers, the superintendent of Three East Seventieth. She dialed his number.

According to Tim, Isabelle Waring was the mother of Heather Landi, a young singer and actress who had just begun to make it in the theater. The daughter as well of famed restaurateur Jimmy Landi, Heather had died the previous winter when her car plunged down an embankment as she was driving home from skiing in Vermont. The apartment had belonged to Heather.

When Lacey got off the phone, she sat for a long moment, remembering that she had seen Heather Landi last year in an off-Broadway musical. In fact, she remembered her in particular.

Heather had it all, Lacey thought—beauty, stage presence, and that marvelous soprano voice. A 10, as Dad would have said.

ON TUESDAY morning Isabelle Waring walked through her daughter's apartment, studying it as if with the critical eye of a real estate agent. She was glad that she had kept Lacey Farrell's business card. The day they'd met in the elevator, she had taken an instant liking to the young woman, who reminded her of Heather.

Admittedly, Lacey didn't *look* like Heather. Heather had had short, curly, light brown hair with golden highlights, and hazel eyes. She had been small, barely five feet four, with a soft, curving body. Lacey, on the other hand, was taller, slimmer, had blue-green eyes and darker, longer, straighter hair, swinging down to her shoulders, but there was something in her smile and manner that brought back a very positive memory of Heather.

After months of brief trips to New York from her home in Cleveland and making stabs at going through the apartment's five huge closets and the many drawers, and after repeatedly meeting with Heather's friends, Isabelle knew she had to put an end to this searching for reasons and get on with her life.

The fact remained, however, that she just didn't believe Heather's death had been an accident. She knew her daughter; Heather simply would not have been foolish enough to start driving home from Stowe in a snowstorm, especially so late at night. The medical examiner had been satisfied, however. And Jimmy Landi, Isabelle's ex-husband, was satisfied. If he hadn't been, he'd have torn up all of Manhattan looking for answers. But he refused to see anything sinister or suspicious in Heather's death.

Isabelle, though, couldn't accept it. At the last of their infrequent lunches, she had told Jimmy about a troubling phone conversation she'd had with their daughter just before her death. "Jimmy, Heather wasn't herself when I spoke to her. She was terribly worried about something. I heard it in her voice."

The lunch ended when Jimmy, in complete exasperation, had burst out, "Isabelle, get *off* it! Stop, please! This whole thing is tough enough without you constantly rehashing everything. Please, let our daughter rest in peace."

Remembering his words, Isabelle shook her head. Jimmy Landi had loved Heather more than anything in the world. And next to her, he loved power, Isabelle thought bitterly—it's what had ended their marriage. His famous restaurant, his investments, now his Atlantic City hotel and casino. No room for me ever, Isabelle thought. Maybe if he had taken on a partner years ago, the way he has Steve Abbott now, our marriage wouldn't have failed. She realized she had been walking through rooms she wasn't really seeing, so she stopped at a window overlooking Fifth Avenue.

New York is especially beautiful in September, Isabelle mused, observing the joggers on the paths that threaded through Central Park, the nannies pushing strollers. When Heather was a baby, I used to take her to the park on days like this, she remembered.

What happened that night, Heather? Isabelle asked herself yet again. What made you take that drive? Or *who* made you? After that accident when you were a child—when you saw that car skid off the road and crash—you were always terrified of icy roads. Why then would you have driven over a snowy mountain at two in the morning?

The buzzing of the intercom jolted Isabelle back from the pangs of hopeless regret. It was the doorman announcing Miss Farrell.

LACEY was not prepared for Isabelle Waring's effusive, if nervous, greeting. "Good heavens, you look younger than I remembered," she said. "How old *are* you? Thirty? My daughter would have been twenty-five next week. This apartment was hers. Terrible reversal, don't you think? The natural order of life is that I'd go first and someday she'd sort through *my* things."

"I have two nephews and a niece," Lacey told her. "I can't imagine anything happening to any of them, so I think I understand something of what you are going through."

Isabelle followed her, as with a practiced eye Lacey made notes on the dimensions of the rooms. The first floor consisted of a foyer, large living and dining rooms, a small library, a kitchen, and a powder room. The second floor, reached by a winding staircase, had a master bedroom, sitting room, dressing room, and bath.

"It was a lot of space for a young woman," Isabelle explained. "Heather's father bought it for her when she came to New York after college. Now he wants me to sell the apartment. It's hard to let it go, though. . . ." Her eyes filled with tears.

"Are you sure you want to sell?" Lacey asked.

She watched helplessly as the stoic expression on Isabelle Waring's face crumbled. "I wanted to find out why my daughter died. I thought I might find an answer here, either in the apartment or from one of her friends. But her father wants me to stop pestering people, and I suppose he's right, that we have to go on, so yes, Lacey, I guess I want to sell."

Lacey covered the woman's hand with her own. "I think Heather would want you to," she said quietly.

THAT night Lacey made the twenty-five-mile drive to Wyckoff, New Jersey, where her sister, Kit, and her mother both lived. She hadn't seen them since early August, when she had left the city for a month away in East Hampton. Kit and her husband, Jay, had a summer home on Nantucket and always urged Lacey to spend her vacation with them instead.

As she crossed the George Washington Bridge, Lacey braced herself for the reproaches she knew would be part of their greeting. "You only spent three days with us," her brother-in-law would be sure to remind her. "What's East Hampton got that Nantucket doesn't?"

For one thing it doesn't have *you,* Lacey thought with a slight grin.

Her brother-in-law, Jay Taylor, owner of a successful restaurant-supply business, had never been one of Lacey's favorite people, but, as she reminded herself, Kit clearly is crazy about him, and between them they've produced three great kids, so who am I to criticize? If only he wasn't so pompous, she thought. Some of his pronouncements sounded like papal bulls.

As she turned onto Route 4, she realized how anxious she was to see her family, especially the kids—Todd, twelve; Andy, ten; and her special pet, shy four-year-old Bonnie. Thinking about her niece, she realized that all day she hadn't been able to shake thoughts about poor Isabelle Waring and the things she had said. The woman's pain was so palpable. She had insisted that Lacey stay for coffee and over it had continued to talk about her daughter. "I moved to Cleveland after the divorce. That's where I was raised. Heather was five at that time. Growing up, she was always back and forth between me and her dad. It worked out fine. I remarried. Bill Waring was much older but a very nice man. He's been gone three years now. I was so in hopes Heather would meet the right man, have children, but she was determined to have a career first. Although just before she died, I did get the sense that maybe she had met someone." Then she had asked, her tone one of motherly concern, "What about you, Lacey? Is there someone special in your life?"

Lacey smiled wryly. Not so you'd notice, she thought. Oh, well. It will happen when it happens.

Her mother answered the door. "Kit's in the kitchen. Jay went to pick up the children," she explained after a warm hug. "And there's someone inside I want you to meet."

Lacey was surprised and somewhat shocked to see that a man she didn't recognize was standing by the massive fireplace in the family room, sipping a drink. Her mother blushingly introduced him as Alex Carbine, explaining that they had known each other years ago and had just met again through Jay, who had sold him the equipment for a restaurant he'd recently opened in the city.

Shaking his hand, Lacey assessed the man. About sixty—Mom's age. Good, solid-looking guy. And Mom's all atwitter. What's up? As soon as she could excuse herself, she went into the state-of-the-art kitchen, where Kit was tossing a salad. "How long has this been going on?" she asked her sister.

Kit, her blond hair pulled back at the nape of her neck, and looking, Lacey thought, for all the world like a Martha Stewart ad, grinned. "About a month. He's nice. Jay brought him by for dinner, and Mom was here. Alex is a widower. He's always been in the restaurant business, but this is the first place he's had on his own. We've been there. He's got a nice setup."

They both jumped at the sound of the front door slamming. "Brace yourself," Kit warned. "Jay and the kids are home."

The boys greeted Lacey with their usual exuberance. Bonnie snuggled up to her shyly. "I missed you," she confided.

At dinner Lacey was asked about the real estate market in New York. "Picking up," she answered. She told them about Isabelle Waring, then noticed that Alex Carbine showed sudden interest. "Do you know her?" Lacey asked.

"No," Alex said, "but I know Jimmy Landi, and I'd met Heather. Jay, you've done business with Landi. You must have met Heather too. She was around her dad's restaurant a lot."

Lacey watched in astonishment as her brother-in-law's face turned a dark red.

"No. Never met her," he said, his tone clipped and carrying an edge of anger. "I used to do business with Jimmy Landi. Who's ready for another slice of lamb?"

IT WAS seven o'clock. The bar was crowded, and the dinner crowd was starting to arrive. Jimmy Landi knew he should go downstairs and greet people, but he just didn't feel like it. This had been one of the bad days, a depression brought on by a call from Isabelle, evoking the image of Heather trapped and burning to death in the overturned car that haunted him long after he had gotten off the phone.

Jimmy sat at his antique Wells Fargo desk in his paneled office in the brownstone he owned on West Fifty-sixth Street that was home to Venezia, the restaurant he had opened thirty years ago. Now Venezia was one of the most popular places to dine in Manhattan.

Jimmy Landi was a swarthy man of sixty-seven, whose hair was still naturally dark and whose brooding eyes under thick unruly brows gave his face a permanently cynical expression. His solid, muscular body gave the impression of animal strength. His detractors joked that despite his custom-tailored suits, he still looked like a day laborer.

He had gotten through the last months by concentrating on the casino and hotel he was building in Atlantic City. "Donald Trump, move over," Heather had said when he'd shown her the model.

Jimmy shook his head and sighed, remembering. A tap at the

door yanked him back to the present. "Come in, Steve," he said.

Thank God I have Steve Abbott as a partner, he thought. Twenty-five years ago the handsome blond Cornell dropout had knocked on the door of the restaurant and announced, "I want to work for you, Mr. Landi. I can learn more here than in college."

Jimmy had been both amused and annoyed by the fresh, know-it-all kid. "You want to work for me?" he had asked, then pointed to the kitchen. "Well, that's where I started."

That was a good day for me, Jimmy thought now. Steve might have looked like a spoiled preppie, but he was an Irish kid whose mother worked as a waitress to raise him, and he had proved that he had much of the same drive. I thought then that he was a dope to give up his scholarship, but I was wrong. He'd been born for this business.

Steve Abbott pushed open the door and turned on the nearest light as he entered the room. "Why so dark, Jimmy?"

Landi looked up with a wry smile, noting the compassion in the younger man's eyes. "Woolgathering, I guess."

"The mayor just came in with a party of four."

Jimmy shoved back his desk chair and stood up. "No one told me he had a reservation."

"He didn't." In long strides Abbott crossed the room and put his hand on Landi's shoulder. "A rough day, I can tell."

"Yeah," Jimmy said. "Isabelle called this morning to say the real estate agent thinks Heather's apartment will sell fast. Of course, every time she gets on the phone, she goes on about how she can't believe Heather's death was an accident. Drives me crazy."

He stared past Abbott. "When I met Isabelle, she was a knock-out, a beauty queen from Cleveland. Engaged to be married. I pulled the rock that guy had given her off her finger and tossed it out the car window." He chuckled. "I had to get a loan to pay the other guy for his ring, but I got the girl."

Abbott knew the story and understood why Jimmy had been thinking about it. "Maybe the marriage didn't last, but you got Heather out of the deal. Come on, Jimmy, the mayor's waiting."

N THE next few weeks Lacey brought eight potential buyers to see the apartment. Two were clearly window-shoppers, the kind whose hobby was wasting real estate agents' time.

"You never know," she said to Rick Parker when he stopped by her desk one evening as she was getting ready to go home. "You take someone around for a year, you want to kill yourself before you go out with her again, then what happens? The person you're ready to give up on writes a check for a million-dollar co-op."

"You have more patience than I do," Rick told her. "I can't tolerate people who waste my time. R.J.P. wants to know if you've had any real nibbles on the Waring apartment." R.J.P. was the way Rick referred to his father.

"I don't think so. But hey, it's still a new listing, and tomorrow is another day."

"Thank you, Scarlett O'Hara. I'll pass that along."

Lacey made a face at his retreating back. It had been one of Rick's edgy, sarcastic days. What's bugging him now? she wondered. And why, when his father is negotiating the sale of The Plaza Hotel, would he give a thought to the Waring apartment?

She locked her desk drawer and rubbed her forehead, suddenly realizing that she was very tired. She had been devoting an awful lot of time to Isabelle Waring. The woman called her daily, frequently inviting her to the apartment. "Come for lunch. You do have to eat, don't you?" she would say. Or, "On your way home, stop by for a glass of wine. The New England settlers used to call twilight 'sober light.' It's a lonesome time of day."

It *is* a lonesome time of day, Lacey thought. And I really don't mind spending time with Isabelle. She's become a friend. But, Lacey admitted to herself, sharing Isabelle's pain brings back everything I felt when Dad died.

She got up. I am going home and collapse, she thought. I need to.

TWO hours later, at nine o'clock, Lacey, fresh from twenty minutes in the Jacuzzi, was happily preparing a BLT when the telephone rang. She let the answering machine take it, then heard Isabelle Waring's familiar voice. I'm not going to pick up, Lacey decided. I simply don't feel like talking to her right now.

Isabelle began to speak in soft but intense tones. "Lacey, guess you're not home. I had to share this. I found Heather's journal in the big storage closet. There's something in the journal that makes me think I'm not crazy for believing her death wasn't an accident. I think I may be able to prove that someone wanted her out of the way. I won't say any more now. Talk to you tomorrow."

Listening, Lacey shook her head, then impulsively turned off the phone. She didn't even want to know if more people tried to reach her. She wanted what was left of the night all to herself.

A quiet evening—a sandwich, a glass of wine, and a book. I've earned it, she told herself.

AS SOON as Lacey got to the office in the morning, Rick appeared in her doorway, looking annoyed. "Isabelle Waring has to talk to you. They put her through to me."

Lacey took the call in Rick's office. "I'm sorry I couldn't get back to you last night, Isabelle," she began.

"That's all right. I shouldn't talk about all this over the phone anyhow. Are you bringing anyone in today?"

"No one is lined up so far."

As she said that, Rick slid a note across the desk: "Curtis Caldwell, a lawyer with Keller, Roland, and Smythe, is being transferred here from Texas. Wants a one-bedroom between 65th and 72nd on Fifth. Can look today."

Lacey said to Isabelle, "Maybe I *will* be bringing someone. Keep your fingers crossed. This could be our sale."

"A MR. Caldwell's waiting for you, Miss Farrell," Patrick, the doorman, told her as she alighted from a cab.

Through the ornate glass door of Three East Seventieth Street, Lacey spotted a slender man in his mid-forties, with tawny skin and light sandy hair, drumming his fingers on the lobby table.

"A problem you need to know about," Patrick said, sighing. "The air-conditioning broke down. They're fixing it, but it's hot inside."

Oh, swell, Lacey thought. No wonder this guy's impatient. But when she introduced herself, a smile brightened the man's face. He even joked. "Tell the truth now, Miss Farrell," he said. "How temperamental *is* the air-conditioning in this building?"

WHEN Lacey had phoned Isabelle Waring to confirm the time of the appointment, the older woman told her she would be busy in the library, that Lacey should just let herself in.

So Lacey had her real estate agent's key in hand when she and Curtis Caldwell stepped off the elevator. She opened the door, called out, "It's me, Isabelle," and went to the library, Caldwell behind her.

Isabelle was at the desk, her back to the door. An open leather loose-leaf binder lay to one side; some of its pages were spread across the desk. Isabelle did not look up. Instead she said, "Just forget I'm here, please."

As Lacey showed Caldwell around, she briefly explained that the apartment had belonged to Isabelle's daughter, who had died last year. He clearly liked the place and did not show any resistance to the six-hundred-thousand-dollar asking price. "You say it will be available next month?" he asked.

"Absolutely," Lacey told him. This is it, she thought.

"I don't haggle, Miss Farrell. I'm willing to pay the asking price, provided I can move in the first of the month."

"Suppose we talk to Mrs. Waring," Lacey said.

The library door was closed. When Isabelle did not answer her knocks, Lacey turned to Caldwell. "If you'll wait a moment in the living room, I'll talk with Mrs. Waring and be right out."

"Of course."

Lacey opened the library door and looked in. Isabelle was still sitting at the desk, but her head was bowed now, her forehead actually touching the pages she had been reading. Her shoulders were shaking. "Go away," she murmured. "I can't deal with this now."

"Isabelle," Lacey said gently, "it's very important. We have an offer on the apartment, but there's a proviso we have to talk about."

"Forget it! I'm not going to sell. I need more time here." Isabelle's voice rose to a high-pitched wail. "Come back later."

Lacey checked her watch. It was nearly four o'clock. "I'll come back at seven," she said, anxious to avoid a scene.

She closed the door and turned. Curtis Caldwell was standing in the foyer between the library and the living room.

"She doesn't want to sell?" His tone was shocked.

"I'm sure it will be all right," Lacey told him. "I'll come back and talk to her this evening. This has been a painful experience for her, but she'll be fine. Where can I call you?"

"I'm at the Waldorf Towers, in the company apartment."

"Don't worry. This will work out," she promised. "You'll see."

His smile was affable, confident. "I'm sure it will," he said.

HE LEFT the apartment building and walked from Seventieth Street to the Essex House on Central Park South, and went immediately to the public phones. "You were right," he said when he had reached his party. "She's found the journal. It's in the leather binder you described. She's also changed her mind about selling the apartment, although the real estate woman is going back tonight to persuade her."

He listened.

"I'll take care of it," he said, and hung up. Then Sandy Savarano, the man who called himself Curtis Caldwell, went into the bar and ordered a Scotch.

LACEY PHONED ISABELLE AT six and was relieved to find her calm.

"Come over and we'll talk about it," she said, "but even if it means sacrificing the sale, I can't leave the apartment yet. There's something in Heather's journal that could be very significant."

"I'll be there at seven," Lacey told her.

"Just let yourself in. I'll be upstairs in the sitting room."

SHE was twenty minutes early but decided to go up anyway. As she opened the door and called Isabelle's name, she heard the scream and the shot. For a split second she froze; then sheer instinct made her slam the door and step into the closet before Caldwell came rushing down the stairs and ran out into the corridor, a pistol in one hand, a leather binder under his arm.

Afterward she wondered if she had imagined that somewhere in her brain she heard her father's voice saying "Close the door, Lacey! Lock him out!" Was it his protective spirit that gave her the strength to force the door closed as Caldwell pushed against it and then to bolt it?

She leaned against the door, hearing the lock click as Caldwell tried to get back into the apartment.

Isabelle! she thought. She stumbled up the winding staircase, then through the ivory-and-peach sitting room and into the bedroom, where Isabelle was lying across the bed. There was so much blood.

Isabelle was moving, pulling at a sheaf of papers that were under a pillow. Blood was on them too.

Lacey wanted to tell Isabelle that she would get help, that it would be all right, but Isabelle began to speak. "Lacey . . . give Heather's journal . . . to her father." She gasped for air. "Only to him. Swear. *You* . . . read it. Show him where . . ." Her voice trailed off. She drew a shuddering breath. With the last of her strength she squeezed Lacey's hand. "Swear . . . please . . . man."

"I do, Isabelle. I do," Lacey said, her voice breaking with a sob.

Suddenly the pressure on her hand was gone. She knew that Isabelle was dead.

"YOU ALL right, Lacey?"

"I guess so." She was in the library of Isabelle's apartment, seated at the desk where Isabelle had sat just hours earlier reading the contents of the leather loose-leaf binder.

Curtis Caldwell had been carrying that binder. He must have grabbed it, not realizing that Isabelle had taken pages out of it.

The pages Lacey had picked up in Isabelle's bedroom were in her briefcase now. Isabelle had made her swear to give them only to Heather's father. But shouldn't she tell the police about them?

"Lacey, drink some coffee. You need it." Rick Parker was crouched beside her, holding out a cup. He had already explained to the detectives that he'd had no reason to question a phone call from a man claiming to be an attorney with Keller, Roland, and Smythe. "We do a lot of business with that firm," Rick had said.

"And you're sure this Caldwell guy is the one you saw running out of here, Ms. Farrell?" asked Detective Ed Sloane, the older of the two detectives from the Nineteenth Precinct. "Ms. Farrell?" An edge of impatience had crept into the man's voice.

Lacey looked back up at Sloane, who was about fifty and heavy-set. What had he asked her? Oh, yes. Was Curtis Caldwell the man she'd seen running down the stairs from Isabelle's bedroom?

"I'm absolutely sure it was the same man," she said. "He was carrying a pistol and the leather binder."

Mentally she gave herself a hard slap. She hadn't meant to talk about the journal.

"The leather binder?" Detective Sloane's tone became sharp. "What leather binder? That's the first you've mentioned it."

Lacey sighed. "It's one of those binders that zips closed. Isabelle was reading it when we were here this afternoon." Lacey knew she should tell them about the pages that *weren't* inside the leather binder when Caldwell took it, but she'd sworn to Isabelle that she would give those pages to Heather's father. She couldn't go back on her word.

Suddenly Lacey felt her legs begin to shake. She tried to hold them still by pressing on her knees, but the shaking wouldn't stop.

"I think we'd better get you a doctor," Sloane said.

"I just want to go home," Lacey whispered. "Let me go home."

Rick was saying something to the detective in a low voice. She rubbed her hands together. Her fingers were sticky. She looked down, then gasped. She hadn't realized that her hands were sticky with Isabelle's blood.

"Mr. Parker is going to take you home, Ms. Farrell," Detective Sloane was saying. "We'll talk to you more tomorrow."

Lacey felt Rick's hands under her arms, urging her to stand. Obediently she got up, allowed herself to be guided through the door, then into the foyer. Curtis Caldwell had stood here in this foyer that afternoon. He had heard what Isabelle said about not selling the apartment.

"He didn't wait in the living room," she said.

"Who didn't?" Rick asked.

Lacey didn't answer. Suddenly she remembered her briefcase. That's where the pages from the journal were. She remembered the feel of the pages in her hand, crumpled, blood soaked. That's where the blood came from. Detective Sloane had asked her if she had touched Isabelle.

She'd told him that she had held Isabelle's hand as she died.

Suddenly Lacey had a moment of total clarity. If she asked Rick to get her briefcase from the closet, Sloane would notice the blood on the handle. She had to get the briefcase herself. And keep them from seeing it until she could wipe it clean.

There were so many people milling around, taking pictures, looking for fingerprints, dusting powder on tables.

Lacey paused at the staircase and looked up. Was Isabelle still lying there crumpled on the bed? she wondered.

"Come on, Lacey," Rick said.

They were passing the closet where she had put her briefcase. Breaking away, Lacey opened the door and grabbed it.

"I'll carry that," Rick told her. Deliberately she sagged against him, weighing down his arm with her right hand, making him support her, tightening her grip on the handle of her briefcase.

She felt as though everyone's eyes were staring at her and the bloody briefcase. Was this the way a thief felt? she wondered. Go back. Give them the journal, said a voice inside her. But it's not mine to give, she thought hopelessly.

LACEY'S apartment was on East End Avenue at Seventy-ninth Street. When they arrived there, Rick wanted to come upstairs, but she demurred. "I just want to go to bed," she said.

"Then I'll call you first thing in the morning," he promised.

Once inside her apartment, the first thing Lacey did was to shove the briefcase under the couch. The living-room windows overlooked the East River. For long minutes Lacey stood at one of the windows watching the lights flicker across the water. Finally the sense of unreality that had overwhelmed her began to dissipate, but in its place was an awareness of being as tired as she had ever felt in her life. She looked at the clock. Ten thirty. Only a little over twenty-four hours earlier she had refused to pick up the phone and talk to Isabelle. Now Isabelle would never call again.

Lacey froze. The door! Had she double-locked the front door? She ran to check it.

Yes, she had, but now she threw the bolt and wedged a chair under the door handle. She was afraid, shaking again.

Her bathroom was large for a New York apartment. Two years ago she had remodeled, adding the wide, deep Jacuzzi. She had never been as happy she had gone to the expense as she was tonight as she sank into the warm water and pushed the button that sent it swirling around her body.

It was only later, when she was snugly wrapped in a terry-cloth robe, that Lacey allowed herself to think about the bloody journal pages in her briefcase. Not now, she thought. Not now.

Still unable to shake the chilling sensation that had haunted her all evening, she poured some Scotch into a cup, filled the cup with water, and microwaved it. Dad used to say there was nothing like a hot toddy to help shake off a chill, she thought. Only his version had cloves and sugar and a cinnamon stick.

Even without the trimmings, however, it did the trick. As she sipped the drink in bed, she felt a calmness settle over her and fell asleep as soon as she turned off the light.

And almost immediately awakened with a shriek. She was opening the door to Isabelle Waring's apartment; she was bending over the dead woman's body; Curtis Caldwell was aiming the pistol at her head. The nightmare was vivid and immediate.

It took her several moments to realize that the shrill sound was the telephone. Still shaking, she picked up the receiver. It was Jay, her brother-in-law. "We heard on the news that Isabelle Waring was shot," he said. "They reported that there was a witness, a young woman. Lacey, it wasn't you, I hope."

The concern in Jay's voice was comforting. "Yes, it was me."

"Kit wants to talk to you," he said.

"I *can't* talk now," Lacey said, knowing that Kit, loving and concerned, would ask her to tell it all again—all about going to the apartment, hearing the scream, seeing Isabelle's killer. "Jay, I can't talk now," she pleaded. "Kit will understand."

She hung up the phone and lay in the darkness, willing herself calm, realizing that her ears were straining to hear another scream, followed by the sound of footsteps. Caldwell's footsteps.

WHEN he had left Lacey in the lobby of her apartment building, Rick Parker had taken a taxi directly to his place on Central Park West and Sixty-seventh Street. By now Isabelle Waring's death would be all over the news. There had been reporters outside her building, and chances were that he had been caught on-camera. If so, his father would have seen it.

As Rick had expected, the light on his telephone answering machine was flashing. There was one message; it was from his father. "No matter what time it is, call me when you get in!"

Rick's palms were so wet that he had to dry them before picking up the phone to return the call. His father answered on the first ring.

"Before you ask," Rick said, his voice ragged and unnaturally high-pitched, "I had no choice. I had to go over there because

Lacey told the police that I'd been the one who'd given her Caldwell's name, so they sent for me."

Rick listened for a minute to his father's angry voice; then he finally managed to break in. "Dad, I've told you not to worry. Nobody knows that I was involved with Heather Landi."

SANDY Savarano, the man known to Lacey as Curtis Caldwell, had raced from Isabelle Waring's apartment, down the fire stairs to the basement, and out through the delivery entrance. Quick strides took him to Madison Avenue, the leather binder tucked under his arm. He took a taxi to the small hotel on Twenty-ninth Street where he was staying. Once in his room, he poured himself a generous Scotch, picked up the binder, and settled in the room's one upholstered chair. Until the last minute the job had been easy enough. He had gotten back into the building while the doorman was helping an old woman into a cab and had let himself into the apartment with the key he'd taken off the table in the foyer.

He had found Isabelle in the master bedroom, propped up on the bed, eyes closed. The leather binder had been on the night table. When she realized he was there, she hadn't screamed. No, she'd been too scared. That was what he'd liked most: the naked fear in her eyes, the awareness that she was going to die. He'd savored that moment. He always liked to take his pistol out slowly, keeping eye contact with his victim while he took careful aim. The chemistry between him and his target in that split second before his finger squeezed the trigger thrilled him.

He pictured Isabelle as she shrank away from him, her lips struggling to form words. Then finally the single scream—*"Don't!"*—mingling with a voice calling her just as he shot her.

Except for the Farrell woman, everything would have been perfect. He had been a fool, he told himself, letting her lock him out, forcing him to run away. But he *did* get the journal, and he did kill the Waring woman, and that was the job he was hired to do. And if necessary he would kill Farrell too.

He unzipped the binder and looked inside. The pages were all neatly clamped in place, but when he thumbed through them, he found they were all blank—none had been used. The actual journal pages must still be in the apartment. It was too late to go back there now. The cops would be all over the place. He'd have to find another way to get them.

But it wasn't too late to make sure that Lacey Farrell never got the chance to ID him in court. That was a chore he'd enjoy.

CHAPTER 3

ACEY woke at quarter of seven, dreading what the day would bring. Detective Sloane wanted her at headquarters to work with a police artist on a composite sketch of Curtis Caldwell.

But as she sat sipping coffee and looking at the barges slowly making their way up the East River, she knew there was something she had to decide about first: the journal.

What am I going to do about it? Lacey asked herself. Isabelle thought there was something in it that proved Heather's death was not an accident. Curtis Caldwell stole the leather binder after he killed Isabelle. Did he kill Isabelle because he was afraid of what she had found in that journal? Did he steal what he thought was the journal to make sure no one else could read it?

The bloodstained pages were still in her briefcase, under the couch. I have to turn them over to the police, Lacey thought, and there's a way I can do it and still keep my promise to Isabelle.

AT TWO o'clock Lacey was in a small office in the police station, sitting across a conference table from Detective Ed Sloane and his assistant, Detective Nick Mars. Sloane seemed a little short of breath, as though he'd been hurrying. Or maybe just smoking too much, Lacey decided. There was an open pack of cigarettes poking out of his breast pocket.

Nick Mars was another story. He was still in his twenties, baby-faced, with innocent blue eyes and an easy smile, and he was nice. She was sure he was the good cop in the good cop–bad cop scenario interrogators play. Sloane would bluster and occasionally rage; Mars would soothe, his manner always solicitous.

Lacey had been at the station for almost three hours, trying to describe Curtis Caldwell to the police artist.

"He didn't have any scars or birthmarks or tattoos," she'd explained to the artist. "At least none that I could see. All I can tell you is that he had a thin face, pale blue eyes, tanned skin, and sandy hair. There was nothing distinguishing about his features—except for his lips, maybe. They were a little thin."

After the artist had failed to come up with a sketch she felt resembled the man she had seen, Lacey had been shown endless mug shots. However, none of them resembled the man she knew as Curtis Caldwell, a fact that clearly upset Sloane.

"Okay, Ms. Farrell," he said brusquely, "we need to go over your story. You were pretty upset when you dialed 911 last night."

Lacey raised her eyebrows. "With good reason," she said.

"And you were virtually in shock when we got there."

"I guess I was." In truth, most of what had happened last evening was a haze to her.

"I didn't escort you to the door when you left, but I understand you had the presence of mind to remember that you'd left your briefcase in the hall closet."

"I remembered it as I passed the closet, yes."

"Do you remember that photographers were taking pictures?"

She thought back. "Yes, I do," she replied.

Sloane slid an eight-by-ten photograph across the desk. "This is an enlargement of a shot taken in the foyer," he explained. He nodded to the younger man. "Detective Mars picked up this little detail."

Lacey stared at the picture. It showed her in profile, gripping her briefcase, holding it away from Rick Parker.

"So you not only remembered to get your briefcase but you insisted on carrying it yourself."

"Well," Lacey explained, "I feel it's important to be self-reliant, especially with my co-workers. In truth, though, I probably was acting on automatic pilot."

"I think you were acting very deliberately," Detective Sloane said. "You see, Ms. Farrell, there were traces of blood in that closet—Isabelle Waring's blood. Now how would it have gotten there, do you suppose?"

Heather's journal, Lacey thought. A couple of the bloody pages had fallen onto the closet carpet as she was jamming them into the briefcase. But she couldn't tell this to the detective yet. She needed time to study the pages.

Sloane leaned across the desk, his manner more aggressive. "Ms. Farrell, I don't know what your game is or what you're not telling us, but clearly this was no ordinary murder. The man who called himself Curtis Caldwell didn't rob that apartment or kill Isabelle Waring at random. The crime was carefully planned. Your appearance on the scene was the only thing that probably did not go according to plan." He paused. "You told us Caldwell was carrying Mrs. Waring's leather binder. Describe it again."

"It was the size of a standard loose-leaf binder," Lacey said, "and had a zipper around it so that nothing would fall out."

"Ms. Farrell, have you ever seen this before?" Sloane shoved a sheet of loose-leaf paper covered with writing across the table.

She skimmed it. Dated three years earlier, it began, "Daddy came to see the show again. Took all of us back to the restaurant for dinner. . . ."

Heather's journal, she thought. I must have missed this page. How many more did I miss? she wondered suddenly.

"Have you ever seen this before?" Sloane asked her again.

"Yesterday afternoon when I brought the man I know as Curtis Caldwell to the apartment, Isabelle was in the library, seated at the desk. The leather binder was open, and she was reading loose-leaf pages she'd taken out of it. This is probably one of them."

At least that much is true, she thought. Suddenly she regretted not taking time this morning to make copies of the journal before going to the station.

That was what she had decided to do—give the original to the police, a copy to Jimmy Landi, and keep a copy for herself.

"We found that page under the bedroom chaise," Sloane told her. "Do you think there were others?" He didn't wait for her to answer. "Let's get back to the smear of Isabelle Waring's blood in the downstairs closet. Do you have any idea how it got there?"

"I had her blood on my hands," Lacey said. "You know that."

"Yes, but your hands weren't dripping with blood when you grabbed that briefcase as you were leaving last night. So what happened? Did you put something in that briefcase before we got there, something you took from Isabelle Waring's bedroom? I think so. Were there perhaps more pages like the one you just read scattered around her room? Can you answer that question?"

Lacey wanted desperately to tell them she had the journal and why she had it. But if I do, she thought, they'll demand I turn it over immediately. They won't let me make copies for Heather's father and myself. They're acting as though I had something to do with Isabelle's death.

She stood up. "No, I can't. Are you finished with me, Detective Sloane?"

"For today. But please keep in mind that being an accessory after the fact in a murder investigation carries criminal penalties. And if you did take any of those pages, I have to wonder just how 'innocent' a bystander you were. After all, you were responsible for bringing the killer into Isabelle Waring's apartment."

Lacey left without responding. She had to get to the office, but first she was going home to get the journal. She would stay at her desk this evening until everyone else had left and make the copies she needed. Tomorrow she'd turn over the original to Sloane. I'll try to make him understand why I took it, she thought nervously.

She started to hail a cab, then decided to walk home. The afternoon sun felt good. She still had the sensation of being chilled to the bone. As she crossed Second Avenue, she sensed someone close behind her and spun around to meet the puzzled eyes of an elderly man. "Sorry," she mumbled as she darted to the curb.

I expected to see Curtis Caldwell, Lacey thought, trembling. If Heather's journal was what he was after, he might come back for it. He knows I can identify him as a murderer. Until the police caught Caldwell—if they caught him—she was in danger.

When she got off the elevator in her building, she hurried down the long corridor to her apartment and dashed inside. She retrieved the briefcase from under the couch and carried it to her desk. Gingerly she removed the journal pages, wincing at the sight of the ones stained with blood. Finally, she put them into a manila envelope and fished around in her closet for a tote bag.

Ten minutes later, that bag firmly under her arm, she stepped out onto the street. As she nervously hailed a cab, she tried to convince herself that whoever Caldwell was, and for whatever reason he had killed Isabelle, he must surely be miles away by now, on the run.

SANDY Savarano, alias Curtis Caldwell, was taking no chances of being recognized as he used a pay phone near Lacey's building. He wore a gray wig, had a graying stubble covering his face, and his lawyer's suit had been replaced by a shapeless sweater over faded jeans. "When Farrell left the police station, she went home," he said as he glanced down the street. "I'm not going to hang around. There's a squad car parked across from her building."

He started walking west, then decided to watch the police car to test his theory that it was there to guard Lacey Farrell. He didn't have to wait long. He watched from half a block away as the familiar figure of a young woman in a black suit, carrying a tote bag, emerged from the building and hailed a cab. As it sped away, he looked to see what the cop car would do. A moment later it leaped from the curb.

Good, Sandy thought. That's one less thing to get in my way.

AFTER THEY RETURNED TO THE restaurant from making arrangements for Isabelle's cremation, Jimmy Landi and his partner, Steve Abbott, went directly to Jimmy's office. Steve poured liberal amounts of Scotch into tumblers, saying, "I think we both need this."

Landi reached for the glass. "I know I do. This has been an awful day. It doesn't make sense, does it, Steve? Some guy claims he's looking to buy an apartment, then comes back and kills Isabelle!" His eyes glistened with tears. "Well, she's with Heather now. Maybe that's where she wanted to be. I don't know."

Abbott, in an effort to change the subject, cleared his throat and said, "Jimmy, Cynthia is coming over for dinner. Will you join us?"

Landi shook his head. "No, but thanks, Steve. I'll be okay. Stop worrying about me and pay attention to your girlfriend. Are you going to marry her?"

"I'm not rushing into anything," Abbott said, smiling.

"You're right. You're young. You've got a long way to go."

"Not so long. Don't forget I turned forty-five last spring."

"Yeah? Well, I turn sixty-eight next month," Jimmy said with a grunt. "And *I've* still got a long way to go before I cash in my chips. Don't you forget it!"

Abbott swallowed the last of his Scotch and stood. "I'm counting on it. When we open our place in Atlantic City, the rest of them might as well close their doors. Right?" Abbott noticed Jimmy glancing at his watch and said, "Well, I'd better get downstairs and do some glad-handing."

Shortly after Abbott left, the receptionist buzzed Jimmy. "Mr. Landi, a Miss Farrell wants to talk to you. She's the real estate agent who was working with Mrs. Waring."

"Put her on," he snapped.

Lacey had waited until everyone in the domestic real estate division left before carrying the tote bag to the copier, where she made two copies of Heather's journal—one for Jimmy Landi, one for herself. Then she called Landi.

The conversation was brief. Jimmy would be waiting for her.

Lacey jumped into a taxi and gave the address of Venezia on West Fifty-sixth Street. Only then did she relax her grip on the tote bag. Why am I so uneasy? she wondered. And why do I have the sensation of being watched?

Once in Landi's office, sitting opposite the brooding, solid-looking man, Lacey was straightforward in telling him Isabelle Waring's dying words. "I promised to give the journal to you," she explained. "And I promised to read it myself. Isabelle wanted me to show you something in it. I suspect she thought I'd find what it was that confirmed her suspicion that your daughter's death was not accidental. I'm trying to obey her wishes." Lacey opened her tote bag and took out the set of pages she had brought with her.

Landi glanced at them, then turned away. Lacey was sure the sight of his daughter's handwriting was painful, but his only comment was a testy "These aren't the originals."

"I'm giving the original pages to the police."

His face flushed with sudden anger. "That's not what Isabelle asked you to do."

Lacey stood up. "Mr. Landi, I don't have a choice. I'm certain that eventually the original pages will be returned to you, but for now I'm afraid you'll have to make do with a copy."

He did not even look up as she walked out.

WHEN Lacey returned to her apartment, she found chaos. Drawers had been spilled, closets ransacked, furniture cushions tossed onto the floor. Even the refrigerator had been emptied and left open. She called the superintendent, and while he dialed 911, she put in a call to Detective Sloane.

He arrived shortly after the local precinct cops. "You know what they were looking for, don't you?" Sloane said.

"Yes," Lacey told him. "Heather Landi's journal. But it's not here. It's in my office. I hope whoever did this hasn't gone there."

In the squad car on the way to her office, Sloane read Lacey her rights. "I was keeping a promise I made to a dying woman," she protested. "She asked me to read the journal and then give it to

Heather's father, and that's what I've done. I took him a copy this evening."

When they got to Lacey's office, Sloane did not leave her side as she unlocked the cabinet and removed the manila envelope in which she had placed the original pages of the journal.

He opened the clasp, pulled out a few of the sheets, then looked at her. "You're sure you're giving me everything?"

"This is everything that was with Mrs. Waring when she died," Lacey said, hoping he wouldn't press her. It wasn't the whole truth: The copy she had made for herself was locked in her desk.

"We'd better go down to headquarters, Ms. Farrell."

At the precinct station house, Sloane said, "All right, Ms. Farrell, let's take this from the top."

The same questions over and over. Had she ever met Heather Landi? Wasn't it odd that on the basis of a chance meeting in an elevator Isabelle Waring had offered her an exclusive on the apartment? How often had she seen Waring in the last weeks? For lunches? Dinners? End-of-day visits?

"She called early evening 'sober light,'" Lacey heard herself saying, searching her mind for anything new to tell him. "She said the Pilgrims called it that. She found it a very lonely time."

Sloane's demeanor didn't give any indication of his reaction. Instead he said, "Let's talk about how Curtis Caldwell got back into the Waring apartment. There was no sign of forced entry. Did you give him a key?"

"No, of course not," Lacey protested. "But Isabelle always left a key in a bowl on the table in the foyer. Caldwell could have seen it there and taken it. But what about my apartment? How did someone get in there? I have a doorman."

"And an active garage in the building and a delivery entrance. These so-called secured buildings are a joke, Ms. Farrell. You're in the realty business. You know that."

Lacey thought of Curtis Caldwell, pistol in hand, rushing to find her, wanting to kill her. She fought back tears. "Please, I want to go home," she said.

Sloane got up. "Okay. You can go now, Ms. Farrell, but I must warn you that formal charges may be pending against you for removing and concealing evidence from a crime scene."

I should have talked to a lawyer, Lacey thought. How could I have been such a fool?

MASCARA and a light lipstick were usually all the cosmetics Lacey wore, but in the morning light when she saw the shadows under her eyes and noted the pallor of her skin, she added blush. It did little, however, to brighten her outlook. Even wearing a favorite brown-and-gold jacket didn't help dispel a sense of gloom.

At the door of the office she took a deep breath and straightened her shoulders. She remembered her father telling her that walking tall made you look confident.

And I *do* need that confidence, she said to herself a few minutes later when she was summoned to Richard Parker, Sr.'s, office.

Rick was in with his father. The elder Parker was obviously angry. "Lacey, according to security, you came here last night with a detective. What was that about?"

She told him as simply as she could, explaining that she had decided she had to turn the journal over to the police, but first she needed to make a copy for Heather's father.

"You kept concealed evidence in this office?" the older Parker asked, raising an eyebrow.

"I intended to give it to Detective Sloane today," she said. She told them about her apartment having been burglarized. "I was only trying to do what Isabelle Waring asked me to do," she said. "Now it seems I may have committed an indictable offense."

"That was really a dumb thing to do," Rick interjected.

"I wasn't thinking straight," she said. "Look, I'm sorry about—"

"I'm sorry about it too," Parker senior told her. "Have you any appointments today?"

"Two this afternoon."

"Liz or Andrew can handle them for you. Rick, see to it. Lacey, you plan on working the phones for the immediate future."

"That's not fair," Lacey said, suddenly angry.

"Nor is it fair to drag this firm into a murder investigation."

"I'm sorry, Lacey," Rick told her.

But you're Daddy's boy on this one, she thought, fighting down the urge to say more.

SLOANE was fond of saying that good detective work begins with a hunch. He expounded the theory to Nick Mars as they studied the pages that comprised Heather Landi's journal.

"I say that Lacey Farrell still isn't coming clean with us," Sloane said angrily. "She's more involved in this thing than she's letting on. We know she took the journal out of the apartment; we know she made a copy of it to give to Jimmy Landi."

"And have you thought of this, Eddie?" Mars asked. "Those pages aren't numbered. So how do we know Farrell hasn't destroyed the ones she didn't want us to see? Her fingerprints aren't just all over these pages. They're all over the whole case."

AN HOUR later Detective Sloane received a call from Matt Reilly, a specialist in the Latent Print Unit. A fingerprint lifted from the front door of Lacey's apartment matched the print of Sandy Savarano, a low-level mobster who had been a suspect in a dozen drug-related murders.

"Sandy Savarano!" Sloane exclaimed. "That's crazy. His boat blew up with him in it two years ago. We covered his funeral."

"We covered someone's funeral," Reilly told him dryly. "Dead men don't break into apartments."

FOR the rest of the day Lacey watched helplessly as clients she had developed were assigned to other agents. She figured that by the end of the afternoon she'd be told to stay away from the office until the investigation was concluded. She also had the feeling that she was being watched, so if she was going to take the copy of Heather's journal out of her desk, she would have to do it when no one was looking.

She finally got her chance at ten minutes of five. She had just slipped the manila envelope into her briefcase when Richard Parker, Sr., summoned her and told her she was being suspended.

"NOT too hungry, I hope, Alex?" Jay Taylor asked as he checked his watch again. "Lacey isn't usually this late." It was obvious that he was irritated.

Mona Farrell jumped to her daughter's defense. "The traffic is always terrible this time of day."

Kit shot her husband a warning glance. "After what Lacey has been through, nobody should be upset that she's a little late."

"I agree," Alex Carbine said. "She's had a rough few days."

Mona Farrell looked at Carbine with a grateful smile. She was never totally at ease with her frequently pompous son-in-law. He usually had little patience with anyone, but she had noticed that he was deferential to Alex.

This evening they were having cocktails in the living room, while the boys were watching television in the den. Bonnie was with the grown-ups, however, having begged to stay up past her bedtime to see Lacey. She was at the window, waiting for her.

It's eight fifteen, Mona thought. Lacey was due here at seven thirty. This really isn't like her. What can be keeping her?

THE full impact of everything that was happening hit Lacey that evening as she was driving out to Kit and Jay's house in Wyckoff, New Jersey, for a family dinner. She suddenly realized that for practical purposes she was out of a job. Parker senior is going to fire me, she thought. He's going to use the excuse that I jeopardized the firm by concealing evidence there. And it was his own son who gave me Curtis Caldwell's name and told me to set up an appointment!

The rush hour was over, but even so, there was a lot of traffic as Lacey inched across the George Washington Bridge, where a blocked lane was creating havoc. Jay must be in a wonderful mood, she thought, smiling ruefully but genuinely worried about keeping her family waiting.

As she drove along Route 4, she debated how much she would tell them about what was going on. Everything, I guess, she finally decided. If Mom or Kit call me at the office and I'm not there, they'll have to know why.

She glanced in her rearview mirror. Was that car following her? Stop it, she warned herself. You're getting paranoid.

KIT and Jay lived on a quiet street in a section of pricey homes. Lacey pulled up to the curb in front of their house, got out of the car, and started up the walk.

"Lacey's here!" Bonnie called joyously. She ran for the door.

"About time," Jay grunted.

Bonnie tugged the door open. As she raised her arms for Lacey's hug, there was the sound of shots, and bullets whistled past them. A flash of pain coursed through Lacey's head, and she threw herself forward, her body covering Bonnie's.

In the sudden quiet that followed the shots, Lacey quickly ran a mental check of the situation. The pain she felt was real, but she realized with a stab of anguish that the gush of blood against her neck was coming from the small body of her niece.

IN THE waiting room on the pediatrics floor of Hackensack Medical Center, a doctor smiled reassuringly at Lacey. "Bonnie had a close call, but she'll make it. She wants to see you."

Lacey was with Alex Carbine. After Bonnie was wheeled out of the operating room, Mona, Kit, and Jay had followed her crib to her room. Lacey had not gone with them.

My fault, my fault—it was all she could think. She was only vaguely aware of the headache caused by the bullet that had creased her skull. In fact, her whole mind and body seemed numb, not yet comprehending the horror of what had happened.

Bonnie was rushing to open the door for me, Lacey thought bitterly. That's all she was doing. And it almost cost her her life.

"Lacey, go on in and see Bonnie," Alex Carbine urged.

Lacey turned to look at him, remembering with gratitude how

he had dialed 911 while her mother tried to stem the blood that was spurting from Bonnie's shoulder.

In her niece's room, Lacey found Jay and Kit on either side of the crib, her mother at the foot.

Bonnie's shoulder and upper arm were heavily bandaged, but when she spotted Lacey, her face brightened. "Lacey!"

Lacey tried to smile. "Snazzy-looking bandage. Where do I sign it?" she asked as she bent over the crib.

"Didn't you have any sense of being followed?" Jay asked.

"For heaven's sake, Jay!" Kit snapped. "Of course she didn't."

Bonnie is hurt, and they're at each other's throats because of me, Lacey thought. I can't let this happen.

Bonnie's eyelids were drooping. Lacey leaned down and kissed her cheek.

"Come back tomorrow, please," Bonnie begged.

"I have some stuff to do, but I'll be back soon," Lacey promised.

Back in the waiting area, Lacey found detectives from the Bergen County prosecutor's office waiting for her. "We've been contacted by New York," they told her.

"Detective Sloane?" she asked.

"No. The U.S. Attorney's office, Miss Farrell. We've been asked to see that you get home safely."

GARY Baldwin, U.S. Attorney for the Southern District of New York, generally wore a benign expression that seemed incongruous to anyone who had ever seen him in action at a trial. Of medium height and slender build, and soft-spoken, he nevertheless could annihilate a witness during cross-examination. Forty-three years old, he was known to have national political ambitions and clearly would like to crown his career in the U.S. Attorney's office with a major headline-grabbing case.

That case might have just landed in his lap. A young woman happens on a murder scene on Manhattan's expensive Upper East Side, the victim the ex-wife of a prominent restaurateur. Most important, the young woman can identify the assailant.

Baldwin knew that if Sandy Savarano had come out of hiding to do this job, it *had* to be tied to drugs. Thought to be dead for the past two years, Savarano had made a career as an enforcer who eliminated anyone who got in the way of the drug cartel he worked for.

But when the police had shown Savarano's mug shots to Lacey Farrell, she had not recognized him. Either her memory was faulty or Savarano had had enough plastic surgery to successfully disguise his identity. Chances are it's the latter, Baldwin thought, and if so, then it means that Lacey Farrell is just about the only person who can actually identify him.

Gary Baldwin's dream was to prosecute Savarano or, better yet, get him to plea-bargain and give evidence against the real bosses.

But the call he had just received from Detective Sloane had infuriated him. The journal that seemed key to this case had been stolen from the precinct. "I was keeping it in my locked cubby in the squad room while Nick Mars and I read it to see if there was anything useful in it," Sloane explained. "It disappeared last night."

Then Sloane had added, "Jimmy Landi has the copy Farrell gave him. I'm on my way to get it from him."

"Make sure you get it before that disappears too," Baldwin said.

He slammed the phone down. Lacey Farrell was due in his office, and he had a lot of questions for her.

LACEY knew that she was being naïve in hoping that turning over Heather Landi's journal to the police would end her involvement in the case. When she finally got home from New Jersey the night before, it was almost dawn, but she'd been unable to sleep.

Now she was sitting in the office of U.S. Attorney Gary Baldwin. Baldwin did not mince words. "Ms. Farrell," he said, "I'm very sorry for the problems you've been having, but the fact is, you seriously impaired a major criminal investigation by removing evidence from a crime scene. For all we know, you may have destroyed some of that evidence. What you did turn over is now missing, which is a stunning sign of its significance."

"I did *not* destroy—" Lacey began in heated protest.

She was interrupted by Baldwin. His voice icy, he said, "Ms. Farrell, we have only your word for that. But you have my word for this: The man you know as Curtis Caldwell is a ruthless killer. We need your testimony to help convict him, and we intend to make sure that nothing happens to prevent that."

He paused. "Ms. Farrell, it is within my power to hold you as a material witness. It would mean keeping you under twenty-four-hour guard in a special facility for however long it takes to apprehend and, with your help, convict the murderer."

"Would I be safe after I testify against him?" Lacey asked. She had a sudden sense of being in a car that was hurtling down a steep hill, out of control, about to crash.

"Yes, you would be," Baldwin said firmly. "Savarano is claustrophobic. He'll do anything to avoid going to prison. Now that we can link him to a murder, he may well be persuaded to turn state's evidence once we've got him, in which case we would not even bring him to trial. But until that happens, we must keep you safe."

Baldwin paused and stared at her. "Have you ever heard of the Witness Protection Program, Ms. Farrell?"

CHAPTER 4

N THE quiet of his locked office he studied Heather's journal again. It was in there, all right. But he had taken care of the problem. The cops were following up all the names they had. Good luck to them. They were on a wild-goose chase.

Lacey Farrell had not been seen for three months. They were either holding her as a material witness or she had disappeared into the Witness Protection Program. She supposedly had made one copy of the journal, for Jimmy Landi, but what would have stopped her from making another copy for herself? Nothing.

By now she would have figured out that if the journal was worth killing for, it had to have something of value in it. Isabelle had talked her head off to Farrell. Who knows what she had said.

Sandy Savarano was back in hiding. He had seemed to be the perfect one to send to retrieve the journal and to take care of Isabelle Waring, but he had been stupidly careless. Twice. He had let Farrell see him at Waring's apartment. Then he had left a fingerprint at Farrell's apartment. Sandy would give everything up in a minute rather than go to prison, he reflected. Farrell had to be tracked down, and Savarano sent to eliminate her.

Then, just maybe, he would be safe at last.

THE name on the bell at the small apartment building on Hennepin Avenue in Minneapolis was Alice Carroll. To the neighbors she was an attractive young woman in her late twenties who didn't have a job and kept pretty much to herself.

For Lacey, after three months, the sensation of sleepwalking was ending and an intense sense of isolation setting in.

I didn't have a choice, she reminded herself when at night she lay awake remembering how she had been told to pack heavy clothing but bring neither family pictures nor items with her name or initials. Kit and her mother had helped her pack.

She had thought of it as temporary. But she soon realized that once she moved and took on her new identity, she could have no involvement with anyone or any part of her life in New York.

It had happened quickly. Two uniformed cops had taken her out in a squad car as though she were going to the precinct for questioning. Her bags were brought down to an unmarked van in the garage. Then she was transferred to an armored van that took her to a safe site and orientation center near Washington, D.C.

Alice in Wonderland, Lacey would think as she passed the next weeks in that enclosure, working with an instructor to create a new background for herself. All the things she had been were gone.

They existed in her memory, of course, but after a time she began to question even that reality. Now there were only weekly phone calls from safe hookups, letters mailed through safe channels. Otherwise there was no contact. None. Nothing. Only the overwhelming loneliness. Her only reality became her new identity. Her instructor had walked her to a mirror. "Look in there, Lacey. You see that young woman? Everything you think you know about her isn't so. Just forget her. It'll be rough for a while. You'll feel like you are playing some kind of game—pretending. There's an old Jerry Vale song that says it all. The lyrics go like this:

"Pretend you don't see her at all . . . it's too late for running . . . look somewhere above her . . . pretend you don't see her at all . . ."

That was when Lacey had chosen her new name, Alice Carroll, after Alice in *Alice's Adventures in Wonderland* and *Through the Looking Glass,* by Lewis Carroll. It fit her situation perfectly.

JANUARY was a lousy month in New York, Rick Parker thought as he walked rapidly along a jogging path in Central Park. A runner brushed into him. "Watch out!" Rick snapped.

The jogger didn't break pace. "Cool it, man," he yelled back over his shoulder.

Cool it! Sure, Rick thought. The old man's finally letting me handle some sales again, and that nosy detective has to show up this morning of all times.

Detective Sloane had come by, going over the same territory. "When you got that call from the man who identified himself as Curtis Caldwell, did it occur to you to check with the law firm he claimed was his employer?" he'd asked for the umpteenth time.

Rick jammed his hands into his pockets, remembering his lame response. "We do a lot of business with Keller, Roland, and Smythe," he'd said. "There was no reason not to take the call on faith."

"Have you any idea how the caller would have *known* his background wouldn't be checked?"

"I have told you before, I have no idea how that caller knew enough to use the law firm's name," Rick had said.

Now he kicked at a ball of crusted, dirty snow that was lying in his path. Were the police getting suspicious of the fact that he had been the one to set up the meeting? Were they starting to suspect that there never had been a phone call?

I should have figured out a better story, he thought, kicking savagely at the frozen earth. Now he was stuck with it.

THE key word in this program is security, Lacey thought as she started a letter to her mother. What do you write about? she asked herself. Not the weather. If I were to mention that it's ten degrees below zero and there's been a record twenty-six-inch snowfall in one day, it would be a dead giveaway that I'm in Minnesota. That's the sort of information they warn you about.

I can't write about a job, because I don't have one yet. I *can* say that my fake birth certificate and my fake Social Security card just came through, so now I can look for a job. I suppose I can tell her that now I have a driver's license, and my adviser, a deputy U.S. marshal, took me to buy a secondhand car. The program pays for it. Isn't that great? But of course I can't say that the marshal's name is George Svenson. Instead she wrote:

My adviser is a good guy. He's got three teenage daughters.

No, take that last part out, she thought. Too specific.

My adviser is a good guy. Very patient. He went with me to buy furniture for the studio.

Too specific. Make that apartment.

But you know me. I didn't want a lot of matched stuff, so he humored me and we went to some garage sales and I found some nice old furniture that at least has character. But I sure miss my own digs.

That was safe enough, Lacey thought.

She was allowed to call home once a week on a secure telephone hookup. The last call she had made, she could hear Jay in the background, hurrying Kit. Well, it *was* a pain in the neck to have to sit and wait for a call at a specific time; she couldn't deny that. And no one could call her back.

It sounds as though the holidays were fun for the kids, and I'm so happy that Bonnie's arm is getting stronger.

Take care of yourself, Mom. Sounds as though you and Alex are having fun. I think he's a nice guy, and I'll never forget how helpful he was that awful night while Bonnie was in surgery.

Love you all. Keep praying that they find and arrest Isabelle Waring's murderer and he plea-bargains and I get off the hook.

Lacey put the letter in an envelope. Svenson would mail it for her through the secure mail-forwarding channel. Writing to her mother and Kit or speaking to them on the phone took away some of the sense of isolation. But when the letter was finished or the phone call completed, the letdown that followed was rough.

Come on, she warned herself, knock off the self-pity. It won't do any good, and, thank God, the holidays are over. To try to break up Christmas Day she had gone to the last Mass at St. Olaf's, the church named for the warrior king of Norway. She then ate a solitary meal at the Northstar Hotel, and tears had welled up as she thought about her mother and Kit and Jay and the children. She and her mother always went to Kit's house on Christmas.

Knock it off! Lacey warned herself as she dropped the envelope into a drawer, where it would await Svenson's pickup.

For lack of something else to do, she reached into the bottom drawer of her desk and pulled out the copy she had made of Heather Landi's journal. What could Isabelle possibly have wanted me to see in it? she asked herself for the hundredth time.

In all, the journal spanned the four years Heather had spent in New York. She wrote in detail about looking for an apartment, about her father insisting she live in a safe building on the East Side. Heather preferred the West Side. As she put it, "It isn't stuffy and has life."

She also wrote about singing lessons, about getting her first part in an Equity showcase revival of *The Boy Friend*. She wrote interestingly about some of the more glamorous parties she attended, many of them apparently through her father's connections.

It was obvious that she had been close to both parents. All the references to them were warm and loving, even though several times she had complained about the need to please her father.

It was clear from the last few entries that Heather was deeply troubled about something. She wrote about being caught "between a rock and a hard place" and not knowing what to do. Unlike the others, those last entries were on unlined paper. There was nothing specific in them, but obviously they had triggered Isabelle Waring's suspicions.

God knows *I'm* between a rock and a hard place right now, Lacey thought hopelessly as she put the pages back into the drawer.

Feeling isolated and overwhelmed, she turned on the radio. A voice was saying, "Hi, I'm Tom Lynch, your host on WCIV."

Tom Lynch! Lacey was shocked out of her homesickness. She had made a list of all the names in Heather Landi's journal, and one of them was Tom Lynch, an out-of-town broadcaster on whom it seemed Heather had once had a mild crush. Was it the same person? And if so, was it possible Lacey could learn something about Heather from him? It was worth pursuing, she decided.

TOM Lynch was a hearty midwesterner. Raised in North Dakota, he was a stalwart who thought twenty degrees was a bracing temperature and believed that only sissies complained about the cold. "But today they've got a point," he said with a smile to Marge Peterson, the receptionist at Minneapolis radio station WCIV.

Marge looked at him with maternal affection. He certainly brightened her day, and since he had taken over the station's afternoon talk show, his mixture of news, interviews, commentary, and irreverent humor had been having the same effect on listeners. She could tell from the fan mail that crossed her desk that the popular thirty-year-old anchorman was headed for big-time broadcasting. And wait until they get a look at him, she thought as she looked up at his hazel eyes, his slightly rumpled brown hair, his warm smile, and his attractively uneven features. He's a natural for television.

"You're off to the gym?" Marge asked.

As Lynch was signing off that afternoon, he had told his listeners that since even a penguin couldn't jog outside in this weather, he would be heading for the Twin Cities Gym as usual, and he hoped to see some of them there. Twin Cities was one of his sponsors.

"You bet. See you later."

"How did you hear about us, Miss Carroll?" Ruth Wilcox asked as Lacey filled out the membership form for the Twin Cities Gym.

"On the Tom Lynch program," Lacey said. The woman was studying her, and she felt the need to elaborate. "I've been thinking of joining a gym for some time."

The prospect of filling out the form had frightened Lacey, since it would be the first time she actually used her new identity. So on the drive to the gym she had reviewed the details: She was Alice Carroll, from Hartford, Connecticut, a graduate of Caldwell College, a safe alma mater because the school was now closed. She had worked as a secretary in a doctor's office in Hartford. When the doctor retired, it seemed like a good time to make a move. She had chosen Minneapolis because she visited there once as a teenager and loved it. She was an only child. Her father was dead, and her mother had remarried and was living in London.

None of which matters at the moment, she thought as she reached into her purse for her new Social Security card. She would have to be careful. She had automatically started to write her real number but caught herself. Address: One East End Avenue, New York, New York 10021 flashed into her mind. No. Five twenty Hennepin Avenue, Minneapolis, Minnesota 55403. Her job? She put a dash through that space. Relative or friend to notify in case of accident: Svenson had provided her with a phony name, address, and telephone number to use in that situation. Any call that was made to the number would go to him.

"Stuck on a question?" Ruth Wilcox asked. "Can I help?"

Lacey was sure she detected a skeptical look in the other woman's eyes. She can *sense* something phony about me, she thought. But she managed a smile. "No, not stuck." She signed "Alice Carroll" and pushed the form across the desk.

"Now let me show you around," Wilcox said.

The place was well equipped, with a jogging track, a large pool, steam and sauna facilities, and an attractive juice bar.

"It gets fairly crowded early in the morning and right after work," Wilcox told her. "Oh, look, there he is," she said, interrupting herself. She called to a broad-shouldered man who was headed toward the men's locker room. "Tom, come here a minute."

A moment later Ms. Wilcox was introducing them. "Tom Lynch, this is Alice Carroll. Alice is joining us because she heard you talk about us on your radio program."

He smiled easily. "I'm glad I'm so persuasive. Nice to meet you, Alice." With a quick nod and another smile he left them.

"WHEN you create someone like the mythical boyfriend, have a real person in mind," Deputy Marshal George Svenson had warned Lacey. "Be able to visualize that guy and the way he talks so that if you have to answer questions about him, it will be easier to be consistent. And remember, develop the trick of answering questions by asking questions of your own."

Lacey had decided that Rick Parker was the mythical boyfriend she had broken up with. She could imagine breaking up with him more easily than having him as a boyfriend, but thinking of him at least did make consistency easier.

She began going to the gym daily, always in the late afternoon. The exercise felt good, and it gave her a chance to focus her thoughts as well. Now that she had the Social Security card, she was anxious to get a job, but Svenson told her the protection program would not provide false references.

"How do I get a job without a reference?" she had asked.

"We suggest you volunteer to work without pay for a couple of weeks, then see if you're hired."

"*I* wouldn't hire someone without references," she had protested.

It was obvious, though, that she would just have to try. Except for the gym, she was without any human contact. Being alone so much, the time was passing too slowly, and Lacey could feel depression settling over her like a heavy blanket. She had even come to dread the weekly talk with her mother. It always ended the same way, with her mother in tears and Lacey ready to scream with frustration.

In the first few days after she started going to the gym, she had managed to make a friend of Ruth Wilcox. It was to her that she first tried out the story of what had happened to bring her to Minneapolis: Her mother had remarried and moved to London, the doctor she worked for retired, and she had ditched her boyfriend. "He had a quick temper and could be very sarcastic," she explained, visualizing Rick Parker.

"I know the type," Wilcox assured her. "But let me tell you something. Tom Lynch has been asking me about you. I think he likes you."

LACEY had been careful not to seem too interested in Tom, but she had been laying the groundwork for a planned encounter. She timed her jogging to be finished just as he was starting. She signed up for an aerobics class close to the jogging track so he would see her as he ran by. Sometimes on his way out he stopped in the juice bar. She began to go into the shop a few minutes before he finished his run and to sit at a table for two.

The second week her plan worked. When he entered the bar, she was alone at a small table and all the other tables were taken. As he looked around, their eyes met. She pointed casually to the empty chair. Lynch hesitated, then came over.

SHE had combed Heather's journal and copied down any mention of Tom. The first time he appeared had been about a year and a half ago, when Heather met him after one of the performances of her show.

The nicest guy came out with us to Barrymore's for a hamburger. Tom Lynch, tall, really attractive, about thirty. He has his own radio program in St. Louis but is moving to Minneapolis soon. Kate, one of the girls in the show, is his cousin, and that's why he came to the show tonight. I talked to him a lot. He said he was going to be in New York for a few days. I hoped he'd ask me out, but no such luck.

An entry four months later read:

Tom Lynch was in town over the weekend. A bunch of us went skiing at Stowe. He's really good. And nice. But he isn't giving me or any of the girls a second look, and anyhow it wouldn't make any difference now.

Three weeks later Heather had died in the accident—if it *was* an accident. Lacey wondered if either Isabelle or the police had ever spoken to Tom Lynch about Heather. And what had Heather meant by writing "anyhow it wouldn't make any difference now"?

Did she mean that Tom Lynch had a serious girlfriend? Or did it mean that Heather was involved with someone herself?

All these thoughts raced through Lacey's head as Lynch settled down across the table from her.

"It's Alice Carroll, isn't it?" he said. "I understand you've just moved to Minneapolis."

"That's right." She hoped her smile did not look forced.

He's going to ask questions, she thought nervously. This could be my first real test. Svenson had told her to answer questions with questions. "Are you a native, Tom?" she asked.

"No. I was born in Fargo, North Dakota. And you?"

Even to her own ears it sounded lame when she tried to explain the move to Minneapolis. "My mother and I visited friends here when I was sixteen. I loved everything about the city."

"It wasn't in weather like this, I trust."

"No, it was in August."

"During the black fly season?"

He was teasing, she knew. But when you're lying, everything takes on a different slant. Next he asked her where she worked.

"I'm settling in," she replied. "But it's time to look for a job."

"What kind?"

"Well, I worked in a doctor's office," she replied.

"What kind of doctor?"

"A pediatrician." Then, anxious to change the subject, she said, "I was listening to you today. I liked your interview with the director of the revival of *Chicago.* I saw it in New York and loved it."

"My cousin, Kate Knowles, is in the road company of *The King and I* that's in town now," Lynch said.

Lacey saw the speculative look in his eyes. He's trying to decide whether to ask me to go with him to see it. Let him, she prayed. His cousin Kate had worked with Heather; she was the one who introduced them.

"It's opening tomorrow night," he said. "Would you like to go?"

In the three months that followed Isabelle's death, Jimmy Landi felt detached, as if his emotions had been anesthetized. All his energy, all his thinking, were channeled into the new casino-hotel in Atlantic City. Situated between Trump Castle and Harrah's Marina, it was designed to outshine them both, a magnificent white showcase with rounded turrets and a golden roof.

And as he stood in the lobby of this new building and watched the final preparations being made for the opening, Jimmy thought, I've done it! I've actually done it! Carpets were being laid, paintings and draperies were being hung, cases and cases of liquor disappeared into the bar.

It was important to outshine everyone else on the strip, to show them up. The street kid who had dropped out of school at thirteen and gone to work as a dishwasher at The Stork Club was on top now, and he was going to rub another success in everyone's face.

Looking through wide, clear-glass doors, he could see gaming tables being set up in the casino. He walked into the massive space. Off to the right, glittering rows of slot machines seemed to be beg-

ging to be tried. Soon, he thought. Another week and they'll be lining up to use them.

Heather. Isabelle. Both gone, Jimmy thought as he stood in the
casino, workmen milling around him. For some reason he had
found himself thinking more and more about Isabelle. As she was
dying, she'd made that real estate woman promise to give him
Heather's journal. He was glad to have it, but what was so important in it? Right after he got it, the cops had asked to take his copy
to compare it with the original.

He had given it to them, although reluctantly. He had looked at
it the night Lacey Farrell gave it to him. Still he was mystified. What
did Isabelle think he would find in it? He had gotten drunk before
he tried to read it. It hurt too much to see Heather's handwriting,
to read her descriptions of things they'd done together.

Isabelle had seen a conspiracy in everything, then ironically ended
up a random victim of a burglar who cased the apartment by pretending to be a potential buyer. It was one of the oldest games
in the world. Isabelle simply had been in the wrong place at the
wrong time.

Or *had* she? Jimmy Landi wondered. Was there even the faintest
chance that she had been right, that Heather's death *hadn't* been an
accident? Could Isabelle have been murdered to silence her?

These were questions Jimmy had avoided. If Isabelle had been
murdered to silence her, it meant someone had deliberately caused
Heather to burn to death in her car at the bottom of that ravine.

Last week the cops had released the apartment, and he had
phoned Parker and Parker, instructing them to put it back on the
market. He needed closure. He would hire a private detective to see
if there was anything the cops had missed. And he would talk to
Lacey Farrell.

The sound of the workmen's hammering finally penetrated his
consciousness. It was time to go. With heavy steps he walked across
the room, opened the glass doors, and went back into the lobby.

Heather, he thought. If I find that someone deliberately hurt you,
baby, I'll kill him myself. I promise you *that*.

IT WAS TIME TO CALL HOME, an event that Lacey both longed for and dreaded. This time the location for the secure phone call was a room in a motel. "Never the same place," she said when George Svenson opened the door in response to her knock.

"No," he agreed, adding, "The line's ready. I'll put the call through for you. Now remember everything I told you, Alice."

He always called her Alice.

"I remember every word. Even to name a supermarket could give away my location," she said. "If I talk about the gym, don't dare refer to it as the Twin Cities Gym. Stay away from the weather. Since I don't have a job, that's a safe subject."

"I'll make the connection; then I'll take a walk," Svenson said.

A moment later she heard the door click behind him as she said, "Hi, Mom. How's everyone?"

"Kit sends her love," her mother said. "The boys are fine. They're both on the school hockey team. You should see how they can skate, Lacey. My heart's in my mouth when I watch them."

I taught them, Lacey thought. I bought ice skates for them when they barely had started to walk.

"Bonnie's a worry, though," her mother added. "Kit takes her to the therapist three times a week, and I work out with her too. But she misses you. So much. She has an idea that you're hiding because someone may try to kill you."

Where did she get that idea? Lacey wondered. Dear Lord, who put that notion in her head?

Her mother answered the unasked question. "I think she overheard Jay talking to Kit. I know he irritates you sometimes, but in fairness, Lace, he's been very good, paying for your apartment. I also learned from Alex that Jay has a big order to sell restaurant supplies to the casino Jimmy Landi is opening in Atlantic City. Apparently Jay's been worried that if Landi knew he was related to you, the order might get canceled. Alex says Landi felt terrible about what happened to his ex-wife, and Jay was afraid he'd start to blame you somehow for her death. You know, for bringing that man to see the apartment without checking on him first."

Maybe it's too bad I wasn't killed along with Isabelle, Lacey thought bitterly.

Trying to sound cheerful, she told her mother that she was going to a gym regularly and really enjoying it. "I'm okay, really I am," she said. "And this won't go on long, I promise. When the man I can identify is arrested, he'll be persuaded to turn state's evidence rather than go to prison. As soon as they make a deal with him, I'll be off the hook. Whoever he fingers will be after him, not me."

Lacey was horrified to hear deep sobs from the other end. "Lacey, I can't live like this," Mona Farrell wailed. "You've got to tell me where you are. You've got to."

"Mom!"

"Lacey, please! I have to know."

"If I tell you, it's between us. You can't repeat it. Even to Kit. They'd throw me out of the program if they knew I told you."

"I have to know."

Looking out the window, Lacey saw George Svenson approaching the motel steps. "Minneapolis," she whispered.

The door was opening. "Mom, have to go. Talk to you next week. Love you. Bye."

"Everything okay at home?" Svenson asked.

"I guess so," Lacey said as a sickening feeling came over her that she had just made a terrible mistake.

LANDI'S restaurant on West Fifty-sixth Street was filled with a sparkling after-theater crowd, and Steve Abbott was going from table to table, greeting diners. Former New York mayor Ed Koch was there, and Calla Robbins, the legendary musical comedy performer who had been coaxed out of retirement to star in a new Broadway show. "Calla, the word is that you're marvelous," Abbott said.

"Actually, the word is that not since Rex Harrison in *My Fair Lady* has anyone faked a song with such flair."

Abbott's eyes crinkled as he bent down and kissed her cheek.

"I hear the new casino will knock everyone dead," said Robbins's escort, a prominent businessman. "Word is that Jimmy is planning to have you run it."

"Jimmy's the principal owner. Jimmy's the boss," Steve said decisively. "And don't you forget it. He sure doesn't let *me* forget it."

From the corner of his eye Steve Abbott saw Jimmy and waved him over.

Landi joined them, his face wreathed in a big smile for Calla.

"Who is boss in Atlantic City, Jimmy?" she asked. "Steve says you are."

"Steve has it right," Jimmy Landi said, smiling. "That's why we get along so good."

As Jimmy and Steve moved away from Robbins's table, Jimmy said, "Did you set up a dinner with that Farrell woman for me?"

Abbott shrugged. "Can't reach her, Jimmy. She's left her job, and her home phone is disconnected."

Jimmy Landi's face darkened. "She can't have gone too far. She's a witness. She can identify Isabelle's killer. That detective who took my copy of Heather's journal must know where she is."

"Want me to talk to him?"

"No, I'll do it. Well, look who's here."

Richard J. Parker was coming through the restaurant doors.

"It's his wife's birthday," Steve explained. "That's why she's with him for a change. They have a reservation for three."

And that punk son of his completes the happy family, Jimmy thought as he hurried across the foyer to welcome them.

The elder Parker regularly brought real estate clients there for dinner, which was the reason Jimmy hadn't banned his son from the restaurant. Last month Rick had gotten drunk and noisy at the bar and had to be escorted to a cab.

R. J. Parker returned Jimmy Landi's hearty handshake. "What more festive place to bring Priscilla than Landi's, right, Jimmy?"

Priscilla Parker gave Jimmy Landi a timid smile. He knew that R.J. not only cheated on his wife but that he bullied her unmercifully as well.

"Hi, Jimmy," Rick said with a slight smirk.

The aristocrat condescending to greet the peasant innkeeper, Jimmy thought. Well, without his father's clout that jerk couldn't get a job cleaning toilets. Smiling, Jimmy escorted them to their table.

LOOKING in the closet for something that would be appropriate for a festive evening out, Lacey reached for a long black wool skirt and evening sweater she had bought at Saks Fifth Avenue.

"You look okay, Alice," she said aloud when she studied herself in the mirror a few minutes later. The skirt and sweater had been an extravagance. But it was worth it, she decided. The effect of understated elegance gave a lift to her spirits.

And I certainly *need* a lift, Lacey thought as she fished in her jewelry box for earrings and her grandmother's pearls.

Promptly at six thirty Tom Lynch called on the intercom from the lobby. She was waiting with the apartment door open when he stepped out of the elevator and walked down the hall.

The obvious admiration in his face as he approached was flattering. "Alice, you look lovely," he said.

"Thanks. You're pretty fancy yourself. Come—"

She never finished saying come in. The door to the elevator was opening again. Had someone followed Tom up? Grabbing his arm, she propelled him into the apartment and bolted the door.

"Alice, is anything wrong?"

She tried to laugh, but knew the effort sounded false and shrill. "I'm so foolish," she stammered. "A—a deliveryman rang the bell a couple of hours ago. He was on the wrong floor. But my apartment was burglarized last year . . . in Hartford," she added hastily. "Then the elevator door opened again behind you and—and I guess I'm just still jumpy," she finished lamely.

There was no deliveryman, she thought. And I'm not just jumpy. I'm terrified that whenever an elevator door opens, I'll see Caldwell standing there.

"I can understand why you'd be nervous," Tom said, his tone serious. "I went to Amherst and used to visit friends in Hartford occasionally. Where did you live, Alice?"

"On Lakewood Drive." Lacey conjured up the pictures of an apartment complex she had studied as part of her preparation in the safe site, praying that Tom wouldn't say his friends lived there too.

"Don't know it," he said, shaking his head. Then, as he looked around the room, he added, "I like what you've done here."

The apartment *had* taken on a mellow, comfortable look. Lacey had painted the walls a soft ivory. The rug she had picked up at a garage sale was old enough to have acquired a soft patina. The dark blue velvet couch and matching love seat were worn but still handsome and comfortable. The shelves next to the television were filled with books and knickknacks, all bought at garage sales.

Lacey started to comment on how much she enjoyed shopping at garage sales but stopped herself. Most people who relocate move their furniture as well. She settled for thanking Tom for his compliment and was glad when he suggested they get started.

An hour later, as they sat companionably sipping wine and eating pizza, Lacey realized she was actually *enjoying* herself. Tom Lynch responded freely to the questions she asked him. "I was raised in North Dakota," he said. "I told you that. After college I moved to New York, fully expecting to set the broadcast industry on fire. It didn't happen, of course, and a very wise man told me that the best way to make it was to create a name for yourself in a smaller broadcast area, then work your way up to larger markets. So in the last nine years I've been in Des Moines, Seattle, St. Louis, and now here."

They had shared one small pizza. Lynch eyed the last piece, then started to put it on her plate.

"You take it," Lacey protested.

"I don't really want—

"You're salivating for it."

They laughed together, and a few minutes later when they left the restaurant and crossed the street to the theater, he put his hand under her elbow. "You have to be careful," he said. "There are patches of black ice everywhere around here."

If only you knew, Lacey thought. My life is a sheet of black ice.

I<small>T WAS THE THIRD TIME SHE</small> had seen *The King and I.* The last time had been on Broadway, and her father had been in the orchestra. Wish you were playing in this one tonight, Jack Farrell, she thought. As the overture began, she felt tears welling in her eyes and forced them back.

"You okay, Alice?" Tom asked quietly.

"I'm fine." How did Tom sense that I was distressed? she wondered. Maybe he's psychic, she thought. I hope not.

Tom's cousin, Kate Knowles, was playing the role of Tuptim, the slave girl who tries to escape from the king's palace. She was a good actress with an exceptional voice. Lacey praised her to Tom during intermission, then asked, "Will she be riding with us to the party?"

"No. She's going over with the cast. She'll meet us there."

I'll be lucky to get any time with her, Lacey worried.

K<small>ATE</small> and the other leads in the play were not the only stars at the party, Lacey realized. Tom Lynch was constantly surrounded by people. She slipped away from him to trade her wine for a Perrier, then did not rejoin him when she saw an attractive young woman from the cast talking animatedly to him.

I don't blame her, Lacey thought. He's good-looking, smart, and nice. Heather Landi apparently had been attracted to him, although the second time she wrote about him there was the suggestion that one of them was involved with someone else.

Lacey walked to a window. The party was in a mansion in Wayzata, an upscale suburb on Lake Minnetonka. She could see that beyond the snow-covered lawn the lake was frozen solid.

Wendell Woods, a prominent banker and the host of the party, came over to her. "It's Miss Carroll, isn't it?"

He was an imposing man of about sixty with steel-gray hair.

He's going to ask me where I'm from, Lacey thought. He did, and she gave the well-rehearsed version of her background. "And now I'm ready to start job-hunting," she told him.

"What kind of job?" he asked.

"I'd like to try my hand at real estate."

"That's mostly commission income, you know. Plus you'd have to learn the area," he said.

"I understand that, Mr. Woods," Lacey said. Then she smiled. "I'm a quick study."

Woods took out a pen and his business card. "Give me your phone number," he said. "I'll pass it on to one of my depositors, Millicent Royce. Her assistant just left to have a baby."

Lacey gladly gave the number to him. I'm being recommended by the president of a bank, she thought. If Millicent Royce is interested in meeting me, she may not bother to check references.

When Wendell Woods turned to speak to another guest, Lacey glanced about the room. Seeing that Kate Knowles was momentarily alone, she quickly made her way to her. "You were wonderful," she said. "I've seen three different productions of The King and I, and your interpretation of Tuptim was great."

Tom joined them. "I see you two have gotten together," he said.

"Tom, I wanted a chance to visit with you," his cousin said. "I've had enough of this party. Let's take off and have a cup of coffee somewhere." Kate smiled at Lacey. "Alice was just telling me how good I was. I want to hear more."

Lacey glanced at her watch. It was one thirty. Not wanting to stay up all night, she suggested having coffee at her place.

"I MADE these cookies this morning," she said as she set a plate on the coffee table. "Try them at your own risk. I haven't baked since high school."

After she poured the coffee, she tried to steer the conversation around so that she could introduce Heather's name. She said, "About a year and a half ago I went down to New York to see a revival of The Boy Friend. I read in your bio in the program tonight that you were in it, but I'm sure I'd remember if I'd seen you."

"You must have gone the week I was out with the flu," Kate said. "Those were the only performances I missed."

Lacey tried to sound offhand. "I do remember that there was a young actress with a really fine voice in the lead."

"Heather Landi," Kate said, turning to her cousin. "Tom, you remember Heather. She had a crush on you. She was killed in a car accident." Kate shook her head. "Such a tragedy."

"What happened?" Lacey asked.

"Oh, she was driving home from skiing in Stowe and went off the road. Her mother, poor thing, couldn't accept it. She came to the theater, talking to all of us, searching for some reason behind the accident. She said that Heather had been upset about something. She wanted to know if we had any idea what it was."

"Did you?" Tom asked.

Kate Knowles shrugged. "I told her that I had noticed that Heather *was* worried about something the week before she died, and I suggested that she may not have been concentrating on driving when she went into the skid."

It's a dead end, Lacey thought. Kate doesn't know anything I don't already know.

Kate put down her coffee cup. "That was great, Alice, but it's very late, and I've got to be on my way." She stood, then turned back to Lacey. "There is one thing about Heather Landi, although it's probably not significant. A guy I've dated, Bill Merrill—you met him, Tom—knew Heather too. Her name came up, and he mentioned that he had seen her the afternoon before she died, in the après-ski bar at the lodge. Bill had gone there with a bunch of guys, including a jerk named Rick Parker who's in real estate in New York and who apparently had pulled something on Heather when she first came to the city. Bill said that when Heather spotted Parker, she practically ran out of the lodge. It's probably nothing, but Heather's mom was so anxious for any information about that weekend that she'd surely want to know. I think I'll write her."

The sound of Lacey's coffee cup shattering on the floor broke the trancelike state she had entered when she heard Rick Parker's name. Refusing their help, Lacey busied herself with cleaning up the mess while calling out her good nights as they headed for the door.

She resisted the urge to tell Kate not to bother with the letter to Isabelle Waring, since it was too late for it to matter to her.

AFTER nearly four months of investigation, U.S. Attorney Gary Baldwin was no nearer to locating Sandy Savarano, though his staff had painstakingly tracked down the people named in Heather Landi's journal.

They also talked to the doorman in the building where the murder took place, but he remembered virtually nothing of the killer. He said he saw too many people come and go.

So that leaves me with only Lacey Farrell to personally finger Savarano, Baldwin thought bitterly. If anything happens to her, there's no case. Sure, we got Savarano's fingerprint off Farrell's door after her apartment was burglarized, but we can't prove he went inside. Farrell's the only one who can tie Savarano to Isabelle Waring's murder. Without her to ID him, forget it.

The only useful information Baldwin's undercover agents had gleaned was that before Savarano had staged his own death, his claustrophobia had become acute and he'd had nightmares about cell doors clanging shut behind him.

So what had brought him out of retirement? Big bucks? A favor he had to repay? Maybe both. And throw in the thrill of the hunt, of course. Savarano was a vicious predator.

Baldwin knew Savarano's rap sheet by heart. Forty-two years old, a suspect in a dozen murders, but hasn't seen the inside of a prison since he was a kid in reform school! A smart guy and a born killer.

If I were Savarano, Baldwin thought, my one purpose in life right now would be to find Lacey Farrell and make sure she never gets the chance to finger me.

Baldwin shook his head, and his forehead creased with concern.

The Witness Protection Program wasn't foolproof; he knew that. People got careless. When they called home, they might say something that gave away their hiding place. One mobster in the program was dumb enough to send a birthday card directly to a girlfriend. He was shot to death a week later.

Gary Baldwin had an uneasy feeling about Lacey Farrell. Her profile made her sound like someone who could find it difficult to be alone for long. Plus she seemed exceptionally trusting, a trait that could get her into real trouble. He shook his head again. Well, there was nothing he could do about it except to send word to her not to let her guard down, even for a minute.

MONA Farrell drove into Manhattan for what had become her standing Saturday dinner date with Alex Carbine at his popular new restaurant, Alex's Place. She always looked forward to the evening with him, even though he left the table frequently to greet customers and the occasional celebrity.

"It's fun," she assured him. "And I really don't mind. Don't forget I was married to a musician. I sat through many Broadway shows alone because Jack was in the orchestra pit."

As Mona exited the George Washington Bridge and turned south onto the West Side Highway, she thought of the flowers that Alex had sent her earlier and smiled.

Alex knew that the weekly phone call from Lacey tore her heart out. The flowers were his way of saying he understood. She had confided to him that Lacey had told her where she was living. "But I haven't even told Kit," she explained.

It's funny, Mona thought as traffic slowed to a crawl, things have always gone smoothly for Kit, but not for Lacey. Kit met Jay when she was at Boston College and he was at Tufts. They fell in love, married, and now had three wonderful kids and a lovely home. Jay might be pontifical and occasionally pompous, but he was a good husband and father. Just the other day he had surprised Kit with an expensive gold-leaf necklace she had admired in the window of Groom's Jewelry in Ridgewood.

Kit said that Jay had told her business suddenly had become very good again. I'm glad, Mona thought. She had been worried for a while that things were not going well. Certainly in the fall it was obvious that he had a lot on his mind.

Lacey *deserves* happiness, Mona told herself. Now's the time for her to meet the right person and get married and start a family. Instead she's alone in a strange city and she has to stay there and pretend to be someone else because her life is in danger.

Mona reached the parking lot on West Forty-sixth Street at seven thirty. Alex didn't expect her until eight, so she had time to check a Times Square newsstand for a Minneapolis newspaper. It would make her feel closer to Lacey if she became familiar with the city.

The night was cold but clear, and Mona enjoyed the five-block walk to the newsstand, where she found a copy of the Minneapolis *Star Tribune.* Lacey may have read this same edition this morning, she thought. Even touching the paper made Lacey seem closer.

Mona fished in her purse for her wallet as the vendor folded the paper and put it into a plastic bag.

When she reached the restaurant, there was a line at the checkroom. Seeing that Alex was already at their table, she hurried over to him. "Sorry. I guess I'm late," she said.

He got up and kissed her cheek. "You're not late, but your face is cold. Did you walk from New Jersey?"

"No. I was early and decided to pick up a newspaper."

Carlos, their usual waiter, was hovering nearby. "Mrs. Farrell, let me take your coat. Do you want to check your package?"

"Why not keep that?" Alex suggested. He took the bag from her and put it on an empty chair at their table.

It was, as always, a pleasant evening. By the time they were sipping espresso, Alex Carbine's hand was covering hers.

"Not too busy a night for you," Mona said teasingly. "You've only been up and down about ten times."

"I thought that might be why you bought a newspaper."

"Not at all, although I did glance at the headlines." Mona reached for her purse. "My turn to get up. I'll be right back."

Alex saw her to her car at eleven thirty. At one o'clock the restaurant closed and the staff went home.

At ten of twelve a phone call was made. The message was simple. "Tell Sandy it looks like she's in Minneapolis."

WHAT had happened between Heather Landi and Rick Parker? Lacey was stunned to learn they had known each other. After Tom Lynch and Kate Knowles had left Friday night, she sat up for hours, trying to make sense of it all. Over the weekend her mind had constantly replayed the night of Isabelle Waring's death. What had Rick been thinking that night as he sat there and listened to the police quizzing her about how well she had known Isabelle and if she had known Heather? Why hadn't Rick *said* something?

According to what Kate had been told, on the last day of her life Heather had been visibly upset at seeing Rick in Stowe. Kate had referred to Rick as a "jerk who's in real estate in New York" and had said that he "had pulled something on Heather when she first came to the city."

Lacey remembered that in her journal Heather alluded to an unpleasant incident when she was looking for an apartment on the West Side. Could it have involved Rick? Lacey wondered.

Rick had been in the West Side office of Parker and Parker at the time Heather was apartment hunting. Did Heather go to Parker and Parker and meet Rick? And if so, what had happened?

Lacey shook her head in anger. Could Rick be involved in *all* of this mess? she wondered. Am I stuck here because of him?

It was because of Rick that I brought Curtis Caldwell to Isabelle's apartment, she reminded herself. If Rick knows Caldwell, then maybe the police would be able to track him down through Rick. Lacey stood up and began to pace the room excitedly. This could be part of what Isabelle had seen in the journal. She had to get this information to Gary Baldwin at the U.S. Attorney's office.

Lacey's fingers itched to pick up the phone and call him, but direct contact was absolutely forbidden. She would have to leave a message for George Svenson to call her.

First, though, I have to talk to Kate again, Lacey thought. I have to find out more about her boyfriend, Bill Merrill, the one who mentioned Heather's reaction to Rick Parker. Baldwin will want to talk to Merrill, I'm sure. He can place Rick Parker in Stowe only hours before Heather died.

Kate had mentioned that the cast was staying at the Radisson Plaza Hotel for the week. When Lacey called her, she seemed pleased at her suggestion that they get together for lunch. They arranged to meet at twelve thirty the next day.

As Lacey replaced the receiver, she felt a surge of hope. She walked to the window and pulled back the curtain. It was a perfect midwestern winter's day. The temperature was only twenty-eight degrees, but the sun was shining.

Until today she had been too nervous to go for a real run, afraid she might look over her shoulder and see Caldwell's pale, icy eyes fixed on her. But suddenly, feeling as though there was the possibility of some sort of breakthrough, she decided that she had to *try* to resume some kind of normal life.

Lacey put on her cold-weather jogging clothes and headed to the door. Just then the phone rang, and she picked it up.

"Ms. Carroll, you don't know me," a crisp voice told her. "I'm Millicent Royce. Wendell Woods suggested we meet. I hear you may be looking for a job in the real estate field."

"I *am* looking, or rather, just about to start," Lacey said.

"Good. Are you free this afternoon by any chance?"

WHEN Lacey left the apartment and jogged down the street, it was with the sense that her luck might be changing at last. If Millicent Royce *did* hire her, it would mean she would have something to do to fill her days until she could go home.

TOM Lynch's program was broadcast weekdays from noon till four o'clock, and his guests ran the spectrum from political figures, authors, and celebrities to local VIPs.

On the Monday morning following the opening of *The King*

and I, Tom sat in his office poring over newspapers from all over the country, looking for unusual subjects to discuss. He had been thinking about Alice Carroll all weekend. There was something so quietly contained about her. She didn't talk much about herself, and something in her told him that she didn't invite questions.

The clothes she had worn to the opening were expensive. A blind man could see that. Also, he had overheard her tell Kate that she had seen *The King and I* three times. And she had talked knowledgeably with Kate about the revival of *The Boy Friend.*

Expensive outfits. Trips in and out of New York from Hartford to go to the theater. These generally weren't the kinds of things one was able to do working for a doctor.

Tom shrugged and reached for the phone. His questions were a sign of his interest in Alice. He was going to call her and ask if she wanted to have dinner tonight. After four rings the answering machine clicked on. Her voice, low and pleasing, said, "You've reached 555-1247. Please leave a message, and I'll get back to you."

Tom hung up, intensely disappointed at not having reached her. He would call back later.

On that Monday morning Sandy Savarano took Northwest flight 1703 from New York to Minneapolis–St. Paul.

He rode first class, as he had on the flight from Costa Rica, where he now lived. He was known to his neighbors there as Charles Austin, a well-to-do U.S. businessman who had sold his company two years ago at age forty and retired to the tropical good life.

His twenty-four-year-old wife had driven him to the airport in Costa Rica and made him promise not to stay away too long. "You're supposed to be retired," she had said, pouting lovingly as she kissed him good-bye.

"That doesn't mean I turn down found money."

It was the same answer he had given her about the several other jobs he had undertaken since he staged his death two years ago.

"Lovely day to fly." The voice was that of a young woman seated next to him.

"Yes, it is," he agreed.

He saw the look of interest in the young woman's eyes and was amused. Women actually found him attractive. Dr. Ivan Yenkel, a Russian immigrant who had given him this new face two years ago, had been a genius. His remolded nose was thinner. The heavy chin was sculpted, his ears smaller and flat against his head. Formerly heavy eyebrows were thinned and spaced farther apart. Yenkel had fixed his drooping eyelids and removed the circles under his eyes.

His dark brown hair was now the color of sand, a whimsy he had chosen in honor of his nickname, Sandy. Pale blue contact lenses completed the transformation.

"You look fabulous, Sandy," Yenkel had boasted when the last bandage came off. "No one would ever recognize you."

"No one ever will."

Sandy always got a thrill remembering the look of astonishment in Yenkel's eyes as he died.

I don't intend to go through plastic surgery again, Sandy thought as, with a dismissive smile to his seatmate, he pointedly picked up a magazine and opened it.

Pretending to read, he reviewed his game plan. He had a two-week reservation at the Radisson Plaza Hotel under the name James Burgess. If he hadn't found Farrell by then, he would move to another hotel. No use arousing curiosity by staying too long.

He had been supplied with some suggestions as to where he might find her. She regularly used a health club in New York. It made sense to assume she would do the same thing in Minneapolis. People didn't change their habits.

She was a theater buff. Well, the Orpheum would be one place to look. The Tyrone Guthrie Theater would be another.

Her only job had been in real estate. If she was working, the odds were she would be in a real estate agency.

Sandy Savarano had located and eliminated two other witnesses in the Witness Protection Program. As the plane began its descent, he was already beginning to anticipate the look he would see in Lacey Farrell's eyes when he shot her.

ROYCE REALTY WAS LOCATED in Edina, about fifteen minutes from downtown Minneapolis. Before leaving the apartment, Lacey studied the map, trying to determine the best way to drive there.

Following the map carefully, she got to the office having made only one wrong turn, parked her car, then stood for a moment in front of the entrance to Royce Realty, looking in through the wide glass door.

She could see that the agency office was small but attractive. The reception room had oak-paneled walls covered with pictures of houses, a red-and-blue-checked carpet, a standard desk, and comfortable-looking leather chairs. A short corridor led to an office where a woman was working at a desk.

Here goes nothing, Lacey thought. If I get through this, I'll be ready for my Broadway debut. As she opened the door, chimes signaled her arrival, and the woman came out to meet her.

"I'm Millicent Royce," she said as she extended her hand, "and you must be Alice Carroll."

Lacey liked her immediately. She was a handsome woman of about seventy whose ample girth was clothed in a well-tailored brown knit suit, and whose clear unlined complexion was devoid of makeup. Her shiny gray-white hair was swept back into a bun.

Her smile was welcoming as she waved Lacey to a chair, but as Lacey sat down, she could see that Millicent Royce's keen blue eyes were studying her intently. She was glad she had decided to wear the maroon jacket and gray slacks. They were conservative, no-nonsense, but with style.

Mrs. Royce sat down opposite her. "It's turning into a terribly busy day," she said apologetically, "so I don't have much time. Tell me about yourself, Alice."

Lacey felt as though she were in an interrogation room with a spotlight shining on her. Millicent Royce's eyes did not leave Lacey's face she answered. "Let's see. I just turned thirty. I'm from Hartford, Connecticut, and after finishing college, I worked for eight years for a doctor who retired."

"What makes you think you'd like real estate?"

Because I love matching people to places, Lacey thought. I love seeing a buyer's eyes light up when I take that person into a house or apartment and know that it's exactly what he or she wants. I love the wheeling and dealing that goes into settling on a price. I love the thrill of closing a sale.

She said, "I don't want to work in a doctor's office anymore, and I've always been intrigued by your business."

"Well, if your retired doctor vouches for you—as I'm sure he will—let's give it a try. Do you have his phone number?"

"No. He changed it and made it unlisted. He was adamant about not wanting to be contacted by his former patients."

Lacey could tell from the slight frown on Millicent Royce's face that she found her answer too evasive.

She remembered what George Svenson had told her: "Offer to work free for a couple of weeks or even a month."

"I have a suggestion," Lacey said. "Don't pay me anything for a month. After that, if you're happy with me, hire me." She met Millicent Royce's steady gaze without flinching. "You won't regret it," she said quietly.

Mrs. Royce shrugged. "That's an offer I can't refuse."

IT WAS Monday afternoon. Steve Abbott had insisted on accompanying Jimmy to a meeting with Detectives Sloane and Mars at the Nineteenth Precinct station house.

"I want to know what's going on!" Landi had said to Abbott that morning, the anger in his voice reflected in his face. "Something's up. The cops have to know where Lacey Farrell is. She can't have just disappeared. She's a witness to a murder!"

"Did you call them?" Steve had asked.

"You bet I did. I told them I was coming to see them and *I wanted answers.*"

"I'm going with you," Abbott had said.

At the station house, Detectives Sloane and Mars took them into the interrogation room. The detectives explained reluctantly that Lacey Farrell had been placed in the federal Witness Protection

Program after an attempt had been made on her life. They also admitted that Heather's journal appeared to be missing.

"You told me you thought Isabelle's death was just a matter of having been at the wrong place at the wrong time," Jimmy said, his anger exploding once again. "Now you're telling me that the Farrell woman is in the Witness Protection Program, *and* you're saying that Heather's journal was stolen from under your noses right here in this station. Don't play games with me. This was no random killing, and you've known it from day one."

Eddie Sloane saw the anger and disgust that flared in Jimmy Landi's eyes. I don't blame him, the detective thought. His ex-wife is dead; we lose something intended for him that may be crucial evidence; the woman who brought the killer into his ex-wife's apartment has disappeared. I know how *I'd* feel.

For both detectives it had been a lousy four months since that October evening when the 911 call from Three East Seventieth had been received. As the case developed, Sloane was grateful that the district attorney had gone toe to toe with U.S. Attorney Baldwin's office. The D.A. had been adamant that the NYPD was not signing off on this one.

"We'll share information with you," the D.A. had told Baldwin, "but you've got to share it with us. When Savarano is collared, we'll cooperate in a plea bargain if you can cut a deal with him. But we'll cooperate *only* if you don't try to upstage us. We intend to stay involved in this case."

"It wasn't a cock-and-bull story, Mr. Landi," Nick Mars said heatedly. "We want to find Mrs. Waring's killer as much as you do. But if Ms. Farrell hadn't taken that journal from Isabelle Waring's apartment, apparently with the idea of giving it to you, we might be a lot further along in this investigation."

"Be honest with us, Detective. You botched this investigation," Abbott snapped. "Come on, Jimmy. I think it's time we hire our own investigator. With the police in charge, I don't think we'll ever find out what's going on."

"That's what I should have done the minute I got the call about

Isabelle!" Jimmy Landi said, getting to his feet. "I want the copy of my daughter's journal I gave you before you lose that one too."

"We ran off extras," Sloane said calmly. "Nick, get the set Mr. Landi gave us."

While they waited, Sloane said, "Mr. Landi, you told us that you read the journal *carefully* before you gave it to us. Thinking back, would you say that's true?"

"What's carefully?" Jimmy asked rather irritably. "I looked through it."

"Look, Mr. Landi," Sloane said, "I can only imagine how difficult all this is for you, but I'm going to ask you to study that journal again. We've gone through it thoroughly, and except for a couple of ambiguous references about an incident that happened on the West Side, we can't find anything even *potentially* helpful. But the fact is that Mrs. Waring told Lacey Farrell that she'd found something in those pages that might help prove your daughter's death was not an accident—"

"Isabelle would have found something suspicious in the Baltimore catechism," Jimmy said, shaking his head.

They sat in silence until Nick Mars returned to the interrogation room with a manila envelope, which he held out to Landi.

Jimmy yanked it from him and pulled out the pages. He glanced through them, then stopped at the last one, read it, then glared at Mars. "What are you trying to pull now?" he asked.

Sloane had the sickening feeling that he was about to hear something he didn't want to know.

"The last couple of pages in the set I gave you weren't written on lined paper," Landi said. "I remember because they were all messed up. The originals of those pages must have had blood-stains. I couldn't stand the sight of them. So where are they? Did you lose those too?"

ARRIVING at the Minneapolis–St. Paul airport, Sandy Savarano went to the baggage area and picked up his suitcase. Then he found a men's room and locked himself in a stall. There he placed the suitcase across the toilet and took out a mirror, a gray wig, thick gray eyebrows, and round glasses with tortoiseshell frames.

He removed his contact lenses, revealing his brown eyes, then with deft movements placed the wig on his head, combed it so that it covered part of his forehead, pasted on the eyebrows, and put on the glasses. With a cosmetic pencil he added age spots to his forehead and the backs of his hands. Reaching into the sides of the suitcase, he took out orthopedic oxfords and exchanged them for the Gucci loafers he had been wearing.

Finally, he unpacked a bulky tweed overcoat with heavily padded shoulders, placing in the bag the Burberry he had worn getting off the plane. The man who left the stall looked twenty years older and totally different from the man who had entered it.

Sandy next went to the car-rental desk, where a car had been reserved for him in the name of James Burgess. He presented a driver's license—a clever fake—and a credit card. The card was legitimate, an account having been set up for him using the Burgess name.

Cold, bracing air greeted him as he exited the terminal and joined a group of people waiting at the curb for the jitney to take them to the car-rental area. While he waited, he studied the map the clerk had marked for him. He liked to plan everything carefully. No surprises—that was his motto. Which made the unexpected arrival of Lacey Farrell at Isabelle Waring's apartment all the more irritating. He'd been surprised and had let her get away.

The jitney approached and stopped. He was anxious to begin the task of finding Lacey Farrell. As long as she was alive, she remained a constant threat to his freedom.

WHEN Millicent Royce agreed to try her out on a volunteer basis, Lacey suggested that she spend the rest of the afternoon familiarizing herself with the files and going through the mail.

At three o'clock Mrs. Royce took a potential buyer to see a condominium and asked Lacey to cover the phone.

The first call was a near disaster. She answered, "Royce Realty,

Lace—" She slammed down the receiver and stared at the phone. She had been about to give her real name.

For the next hour the phone continued to ring, and Lacey carefully managed each call. She asked the usual real estate broker questions: Price range? How many bedrooms? Was school district a factor? Would purchase be contingent on sale of present home? She even put the answers in real estate shorthand: "min. 4BR/3b/fpl/cen air."

Later she realized that being back in her own milieu could be a trap. As a precaution she went through all the messages she had taken, rewording them to disguise her knowledge of the business.

When Mrs. Royce returned, she was pleased to get the messages Lacey had taken. It was nearly five o'clock. "I *will* see you in the morning, Alice?" There was a hopeful note in her voice.

"Absolutely," Lacey said. "But I have a lunch date I can't break."

WHEN she got home, the answering machine was blinking. Tom had phoned at four thirty. "Thought I might see you at the gym, Alice. I enjoyed Friday night. If you pick this up by seven and feel like having dinner tonight, give me a call. My number is—"

Lacey pushed the STOP button on the machine and erased the message without waiting to hear Tom's phone number. It was easier to do that than spend another evening lying to someone who in different circumstances she would have enjoyed dating.

AFTER checking into the Radisson Plaza Hotel, Sandy Savarano spent the rest of the day poring over the phone book and making a list of the health clubs and gyms in the metropolitan area.

He also made a list of all the real estate agencies in Minneapolis. His plan was simple. He'd say he was conducting a survey for the National Association of Realtors because there was growing evidence that adults in the twenty-five to thirty-five age group were not entering the real estate field. He would ask two questions: Had the agency hired anyone in that age group as agent, secretary, or receptionist in the last six months? If so, were they male or female?

He'd need another plan for checking out health clubs and gyms, since most people who joined them were in that age group.

He would have to actually go to them, pretend he was interested in joining, then flash Farrell's picture. It was an old photo, cut from her college yearbook, but it still looked like her. He would claim that she was his daughter and had left home after a family misunderstanding. He was trying to find her.

Suddenly Sandy began to experience the curious thrill that came to him whenever he began to stalk a victim and sensed that he was approaching the habitat of the hunted.

CHAPTER 6

N TUESDAY morning Lacey was waiting in front of Royce Realty when Millicent Royce arrived at nine o'clock.

"The pay isn't *that* good," Mrs. Royce said with a laugh. She unlocked and opened the door. The warmth of the interior greeted them. "A Minnesota chill in the air," Royce said. "First things first. I'll put coffee on. How do you like yours?"

"Black, please."

"Regina, my assistant who just left to have a baby, used two heaping teaspoonfuls of sugar and never gained an ounce. I told her it was serious cause for simple hatred."

Lacey thought of Janey Boyd, a secretary at Parker and Parker, who was always munching a cookie or a chocolate bar but remained a size six. "There was a girl like that at—" She stopped herself. "At the doctor's office," she finished. The first phone call of the day came right then and was a welcome interruption.

At twelve Lacey left for the luncheon date with Kate Knowles.

SHE ARRIVED AT THE RADISSON at twelve twenty-five to find Kate already at the table, munching on a roll. "This is breakfast and lunch for me," she told Lacey, "so I started. Hope you don't mind."

Lacey slid into the seat opposite her. "Not at all. How's the show going?"

"Great."

They both ordered omelettes, salads, and coffee. "I have to admit I'm getting curious," Kate said. "I was talking to Tom this morning and told him we were having lunch. He said he wished he could join us and sent his best to you." Kate reached for another roll. "Tom was telling me that you just decided to pick up and move here after visiting once as a kid. What makes a place stick in your mind like that?"

Answer a question with a question, Svenson had taught her.

"You're on the road a lot with shows," Lacey said. "Don't you remember some cities better than others?"

"Oh, sure. The good ones, like here, and the not-so-good ones. Let me tell you about the all-time not-so-good one. . . ."

Lacey found herself relaxing as Kate told her story, her timing perfect. So many show business people had the same talent; they could make a grocery list sound interesting.

Over a second cup of coffee Lacey said, "You talked the other night about someone you're dating. Bill something, wasn't it?"

"Bill Merrill. Could even be Mr. Right."

"What does he do?"

"He's an investment banker."

"Which bank is he with, Kate?"

"Chase."

Kate appeared to sense that she was being probed for information. I've got what I need to know, Lacey thought. Get back to letting Kate do the talking.

"I guess the best of all possible worlds for you is to get a Broadway hit that runs for ten years," Lacey suggested.

"Now you're talking," Kate said with a grin. "I'd love to be able to stay put in New York. Primarily because of Bill, of course, but there's no question that Tom's going to end up there in the next few years. That really would be the icing on the cake for me. We're both only children, so we've been more like siblings than cousins. He's always been there for me. Plus Tom's just naturally the kind of guy who seems to sense when people need help."

I wonder if that's why he asked me out last week and called me last night? Lacey thought. She signaled for a check. "I've got to run," she explained quickly. "First full day on the job."

AT A pay phone in the lobby she called and left a message for George Svenson. "I have new information concerning the Heather Landi case that I must give directly to Mr. Baldwin at the U.S. Attorney's office." When she hung up, she hurried through the lobby, aware she was already late getting back to the agency.

Less than a minute later a hand with brown age spots picked up the receiver that was still warm from her touch.

Sandy Savarano never made phone calls that could be traced. His pockets were filled with quarters. His plan was to make five calls here, then go to a different location and make five more until his list of local real estate offices was exhausted.

He dialed, and when someone answered, "Downtown Realty," he began his spiel. "I'm with the National Association of Realtors," he said. "We're conducting an informal survey. . . ."

U.S. ATTORNEY Gary Baldwin had been infuriated by Detective Sloane's phone call the previous afternoon informing him that several pages of Jimmy Landi's copy of his daughter's journal had vanished from the police station.

"How is it you managed to not lose the whole thing?" Baldwin had raged. "That's what happened to the original."

When Sloane phoned again twenty-four hours later, it gave Baldwin a second chance to air his grievances. "We're busting our chops going over the copy you gave us and find we don't have several pages that obviously were of some importance. Where'd you leave this evidence? On the bulletin board?"

Sloane too was incensed by the fact that the journal, as well as several pages from the copy, had disappeared from *his* locked evidence box in *his* cubby in the squad room.

He carried the keys to both on the key ring he kept in his jacket pocket. But he was always leaving the jacket draped on the back of his desk chair. Anybody could have taken the key ring, made duplicates, then returned the keys without his noticing.

After the original journal vanished, the locks had been changed. But he hadn't changed his habit of leaving his keys in his jacket.

Sloane focused once more on the phone conversation, grabbing the opportunity to get in a word. "Sir, I reported this yesterday because you should know about it. I'm calling now because, frankly, I'm not sure Jimmy Landi is a reliable witness in this instance. He admitted yesterday that he barely even scanned the journal when he had it. He's also threatening to bring in his own investigator. And his partner, Steve Abbott, came with him and was throwing his weight around on Jimmy's behalf."

"I don't blame Landi," Baldwin snapped. "And another investigator on this case could be a good idea, especially since you don't seem to be getting anywhere."

"You know that's not so. He'd just get in the way. But at this point it looks like it's not going to happen," Sloane said. "Abbott just called me. In a way, he apologized. He said that, thinking it over, it's possible that Landi was mistaken about the unlined pages he thinks are missing. He said the night Jimmy got the journal from Lacey Farrell, it was too tough on him to read it and he put it aside. The next night he got smashed before he looked at it. Then a day later we took his copy from him."

"It's possible he's mistaken about the missing pages, but we'll never know, will we?" Baldwin said, his voice cold. "And even if he *is* wrong, the original journal was taken while in your possession, which means someone in your precinct's working both sides of the street. I suggest you do some housecleaning there."

"As I remember it, sir, *we* were the ones who found and identified Savarano's fingerprint on the door to Farrell's apartment,"

Sloane shot back. "*Your* investigators certified that he was dead."

A click of the phone in the U.S. Attorney's office proved to Detective Ed Sloane that he had succeeded in getting to the thin-skinned Baldwin. But it was a hollow victory, and Sloane knew it.

FOR the rest of the afternoon Gary Baldwin's staff endured the fallout from his frustration over the bungled investigation. Then his mood changed when he received word that Lacey Farrell had new information for him.

She called him that night over a secure line that Svenson had set up in a Minneapolis hotel room.

"Mr. Baldwin," Lacey began, "I have some information that I think may be very important. I've learned that Rick Parker—of the Parker and Parker I used to work for—was in the same ski lodge as Heather Landi only hours before she died and that she seemed frightened when she saw him."

There was a long pause; then Baldwin asked, "How did you possibly come by that information in Minnesota, Ms. Farrell?"

Lacey realized suddenly that she had not thought this revelation through before making the call. She had never admitted to anyone that she had made herself a copy of Heather's journal before turning it over to Detective Sloane. She already had been threatened with prosecution for taking the original journal pages from Isabelle's apartment. She knew they'd never believe that she had made a secret copy of it only to honor her promise to Isabelle to read it.

"I asked you how you came by that information, Ms. Farrell."

Lacey spoke carefully. "I have made a few friends out here, Mr. Baldwin. One of them invited me to a cast party for the road company of *The King and I*. I chatted with Kate Knowles, an actress in the group, and—"

"And she just *happened* to say that Rick Parker was in a skiing lodge in Vermont just hours before Heather Landi died. Is *that* what you're telling me, Ms. Farrell?"

"Mr. Baldwin," Lacey said, her voice rising, "when I spoke to Kate Knowles, it came up that she had been in an off-Broadway revival of *The Boy Friend* two years ago. We talked about it. I saw that show, with Heather Landi in the lead."

"You never said you knew Heather," Baldwin interrupted.

"I didn't *know* her," Lacey protested. "I, like hundreds of other theatergoers, saw her perform in a musical. If I see Robert De Niro in a film tonight, should I tell you that I *know* him?"

"All right, Ms. Farrell, you've made your point," Baldwin said. "So the subject of *The Boy Friend* came up. Then what?"

Lacey reminded herself to stay calm. "Since Kate was in the cast, I figured she must have known Heather. So I got her to talk about Heather. She freely told me that Isabelle Waring had asked everyone in the cast if Heather had seemed upset in the days before she died, and if so, did they have any idea why."

Baldwin sounded somewhat mollified. "That was smart of you. What did she say?"

"She said that, yes, Heather *was* troubled. No, she never told anyone why. But then—and this is the reason for my call—Kate told me that she was thinking of writing Heather's mother with one thing she had remembered. Of course, Kate's been on the road and doesn't know that Isabelle is dead."

Once again Lacey spoke slowly and deliberately. "Kate Knowles has a boyfriend in New York. His name is Bill Merrill. He's an investment banker with Chase. He knows Rick Parker. Bill told Kate he had been chatting with Heather in the bar of the lodge in Stowe the afternoon before she died. When Rick came in, though, Heather broke off their conversation and left."

"He's sure this was the afternoon before Heather died?"

"That's what Kate said. Her understanding is that Heather was very upset when she spotted Rick. I asked Kate if she had any idea why, and she said that apparently Rick had pulled something on Heather when she moved to New York five years ago."

"Ms. Farrell, let me ask you something. You worked for Parker and Parker for eight years. With Rick Parker, right?"

"Yes. But Rick was in the West Side office until three years ago."

"I see. And through this whole thing with Isabelle Waring he never communicated to you that he might have known Heather Landi?"

"No, he did not. May I remind you, Mr. Baldwin, that I'm where I am because Rick Parker gave me the name of Curtis Caldwell. Rick is the only one in the office who spoke, or *supposedly* spoke, to that man who turned out to be Isabelle Waring's killer. Wouldn't it have been natural in the weeks I was showing that apartment, and telling Rick about Isabelle Waring and her obsession over her daughter's death, for him to have said he knew Heather? I certainly think so," she said emphatically.

"Let me get this straight," Baldwin said. "You say the man who saw Rick Parker in Stowe is a banker named Bill Merrill?"

"Yes."

"Was all this information just volunteered at this casual meeting with Ms. Knowles?"

Lacey's patience snapped. "Mr. Baldwin, in my effort to get this information for you, I manipulated a luncheon with a very nice actress whom I would enjoy having as a friend. I've lied to her as I have to every living soul I've met in Minneapolis other than George Svenson. It's in my best interests to pick up any information I can that might lead to my having the chance to become a normal human being again. If I were you, I'd be much more concerned with investigating Rick Parker's link to Heather Landi than acting as if I'm making things up."

"I wasn't suggesting anything of the sort, Ms. Farrell. We'll follow up on this information immediately. However, you must admit that not too many witnesses in the protection program manage to bump into the friend of a dead woman whose mother's murder was the cause of their being in the program."

"And not too many mothers get murdered because they're not convinced their daughter's death was an accident."

"We'll look into this, Ms. Farrell. And remember not to let your guard down. Watch what you say. If even *one* person knows where you are, we'll have to relocate you."

"Don't worry, Mr. Baldwin," Lacey said as with a sinking heart she thought again about telling her mother where she was.

TOM LYNCH WAS THINKING about Alice as he showered after working out at the Twin Cities Gym. For the second day in a row she had not shown up at the gym. Nor had she returned his call.

He stepped out of the shower and vigorously toweled himself dry. On the other hand, Kate had called him after her lunch with Alice and mentioned that Alice was starting a new job. Maybe that's why she hadn't gotten back to him, he decided. Or maybe there was another guy in the picture.

Knowing that Ruth Wilcox missed nothing, Tom stopped at her office on the way out. "No sign of Alice Carroll again today," he said, trying to sound casual.

He saw the spark of interest in Ruth's eyes. "As a matter of fact, I was just about to call her to see if something was wrong," she said. "She's been so faithful that I figure something must be up." Ruth smiled slyly. "Why don't I call her right now?"

After four rings Ruth said, "What a shame. She must be out, but the answering machine is on. I'll leave a message."

Her message was that she and a certain very attractive gentleman were wondering where Alice was keeping herself.

Well, at least that will smoke her out, Tom thought. If she's not interested in going out with me, I'd like to know it. I wonder if there is some kind of problem in her life.

When he left the gym, he decided to drive over to where Alice lived. With luck she would be there, and he would ask her if she wanted to go to a movie.

He parked at the curb outside her building and studied it, remembering that Alice lived on the fourth floor. But her windows were dark. I'll wait awhile, Tom decided.

Forty minutes passed. He was about to leave when a car pulled into the driveway. The passenger door opened, and he saw Alice get out and dart into the building. For a moment the car was illuminated by the overhead light. He caught a glimpse of the driver, an older man. Certainly an unlikely romantic partner.

After the car left, Tom walked over to the building. The intercom was in the foyer. He pushed 4F.

When Alice answered, she obviously thought it was the man who had just dropped her off. "Mr. Svenson?"

"No, Alice, it's Mr. Lynch," Tom said, his tone one of mock formality. "May I come up?"

WHEN Lacey opened the door, Tom could see that she looked drained, even stunned. Her skin was pale, almost alabaster white. The pupils of her eyes seemed enormous. "Obviously, something's terribly wrong," he said. "What is it, Alice?"

The sight of his tall, rangy figure filling the doorway, his concern, the realization that he had sought her out when she ignored his call, almost unhinged Lacey.

It was when he called her Alice that she managed to rein herself in, regain a modicum of control. In the twenty-minute ride from the secure phone back to the apartment she had exploded at George Svenson. "What is the *matter* with that Baldwin? I give him information that *has* to be useful in this case, and he treats me as if I'm a criminal! He just dismissed me, treated me like a child."

Svenson's response had been, "Take it easy, Alice. Calm down." And in fact, he had the kind of voice that could soothe a lioness, let alone Lacey. It came with the job, of course.

During the drive home a new fear had hit Lacey. Suppose Baldwin had someone on his staff talk to her mother to be sure Lacey hadn't told her where she was living. They would see through Mom in a minute, she thought. She'd never be able to fool them. If Baldwin thought Mom knew, he would relocate me, I know it. I can't go through the business of starting over again.

After all, here in Minneapolis she had a semblance of a job and the beginnings of something resembling a personal life.

"Alice, you haven't invited me in. You might as well. I have no intention of leaving."

Lacey attempted a smile. "Please come in, Tom. I was just about to pour myself a glass of wine. Will you join me?"

"I'd be glad to." Tom took off his coat and tossed it onto a chair. "How about I do the honors?" he asked. "Wine in the fridge?"

"No, as a matter of fact, it's in the wine cellar. That's just beyond my state-of-the-art kitchen."

The pullman kitchen in the tiny apartment consisted of a small stove and oven, a miniature sink, and a bar-size refrigerator.

Tom raised his eyebrows. "Shall I lay a fire in the great room?"

"That would be nice. I'll wait on the veranda." Lacey opened a cabinet and poured cashews into a bowl. Two minutes ago I was about to go to pieces, she thought. Here I am, actually joking with someone. Clearly Tom's presence had made the difference.

She sat in a corner of the couch; he settled in the overstuffed chair and stretched out his long legs. He lifted his glass to her in a toast. "Good to be with you, Alice." His expression became serious. "I have to ask you a question, and please be honest. Is there another man in your life?"

Yes, there is, Lacey thought, but not the way you're thinking. The man in my life is a killer who's stalking me. She looked at Tom for a long minute. I could love you, she thought. Maybe I've already started to. She remembered the bullets whistling past her head, the blood spurting from Bonnie's shoulder. No, I can't risk it, she thought. I can't expose Tom to danger.

"Yes, I'm afraid there *is* someone in my life," she told him, struggling to keep her voice steady.

He left ten minutes later.

RICK Parker had taken more than a dozen prospects to look at the Waring apartment, but no one had actually made an offer. Now he had a potential buyer, Shirley Forbes, a fiftyish divorcée. She had seen the place three times, and he had arranged to meet her there again at ten thirty.

This morning, as he had walked in the door of the office, his phone was ringing. It was Detective Sloane. "Rick, we haven't talked in a couple of weeks," Sloane said. "I think you'd better come in today. I want to see if your memory has improved."

"I have nothing to remember," Rick snapped.

"Oh yes you do. Twelve o'clock. Be here."

Rick jumped as Sloane abruptly broke off their connection. He sat heavily in his chair and began rubbing his forehead. The savage pounding inside his head made him feel as though his skull were about to explode. I'm drinking too much, he told himself.

He had made the rounds of his favorite bars last night and vaguely remembered that he had ended up at Landi's for a nightcap. Did I do something stupid while I was there? he wondered. Did I say anything to Jimmy about Heather?

The last thing he needed now was to go back into Heather's apartment just before he had to go talk to Sloane, but there was no way he could postpone the appointment with Shirley Forbes. All his father would need to hear was that he had let a potential sale of that apartment slip through his fingers.

"Rick." R. J. Parker, Sr., was standing over his desk, scowling at him. "I talked to Jimmy Landi. He wants that apartment sold. I said you had someone who's definitely interested. He said he'd take a hundred thousand less than he's been asking."

"I'm on my way to meet Mrs. Forbes now, Dad," Rick said.

"Rick," his father said, "I don't think I have to tell you that the sooner that place is off our hands, the less chance Jimmy has of finding out—"

"I *know*." Rick pushed his desk chair back. "I've got to go."

"It's exactly what I want, but I know I'd never spend a comfortable moment here. I'd keep thinking of that poor woman."

Shirley Forbes announced her decision as she and Rick stood in the bedroom where Isabelle Waring had died. The apartment had been left with everything still in place. Forbes looked around the room. Her eyes unnaturally wide behind oversized glasses, she pointed to the bed. "I've read all about it. Mrs. Waring was resting right here in the bedroom, and someone came in and shot her. The real estate agent came in just in time to hear her beg for her life. Just think, that agent could have been killed too. That would have been two murders in this apartment."

Rick turned abruptly. "Okay, you've made your point. Let's go."

The woman followed him through the sitting room and down the stairs. "I'm afraid I've upset you, Mr. Parker. I'm so sorry. Did you know either Heather Landi or Mrs. Waring?"

Rick wanted to rip off those idiotic glasses and grind them under his feet. He wanted to push this stupid woman down the stairs. He had other listings to offer her, but to hell with them, he decided.

She saved him the trouble of telling her to get out by saying, "I really must rush now. I'll call you in a few days to see if anything else has come up."

She was gone. Rick went into the powder room, opened the door of the linen closet, and extracted a bottle from its hiding place. He carried the bottle into the kitchen, got out a glass, and filled it with vodka. Taking a deep sip, he sat on a stool at the counter.

His attention became riveted on a small lamp at the end of the counter. The base was a teapot. He remembered it all too well.

"It's my Aladdin's lamp," Heather had said that day she spotted it in a secondhand store on West Eightieth. "I'll rub it for luck." Holding it up, she had closed her eyes and chanted in a somber voice, "Powerful genie, let me get the part I auditioned for." Then in a worried voice she had added, "And don't let Daddy be too mad when I tell him I bought a co-op without his permission."

She had turned to Rick and said, "It's my money to use as I want, but I know my father wanted to have a say in where I live. He's worried enough about my deciding to be on my own."

Then she had smiled—she had a wonderful smile, he remembered. "Maybe finding this lamp is a sign that everything will be fine."

The next week Heather had begged Rick to cancel the co-op sale. "I told my mother that I'd seen a place I loved. She was so upset. She told me that as a surprise my father had already bought an apartment for me on East Seventieth at Fifth Avenue. I can't let him know that I've bought another one without his permission. Rick, please," she pleaded, "your family *owns* the agency. Help me."

Rick looked at the lamp, now sitting on the counter. Reaching for it, he yanked out the cord as he picked it up and threw it with all the force he could muster.

The genie in the lamp had gotten Heather the part in the show. After that he hadn't helped her very much.

UNDERCOVER detective Betty Ponds, the woman Rick Parker knew as Shirley Forbes, reported to Detective Sloane, "Parker's so jumpy he's twitching. Before long he'll crack."

"He has a lot to be worried about," Sloane told her. "The feds are talking right now to a guy who can place Parker in Stowe the afternoon before Heather Landi died."

"What time do you expect Parker?" Ponds asked.

"Noon."

"It's almost that now. I'm out of here. I don't want him to see me." With a wave she left the squad room.

Noon came and went. At one o'clock Sloane phoned Parker and Parker. He was told that Rick had not returned to the office since leaving for a ten-thirty appointment. By the next morning it was clear that Rick Parker had disappeared.

LACEY knew she could not continue to go to the Twin Cities Gym. Even though she had told Tom Lynch there was someone else in her life, she was sure that if they saw each other day after day, they would end up going out together, and there was just no way she could tolerate the web of lies she would have to spin.

There was no question she liked him and no question that she would like to get to know him. She could imagine sitting across a table from him and over a plate of pasta and a glass of red wine telling him about her mother and father, about Kit and Jay and the children. What she could *not* imagine was inventing stories about a mother who supposedly lived in England, about the school she never attended, about her nonexistent boyfriend.

Given her distressed state, the job with Millicent Royce was a life-saver. At Millicent's invitation, Lacey had been out with her on several sales calls, either to show houses to a prospective client or to obtain new listings.

"It will be more interesting for you if you get to know the area well," Mrs. Royce told her. "Did you ever hear it said that real estate is all about location?"

Location, location, location. In Manhattan a park or river view dramatically increased the price of an apartment. Lacey found herself longing to swap stories with Millicent about some of the eccentric clients she had dealt with over the years.

The evenings were the hardest times for Lacey. They stretched long and empty in front of her. On Thursday night she made herself go to a movie. The theater was half empty, with rows of unoccupied seats, but just before the film began, a man came down the aisle, went past her row, turned, looked around, and chose the seat directly behind her. In the semidarkness she could tell only that he was of medium height and slender. Her heart began to race.

As the credits rolled, she could hear the seat behind her creaking as he settled in; she could smell the popcorn he was carrying. Then suddenly she felt his hand tap her shoulder. Almost paralyzed with fright, she turned her head. He was holding a glove.

"This yours, ma'am?" he asked. "It was under your chair."

Lacey did not stay to see the film.

ON FRIDAY morning Millicent asked Lacey what she would be doing over the weekend.

"Mostly hunting for a gym," Lacey said. "The one I joined is fine, but it doesn't have a squash court, and I really miss that."

"I've heard the new health club in Edina has a great squash court," Millicent told her. "And because they're new, there's a discount for joining right now."

When Millicent left later for an appointment, Lacey called George Svenson. She had two requests for him: She wanted to speak to U.S. Attorney Gary Baldwin again. "I deserve to know what's happening," she said. Then she added, "People are getting too curious at the Twin Cities Gym. I'm afraid I've got to ask you to advance the registration fee for a different one."

Svenson did not hesitate. "I can okay that. The change will do you good."

OTTIE Hoffman read the New York papers every morning over her solitary breakfast. For forty-five years, until a little over a year ago, she and Max had shared them. It was still unreal to Lottie that on that day in early December, Max had gone out for his usual early morning walk and never returned.

An item on page 3 of the *Daily News* caught her eye. Richard J. Parker, Jr., wanted for questioning in the murder of Isabelle Waring, had disappeared. What had happened to him? Lottie wondered nervously.

She went to the desk in the living room. From the middle drawer she took out the letter Isabelle Waring had written Max the very day before she had been murdered.

Dear Max,

I tried to phone you today, but your number is unlisted, which is why I am writing. I am sure that you must have heard that Heather died in an accident last December. Her death was a tremendous loss to me, of course, but the circumstances of her death have been especially troublesome.

In clearing out her apartment I have come across her journal. In it, only five days before her death, she refers to her intention of meeting you for lunch. She does not mention you after that, but entries in the journal indicate she was clearly distraught.

Max, you worked at Jimmy's restaurant for the first fifteen years of Heather's life. You were the best captain he ever had. Remember how you used to do magic tricks to entertain

Heather? She loved and trusted you, and it is my hope that she may have confided in you when you saw her.

In any event, will you please phone me? I'm staying in Heather's apartment. The number is 555-2437.

Lottie returned the letter to the drawer and went back to the table. She picked up her coffee cup, then realized that her hand was trembling. I called Isabelle Waring, she remembered nervously. She was so shocked when I told her that Max had been killed by a hit-and-run driver only two days before Heather's death. At that time I still thought his death was an accident.

She remembered that Isabelle had asked if she had any idea what Max and Heather might have talked about.

Max had always said that in the restaurant business you heard a lot but you learned to keep your mouth shut. Lottie shook her head. Well, he must have broken that rule when he talked to Heather, she decided, and now I know it cost him his life.

I tried to help Isabelle, Lottie thought. I told her what I knew. I told her that I'd never met Heather, although I had gone with my senior citizen group to see *The Boy Friend* when she was in it. Then soon after that, on a day outing with the same group to Mohonk Mountain House, the resort in the Catskill Mountains, Lottie had seen Heather a second—and last—time. I took a walk along the trails, she remembered, and I saw a couple with their arms around each other. I recognized Heather but not the guy. That night she had told Max about it.

He asked about Heather's boyfriend, she remembered. When I described him, Max knew who I was talking about and became terribly upset. He said that what he knew about that man would curl my hair. He said the man was a racketeer and a drug dealer.

Max didn't tell me the man's name, Lottie thought, and before I could describe him to Isabelle Waring when I called that night, Isabelle had said, "I hear someone downstairs. It must be the real estate agent. Give me your number. I'll call you back."

I waited for Isabelle's call all evening, Lottie remembered, and then I heard the eleven-o'clock news. It was only then that the full impact of what must have happened had hit her. Whoever had come in while she and Isabelle were on the phone must have been Isabelle's murderer. And now Lottie was convinced that Max was dead because he had warned Heather away from the man she was seeing.

And if I saw that man, I could identify him, Lottie thought, but thank the Lord no one knows that. Suppose the police should ever come to me, she wondered suddenly. What would Max want me to do? She knew he would never have put her in danger.

The answer was very calming, and it came to her as clearly as if he were sitting across the table. "Do absolutely nothing, Lottie," Max cautioned. "Keep your mouth shut."

SANDY Savarano's search was taking more time than he had expected. In the mornings he checked out real estate agencies, giving the most attention to small businesses, usually storefront offices, where he could walk past and see what was going on inside. To the more prosperous-looking setups he gave scant attention. They wouldn't be likely to take on someone without a thorough background check. Afternoons he spent covering health clubs and gyms.

Sandy had no doubt that eventually he would find Lacey Farrell. A person didn't change her habits just because she changed her name. He'd tracked down quarry in the past with a lot less to go on.

LATE Friday morning Sandy drove to Edina to check out Royce Realty. The woman he had spoken to on the phone had answered his initial questions freely enough. Yes, she had a young woman working for her, age twenty-six, who was planning to take her Realtor certification test but had left to have a baby.

Sandy had asked if that young woman had been replaced.

It was the pause that interested him. It indicated neither denial nor confirmation. "I have a candidate in mind," was what Mrs. Royce finally told him. And yes, she was in the right age category.

When Sandy reached Edina, he parked his car in the supermarket lot across the street from the Royce office. He got out, crossed the street, and sauntered past the agency, stopping as if to examine the contents of a flyer displayed in the window.

He could see there was a desk in the reception area. Neatly stacked papers suggested that it was usually occupied. He could see beyond to where a largish woman with gray hair was sitting at a desk in a private office. Sandy decided to go in.

MILLICENT Royce looked up as the door chimes signaled the arrival of a conservatively dressed gray-haired man in what she judged to be his late fifties. She went to greet him.

He said he was Paul Gilbert, visiting the Twin Cities on business for 3M. "That's Minnesota Mining and Manufacturing," he explained. "My daughter's husband is being transferred here, and my daughter was told that Edina is a lovely place to live. She's pregnant, so I thought that while I'm here, I could do a little house hunting for her."

"Aren't you the good father!" Millicent said. "Now let me just ask you a few questions so I can get some idea of what your daughter is hoping to find."

Sandy gave answers about his supposed daughter's needs, which included "a nearby kindergarten for her four-year-old, a backyard, and a large kitchen—she loves to cook." He left half an hour later with Mrs. Royce's promise to find just the right house.

Sandy went back and sat in the car, his eyes fixed on the entrance to the agency. If someone was using the reception desk, she was probably at lunch, he figured, and would return soon.

Ten minutes later a young blond woman in her twenties went into the agency. Customer or receptionist? Sandy wondered. He got out of the car and again crossed the street, taking care to stay out of view of anyone inside the office. For several minutes he stood in front of the delicatessen next door, reading the lunch specials. From the corner of his eye he could see into the Royce agency.

The young blond woman was sitting at the reception desk, talking animatedly to Mrs. Royce. Unfortunately for Sandy, he could not read lips or he would have heard Regina saying, "Millicent, you have no idea how much easier it was to sit behind this desk than to take care of a colicky baby!"

Sandy walked quickly back to his car and drove away. Since there were other possibilities to track down in the area, he decided to continue making the rounds of suburban agencies, but he wanted to be back downtown by late afternoon to look into the health clubs.

The next club on his list was the Twin Cities Gym.

MONA Farrell had carried the phone to the window so she could see the car pull up. "I've got to go, Lacey," she said. "Jay and Kit are here to pick me up. We're going to dinner in New York."

Lacey and her mother had been talking for nearly forty minutes, but Lacey was especially reluctant to break the connection tonight. It had been such a long day, and the weekend stretched endlessly before her.

Last Friday at this time she had been looking forward to her date with Tom Lynch. There was nothing for her to look forward to now.

When she had asked about Bonnie, she could tell from her mother's overly cheerful reassurances that Bonnie was still not doing well. Even less reassuring had been the news that her mother, Kit, and Jay were about to drive into the city to have dinner with Jimmy Landi at Alex Carbine's restaurant. Landi had found out from the private detective he had hired that Jay was Lacey's brother-in-law and that Alex was dating Lacey's mother.

As she said good-bye, Lacey cautioned, "Mom, be careful not to tell anyone where I am."

"Lacey, don't worry. No one will learn anything from me. Now I really do have to go. What have you got on for tonight?"

"I'm signed up at a new gym. It has a great squash court."

"Oh, I know how much you love to play squash." Mona Farrell was genuinely pleased. "Love and miss you, dear. Good-bye."

She hurried down to the car, thinking that at least she could tell Kit and Jay and Alex what Lacey was doing for recreation.

ON FRIDAY EVENING TOM Lynch was planning to have an after-theater drink with his cousin, Kate. Her show was completing its Minneapolis engagement, and he wanted to say good-bye to her. He was also hoping she'd pick up his spirits; ever since Alice Carroll had told him that there was another man in her life, he had been depressed.

He had decided to come over to the gym and work out. He wasn't meeting Kate until eleven o'clock, and there was absolutely nothing else he could think of to do with his time.

He admitted to himself that he actually was harboring the secret hope that Alice might come into the gym. However, when he emerged from the men's locker room and looked around, it was clear that she wasn't there.

Through the glass that surrounded the manager's office, Tom could see Ruth Wilcox in conversation with a gray-haired man. When the man left, Tom went in to ask Ruth if she had heard anything from Alice.

"Have I got news, Tom!" Ruth confided. "Close the door."

Somehow Tom knew that the news had to do with Alice Carroll and the gray-haired man who had just left.

"That guy is looking for Alice," Ruth told him, her voice snapping with excitement. "He's her father."

"That's crazy! Alice told me her father died years ago."

"Maybe that's what she told you, but that man says he's her father. He even showed me her picture and asked if I'd seen her."

Tom's instincts as a newsman were aroused. "What did you tell him?" he asked cautiously.

"I didn't say anything. How do I know he wasn't a bill collector? I said that I couldn't be sure. Then he told me that his daughter and his wife had had a terrible misunderstanding and that he knew his daughter had moved to Minneapolis four months ago. His wife is very sick and desperate to make amends before she dies. He said that he'd appreciate it if I didn't tell Alice he was looking for her. He doesn't want her to disappear again. I felt sorry for him. He had tears in his eyes."

If there's one thing I know about Alice Carroll, Tom thought, it is that no matter how big a misunderstanding she's not the kind who would turn her back on a terminally ill mother.

Then another possibility occurred to him, one that he found enticing. If she wasn't telling the truth about her background, maybe the man she claimed to be involved with doesn't exist, he thought. He felt better already.

DETECTIVE Ed Sloane worked the eight-to-four day shift, but at five thirty on Friday evening he was still in his office at the Nineteenth Precinct with Rick Parker's file spread out on his desk.

He was glad it was Friday. Over the weekend at least he might get some peace from the feds. It had been a grueling couple of days. Since Tuesday, when Rick Parker had not shown up for his appointment, the rocky relationship between the NYPD and the U.S. Attorney's office had become openly hostile.

It drove Sloane nuts that it was only when two federal agents showed up looking for Parker that Gary Baldwin finally admitted they had a witness who could place Rick at a ski lodge in Stowe the afternoon before Heather Landi died.

Baldwin didn't share that information, Sloane thought, but when he learned that I was putting heavy pressure on Parker, he had the nerve to complain to the district attorney.

Fortunately the D.A. stood by me, Sloane thought grimly. The D.A. had reminded Baldwin that the NYPD had an unsolved homicide that had occurred in the Nineteenth Precinct, and it was their intention to solve it. He also made it clear the NYPD was running the case, not the feds.

The fact that the D.A. had gone to bat for him had given Sloane a driving need to be the one who eventually pulled Rick Parker in. Unless Rick was already dead, of course, Sloane reminded himself, which was a distinct possibility.

In the four months since Isabelle Waring's murder, Sloane had put together an extensive curriculum vitae on Rick Parker. Now, once again, he read through the thick file.

Richard J. Parker Jr. Only child. Thirty-one years old. Kicked out of two prestigious prep schools for possession of drugs. Suspicion, but no proof, of selling drugs—witness probably paid off to recant. Took six years to finally finish college. Father paid for damages to fraternity house during wild party.

Always plenty of spending money through school years, Mercedes convertible as a 17th birthday present, Central Park West apartment as college graduation gift.

First and only job at Parker and Parker. Five years in the West 67th Street branch office, three years to present in East 62nd Street main office.

It hadn't been hard for Sloane to learn that Rick's co-workers on the West Side had despised him. One former employee of Parker and Parker told Sloane, "Rick would be out partying all night, show up with a hangover or still high on coke, and then start throwing his weight around in the office."

Five years ago Rick's father had elected to settle a sexual assault complaint brought against Rick by a young secretary rather than have a public scandal. Following that episode, Parker had frozen the income from Rick's trust fund and put him on the same base salary plus sales commission as his fellow employees.

Papa must have taken a course on tough love, Sloane thought with a touch of sarcasm. However, tough love doesn't support a cocaine habit. So where's Rick been getting his drug money, and if he's still alive, who's paying for him to hide out?

Sloane pulled another cigarette from the ever-present pack in his shirt pocket. The file revealed one consistent pattern. Parker senior always came through when his son was in real trouble. Like now.

Ed Sloane grunted and got up. He was going to drive up to Greenwich, Connecticut, and have a chat with R. J. Parker, Sr.

As usual after speaking with Lacey, Mona Farrell had been on the verge of tears. When she got into Kit and Jay's car for the drive to the city, Kit asked, "How's it going, Mom?"

Mona attempted a smile. "I'm all right, dear."

"Did you tell Lacey we were meeting Jimmy Landi?" Jay asked.

"Yes."

"What did she say?"

"She said—" Mona Farrell stopped herself before she blurted out that Lacey had cautioned her not to tell where she was living. Kit and Jay did not know that Lacey had confided that information to her. "She said that she was surprised," Mona finished lamely, feeling uncomfortable.

"SO ALEX has made you a captain, Carlos?" Jimmy Landi greeted his former employee as he sat down at the table in Alex's Place.

"Yes, he did, Mr. Landi," Carlos said with a big smile.

"If you'd waited awhile, Jimmy would have promoted you," Steve Abbott said.

"Or maybe I wouldn't," Jimmy said shortly.

"In any case, it's a moot point," Alex Carbine told him. "Jimmy, this is your first time here. Tell me what you think of the place."

Jimmy Landi looked around him, studying the attractive dining room with its dark green walls brightened by colorful paintings in ornate gold frames.

"Looks like you got your inspiration from the Russian Tea Room, Alex," he commented.

"I did," Alex Carbine agreed pleasantly. "Now, Jimmy, what are you having to drink? I want you to try my wine."

JIMMY Landi isn't the kind of man I had anticipated, Kit thought as she sipped a glass of chardonnay. Despite his apparent good humor, however, she sensed that Landi was extremely tense. There was a drawn look to his face and an unhealthy pallor. Perhaps it's grief over his daughter's death, she decided.

Kit instinctively liked Jimmy's partner, Steve Abbott. Alex had told them that he had become something of a surrogate son to Jimmy and that they were very close. Not in appearance, though, Kit decided. Abbott is *really* good-looking.

As dinner progressed, Kit could see that Steve and Alex were deliberately keeping the conversation away from any mention of either Lacey or Isabelle Waring. Between them they got Landi to tell some amusing stories about encounters with some of his celebrity clients. He was a first-class raconteur, a trait that Kit decided combined with his earthy, peasant appearance to make him oddly attractive. He also seemed genuinely warm and interested in them.

On the other hand, when he noticed a waiter's impatience with a woman who was hemming and hawing over her entrée selection, his face darkened. "Fire him, Alex," he said sharply. "He's no good."

Wow, Kit thought. He *is* tough!

Finally Jimmy began to discuss Lacey and Isabelle Waring. As soon as coffee was served, he said abruptly, "Mrs. Farrell, I met your daughter once. She was trying to keep her promise to my ex-wife by delivering my daughter's journal to me."

"I know that," Mona said quietly.

"I wasn't very nice to her. She'd brought me a copy of the journal instead of the original, and at the time I thought she had some nerve to give the original to the cops."

"Mr. Landi, my daughter has been threatened with prosecution for withholding evidence, because she tried to fulfill Isabelle Waring's dying wish," Mona retorted.

"I learned about this only two days ago," Landi said brusquely. "I hired a private detective when I saw that I'd been given the runaround by the cops. He's the one who found out that the story they'd given me about a professional thief unintentionally killing Isabelle was so much hogwash."

Kit watched as Landi's complexion darkened to beet red.

Steve Abbott had noticed too. "Calm down, Jimmy," he urged. "You'll make a lousy patient if you have a stroke."

Jimmy shot a wry glance at him, then looked back at Mona. "I know your daughter's in that witness protection plan," he said. "Pretty lousy for her and for all of you."

"Yes, it is," Mona said, nodding in agreement.

"How do you stay in touch with her?"

"She calls once a week," Mona said. "In fact, I was talking to her just before Jay and Kit picked me up."

"You can't call her?" Jimmy asked.

"Absolutely not. I wouldn't know where to reach her."

"*I* want to talk to her," Jimmy said. "Tell her that. The detective I hired tells me your daughter spent a lot of time with Isabelle in the days before she died. I have a lot of questions I want to ask her."

"Mr. Landi, that request would have to be made through the U.S. Attorney's office," Jay said.

"They'll probably turn me down," Jimmy growled. "But maybe there's another way. You ask her this question for me. Ask her if she remembers if there were a couple of unlined pages with writing on them at the end of Heather's journal."

"Why is that important, Jimmy?" Alex Carbine asked.

"Because if there *were,* it means that none of the evidence delivered to that precinct is safe. It's going to be doctored or disappear."

Jimmy waved away Carlos, who was standing behind him with the coffee carafe. Then he stood and extended his hand to Mona. "Well, that's it, I guess. I'm sorry for you, Mrs. Farrell. I'm sorry for your daughter. From what I hear she was very nice to Isabelle, and she tried to be helpful to me. I owe her an apology. How is she doing?"

"Lacey is a trouper," Mona said. "She never complains. In fact, she's always trying to cheer me up." Mona turned to Kit and Jay. "I forgot to tell you two in the car that Lacey just joined a new health club with a fabulous squash court." She turned back to Landi. "She's always been a demon for exercise."

AFTER completing her call to her mother and hanging up, Lacey met George Svenson in the lobby of the motel where she'd made the call and walked wordlessly with him to the car.

She thought briefly about what she would do for the rest of the evening. She simply could not spend it alone in the empty apartment. Ever since she'd told her mother where she was, she admitted to herself ruefully, she'd felt afraid.

The warnings Lacey had received in the safe site echoed in her head. It's not that your family would knowingly give you away, she was told. It's remarks they might unconsciously make that could jeopardize your safety.

She remembered how her dad had always joked that if Mom ever wrote her memoirs, they ought to title the book *In Deepest Confidence,* because Mom never could keep a secret.

Then she thought of how shocked her mother had sounded when Lacey warned her not to drop anything to Jimmy Landi about where she was living. Maybe it will be okay, Lacey thought, praying that her mother had taken the warning seriously.

Svenson was silent the entire drive home, leaving Lacey to her thoughts. Finally she asked him if he had heard anything more from Gary Baldwin.

"No, I haven't, Alice," he replied.

"Then kindly pass the word to the Great One that I want to know what is going on. I gave him some important information Tuesday night. As a simple courtesy, he could keep me informed of developments. I don't think I can live like this much longer."

Lacey bit her lip and slumped back in the seat. As always when she vented her anger on Svenson, she felt embarrassed.

"I had money put in your account, Alice. You can join the new health club tomorrow morning."

It was Svenson's way of telling her he understood how she felt.

"Thanks," she murmured, then realized she wanted to shout, "Please, just once, call me Lacey! My name is Lacey Farrell!"

TOM Lynch had left her a message. "Alice, it's imperative that I see you tomorrow. Please call me back." He left his number.

If only I could call him, Lacey thought.

Ruth Wilcox had phoned as well. "Alice, we miss you. Please come in over the weekend. I want to talk to you about a gentleman who was inquiring about you."

Ruth, still playing the matchmaker, Lacey thought wryly.

She went to bed and managed to fall asleep, but then drifted promptly into a nightmare. In it she was kneeling beside Isabelle's body. A hand touched her shoulder. She looked up and saw Isabelle's murderer, his pale blue eyes staring down at her, the pistol he was holding pointed at her head.

She bolted up in bed, trying to scream. After that it was no use. There was no more sleep for the rest of the night.

Early in the morning Lacey made herself go out for a jog but found she could not resist casting frequent glances over her shoulder to make certain she was not being followed.

I'm turning into a basket case, she acknowledged when she got back to the apartment and bolted the door. It was only nine o'clock in the morning, and she had absolutely no plans for the rest of the day. *I'll have some breakfast, then try the new club*, she decided. *It will be something to do.*

Lacey got to the Edina Health Club at ten fifteen and was waved to a seat in the business office. She fished in her tote bag for her completed registration forms as the manager wound up a phone call by saying, "Yes, sir. We're a new facility and have a wonderful squash court. Do come right over and take a look."

CHAPTER 8

N SATURDAY morning Ed Sloane drove from his home in the Bronx to the meeting he had insisted on having with Richard J. Parker, Sr., in Greenwich, Connecticut. It haunted Sloane that evidence that might have been crucial to solving the murder of Isabelle Waring had been lost, stolen by some unknown perpetrator—most likely a bad cop—from his own cubby.

As he turned off the Merritt Parkway at exit 31, Sloane thought about the sting he had set in motion in the squad room, aimed at catching whoever had been taking things out of the evidence box. With the captain's help he had concocted the story that a piece of evidence locked in his cubby might be the key to solving Isabelle Waring's murder. His entry describing the supposed evidence in the precinct's evidence log was deliberately ambiguous.

A hidden ceiling camera was now trained on Sloane's desk. He had begun to make a production out of taking his keys out of his suit jacket and locking them in his desk, but next week he would start reverting to his old habit of leaving his keys in his jacket. He had a feeling that with the kind of fake information he was passing around, there was a good chance he would smoke out the thief. Surely whoever killed Isabelle Waring had to be behind the thefts from the squad room and would be seriously worried about potential new evidence. Sloane found it hard to believe, though, that someone like Sandy Savarano would be behind the thefts himself. He was just a triggerman. No, Sloane thought, chances were that somebody with clout and lots of money was calling the shots.

THE Parker estate was situated on Long Island Sound. The handsome red brick mansion was turreted at either end and old enough to have acquired a mellow patina, set off by the patches of snow still covering the extensive grounds.

Sloane drove through the open gates and parked to the side of the semicircle at the main entrance.

An attractive young woman in a maid's uniform told him he was expected. "Mr. Parker is in his study," she said.

Parker was sitting on a leather couch, sipping coffee. He neither got up to greet Sloane nor did he offer him coffee. "Sit down, Detective," he said. It was not so much an invitation as an order.

"Mr. Parker," Sloane said, "I think you should know from the outset that I'm not one of your lackeys. This is not some real estate transaction, some big deal that you're running. I am here to talk to you about your son, who is well on the way to being considered a suspect in not one, but *two* murder cases."

Sloane leaned forward and tapped the coffee table for emphasis. "You are certainly aware that your son was the one who cleared the way for the killer to get into Isabelle Waring's apartment. That alone makes him an accessory before the fact. A bench warrant on that charge is about to be issued for his arrest.

"But here's another piece of information you should know. Rick was in Stowe the afternoon before Heather Landi died, and we have an eyewitness who can testify that she appeared frightened of him and ran out of the lodge when he showed up." Sloane stopped and looked at the man sitting tensely before him.

Red patches mottled Parker's face, revealing his agitation, but his voice was icy calm when he said, "Is that all, Detective?"

"Not quite. Your son is a drug addict. You've apparently stopped paying his bills, but he's still getting the drugs somehow. Chances are that means he owes someone a lot of money. That could be a very dangerous situation. My advice to you is to hire a criminal lawyer for him and tell him to surrender to us. Otherwise you might face charges yourself."

"I don't know where he is." Parker spat out the words.

Sloane stood up. "I think you do. I warn you. He's potentially in great danger. He wouldn't be the first person who got in over his head and paid the price by disappearing. Permanently."

"My son is in a drug rehabilitation clinic in Hartford," Priscilla Parker said. "I drove him there last Wednesday."

Detective Sloane turned, startled by the unexpected voice.

Mrs. Parker had suddenly materialized in the doorway. "My husband is being honest when he says he doesn't know where Rick is," she said. "Rick came to me for help. His father was otherwise occupied that day." She looked at her husband, contempt and loathing written clearly on her face.

AFTER she had given the manager at the Edina Health Club the completed registration forms and her check, Lacey went directly to the squash court and began hitting balls against the wall. She quickly realized that the combination of the previous sleepless night and her earlier jog had left her exhausted. She kept missing easy returns, and then she fell, badly wrenching her ankle.

Disgusted with herself and close to tears, she limped off the court and collected her coat and tote bag from the locker.

The door to the office was partially open. Inside, a gray-haired man was waiting to speak to the manager.

Lacey could feel her ankle swelling already. For a moment she paused in front of the open door, debating whether to ask the manager if the club kept elastic bandages in its medical supply kit. Then she decided to go home and put ice on her ankle instead.

Earlier that morning a smattering of clouds had dotted the sky, but driving from Edina to Minneapolis, Lacey could tell that a heavy snowfall was imminent.

She had a designated parking spot behind her apartment building. She pulled into the space, turned off the engine, and sat for a moment. Her life was a mess. Here she was, hundreds of miles away from her family, trapped in a lie, having to pretend to be someone other than herself—and why? Why? Just because she had been a witness to a crime.

She got out of the car, favoring her throbbing ankle. As she turned to lock the door, she felt a hand on her shoulder.

Life seemed to be moving in slow motion as she tried to scream, but no sound would come. She lunged forward, trying to break away, then gasped and stumbled as a flash of pain like the sting of a hot branding iron seared her ankle.

An arm went around her, steadying her. A familiar voice said contritely, "Alice, I'm sorry. I didn't mean to frighten you."

It was Tom Lynch.

Limp with relief, Lacey sagged against him. "Oh, Tom. Oh, I— I'm all right. I just— I guess you startled me."

She started to cry. It was so good to feel herself firmly encircled and protected by his arm. She stood there for several moments, not moving, a sense of relief washing over her. Then she straightened and turned to face him. She couldn't do this—not to him, not to herself. "I'm sorry you bothered to come, Tom. I'm going upstairs," she said, making herself breathe normally, wiping away the tears.

"I'm coming with you," he told her. "We have to talk."

"We have nothing to talk about."

"Oh, but we do," he said. "Starting with the fact that your father is looking all over Minneapolis for you because your mother is dying and wants to make up with you."

"What . . . are . . . you . . . talking . . . about?" Lacey's lips felt rubbery. Her throat constricted to the point where she could barely force the words out of her mouth.

"I'm talking about the fact that yesterday some guy showed up at the gym with your picture, claiming to be your father."

He's in Minneapolis! Lacey thought. He's going to find me!

"Alice, look at me! Is it *true?* Was that your father?"

She was desperate now to be free of Tom. "Please go away."

"I will *not* go away." He cupped her face in his hands, forcing her to look up at him.

She saw the way his forehead was creased with concern for her, the expression in his eyes. The look you give someone special.

If Isabelle Waring's murderer had been able to coax my address out of Ruth Wilcox at Twin Cities Gym, she thought, I probably wouldn't be alive right now. So far, so good. But where else was he showing her picture?

"Alice, I know you're in trouble, and no matter what it is, I'll stand by you. But I can't be in the dark anymore," Tom's voice urged. "Can't you understand that?"

She looked at him. He was exactly the person she had hoped to meet someday. But not now! Not here! Not in this situation. I cannot do this to him, she thought.

A car drove into the parking area. Lacey's instinct was to pull Tom down, to hide with him behind her car. I have to get away, she thought. And I have to get Tom away from me.

As the approaching car came into full view, she saw that the driver was a woman who lived in the building.

But who would be driving the next car to come into the parking lot? she wondered angrily. It could be him.

The first flakes of snow were beginning to fall.

"Tom, please go," she begged. "I have to call home and talk to my mother."

"Then that story is true."

She nodded, careful not to look at him. "I have to straighten some things out. Can I phone you later?"

His eyes, troubled and questioning, lingered on her face. "Will you tell me one thing? Is there another man in your life?"

"No, there is not."

He nodded. "That's all I need to know."

Another car was driving into the parking area. Get away from me, her mind screamed. "Tom, I have to call home."

"At least let me walk you to the door." He took her arm. After they had gone a few steps, he stopped. "You're limping."

"It's nothing. I stumbled over my own feet." Lacey prayed her face wasn't showing the pain she felt when she walked.

Tom opened the door to the lobby for her. "When will I hear from you?"

"In an hour or so." She looked at him, forcing a smile.

His lips touched her cheek. "I'll be waiting for your call."

She waited in the lobby until she saw his dark blue BMW drive away. Then she rushed to the elevator.

LACEY did not wait to take off her coat before she called the health club. The gratingly cheerful voice of the manager answered. "Edina Health Club. Hold on, please."

A minute, then a second minute went by. Damn her, Lacey thought, slamming her hand down to break the connection.

It was Saturday. There was a chance her mother was home. For the first time in months Lacey dialed the familiar number directly. Her mother picked up on the first ring.

Lacey knew she could not waste time. "Mom, who did you tell I was here?"

"Lacey? I didn't tell a soul. Why?" Her mother's voice went up in alarm.

Didn't *deliberately* tell a soul, Lacey thought. "Mom, that dinner last night. Who all was there?"

"Alex and Kit and Jay and Jimmy Landi and his partner, Steve Abbott, and I. Why?"

"Did you say *anything* about me?"

"Nothing significant. Only that you'd joined a new health club with a squash court. That was all right, wasn't it?"

My God, Lacey thought.

"Lacey, Mr. Landi wants very much to talk to you. He asked me to find out if you knew whether the last few pages of his daughter's journal were written on unlined paper."

"Why does he want to know that? I gave him a complete copy."

"Because he said that if they were, somebody stole those pages from the copy while it was at the police station, and they also stole the *whole* original copy. Lacey, are you telling me that whoever tried to kill you knows you're in Minneapolis?"

"Mom, I can't talk. I'll call you later."

Lacey hung up and called the health club again. The manager was solicitous. "Oh, Alice, your dad came in looking for you. Someone told us you gave your ankle a nasty wrench on the squash court. Your dad was so worried. I gave him your address. That was all right, wasn't it? He left just a couple of minutes ago."

LACEY stopped only long enough to jam her copy of Heather Landi's journal into her tote bag before she half ran, half hopped to the car and headed for the airport. A sharp wind slapped snow against the windshield. Hopefully he won't figure out right away that I've left, she told herself. I'll have a little time.

There was a plane leaving for Chicago twelve minutes after she reached the ticket counter. She managed to get on it just before the gates closed. Then she sat in the plane for three hours on the runway while they waited for clearance to take off.

SANDY Savarano sat in his rental car, the street map of the city unfolded in front of him, the thrill of the chase warming him. He had found 520 Hennepin Avenue on the map. It was just ten minutes from the Radisson Plaza, where he was staying. He took the car out of park and stepped on the accelerator.

He felt adrenaline pumping through his body, accelerating his heartbeat, quickening his breath. He would have her taken care of soon. He was close. This was the part he liked most.

The attendant had said that Farrell was limping when she left the health club. Chances were she went directly home.

Alice Carroll was the name she had taken—he knew that now. Shouldn't be too difficult to find out her apartment number—probably would be on her mailbox in the lobby.

The snow was getting heavier. Savarano frowned. He didn't want to have to deal with any weather problems.

He reached 520 Hennepin Avenue. It was a nondescript corner building, seven stories high—not large, which was better for him. He was sure the building would have little in the way of security.

He parked across the street and walked to the building entrance. The door to the small outer vestibule was unlocked. The names and apartment numbers of the residents were on the wall above the mailboxes. Alice Carroll was in apartment 4F. Typical of such buildings, in order to gain admittance to the lobby, it was necessary to either have a key or to use the intercom to get a resident to buzz down and release the lock.

Savarano waited impatiently until he saw someone coming up the walk, an elderly woman. As she opened the outer door, he dropped a key ring on the floor and bent down to retrieve it. When the woman unlocked the door that opened to the lobby, he straightened up and held it for her, then followed her in.

She gave him a grateful smile. He followed her to the elevator, then waited until she had pushed the button for the seventh floor before he pushed 4—the kind of attention to detail that made Sandy Savarano so successful. He didn't want to find himself getting off the elevator with Farrell's next-door neighbor. The less he was seen, the better.

Four F was the last apartment on the left. Sandy's right hand was in his pocket, holding his pistol, as he rang the bell with his left hand. He had his story ready if Farrell wanted to know who was there. "Emergency Services, checking a gas leak," he would say. It always worked.

There was no answer.

The lock was new, but he had never seen a lock he couldn't take apart. The tools were in a kit he kept around his waist. It looked just like a money belt. In less than four minutes he was inside 4F, the lock securely back in place. He would wait for her here. Maybe she's gone to have her ankle x-rayed, he thought.

He had been told to search this apartment to be sure Farrell hadn't made a copy of Heather Landi's journal for herself. He started toward the desk just as the phone rang.

Farrell's voice on the tape was low and reserved. "You have reached 555-1247. Please leave a message," was all it said.

"Alice, this is George Svenson," the caller said, his voice urgent and authoritative. "Your mother just phoned the emergency number in New York to report you were in trouble. We're on the way. Bolt your door. Don't let anyone in until I get there."

Savarano froze. They were on the way! If he didn't get out of there immediately, he was the one who would be trapped. In seconds he was out of the apartment and on the fire stairs.

Safely back in his car, he had just joined the traffic on Hennepin Avenue when police cars, lights flashing, roared past him.

That had been as near a miss as any he had ever had. For a few moments he drove aimlessly, forcing himself to calm down. Where would Farrell go? he asked himself. Would she hide at a friend's place? Would she hole up in a motel somewhere?

Wherever she was, he figured she wasn't more than thirty minutes ahead of him. What would *he* do if he were in the Witness Protection Program and had been tracked down?

I wouldn't trust the marshals anymore, Sandy told himself. I wouldn't move to another city for them and wonder how long it would take to be found again.

Usually people who left the Witness Protection Program voluntarily did so because they missed their families. They usually went back home. That's where Farrell was headed, Sandy decided. She was on her way to New York. He was going there too.

HE WENT to the Northwest Airlines counter first. It was obviously the busiest carrier in Minneapolis. He was told that at present all flights were grounded by the snow. "Then maybe I'll be able to join my wife," he said. "She left about forty minutes ago. Her mother was in an accident in New York, and I imagine she took whatever flight she could get. The name is Alice Carroll."

The ticket agent was warmly helpful. "No direct flight to New York left in the last hour, Mr. Carroll. She might have made a connection through Chicago, though. Let's check." The agent's fingers tapped the computer keys. "Here we are. Your wife is on flight sixty-two to Chicago, which departed at eleven forty-eight." She sighed. "Actually, it's still on the runway. I'm afraid I can't put you on it, but you could meet her in Chicago. There's a plane boarding right now. Chances are they'll arrive only minutes apart."

DETECTIVE Ed Sloane and Priscilla Parker waited for her son, Rick, in the comfortable sitting room of Harding Manor. The estate was a private home that had been donated as a rehabilitation center by a couple whose only son died of a drug overdose.

As they waited, Mrs. Parker nervously explained, "I know what you must think of my son. But you don't realize how much promise there is in him. Rick could still do so much with his life. I *know* he could. His father has always spoiled him, taught him to think of himself as above any discipline. When he got into trouble, I pleaded with my husband to make Rick face the consequences. But instead he bought people off."

"Why did your husband change his mind about Rick?" Sloane asked. "We know that he cut off his trust fund income."

"Let Rick tell you," Priscilla Parker replied. "That's his voice. He's coming. Mr. Sloane, is he in a lot of trouble?"

"Not if he's innocent, Mrs. Parker. And not if he cooperates."

SLOANE REPEATED THOSE WORDS to Rick Parker as he waited for him to sign a Miranda warning. Rick's appearance shocked him. His face was pale, and there were dark circles under his eyes. Kicking a drug habit isn't fun, Sloane reminded himself.

Rick handed Sloane the signed release. "All right, Detective," he said. "What do you want to know?" He was seated next to his mother on the sofa.

"Why did you send Curtis Caldwell—I'll call him that since it's the name he was using—to Isabelle Waring's apartment?"

Beads of perspiration appeared on Rick Parker's forehead as he spoke. "You know the reason I'm here. I've got an *expensive* drug habit. And I simply haven't been able to cover it. I've been buying more and more on credit. In early October I got a call from my dealer saying he knew someone who wanted to see the apartment. He also said he knew this guy might not meet our standards."

"Were you threatened in case you didn't go along with that?" Sloane asked.

Parker rubbed his forehead. "Look, all I can tell you is I *knew* I wasn't being asked for a favor; I was being told what to do. So I made up the name Curtis Caldwell and said he was from Keller, Roland, and Smythe. We'd just finished selling several co-ops to some lawyers the firm had transferred to Manhattan. No one questioned it. That's all I did," he burst out. "*Nothing* more. When Lacey Farrell told me that guy was the one who killed Heather's mother, I didn't know what to do."

Sloane noted immediately the familiar way in which Rick Parker referred to Heather Landi.

"Okay. Now, what had been going on between you and Heather?"

Rick looked directly at Sloane. The misery in Parker's eyes seemed genuine. "I met Heather nearly five years ago," he said, "when she came to our office looking for a West Side apartment. I started taking her around. She was beautiful, vivacious, fun."

"You knew Jimmy Landi was her father?" Sloane asked.

"Yes, and that was part of what made me enjoy the situation so much. Jimmy had barred me from going into his place one night because I was drunk. It made me angry. So when Heather wanted to get out of her contract for a co-op on West Seventy-seventh Street, I saw my chance to have some fun, at least indirectly, at Jimmy Landi's expense."

"She signed a contract?"

"An airtight one. Then she came to me in a panic. She found out her father had already bought her a place on East Seventieth. She begged me to tear up the contract."

"What happened?"

"I told her I would tear it up if I could take it out in trade."

You slime, Sloane thought. She was a kid, new to New York, and you pulled that.

"You see"—Rick paused and looked down at his hands—"I didn't have the brains to realize what I really felt for Heather. I had been able to crook my finger, and any number of girls would come running. Heather had ignored my attempts to seduce her. So in the deal we made over the co-op contract, I saw a chance to get what I wanted and to even the score with her father. But the night she came to my apartment, she was clearly terrified, so I decided to back off. She really was a sweet kid, the kind I could actually fall in love with. In fact, maybe I *did*. I teased her a little bit, and she started crying. So I told her to grow up and to leave, that I was too old for babies. I guess I succeeded in humiliating her enough to scare her away from me for good."

Rick got up and walked to the fireplace as if he needed the warmth of the flames. "That night, after she had been to my apartment, I went out drinking. When I left a bar in the Village, I was suddenly hustled into a car. Two guys worked me over. They said if I didn't tear up that contract and stay away from Heather, I wouldn't live to see my next birthday. I had three broken ribs."

"Did you tear up the contract?"

"I *had* torn it up. But not before my father got wind of it and forced me to tell him what had happened. Our main office had sold the East Side apartment to Jimmy Landi, for Heather, but that deal was peanuts compared to another deal that I found out was in the works. At that same time, my father was brokering the sale of the Atlantic City property to Jimmy Landi. If Landi had found out what I pulled on Heather, it could have cost my father millions. Don't forget, for my father, if there's a business deal involved, it doesn't matter that I'm his son."

"We have an eyewitness who claims that Heather ran from the après-ski lounge in Stowe the afternoon before she died because she saw you there," Sloane told him.

"I never saw her that day," Rick Parker said. He seemed sincere. "But the few times I had run into her, that was the reaction I got. She couldn't get away from me fast enough."

"Heather obviously confided in someone, who ordered you roughed up. Was it her father?"

"Never!" Rick almost laughed. "And tell him she had signed that contract! Are you kidding? She wouldn't have dared."

"Then who?"

"My father has been a regular at Landi's for thirty years," Rick said. "He always made a fuss over Heather. I think Dad was the one who set the goons on me."

WHEN her plane finally took off at three p.m., Lacey leaned back and closed her eyes, sensing that the choke collar of terror she had felt tightening around her neck was easing. For three hours she had been terrified that the flight would be canceled, that the plane would taxi from the runway back to the gate, that she would find Curtis Caldwell waiting for her.

Finally they were in the air. For the next hour or so—at least until they reached Chicago—she was safe.

She was still wearing the same sweat suit and sneakers she had worn to the health club that morning. She had loosened the sneaker on her right foot but had not taken it off for fear she would not be able to get it on again. Her ankle was now twice its normal size, and the pain was shooting up as far as her knee.

Forget it, she told herself. You can't let it stop you. You're lucky you're alive to feel pain. You've got to *plan*.

In Chicago she would get on the first available flight to New York. But what do I do when I get there? Where do I go?

She already had put one full-fare coach flight on her Alice Carroll credit card. Now she would have to book a second full-fare flight to New York. Her card had a three-thousand-dollar limit, and there might not be enough left to cover a hotel room in Manhattan. Besides, she was sure that when the U.S. Attorney's office became aware she was missing, a trace would be put on that card.

No, she had to find a place to stay, one that wouldn't put anyone else in danger, and where no one would think to look for her.

As the plane flew over the Midwest, Lacey considered her options. She could call Gary Baldwin and agree to go back into the Witness Protection Program. The marshals would whisk her away again; she would stay in a safe house for a few weeks before being sent to another unfamiliar city, where she would emerge as a newly created entity. No way, she vowed silently. I'd rather be dead.

Lacey thought back to the chain of circumstances that had led her to this point. Could her mother have given her away? Mom had dinner last night at Alex Carbine's restaurant, Lacey thought. I like Alex a lot. He was especially wonderful the night Bonnie was injured. But what do we really know about him? The first time I met him, when he came to dinner at Jay and Kit's, he told us that he'd met Heather.

Jay may have known Heather too, a voice whispered to her. He denied it. But for some reason when her name came up, he was upset. Don't even think that Kit's husband might be involved in this, Lacey told herself. Jay may have his quirks, but he's basically a very good and solid person.

What about Jimmy Landi? No, it couldn't be him. She had seen the grief in his eyes when he took the copy of Heather's journal from her.

What about the cops? Heather's handwritten journal disappeared after I gave it to them, Lacey thought. Now Jimmy Landi wants to know if there were entries written on unlined paper at the end of the journal. I remember those three pages. They had blood on them. If copies of those pages disappeared while in police custody, then there had to be something important on them.

Her copy of the journal was in the tote bag pushed under the seat in front of her. Lacey was tempted to take it out and look at it but decided to wait until she could study the unlined pages alone.

"We are beginning our descent . . ."

Chicago, she thought. Then New York. Home!

The flight attendant finished the speech about seats upright and buckling up, then added, "Northwest apologizes for the weather-related delay you encountered. You may be interested to learn that the visibility lowered immediately after we took off. We were the last plane to leave the airport until flights resumed only a few minutes ago."

Then I'm at least an hour or so ahead of anyone who may be following me, Lacey told herself.

Whatever comfort that thought provided was driven away by another possibility. If Caldwell was following her and thought she was planning to go to New York, wouldn't it be smart for him to have taken a direct flight and be waiting for her there?

EVERY nerve in Tom Lynch's body had shouted at him not to leave Alice alone. He drove five miles in the direction of his apartment in St. Paul before he made a fast U-turn and headed back. He would make it clear to Alice that he had no intention of getting in her way while she spoke to her mother and whatever other family members might be involved in their rift. But surely she could have no objection to his waiting in the lobby of her building until she was ready for him to come up. I want to be there for her, he thought.

Tom's first indication of trouble came at the sight of police cars parked at Alice's building, lights flashing. A sickening sense of inevitability warned him that the police presence had to do with Alice. He managed to find a parking spot a block away and jogged back to her building. A policeman stopped him at the entrance.

"I'm going up," he told the cop. "My girlfriend lives here, and I want to see if she's all right."

"Who's your girlfriend?"

"Alice Carroll, in four F."

The change in the police officer's attitude confirmed Tom's suspicion that something had happened to Alice. "Come with me. I'll take you upstairs," the officer told him.

In the elevator, Tom forced himself to ask the question he dreaded to put into words. "Is she all right?"

"Why don't you wait till you talk to the guy in charge, sir?"

The door to Alice's apartment was open. Inside, Tom saw three cops taking instructions from an older man whom he recognized as the one who had driven Alice home the other evening.

Tom interrupted him. "What's happened to Alice?" he demanded. "Where is she?"

He could see from the surprise on the other man's face that he had been recognized, but there was no time wasted in greeting him. "How do you know Alice, Mr. Lynch?" George Svenson asked.

"Look," Tom said, "I'm not going to answer your questions until you answer mine. Where is Alice? Who are you?"

Svenson responded succinctly. "I'm a deputy federal marshal. We don't know where Ms. Carroll is. We do know that she had been getting threats."

"Then that guy at the gym yesterday who claimed to be her father was a phony," Tom said heatedly. "I thought so, but when I told Alice about him, she didn't say anything except that she had to go and call her mother."

"What guy?" Svenson demanded. "Tell me everything you know about him, Mr. Lynch. It may save Alice Carroll's life."

WHEN Tom finally got home, it was after four thirty. The flashing light on the answering machine indicated he had four messages. As he had expected, none of them were from Alice.

He sat at the table by the phone, his head in his hands. All Svenson had told him was that Alice had been receiving threatening phone calls and had contacted his office, which was why they were there. "She may have gone out to visit a friend," Svenson told him.

Or she may have been abducted, Tom thought. A child could see that they were avoiding telling him what was really going on. The police were also trying to find Ruth Wilcox from Twin Cities Gym, but she was off-duty over the weekend. They said they hoped to get a fuller description of the man claiming to be Alice's father.

Tom had told Svenson that Alice had promised to call. "If you hear from her, tell her to call me immediately," Svenson ordered.

In his mind Tom could see Alice, quiet and lovely, standing at the window of the banker's home in Wayzata only a week ago. Why didn't you trust me? he raged at that image. You couldn't wait to get rid of me this morning!

There was one possible lead that the police had shared with him. A neighbor reported that she thought she had seen Alice getting into her car around eleven o'clock. I only left her at quarter of eleven, Tom thought. If that neighbor was right, then she left only ten minutes after I did.

Where would she go? Tom wondered. Who was she, really?

LACEY arrived in Chicago at four thirty. There she bought a ticket for a five-fifteen plane to Boston. Once again she used her credit card, but she planned to pay cash for the Delta shuttle from Boston to New York. That plane landed at the Marine Air Terminal, a mile from the main terminals at La Guardia Airport. She was sure anyone who followed her to New York wouldn't look for her there, and by not using her credit card for the shuttle, she might lead Baldwin's office to think she had stayed in Boston.

Before she boarded the plane from Chicago, she bought a copy of *The New York Times.* Midway through the flight she glanced through the paper and gasped. Rick Parker's face was looking up at her. It was an update on an earlier story. Richard J. Parker, Jr., who, police now confirmed, was a suspect in Isabelle Waring's death, was missing.

It was only as the plane was landing in Boston that Lacey realized she had finally figured out the one place she could stay in New York where no one would ever think of looking for her.

It was five minutes past eight when she got off the plane at Logan Airport. Praying that he would be home, Lacey made a phone call to Tim Powers, the superintendent of Isabelle Waring's building.

Four years earlier, after showing an apartment, Lacey had been instrumental in preventing what surely would have been a terrible accident, and one for which Tim Powers would have been blamed. It had all happened so quickly. A child broke free from his nanny and raced into the street through the building's front door, which Tim had left open. Lacey's quick action had kept the child from being hit by a passing delivery truck.

Tim, trembling from the shock of the near disaster, had vowed, "Lacey, it would have been my fault. If you ever need *anything*—anything at all—you can count on me."

I need it now, Tim, she thought as she waited for him to answer.

Tim was astonished to hear from her. "Lacey Farrell," he said. "I thought you'd disappeared off the face of the earth."

That's almost exactly what I've done, Lacey thought. "Tim," she said, "I need help. You once promised—"

He interrupted her. "Anything, Lacey."

She looked around, fearful of being overheard. "Tim," she said hurriedly, "I'm being followed. I think it's the man who killed Isabelle Waring. I need a place to stay. He'd never look for me in Isabelle's apartment. And please, Tim—this is *very* important—don't tell anyone."

AFTER leaving Rick Parker at the rehabilitation center, Detective Sloane rode with Priscilla Parker to her Greenwich estate, where he picked up his own car to drive to Manhattan. On the way he phoned the precinct to check in. Nick Mars was there. "Baldwin's been calling for you," Mars told Sloane. "All hell is breaking loose. Lacey Farrell almost got nailed in Minneapolis, where the feds had her stashed. She's disappeared, and Baldwin thinks she's headed for New York. He wants to coordinate with us to find her before she gets nailed here. He wants to take her into custody as a material witness." Then he added, "How did you make out, Ed? Any luck finding Parker?"

"I found him," Sloane said. "Call Baldwin and arrange a meeting. I'll be there by seven."

WHEN Sloane arrived at the Nineteenth Precinct, he stopped at his desk and took off his jacket. Then, with Mars in tow, he went to see U.S. Attorney Baldwin, who was in the interrogation room.

Baldwin congratulated Sloane on finding Rick Parker. "What did Parker tell you?" he asked.

Sloane gave a full report.

"Do you believe him?" Baldwin asked.

"I think he's telling the truth," Sloane said. "I know the guy who sells him drugs. If he was the one who told Parker to set up the appointment that got Savarano into Waring's apartment, it was nothing Parker actually planned himself. He was just a messenger. Parker's a jerk but not a criminal."

"Do you believe that his father ordered him roughed up when he tried to hit on Heather Landi?" Baldwin asked.

"I think it's possible," Sloane said. He reached for a cigarette, then frowned. "They're in my jacket. Nick, would you?"

"Sure, Ed."

The round-trip took Mars about a minute. He plunked the cigarette pack and a grimy ashtray on the table in front of Sloane.

"Has it ever occurred to you to give up smoking?" Baldwin asked, eyeing both cigarettes and ashtray with disdain.

"Many times," Sloane responded. "What's the latest on Farrell?"

As soon as Baldwin opened his mouth, it was obvious to Ed Sloane that he was furious with Lacey. "Her mother admits she knew Farrell was in Minneapolis, but she swears she didn't tell anyone. Although I don't believe *that* for a minute."

"Maybe there was a leak somewhere else," Sloane suggested.

"There was no leak from my office or from the federal marshal's office," Baldwin said, his tone icy. "We maintain security. Unlike this precinct," he added.

I let myself in for that one, Sloane acknowledged silently. "What's your game plan?" he asked.

"We've flagged the credit card we gave Farrell. We know she used it to fly to Chicago, then to Boston. She's got to be on her way to New York.

"We have a tap on the phone in her apartment, not that I think she'd be stupid enough to go there," Baldwin continued. "We've got that building under surveillance. We also have taps on her mother's phone, her sister's phone, and Monday there'll be taps on the phones in her brother-in-law's office. We've got a tail assigned to each family member in case they try to meet her."

Baldwin paused and looked at Sloane appraisingly. "It also occurred to me that Lacey Farrell just might try to call you directly," he said. "What do you think?"

"I doubt it. I didn't exactly treat her with kid gloves."

"She doesn't deserve kid gloves," Baldwin said flatly. "She concealed evidence in a murder case. She gave away her location when we had her protected. And now she's putting herself in an extremely risky position. We've invested a lot of time and money in keeping Ms. Farrell alive, and we've gotten nothing much back except complaints and lack of cooperation on her part. You'd think she'd at least be grateful."

"I'm sure she's eternally grateful," Sloane said as he got up. "I'm also sure that even if you hadn't spent all that time and money, she'd probably like to stay alive."

As THEY had agreed, Lacey called Tim Powers from the Marine Air Terminal. "I should be there in twenty minutes, a half hour at the most," she told the superintendent. "Be watching for me, please, Tim. It is very important that nobody sees me."

"I'll give the doorman a coffee break," Tim promised, "and I'll have the key ready to hand you."

It feels so strange to be back in New York, Lacey thought as the cab sped into Manhattan and headed south on the FDR Drive. When the plane had made its final approach before landing, she had pressed her face against the window, drinking in the New York skyline, realizing how much she had missed it.

The driver got off the Drive at Seventy-first Street and headed west to Fifth Avenue. He turned left on Fifth, then left again on Seventieth, and stopped outside the building.

Tim Powers was waiting for her. He opened the door and greeted her with a pleasant "Good evening, miss," but no sign of recognition. Lacey paid the driver and hobbled out of the cab, thankful she would finally be able to stop moving around. It was just in time, because she could no longer deny the pain of her wrenched ankle. Tim slipped her the key to the Waring apartment. He assisted her to the elevator, put his master key in the control, and pushed 10. "I fixed it so you'll go straight up," he said. "That way there'll be no risk of running into anyone who knows you."

"Tim, I can't tell you how much—"

He interrupted her. "Lacey, get upstairs fast and lock the door. There's food in the fridge."

THE apartment seemed to have been kept in pristine order. The framed pictures of Heather that had been scattered through the living room were still there. In fact, everything seemed to be much as Isabelle had left it. Lacey shivered. She almost expected to see Isabelle walk down the stairs. She suddenly felt as if she were an intruder, moving in with ghosts.

In the library there was a leather sofa that converted into a bed, and adjacent to the library was the powder room. Those were the rooms she would use. There was no way that she could ever sleep in the bed in which Isabelle had been shot.

As Lacey hung her jacket in the foyer closet, she remembered hiding there and watching as Caldwell rushed past.

"Upstairs," Lacey said aloud, knowing that she had to see the bedroom just to be rid of the feeling that Isabelle's body was still there. She half hopped her way up the staircase. She went through the sitting room to the bedroom and turned on the light.

The place looked exactly as it had when she had been there with

Curtis Caldwell. Where was he now? she wondered suddenly, panic washing over her. Had he followed her to New York?

Lacey looked at the bed and visualized Isabelle's bloodied hand, trying to pull the journal pages from under the pillow. She could almost hear Isabelle's dying plea: *Lacey . . . give Heather's journal . . . to her father. Only to him. Swear. You . . . read it. Show him where . . .* Then Isabelle had made one last effort to breathe and speak. She'd died as she exhaled, whispering, *man.*

Lacey turned and hobbled through the sitting room and eased her way down the stairs. Get something to eat, she told herself. You're hungry, and the irritation from that is just making everything else worse.

Tim had done a good job of putting together a meal for her. There was a small roast chicken, salad greens, rolls, a wedge of cheddar cheese, fruit, instant coffee.

Forty minutes later she was sitting wrapped in blankets on the library couch. The copy she had made of Heather's journal was on the desk. The three unlined pages were spread out side by side, with the bloodstains that had smeared the original pages resembling a Rorschach test blot. She reached for those pages.

A thought came to her. Was it possible that Isabelle had been making a special effort to touch these particular pages in her last moments of life?

Once again Lacey began to read the pages, searching for some clue as to why they were so important that someone had stolen the only other copies that existed. She had no doubt that these were the pages that Caldwell had found it worth killing for, but *why?* What was the hidden secret in them?

The last entry that seemed upbeat was on the top of the first unlined page, where Heather wrote that she was going to have lunch with Mr. or Max or Mac Hufner—it was impossible to tell.

I wonder if the police talked to him, Lacey thought. She also wondered if the police had made a list of the people mentioned in the journal before it was stolen.

She looked at the pages again. Neither Jimmy Landi nor the

police have these three pages now, she reminded herself. Mine are the only copies.

She knew she had to get to work on trying to solve the mystery hidden in these pages. If anyone was going to unravel the secret, clearly it would have to be her. But could she do it in time to save her own life?

CHAPTER 9

HEN flights from Minneapolis resumed, Sandy Savarano took the first direct flight to New York. He reasoned that from Chicago, Lacey would connect to New York. Where else would she go? Once in New York, Sandy managed to cover most of the areas through which deplaning passengers would have to pass. Finding and gunning down Lacey Farrell had become more than a mere job for him. At this point it was consuming him. The stakes had become higher than he wanted to play for. He liked his new life in Costa Rica. The money he was being paid to get rid of Farrell was impressive but not necessary to his lifestyle.

What *was* necessary to him was not having to live with the knowledge that he had botched his final job—that, and eliminating someone who could send him to prison for life.

After checking flight arrivals for a stretch of five hours, Sandy decided he would only draw attention to himself if he hung around any longer. He took a cab to the brownstone apartment on West Tenth Street that had been rented for him. He would wait there for further information on Lacey Farrell.

He did not have the slightest doubt that by midafternoon tomorrow he would once again be closing in on his quarry.

JIMMY LANDI HAD INTENDED to go to Atlantic City for the weekend to see that everything was ready for the casino's opening. It was an exciting time for him, and he found it difficult to stay away.

He felt it was always important for a person to have a challenge, but it was never more important to him than now. Steve Abbott was taking care of the day-to-day running of the operation, which freed Jimmy for the big picture. Still, he didn't seem to be able to keep his mind on the casino, no matter how hard he tried. The problem was that since he had gotten back the copy of Heather's journal last Monday, he had become obsessed with it. It was like a gateway to memories he wasn't sure he wanted to revisit.

What had happened five years ago that Heather was so anxious to keep from him? he wondered. He couldn't help dwelling on that part of her journal. The thought that somebody had pulled something on Heather and gotten away with it was driving him crazy. Even after all this time he still needed to get to the bottom of it.

The question of those unlined pages from the journal was also gnawing at him. He could swear he had seen them.

Maybe there weren't any unlined pages, he told himself. But assuming that I'm not wrong and that the pages were there originally, then chances are they wouldn't have disappeared unless someone thought they were important. There is only one person who might be able to tell me the truth, he thought: Lacey Farrell. When she made the copy of the journal for me, surely she would have noticed if some of the last pages were different from the others. There were stains on them, he vaguely recalled.

He decided to call Lacey Farrell's mother and again ask her to pass on to Lacey the question he needed to have answered: Do those pages exist?

LACEY glanced at the clock when she woke up. She must have been asleep for about three hours. She pushed back the blankets and got out of bed, automatically putting most of her weight on her left foot, biting her lip at the throbbing discomfort of the swollen right ankle.

She put her hands on the desk to steady herself. The three un-lined pages still lay there, commanding her immediate attention. Once again she read the first line of the first page. "Lunch with Mr."—or was it Max or Mac?—"Hufner. It should be fun. He says he's grown old and I've grown up."

It sounds like Heather was referring to someone she had known for a long time, Lacey thought. Who could I ask? There was only one obvious answer: Heather's father.

He's the key to all this, Lacey thought.

She decided that a quick shower now would help to wake her up. She wanted to get dressed, to get out of the nightshirt she had taken from Heather Landi's closet. But what do I wear? she asked herself. I can't wear my sweat suit. I might be too easy to spot. She felt ghoulish going through Heather's clothes.

She fixed herself coffee and a toasted roll, and then showered. At eight o'clock Tim Powers called on the apartment intercom. "Can I come up?"

They had coffee together in the library. "How can I help you, Lacey?" Tim asked.

"You already have," she replied with an appreciative smile. "Is Parker and Parker still handling the sale of the apartment?"

"As far as I know. You've heard that Junior is missing?"

"I read that. Has anyone else from their office brought somebody in to look at the place?"

"No, and Jimmy Landi phoned the other day. He wants the apartment sold, and soon. I told him straight that I thought it would have a better chance if we cleared everything out."

"Do you have his personal number, Tim?"

"Sure. You know this phone is still on. They never bothered to disconnect it."

Lacey knew it would cost Tim his job if she was discovered using this place, so she couldn't risk staying much longer. Still, there was one other thing she had to ask him to do. "Tim, I've got to get word to my mother that I'm all right. I'm sure her phone is tapped, so would you go to a public phone and call her? Don't identify yourself, and don't stay on for more than a few seconds or they'll be able to trace the call, although even if they do, at least it won't be coming from here. Tell her I'm safe and will call her as soon as I can."

"Sure," Tim Powers said as he stood. He glanced at the pages on the desk, then looked startled. "Is that a copy of Heather Landi's journal?"

Lacey stared at him. "Yes, it is. How do you know that, Tim?"

"The day before Mrs. Waring died, I was up here changing the filters in the radiators. She was reading the journal. I guess she'd just found it that day, because she was clearly upset."

"Did she talk to you about it, Tim?" Lacey asked.

"Not really. She got right on the phone, but whoever she tried to call has an unlisted number."

"You don't know who it was?"

"No, but I think I saw her circle the name. I remember it was near the end. Lacey, I've gotta go. Give me your mother's phone number. I'll call on the intercom and give you Landi's."

When Tim left, Lacey picked up the first of the unlined pages and brought it to the window. Blotched as the page was, she could detect a faint line around the name Hufner.

Who *was* he? How could she find out?

Talk to Jimmy Landi, she decided. That was the only way.

TIM Powers gave Landi's phone number to Lacey, then went looking for a public phone. He had a supply of quarters with him.

Twenty-seven miles away in New Jersey, Mona Farrell jumped at the sound of the telephone. Let it be Lacey, she prayed.

A hearty, reassuring man's voice said, "Mrs. Farrell, I'm calling for Lacey. She wants you to know that she's okay and will get in touch as soon as she can."

"Where is she?" Mona demanded. "Why can't she talk to me?"

Tim knew that he should break the connection, but Lacey's mother sounded so distraught he couldn't just hang up on her. Helplessly he let her pour out her anxiety as he kept interjecting, "She's okay, Mrs. Farrell. Trust me, she's okay."

When he replaced the receiver, Mona Farrell was still pleading for him to tell her more. He started home, unaware of the unmarked police car that raced to the phone booth he had just used. Nor did he know that the phone was immediately dusted for his fingerprints.

EVERY hour that I'm here doing nothing means that I'm an hour closer to being tracked down by Caldwell or taken into custody by Baldwin, Lacey thought. If only I could talk to Kit. Kit has a good head on her shoulders. Lacey walked over to the window and pulled the curtains back just enough to see out.

Central Park was crowded with joggers, in-line skaters, people strolling or pushing carriages. Of course, she thought. It was Sunday. Almost ten o'clock on Sunday morning. Kit and Jay would be in church now. They always went to the ten-o'clock Mass.

"I *can* talk to Kit!" Lacey said aloud. Kit and Jay attended St. Elizabeth's. Everyone knew them. Her spirits suddenly buoyed, she dialed New Jersey information for the number of the rectory.

Somebody be there, she prayed, but then she heard an answering machine click on. The only thing she could do was to leave a message and hope that Kit would get it before they left the church. Leaving her phone number, even at a rectory, would be too great a risk.

Lacey spoke clearly and slowly. "It is urgent that I speak with Kit Taylor. I believe she is at the ten-o'clock Mass. I'll call this number again at eleven fifteen. Please try to locate her."

She hung up and dialed Jimmy Landi's number. When his machine picked up, she decided not to leave a message.

DETECTIVE Sloane was at home, off-duty, on Sunday when the desk sergeant at the precinct phoned to say that a friend of Lacey Farrell's had called her mother from a pay phone.

When Sloane reached the precinct, the sergeant nodded toward the captain's office. "The boss wants to talk to you," he said.

Captain Frank Deleo's cheeks were flushed, usually a sign that something or someone had incurred his wrath. Today, however, Sloane saw immediately that Deleo's eyes were troubled and sad. He knew what that combination meant. The sting had worked. They had pinned down the identity of the rogue cop.

"The guys in the lab sent over the tape late last night," Deleo told him. "You're not going to like it."

Ed Sloane looked at the TV screen. Deleo pressed the PLAY button. Sloane leaned forward. He was looking at his own desk, with his jacket on the back of the chair, the keys deliberately left dangling from the pocket in an effort to tempt the thief who was removing evidence from his cubby.

On the upper-left section of the screen he could see the back of his own head as he sat in the interrogation room. "This was filmed last night!" he exclaimed.

"I know it was. Watch what happens now."

Sloane stared intently at the screen as Nick Mars scurried out of the interrogation room and looked around. There were only two other detectives in the squad room. One was on the phone with his back to Nick; the other was dozing.

As they watched, Mars reached into Sloane's jacket pocket and slid out his key ring, cupping it in his palm to conceal it. He turned toward the cabinet containing the locked private cubbies, then spun swiftly around, quickly replacing the keys. He then pulled a pack of cigarettes out of the breast pocket of Sloane's jacket.

"This is where I made my untimely entrance," Deleo said dryly. "He went back to the interrogation room."

Sloane was numb. "His father's a cop; his grandfather was a cop; he's been given every break. Why?"

"Why *any* bad cop?" Deleo asked. "Ed, this has to remain between you and me for now. That piece of film alone isn't enough to convict Mars."

"We have to do something. He's my partner. I don't want to have to sit across the table from him and work a case together," Sloane said flatly.

"Oh yes you do. Baldwin's on his way here again. He thinks Lacey Farrell is in the neighborhood. There's nothing I'd like better than for us to be able to crack this case and rub Baldwin's face in it. Your job is to make sure that Nick doesn't get the chance to lift or destroy any more evidence."

"If you promise me ten minutes alone with the jerk once we nail him."

The captain stood up. "Come on, Ed. Baldwin will be here any minute."

IT'S a day for show-and-tell, Ed Sloane thought bitterly as an assistant U.S. attorney prepared to replay the conversation they had taped between Lacey Farrell's mother and her unknown caller.

When the recording began to play, Sloane's raised eyebrows were the only sign of the shock he was experiencing. He knew that voice from the countless times he had been in and out of Three East Seventieth. It was Tim Powers, the superintendent.

And he's hiding Farrell in that building! Sloane thought.

The others sat silently, listening intently to the conversation. Baldwin had a cat-who-ate-the-canary expression. He thinks he's showing us what good police work is all about, Sloane thought angrily. Nick Mars was sitting with his hands folded in his lap, frowning— Dick Tracy incarnate, Sloane said to himself. Who would that rat tip off if he got wind that Powers was Lacey Farrell's guardian angel?

Ed Sloane decided that for now, at least, only one person besides Tim Powers was going to know where Lacey Farrell was staying. Himself.

LACEY put the pages of Heather's journal into her tote bag. Tim had told her that a real estate agent was showing the apartment at eleven thirty. She would make one more attempt to reach Kit at St. Elizabeth's, but then she had to get out of there. She looked at her watch. It was ten thirty. Just enough time to try Jimmy Landi's number once more.

This time he answered on the fourth ring. Lacey knew she could not waste time. "Mr. Landi, this is Lacey Farrell. I'm so glad I reached you. I tried a little while ago."

"I was downstairs," Jimmy explained.

"I know there's a lot to explain, Mr. Landi, but I don't have time, so just let me talk. I know why you wanted to talk to me. The answer is yes, there were three unlined pages at the end of Heather's journal. Those pages were filled with her worries about hurting you. The only happy reference was right at the beginning, where she wrote about having lunch with some man who must have been an old friend. She wrote that he said something to her about her growing up and his growing old."

"What's his name?" Jimmy demanded.

"It looks like Mac or Max Hufner."

"I don't know the guy. Maybe he's someone her mother knew." He paused. "You're in a lot of trouble, aren't you, Miss Farrell?"

"Yes, I am."

"What are you going to do?"

"I don't know."

"Where are you now?"

"I can't tell you. But I'm convinced Isabelle was onto something and that's why she was killed. I'm sorry. I've got to go."

Jimmy Landi heard the click as Lacey hung up. He laid down the receiver as Steve Abbott came into his office.

"Who was that?" Abbott asked.

"Lacey Farrell. I guess her mother got my message to her."

"Farrell! I thought she was in the witness protection plan."

"She was, but not anymore, I guess."

"Where is she now?"

Jimmy looked at his caller ID. "She didn't say, and I guess I didn't have this on. Steve, did we ever have a guy with a name like Hufner work for us?"

Abbott considered for a moment, then shook his head. "I don't think so, Jimmy, unless it was a kitchen helper."

Landi glanced toward the open door that led to a waiting room. Someone was pacing outside. "Who's that?" he asked.

"Carlos. He wants to come back. He says working for Alex Carbine is too quiet for him."

"Get that bum out of here. I never liked the guy in the first place."

AT TEN past eleven Lacey phoned St. Elizabeth's rectory again. This time the phone was answered on the first ring. "Father Edwards," a voice said.

"Good morning, Father," Lacey said. "I called earlier and left a message asking that Kit Taylor be—"

She was interrupted. "She's right here. Just a moment."

It had been two weeks since they had spoken. "Kit," Lacey said, then stopped, her throat tight with emotion.

"Lacey, we miss you. We're so scared for you. Where are you?"

Lacey managed a tremulous laugh. "Trust me. It's better you don't know. But I *can* tell you that I have to be out of here in five minutes. Kit, is Jay with you?"

"Yes, of course."

"Put him on, please."

Jay's greeting was a firm pronouncement. "Lacey, this can't go on. I'll hire an around-the-clock bodyguard for you, but you've got to stop running and let us help you."

"Jay, I can't go on living like I have been. I won't stay in the Witness Protection Program. I'm sure now that the key to this whole terrible mess is to find out who was responsible for Heather Landi's death. Like her mother, I'm convinced she was murdered. And the clues to who did it have got to be in her journal, if I can just figure them out. I think Isabelle Waring tried to find out what happened, and that's why she died."

"Lacey—"

"Let me finish, Jay. About a week before she died, Heather had lunch with an older man whom she'd apparently known for a long time. My hope is that he was somehow connected to the restaurant business and that you may know him."

"What's his name?"

"It's hard to make it out, but it looks like Mac or Max Hufner."

"Max Hoffman," Jay said. "Sure I knew him. He worked for Jimmy Landi for years."

Isabelle's last words. *"Read it. . . . Show him . . ."* Then that long, shuddering gasp, *". . . man."* Isabelle died trying to tell me his name, Lacey realized suddenly.

Then she realized what Jay had just said, and it sent a chill through her. "Jay, why did you say you *knew* him?"

"Lacey, Max died over a year ago in a hit-and-run accident near his home in Great Neck. I went to his funeral."

"How *much* over a year ago?" Lacey asked.

"Well, let me think," Jay said. "It was about the time I bid on the Red Roof Inn job in Southampton, so that would have made it about fourteen months ago. It was the first week in December."

"That's when Heather Landi was killed!" Lacey exclaimed. "Two car accidents within days of each other . . ." Her voice trailed off.

The apartment intercom was buzzing—Tim Powers signaling her to get out. "Jay, I've got to leave. Stay there. I'll call you back. Just one thing. Was Max Hoffman married?"

"For forty-five years."

"Jay, get his wife's address for me. I *have* to have it."

Lacey grabbed her tote bag and a black hooded coat she had taken from Heather's closet. She left the apartment and hobbled to the fire stairs.

Tim Powers met her inside the staircase at the lobby level. He pressed bills into her hand and dropped a cellular phone into her pocket. "It'll take a while to trace any calls made on this."

"Tim, I can't thank you enough." Lacey's heart was pounding.

"There's a cab waiting out in front with the door open," Tim said. "Keep that hood up." He squeezed her hand.

"Where to, miss?" the cabdriver demanded.

"Great Neck, Long Island," Lacey said.

HAD she been followed? Lacey wondered. She couldn't be sure. There was a black Toyota sedan that seemed to be maintaining a constant distance behind the cab.

Maybe not, she thought, breathing a slight sigh of relief. The car had turned off the expressway at the first exit after they came out of the Midtown Tunnel.

Lacey knew Kit and Jay were waiting in the rectory for her call. She had to get the street address where Max Hoffman had lived, and where, please God, his wife still lived. She had to go there and talk to Mrs. Hoffman and get from her anything she might know about her husband's conversation with Heather Landi.

The traffic was fairly light, and Lacey realized that they were getting close to Great Neck. What would she do if she arrived there without an address to give the driver? He hadn't wanted to drive so far out of Manhattan in the first place. If she *did* get to where Mrs. Hoffman lived and the woman wasn't home or wouldn't open the door, what would she do then?

And what if she was being followed?

She removed the cellular phone from her pocket and called the rectory again. Kit answered immediately. "Mom just got here, Lacey. She's dying to talk to you."

"Kit, please . . ."

Her mother was on the phone. "Lacey, I didn't tell a soul where you live!"

She's upset, Lacey thought. It's so hard for her, but I just can't talk to her about all this now.

Then mercifully her mother said, "Jay has to speak to you."

They were entering Great Neck. "What's the address?" the driver asked.

"Pull over for a minute," Lacey told him.

She felt her nerves tingle. A black Toyota sedan had slowed down and driven into a parking lot. She *was* being followed. She felt her body go clammy. Then she allowed herself a sigh of relief as she saw a young man with a child get out of that car.

"Lacey?" Jay was saying, his tone questioning.

"Jay, did you get the Hoffmans' street address?"

"Lacey, I haven't a clue where to get it. I'd have to go into the office and make phone calls to see if anyone knows. I did call Alex.

He knew Max very well. He says he has the address in a Christmas card file somewhere. He's looking for it."

For the first time in her horrible months-long ordeal Lacey felt total despair. Then she heard Jay ask, "What can you do, Father? No, I don't know which funeral home."

Father Edwards took over. While Lacey talked with her mother, the pastor called two funeral homes in Great Neck. He introduced himself and said that one of his parishioners wanted to send a Mass card for Mr. Max Hoffman, who had died a year ago. The second funeral home acknowledged having made the arrangements for Mr. Hoffman and furnished Mrs. Hoffman's address. Jay passed it on to Lacey.

"I'll talk to all of you later," she said. "For God's sake, don't tell anyone where I'm going."

At least I *hope* I'll talk to you later, she thought as the cab pulled out from the curb on its way to Ten Adams Place.

CHAPTER 10

T MADE Detective Ed Sloane's flesh crawl to be sitting next to Nick Mars, having to act as if everything were fine.

Sloane knew he had to be on guard against sending out hostile signals that Nick might pick up, but he promised himself that he would have his full say when everything was out in the open.

They began their vigil of watching the apartment building at Three East Seventieth Street at about eleven fifteen, immediately after the meeting with Baldwin broke up. Nick, of course, didn't understand. "We're wasting our time," he complained.

"Just call it an old dog's hunch, okay, Nick?"

They were there only a few minutes when a woman in a long hooded coat walked out of the building and got into a waiting cab. Sloane couldn't see the woman's face, but as he watched her move, he sensed something familiar about her that raised the hairs on the back of his neck. And she was favoring her right leg. The report from Minnesota mentioned that Farrell had an injured ankle.

"Let's go," Sloane told Mars. "She's in that cab."

"You're kidding! Are you psychic or holding back on me?"

"Just a hunch. The phone call to her mother was made five blocks from here."

"I'll call it in," Nick said.

"Not yet you won't."

They followed the cab through the Midtown Tunnel onto the Long Island Expressway. "Where do you think she's going?" Nick asked.

"I don't know any more than you do," Sloane replied. Then he decided to lay it on. "You know, I've always thought that Lacey Farrell might have made a copy of Heather Landi's journal for herself. If so, she may be the only one with the complete journal. Maybe there's something important in those three pages that Jimmy Landi says we're missing. What do you think?"

It was Nick's turn to say, "I don't know any more than you do."

In Great Neck, the cab pulled over to the curb. Was Lacey Farrell getting out? Sloane wondered. He got ready to follow her on foot if necessary.

Instead she stayed in the cab. After a few minutes it pulled out.

They followed her through town, past some obviously expensive houses. "Which one do you want?" Nick asked.

Is that what you're about? Sloane wondered. A cop's salary not good enough for you? You could have changed jobs, kid, he thought. You didn't need to change sides.

Gradually the neighborhood they were driving through changed. The houses were much smaller, closer together but well kept, the kind of neighborhood Ed Sloane felt comfortable in. "Take it easy," he cautioned Nick. "The cab's looking for a house number."

They were on Adams Place. The cab stopped in front of Number Ten. There was a parking spot across the street, about five car lengths down, behind an RV. Perfect, Sloane thought.

He watched as Lacey Farrell got out of the cab. She seemed to be pleading with the driver, who kept shaking his head. Then he rolled up the window and drove away.

Farrell watched the cab until it was out of sight. For the first time Sloane could see her face. He thought she looked vulnerable and scared as she limped up the walk and rang the bell.

It didn't look as if the woman who opened the door a crack was going to let her in. Lacey kept pointing to her ankle.

It was time to call in a report. Sloane found it very satisfying that he would be the one to bring Lacey Farrell in, even though it meant turning her over to Baldwin's custody.

He did not know that an equally satisfied Sandy Savarano was watching from a second-story bedroom in Ten Adams Place, where he had been patiently awaiting Lacey's arrival.

"WHY did you come here?" Lottie Hoffman demanded after reluctantly admitting Lacey into her home. "You can't stay here. I'll call another cab for you. Where do you want to go?"

Now that she was face to face with the one person who might be able to help her, Lacey felt as though she were bordering on hysteria. She still wasn't sure whether or not she had been followed, but she knew she couldn't keep running.

"Mrs. Hoffman, I haven't *got* anyplace to go," she declared passionately. "Someone is trying to kill me, and I think he's been sent by the same person who ordered your husband, Isabelle Waring, and Heather Landi killed. It has to stop, and I think you can make it stop, Mrs. Hoffman. Please help me!"

Lottie Hoffman's eyes softened. She noticed Lacey's stance, how she favored one foot. "You're in pain. Come in. Sit down."

The living room was small but exquisitely neat. Lacey sat on the couch and slipped off her coat. "This isn't mine," she said. "I can't go to my own home or reach into my own closet. I can't go near my family. My little niece was shot and almost killed because of me. I'm going to live like this for the rest of my life if whoever is behind all this isn't identified and arrested. Please, Mrs. Hoffman, tell me. Did your husband know who is behind it?"

"I'm afraid. I can't talk about it." Lottie Hoffman kept her head down as she spoke. "If Max had kept his mouth shut, he'd still be alive. So would Heather. And her mother." Lottie raised her head. "Is the truth worth all those deaths? I don't think so."

"You wake up scared every morning, don't you?" Lacey asked. She reached over and took the elderly woman's thin, heavily veined hand. "Tell me what you know, please, Mrs. Hoffman. Who is behind all this?"

"The truth is, I don't know his name. Max did. Max worked for Jimmy Landi. He knew Heather. If only I hadn't seen her that day at Mohonk. I told Max about it and described the man she was with. He got so upset. He said that the man was a drug dealer and a racketeer, but that no one knew it. So Max made the lunch date with Heather to warn her—and two days later he was dead." Tears welled in Lottie Hoffman's eyes. "I miss Max so much, and I'm so scared."

"You're right to be," Lacey told her gently. "But keeping your door locked isn't the solution. Someday, whoever this person is, he'll decide that you're a potential threat too."

SANDY Savarano attached the silencer to his pistol. It had been child's play to get into this house. He could leave the same way he had come in—through the back window of this bedroom. The tree outside was like a staircase. His car was on the next street, directly accessible through the neighbor's yard. He would be miles away before the cops sitting outside even suspected something was wrong. He looked at his watch. It was time.

The old woman would be first. She was only a nuisance. What he wanted most was to see the expression in Lacey Farrell's eyes when he pointed the pistol at her. He wouldn't give her time to scream. No, there would be just long enough for her to make that whimpering little sound of recognition that was so thrilling to hear, as she realized that she was about to die.

Sandy put his right foot on the first step of the staircase, then with infinite caution began his descent.

ALEX Carbine called Landi's restaurant and asked to speak to Jimmy. He waited, then heard Steve Abbott's voice. "Alex, is there anything I can do for you? Jimmy's feeling awfully down today."

"I'm sorry about that, but I need to talk to him," Carbine said. "By the way, Steve, has Carlos come to you guys for a job?"

"As a matter of fact, he has. Why?"

"Because if he's still there, you can tell him he doesn't have one here anymore. Now put me through to Jimmy."

Alex waited until Landi picked up his phone. "Look, I'm sorry to bother you, but I wanted to pass something on. I understand Carlos is sniffing around for a job. Don't take him back!"

"I don't intend to, but why not?" Jimmy responded.

"Because I think he's on the take somehow. It's been driving me nuts that Lacey Farrell was tracked down by this killer to where they had her hiding in Minneapolis."

"Oh, is that where she was?" Jimmy said. "I hadn't heard."

"Yes, but only her mother knew it. Anyway, the night Mona Farrell learned that Lacey was in Minneapolis, she bought a copy of the Minneapolis *Star Tribune* and had it with her at dinner. I saw her slip it back into the bag when I came to the table. But here's what I'm getting at: I noticed that at one point, when Mona was off to the powder room and I was glad-handing a customer, Carlos was at our table, supposedly straightening our napkins. I saw him move the bag, and it's entirely possible that he looked inside."

"It's just the sort of thing Carlos would do," Landi replied.

"And then he was our waiter again on Friday night when Mona talked about Lacey joining a health club."

"Hmmm," Jimmy murmured, "it sounds like maybe Carlos was working to earn more than a tip Friday night. I gotta go, Alex. Talk to you soon."

THE INSTINCT THAT HAD NEVER failed him told Sloane that something was going terribly wrong. "I think it's time we go in and collect Ms. Farrell," he said.

"Why do that, Ed?" Nick Mars asked, surprised. "We'll pick her up when she comes out."

Sloane opened the car door and drew his pistol. "Let's go."

LACEY wasn't sure if she actually heard a sound on the staircase. Old houses seem sometimes to have a life of their own. She was aware, however, that the atmosphere in the room had changed, like a thermometer suddenly plummeting. Lottie Hoffman felt it too; Lacey could see it in her eyes.

Later she realized that it was the presence of evil, creeping, insidious, enveloping her, so real it was almost tangible. She had felt this same chill when she hid in the closet as Curtis Caldwell came down the stairs after killing Isabelle.

Then she heard it again. The faintest of sounds, but very real. It wasn't her imagination. There was someone on the staircase. I'm going to die, she thought.

She saw terror creep into Mrs. Hoffman's eyes, so she put a warning finger to her own lips, urging her to remain quiet. He was coming down the stairs so slowly, playing cat and mouse with them. Lacey looked around the room. There was no way out. They were trapped.

Her eyes fastened on a glass paperweight on the coffee table. It was about the size of a baseball, and it appeared to be heavy. She couldn't reach it without getting up, something she was afraid to risk. Instead she touched Mrs. Hoffman's hand and pointed to the paperweight.

The staircase became exposed to Lacey's view halfway down. That's where he was now. Through the wooden spindles she could see one well-polished shoe.

A frail and trembling hand grasped the paperweight and slid it into Lacey's hand. Lacey stood up, swung her arm back, and as the assassin she knew as Curtis Caldwell came into full view, threw the paperweight, with all the strength she could muster, at his chest.

The heavy piece of glass struck him right above the stomach just as he prepared to move quickly down the remaining steps. The impact caused him to stumble and drop the pistol. Lacey immediately lunged to try to kick it away from his reach as Mrs. Hoffman, with faltering steps, made her way to the front door and flung it open. She screamed.

Detective Sloane rushed past her into the entry hall. Just as Savarano's fingers were closing on the pistol, Sloane smashed his foot down on Savarano's wrist. Behind him, Nick Mars aimed his pistol at Savarano's head and started to pull the trigger.

"Don't!" Lacey screamed.

Sloane whirled and slapped his partner's hand, causing the bullet intended for Savarano's head to go through his leg instead. He let out a howl of pain.

Dazed, Lacey watched as Sloane handcuffed Isabelle Waring's murderer, the sound of approaching sirens shrilling outside. Finally she looked down into the eyes that had haunted her these past few months. Ice-blue irises, dead black pupils—the eyes of a killer. But there was something new in them: fear.

U.S. Attorney Gary Baldwin appeared suddenly, surrounded by his agents. He looked at Sloane, at Lacey, then at Savarano.

"So you beat us to him," he said, grudging respect evident in his voice. "Congratulations."

He leaned over Savarano. "Hi, Sandy," he said softly. "I'm preparing a cage that's got your name on it—the darkest, smallest cell at Marion, the roughest federal prison in the country. Locked down twenty-three hours a day. Solitary, of course. Chances are you won't like it, but some people don't stay sane long enough in solitary for it to matter. Anyway, you think about it, Sandy. A tiny little cage. Just for you. For the rest of your life."

He turned to Lacey. "You all right, Ms. Farrell?"

She nodded.

"Someone isn't." Sloane went over to Nick Mars, whose face was chalk white. He took his partner's pistol, then his handcuffs. "Stealing evidence is bad enough. Attempted murder is a lot worse. You know what to do, Nick."

Nick put his hands behind his back and turned. Sloane snapped Nick's own cuffs on him.

JIMMY Landi did not emerge from his office all afternoon. Steve Abbott looked in on him several times. "Jimmy, you okay?" he asked.

"Never better, Steve," he said shortly.

"You don't look it. I wish you'd stop reading Heather's journal. It's just getting you down."

"I wish you'd stop telling me to stop reading it."

"Touché. I promise I won't bother you again, but remember this, Jimmy—I'm always here for you."

"Yes, you are, Steve. I know."

At five o'clock Landi received a phone call from Detective Sloane. "Mr. Landi," he said, "I'm at headquarters. I felt we ought to fill you in. Your ex-wife's murderer is in custody. Ms. Farrell has identified him. He's also being charged with the death of Max Hoffman. And we may be able to prove that he was the one who ran your daughter's car off the road too."

"Who is he?" Jimmy asked.

"Sandy Savarano. He's a paid hit man. We expect him to cooperate fully in the investigation. He doesn't want to go to prison."

"None of them do," Jimmy said. "Who hired him?"

"We expect to know that very soon. We're just waiting for Sandy to come to Jesus. Of much less magnitude, by the way, we have a suspect in the theft of your daughter's journal."

"Suspect?"

"Yes, in the legal sense, even though he admitted it. But he swears he didn't take the three unlined pages you thought we lost. I guess Steve Abbott was right. We never had them."

"Steve seems to have a lot of the answers," Jimmy agreed.

"Ms. Farrell is here. She'd like to talk to you."

"Put her on."

"Mr. Landi," Lacey said, "I'm awfully glad this is over. It's been an ordeal for me, and I know it's been terrible for you as well. Mrs. Hoffman is with me. She has something to tell you."

"Put her on."

"I saw Heather at Mohonk," Lottie Hoffman began. "She was with a man, and when I described him to Max, he was so upset. He said the guy was a racketeer, a drug dealer, and that no one suspected him, least of all Heather. She had no idea that . . ."

Even though she had heard it all before, it was chilling to Lacey to consider the appalling crimes committed after Max Hoffman warned Heather away from the man she was dating.

She listened as Mrs. Hoffman described the man she had seen that day. Clearly it was no one *she* knew, Lacey thought.

Sloane took the phone from Mrs. Hoffman. "Mr. Landi, does the man she described sound like anyone you know?"

The detective listened for a moment, then turned to Lacey and Mrs. Hoffman. "Mr. Landi would be very appreciative if you'd stop by his office now."

All Lacey wanted to do was to go to Kit's house to see everyone. "As long as it's just a few minutes there," she said.

"That's all," Sloane promised. "Then I'll drive Mrs. Hoffman home." Sloane was called to the phone as they were leaving the station house. When he returned, he said, "We're going to have company at Landi's restaurant. Baldwin is on his way."

THE receptionist took them upstairs to where Jimmy was waiting. Landi said, "Mrs. Hoffman, please describe again exactly the man you saw with my daughter."

"He was very handsome. He—"

"Wait. I'd like my partner to hear this." Landi turned on the intercom. "Steve, got a minute?"

Steve Abbott came into the office smiling. "Oh. I didn't realize you had company."

"*Interesting* company, Steve. Mrs. Hoffman, what's wrong?"

Lottie Hoffman was pointing at Abbott. Her face was ghastly

white. "You're the one I saw with Heather. You're the one Max said was a drug dealer and a racketeer and a thief. You're the reason I'm alone."

"What are you talking about?" Abbott said, his brows knitting fiercely, the mask of geniality momentarily fallen from his face. All of a sudden Lacey thought it was possible to imagine this handsome, debonair man as a killer.

Accompanied by a half-dozen agents, U.S. Attorney Gary Baldwin came into the room.

"What Mrs. Hoffman is saying, Mr. Abbott, is that you are a murderer, that you ordered her husband killed because he knew too much. Max Hoffman quit working here because he had seen what you were doing and knew his life wouldn't be worth a plugged nickel if you knew. You've been dropping old suppliers like Jay Taylor and buying from Mob-owned businesses, most of the stuff stolen. You've done it in the casino too. And that's only one of your activities.

"Max had to tell Heather what you are. And she had to decide whether to let you keep cheating her father or tell him how she found out about you.

"You didn't take the chance. Savarano told us you called Heather in Vermont and said Jimmy had had a heart attack and she should get right home. Savarano was waiting for her. When Isabelle Waring wouldn't stop looking for reasons to prove Heather's death wasn't an accident, she became too dangerous."

"That's a lie," Abbott shouted. "Jimmy, I never—"

"Yes, you did," Jimmy said calmly. "You killed Max Hoffman, and you did the same to my daughter's mother. And to Heather. You killed her." Jimmy's eyes blazed with anger; his hands formed into giant fists; his cry of agony exploded through the room. "You let my baby burn to death," he howled. "You—you—" He lunged across the desk and wrapped his powerful hands around Abbott's throat. It took Sloane and the team of agents to pry his fingers loose.

Jimmy's racking sobs echoed throughout the building as Baldwin took Steve Abbott into custody.

AT EIGHT O'CLOCK THE DRIVER Jay had sent to pick up Lacey at her apartment called to say he was downstairs. Lacey was frantic to see her family, but there was a phone call she still had to make. There was so much to tell Tom, so much to explain. Baldwin, now suddenly her friend and ally, had told her, "You're out of the loop now. We've plea-bargained with Savarano, so we won't need your testimony to get Abbott. So you'll be okay. But keep a low profile for a while. Why not take a vacation until things settle down?"

She had replied only half jokingly, "I *do* have an apartment and a job in Minnesota. Maybe I should go back there."

She dialed Tom's number. The now familiar voice sounded strained and anxious. "Hello," he said.

"Tom?"

A whoop of joy. "Alice, where *are* you? Are you all right?"

"Never better, Tom. And you?"

"Worried sick! I've been going out of my mind since you disappeared."

"It's a long story. You'll hear it all." She paused. "There's just one thing. Alice doesn't live here anymore. Do you think you could possibly get used to calling me Lacey? My name is Lacey Farrell."

THE
BIG
PICTURE

DOUGLAS
KENNEDY

The big picture—
sometimes you don't see it.
Until it's too late. . . .

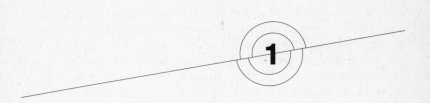

1

IT WAS four in the morning, I hadn't slept in weeks, and the baby was crying again.

The baby didn't wake me, because I'd been staring at the ceiling for hours when he started bawling. But I was so shell-shocked from lack of rest that I couldn't move from the bed. I just lay there, rigid, as Josh pushed his five-month-old lungs to new extremes.

Eventually his repetitive shrieks prodded my wife, Beth, into a half-awake state. Nudging me with her elbow, she spoke to me for the first time in two days. "You deal with him." Then she rolled over and covered her head with a pillow.

I did as ordered, my movements mechanical. I sat up. I put my feet on the floor. I reached for the striped bathrobe on the bedside chair. I walked to the door and opened it. My day had begun—though in reality it had never really ended.

The nursery was opposite our room. Unlike our other son—four-year-old Adam, who started sleeping through the night after he passed the eight-week mark—Josh was a serious insomniac. He refused to collapse for more than two hours at a stretch. Twenty weeks into his little life Beth and I had yet to experience a night of unbroken sleep. Recently I'd been trying to convince myself that exhaustion was the main source of the disharmony between us—a disharmony that turned rather nasty two nights ago, when Beth let fly with some pent-up venom and called me totally self-absorbed. Naturally, I counterpunched and told her she was a suburban shrew.

Forty-eight hours after that exchange, she still wasn't talking to me. So it wasn't just Baby Josh's cries that were keeping me awake at night. It was lots of other things. Like this house. I now hated this house. Not that there is anything hateful about my house. On the contrary, it is the sort of suburban American classic that many a citizen would be proud to own—a two-story colonial with dark green shutters, four bedrooms, eat-in kitchen, basement family room, and a separate, two-car garage. Asking price: $485,000. But this corner of Connecticut took a beating during the recession, so we snagged it for $413,000 in 1991. At the time, several colleagues at the law firm where I work told me I had made a "killer deal." But when I was signing the contract, all I could think was, We really are the architects of our own incarceration.

Like every room in the house, Josh's nursery is Early American. He sleeps in a mahogany crib, circa 1782. He gets his diapers changed on top of a pine chest from an old York, Maine, inn. When he gets older, he'll be able to sit in a tiny rocking chair that once housed the backside of little Nathaniel Hawthorne.

How do I know all this about my kid's furniture? Beth, of course. Two years after we moved here from the city, she got rid of all that functional stuff we once acquired at the Pottery Barn and announced: We're going Colonial. To Beth this didn't mean buying some leatherette Williamsburg wing chairs at Ethan Allen. Instead, everything in our new home was going to be one hundred percent Guaranteed Federalist. And for months she went on an authenticity binge—scouring every antiques shop from here to New London. When the house was fully furnished, it was a triumph. Though Beth never said anything, I knew that she secretly despised what she had created, that she realized it was a diversionary tactic, designed to deflect her attention from certain uncomfortable truths. Like me, she too now hated this house and all that it implied.

Josh had gone ballistic by the time I reached his crib. I combed the floor for the pacifier he had flung away. When I found it, I sterilized it by popping it between my lips and then shoved it back into his mouth. I picked him up and slung him across my shoulder. Halfway down the stairs he spit out the pacifier and returned to wailing mode. And when he saw the bottle of formula by the microwave in the kitchen, he really did some ear damage during the twenty seconds it took to heat it.

Adam was a real designer baby, the sort of cute charmer you'd see in a diaper commercial. But Josh is a little bruiser, with an oversized head and a boxer's nose and the disposition of a pit bull. Naturally, I love him, but I'm not sure if I like him yet. Of course, I have a theory about why he cries so much: He's reacting to the enmity between his parents. Kids sense these things. Adam too is very aware that his parents haven't been getting along. Whenever Beth and I have a nasty exchange, his big gray eyes plead with us to like each other again. It guts me, seeing his concern; it also brings me back to when I was Adam's age and I too watched helplessly as my parents pulled each other apart.

As soon as Josh saw me retrieve the heated formula from the microwave, his hands began to flap until I turned it over to him. Then I pulled out a kitchen chair and sat down, cradling him against me while he slurped away. There was at least five minutes of quiet ahead while he finished the bottle. So with my free hand I reached out and hit the remote control for the little nine-inch television tucked away on a countertop and flipped to CNN.

As the screen flickered to life, I saw something that made me flinch. Not something, actually. Someone. Her name was Kate Brymer—CNN's star war correspondent. She was dressed in designer fatigues and a flak jacket, reporting from some bombed-out hospital in Sarajevo. I noticed that her bobbed chestnut hair was well coiffed for someone in a war zone. Then again, she always had a thing about her hair. When we lived together at college, she used to brush it incessantly. Even then she understood that her looks would be a necessary weapon in her quest for importance.

I remember her lying in bed one wet Sunday afternoon, browsing through a book by war correspondent Martha Gellhorn. "I'll write a memoir like this one day," she said, certain about her professional destiny. Then she held up a collection of battlefield photos by the great Robert Capa, adding, "And you'll be this guy." But Kate was wrong about me. I've never been anywhere near a war zone, and I now knew that I never would.

Josh suddenly flung the bottle to the floor. Within seconds the crying game started. I tossed him back over my shoulder, opened the door next to the fridge, and walked down five steps to the basement, which had become my haven.

It's not a big area—around sixteen feet by twelve feet—with two small rooms off the main area, but I've managed to use the space shrewdly. It's also the one corner of the house that Beth hasn't managed to Martha Washingtonize. As you come down the stairs, you immediately see my exercise area—a NordicTrack, a StairMaster, and a set of free weights. I try to do a forty-minute workout every morning to keep my body trim at a constant one hundred and seventy-five pounds. My doctor tells me it is the perfect weight for a five-foot-eleven nonsmoking thirty-eight-year-old. But perhaps the real reason I'm so fit is because any time I feel like punching a wall with my fist, I come down here and drain the rage with bench presses.

Or I bury myself in the one place where I am truly content—my darkroom. It used to be the laundry room, but one of the first things we did after moving in was to transfer the washer and dryer to a pantry off the kitchen. Then the carpenter and plumber got to work. All existing cabinets and fixtures were torn out. A pair of professional stainless steel sinks were installed. The walls were replastered and painted light gray; then a sleek unit of customized steel-gray cabinets and work tops was built into one wall. And I dropped $2300 on a real indulgence—the latest light-trap revolving door, a cylinder within a cylinder, guaranteed to create the perfect darkroom blackout.

Following the advice of a photojournalist I know at *Newsweek,* I also invested in top-range reproduction equipment: a Beseler 45mx enlarger, a Kindermann film dryer, a mechanized Kodak tray rocker.

I only use top Ilford-brand laboratory chemicals; I only print on Galleria bromide paper. And like most serious photographers, I favor two top-grade monochrome films: Kodak Tri-X and Ilford HP4.

Opposite this work area is a floor-to-ceiling locker, secured by two pickproof locks. If you have a camera collection valued at over $45,000, you cannot afford to take chances.

I started collecting cameras in 1962. I was six years old, visiting my maternal grandparents in Fort Lauderdale. I picked up an old Brownie that had been left on a side table, looked through the viewfinder, and was captivated. Here was a whole new way of seeing things. But most pleasing to my six-year-old sensibility was the discovery that you could hide behind the lens. And for the remainder of our stay—during which my parents squabbled, my grandparents squabbled, and then each couple turned on the other—I spent much of the time with that Brownie in front of my face. My father was not amused. At the dinner table one night, when I tried to eat a shrimp cocktail while keeping the Brownie at eye level, he snatched the camera from me. My grandfather Morris thought his son-in-law was being unduly harsh, and came to my defense. "Let the kid have his fun. Betcha he's gonna be a photographer when he grows up."

"Only if he wants to starve," my father said, a hint of old Yalie contempt in his voice.

That was the first of many confrontations I would have with my father on the subject of photography. But at the airport, at the end of that brief, shrill visit to Fort Lauderdale, my grandfather handed me the Brownie. I still have it. It's stored in my cabinet, next to my first Instamatic (Christmas 1967), my first Nikon (high school graduation), my first Leica (college graduation, 1978—a present from my mother six months before an embolism snuffed out her life at the age of fifty-one).

One wall of the basement is filled with a selection of my landscapes—rather moody Ansel Adams–style vistas of the Connecticut coast. Another wall is all portraits—Beth and the kids in a variety of poses, using only available light and an open aperture to give them a grainy, naturalistic tone. And the final wall is what I call my Diane Arbus phase: a man with no legs and an eye patch begging in front of Bloomingdale's, a drunk on the Bowery pulling out a half-eaten Big Mac from a garbage can. Adam loves my collection of urban sickos. Every time he visits me down here while I'm working, he climbs onto the gray studio couch beneath them, points to the Bowery dipso, giggles with delight, and says, "Yucky man! Yucky man!" He's my kind of critic. And Baby Josh? He notices nothing. He just cries.

He was certainly crying that morning. Since I'd brought him down from the kitchen, he hadn't let up. Maybe his diaper was the problem. I laid him down on the couch, undid the snaps at the bottom of his onesie, and peered into his Pampers. A full load.

So it was back upstairs to the nursery. I deposited Josh on the plastic changing mat that covers the top of his pine chest and once again undid the snaps of his onesie. When this was achieved (after considerable effort), I pulled back the lower part of his suit, ripped off the plastic fasteners on his Pampers, and stared into a diaper from hell. I turned away from him for a moment to grab a handful of Baby Wipes from the windowsill.

In the three seconds that my hand was off his chest, the unthinkable happened: Josh dislodged himself from the changing mat. When I turned back, he was about to roll off the chest. I roared his name and dove toward him just as he toppled off the edge. Somehow I got myself under him, my head crashing into the chest as he landed on top of me. He screamed in shock.

And then the nursery door flew open, and Beth was bearing down on me, yelling, "I told you *never* let him go."

She snatched Josh from me. As she picked him up, his diaper fell off, landing on my stomach. I didn't care that my robe was now smeared with diarrhea, as I was more preoccupied with Beth's unforgiving voice: "You never listen, do you?"

"It was an accident," I said. "He's not hurt."

"But I told you over and over . . ."

"All right, all right. I was—"

"Wrong."

"Fine." I was on my feet. As I stood up, the diaper slid off me and, with a soft plop, landed facedown on the rug—a hand-loomed 1775 rug from a boardinghouse where John Adams once stayed.

"Terrific," Beth muttered, her voice weary. "Just terrific."

"I'm sorry, Beth."

"Just go, Ben. Go get a shower. I'll deal with this. As usual."

I beat a fast retreat. But as I entered the hallway, I saw Adam standing by his door, his favorite stuffed toy—a koala bear—clutched against him, his eyes wide. I knelt down and kissed his blond head, saying, "It's okay now. Go back to sleep."

He pointed to my splattered robe, wrinkling his nose as the smell hit him. "Yucky man, yucky man."

I managed a small smile. "Yeah, real yucky man."

When I came downstairs showered and dressed for work, Beth was in the kitchen feeding Josh and Adam. She had changed into a pair of leggings and a black sweatshirt that didn't disguise her new-found leanness. Beth was never fleshy, but when I first met her seven years ago, she did look like the captain of some hard-drinking field hockey team: an exuberant, big-boned blonde who liked to talk football and guzzle beer. She also had the most mischievous of laughs. Now, at thirty-five, she had become aerobically gaunt. Her cheekbones were sharply defined, she had no waist, and her once long hair was cut short in that chic mannish style favored by French movie actresses. I still found her enticing, and she still turned heads. But most of the time the tough-girl ebullience had been replaced by all-purpose world-weariness.

I put my hand on her shoulder and tried to plant a kiss on her head. But as soon as I touched her, she flinched, shrugging me off. So I kissed my two sons good-bye and picked up my briefcase. "I might have a meeting at five thirty," I said.

"Doesn't matter. Fiona's working late tonight," Beth said, mentioning the Irish nanny who looked after Adam and Josh.

I opened the back door. "See you," I said. She didn't respond.

It is a seven-minute walk to the train. As I pulled up the collar of my Burberry against the October chill, I remembered the sales pitch of the real estate broker who sold us the house: "You're not just buying a great house, you're also buying a great commute."

Our road is called Constitution Crescent. There are twenty-four houses—eleven colonials, seven Cape Codders, four split-level ranches, and two red brick Monticellos. Each house has a half-acre front lawn and a driveway. The favored car is the Volvo station wagon. There is also a handful of sports cars: a Porsche 911, owned by Chuck Bailey, a creative director at some big ad agency; a battered MG that belongs to a local, and not very good, photographer named Gary Summers; and a Mazda Miata that sits in my driveway, next to the Volvo that Beth uses.

At the end of Constitution Crescent is a clapboard Episcopalian church. In front of it is a town sign: NEW CROYDON, EST. 1763.

I turned left at the church to reach New Croydon's central drag, Adams Avenue. Making a right on Adams, I cut across a parking lot and climbed the steps to the bridge that spans the railway tracks. The 6:47 was due in three minutes. I hurried toward the southbound platform. It was already black with suits. There must have been eighty of us waiting for that dawn express.

As I bought *The New York Times* and *Vanity Fair* from the station shop, I felt a drop of acid hit my stomach. I winced. More bile trickled down, scorching my gut. When the train rolled into the station, I staggered on board, almost doubled over. Falling into the first available seat, I dug out a bottle of Maalox from my attaché case and downed a third of it in one long slurp. In the five minutes it took the train to rumble to its next stop—Riverside—the agony abated.

First Riverside, then Cos Cob, then Greenwich, followed by Port Chester, Rye, Harrison, Mamaroneck, Larchmont, New Rochelle, Pelham, Mount Vernon, 125th Street, and, finally, Grand Central station. My morning litany. Similar to the one my late father sang for thirty-five years. Only whereas I travel Metro North, his beat was the old Hudson River Line.

He too had a good commute. His brokerage firm was on Madison and Forty-eighth, a ten-minute walk from Grand Central.

Once, when I was eleven, I accompanied him into the city. At his office, I was shown the executive suite, where he had one of four offices. It was a plush world of big desks and overstuffed leather armchairs. Just like the India Club, where he took me for lunch. It was down in the financial district, near the Stock Exchange. The atmosphere was very Bostonian, very old Yankee—lots of wood paneling. The dining room was high-vaulted and formal. The waiters wore starched white livery. And all around us was a landscape of pinstripes and horn-rimmed glasses: Wall Street at lunch.

"You'll be a member here one day," my father said. And I remember thinking that having a big office and eating every day at the India Club must be the pinnacle of adulthood.

Eight years later I vowed never to set foot in the India Club again. It was the summer of '75; I had just finished my freshman year at Bowdoin College and had landed a vacation job as a salesman at a camera shop. My father was appalled that I had turned down his offer to "learn the bond business" as a runner on the floor of the Exchange. He summoned me to lunch.

As soon as I sat down at his table, he told me that if I didn't take the job he'd offered me, I could forget about going back to Bowdoin in the fall, as he wouldn't pay the tuition.

I capitulated. And for the next three summers I did as my dad demanded and worked for his firm as a runner on the floor of the Exchange.

Why did I wimp out? Because when you've been raised and educated in a select East Coast realm (private day school in Ossining, New York, four years at Andover, acceptance at an elite New England college like Bowdoin), you don't throw it all away to sell Nikons. Not unless you want to be considered a total loser—someone who was offered all the breaks but still couldn't achieve.

Achieve. That most American of verbs. To my father it meant one thing: making serious money. The sort of money you can most readily obtain by climbing the corporate ladder or embedding yourself in one of the safer professions. But though I did take the prelaw courses my father suggested, I always told myself that when I finished college and was no longer economically beholden to him, I would kiss his achieving world good-bye.

"Don't let him intimidate you," Kate Brymer always told me.

Kate Brymer. As the train pulled out of Harrison, I found myself flicking through the glossy pages of *Vanity Fair.* And there she was, standing in front of some Bosnian killing field. As always, she was wearing stylish fatigues and stared at the camera with her now predictable Mother-Courage-Dressed-by-Armani look. The article headline read IN THE REAL LINE OF FIRE: CNN'S KATE BRYMER BRINGS GUTSY CHIC TO BOSNIA.

I'm envious of Kate. Always was. Especially after we left Bowdoin in the summer of '78 and moved to Paris. Though my father refused to support me while I tried to get established there as a photographer, Kate had a sizable trust fund that enabled us to rent a studio apartment in the Marais district. Within a fortnight of arriving in the city, she had a job working as a gofer for *Newsweek.* After three months she was taken on as a production assistant at the Paris bureau of CBS News. Eight weeks later she arrived home one evening and announced that she was moving in with her boss, the CBS bureau chief. She was packed and gone by morning.

Within two months so was I. I couldn't afford to continue living in Paris. I was broke, having struck out on the job front. "These shots aren't bad, but they're nothing special," the photo editor of the *International Herald Tribune* told me after I showed him my portfolio.

Back in New York, every picture editor I met told me the same thing. My photos were "all right," but being just all right wouldn't get me far in the Big Apple.

It was a miserable time. Still reeling from the abrupt way Kate had kicked me in the teeth, I ended up crashing in the cramped Morningside Heights apartment of a friend who was doing graduate work at Columbia. While I desperately hunted for some sort of start in the photographic game, I kept myself fed by working as a salesman at Willoughby's Cameras on West Thirty-second Street. And then my mother died. And panic set in. I was a failure. A nohoper. Opening up magazines like *GQ* and *Esquire* and *Rolling*

Stone only underscored my status as a failure, for their pages were filled with guys my own age who were already big-deal success stories. And I began to convince myself that I would never make it as a photographer, that I would end up fossilizing behind the counter of Willoughby's—a middle-aged clerk with terminal dandruff.

Panic, of course, has its own crazy momentum. Once you're in its grasp, you surrender to the melodramatic. Your situation is hopeless. There is No Way Out. You must find a solution *now.* And you end up making wrong decisions that alter everything. Decisions that you come to loathe.

I look back on those few months of mid-twenties angst and wonder, Why didn't I have more confidence in my photographic abilities? But when you've been schooled in the achieving ethic, you think that if you don't move upward at the speed you believe you deserve, you must be doing something wrong. I fell victim to this delusion.

Four months after I started work at Willoughby's, my father paid me a surprise visit around lunchtime. As soon as he saw me in my salesman uniform (a cheap blue jacket emblazoned with the name of the store), he had to work hard at containing his disdain.

"Here to buy a camera?" I asked him.

"Here to buy you lunch," he said.

We retreated to a little coffee shop on Sixth and Thirty-second.

"Not the India Club, Dad? Or would the jacket embarrass you?"

"Always the smart aleck," he said.

"So the jacket *does* embarrass you. . . ."

"You really don't like me, do you?" he replied.

"Maybe that's because you've never particularly liked me."

"Stop talking nonsense. You're my only child."

"But I'm a disappointment. A professional disappointment."

"If you're happy doing what you do, then I'm happy for you."

I looked at him carefully. "You don't mean that," I said.

He laughed a bronchial laugh. "You're right," he said. "I don't. I think you're wasting time. But you're twenty-three. If this is what you want, I won't say a word against it."

Silence. We ordered.

"But I will tell you this. There will come a point when you'll wake up one day and rue the fact that you have no money. If you had a law degree behind you, you'd be able to live the way you want *and* use your free time to concentrate on photography. Money is freedom, Ben. If you decide to go back to school—get a law degree or an M.B.A.—I'll pay for it."

I refused to consider his Faustian bargain for at least a month. It was early August. I'd just had four job applications rejected from assorted newspapers. One Sunday afternoon a tall, angular man in his sixties wandered into Willoughby's and asked for a half-dozen rolls of Tri-X. He handed over his Amex card, and I saw the name: RICHARD AVEDON.

"*The* Richard Avedon?" I asked, sounding far too starstruck.

"Maybe," he said, a little bored.

"Richard Avedon . . ." I said, making an imprint of his credit card. "I am just the biggest fan of your Texas drifters photographs. Really amazing stuff. I'm shooting a sequence right now in Times Square. Drifters, hookers, general lowlife. And, like, I'm trying to adopt your 'the face is the landscape' separation of subject from vista. But what I was going to ask was—"

Avedon interrupted my manic monologue. "We finished here?"

I felt as if I had taken a left to the jaw. "Sorry," I croaked, and handed him the credit card slip. He scribbled his name, picked up his film, and left, shaking his head toward the leggy blonde waiting for him at an adjoining counter.

"What was he going on about?" I heard her ask him.

"Just some no-hope camera geek," he said.

A few days later I signed up to take a review course for the LSATs. To my amazement I scored high—695 high. Good enough to get me accepted at three of the top law schools in the country: N.Y.U., Berkeley, and Virginia. I was jubilant. I finally felt like a winner, the class act I was supposed to be. And I convinced myself I had done the right thing. Especially since for the first time in my life I had actually made my father happy. So happy that after I told him I had decided to enter N.Y.U. Law that autumn, he sent me a check for $5000, accompanied by a note telling me to "go have some fun before buckling down."

So I quit my job at Willoughby's and hit the road. I roamed the Pacific Northwest for a month in a battered Toyota, a camera on the seat beside me. And at the end of that indolent road movie of a summer, I sped back to New York, sold my car, put my camera on a shelf, and began my study of the law.

The year after I passed my bar exam—and was already comfortably positioned in a major Wall Street firm—my father died. A massive coronary after a massive lunch at the India Club.

Money is freedom, Ben. Sure it is, Dad. Until you buckle down. And find yourself singing a morning litany that goes: Riverside, Cos Cob, Greenwich, Port Chester, Rye, Harrison, Mamaroneck, Larchmont, New Rochelle, Pelham, Mount Vernon . . .

"One hundred Twenty-fifth Street. Grand Central next stop." The conductor's voice jolted me awake. I had slept through the suburbs. And for a few befogged moments I wasn't sure where I was. Or how I'd ended up on this commuter express. Surrounded by suits. Wearing a suit. This can't be right. I must have made a big mistake. I am the wrong man on the wrong train.

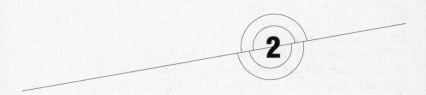

2

THERE were nine pills laid out across my office desk. One Zantac for gastric acid, two ginseng softgels for natural energy, two tabs of Dexedrine for chemical energy, a Valium for stress, and three tabs of beta carotene to keep my system detoxified.

"It's the big jolt of beta that really gets me," Estelle said, eyeing my morning pharmaceutical intake.

"Keeps me clean and pure," I said, popping the pills into my mouth and washing them down with a Maalox chaser.

"Now I suppose you want your morning coffee?" she asked.

"Please. And the Berkowitz file, while you're at it."

"It's already on your desk. Look at article five, subdivision A of the will. There was a violation of the rule against perpetuities because the trust never ended."

I looked up at Estelle and smiled. "You're the one who should be sitting behind this desk."

"Don't want to be drinking Maalox for breakfast." She opened the door to her outer office. "Anything else, Mr. Bradford?"

"My wife . . . would you get her on the phone, please."

A quick glance at her watch. I could tell what she was thinking and what she would tell her colleagues come lunchtime: "Calling his wife fifteen minutes after he reaches the office, and it's, like, the eighth time in two weeks." But being the consummate legal secretary that she is, Estelle said nothing except, "I'll buzz you when I reach her."

Estelle. Forty-seven years old, divorced, built like a Buick. She'd joined the firm twenty-five years ago, and now she could be running this division, because nobody in Lawrence, Cameron and Thomas knows more about inheritance law. She has a microchip mind; once she has processed even the most obscure morsel of information, she can call it up at random years later. And she is probably the world's leading expert on the rule of perpetuities—a law that makes sense only to a T&E lawyer.

T&E. Trusts and estates. We're the folks who are here to remind you that, alas, you can't take it with you. So with an eye toward your inevitable demise, we help you plan how to disburse your accumulated temporal booty. Of course, Lawrence, Cameron and Thomas will not represent you unless your net worth is more than $2 million. We're a small department, T&E. One senior partner (Jack Mayle), one junior partner (*moi*), three associates, five secretaries. And since T&E is considered a decidedly nerdish branch of the law, we're tucked away at the back of corporate headquarters, with only one corner office to our name.

The offices of Lawrence, Cameron and Thomas are located on the eighteenth and nineteenth floors of 120 Broadway in lower Manhattan. The building is one of those Roaring Twenties testaments to boom capitalism, the skyscraper equivalent of a Wurlitzer organ.

People in the firm consider a corner office to be a big deal. Only full partners are allocated them, but since there are just eight corner offices, senior lawyers spend years fretting about when they'll finally get one. Personally, I don't fret about the position of my office (nineteenth floor, nice view of the Brooklyn Bridge, adjoining the corner suite occupied by Jack Mayle). And I certainly don't fret about the cash they throw at me—around $315,000 a year (depending on bonuses). In fact, I can't complain about anything to do with Lawrence, Cameron and Thomas. Except the work. I really fret a lot about the work. Because it bores me. Bores me stupid.

Of course, I knew that T&E was Dullsville when I joined the firm in September 1983. But that was the mid-'80s, and Wall Street was the place to be. So I developed a master plan. I'd stay five years max, save like an idiot, and then, while still in my early thirties, devote my time to photography. After all, America was brimming with famous lawyer-novelists. Why couldn't I be the first famous lawyer-photographer?

Like all new associates at Lawrence, Cameron and Thomas, I did time in each of the firm's heavyweight divisions—litigation, corporate law, and tax—but discovered they were filled with guys who delighted in gutting the opposition and sticking knives into each other. Of course, this breed dominates so much of American corporate life. They've been educated in a play-to-win philosophy, and they love using the language of the gridiron. "We want you to play the tough linebacker here. . . . We don't like field goals in this department, only touchdowns." After months of dismal football metaphors I realized that to survive the cutthroat theatrics of a sexy legal division, you had to buy into their gladiatorial belief that business is war. Since I simply looked upon the law as a means by which to subsidize my future photographic career, I decided to seek out a quiet niche. And when I met Jack Mayle, I knew I had found my mentor, my rabbi.

"If you're one of those prep school Apaches who wants to collect scalps, I've got no use for you here," he said during our first interview. "There's no glamour in T and E. This is Nebbish Town, *capisce?* Our motto is, Let the goys have the coronaries."

"But Mr. Mayle," I said, "I'm a goy."

He threaded his liver-spotted fingers together and cracked his knuckles. "This has crossed my mind," he said with a hint of rabbinical mischief in his voice. "But at least you're a *quiet* goy."

Jack Mayle bought handmade suits from Dunhill. His fine gray hair was always well oiled and combed back. He looked like George Raft—a diminutive dandy who decided that dressing well was the best defense against his five-foot-four stature and the fact that he was the only Jewish senior partner in a deeply WASP firm. I think one of the reasons Jack took to me was that he sensed (and approved of) my outsider status. He'd done a stint as a would-be abstract painter in Greenwich Village before bowing to family pressure and winning a scholarship to Brooklyn Law. So watching me back-seat my photographic ambitions to play the corporate game must have triggered some protective instinct in him, because within two weeks of my arrival in T&E he let it be known that after twenty-four years at Lawrence, Cameron, he had found his successor. "You play your cards right, I'll get you a junior partnership in five years," he told me.

Another Faustian bargain dangled in front of me. Partnership? At the premature age of thirty-three? That would have amazed the old man. All right, T&E wasn't exactly a thrill a minute, but I started convincing myself that the minutiae of legal work suited my nature. I mean, if I loved the minute technicalities involved in printing a photograph, surely I could come to enjoy the detailed craftsmanship of will writing. Couldn't I?

The phone buzzed on my desk. I hit the SPEAKER button and got a nasal blast of Estelle. "Your wife doesn't answer, Mr. Bradford. And Mr. Mayle was wondering if you had a minute."

"Tell him I'll drop by in fifteen. Finishing up a few adjustments to the Berkowitz document."

These adjustments took all of five minutes. Then I picked up the phone, hit the first button on my speed dialer, and was connected with my home number. It answered.

"Hola? Quién es?" said Perdita, our Guatemalan housekeeper.

"Hola, Perdita," I said. *"Dónde está señora Bradford?"*

"Ha salido. Para todo el día."

"Te ha dado un número de teléfono dónde está?"

"No, señor."

"Y los niños?"

"Han salido con Fiona."

Out all day. No telephone contact number. And the kids were off with the nanny. I bit my lower lip. That was the third weekday in a row Beth had been out of the house by nine. I know because on each of those mornings I had tried to reach her from the office, hoping somehow to broker a cease-fire between us.

I flipped open my address book and dialed the number of Wendy Waggoner, a local cookbook writer (I'm sure you've read *Wendy's Waistline Wonders: The Ultimate Foodie Diet*) and the only forty-year-old woman I knew who still wore plaid skirts with big safety pins. Beth played tennis with Wendy one morning a week. Maybe this was that morning.

"Residencia de Waggoner." Another Latin American maid.

"Is Wendy there?" I asked, suddenly tired of bilingual calls to Connecticut.

"Senora Waggoner is in city today. Message?"

"No, *gracias.*" I hung up. No need to make Wendy wonder why I was phoning her on a weekday morning in search of my wife.

Estelle buzzed me again. "Mr. Mayle was wondering . . ."

"I'm on my way," I said.

Jack's office was next to mine. I knocked and entered. He was sitting in his vast leather desk chair, looking more dwarfed than usual. He smiled a weary, cheerless smile, a smile I didn't like. "Sit down, Ben," he said.

I did as ordered.

He looked at me carefully. "Everything okay on the home front?"

"Fine, Jack. Just fine."

"Liar."

"That obvious?"

"You look like hell, Ben."

"Nothing twenty straight hours of sleep won't cure. But you . . . you look like a guy who's just spent two weeks in Palm Springs."

"No, I do not," he said.

"Sorry," I said, taken aback by his irritated tone.

He gazed blankly at his desk blotter for what seemed like minutes. Finally he spoke. "I'm dying, Ben."

LATER, back in my office, I sat down at my desk and put my head in my hands. Jack. My mentor, my surrogate father.

I'm dying, Ben.

Inoperable stomach cancer. He'd found out two weeks ago but hadn't told anyone, not even his wife.

"They say eight months, a year max," he'd said.

He wanted the news kept quiet within the firm. "I'm not submitting to chemo. If it's terminal, it's terminal. So I'll take their painkillers and keep going to the office until—"

He broke off, tightened his lips, and stared out his window at the frantic pedestrian parade on Wall Street—everyone looking so purposeful, everyone so preoccupied with getting somewhere.

"You know what's hardest about all this?" he said quietly. "It's realizing that there's no future possibility for change, for exploring other options, for even dreaming about another life, because you've run out of road."

Then he turned around. Staring me straight in the eyes, he said, "You're going to be the new senior partner, Ben."

I flinched. An involuntary movement, but Jack saw it. And said nothing. Because he knew. He knew exactly what this meant for me. A half mil a year minimum, plenty of corporate prestige . . . and the death of my other life. That unrealized life behind a viewfinder.

A life that—like Jack's stint long ago in some MacDougal Street garret—becomes the stuff of daydream.

Sitting there at my desk, I suddenly felt light-headed, shaky. I needed to talk to Beth. I grabbed the phone. It trembled in my hand as I hit the speed dialer and called home. It rang four times. Then I heard my upbeat voice on the answering machine.

"Hi there. You've reached Ben and Beth Bradford. We can't come to the phone right now. . . ."

Ben and Beth Bradford. I always told her that if we ever got married, she should keep her own name.

"I'll live with you forever," she said one evening in January of 1988, when we were killing a second bottle of wine down at the Odeon, "but we're never getting married."

"But if we did . . ."

"Then I'd take your name."

"That's kind of old-fashioned of you," I said.

"Nah," Beth said, "just being practical. Beth Bradford would look a lot better on a dust jacket than Beth Schnitzler."

1988. We'd been living together for just a few months in a loft-style apartment in SoHo. We were artists-in-waiting. At least that's what Beth dubbed us. There was always a touch of archness in her voice when she used that phrase, but we both believed it was only a matter of a year or two before we liberated ourselves from the wage-slave world. And every weekday morning, before heading off to her job as an assistant fiction editor at *Cosmopolitan,* Beth would get up at six and work on the novel she hoped would make her literary name. She refused to let me see it until one Saturday in March of '89, when she handed me the 438-page manuscript and said, "It's called *The Playpen of Ambition.*"

Written in a style that could be described as sensitive-girl lyricism, it was about a young, gawky girl from Westchester County attempting to cope with her mother's agonizing death from breast cancer. When Mama eventually expires, the girl moves to the Big City determined to become a Great Painter. She takes a job in the art department of a glossy magazine, falls in love with a dermatologist, and finds herself torn between the temptations of domesticity and the "inner voice" of her muse. It was, give or take a few details, the large-print edition of Beth's life.

In the five months after she finished it, twenty-two publishers rejected *The Playpen of Ambition.*

That autumn Beth discovered she was pregnant.

The idea of fatherhood—and all its incumbent responsibilities—terrified me. But I was desperate to keep Beth, and I convinced myself that a child would *permanently* cement us together. Beth raised all sorts of fears about becoming a facsimile of her mother, who had been a highflier in public relations at one of the big New York firms before she got married and had Beth. Then it was off to Ossining and a life of PTA meetings and coffee mornings.

I assuaged Beth's fears. We would keep on living in the city. She would keep on working. A nanny would be hired to look after the child. Life, I assured her, would go on as before.

"It never works that way," she said.

"It can. It will. And after we're married . . ." I pulled her toward me. I kissed her deeply.

Then she took my face in her hands and looked at me carefully. "So much for our artist-in-waiting fantasy."

"We'll get there."

"Maybe, but if I *ever* suggest moving to the burbs, shoot me."

I didn't remind her of that comment thirteen months later when she called my office one afternoon in a state of shock. "You've got to get home *now,*" she said, sounding totally panicked.

My heart stopped. Adam was just four months old. Crib death, meningitis . . . "Tell me," I finally said.

"Vomit," she sobbed. "He's covered in vomit."

The vomit in question was from a homeless guy camped out in an alley opposite our apartment. Beth, home early that day from *Cosmo,* was heading out with Adam for a walk. Suddenly this bum veered into her path.

"Give a guy a dollar, huh? Jus' one little—" But he didn't finish the sentence, as he suddenly turned green and blew lunch all over

Adam. That weekend I suggested we house-hunt in Connecticut.

"I can't believe we're doing this," Beth said after I made an offer on the house on Constitution Crescent.

"Nor can I. But hey, we'll both be in the city every day, right? And New Croydon is a great town for kids. I mean, as you said yourself, you don't want to raise your son in Calcutta."

"I know what I said. I know *all* the arguments."

"Lookit, if we can't stand it, we'll move back to town."

"We'll never move back," she said bleakly.

The Picket Fence, Beth's next novel, was started a few months after we set up house in New Croydon. My junior partnership had come through, and brimming with arrogant largesse, I made a dumb but well-intentioned mistake: I convinced Beth to give up her job and devote herself full-time to writing.

The Picket Fence took Beth nearly two years to write. By the time the final rejection letter arrived, she was pregnant with Josh, and feeling even more trapped by domestic routine, she started to withdraw from me. She also stopped writing and turned her attention to Colonial American furnishings. Josh was born; he refused to sleep; Beth refused to have sex with me and also refused to talk about why she refused to have sex with me. She kept buying eighteenth-century bric-a-brac; I kept buying darkroom equipment; we kept dodging the issue of why our marriage had become so deadlocked. But we both understood why. Because she blamed me for turning her into her mother—a talented, independent woman slowly atrophying in commuter land.

I SNAPPED out of my reverie about the state of my marriage and glanced at my watch. Lunchtime. I decided to get out of the office and cheer myself up with a taxi ride up to West Thirty-third Street and a visit to Upton Cameras, purveyors of high-end photographic equipment.

Ted, the manager, greeted me with a smile. Ted was always super-friendly toward me because over the past two years I had spent around $20,000 in his shop.

"Well, it's here, Mr. Bradford," he said.

"It" was the new Canon EOS-1N top-of-the-line pro camera. Just the sort of camera you'd want for covering a fast-moving news story. I had no real use for this camera, but I still wanted it. After all, I am still an artist-in-waiting, albeit one who can afford to drop $2499 plus tax on a Japanese toy.

Ted had the camera unpackaged for me on a display counter. "Try the shutter release," he said.

I depressed the black button. It was like pulling the trigger on a submachine gun—a ferocious rat-tat-tat-tat as the motor drive revved into action. "You think I should consider an autozoom flash to go with this?"

"Funny you should mention that," Ted said. "Ordered one just in case you might be considering it."

"Mind reader. How much will it set me back?"

"It lists for three hundred and thirty-four dollars, but I'll give you the twenty percent professional discount."

"Sold," I said.

The twenty percent professional discount. Ted was one shrewd salesman. In the three years since I'd discovered Upton Cameras, he'd never once asked me what I did for a living. Instead, he treated me as a pro. But I wondered if he saw me as a spoiled rich suit who bought whatever overpriced gear he fancied.

"With tax, that's two thousand nine hundred and forty-seven dollars," Ted said as the credit card machine whirred to life and a voucher sprouted out.

"Fine," I said, and signed on the dotted line.

Ted, meanwhile, unwrapped a Tenba Venture Pak—the best camera bag in the world, if you believe their advertising. He packed it with my new camera and assorted accessories.

"Uh, I didn't buy that bag," I said.

"Let's just say it's on the house."

"Thanks, Ted."

"No, thank *you*, Mr. Bradford, as always. And you know we're always here if you need us."

We're always here if you need us. Retail therapy. But walking east down Thirty-third, I didn't feel that buzz of therapeutic bliss. Just anxiety. Especially as I saw Wendy Waggoner walking toward me. No plaid skirts today. Instead, she was power-dressed to kill in a black Armani suit. Her blond hair was stylishly cropped, and she was accompanied by some super-tall trendy with oval designer specs and a gray ponytail. Wendy air-kissed my cheeks.

"Ben, meet Jordan Longfellow, my editor. Ben's a neighbor in New Croydon. A photographer who just happens to be a lawyer too. You publish lawyers, don't you, Jordan?"

A flash of his teeth. "Some of my best writers are lawyers," Jordan said. "You a writer, Ben?"

"He writes wills," Wendy said.

I wanted to garrote her. Instead, I managed a thin smile. Jordan glanced at his watch.

"Must fly, Ben," Wendy said. "Big editorial meeting on the new book. You and Beth coming to the Hartleys' on Saturday?"

In the taxi back to the office, I felt like punching out a window. *Big editorial meeting on the new book.* And a Pulitzer Prize goes to Wendy Waggoner for *365 Ways to Cook Meat Loaf.*

I finally stopped seething around five o'clock, when, after three action-packed hours analyzing a residuary trust, Estelle buzzed me.

"Your wife on line two, Mr. Bradford."

An adrenaline rush of nerves. Try to sound nice and relaxed and upbeat. "Hey there," I said.

"Getting you at a bad time?" she asked, sounding surprisingly pleasant.

"Not at all."

"It's just . . . the kids and I have been invited to Jane Seagrave's for dinner."

"No problem. I was thinking about working late, maybe catching the seven forty-eight."

"I'll have something ready for you if you like."

Hang on, we're talking civilly. "A Bud will do," I said.

A laugh from Beth Bradford. This *was* promising.

"Good day?" she asked.

It was the first time in weeks that she had thrown a pleasantry in my direction. I decided to say nothing about Jack Mayle. "Average. How 'bout you?" I asked. "What did you get up to?"

"Not much. Nice lunch with Wendy in Greenwich."

"Wendy Waggoner?" I said.

"The one and only," Beth said with a giggle.

I tried to sound calm. "And how was Wendy?"

I ARRIVED home that night to a kiss and the offer of a very dry martini. I accepted. Beth was extremely solicitous when I told her about Jack. She talked about a divan she'd just discovered that once graced the study of Ralph Waldo Emerson. Everything about the evening was civility itself. So civil, in fact, that I never asked about her "lunch" with Wendy Waggoner.

We went to bed. An uninterrupted night's sleep (miracle of miracles)! A kiss in the morning when she got up. More civil chat over our muesli and fresh mangoes. An upbeat reminder of our weekend schedule: "I want to hit Gap Kids in Greenwich. . . . The Hartleys' party starts at seven. . . . There's a special on wild Nova Scotia salmon at DeMarco's. I thought that would go well with a fantastic New Zealand white wine I've just discovered." A kiss on the lips as I walked out the door.

I should have felt relief. Delight that after months of domestic frost a thaw was in progress. But. But. But. I knew this sudden turnaround was no Pauline conversion. *I knew . . .*

"Anything up for today?" I asked before leaving the house.

For a nanosecond Beth averted her eyes. That's when I really knew. "I might tootle on up to the Colonial Barn," she said, mentioning an antiques dealer in Westport. "Steve has that divan from Emerson's study I was telling you about. There's a lot of interest in it, so he can only hold it for me until the end of today."

"How much?" I asked.

She looked away from me again. "Fourteen fifty."

"Buy it," I said.

"Darling," she said sweetly. "You're too good."

So good, in fact, that as soon as I reached the office, I called directory assistance and obtained the number for the Colonial Barn. I phoned but got a recorded message telling me to call back after ten. An hour went by, during which I tried to concentrate on work—specifically, objections filed by the disgruntled stepdaughter of some big-deal Merrill Lynch stockbroker who suffered a coronary while playing squash at the New York Athletic Club.

Finally it was time to call Westport again.

"The Colonial Barn. Good morning. Steve here."

I lowered my voice an octave or two and said, "Morning. Perhaps you could help me. I'm trying to find a divan for my study. Something mid-nineteenth century, preferably American."

"Well, you are in luck, sir. I have the most fabulous divan. Boston handmade, 1853. Once belonged to Ralph Waldo Emerson."

"Ralph Waldo Emerson," I said. "That *is* impressive. What would we be talking about?"

"Twenty-two hundred. But I must warn you that one of my very best customers has expressed an interest in buying it."

For fourteen fifty, or so she said. Who's the liar here? "You mean, it's reserved?" I asked.

"Well . . . not exactly. But she is *very* interested."

"So if I didn't come in today, it would be gone?"

A pause. "I don't think she'll be in today. She told me the earliest she could come back was next Wednesday."

Bingo. "I'll think about it," I said, and hung up.

Anything up for today? One lie raises your suspicions. Two lies verify them. And there was only one thing she could be hiding from me, only one activity that would suddenly have made her cordial toward me again.

But *who?* Who was the bastard? My brain sped, Rolodex style, through friends, acquaintances. The culprit had to be someone who didn't commute into the city every day, who was therefore available to see Beth during business hours.

Another mental Rolodex flip through all the work-at-home guys we knew in the area. Bill Purcell, freelance writer *extraordinaire?* Not a chance. He was a geek deluxe, with a nightmare wife who treated him like a schnauzer on a short lead. Gary Summers, that would-be photographer who lived near us on Constitution Crescent? Shaggy-haired with a wispy beard and a smirk so charged with self-satisfaction it could light up Alaska. Beth loathed him. Strike him off the list.

And those were the only two self-employed men I could think of. Maybe someone she met in a local shop? Steve in the Colonial Barn? Tony the fishmonger? *Who?* She was probably with him right now.

I decided to leave the office. I grabbed my briefcase and my Burberry and headed out the door. Estelle looked up in surprise.

"I'm feeling lousy," I said. "Touch of the stomach flu or something. Decided to call it a day."

The 12:46 from Grand Central was deserted. So too was the station platform at New Croydon. I walked quickly down Adams Avenue, feeling curiously out of place. Because at 1:30 on a weekday it was hard to find a man between the ages of twenty-five and fifty on the streets of the town.

As I turned into Constitution Crescent, I could hear my heart pummel my chest. What if she was there with the guy? *In our bed.*

I reached my front door and silently inserted the key. Opening the door, I crept inside. I dumped my coat, sat down on a little 1768 Providence guesthouse footstool, and took off my heavy black wing tips. Then, holding my shoes in one hand, I crept up the stairs and down the corridor, my eyes focused on our bedroom door at the end of the hall. When I reached it, my hand shook as I touched the knob. I flung the door open.

Nothing. Nothing except our perfectly made bed with its perfectly made Colonial patchwork quilt. I sat down on the edge of the bed, tried to collect myself. I felt no relief. Where could she be? His place, obviously. But where did he live? How had they met? What were they doing right now? Fear kicked in. A helpless fear. I knew I could do nothing except await Beth's return.

She found me in the basement on the NordicTrack. "What are you doing here?" she said, startled to find me home so early.

"Felt sick. Came home," I answered, panting.

"Sick? Then what are you doing working out?"

"Felt better by the time I was on the train. So tell me . . . you do it?"

"Do what?" She looked alarmed.

"Get Emerson's divan."

"Oh, *that.*" Her relief was tangible. "I decided it was too expensive. But I picked up the Nova Scotia salmon from DeMarco's. And a bottle of that amazing New Zealand sauvignon blanc I told you about. Cloudy Bay, it's called."

"Where'd you hear about it?"

"Herb at the liquor store was giving it raves."

An awkward silence broken by the sound of the front door opening and Adam yelling at Fiona, "I watch *Sesame Street!*"

"Hey, big guy!" I shouted up the stairs.

"Daddy!" Adam shouted back, his voice filled with little-boy excitement. As he bounded down the stairs, I crouched to let him throw himself into my arms. "You bring me a present?" he asked.

Beth and I exchanged an amused smile. Adam was always in the market for a present. "I brought you me," I said.

"No presents?"

I laughed. "Maybe a present tomorrow."

"I want a present *now,*" he whined.

"How 'bout McDonald's now?"

Beth didn't like this. "No, Ben. He's eating too much junk as it is. I really wish you'd think before—"

"Leave it," I said, my tone suddenly curt.

Beth was about to counterpunch but thought better of it. "Do what you like. You always do." She headed up the stairs.

"McDonald's?" I asked Adam again.

"I want french fries," he said with a smile.

We took the Volvo. En route Adam began to sing, and I couldn't help but smile as his four-year-old voice chirped away.

At McDonald's, he was an absolute delight, concentrating all his attention on the business of eating his Chicken McNuggets and french fries, but glancing up at me occasionally with a big smile and saying "Delish-ous," this week's new word.

At Talley's Toys, I let him choose two new coaches to go with his Thomas the Tank Engine train set. Then we made a stop at "Daddy's toy shop"—New Croydon Fine Wines and Liquors. Herb, the bald old-timer who'd been running the store since the Eisenhower era, was behind the counter.

"How you doing, Mr. Bradford?" he said.

"It's Friday, Herb. That's how I'm doing."

"I hear ya. What can I get you?"

"Bottle of Bombay Sapphire. A liter."

Herb turned around, grabbed a bottle of that very overpriced gin, and set it down in front of me. "Anything else?"

"How about a bottle of Cloudy Bay sauvignon blanc."

"Cloudy *what?*"

"Cloudy Bay. New Zealand wine. Been getting rave reviews. You do stock it, don't you?"

"Sorry, Mr. Bradford. Never heard of it. But if you've got a minute, I'll call my wholesaler."

He picked up the phone, and I played a game with Adam—how many bottles of Gallo wine can you count?—until Herb finished his call. "Cloudy Bay is available in the States," he said, "but only through special order. If you want it, you're gonna have to pay for it. Eighteen ninety-nine a bottle."

"I'll think about it," I said.

Back home, Beth was surprised to see me walk in with the Bombay Sapphire. "We've already got gin," she said.

"Yeah, Gilbey's. What I want is a good martini."

"You buy it at Herb's?" she asked casually.

I felt like saying, "Yeah, and I discovered he has never stocked Cloudy Bay." Instead, I lied. "Nah, got it at the package store on the Post Road."

I saw her eyes flicker down to the shopping bag that Adam had clutched in his hands: Talley's Toys. Located right near Herb's shop. Dumb, Bradford, dumb. Now she knew I was lying. But she said nothing, because she was probably wondering whether I knew she was lying too.

"I think I could use a martini," Beth said.

We drank one, put the kids to bed, then drank a second. Perfect mental novocaine. So perfect that we actually had another rather cheery evening. The salmon was first-rate. And the Cloudy Bay . . . well, it was sublime. So transcendentally good that I temporarily stopped obsessing about who might have supplied it to Beth, and instead made her laugh. I liked seeing her laugh. Liked seeing her enjoy my company again. And hoped this was a sign that perhaps nothing was happening—that I was letting my midlife paranoias invent fantasies about another guy, with (it has to be said) excellent taste in esoteric kiwi wines.

I covered Beth's hand with mine. "This is nice," I said.

I felt her stiffen. "Yes," she said, "it is."

"We should do this more often."

"You mean, get drunk?"

"I mean, get along."

She pulled her hand away. "Don't spoil—"

"I'm not trying to spoil anything. It's just, we haven't been getting along for months."

"But we are *now*," she said.

"Yeah, now, tonight, after a lot of booze."

"You don't want to get along. You want to fight, is that it?"

"Of course I don't—"

"Then stop. Drop it."

"You don't understand what I'm trying to say here."

"Ben, why can't you just shut up and let—"

"Don't tell me to shut up."

"That's it. I'm going to bed."

"Go to bed," I taunted. "Walk away. That's just your style—"

But I didn't get to finish that sentence, as she slammed the dining-room door behind her. So much for our cease-fire.

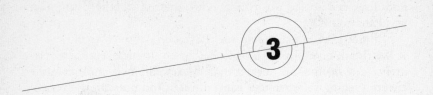

3

THE next morning Beth wouldn't speak to me. As it was Saturday, she engaged in that most American of activities: She went shopping. She took Adam and Josh to Gap Kids while I stayed home, slurping Maalox to help calm the waterfall of acid that was drenching the walls of my gut.

After lunch, when Beth and the kids came home, she still wouldn't speak to me.

I tried to apologize. Silence. Silence when I announced that, as Adam was happily watching *The Jungle Book* for the thirty-second time, I'd sneak off to my darkroom for an hour or two.

I powered up the enlarger, loaded a negative into its carrier, snapped on the safelight, and began to finger the electronic auto-focus button. Slowly an image emerged: a hefty middle-aged man—trebled-chinned, suit crumpled—emerging from the doors of the New York Stock Exchange, his eyes wide and fearful.

I caught this shot a few weeks ago. Sneaking out of the office early one afternoon with my Nikon in my briefcase, I loitered for an hour or two in a Wall Street doorway, shooting four rolls of Tri-X as I watched the comings and goings of brokers and Exchange personnel. The one hundred and forty-four exposures managed to yield three or four interesting pictures—not a bad return for me, as I'm ferociously selective about what I'll even bother to print. And from the moment I hung up the negatives to dry, I knew that this image of bloated midlife anxiety had hit the bull's-eye, that it transcended mere clever composition and had accidentally stumbled into the realm of uncomfortable truth.

That's the thing about photography: The best shots are always accidents. Happenstance is *all* in photography. You can spend hours waiting for the right moment. Ultimately, though, you never get what you're lingering for and instead discover that a few shots you rattled off while hanging about have a spontaneity that is lacking in your attempts at consummate composition. Rule number one of art: You can never pick the right moment. You just stumble into it and hope that your finger is on the shutter release at the time.

I cropped some background in order to tighten up the image of that world-battered broker staggering out of the portals of the Stock Exchange. Then, sliding an eight-by-ten piece of Galleria bromide paper into the frame, I clicked off the enlarger lamp, pressed the autoprint button, and watched as the image beamed on for three seconds. Red light. A sixty-second dunk into developer, followed by stopper, then fixer, then a switch back to normal fluorescent light. Just as I pulled the paper out of this final chemical bath and hung it up to dry, there was a knock on the door.

"Baby-sitter's here," Beth said.

"Coming," I said.

Bill and Ruth Hartley lived less than a mile from us. Their house was a Cape Codder with an array of children's playthings on the lawn. I found those swings and slides a little spooky, because their only son, Theo, had Down's syndrome and spent most of the year boarding at a special school near New Haven. Bill was a stockbroker at a small Wall Street brokerage firm. Ruth was a successful public relations executive. They made good money. They had a pleasant house, a pleasant thirty-foot sloop moored nearby, a pleasant way of appearing close, yet never cramping each other's style.

When the tragedy that was Theo happened, they managed to hang together. I envied them. Unlike Beth and myself, they had embraced their limitations. Instead of looking upon their suburban life as a terrible compromise, they accepted the cards that had been dealt them. In the process, they had discovered something that had eluded the two of us—a degree of contentment.

I didn't envy Bill the inner tube of flab around his waist, however.

Or his taste in sweaters. As he greeted us at the door, he was wearing a dark green crew neck decorated with small penguins. "Who
gave you *that?*" I asked him. "Nanook of the North?"

Ruth popped her head around the doorway. "I did."

Beth gave me an exasperated look, muttered "Jerk" under her
breath, and headed off into the already crowded living room.

"More fun on the home front?" Bill asked. He was the closest
thing I had to a good friend.

"Don't ask."

"Double Scotch, then? Got some twenty-five-year-old Macallan
with your name on it." He was about to lead me to the kitchen. But
the doorbell rang, and he turned back to answer it.

I spun around. Standing in the doorway was Gary Summers. Our
neighbor, the would-be photographer. His long, dirty-blond hair
was tied in a ponytail. His stubble seemed even more designer than
usual. And his smirk was as wide as a 70-mm screen. But it was his
clothes that really got me. They were so *downtown.* Black linen
shirt, black baggy trousers, black leather suspenders. Standard
operating gear for downtown Manhattan but attention seeking amid
the Ralph Lauren suburbanites of New Croydon. Then again, the
only reason Gary lived among us was because he could never cut it
downtown. I knew he'd tried to make it as a photographer in New
York but had never gotten anywhere. And after his parents died, he
retreated to the family home in New Croydon and lived off the
modest inheritance he'd been left. But though he was widely considered something of a loser, he still talked a great game—always
going on about forthcoming magazine assignments, which never
materialized; always saying it was just a matter of time before he
moved to L.A.; always regarding us suits and our pert, button-nosed
wives with smirky contempt. I loathed him.

"Brought you a special little number." He handed Bill a rectangular gift box.

Bill opened it, appeared impressed. "Well, you can stay," he said.
"Go find yourself a drink." Gary gave me a smarmy nod and
headed off in search of the bar. As soon as he was out of earshot,

Bill whispered, "He may be a pretentious bozo, but he really knows his wine. Ever heard of this stuff?" He handed me the bottle. Cloudy Bay sauvignon blanc, 1993.

"Yes," I said, "I've heard of it."

THE rest of the party was a blur. No doubt Bill's liter of twenty-five-year-old Macallan had something to do with this. It was rarely out of my company for the entire evening. And by the time I called Wendy Waggoner "Meat Loaf," more than half the bottle was sluicing around my bloodstream.

For some curious reason Wendy didn't like that nickname. Her husband, Lewis, also took umbrage. Fortunately, I managed to dodge the left hook he swung at me. Unfortunately, it landed on the jaw of Peggy Wertheimer, the most seriously neurotic woman in New Croydon. Thankfully, the blow did not fracture or dislocate anything, but it did break up the party. Peggy began to shriek in shock. Wendy shrieked at Lewis for being such a hothead. Lewis shrieked at me for allegedly provoking him. Beth stormed off for home without me. And Gary Summers smugly turned to me and said, "Remind me to invite you over the next time a couple of my Serb and Croat friends are in town."

Gary. Impossible. Unbelievable. Beth abhorred him. Hated his arrogance, his vanity. *Picked up the Nova Scotia salmon and a bottle of that amazing New Zealand sauvignon blanc.* Cloudy Bay sauvignon blanc, 1993, to be exact. Just a coincidence, right? Then why did Beth lie about where she obtained the bottle?

Even though I spent most of the party throwing back shot after shot of the Macallan, I managed to keep Beth under surveillance. For the first two hours she studiously ignored Gary, and I began to think, Stop being a paranoid. Then I glanced in her direction while she was standing on the staircase chatting with Chuck Bailey, the Porsche-driving ad man. As Gary squeezed by them on his way up to the second-floor bathroom, he managed to lay his hand atop Beth's fingers. A blush colored her cheekbones, a dreamy smile flickered across her lips, and I felt as if three Pershing missiles had just landed in my gut. Shortly thereafter I was inspired to call Wendy Waggoner "Meat Loaf."

"Blame it on Madame Beth Bovary and that creep," I felt like screaming. But some modicum of lawyerly restraint kicked in, and I avoided the sort of appalling *j'accuse* scene that would've had tongues wagging in New Croydon for months. Instead, I shook Gary's hand good-bye after he proffered it, and nodded politely when he said, "Any time you're in the mood, drop over and we can talk cameras." Talk about chutzpah.

As soon as Gary made his good-byes, I staggered toward the door, having decided that I must get home, must confront Beth.

"Ben." It was Ruth, blocking my path.

"Ruthie, Ruthie." My words were slurred. "I—I'm . . ."

"Drunk," she said gently. "In no condition to go home."

"But—but—I gotta . . ." I tried to lean against a wall for support and slid to the floor.

The next thing I knew, it was morning, and the inside of my head was my own private Nagasaki. A knock on the door and Bill waltzed in carrying a glass of orange juice. "Room service," he said brightly.

"What's the time?" I muttered.

"Noon."

"Noon! I've got to call Beth."

"Ruth already has. Everything's fine. Beth's taken the kids to see her sister, Lucy, in Darien. You up for an afternoon on the Sound?"

"I've got to call Beth at Lucy's."

"Don't bother."

"It's that bad?" The alarm in my voice was tangible.

"You'll sort it out. But not on the phone. And not this afternoon. So hit the shower. I want to be out on the water in an hour."

We made it to the boat in forty-five minutes. It was a peerless autumn day on Long Island Sound, the wind steady and bracing. Bill's boat, christened the *Blue Chip,* was a thing of beauty. A white fiberglass hull, scrubbed wooden decks, a two-bunk cabin, and a compact head. The full galley kitchen contained a little icebox and a small gas stove that was hooked up by rubber tubing to a large natural-gas canister. There was an engine if you wanted to go off sail. And stored in a little closet near the head were two jerry cans full of motor diesel. Bill was taking no chances of running out of gas. The *Blue Chip* also boasted just about every mod-con navigational device imaginable.

"Feel like heading east to Sheffield Island?" Bill asked. "It's an easy two-hour run from here."

"And it's right off the coast from Darien too."

"You want to go pick trouble with your wife, you swim ashore."

"All right, I'll shut up."

"You're learning."

As soon as the sail was hoisted, Bill cast off the mooring. Then he trimmed the mainsail. With a decisive whoosh it grabbed the wind and sent the boat sharply to port. He spun the wheel, and the *Blue Chip* steadied; within minutes we cleared New Croydon harbor. Bill shouted, "Coming about"; I ducked as the boom swung over to starboard, and with the sail trimmed down, another whoosh of wind sent us east.

"Take over," Bill yelled over the sudden gust. As soon as I had the wheel in my hands, the wind picked up another five knots, and we whipped along, sailing due east into open seas. "Where d'you think you're heading?" Bill yelled.

"Europe," I shouted back. I squinted into that burnished autumn sun, the mounting gale at my back. And for a few tantalizing minutes my head emptied. I was racing, leaving everything behind, and nothing, no one, could catch up with me.

For nearly an hour Bill and I didn't exchange a word. I knew he was thinking what I was thinking: Why stop? Why not make a dash across the Atlantic? Why not make a run for it? We all crave latitude in life yet simultaneously dig ourselves deeper into domestic entrapment. We may dream of traveling light but accumulate as much as we can to keep us burdened and rooted to one spot. And we have no one to blame but ourselves. Because, though we all muse on the theme of escape, we still find the notion of responsibility irresistible. The career, the house, the dependents, the debt—

it grounds us. Provides us with a necessary security, a reason to get up in the morning. It narrows the choice and, ergo, gives us certainty. And though just about every man I know rails against being so cul-de-saced by domestic burden, we all embrace it with a vengeance.

"You wanted to keep going, didn't you?" Bill asked as we dropped anchor off Sheffield Island.

"Wanted to? Sure. Would've?" I paused, then shrugged. "Nah."

"Why not?"

"You can run, but you can't hide," I said.

"But you *do* want to run?"

"All the time. Don't you?"

"No one's ever totally satisfied with their situation, Ben. But some of us are a little more accepting of their circumstances."

I cracked open a beer and turned my gaze toward the wooded Connecticut coast. It seemed so pastoral from this perspective, with not a swimming pool or station wagon in sight.

"Do you know how mind-numbingly dull T and E can be?"

"You may not be doing exactly what you want to be doing, Ben. But I'll tell you something, chum. Life is *here.* And if you keep hating where you are, you're going to wind up losing it all. And believe me, once you lose it, you'll desperately want it all back again. It's how it works."

I took another long swig of beer, then asked, "Say Beth has already decided that it's gone beyond the point of no return?"

"With two kids in the picture and no career of her own? Trust me. She's not that self-destructive."

"Then what's she doing with Gary?" I felt like shouting. But I didn't want to appear paranoid. And I feared the truth.

Instead, I simply said, "I'll see if I can talk to her."

"Try talking to yourself while you're at it too."

I threw my eyes heavenward. "Thanks, Dad," I said.

"All right, end of homily," Bill said. "Take us home."

We made New Croydon by nightfall. I navigated us back into the harbor without the use of any of Bill's fancy technology.

"Impressive," Bill said as we docked. "The old Bowdoin training?" He knew I'd spent three years on my college sailing team.

"Never leaves you."

Bill drove me back to my house. It was dark. I checked my watch: seven p.m. No cause for alarm. Yet.

"Hang in there," he said, proffering his hand.

How strange it was to enter an empty house. I would have enjoyed this respite from domestic din had I not noticed the flashing light on our answering machine. I hit the playback button.

"Ben, it's me. I've decided to stay up here with the kids for the next few days. I'd appreciate it if you didn't try to contact me. I will be consulting a lawyer. I think you should do the same."

Click. I sat down slowly on the sofa and shut my eyes. She really meant business this time. I picked up the phone and dialed my sister-in-law. She answered. "Ben, Beth doesn't want to—"

"I have to speak with her."

Click. I hit the redial button. Phil, my laconic cost accountant brother-in-law, now answered. "Not the right moment, Ben."

"Phil, you don't under—"

"Yeah, I do."

"I am about to lose my family, Phil."

"Yeah, so Beth said. When she gets back, I'll tell her you—"

"Beth is out?"

"Yeah, left around an hour ago. Said she was going to see Wendy somebody . . ."

I hung up, stormed out of the house, jumped into my Miata, and pulled out to Constitution Crescent. I knew what I was going to do: charge up Gary's front lawn at full speed, ram my Miata through his front door, and crash right into his living room. But a little voice in my head whispered, Prudence. I slowed down. And cruised the back streets until I found our Volvo parked on the road running parallel to Constitution Crescent. Smart move, Beth. Leaving the Volvo in Gary's driveway might raise a suspicion or two.

I steered back into Constitution Crescent. Cutting my headlights, I slid the Miata into my driveway and killed the engine. Then, walking around to the backyard, I unlocked the door to my basement.

Once inside, I grabbed my new Canon, a roll of Tri-X, a telephoto lens, and a tripod, then headed upstairs to Adam's bedroom, which faced Constitution Crescent. The curtains were open; the lights were out. I unfolded the tripod, attached the Canon at its base, loaded the film, twisted on the telephoto lens. Pulling a chair over to the window, I sat down, peered through the viewfinder, aimed it across the road at Gary's front door, and waited.

An hour went by. Then, just after 8:30, the door opened. Gary poked his head out, looked up and down the road, and nodded behind him. Beth stepped into the doorway. Gary pulled her toward him and kissed her deeply. I flinched, jerking my head back from the viewfinder as my finger depressed the shutter release. The motor whizzed through the thirty-six exposures. When I put my face back to the camera, the embrace was ending. Looking nervous, Beth glanced in the direction of our house. Seeing nothing but the lights behind the drawn curtains of our living room, she turned back to Gary. A final full, deep kiss on his lips. Then, head lowered, she hurried off into the night.

I was on my feet, running down the stairs, about to make a dash up the road and catch her before she reached the Volvo. Instead, I flopped onto the living-room sofa. That kiss. It was so ardent. So serious. What did Beth see in the creep? But I knew if I ran up to her now and staged a scene, she'd use the fact I'd spied on her as further proof that our marriage was a sham. We would cross the frontier of no return—and never find our way back again.

I began to pace up and down the living room. Images flooded my brain: a divorce judge granting Beth full custody of the two boys, the house, and three quarters of my income. Adam and Josh developing Gary's world-class smirk.

Gary. Suddenly I found myself on autopilot, marching across the road toward his front door. I didn't know what I was going to say to him, but there I was on his doorstep ringing the bell. Beth couldn't have been gone for more than five minutes, so when Gary swung the door open, he blanched in shock.

"Ben . . ."

I managed one word. "Cameras."

"What?"

"Cameras. You said I should drop by, we'd talk cameras."

I could see him studying me, trying to gauge whether or not my arrival on his doorstep was just coincidence. "Yeah, guess I did. But . . ." He hesitated, and I could almost hear him deciding: Can I handle this? The telltale smirk that crossed his face gave me his answer. He gestured grandly with his right hand. "*Entrez,* dude."

I stepped inside. Though Gary's house was a Cape Codder, crossing its portals took you out of New England and into some ersatz Tribeca environment. Walls had been distressed in a gray-blue tint. Carpets had been pulled up, floorboards painted black. Four pinpoint spotlights dangled from the ceiling. The only piece of furniture was a long black leather couch. "Quite a place," I said. "Who was your decorator? Robert Mapplethorpe?"

"Very witty. Actually, I did all the work myself. Drink?" He motioned for me to follow him into the kitchen. Like the living room, it appeared half finished. For a moment I felt sorry for Gary and his desperate attempt to replicate Tribeca cool in the suburbs. But my empathy ended as soon as I saw two wineglasses on a countertop, one dappled by the pink lipstick Beth wore.

Nodding at the glasses, I managed to mutter, "Been entertaining?"

He worked hard at suppressing a smile. "Yeah, guess you could say that." He opened the fridge and pulled out a bottle of Cloudy Bay sauvignon blanc. "Ever try this stuff?" he asked.

"Beth brought a bottle home once."

Another little smile as he uncorked the wine. "She's got good taste, your wife." He grabbed the bottle, two glasses. "Darkroom's this way." He led me down a narrow flight of stairs to the basement. It was a cramped, dark space. One wall was taken up with domestic appliances—a washer, a dryer, a large freezer. The other held his printing equipment: an old Kodak enlarger, battered chemical trays, and clotheslines on which were pinned several dozen prints.

"Compared to your setup, it's kind of third world," Gary said, flicking on the fluorescent overhead light.

"Don't remember ever showing you my darkroom, Gary."

He turned away and busied himself pulling a few prints down from the clothesline. "Just conjecturing, counselor."

"Conjecturing *what?*"

"That you have a spiffy darkroom with spiffy equipment."

"But you've never seen it. Have you?"

"Nope. Never have."

Liar. Beth must have given him a guided tour of my basement. "Then why do you automatically presume—"

"Because a spiffy Wall Street guy like you can afford the best and therefore probably *has* the best." He dropped a stack of prints into my hands. "Here. Tell me what you think of these."

I shuffled through the half-dozen prints, all of them bleak monochromatic portraits of assorted lowlifes. "Impressive," I said. "Arbus meets Avedon."

"You're saying they're derivative?"

"Not derivative. Studied. Too self-consciously artful. Not enough of the passive spectator."

"The photographer can *never* be a passive spectator."

"Says who?" I asked.

"Says Cartier-Bresson."

"A friend of yours?"

"I met him once or twice, yeah."

"And I suppose he personally told you, 'Gary, ze photographer, he must never be ze passive spect-a-tor.' "

"He wrote it." Reaching behind him, Gary grabbed a Cartier-Bresson book off a shelf, riffled through some pages, then read out loud: " 'The photographer cannot be a passive spectator; he can be really lucid only if he is caught up in the event.' "

"Well, how 'bout that," I said. "He autograph that book for you?"

Gary ignored the sarcasm and read on.

"We are faced with two moments of selection and thus of possible regret: the first and more serious when actuality is there, staring us in the viewfinder; and the second when all the shots have been developed and printed and we have to reject the less effective one. It is then—too late—that we see exactly where we failed."

He looked up at me, his face flushed with acrimony. "That touch a chord with you, counselor?" he asked. "Not that you'd know anything about failure. Especially when it comes to photography. And your wasted year in Paris. And your stint behind the counter at Willoughby's, and . . ."

I heard myself whispering, "How the . . ."

The smirk was now epic, triumphant. "Guess," he said.

I stared at the linoleum floor. Finally I muttered, "How long?"

"You mean, Beth and me? Couple of weeks."

"And is it . . ."

He cackled. "Love? That's what *she's* calling it."

Another punch to the gut. "And you?"

"Me?" he said brightly. "Well, I'm having fun. A lot of fun."

"Shut up."

"No, no, no. *You* shut up. And listen good. She loves me. And hates you."

"She doesn't—"

"Oh yes she does. Hates you big time. Hates your job. Hates her life up here. But what she really really hates is your self-pity. The way you act so entrapped, while all the time refusing to accept that it was you who couldn't cut it as a photog—"

"And *you've* cut it, loser?"

"At least I'm still out there pitching. You're just some corporate stain who can't even—"

And that's when I lashed out. And hit him. With the Cloudy Bay bottle. Grabbing it. Swinging it wildly and catching him on the side of the skull. The bottle shattered in two, the broken stem still in my hand. Gary was knocked sideways. As he fell away from me, I lashed out again, and suddenly the jagged glass was in the back of his neck. It all couldn't have taken more than five seconds—and I was drenched in blood.

When I managed to wipe the blood from my face, I saw Gary staggering around the darkroom, the bottle protruding from his neck. He turned toward me, his face a chalky mask of shocked bemusement. His lips formed a word: "What?" Then he fell forward, facedown into a tray of developer fluid. The tray upended. His head slammed into the floor.

Silence. My legs gave out. I slumped to the linoleum. A curious echo reverberated between my ears. Time seemed swollen, distended. My mouth felt dry. So dry that I licked my lips. And tasted that sweet sticky liquid running down my face. A taste that told me: Life as I knew it would never be the same again.

I looked at Gary carefully. Blood was still leaking from the wound, mixing with the developer fluid to form a reservoir beneath his outstretched arms. No signs of life.

Just seconds ago I was a model American: an industrious, economically productive, child-rearing, mortgage-paying, Gold Card–carrying resident of the top-income echelon. One moment a perfect citizen, the next . . .

A murderer? *Me?*

My tan Shetland sweater was sodden, crimson. So too my khakis and Docksiders. And though I was in deep netherworldly shock—though I still couldn't exactly fathom what had happened and stared at Gary's ever stiffening body with disbelief—a curious lucidity began to undercut the free-floating trauma and fear. And in those moments of pure clarity a scenario of future horrors began to unspool in my head.

They would come for me at the office. There'd be two of them. Homicide detectives with the Stamford Police Department. "Benjamin Thomas Bradford," cop one would say while cop two cuffed my hands behind my back, "you are under arrest for the murder of Gary Summers. . . ."

I'd be led out of the office. Estelle would be in tears. Jack, looking apoplectic, would still manage to yell, "Ben, don't tell 'em anything until Harris Fisher gets there"—Harris being Wall Street's leading white-collar criminal lawyer.

After reaching Stamford, I'd be fingerprinted and booked. At last Harris would arrive. "A bad business, counselor," he'd say as soon as the two detectives were out of the room.

"How bad?" I'd manage to croak.

"Seems your fingerprints are all over Mr. Summers's house, no one can vouch for your whereabouts at the time of his murder, your wife has made a statement that she and Mr. Summers were, uh, *involved,* and there is the unfortunate matter of those photographs you took of your wife and Mr. Summers in mid-embrace. Pity you forgot about the camera in the window. First thing the police found when they searched your house."

Hanging my head, I'd ask, "Any plea-bargain possibilities?"

"Man one—eighteen to twenty-five."

Twenty-five years? I can't do twenty-five years. Think. Think of a way out of this. You're a lawyer, after all.

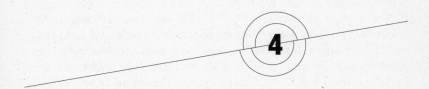

FINDING the basement bathroom was my first bit of luck. It was tucked away next to the freezer—a grubby little toilet and shower stall that was stacked with half-filled paint cans, turpentine bottles, and other home-decorating detritus. I didn't care about the mess. A shower in the basement meant I wouldn't have to go upstairs in my bloodied clothes and leave smudges of DNA-rich evidence around the house. I stripped off everything and dumped it all into a black plastic bag I found among the cleaning supplies. Then I stepped into the shower and stayed there for over ten minutes. There was a lot to wash away.

The only towel in the bathroom had once belonged to a Motel 6.

After turning it into a makeshift toga, I went upstairs in search of Gary's bedroom. I found it at the rear of the second floor. The room continued the house's crash-pad theme, with half-stripped floorboards, strewn clothes, and an expensive futon on a varnished frame. I found what I was looking for near the bed. A pair of black sweats, top and bottom. Gary was about my height and had the same lanky frame, which meant that his clothes fit reasonably well. So too did a pair of his black Nikes. I checked my watch: 9:30. Around forty minutes since . . .

I sat down on the bed, woozy, my adrenaline in overdrive. Did someone see me knock on Gary's door, go inside? If they did, I'm toast. Easy now. Easy. Don't go Dostoevskian. It's not the moment for guilt, remorse, shame, existential soul-searching—unless you really want to walk the plank. Forget the crime. Think of it as . . . a problem. Problems can be solved. One step at a time.

Alibi? You called Darien twice around seven. And then? There are two hours to account for. You could say you were watching television. *All right, Mr. Bradford, can you remember what Murphy Brown was up to that night? . . . Oh, you were watching CNN. What was the lead story?* Forget television. You could always say you were reading, but how are you going to prove you were home all the time? The phone bill will show those early calls to your in-laws. But after that . . . ? I had to get on the phone now, call Beth, and have some sort of record on my telephone bill to show I was in our house around the hour the murder was committed. It wouldn't totally clear me, but it might toss up some reasonable doubt.

But before I made the dash home, I needed to get rid of evidence here. Motel 6 towel in hand, I crept downstairs to the kitchen. It was dark, so I pulled down the venetian blinds and hit the lights. Beneath the sink I found a pair of rubber gloves, a rag, and an aerosol can of Pledge. Donning the gloves, I sprayed every surface I could find, in case I'd inadvertently fingered any of them. Then I went back to the basement.

As I descended the stairs, I saw his face. Half his face. The other side rested against the linoleum. One eye stared up at me with glassy reproach. I noticed that the flow of blood had ceased. First things first. The bottle. I approached the body, steeling myself for the task ahead. Crouching down, I grabbed the bottle neck and pulled hard. The bottle escaped from Gary's neck with a loud, repulsive slurp.

Grabbing both his arms, I pulled him out of the small crimson pool surrounding his body. Blood and developer fluid streaked the linoleum as I tugged. Then I turned him over. Reaching into his pockets, I found his keys and wallet. I pocketed them. As I stood up, my back bumped against the freezer. A large old chest-style model. I opened it. Bachelor provisions: a couple of pizzas, four tubs of Ben & Jerry's Cherry Garcia, nothing more. Perfect. My second bit of luck. I dumped the food into the black plastic bag. Then I sat Gary up and leaned him against the freezer. Bending down, I took a deep, steadying breath and pulled him toward me, wrapping my arms beneath his arms. When he was standing, I let go and pushed him backward. His skull landed in the middle of the freezer. Using his legs as a rudder, I maneuvered his body, steering his head into one corner of the compartment. I then folded his legs back on top of him and jammed the freezer lid closed. He could stay there until I decided what to do with him.

It was now almost ten o'clock. I grabbed a mop from the bathroom, dumped the remaining contents of a Mr. Clean bottle into a bucket, and got to work on the floor. Within twenty minutes the blood and developer fluid were gone. I snapped the mop in two and tossed it into the plastic bag. The bucket followed, along with the developer tray and the smashed Cloudy Bay bottle. I worked fast but thoroughly. I was taking no chances. Two rinses of the basement sink and shower. A comprehensive rubdown of all basement surfaces and everything I'd touched in Gary's bedroom. Finally it was time to leave.

A fast peek out the door. Constitution Crescent was silent. I pulled my head back in, hoisted the bag, and let myself out. My first instinct was to run, but the lawyer in me counseled calm. Don't run. Walk. Just don't look back.

I walked briskly across the road, fully expecting to hear the "Hey you! Stop!" that would signal the end. But all I heard was the sound of my own footsteps moving from paved road to graveled driveway as I made my way to my back door. Reaching into the sweats' pocket for my keys, I found Gary's. Mine were missing. Immediately I was on my knees, scrambling through the plastic bag until I found my khakis. I dug into the pockets. No keys. All the bloodied clothes now came tumbling out. No keys. Then I saw the hole in the bag.

I quickly repacked the bag and left it by my basement door. Then I retraced my footsteps, eyes rooted on the ground. I didn't have to walk far. Just to the edge of the road, where the keys lay a few inches from the curb. Reaching down to grab them, my relief was huge. Until I heard a voice. "Something wrong?"

I looked up. It was Chuck Bailey, the ad man, dressed for jogging with a battery-operated lamp strapped to each biceps.

"Chuck," I said, trying to sound collected. "Dropped my keys."

He jogged in place. "You have a death wish?"

I was more than a little nervous. "I don't under—"

"The sweats, Ben. The shoes. All black. Makes you kind of invisible. Car comes along, you're toast. Who you trying to be? Zorro?"

I managed a laugh.

"Just like Gary. Always jogs at night, dressed like you. The invisible man." He glanced at my feet. "Same Nikes too."

"How's biz?" I asked, trying to change the subject.

"One long panic attack. Just lost the Frosty Whip account." He checked his watch. "Gotta go. Knicks versus the Clippers tonight from L.A. Buy yourself some lights, you gonna jog in the dark. You're a family man."

"Tell me about it."

A male-bonding laugh from Chuck Bailey. "I hear ya."

I watched him jog up the road. That went well. More than well. *And Mr. Bailey, you say Mr. Bradford was wearing black Nikes, the same sort of Nikes that Mr. Summers usually wore? And—let me get this straight—before that night you'd never seen Mr. Bradford in black Nikes?*

Mental note: Buy a pair of black Nikes tomorrow. And get that camera out of the window now.

I walked to the back door, turned the key in the lock, grabbed the plastic bag, and ducked inside. Leaving the bag near my gym equipment, I raced upstairs, snatched the camera and tripod from the bedroom, and returned to the basement. Flipping open the back of the Canon, I yanked out the film, exposing all thirty-six frames. That additional evidence destroyed and laid to rest in the bag, I reached for the phone and dialed Darien. Phil answered.

"Put her on," I ordered.

He hung up. When I redialed, the answering machine was on. So I left a message. "Beth, it's me. I am upset. Very upset. I think we should try to talk it out, see if we can—"

She suddenly came on the line. "There is nothing to talk about," she said quietly. "I've decided to remain up here with the boys for the week. I've also called Fiona and informed her that she has the week off. And I'd like you to find somewhere else to stay by the time we're back next Sunday."

"It's not just *your* house—"

"There are two ways we can handle this, Ben. Politely or with injunctions."

The phone shook in my hand. "They're my boys too," I said.

"And I won't keep them from you. If you'd like to drop by some evening this week and see them, that would be nice. But don't call back tonight. We won't answer." And she hung up.

I put the phone back in the cradle and covered the back of my head with my hands. I stayed in that cowed position for what seemed like an hour, replaying over and over that moment when I reached for the bottle.

Go on. Get it over with. Grab the garden hose, a bottle of Irish, a bottle of tranquilizers. Then drive off to some secluded spot, insert the hose in the exhaust, thread it through the window, turn on the ignition, and surrender to the inevitable. You'll pass out, won't feel a thing. Face it, you'd never be able to live with the guilt. Every waking hour would be overshadowed by the fear: Today they'll find out. . . . Today they'll come for me. . . . Today is the last time you'll ever see your boys. You're going to lose everything anyway. End the agony now.

I stood up. My legs buckled. I fell back on the couch, weeping uncontrollably. Crying for my sons. And for myself. I was guilty not just of murder but of self-hatred—a loathing that had made me despise the life I'd built for myself. And now, in the final hour or two of that existence, I would bear witness to the cruelest of ironies—the fact that I so desperately wanted to keep what I once so wanted to flee. Had I believed in some sort of supreme being— some Mr. Fixit in the sky—I would have sunk to my knees and pleaded: Give me back everything that I once found so stifling. Give me back the drudgery, the marital squabbles, the sleepless nights. Give me back my kids. No more would I think life was else- where. Just give me one more chance.

I was on my feet, lurching through the house. I grabbed a bottle of whiskey before bolting up the stairs. In the bathroom I flushed a dozen Valium down with as much Black Bush as I could swig. But the excessive overdose of whiskey set my gut aflame. I was sud- denly, convulsively sick.

I remember little beyond staggering, fully clothed, into the shower and turning on the water. I shoved my face under the spray, blasting away the noxious tang of a botched suicide.

I stripped off the sweats, leaving them in the shower. Without bothering to towel off, I fell out of the bathroom and into bed.

And then it was Monday morning. And the phone was ringing. I answered it with a grunt.

"Mr. Bradford, is that you?"

Estelle. My eyes tried to focus on the bedside clock: 10:47.

"Mr. Bradford, you there?" Her voice was thick with worry.

"Sick. I'm sick."

"You sound it, Mr. Bradford. You sound like death."

"Food poisoning, that's all. Bad can of soup."

"Could be botulism. Or hepatitis. Have you called the doctor?"

"Estelle, the worst is over. A day in bed is all I need. Cancel my appointments. Tell Jack. And I'll call in later. I'm going back to sleep now."

I hung up. And spent an hour staring at the ceiling, cursing my bile-filled gut for failing me. A nice, calm gut, and I would have been happily dead by now. I started to cry and slammed my fist against the bedside table. It connected with the television remote control, and the picture tube blurred into life.

On the screen was a televangelist in a polyester suit. "And then," thundered the reverend, "Jesus said to Nicodemus, *Except a man be born again, he cannot see the kingdom of God.* When you're born again, it's like you're being given a second chance. You walk new; you talk new; you *are* new. It's as if you've killed off your old life and come back with a second chance. Reborn a new man. . . ."

I sat bolt upright. My tears subsided, and a wave of calm descended over me. And I found myself thinking, Yes, I must die. For there is no other way out. But after I am dead, why can't I begin life anew? Why can't I have that second chance? Why shouldn't I be born again?

The more I considered it, the more clearly I realized, You don't need Jesus to be reborn. You just need a lot of careful planning.

THINK of it as a moonwalk, I kept telling myself. Take one slow, calculated step at a time. And don't chance anything.

So I didn't return to Gary's house until after dark on that Monday night. Before leaving my house, I locked the plastic bag of evidence in my darkroom, shoved a penlight in my pocket, and put on a pair of surgical gloves. (I buy them in bulk to use while handling photographic chemicals.) Then, making certain the coast was absolutely clear, I light-footed it across the road to Gary's.

Once inside, I found my way upstairs to a spare bedroom that Gary used as an office. The blinds were closed. I turned on a desk lamp. Chaos. Dirty clothes were thrown everywhere; papers littered the floor; his desk and IBM ThinkPad were covered with dust. I shuffled through his bills and bank statements. His Amex and MasterCard accounts were long overdue. Southern New England Tele-

phone had sent out a final notice for $484.70. When I inspected his
Chemical Bank statement, there was a balance of only $620 in his
checking account. But judging from previous deposits, he was due
a quarterly trust fund installment of $6900 tomorrow.

I opened his IBM ThinkPad, powered it up, and accessed my
way into his files. There was a directory named PROFCOR. It contained three dozen or so PROFessional CORrespondences, letters
offering his services to just about every magazine in New York. The
last one, dated six days ago, was to a Jules Rossen, photo editor of
a new travel magazine called *Destinations*.

> Dear Jules,
>   Great seeing you last week. I love the idea of a photo essay
> covering the California/Baja California border. The fee you
> mentioned—$1000, including expenses—is considerably lower
> than what I'm usually paid. But I do appreciate that as a new
> publication, *Destinations* does not yet have the wherewithal to
> match the fees paid by established magazines. And as I was
> dead impressed by the dummy issue you showed me, I'd be
> willing to accept the terms you offered.
>   I have a small gap in my schedule at the moment and could
> head west as soon as you give me the green light.

*The fee you mentioned is considerably lower than what I'm usually
paid.* By whom? *The New Croydon Shopping Gazette?* I switched
out of PROFCOR and went into a directory labeled B.

                                                    9-15-94
> B: Can't do Monday. Tuesday, lunchtime? Await your call.
>   G.

                                                    9-21-94
> B: I leave another of these notes in my letter box, I'm gonna
> start thinking I'm in a bad le Carré novel. Tomorrow at two
> works.
>   G.

9-24-94

B: Off to Boston on biz. Don't worry—I won't call, though I think you're being a little paranoid about me phoning. He's not there during the day, and if the nanny answers, I can always say I'm the plumber. I'll miss you.

G.

10-5-94

B: Thinking about what you said yesterday. Stop worrying— he's too preoccupied to suspect anything. And when you do finally give him the heave-ho, we can keep playing it low-key for a while. Does that calm your bourgeois conscience?

G.

10-27-94

B: Great news. Assignment in the offing to Baja California. Might have to head west in a hurry. Yeah, I've been invited to the Hartley thing on Saturday. If you're uncomfortable with me being there in the presence of hubby, missing it won't kill me. We can talk it through on Friday.

G.

She loves me. And hates you. I didn't believe it then, but after reading the B files, I felt that Gary had been speaking the truth. If Beth was that smitten with him, she'd be curious if he just disappeared. Gary would have to be called out of town and then decide to stay away permanently. And sometime after Sunday—when Beth returned home with the kids—I would have to be dead.

I was beginning the last week of my life.

DURING my first year at Lawrence, Cameron and Thomas a junior associate in the mergers and acquisitions division was nabbed after forging the signature of a vacationing senior partner on an urgent contract.

"Dumb," Jack Mayle said. "He should've known that if you want to fake a signature, you copy it upside down. Oldest trick in the forger's book."

Good advice, Jack. Pulling Gary's Amex card out of his wallet, I turned the signature side upside down, reached for a yellow legal pad and a Bic pen, then began to practice copying his signature. After ten or so attempts I had it reasonably perfected. Then I went back to the ThinkPad, opened the directory named MONEYBIZ, and found out about Gary's banking arrangements.

Next, turning to a gray filing cabinet near his desk, I hit gold: a fat, dirty manila file that contained his birth certificate, his Social Security card, the title to his house, his will, and the all-important trust documents. More good news here. The house was fully paid off, and Gary was sole owner. He was also the sole beneficiary of the trust, currently yielding an annual income of $27,600, paid quarterly to his Chemical Bank checking account. There were no conditions attached to the trust, barring the fact that the principal was inviolate. Gary's will was also straightforward. He had never married and was an only child. In the event of his death, his estate was to be left to Bard College, his alma mater, on the stipulation that—I couldn't believe this—a chaired professorship in photography be created in his name. I had to laugh. The guy's vanity knew no limits. The Gary Summers Professor of Photography!

For the next few hours I sorted Gary's paperwork. By five in the morning I had brought some order to his office but couldn't risk working on, as Constitution Crescent's early risers would soon be out for their predawn jogs. Grabbing the legal pad on which I'd practiced his signature, I moved quickly around the house, turning off lights. Then I slipped back across the street.

Once I was inside my house, the legal pad and surgical gloves joined the other evidence in the black plastic bag. I chased three large tabs of Dexedrine with a long slurp of Maalox, then showered and shaved and dressed for work.

I made a trip to the laundry room with some dirty clothes, and once the washing machine was operating, I tossed the bag of evidence into the Miata's minuscule trunk. On Tuesday mornings I always paid a precommute visit to the recycling plant, so I also stuffed three bags of empty bottles, cans, and newspapers into the passenger seat.

New Croydon was far too high tax bracket to allow a dump within its municipal limits. Its good citizens used the Stamford dump, ten miles up the road. The sun was just gaining altitude by the time I got there. I was relieved to see five cars in front of me, waiting for the gates to open at 6:30, as I didn't want to be the first face that the dump employees saw at the start of the day. I only had to wait five minutes before some guy in overalls lifted the barricades and waved us through. After tossing the recycling bags into their respective bins, I drove over to the area earmarked for household garbage.

"Anything inflammable?" asked the guy at the Dumpster.

I shook my head and suffered a nervous moment because sometimes they actually checked the bags. But it must have been too early to start inspecting garbage, as the guy grabbed the bag and tossed it into a Dumpster overflowing with last night's debris.

I made it back to New Croydon in fifteen minutes, parked my car at the station, and caught the 7:02 into the city. I was in my office by 8:30. Estelle would arrive at nine.

I went to my desk, reached into a lower drawer, and pulled out a file containing my own last will and testament. Naturally, I'd drafted it myself—an airtight document leaving my entire estate to Beth and the kids. She'd do well out of my death. All told, she could expect around $1.4 million—enough to keep her and the boys in relative New Croydon comfort.

I also did a thorough inspection of my insurance policies. They covered every possibility for my demise (barring death in a war zone), so there was no chance the insurance company would renege on the payout.

Locking the documents back in my desk, I found a sheet of stationery, picked up a pen, and wrote Estelle a note telling her that I still wasn't feeling well and that, on my doctor's advice, I'd be taking the next few days off but would check in from time to time just in case any urgent business was pending. Folding the letter into an envelope marked ESTELLE, I left it in a prominent position on the front of my desk. Then I grabbed my coat and briefcase and beat a fast retreat out of the office.

I hailed a cab and told the driver to take me to Columbia University, my old turf during the six-month lost-soul period following Paris. It took twenty minutes to reach Broadway and 116th Street. I got out, walked south three blocks, and entered a sprawling old bookshop I used to frequent all those years ago.

I made my way to the shelves marked ALTERNATIVE & ANARCHIST. After a few minutes' browsing, I found what I was looking for: *The Anarchist's Cookbook,* which contained everything you needed to know to make homemade explosives. I riffled through a chapter entitled "Explosives and Booby Traps" until I found the recipe I was after and copied it down in a little notebook. I then returned the "cookbook" to the shelf and went digging around until I encountered a paperback entitled *Directory of Mail Drops in the United States and Canada.* According to its back-cover blurb, the book provided "a listing of over 700 mail drops and remailing services with tips on using them." Under "California, Bay Area," I found the phone number of a service in Berkeley and added it to my notebook.

My next stop was a bank, where I withdrew $500 from a cash machine and handed over a ten-dollar bill to a teller in exchange for a roll of forty quarters. I found a phone booth, dialed the Berkeley number, and deposited $5.25 for three minutes when requested to by the operator. After three rings a guy answered. His voice was beyond laconic. "Berkeley. Alternative. Post. Office. Yeah?"

"Hi," I said. "Are you the people who provide mailing addresses?"

"Yeah. We're. Those. People." It was like listening to maple syrup being poured.

"How does it work?"

"Twenty dollars a month. Minimum six months. Payment in advance. You give me your name now. When you have a new address, you call us. And we remail everything. To you."

"You never give out that new address to anyone, do you?"

"No. We're the Alternative Post Office. We keep. Cool."

"I want the service to start tomorrow."

"You gotta wire us. The money. Via Western Union." He gave me their Western Union number and the Berkeley address to which mail was to be redirected. Then he asked, "You got a name?"

"Gary Summers," I said.

"Okay. Gary. Wire me the money. Then we take care. Of the rest. Later, dude." And he hung up.

I wondered how many brain cells he'd lost during the '60s. The guy had spoken so slowly I'd used up most of my quarters, but I did have enough left to call directory assistance and discover that there was a Western Union office in a drugstore on Fifty-first and Second. Perfect. I jumped in a cab, got to the pharmacy, and wired $240 to the Berkeley Alternative Post Office with a terse note: "12 months' payment. Re Gary Summers."

That business concluded, I walked to Grand Central and caught the 1:46 back to New Croydon. When I reached the station, I collected my car, drove the ten miles to Stamford, and paid a visit to the large central post office downtown. I filled out a change of address card indicating that as of tomorrow Gary Summers of 44 Constitution Crescent, New Croydon, Connecticut, would like his mail rerouted to 10025-48 Telegraph Avenue, Berkeley, California. Quickly slipping Gary's wallet out of my pocket, I turned his Amex card upside down, then inverted the postal form and copied his scrawl on the line marked SIGNATURE. I wrote "New Croydon P.O." on the front of the prepaid change of address card, then popped it into the mailbox.

I spent the next fifteen minutes cruising around Stamford until I found a large multistory parking garage on Broad Street. According to a sign out front, it was open twenty-four hours. It offered long-term weekly rates. It had one thousand spaces. It was a low-rent operation with no video surveillance—not the sort of place, I figured, where they took much notice of cars left for several days.

I drove on to the Stamford Town Center Mall, parked the Miata on the eighth level of their garage, and fed the meter with enough quarters to cover the maximum one-day parking allowed there. Hiking down Atlantic Street to the train station, I waited fifteen minutes for the southbound local. Boarding it, I was back in New Croydon in six minutes. It was now 4:15. If anyone noticed me walking home, they would simply think I was making an early day of it from work.

No messages on the answering machine. No mail of interest. I changed out of my suit and dressed for my next outing. Gary's standard around-town outfit was Levi's, denim shirt, leather jacket, black baseball cap. I had reasonable facsimiles of all these clothes in my closet (we all shop at the Gap). I put them on, then waited forty minutes for the early evening darkness. The next maneuver was going to be tricky.

Just after five I let myself out the back door, banking on the fact that most of my commuting neighbors never got home before six. I guessed right. No beleaguered daddies slouching home from the station. I pulled the cap down until it almost touched my nose. Crossing the road, I approached Gary's MG, parked in the driveway, and climbed inside. The interior was a disaster. There was a big gash in the driver's seat; empty Budweiser cans littered the floor. But I was relieved to discover the all-important car registration in the glove compartment. And though Gary may have been a slob, he kept his twenty-five-year-old car in perfect under-the-hood condition. The engine fired on the first go.

Heading away from the direction of the station, I drove at low speed through assorted back streets, avoiding any of New Croydon's main thoroughfares. Finally reaching I-95, I stayed well within the speed limit all the way to Stamford and the parking garage I had cased earlier.

Entering it, I didn't make eye contact with the attendant as his hand shot out from his booth, giving me a ticket. I slipped it under the sun visor and found a space on the third floor. I took the stairs down and exited through a side door.

It was a fast, nervous walk through some very dark mean streets to the Town Center Mall. Immediately I headed to the multiplex cinema and bought a ticket for the next film. I had fifteen minutes to kill, so I went to a pay phone and called Darien. Beth answered.

"Oh," she said, her tone glacial. "Where're you?"

"Stamford. The mall. Made it an early day, decided to hit a movie. Want to join me?"

"Ben . . ."

"Leave the kids with Lucy and Phil; you could be here in ten minutes."

"*Ben,* I told you—"

"I just thought, maybe—"

"No. I don't want to see you. I'm hanging up now, Ben."

"Hang on. I'm coming up to see the boys on Saturday afternoon. That's the least—"

"Saturday will be fine," she said, cutting me off. "Good night."

I staggered into the movie. Some "cop on the edge protecting some woman on the run" thing. I couldn't engage with it, because all I saw in front of me was Adam and Josh. And all I could think was, After Saturday you will never see them again.

The end credits rolled. The brightening houselights disoriented me. But outside in the mall, the fluorescent glare was even worse. When I heard my name being called, it took a moment before Bill and Ruth Hartley came into proper focus.

"Hey, life of the party," Ruth said, kissing my cheek.

"Night off alone?" Bill asked.

"Yeah. Thought I'd kill it in a movie."

"What'd you see?" Ruth asked.

"Some action junk. You?"

"Ruth's dragging me to some arty English film. Cultural enlightenment." He flashed Ruth a smile. "How's Beth?"

"Still in Darien with the kids."

"Oh," Bill said. "Everything okay?"

"Uh, no."

"Bad?" he asked.

"Very bad," I said. "Kind of irreparable, I think."

"Oh, Ben," Ruth said, taking my arm and gripping it tight.

"We'll forget the movie," Bill said. "Let's—"

"No, really—"

"Ben," Ruth added, "you can't be on your own. Come on home with us."

"I'm fine. Honestly. All I need is sleep. I haven't—"

"That's pretty obvious," Bill said. "Why don't you—"

"Not tonight. Please. I'm handling it. And after eight hours' sleep I'll probably be handling it even better."

"Tomorrow, then," Ruth said.

"All right."

"Right after work. You promise?" she asked.

"I'll be there," I said. "And thanks."

Then I walked off, not turning back. I didn't want to see their concerned faces and hoped they wouldn't call me late tonight at home to check on me. Because I wouldn't be there.

I drove the Miata back to New Croydon and was home by nine. I hadn't eaten in about a day, so I forced myself to ingest a plate of scrambled eggs and toast. And four cups of coffee. I returned to my darkroom, changed into Gary's sweats and Nikes, and covered my hands with a fresh pair of surgical gloves.

Just after ten I let myself into Gary's after first grabbing a pile of mail from the box on his front lawn. Using the penlight, I headed upstairs to his office and leafed through the mail. There was a letter from *Destinations* magazine.

Dear Gary,

    I hate to be the bearer of bad news, but we've decided to go with a San Diego–based photographer for the Baja California story. Sorry for the disappointment. Keep in touch.

                            Sincerely,

                            Jules Rossen

Poor Gary. They told him he was a virtual cert for the job, when all the time they knew this San Diego hack was their ace in the hole. Suddenly I was taking Gary's side. Defending his corner. Wanting to fire back a letter to Jules "Judas" Rossen, informing him that he didn't deserve a photographer of my talents.

My talents? It was starting already.

This rejection letter did fit in very neatly with my plan. No one at *Destinations* would be chasing after Gary, wondering when he'd be delivering the photographs. No one would be looking for him at all. Except Beth. I opened up his ThinkPad, switched into the B directory, created a new file, and wrote:

> B: Big news. Landed the Baja California gig. They want me on the border pronto, so I'm hitting the road tonight. Be gone two, three weeks. Gonna miss you big time.
>
> G.

I hit the PRINT key, then popped the letter into an envelope.

I now turned to the pile of debt demands on his desk. Altogether he owed $2485.73. Switching into his MONEYBIZ directory, I discovered that he paid all bills via his bank. Whenever his creditors started threatening legal action, he'd simply fax a letter to Chemical Bank authorizing a list of transfer payments from his checking account.

Opening up a new file in MONEYBIZ, I wrote a terse communiqué to the bank, informing them that they should pay the designated amounts listed below to Amex, Visa, MasterCard, Southern New England Telephone, and Yankee Power and Electric. I retrieved the bank's fax number from a previous letter. I hit the PRINT button. I did another ever improving rendition of Gary's signature. I fed the letter into the fax machine and pressed SEND. Gary Summers was now out of debt.

There were more letters to write. Every credit card and utility company received faxed instructions to set up a direct billing arrangement with Gary's bank. Chemical Bank was dispatched copies of these letters. Any debts he ran up in the future would be cleared automatically. When it came to paying his bills, he would now be a model citizen.

Correspondence completed, my eye fell on a file marked NUMB.

Hitting the ENTER button, I couldn't believe my dumb luck. NUMB was for "numbers," and here was a list of PIN numbers for all his cards—most important, his ATM bank card. I had really struck pay dirt. It would now be possible to call on Gary's trust fund money at any cash machine in the country.

MONEYBIZ completed, I turned my attention to the anarchic state of his office and bedroom. If he was leaving town for a while, surely he would have made some effort to tidy up. So, finding a couple of empty boxes in a closet and some black plastic garbage bags, I spent several hours sorting through his papers. Anything of reasonable importance went into the boxes. Everything else was bagged. Moving on to his bedroom, I folded and stored clothes. Then I did a basic cleanup of the living room, before returning to the office for the manila file containing Gary's birth certificate and other vital documents. It was almost four thirty. Time to finish business for the night. Slipping quickly out the back door, I deposited two bags of trash in the bins at the side of his house, then popped the note to Beth inside his mailbox.

Back at my house, the effects of a sleepless night finally hit me. I lay down on my bed, shut my eyes, and didn't open them again until 11:08 Wednesday morning. After a shower I dressed again in Gary-style clothes, pocketed his birth certificate, and headed for the highway.

It was a little after twelve. Five hours of available light. Just about enough time to run a few crucial errands before dinner at the Hartleys'.

The first errand involved a trip to the motor vehicle bureau in Norwalk. Before reaching it, I stopped in a gas station and used the phone. I dialed information, obtained the number for the Connecticut Department of Motor Vehicles, and punched it in. After waiting five minutes, I finally spoke with a civil servant named Judy. I explained that I had lost my license and wondered if I needed a new photograph for the replacement.

"Of course you'll need a new photograph," Judy said.

"Now I know this sounds kind of silly," I said, "but I really liked my old photograph and was wondering if you might have it on file."

"Can't help you out there, sir. The state of Connecticut doesn't keep computerized photo records of driver's licenses."

It was the news I was hoping to hear. I retreated to the station rest room, pulled out Gary's license, noted the number in my notebook, then extracted the scissors on my Swiss army knife and turned the license into confetti. Three flushes and it had vanished.

I'd chosen the motor vehicle bureau in Norwalk because it was never particularly crowded. Indeed, there were only five people in line ahead of me. While waiting, I filled in a lost-license form, noting the number of Gary's "misplaced" driver's license.

"Got your birth certificate and Social Security card?" asked the buck-toothed nerd behind the desk. I handed them over. "Over there for the eye test," he said, pointing to another line.

It took two minutes to call out the letters on the eye chart. Then I was shunted along to a photo machine. Ten minutes later, when someone called out "Gary Summers," it took me a moment to realize: That's me. I approached the counter.

"Here you go, Mr. Summers," said the clerk, handing over a new license and counting the cash I pushed toward him. "Try not to lose it again."

As I rolled north up I-95, I gave thanks to the overbureaucratized state of Connecticut for not having the software necessary for keeping a record of license photos.

The rest of the afternoon was spent shopping. Heading first to a big mall in Bridgeport, I used my own ATM card to withdraw another $500 from a cash machine. Then I entered an auto-supply place and bought two plastic gas cans. Now north to New Haven, where I found a large sporting goods store and dropped $195 on an inflatable rubber dinghy, a foot pump, and a pair of oars. A forty-minute drive onward to Hartford. I used the yellow pages to find a chemical-supply company, where I bought a four-ounce bottle of acid. Moving south to Waterbury, I hit a gardening outlet that sold weed-killing chemicals. Then I shot farther south to Danbury, where I bought black plastic sheeting and a lunchbox. Back now to

Stamford and a mall on the outskirts of town. Here I stopped at three different shops to pick up black sweats and sneakers, a green car tarpaulin, two giant duffel bags, a roll of industrial-strength tape, two foot-long cardboard tubes, and two glass vials with cork stoppers. I considered this extended tour of Connecticut a safety precaution. One-stop shopping—especially for a mass purchase that included inflammatory chemicals and a rubber boat—might have raised a few eyebrows.

I was back in New Croydon by seven. I stored my purchases in assorted locked corners of my darkroom. Then I drove to the Hartleys'. They plied me with good Scotch and good chablis. They fed me Dover sole. They listened with attentive sympathy as I gave them the large-print edition of the disintegration of my marriage. They made all the usual kind/practical noises about counseling, mediation, the potential for reconciliation. They looked at each other when I mentioned that Beth wanted me out of the house by Sunday.

"Take our spare room for a while," Ruth said.

"I couldn't," I said.

"You must," Bill said.

"I don't know what to say."

"Say nothing," Bill said. "Just keep drinking."

He refilled my glass. I sipped the wine and then dropped a question I'd been waiting to drop all evening. "I'm thinking of staying out of the office until the middle of next week. Don't suppose you're up for a day or two on the Sound?"

"Love to," Bill said, "but we're visiting Theo at his school in New Haven on Sunday. How about Saturday?"

"Up seeing Adam and Josh in Darien."

"Well, if you want to go by yourself on Sunday, you're welcome to the boat. Head off for a night or so if you like. From what I saw last week, you certainly seemed to know what you were doing. A few days out alone might do you some good."

"Wouldn't want to risk anything happening to the *Blue Chip*."

"It's insured."

"Heavily," Ruth added. And we all laughed.

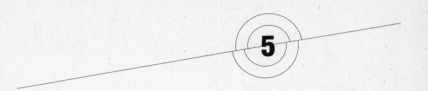

MY BEDTIME reading was supplied by Bill. Three large navigational charts of the Connecticut coast. I glanced at them for around five minutes before sleep caught me like a sucker punch. When I stirred nine hours later, it took me a moment to realize that it was eleven a.m. on Thursday and I was in the Hartleys' spare room, having been far too smashed to drive home last night. A note and a batch of keys were on the bedside table.

> We've gone to work. Make yourself at home. Hang on to these keys. The little one unlocks the *Blue Chip*'s cabin, in case you want to have a look around. Hang in there.
>
> > Love,
> > R. & B.

I didn't deserve friends like Ruth and Bill. They were too decent, too trusting. And I was going to take advantage of their hospitality in a very big way.

After a fast shower I took a closer look at Bill's charts. Running my finger along the jagged teeth of the Connecticut coastline, I found a tiny spit of land east of New London called Harkness Memorial State Park.

It was a hundred miles northeast of New Croydon. And two hours later I was there. Rolling acres of green lawn, picnic tables, and the old Harkness mansion, now a museum and looking like a haunted house from a Vincent Price movie. There were low gates at the park entrance. As it was the third day of November, it was the off-season, and I had the place to myself. Strolling down to the beach, I saw a few pleasure boats out on the water and a clear, unimpeded stretch of sea that, fifteen miles due east, would become the Atlantic Ocean.

Making my way back to the Miata, I left the park and turned left. A half mile down the road I braked suddenly in front of a dilapidated farmyard gate. Behind it was a field with a large clump of trees. The nearest dwelling—a red clapboard house—was around a quarter of a mile away. The field was perfect for my needs.

Returning to New London, I clocked the mileage to the train station, then followed signs to I-95 and headed for New Croydon.

Back at my house that evening, I called my mentor, Jack Mayle, at home in Scarsdale. He sounded depleted. "Little fuzzy tonight," he said. "Must be the pills the doc has got me popping. You all right?"

"Still feeling pretty shaky," I said.

"Well, stay home. Try to get some rest. Best thing for you. You can't be too careful with food poisoning. But lookit, I gotta have you back on Wednesday."

"I'll be there," I lied. "And thanks for everything, Jack. You've been the best."

He detected the note of finality in my voice. "You sure you're okay, Ben?"

"Just tired." I hung up. And realized we would never speak again. The first good-bye. With harder ones to come.

A covert dash to Gary's house. I made my way to the basement and opened the freezer. He was still there. Then I turned my attention to his darkroom. Unlike me, he had only three cameras: a Rolleiflex, a Nikkormat, and a pocket-size Leica. I packed them all into his camera bag, along with two extra lenses and a small tripod.

Carrying the bag upstairs to his bedroom, I found a black travel bag in his closet and filled it with clothes. I also grabbed his Filofax, his shaving kit, and a pair of Ray Ban Wayfarers he always wore. One last item: his IBM ThinkPad. The carrying case also contained a portable Canon printer. How convenient. I slotted the ThinkPad into the case and hoisted the bags.

A fast, nervous hobble across the road. Once I was in my driveway, the bags were stored in the trunk of the Miata. After a trip to my darkroom, they were joined by the green car tarpaulin and the file of Gary's documents.

Then it was off to Stamford. The attendant in the parking garage didn't look up from his *Sports Illustrated* as I collected my ticket. I found a space three cars from Gary's MG. The garage was empty of drivers, so no one saw me as I transferred everything from the trunk of the Miata to that of the MG. Needing to kill time (I didn't want to prod the attendant's attention by driving out five minutes after arriving), I walked over to an Indian restaurant nearby. I killed an hour over tandoori chicken and a few beers.

No notice was taken of me when, at 11:15, I drove out of the garage in the Miata. And there was a new attendant on duty when I arrived back on foot early the next morning, having caught the 6:08 local from New Croydon. It was Friday, and I looked like I was starting the weekend early, dressed for a country walk: hiking boots, a daypack on my back. Gary's MG fired on the first turn of the ignition key. I forked over $24 for the parking fee and yawned my way up I-95.

Bypassing the entrance to Harkness State Park, I traveled on to the farmyard gate. I jumped out, threw open the gate, drove in, closed the gate, then headed for the trees. Creeping along, I drove the MG as far as possible into the cluster of elms and oaks, turned off the motor, unwrapped the tarpaulin, and covered the car. Then I piled the tarpaulin high with leaves. When I hiked back to the main road, I could just about make out a mound of leaves deep within this forest.

Pulling a baseball cap and a pair of shades out of my daypack, I began the five-mile trek back to the New London train station. Only a few cars passed me, and no one paid me the slightest attention. I was just a fresh air freak out for a hike.

When I got on the southbound train, I took a seat near the bathroom, just in case I needed to hide from a familiar face.

A hazardous job awaited me upon my return to New Croydon. Opening a locked cabinet in my darkroom, I extracted the chemicals I'd purchased. Then I dug out my notebook containing the recipe from *The Anarchist's Cookbook* and went to work. Playing mad scientist, I measured out assorted doses of each chemical before blending them together. Retrieving one of the foot-long cardboard tubes I'd bought, I secured the plastic cover on the bottom end with electrical tape. After filling the tube with the chemical compound, I taped shut the top end and employed scissors to bore a small hole in the plastic cover. Two pieces of Scotch tape were then placed over this aperture. Picking up the second tube, I repeated the process. When I was finished, I packed the tubes in a carry-on bag, tore up the recipe, and gave it a burial at sea via the toilet.

Using a tiny funnel, I now filled two vials with acid, sealed them both with Blu-tack, a nonflammable substance, then taped a cork stopper to the side of each bottle. Bringing out a lunchbox, I used electrical tape to secure the bottles to opposite ends of the box. Once they were fastened in place, I shut the box and gave it a vigorous, nerve-racking shake. The two vials didn't move; the acid didn't leak. And I didn't go up in flames.

The next morning, Saturday, I stored the vials aboard the *Blue Chip*. I'd rung Bill the previous night, telling him I wanted to get my supplies on the boat before sailing off on Sunday. Bill promised to give the harbormaster a call—in case he wondered what a stranger was doing snooping around the sloop.

"How do," the harbormaster said as he walked down the dock toward me. He was around sixty, with a face as craggy as granite. "You're Hartley's friend, right?"

"Ben Bradford," I said, proffering my hand.

He gave it a stern shake, then stared at the bag of groceries and the large duffel I had already loaded on deck. "Amount you're stowing aboard, looks like you're planning to do the Atlantic."

"You never know," I bantered.

He noticed another giant duffel still on the dock. "What you got in that?" he asked.

My palms began to sweat. "Scuba gear."

"Ain't nothing to look at in these waters 'cept sewage," he said. "Need a hand?" Before I could decline the favor, he grabbed one end of the duffel. I jumped down onto the dock and grabbed the opposite side. "Weighs a ton," he said, helping me hoist it. "Feels cold as hell too."

"Keep the tanks in my garage. It's like an icebox in there."

We managed to lift the duffel onto the boat, then lowered it gently. He kept staring at it. I tried to remain calm.

"Scuba diving in November?" he said. "Better you than me." He kicked the bag with his left shoe. Thankfully, it connected with the steel tank, making a muffled bong. "Sounds like a big tank," he said. "How long can you stay under with it?"

" 'Bout an hour."

"Guess that's long enough. Well, happy sailing."

"Appreciate the hand," I said.

He nodded curtly, climbed down to the dock, and strolled off.

I went below into the cabin, flopped on a bunk, and tried to stop hyperventilating. Why was the harbormaster being so nosy? Did he suspect something? Or was he just a prying old man with nothing better to do than make my business his business? I decided to go with the nosy-old-man scenario. He had no reason to distrust me, after all. And he certainly didn't realize that he had just helped bring aboard the frozen body of Gary Summers. Thank goodness I had tossed the scuba tank into the same bag with the body.

Getting Gary into the bag had been quite a job. Around one this morning—after I'd completed the *Anarchist's Cookbook* recipe—I'd backed my Miata into Gary's garage, closing the door behind me. Carrying the largest of the duffels I'd bought on Wednesday, I went down to the basement and got straight to work, unzipping the duffel and laying out black plastic sheeting on the floor. Opening the chest freezer, I managed to get Gary sitting upright, but nearly slipped a disk trying to hoist him out. He was rock solid and so cold that when I wrapped my arms around his midsection, I could barely hold him for more than a few seconds. But after several attempts I finally had him out of the freezer and onto the plastic sheeting.

Twenty minutes later Gary's body was inside the duffel bag, and the bag was in the trunk of my Miata. I decided I'd load the duffel up with scuba gear as soon as I got back to my house, in an attempt to mask its actual contents.

I eased the Miata out into the driveway, locked Gary's garage behind me, and drove without lights across the road. I didn't look back. I didn't want to lay eyes on that house ever again.

A few hours later I was at the New Croydon docks unloading my gear. Once I bade the harbormaster farewell and retreated to the cabin, I waited a good fifteen minutes before going back on deck. Hauling the duffel below, I unpacked the scuba equipment, then stored Gary in a cabinet beneath the portside bunk. The second duffel, containing the inflatable dinghy, went into the fuel stores.

It was now early afternoon and time to head to Darien.

PHIL and Lucy's house was a throwback to the Eisenhower era, with a red brick porch adorned with thin white columns. A large American flag drooped from a pole above the front door. I steered my car into the driveway and spent a moment or two trying to control my dread. Then I got out and rang the doorbell.

Lucy answered. "Ben," she said tonelessly.

"Hi, Lucy." The anxiety in my voice was palpable.

"He's here," she yelled over her shoulder. Then, turning back to me, she said, "You might as well come in."

As soon as I was in the door, Adam came charging up from the basement playroom and threw himself at me.

"Daddy! Daddy!" he cried.

I grabbed him and held on tight.

"Daddy's here, Mommy," he announced loudly.

"So he is." Beth was standing on the opposite side of the room, with Josh asleep against her shoulder. She gave me a fast nod.

"You well?" I asked.

"Okay," she said quietly.

"We're going to McDonald's," Adam said.

"Go get your coat, big guy," I said. Adam ran off. An awkward silence. I broke it. "Josh keeping you awake much?"

"He went down for five hours last night."

"Something of a record. Can I . . ."

"Of course," she said, and gently handed Josh to me. His head nuzzled against my neck. I rocked him back and forth. Adam came running back into the room, dragging his brown duffel coat behind him. I handed Josh back to Beth with reluctance, a chill running through me. Adam took my hand.

"Can you have him back by five?" Beth asked. "He's been invited to a party."

"Fine. Can I take the Volvo? I won't have to transfer the booster seat."

"Here," she said, handing me the keys. "Five, please. No later."

At McDonald's, Adam had his usual Chicken McNuggets and french fries. He played with the little Disney toy that accompanied his meal. "When are we going to Disney World?" he asked.

"We'll get there sometime," I said, reaching into my pocket for a bottle of pills. I popped two, washing them down with Coke.

"Daddy takes medicine," Adam observed.

Daddy's taking Dexedrine. Daddy also wishes he had some Valium on him. Because this talk of Disney World is about to make Daddy fall apart. "Where to next?" I asked.

"Toys! You buy me a present?"

"A big present."

We drove into Stamford and parked in front of the Baby and Toy Superstore on Forest Street. Adam tore into the shop. Within moments he had found the bicycle section and mounted a pint-size red Schwinn with training wheels.

"Please, Daddy. Buy me this." He pressed down on the wheels and started riding in circles.

"Only if you wear a helmet."

A saleswoman chimed in, "We have them in different colors."

"Red, I think," I said. "It'll match the bike."

She returned a few moments later with a box.

"I wear it!" Adam said, halting momentarily while the saleswoman strapped on the helmet. Then he was off again, wheeling around the bike department.

"A lovely boy," the saleswoman said.

"He is that," I said. Adam looked up for a moment and gave me a grin of utter delight. My son. My beautiful son.

"You know the bike is self-assembly," the saleswoman said. "But it shouldn't take you more than an hour."

My heart sank. "Don't you have one already assembled? I don't have much time with him today."

She nodded understandingly as she categorized me as another divorced dad, trying to assuage his guilt with another expensive gift. "I'm sure the manager will let you take the one he's riding," she said.

Before we left the store, Adam also scored a remote control Cookie Monster car and a Lego fire station. There was so much booty that a shop assistant helped me carry it out to the Volvo. It was now 3:30. Just ninety minutes left. And a cold drizzle was leaking down from a dingy sky. "Can we go to the park?" Adam asked as I strapped him into his seat.

"It's raining, big guy. Parks aren't fun when it's wet."

"I want to ride my bicycle!"

"Not in the park. You'll catch a cold—"

"Please, Daddy. I ride my bicycle!"

And that's how we ended up inaugurating Adam's bicycle on the top floor of the Stamford Town Center Mall. It was the quietest corner of the complex—there were only a couple of fast-food joints up here—so Adam was able to bike up and down without too many disapproving looks. I followed him at first. But after twenty minutes of chasing Adam's bicycle, fatigue hit, so I parked myself at a snack bar counter and watched him. Twice I tried to convince him to give the bike a rest, enticing him with the offer of an ice cream. Twice he said, "I ride my bike, Daddy."

Eventually he did tire of this cycling marathon and accepted a vanilla cone. Four twenty. Down to just forty minutes. We moved to a table. His free hand was proprietorially gripped around the handlebars of the Schwinn.

"You're really good on the bike, Adam."

"I want to ride without the little wheels."

"Maybe in a year or so you can take them off."

"You teach me, Daddy?"

I bit hard on my lip. "I'll teach you, big guy."

"We take the bike to Disney World. And to the zoo . . ."

As he sang this sweet litany of future times together, I lost a battle I had been fighting for hours.

"Why are you crying, Daddy?" His eyes were wide with fear. They grew wider as my sobbing became uncontrollable. I clutched him against me. And held on tight, as if he could somehow lead me back to the life I was about to lose.

"Stop it, Daddy. *Stop.*"

He stiffened in my arms, terrified. But I couldn't stop. I had lost everything. I was now in free fall.

"Hey, hey? *Hey?*" I felt a hand clutch my shoulder. I relaxed my grip for a moment, and Adam sprang out of my arms, running down the corridor. I looked up. The manager of the snack bar was standing over me, his face aghast. "You okay?" he asked.

I shook with disorientation, my vision blurred by tears.

"Hang on, I'm gonna call for a doc—"

"No need, no need," I managed to say. "Upset, that's all."

"So's your little boy."

"Adam . . ." I stood up in panic, unable to see where he was. Then I heard him crying. He was cowering against a nearby wall. I tried to move toward him, but the snack bar manager—a beefy man in his forties—held me back.

"Is that really your kid?" he asked. I tried to shrug him off, but his hand grabbed my collar and yanked hard. "I'm asking you again, pal. Is that your kid?"

"Of course it's my—" I struggled against him, but he had me in a menacing grip. I was marched over to Adam, who was white with fear.

"Is this your daddy?" the manager asked him.

Adam managed a terrified nod.

"You sure? You don't have to be afraid, son."

Adam stood, paralyzed for a moment, then threw himself against my legs, weeping. The manager finally let go of my collar. I knelt down and gathered Adam in my arms, whispering, "I'm sorry, I'm sorry." I rocked him gently until his tears subsided.

Post-shopping traffic was heavy, and we didn't reach Phil and Lucy's house until 5:40.

The moment I pulled into the driveway, Beth was storming out the door into the rain. "Congratulations. Well done," she said.

"The traffic was terrible," I said, getting out of the car.

"I told you five o'clock. He's missed the party now," Beth said, lifting Adam out of his seat. She finally caught sight of all the booty in the car. "Are you crazy?"

"He wanted a bike, so—"

"No way, no way. We're not accepting it. I don't want your guilt. I don't want anything from—"

"Please, Beth. Let him keep—"

She snatched the car keys from my hand. "Just go, will you? *Go.*"

She turned and ran with Adam through the driving rain into the house. I gave chase, but she slammed the door just as I reached the step. The rain was now frenzied. But I didn't care. I kept pounding on the door, screaming, begging to be let in. There was only silence from within. I backed away from the door, defeated. And then I saw her. Staring out at me through a window, looking forlorn. For one brief moment our eyes locked. A moment of terrible indecision. A moment when the veil of enmity lifted, and all we could behold was sadness.

But then the moment ended. She mouthed two words, "I'm sorry." Not an apology. Just a statement of finality.

It was over. All over. It was time to end it all.

I MOVED out of the house that night. I scribbled a note to Beth and left it on the kitchen table. I kept it straightforward:

Borrowed Bill's boat for the weekend. Back Tuesday night. I'll be staying at Bill and Ruth's for the next few weeks. Will drop over to see the boys on Wednesday. I love you all.

I took a shower and changed into the clothes I'd be wearing tomorrow: khakis, a button-down shirt, a heavy sweater, deck shoes, a Nautica windbreaker. I rechecked my pockets to be sure that Gary's wallet and keys were stowed separately from my own.

It was time to leave. To slam the door behind me. To make that final move. I stared at the family photos pinned to a bulletin board in the kitchen. I walked over and took down a picture of Josh sitting on Adam's lap. I'd always loved it—and for one brief moment decided I had to have it. But no evidence of the past was allowed where I was going, so I quickly pinned the photo back to the board.

Bill and Ruth were already asleep when I arrived at their place. A bottle of Laphroaig and a glass had been left on the bedside table, along with a note: "Guaranteed cure for insomnia." I climbed between the sheets, downed a glass, poured another. Surely Beth would let Adam have the bicycle, wouldn't she? If she was stubborn about it, she'd change her mind by Tuesday. When the phone rang at home and she heard the news.

The next thing I knew, Bill was shaking me.

"Rise and shine, sailor," he said.

"I'll rise, but I won't shine," I muttered.

"Half a bottle of malt does have that effect."

Ruth was still asleep as Bill and I drove to the harbor in his Jeep. "Listen," he said, "are you sure you're up to being by yourself at sea for two nights? You have us both worried. I mean . . ."

"I'm not going to jump overboard, if that's what you mean."

"That's what I mean."

"Not my style."

"Good."

It was eight o'clock when we arrived at the harbor. The sky was a deep azure blue. There was a nippy northwesterly blowing. A perfect day for sailing.

"Well," Bill said, "I better shove off. Theo is expecting us by ten. When you dock on Tuesday, give me a call. I'll come pick you up. And of course, if there are any problems, use ship-to-shore to reach my mobile."

"There won't be any problems." I tossed him my car keys, in case he needed to move the Miata out of his driveway. We shook hands.

"Go easy," he said.

"Thanks again, friend," I said.

I boarded, moved to the wheel, turned the ignition key. The motor hummed to life. Bill untied the *Blue Chip* from the dock and tossed the docking line back aboard. I pulled down on the gearshift, raised the throttle, and slowly began to power out of New Croydon harbor. I gave Bill a final nod. He raised a hand slowly, a somber, apprehensive gesture of farewell.

I motored for around half a mile; then I cranked up the mainsail and the jib and set an easterly course down Long Island Sound.

I sailed all day. Near Old Lyme Shores light began to dim. By the time I dropped anchor a mile off Harkness State Park, day had become night. Scanning the shore with my binoculars, I saw no hints of campfires. Thank goodness it wasn't summer, when the park would have been filled with vacationers.

After stowing the sails, I went below. It was time to begin. I could feel my stomach caving in, but I steadied myself, thinking, Just take it step by step.

One. I pulled on surgical gloves, then dug out the duffel containing the dinghy. After inflating it with the foot pump, I attached a line to its bow, stowed its oars aboard, and carted it out on deck.

Two. I changed into a pair of black sweats and black sneakers. Then I shoved Gary's wallet and keys into a back pocket.

Three. I unwrapped Gary. He was still cold to the touch. Using heavy-duty scissors, I cut off his clothes and dumped them into a black plastic garbage bag. Balancing him on the edge of the port bunk, I dressed him in the clothes I'd just taken off. Then, after stripping off the blankets, I laid him on the bunk. I shoved my wallet and house keys into his pocket and tucked the blankets in. He looked like he was enjoying a sweet sleep.

Four. I excavated the two jerry cans of diesel. I drenched Gary's head, hands, and body. Then I doused the cabin walls and floors with the remaining diesel before tossing the two cans into the plastic bag.

Five. I taped the two prefilled cardboard tubes to the port and starboard walls. I inverted both vials of acid and inserted them, cork first, into the top of each tube. I had now primed an incendiary device known as a nipple bomb. In around seven hours—according to *The Anarchist's Cookbook*—the acid would eat through the cork and flow into that most inflammable compound of chemicals. The result would be two huge fireballs quickly engulfing Gary.

Six. Using the *Blue Chip*'s global positioning system, I charted a southeasterly course at a speed of seven nautical miles per hour. The boat would travel by autopilot across the Sound, then ride the ebb tide through the Race—a narrow passage of water with strong tidal currents south of Fishers Island. After clearing this passage, it would leave Montauk Point to starboard and Block Island to port, eventually entering the Atlantic. By the time the nipple bombs kicked in, the craft would be thirty miles from the nearest landfall. The fire would rage. Gary would be cremated. The gas-stove canister would detonate. And, given that it was the middle of the night, it would be at least five hours before any forensic experts were on the scene to inspect whatever wreckage still remained. Five hours in seawater was enough time to mask the excessive amounts of diesel used to destroy the boat and scatter evidence. In short, it would look like a very bad accident.

Seven. I stuffed the plastic bag into one of the duffels and went on deck. Placing the duffel in the dinghy, I lowered the inflatable boat into the water, tying it to the stern of the *Blue Chip*. I pulled up the anchor, stowing it on board. Then I powered up the engine and raced to the stern as the sloop began to move.

But as I tried to board the dinghy, I slipped and plunged into the arctic waters of the Sound. I hung on to the side of the dinghy, gasping for air. The *Blue Chip* was now moving quickly. I swam madly toward its stern. A fast unscrambling of the knot, and I fell back into the Sound. As the *Blue Chip* left me behind, I gripped the rope as if it were a life raft, yanking the dinghy toward me. When I had finally reeled it in, I hoisted myself on board. It nearly capsized under my angled weight. Using my hands, I bailed out as much water as possible, but there was still a good foot sloshing around. Grabbing the oars, I rowed for shore, shivering with cold.

It took a half hour to reach the beach. Along with everything else in the duffel, my flashlight was waterlogged, dead. A wind was blowing, my sweats were sodden, and I had no light to guide me through the park to the road. I deflated the dinghy, folded it up, and added it to the duffel. Then I started to walk, the heavy duffel hoisted atop my right shoulder. I reached a paved path and followed it through the pitch-black park, the duffel's weight becoming heavier with every step. It took me twenty minutes to reach the park gates. They were only four feet high. Tossing the duffel before me, I climbed over and continued my slow hike.

The final quarter mile was agony, the duffel now a torturous deadweight. It landed at my feet when I reached the farmyard gate. I tossed it over, followed it, and headed for the trees. When I reached them, I kept colliding with branches. But I kept going until I suddenly connected with something hard. I dug through the leaves and found the car tarpaulin. Pulling it off, I reached into my sweats for the keys. Springing open the trunk of the MG, I grabbed a clean set of clothes and a towel from Gary's travel bag, then flung the duffel inside. I unlocked the driver's-side door, hit the ignition, set the heater on maximum, and climbed out again. As the car interior heated up, I stripped out of my wet clothes. After changing into Gary's clothes, I jumped into the now warm MG.

I still stank of the sea. I tried to comb my hair with my fingers but ended up looking like a haunted, waterlogged refugee. If a cop were to stop me, I wouldn't exactly inspire confidence. Nervously I put the car in reverse. But as soon as I had backed up a few feet, I screeched to a halt and jumped out. I had forgotten my sodden clothes and the tarpaulin. Brilliant. Nothing like leaving evidence in your wake. Wrapping them up in a big ball, I tossed them next to the duffel in the trunk. Driving without lights, I inched my way through the trees until I reached the open field. A quick opening and closing of the farmyard gate, and I was on the road, headlights now aglow. Thinking, My name is Gary Summers. I am a photographer.

6

I DROVE all night. I drove all day. I concentrated on numbers. Interstate numbers: 95 to 78 to 76 to 70. On the outskirts of Kansas City my brain went haywire. Triple vision, a surge of nausea, Dexedrine overload. I needed a bed fast. I sidestepped two small mom-and-pop motels and checked into a large, anonymous Days Inn, where I registered under G. Summers. The room was a little tatty. I didn't care. I hung out the DO NOT DISTURB sign, climbed in between the stiff, frosty sheets, and died.

I didn't stir for twelve hours. The digital bedside clock said 6:07 a.m. For a few befuddled minutes I wondered, Why isn't Josh crying? But then reality hit. Good morning, you're dead. I fumbled for the remote control and stared, half awake, at *CNN Headline News*. A White House cabinet resignation. More fun in Bosnia. Nothing about an explosion aboard a small boat off Montauk Point.

I showered but didn't shave; I was trying to camouflage my features under some stubble. I put on dark glasses and a baseball hat. I checked out and hit the road.

The hours clicked by. Night. The Colorado state line. And, coming up fast on my rear, the blue lights of a highway patrolman. My pulse went berserk. They'd found the boat. Intact. With Gary's body. And two dud nipple bombs. They'd searched Gary's house, realized his car was missing, issued a bulletin for an MG with Connecticut plates. And now the Colorado cops were going to make the collar. The sirens shrieked. The lights of the patrol car filled my rearview. I knew what I was going to do. As soon as they were on my bumper, I'd veer left, cross the divider, and go right into the path of an oncoming truck. But just as the cop car closed in on my tail, it swerved left and sped off in pursuit of a pickup doing ninety in front of me. I took the next exit and checked into the first motel I could find. But I couldn't sleep, convinced that it was just a matter of time before the knock came on the door.

I was back on the interstate just after sunrise. I reached the outskirts of Denver by ten. I stopped at a McDonald's and bought a *New York Times*. In the second section, on the bottom corner of page 4, I saw the story:

> LAWYER MISSING, FEARED DEAD AFTER BOAT EXPLOSION
> Benjamin Bradford, a junior partner at the Wall Street law firm of Lawrence, Cameron and Thomas, is feared dead after the sailboat he was piloting went ablaze seventeen miles east of Montauk Point, L.I. "From what we can ascertain so far, a fire engulfed the cabin of the craft and quickly combusted," said coast guard spokesman L. Jeffrey Hart. "Though we can't rule anything out, we are currently treating this as an accident."

I reread the story several times. It took a while to sink in. "We are currently treating this as an accident." My mind shifted into overdrive. After the cops ascertained that I didn't have any homicidal enemies and would have jumped overboard if I'd been suicidal, they would file my death away under misadventure. I was going to get away with it. And yet I didn't feel triumphant. Just numb.

My past had been eradicated. No responsibilities, no ties, no former life. Question: When you wipe a slate clean, what do you end up with? Answer: a blank slate. Alternative answer: freedom. The burdenless life you've always craved. But when you're finally confronted with that freedom—that blank slate—you feel nothing but fear. Because freedom of the absolute, no-strings variety is like staring into an uncharted void, a realm without structure. I left my Big Mac untouched. I went back to the car. I drove. Direction: nowhere.

For the next few weeks I just drifted, wandering the interstates like some motorized Flying Dutchman. A pattern developed. A day on the road, a night in a motel. Cash only. No conversations. Just a few phrases: "Fill 'er up. . . ." "Can I have a shake with the cheese-burger." I never stayed more than one night anywhere. I never left the interstate system, because I feared small towns where people might be interested in a stranger passing through. Every day I scoured *The New York Times*. Finally, when I was somewhere outside Provo, Utah, the *Times* ran another Ben Bradford story.

FOUL PLAY RULED OUT IN BRADFORD DEATH

Twelve days after the boat he was piloting caught fire and exploded in the Atlantic, police investigators have ruled out foul play in the death of Wall Street lawyer Ben Bradford. No further investigation of the case will be undertaken.

It was the news I had been waiting to read. The all-clear had sounded. But I still roamed the interstates. All journeys have a logical structure. You depart, you return. But mine had become an endless ride down a concrete corridor.

On the last Tuesday in November, I reached Rock Springs, Wyoming, a nowhere town on I-80. I checked into the Holiday Inn, opened up the IBM ThinkPad, and composed a letter to Beth.

December 2, 1994
Berkeley, CA

B: Greetings from the People's Republic of Berkeley. The Baja assignment didn't go as well as expected. The photo editor at the mag thought my work too hard-edged and graphic. Everyone wants gloss these days.

I know I shouldn't be writing you at home, but I thought I'd better come clean straightaway. While hanging out in San Felipe, I hooked up with a photographer from the Bay Area named Laura. She was on vacation, and what we both thought was just a weekend thing turned into something more. So much so that I followed her back to Berkeley, where she lives. Sorry to end it this way, but let's face it, it was always just a fling. It will be a nice memory—and they're few and far between. Take care.

G.

The letter was a little harsh, but the whole point of it was to so enrage Beth that she would never want anything to do with Gary again. Satisfied with my handiwork, I fed a sheet of paper into the Canon Bubble-Jet and hit the PRINT button. Then I typed Beth's name and address on the computer screen and printed out an envelope. I folded the letter into the envelope and shoved it into a larger envelope, already stamped and addressed to the Alternative Post Office in Berkeley. I also enclosed a ten-dollar bill paper-clipped to a note: "Please mail this for me. Gary Summers."

The next morning, after checking out, I tossed the envelope into the motel mailbox. It would take at least forty-eight hours to reach California, which is why I dated Gary's letter December 2. Once received, the Alternative Post Office folk would dispatch Gary's letter to Beth with the necessary Berkeley postmark.

I found the MG in the motel parking lot, climbed in, and opened my Rand McNally road atlas. Driving west on I-80 would bring me into Salt Lake City. East would eventually edge me into Nebraska. Terrific options. The only other route out of town was 191, a two-lane blacktop heading north into mountain country. I had been dodging back roads for weeks, sticking to the anonymity of the highway. But with Ben Bradford's death now ruled accidental, I no longer had to live as a fly-by-night. I opted for the back road.

I spent that night in Jackson, Wyoming. At first light the next morning I was heading west on Route 22. It had snowed heavily during the night. Although the road was freshly plowed, it was still a little tricky. Twice the MG went into a skid. Twice I just managed to gain control of the car before it swan-songed into a ravine. I crept along at twenty miles per hour, my teeth chattering. The car heater tried hard but wasn't really effective against an outside temperature of eight degrees Fahrenheit.

In Idaho, I took Route 33. The hours crept by. Around one o'clock that afternoon of December 1, I passed a road sign welcoming me to Big Sky Country. The state of Montana. There was no sky. There was just an ashen dome of snow. I was on Route 287. In front of me I could see the flashing lights of a plow-cum-sander. I trailed behind it as it opened the road for me. For three slow hours I followed in its wake. Until it led me safe and secure onto Interstate 90. It was now around four. I had been driving since dawn, but the snow was starting to ease and I couldn't face an early retreat to another motel room. So I turned west. Fifty miles down I-90 the snow turned to freezing rain. Seventy-five miles down I-90, and I was in a near collision with a moose as the snow started again. One hundred and fifty miles down I-90 the blizzard was so encompassing that I could just about see the exit sign for the town of Mountain Falls.

I stopped at a Holiday Inn because it was the first place I saw. "Is early December always like this?" I asked the receptionist at the front desk.

"Yep," she said. "Winter in Montana."

By morning the snow clouds had headed south. Light streamed through the plastic curtains of my motel room. I left the Holiday Inn in search of breakfast. Maybe it was the sight of all that pristine snow. Or maybe I was simply ready to get off the road. Whatever the reason, after a five-minute walk through Mountain Falls, I knew I was going to stay awhile.

The main street was called Main Street. At its northern end the mountains began. Due south there was a river called the Copperhead. In between there was a half-mile stretch of old red brick buildings, including a bar and grill called the Mountain Pass.

When I ambled in for breakfast, there were five hard men drinking beer at the bar. They looked up as I entered and did not favor me with a smile. But the waitress—a plump woman with permed hair and a serious mustache—did offer me a welcoming half grin as I slid into a booth near the kitchen.

"Y'hungry?" she asked. I nodded. "Then our Mountain Man $4.95 breakfast special's for you."

It arrived a few minutes later. A steak, two eggs, three pancakes, a huge lump of home fries. I could finish only half of it.

"Thought you was hungry," the waitress said when she came by with a coffeepot.

"Not that hungry."

Suddenly the door flew open, and a thickset man in a battered duffel coat staggered in. He was around forty, with a drinker's face: red and blue veins crisscrossing his cheeks, a bulbous nose.

"Rudy," the waitress shouted, "you git right now."

"Ah c'mon, Joan," Rudy said. "You can't bar me forever."

"Wanna bet?"

"Just a cup of coffee."

"Charlie!" the waitress shouted. A hulk appeared from the kitchen. Around six five, with tree trunks for arms. He had a baseball bat in one hand. Rudy backed off toward the door.

"Got the message," he said. And he was gone.

"Who's your friend?" I asked the waitress.

"You mean you don't know him?"

"I'm new in town."

"Must be, 'cause if you live in Mountain Falls, you know Rudy Warren. Especially if you read the local paper."

"He's a journalist?"

"Yeah. Writes for *The Montanan.* He's also a drunk. Six weeks ago he comes in, throws back a dozen drafts, grabs a stool, tosses it into the bar, walks out. Four hundred bucks' worth of damage."

"He pay?"

"Yeah. But he ain't drinking here again. No way."

I left the Mountain Pass and took a wander up Main Street. I passed three espresso joints, two decent bookshops, a contemporary art gallery, and Fred's Hole—a suspect-looking bar advertising an "Amateur Striptease Night" that evening. I took to the town's mixture of western sleaze and bookish cosmopolitanism. I liked the fact that it was a town of around 30,000, according to the signs—cozy, yet still big enough to get lost in.

The cold was beginning to penetrate my bones. I moved on to a cash machine and withdrew $250 from Gary's account. Then I headed to a sporting goods store and bought a thick down parka and a pair of insulated boots. Next door to the shop was a real estate agency, open all day Saturday, according to the hours posted on the front door. I walked in. A woman in her late forties—blond, dressed in a blazer and a tweed skirt—was seated behind a desk.

"Hi there," she said. "And how are you today?"

"I'm fine, thanks," I said, taken aback by her overfriendly tone. "Do you rent apartments?"

"We sure do, Mr. . . ."

"Summers. Gary Summers."

She proffered her hand. "Meg Greenwood. What sort of place were you looking for, Gary?"

"One bedroom. Something central."

"For you and your wife?"

"I'm single."

A smile crossed her lips. "How did you slip through the net?"

"Sorry?"

"Just a joke. Price range?"

"I'm sort of new in town, so I don't exactly know . . ."

"One beds go from four hundred and fifty to seven hundred dollars a month. I've got a one-and-a-half for six hundred in Frontier Apartments. Know the building?"

"Like I said, I'm new in Mountain Falls."

"From back east, are you?"

"Uh, yeah. How'd you—"

"Takes one to know one. Connecticut girl myself. And you?"

"Connecticut."

"No kidding! Whereabouts?"

"New Croydon."

"I don't believe it. I'm Darien born and bred."

I wanted to run out the door.

"Well, New Croydon guy, what brings you to Montana?"

"A photographic assignment."

"You're a photographer?"

I really needed to kill this conversation quickly. "Yeah. Now about this place at the Frontier Apartments . . ."

"Well, it's just two blocks from here. Got ten minutes?"

"Sure."

Walking to the apartment, she bombarded me with questions.

"So, what magazines you work for?"

"I'm working on a book," I lied. "About Montana."

"So you're looking for a base for a few months?"

"Exactly."

We reached the Frontier Apartments and rode the tiny elevator up to the third floor. "Lived here myself for a month after my divorce," she said. "Course, once the money came through from the sale of our house, I was able to buy a nice two-bedroom A-frame in Shawmut Valley. Have to get you out there sometime."

Another of her little smiles. The elevator stopped with a jolt.

"Well, here we are," she said, stopping in front of a battered wood door. "Now before we go inside, I have to tell you that the decor is a bit tired. But the space is great."

Tired was the operative word. Elderly floral wallpaper, threadbare rust-colored carpet, sagging double bed. "This is what six hundred a month buys in Mountain Falls?" I asked.

"The location is fantastic. And look at all the space."

She had a point. The living room and master bedroom were spacious, and there was a small, narrow bedroom that would make a nice darkroom. But the grim decor would have to go. "You'd have no objections to me fixing it up, would you?" I asked.

"We just manage the property. The owners live in Seattle. They use it as an investment, so yeah, I think I could talk them into it. As long as you're not planning anything radical."

"I'm from Connecticut. Radical isn't part of my vocabulary."

She laughed, then added, "The minimum lease is six months."

"That shouldn't be a problem . . . at five fifty a month."

"You *are* from Connecticut."

We returned to her office. She made the phone call to Seattle and blathered on to the owner about this wonderful new tenant she'd found and how he was willing to renovate the apartment in exchange for a rental reduction of $50 a month. The owner seemed to take a lot of convincing, but Meg Greenwood won him over.

"Took some talking, but it's yours," she said to me after hanging up. "A month's security deposit and a month's rent in advance, of course. Plus our finder's fee of two hundred and seventy-five dollars."

I did some fast math. After the withdrawal I made today, Gary's checking account had a balance of $3165. Moving in was going to cost me $1375. There would be another $550 due a month from now, leaving me with a grand total of $1240 to cover the eight weeks until the next trust fund payment hit the account. I would have to live cheap. "When can I move in?" I asked.

"Monday morning, I guess, if that's good by you."

"Fine. I'll be here to sign the lease at ten, if that suits."

"Sounds good to me. Uh, you wouldn't be able to supply us with some references, would you?"

That stopped me short. "Might take a couple of days," I said. "My bank's back east and . . ."

"No one here can give you a character reference?"

I gave her a big flirty smile. And said, "Only you."

She upped the coquettish ante. "Guess I'll just have to accept your New Croydon word of honor that you're good for the rent."

I fretted the rest of the weekend about Meg Greenwood. I envisaged her making calls to her pals in Darien, telling them how she had stumbled upon that rarest of species: an unattached man. I needed to throw a barricade around myself fast.

"Hey there, New Croydon guy," Meg said as I entered her office on Monday morning.

"Morning." Taking a seat, I reached into the inside pocket of my parka and brought out a stack of notes retrieved from an ATM machine. I counted out the bills and stacked them neatly on her desk.

"A check would have been fine," she said, eyeing the cash.

"Yeah, but it would've taken a couple of days to clear my New York bank. You have the lease?"

She handed me a three-page document. I perused it, then called her attention to a specific sentence. "Uh, clause four kind of worries me," I said. "It's the phrase 'residual ownership rights.' Does this imply that the lessee can have his tenancy terminated if the landlord decides to assert his absolute privileges of householdership as guaranteed by the freehold title deeds?"

She looked bemused. "I thought you were a photographer."

You idiot. Damage limitation bells went off in my head. "My dad was in real estate," I said, trying to smile. "Spent summers working in his office. So leases are a useless specialty of mine."

"He obviously taught you well. But we don't have tenant-right guarantees out here, so all leasing agreements come with a residual ownership clause."

"Fine," I said, not wanting to pursue this issue further. I picked up a pen and signed both copies of the lease. She handed me the keys. I shook her hand. "You've been great, Meg." I stood up.

"One last thing," she said. "You free for dinner some night?"

"Love to," I said, moving toward the door. "But how about in a couple weeks' time, when I've settled in and Rachel's in town?"

"Rachel. Who's Rachel?"

"My girlfriend."

"You said you were single."

"I am. But I do have a girlfriend in New York. Coming out to visit me over Christmas, so if you're around, we'd love to . . ."

She looked at me as if I'd just duped her. Which, of course, I had.

ON MY first night in the apartment, it started to snow again. It didn't stop for ten days. This suited me fine. It kept me indoors. Kept me working. Distanced me from the preparations for Christmas that were everywhere to be seen on the streets of Mountain Falls. Christmas was a holiday I was dreading.

I slept badly that first night. The bed sagged in four different places; the sheets were mildewy. The next morning I threw out the bed and spent $150 on a futon. I dropped an additional $200 on a duvet, a fitted sheet, pillows.

The carpets went next. I rented a sander for $75 and spent a week eradicating the paint that covered the pine floors. Then I turned my attention to the walls. My initial attempts at repapering were moronic. Several rolls buckled, and I had to strip them off and start again. I didn't finish the job until Christmas Eve.

I woke up Christmas morning haunted by images of Adam and Josh. I saw Adam diving into a pile of presents under the tree. "Where my present from Daddy?" he'd ask Beth. And Beth would try to explain yet again that Daddy was . . .

I felt myself getting shaky, so I went to work, spending eighteen hours in the company of a brush and several cans of white paint. Christmas dinner was a cheese omelet and three bottles of beer.

By New Year's Day the apartment was repainted, the floors were varnished, and I was almost broke. After I paid the next month's rent (slipping it under the door of Greenwood Realtors late one night to avoid meeting Meg), I had exactly $250 left. There was still a month to go before the next trust fund payment. I would have to live on $9 a day.

It didn't prove difficult. I shopped carefully at the supermarket; I bought dollar paperbacks; I lay low. On February 2, when my net worth was $7.75, I went to a cash machine on Main Street and hit the button for balance information. The figure $6900.00 popped up on the screen. Relieved, I withdrew $750 and went shopping.

Petrie's Cameras was located opposite the Holiday Inn. I'd passed it many times but had kept away from its temptations. Until now. "How do," said the guy behind the counter. He was in his late thirties—tall, shaggy-haired, with a plaid lumberjack shirt.

"I'm in the market for an enlarger," I said. "Probably something used, if you do secondhand equipment."

"We most certainly do," he said. "Got a great buy in the back— a Durst AC707 autocolor. In perfect shape, a bargain at four hundred and seventy-five dollars. Want to see it?"

I nodded, and he disappeared into the storeroom. Four hundred and seventy-five dollars for an enlarger—it had to be a piece of junk. My Beseler 45mx had cost me $3750 two years ago. Still, I was not in a position to be cavalier with money.

The salesman returned with the enlarger, plugged it in, and demonstrated the autofocus. "It's not top of the line," he said, "but it does the job nicely. Comes with a six-month guarantee."

"Sold," I said. "I need some chemicals. You stock Ilford?"

"Of course."

"Galleria bromide paper?"

"Naturally."

"And I'll also need an easel, three trays, a safety light, a neg focuser, a developing canister, a changing bag, and a timer."

"You got it. The name's Dave Petrie, by the way."

I shook his hand and introduced myself.

"New in town, Gary?"

"Yeah."

"This a hobby of yours?"

"No. I get paid for it."

"Thought so. We offer a fifteen percent professional discount."

"Then I'll take a dozen rolls of Tri-X and Ilford HP4."

After he returned with all the goods, he spent several minutes writing up an invoice. "With tax, that's seven hundred forty-two dollars and fifty cents."

I withdrew my wad of notes.

"We do take credit cards, if you prefer," he said.

"I always pay in cash."

"Fine by me. You know, we've got an amateur photographic society in Mountain Falls. Meets twice a month. I'm sure they'd love to hear about your work. . . ."

"Kind of busy right now," I lied.

"I understand. Want me to deliver this stuff for you?"

"No need. I'll drop by later in my car."

I walked across Main Street, thinking that Mountain Falls was just a little too friendly for my liking. I had the strong urge to flee. But if I ran out on the lease, Meg Greenwood would be on the phone to

Connecticut. I had no option but to stay and adjust to the inquisitive cordiality of small-town life. Because if I didn't start relaxing here, if I kept regarding every question as a potential threat, I would call attention to myself as a cryptic crank with something to hide.

So when I returned to Petrie's Cameras later that morning to collect my purchases, I accepted Dave's offer of a cup of coffee, over which he told me a bit about himself—a refugee from Phoenix who drifted up here after college and was now married with two kids.

"Running a shop wasn't what I had in mind when I came to Montana," he said. "But the big problem with Mountain Falls is that though the lifestyle is great, you can't support a family as a photographer. Not enough work. Still, Beth and I—"

"You wife's named Beth?" I said.

"Yeah. Anyway, the way Beth and I see it, you want to live in a place like Montana, you've got to make some trade-offs."

As I left Petrie's Cameras, I regretted the fact that Dave wanted to be my friend and I couldn't afford friends.

I spent the next few days assembling my darkroom. Then I grabbed my camera and a half-dozen rolls of Tri-X and headed east on a back road marked RTE. 200. Outside the town of Lincoln, I stopped at a roadhouse and entered a forgotten era. Sawdust floors, a soda fountain with hand-action syrup pumps, a zinc bar where a couple of men with lined faces sat drinking. Behind the bar was a gnarled woman in a floral-print smock. She noticed the camera.

"Photographer?" she asked as I took a seat at the bar.

I nodded. "Mind if I take a few shots here?"

She glanced at her customers. "Buy 'em a round. There should be no problem."

I tossed $10 on the bar and went to work. The light was terrific—slanting shafts of winter sun beaming through the grimy windows. I worked quickly, concentrating on the faces of the drinkers. I also shot a dead-on portrait of the manageress.

"You git what you want?" she asked after I finished.

"Yes, ma'am. Much obliged."

She picked up a pencil stub, licked it, and scribbled something on a slip of paper. "Gonna expect a copy of my picture," she said, handing me the paper. "A deal?"

"A deal," I said.

I drove farther east, crossed the Continental Divide, and entered Lewis and Clark County. The road was devoid of any hint of late-twentieth-century life. Just a long strip of blacktop snaking its way through high country. Eventually I did come across a gas station. Two ancient pumps, a battered garage. A kid around seventeen came out to fill my car. He had a frizzy beard, bad acne, a baseball cap, and a battered parka worn over oil-splattered overalls. I convinced him to pose in front of the pumps. He obliged, then asked if his wife and baby son could be part of a picture.

"Great idea," I said.

He disappeared into the garage. A moment later this wisp of an adolescent—she couldn't have been more than sixteen—came out cradling a tiny infant, bundled up against the cold.

"My wife, Delores," the pump jockey said.

Delores chewed gum. She wore a faded Michael Jackson sweatshirt. I found it hard to look at the little boy, so I quickly posed the family between the two pumps, the background framed by that decrepit garage and the empty snowbound terrain beyond. I shot a dozen exposures, paid for my gas, wrote down their address, and promised to send them a print.

I returned to Mountain Falls just before sundown and went straight to my darkroom. By late evening I was poring over the developed negatives and circled nine frames with a red china marker. I printed them. When they were dry, I rejected four outright. But the five that remained pleased me. The barroom faces were strongly delineated. You saw hard, creased features tempered by an all-purpose weariness. The roadhouse manageress looked like the original wizened, tough broad, but the surrounding detail made the picture. Her gnarled hand pulling down an old soda spray. A bottle of Hiram Walker at her elbow.

One of the gas station shots also made the cut. It showed the pump jockey and his wife standing side by side. The baby was cradled low in his arms. They were trying to smile, but the rusty pumps, the forsaken terrain emphasized the bleakness of their prospects.

The five that worked did so because they didn't impose an artful eye on the subject matter. When I concentrated on faces—and let them define the composition—everything else fell into place. So why not keep concentrating on faces?

The next morning I mailed the promised prints to the manageress and the gas station couple. And for the next three weeks I took constant day trips out of Mountain Falls. I went to Whitefish and shot gamblers working the slots at a local casino. I went to Kalispell and photographed the owner of an auto wrecker's. I roamed everywhere west of the Continental Divide. I ignored landscapes. I concentrated on pictures where the faces dominated, where they told you everything you needed to know about the individual and his milieu.

By the beginning of March, I had sixty prints I could live with. I also had a cash-flow problem, as I had shot over a hundred and fifty rolls of film. After I paid April's rent, I would be left with just $1350 until the next trust fund payment.

"Sure you don't feel like opening an account with us?" Dave Petrie asked me one morning.

"Thanks for the offer, but I'm a cash guy."

"You're also my best customer. When are you gonna have a night free to come over, meet Beth and the kids?"

"When this project is wrapped."

"Must be a biggie, considering the amount of film you're buying. Gonna make you some big money?"

"I doubt it."

There was a blizzard in the middle of March. Ten straight days of whiteout. It kept me confined to the Frontier Apartments, gave me cabin fever. So one night I braved the snow and walked up Main Street in search of liquid entertainment. I found Eddie's Place. It was a loud joint: a huge horseshoe bar three-deep with drinkers.

I managed to secure a stool at the bar. I ordered a Bud Light.

"You always drink low octane?" asked the guy next to me. Middle-aged, hangdog eyes, a face I'd seen before. He shouted to the woman working the bar. "Linda, honey, another J&B. And pour my friend here a shot of something while you're at it."

"What's it going to be?" she asked me.

"You have Black Bush?" I asked.

"We got it," she said, filling a glass.

"Man's got expensive taste in whiskey," the guy said as Linda lifted a ten-dollar note from the pile of cash in front of him.

"Next round's mine," I said.

"Fine by me," he said. "Rudy Warren."

Yes, I *had* seen his face before. When he was being thrown out of the Mountain Pass. "Gary," I said.

"Passing through Mountain Falls?"

"Living here." I gave him my spiel about being on a photographic assignment.

"Oh, you're one of those," he said.

"One of what?"

"An *artiste*. We attract 'em in Mountain Falls. You ask around this bar, you'll find at least a dozen guys writing the great Rocky Mountain novel or pretending they're Ansel Adams."

"Thank you for turning me into a cultural cliché."

"You offended?"

"Not really."

"I'm disappointed. I usually manage to offend everyone."

We drank four more rounds, during which Rudy talked nonstop about Montana and Mountain Falls. He said he was a Mountain Falls lifer. Born here. Never worked or lived anywhere else.

Linda the barkeep kicked us out at two. We fell into the street. It was still snowing. "How're you going to get home?" I asked.

He reached into his pocket, pulled out his keys. "In my car."

"No way. Give me the keys, Rudy."

"Who are you? My nanny, Mary Poppins?"

I snatched the keys out of his hand. "I'm going home," I said. "You want your car keys, follow me."

I turned and headed up Main Street, Rudy staggering behind me. The cold was brutal, but it did serve as an antidote to all the booze we'd imbibed. When I reached the Frontier Apartments, I waited inside the lobby for Rudy.

"You live here?" he asked as he entered the foyer.

I nodded.

"Think I got up to no good here once with a real estate broker named Meg Greenwood. You ever meet that crazy in a bar, at a party, you take a walk. Like fast."

I laughed. "Come on up. I'll call you a cab."

When we walked into my living room, Rudy emitted a low whistle. "Will you look at this," he said. "SoHo, Montana."

"Glad you approve," I said. "Know the number of the local cab company?"

"Buy me a beer; then you can kick me out."

I staggered into the kitchen. Rudy followed. I extracted two bottles of Rolling Rock from the fridge. I handed him one.

"Much obliged," he said. After taking a long swig, he stared at me long and hard. "I sure wouldn't want to play poker with you, 'cause I bet you're one heck of a bluffer."

I felt the onset of unease. "I always lose at poker," I said.

"Don't believe it," he said. "I've spent the last five hours drinking with you, and you've told me nothing about yourself. Being the nosy journo that I am, it makes me wonder, Why?"

"Maybe because, unlike you, I don't need to give everyone the story of my life after the second drink. Let's see about that cab."

I walked back into the living room and picked up the phone. I dialed information. The operator gave me the number of the taxi company. I called them. After forty rings I put down the phone. "They don't answer," I said, heading toward the kitchen.

"After twelve on a snowy night they always call it quits."

He was no longer in my kitchen. He was in my darkroom, leafing through a stack of my Montana portraits. He looked up as I entered. "All your own stuff?" he asked.

I nodded. He said nothing; he just kept flipping through the pile of prints, a smile occasionally crossing his lips. "It's Madge the Menace," he said at last, holding up a shot of the roadhouse manageress.

"You know her?"

"She's barred me from her place at least twice." He held up his empty bottle. "Could you score me another Rolling Rock?"

"Getting kind of late," I said. "How are you gonna get home?"

"You got a couch?"

"I guess . . ."

"Then you've got a guest."

"I'll get you the beer," I said.

Still holding the stack of pictures, he reeled into the living room and flopped on the couch. I extracted the last two Rolling Rocks from the icebox, handed him a bottle, and collapsed in an armchair opposite him. He drank the beer while working his way back through the photographs.

He finally looked up. "Best gallery of Montana faces I've ever seen."

"You serious?"

"I look at these faces and I think, *My* people, my Montana." He kicked off his shoes, stretched out on the couch, handed me the photos. "Now get me a blanket," he said.

I dropped the prints in the darkroom, then dug out the ancient mildewed bedspread that came with the bed I threw out.

"Gracious living," Rudy said as I threw it over him. "How 'bout a glass of water. Just half full."

"Okay, Your Highness."

When I came back from the kitchen, Rudy reached into his mouth and extracted a full set of dentures—uppers and lowers. He dropped them into the glass and set it down by the couch. I flinched. He noticed. "You sure I haven't offended you yet?" he said, his toothless mouth making him sound rubber-voiced.

"Night," I said. "Thanks for the kind words about the photos."

"I'm never kind," Rudy Warren said. "Just accurate."

I flicked off the room light and pitched into bed.

I woke at eleven, vowing to convert to Mormonism, Islam, or any other faith that proscribed the use of alcohol. A shower helped, but I was still feeling shaky when I lurched into the living room.

The couch was empty. So too was the glass that had contained Rudy Warren's teeth. "Rudy?" I said, thinking he might be in the kitchen. No response. I made myself a mug of coffee and carried it with me into the darkroom, flipping on a light as I entered.

I blinked with shock. My stack of Montana prints was gone.

I cursed myself for playing the good Samaritan and inviting Rudy back here. Why did he take the prints? A dozen story lines raced around my skull. Sensing that I was a man with a past, he'd absconded with the photos and would demand a ransom for their return. Maybe he had a friend who was a cop—some drinking buddy. "Check this new guy out," Rudy would say, spreading my prints out on the bar. "Dude says he's a photographer, but the minute you give him the third degree, he breaks out in a sweat."

I picked up the phone. I dialed *The Montanan* and asked for Rudolph Warren. I got an answering machine. "Hi. Rudy Warren here. You know what to do: name and number after the beep."

I forced myself to sound calm, friendly. "Rudy, Gary Summers calling. Hope you got over your hangover. Could you give me a ring at 555-8809 when you have a chance. Thanks."

I hung up and immediately dialed information in search of his home number. It was unlisted. Damn. Over the next two hours I called *The Montanan* three times. I kept getting connected to his answering machine. I left no further messages. Eventually, around four, the phone rang. I dove for it.

"Gary Summers?" It was a woman's voice.

"Yes."

"Hi. I'm Anne Ames, the photo editor at *The Montanan*. Rudy Warren walked into my office this morning, tossed a bundle of your prints on my desk, and said I should hire you on the spot."

I let out a laugh of immense relief.

"So that's what he wanted with the prints," I said.

"He didn't tell you he was going to show them to me?"

"No. But from what I gather, Rudy is a man of surprises."

Now it was her turn to laugh. "That is the understatement of the year," she said. "Anyway, I think they're great. I was just wondering if they were already promised to another paper or periodical?"

"Not yet."

"Great. Then maybe we can do some business. You free tomorrow around noon?"

As soon as I agreed to the appointment, I wanted to cancel it. But my free-floating fears were tempered by vanity. Someone in the professional photographic game liked my work. So I showed up at the offices of *The Montanan* at noon the next day.

Anne Ames was in her mid-thirties. Tall, willowy, with stylishly cut strawberry-blond hair, and clear skin, free of makeup. She wore well-pressed denim jeans and a denim shirt. I glanced at her hands. No wedding ring. Her handshake was firm. I could see her sizing me up. I'd gotten used to tying my now shoulder-length hair into a ponytail and had even learned to live with designer stubble. When I stared at myself in the mirror, I no longer saw Ben Bradford; rather, an emergency edition of Gary Summers.

Anne's office was a chaotic jumble of prints and marked-up page proofs. There was something reassuring about its untidiness—a hint of a rebellious streak lurking behind her well-scrubbed appearance.

"Welcome to the photo junkyard," she said, motioning me toward a chair. She dug through a pile of papers and found my photos. "So, Gary, on the basis of these, you are one terrific photographer. Which leads me to ask, What are you doing in Mountain Falls, Montana?"

I was about to give her my usual spiel about the book I was allegedly working on, but sensed she might see through it. So I decided to play it straight. Well, sort of straight. "I was freelancing in New York. I wasn't scoring much in the way of work, so I headed west. I pulled in here for a night, liked what I saw, thought, Why not stay awhile? End of story." I could tell she liked the fact that I didn't gloss over my failure to cut it in Manhattan.

"And what made you decide to start shooting faces?"

"An accident." I told her about stopping at the roadhouse.

"Best ideas always start as accidents," she said. "And we'd like to benefit from this one. I've shown your pictures to the editor. He suggests running a photographic feature every Saturday. We'll call it

Montana Faces and use one of your prints each week. Initially, we're going to try it for six weeks, and we'll pay a hundred and twenty-five dollars a picture."

"That's kind of low, isn't it?" I said.

"Welcome to Montana," she said. "What I'm offering is well above our normal rates."

"It's still below what I'd be prepared to accept," I said.

"Which is what?"

I plucked a figure out of the air. "Two fifty a print."

"In your dreams," she said. "One seventy. Final offer."

"One seventy-*five*."

"What are you, a lawyer?" she said.

I managed a laugh. "Absolutely," I said. "Can't you tell? One seventy-five, then?"

"You push a hard bargain, Gary, but I'm not going to argue over five bucks. One seventy-five. Done deal."

I stood up.

"One last thing," she said. "Are you really from New Croydon, Connecticut?"

I suddenly wanted to evaporate. "How did you know that?"

"Meg Greenwood."

"Friend of yours?"

"Everyone knows each other in Mountain Falls," she said. "Well, nice doing business with you. I'll be in touch in a day or two."

On my way back to the apartment, I found myself in the pincer grip of major anxiety. How much had Meg Greenwood told her? Did she call me a sleaze? Had she informed Anne how I'd charmed her until the lease was signed, then fed her some garbage about a girlfriend in New York?

Late that afternoon the phone rang. "Gary Summers?"

"That's right," I said.

"This is Judy Wilmers. I run the New West Gallery. Anne Ames dropped over this afternoon with your photographs. Very impressive. Might we be able to meet tomorrow for coffee?"

Why, oh why, did I land myself in a small town?

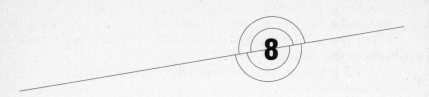

8

THE New West Gallery was located on a narrow side street off Main. It was decorated to look like the sort of art emporium you now found in SoHo or Tribeca. A concrete floor painted black. Stark white walls, spot lighting, a café with chrome tables and chairs. A collection of abstract canvases, under the collective title "Prairie Earth Dreams," was currently on view.

Judy Wilmers wore a long denim skirt and a lot of Native American bangles. She had gray hair that cascaded down to her waist. We sat in the café. She drank rose hip tea; I slurped down a double espresso. She was from the Bay Area and used to run a small gallery in Pacific Heights, but moved here in '86, when her first marriage broke up and she needed to "re-alter the parameters" of her middle age. She thought my photos had "far-reaching potential."

"You mean, you think they'll sell?"

"Like hotcakes."

Judy quickly got down to business—a negotiating game she played with karmic ruthlessness. A show had just fallen through; she had a slot in six weeks' time, but she needed a wider range of prints from which to "compose" the exhibition. The gallery would pay for framing. She was gauging a price of around $150 per print and wanted a fifty-fifty split on all sales, plus thirty-five percent of all subsidiary rights—books, postcards, even reproduction on the Internet.

You want the show, I said, you agree to a sixty-forty split, with no future hold on subsidiary rights. She wouldn't budge. I stood up, picking up my prints. "Thanks for the coffee."

"Aren't you being a little vain, Gary? Anne told me you admitted you came to Mountain Falls because things weren't working out workwise in New York. Don't you want this show?"

"Not if I'm going to be manipulated out of future terrestrial copyright—" I caught myself before I descended into further legal jargon. "If you want to renegotiate terms," I said, "you have my number." With that, I left.

I was at first relieved to have blown off Judy Wilmers. It would have been far too much exposure. But a vainglorious voice inside my skull kept niggling me: She offered you a show . . . and what do you do? Throw it away by getting legalistic.

On my way back to the apartment I stopped at Benson's, the department store on Main Street, and shelled out $70 for an answering machine. I rigged it up as soon as I was home; then I picked up a camera and hit the road.

When I returned just before sunset, there were three messages on my new machine. The first and third were from Judy Wilmers. "I am sure we can reach détente, Gary," she said in message number one. "Muse on the nature of potential and call me back." In her second message she got down to brass tacks. "Here's the deal. I agree to a sixty-forty split in your favor; you give me a twelve-month option to act as your agent and handle subsidiary rights for thirty-five percent of sales. At the end of the year all rights revert to you. Believe me, as a friend, you'd never land such a deal in New York."

"As a friend." Did this woman have any sense of irony?

In between the two sales shticks from Judy there was a message from Anne Ames, asking me to call her mobile phone. She was in her car when she answered.

"Don't the natives here take a dim view of cellular phones?" I asked.

"Yeah, but they all have them. Listen, I've chosen the six prints we're going to use. Want to see what I've picked and scam dinner off *The Montanan* at the same time?"

"Didn't know the photo editor had an expense account."

"Two hundred bucks a year, which means I'm going to blow half of it tonight. Be outside your door in five minutes."

She took me to Le Petit Place. It was the best restaurant in Mountain Falls, with a menu that described itself as New Pacific, even though we were around five hundred miles from that body of water. Our "waitperson" was called Calvin. He recommended the sea bass with shiitake mushrooms. The wine of the week was an Oregon chardonnay "with just the right oaky atmospherics."

"You know how to make a martini?" I asked.

"Of course," he said, sounding slightly offended.

"A Bombay Gin martini, then, very dry, with four olives."

"And Madame?" Calvin asked.

"Madame would like the same," Anne said.

The drinks arrived; we ordered our food. Anne lifted her glass. "To our collaboration," she said. We clinked glasses.

Over dinner she told me a little bit about herself. She'd grown up in Armonk, New York, and had gone to Skidmore. After graduating, she worked as a photo researcher for a glossy magazine in Boston.

"I was living in Cambridge," she said, "and the guy in the apartment next to mine was named Gregg. Finishing a doctorate in English. Within a year we were married. Within two we were yanked out of Boston and plopped down in Bozeman, when Gregg got a job at Montana State."

"How long did the marriage last?" I asked.

"Five years."

"Why'd it end?"

"Something happened."

"What?"

"Something." Her tone hinted that it would not be wise to pursue this line of questioning. "Anyway, after we split, I didn't want to stay in Bozeman, but I also didn't want to leave Montana. I paid a visit to Mountain Falls and had a friend get me an interview with Stu Simmons, the editor of *The Montanan.* Timing was on my side. A week earlier his photo editor had quit. I got the job. I moved here."

I could see that she now expected me to fess up and give her the rundown on my failure to cut it in Manhattan. So I essentially took some of the details of Gary's life and embellished them. I was surprised at just how fluid I was. I even mentioned the affair with Beth.

"Was it serious?" Anne asked.

"Nah. Just self-destructive. You seeing anyone right now?"

"There was a guy—a journalist on the paper—but he left town three years ago. Since then just a couple of dumb mistakes."

"I'm surprised," I said.

"Don't be. The pickings are slim in Mountain Falls."

"There's always Rudy Warren."

"Give me a break."

We drank the wine, ate the sea bass, ordered another bottle of wine, and began to laugh a little too loudly.

We lurched out of Le Petit Place around midnight. "I hope you're not planning to drive home," I said.

"No way," Anne said, linking her arm with mine. "Because you're going to walk me back."

We said nothing as we strolled the three blocks to her house. Anne lived on a quiet treelined cul-de-sac of 1920s shingle homes. When we reached the front steps, she turned and gave me a hundred-watt smile. The glow of lamplight fell across her face. I thought, She is beautiful.

"Well . . ." I said. "That was fun."

"A lot of fun."

I leaned forward to peck her cheek but suddenly kissed her fully on the lips. She threw her arms around me, and we started lurching backward, falling into the house.

Later, in bed, she said, "I could get used to this."

"I could get used to this too," I said.

When I woke in the morning, Anne was gone. A note had been left on the pillow.

> Gary:
>   Some of us have to work. Call me later. I could be persuaded to cook you dinner tonight. Coffee, tea, gin in the kitchen.
>
> Love,
A.

I wandered through her house. It was simply decorated, with bleached floorboards and New Mexican throw rugs. There was a small darkroom in what was once a second bathroom, where two recent prints were clipped to a clothesline. The first showed a billboard—BUTTE ELEGANT MOTEL . . . HONEYMOON SUITES . . . HEIR CONDITIONED—riddled with bullet holes. The second was of a small backwoods church buried in snow, its steeple adorned with the slogan JESUS IS COMING. I smiled. Anne Ames had a splendidly sardonic eye. She also knew what she was doing with a camera.

There was a phone in the darkroom. I picked it up and rang her at the paper. "I really like the shot of the buried church," I said.

"You've been snooping."

"You leave me alone in your house, of course I'll snoop around. The photos are great. You going to show me more?"

"If you like."

"I like."

"Dinner invitation accepted, then?"

"Absolutely."

"See you around seven," she said. "Bring plenty of wine."

You shouldn't be doing this, I told myself. I know, I know, another voice said. But do me a favor. Stop talking.

I made myself a cup of coffee and wandered into the living room. There was a photo on the mantelpiece—Anne cradling a tiny infant in her lap. Must be a niece or a nephew, I thought, as she'd mentioned nothing about children. I checked out the magazines and newspapers. *The New Yorker, The Atlantic Monthly, The New York Times.* I leafed through the *Times.* When I reached the obituary page, my eye fell upon a story:

JACK MAYLE, LAWYER, DEAD AT 63

Jack Mayle, a senior partner at the Wall Street firm of Lawrence, Cameron and Thomas, died on Saturday at Mount Sinai Hospital after a long illness. He was 63.

Poor Jack. He'd been my surrogate father. Someone who *understood.* Because, like him, I was an outsider. We were two corporate types who played the Wall Street game, yet secretly abhorred everything to do with it. I probably hastened his death with my own. Another of my victims.

I closed up Anne's house and walked back to my apartment. When I opened the front door, a stale aroma of cigarette smoke hung in the air. Someone was there, and I was suddenly very scared. Until I heard a half-awake voice. "That you, photographer?"

I poked my head into the living room, and there, sprawled on my sofa, was Rudy Warren, three dead bottles of beer lined up by his mud-caked shoes. His teeth were sunk in a glass of water.

"Morning," he said. Then, hoisting the glass, he downed the water before shoving his teeth back in his mouth.

"Charming," I said. "How did you get in here?"

"The keys I stole the other night. You know, the spare set you keep in the kitchen." He reached into his pocket and tossed them to me.

"You make copies of these?" I asked.

"Don't be a jerk. Just took 'em in case I needed an emergency bed sometime."

"Which you did last night?"

"Yep. Couldn't drive a tricycle, let alone my car."

"You could've called me first."

"Check your answering machine. You'll see there's at least three messages from me. But you were out, romancing Ms. Ames."

"You have no other friends in town?"

"None that'll talk to me anymore. You wouldn't put a pot of coffee on the stove, would you?"

"Rudy, I want you out of here now."

"You're kind of pissed off at me, aren't you?"

"Very perceptive."

"You should learn a thing or two about friendship, photographer. And about small towns. You want to play Mr. Aloof, buy yourself a ticket back to New York. Out here we like living in each other's pocket. And having a sense of who—and *what*—we're dealing with. I mean, Dave at the camera shop tells me you're a great customer, always pleasant, always polite. But he must have asked you to dinner half a dozen times. Every time you've dodged it. Now why's that?"

Because he has a wife named Beth, that's why. And two sons. "I don't like mixing business with pleasure."

"Okay," Rudy said. "Remain a closed book." He stood up, grabbing his coat off the floor. "One last thing. I've got a real soft spot for Anne Ames. We all do at the paper. So don't mess her around. She's a great kid, and she's been through enough."

"What, exactly?"

"I'm sure she'll tell you about it. In time." He opened the door. And said, "See you at Eddie's sometime."

LATER that afternoon Judy Wilmers and I achieved closure. I told her the sixty-forty split was acceptable, but I would only allow her a six-month period in which to market my work and wanted to give her only twenty-five percent of subsidiary sales. She dug her heels in, saying that if she could only have six months, she would insist on a thirty percent cut. I conceded. The exhibition would open on May 18 and run until July 1. There would be an opening launch party attended by "important dealers." She wanted another thirty portraits within two weeks. "That'll make eighty all together. I'll choose forty for the show."

When I visited Anne that evening, I arrived armed with two bottles of Washington State shiraz. After dinner I mentioned that our previous night together seemed to be the stuff of public knowledge around Mountain Falls.

"Don't look at me," Anne said. "Advertising my private life isn't exactly my idea of a good time."

"Well, how is it that the walls have ears and eyes here?"

"Not a lot else to do," Anne said. "But hey, are you worried that people know you spent a night here? I mean, it was just a night. Tonight's just another night."

I returned her smile. "And tomorrow," I said, "is also just another night."

She leaned over and kissed me deeply.

"That is exactly what I wanted to hear."

THE NEXT TWO WEEKS WERE frantic as I rushed to shoot more portraits. Every morning I was on the road at first light. Every afternoon I would spend a few hours developing film in my darkroom before heading over to Anne's for dinner. I would always show up with wine and just-dried contact sheets.

"What sort of flash did you use for the picture of the gun salesman?" she asked one evening after studying my portrait of the proud proprietor of Ferdie's Firearms in Butte.

"None," I said. "Just available light."

"No kidding. How'd you get that spectral glow on his face?"

"Got lucky with the late afternoon sun."

"Luck has nothing to do with it. You manage to make your portraits look happenstantial, even though it's clear that each shot is carefully thought out. That's a neat trick."

"I only learned it recently."

"I figured as much. So when you get big, you'll be able to say that coming to Montana was the moment you found your eye."

"Yeah. Montana was my liberation."

"From what?"

"Professional failure. Self-doubt."

"Anything else?"

I chose my words carefully. "Everyone has a history, Anne."

"I know. It's just you're selective about telling me yours."

"It's only been ten days."

"True."

"And you've been a bit selective about your own past."

She looked at me squarely. "You want to know why my marriage ended?"

"Yes, I do."

She fell quiet for a few moments. "You see the photograph on the mantelpiece with me and the baby?"

I nodded.

"My son," she said. "Charlie." She paused. "He died."

I shut my eyes. Her voice remained calm. "It happened around a month after that photo was taken. He was just four and a half months old. Still waking up two, three times a night. Only on that night he didn't stir. Gregg and I were so tired from weeks of broken sleep we crashed right out, didn't move until seven the next morning. I was up first. And when I didn't hear a sound from his crib, I knew immediately—" She broke off, avoided my gaze. "Sudden infant death syndrome. That's what they call it. The doctors told us there was no rhyme or reason to this . . . syndrome. It simply happened. We mustn't blame ourselves. But of course, we did. If only we'd checked on him. If only we hadn't been so tired. If only . . ."

I closed my eyes again. In that darkroom of my brain Adam and Josh came into sharp focus.

"A marriage has to be rock solid to survive a child dying," she said. "Ours wasn't. Within eight months I'd moved to Mountain Falls. And y'know, seven years later, I've never made contact with Gregg again. I can't. You don't get over it. You just learn to *deal* with it. To keep it hidden from view. Tucked away in a room of your own—a place only you know exists and which you visit every waking hour of every day. And no matter how hard you try, you know that you'll never rid yourself of that room. It's with you now forever." She looked back up at me. "You're crying," she said.

I said nothing, rubbing my eyes with my shirtsleeve. Anne put her head on my shoulder and began to sob. I held her until she stopped. "Never ask me about that again," she finally said.

Later that night I woke suddenly. The digital clock by the bed said 3:07. The room was black. Anne was curled up, dead to the world. I stared at the ceiling. Adam and Josh appeared before me again. My lost sons. Anne was right: Grief is a dark room all your own. Only unlike hers, my loss was self-inflicted. When I killed Gary, I killed my life, a life I didn't want. Until it was dead.

The next morning—a Saturday—Anne roused me out of bed by dangling a copy of *The Montanan* in front of my face. "Rise and shine," she said. "You're in print."

I was awake in seconds. And there, on the second page of the Weekend section, was my picture of the gas station couple and their baby. There was no editorial comment, no caption beneath the photo.

There was just a headline: FACES OF MONTANA BY GARY SUMMERS.

"Pleased?" she asked.

"Amazed. It's the first picture of mine ever to make it into print. You did a great job with the layout and the reproduction. The clarity's first-rate. Thanks."

She kissed me. "Anytime, toots. Got any plans today?"

"I'm yours."

"I like the sound of that. Feel like an overnight jaunt out of town?"

"You're on."

We took my car and first stopped at my apartment so I could pick up a change of clothes and a camera.

Back in the car, Anne told me to take Route 200, heading east.

"Where are we going, by the way?" I asked.

"You'll see."

Around thirty miles down Route 200 Anne directed me onto a narrow, winding strip of blacktop that snaked its way through a forest of towering pines. They were so densely packed together, so vertiginous, that the sky seemed to disappear. It was like being in a vast, lofty cathedral. Ten minutes into this timberland Anne told me to make a left turn onto a tiny paved road, the surface of which was so jagged that I had to slow down to fifteen miles per hour.

"Hope this is worth it," I said.

"Believe me, it is."

Five minutes later the blue began. Not blue, exactly, more of an aquamarine. In front of us was a boundless lake. Two tiny islands floated in the middle of its expanse, both empty of habitation. We parked the car near the water's edge and got out. This was an Eden freshly minted, unsullied, enveloped within a giant primeval forest.

"Moose Lake," Anne said. "Second biggest in the state."

I asked her how long she had been coming here.

"Ever since I bought that."

She pointed to a tiny cabin about two hundred yards from us, tucked within the pines. It was something of a shack. Weather-beaten wood, small aerielike windows, stone chimney. We walked over to the cabin and entered. The inside consisted of one large room. Wood-burning stove, an old tin sink, an iron double bed, shelves piled high with tins of food, a wine rack with a dozen dusty bottles. A transistor radio provided the only link with the outside world.

"There's no electricity," Anne said. "Just kerosene lamps. It does have a toilet, however, and a bathtub, but the only way you get hot water is by boiling it on the stove. It's my escape hatch."

"You do amaze me, Ms. Ames. How long have you had it?"

"Four, five years." She opened the door of the stove and lit it. "I always lay a new fire before leaving. It means I don't have to spend an hour chopping wood when I return. Two hours from now this place should be tolerable. C'mon, let's take a hike."

We set off down a narrow path that fronted the water's edge. The air was champagne crisp, and a light wind swayed the pines. The calm was enveloping. As we trekked along, it struck me that what I loved most about this state wasn't only its lonely roads and grand skies but also its respect for stillness.

It was almost dark by the time we returned from our hike. The stove had done its work; the cabin had lost its meat-locker chill. Anne pulled some olive oil from a shelf, poured it into a hefty frying pan, and placed the pan on the stove. "You're about to discover the wonder of my backwoods pasta sauce," she said. "How about opening some wine?"

She added two tins of tomatoes to the pan, then filled a pot with water and placed it at the rear of the stove.

"You've got yourself a pretty impressive larder," I said, eyeing the vast array of tinned goods. "You really could disappear without a trace if you wanted."

"Not anymore," she said.

"Why's that?"

A hint of a grin. "You'd know where to find me now." She added a tin of clams to the tomatoes and tossed a handful of pasta into the boiling water. I uncorked a bottle of shiraz, lit candles, set the table.

"Linguine alle vongole," she said, placing a steaming bowl of pasta on the table. "An old Montana favorite."

We ate. We drained the bottle of shiraz. The candlelight flickered. She leaned over to cover my hand with hers. The glow of the flame radiated across her face. "Happy?" she asked.

"Very happy."

"Me too."

We fell silent. Then she asked, "Do you have a kid somewhere?"

Without thinking, my free hand clenched. Thankfully, it was under the table. "No."

"I'm surprised."

"Why?"

"Because when I told you about Charlie, you got very upset."

"It's a very upsetting story," I said.

"Yeah. But of the few people I've told, the ones who don't have kids usually don't react so emotionally, whereas anyone who is a parent finds the story unbearable. Like you did."

I shrugged. I figured it was the safest response.

"Don't get me wrong," she said. "I was very touched by your reaction. It just surprised me." She paused, stared me straight in the eye. "You want kids?"

I returned her gaze. "I might. And you?"

"I might too."

I FELT a hand clasping my shoulder, shaking me. "Gary . . ."

I snapped awake. Anne was standing over me, dressed and looking anxious. "We've got to go," she said.

"What . . ." My brain was blurry. I glanced at my watch. Nearly noon. No wonder I was fogged in.

"We've got to leave right now," Anne said.

"Why?"

"I'll show you when you get up. But you've got to get up *now*." She all but pulled me out of bed. "Move!"

I did as instructed, throwing on my clothes, tossing some things into my overnight bag. "Why all this drama?"

"Step outside," she said.

I hoisted my bag and opened the door. A fire was raging. It had engulfed part of the forest. It was less than a mile away from us, and flames were licking the treetops. A strong wind was blowing, fanning the blaze. I raced to the car and grabbed my Rolleiflex.

"Are you crazy?" Anne said.

"Just a couple of shots."

"Use Ilford HP4. It has sharper definition."

I grinned at her. "Yes, boss."

"And be fast about it. We've only got a few minutes."

I twisted on a telephoto lens and squeezed off a dozen shots of the pines in full blaze. Seen through the sniper sight of the telephoto lens, they looked like oversized birthday candles burning brightly. But then there was an ominous whoosh, and the flames seemed to erupt, spreading closer toward us.

"We're out of here," Anne said. "I'll drive."

I tossed her the keys, and we jumped into the MG. She turned on the ignition. Nothing. She turned the key again. Still no sound.

"Pump the accelerator," I said.

She hit the pedal several times, then tried the ignition. Silence.

We could smell the burning pines. "If it doesn't start, we die," Anne said, desperately pumping the pedal again.

"Stop," I said. "You'll flood it. Throw it into second. Now turn the key and put the clutch to the floor."

She did as ordered. I jumped out of the car, ran to the back, and pushed. At first it wouldn't budge, but once I shoved it over a small bump, it began to roll downhill. "Let out the clutch," I yelled. Suddenly the engine turned over. "Pump it," I shouted as Anne tried to sustain the engine blast. But within seconds it was silent again.

"Damn!" Anne turned the ignition again in frustration. It made a grinding noise. The smoke from the fire was now thickening.

"Get back into second," I yelled. "Clutch down?"

"Yeah," she shouted back. "Go."

Using all the weight I could muster, I shoved the MG again and ran behind it until it developed its own momentum and slid away from me. There was a convulsive burp, followed by the reassuring roar of the engine. I raced to the car and jumped in.

Anne gunned the accelerator, shifted into first, and we took off. The wind whipped up again, and a thick, toxic cloud of smoke blew in through the window, making us gag, covering us both in soot. We struggled to roll up the windows, coughing violently. Visibility was minimal—ten feet, at most. Anne was leaning halfway over the wheel, trying to keep her vision fixed on whatever she could see of the road. For a quarter of an hour we didn't exchange a word. We both knew if we didn't clear this part of the woods soon, the fire would swallow us whole.

The smoke was terrifying. Anne looked white-faced, but she kept the car moving as fast as possible over the potholed track. Just as the fog momentarily parted to reveal the main road, there was a bang as the fire closed in behind us. Anne screamed as a large pine cracked in half and dangled over the road, its branches ablaze. But just when it looked as if it was about to collapse across our path, a blast of water flooded the windshield, blinding us. When the water cleared away, we discovered we had reached the main road and had been saved from immolation by the local fire brigade.

Two uniformed officers ran to the car and pulled us both out. Anne was gagging loudly. One of the firemen shoved an oxygen mask across her face. I grabbed my camera and went running to her side. "You okay?" I asked.

She nodded, then pulled the mask off and said, "Go to work."

"Gotcha."

"And I want color as well as black and white."

I leaned over and kissed her.

"Miss," one of the firemen said, "put the mask back on."

But she was digging in the pocket of her jacket for her mobile phone. "Not until I call my paper. Gary, get on with it."

I ran up the road. Overhead, seaplanes were bombarding the fire with water, then returning to the lake to restock their pontoons with more water.

I switched over to Fujicolor and nabbed a close-up of an older officer—his skin as cracked as petrified cement—wide-eyed with disbelief as the red glow of the flames bathed his face. The heat around me was so acute that I was drenched in sweat. But I kept working, my brain running on high octane. The extremity of the situation—the fact that Anne and I had escaped immolation by seconds—was overridden by the kick of danger, of finally being in the picture. I now understood why combat photographers run toward gunfire. There was something irresistible about edging so close to death. Yet you actually believed that because you were looking at everything through a viewfinder, you were immune to danger. The camera became something of a shield. It granted you absolution from jeopardy. Or at least that's what I thought as I raced up and down the forest road, reeling off shots, oblivious to the flames.

"You, photographer!" I spun around and saw the officer in charge pointing directly at me. "I want you out—"

The officer didn't get to complete his sentence, as a sheet of flame suddenly leaped out from the trees, enveloping a firefighter standing ten feet in front of him. Immediately three of the man's colleagues were charging toward him. I trained my camera on his torched body. My finger kept squeezing the shutter release as the firefighter spun around in agony—his clothes and hair aglow—while his colleagues desperately attempted to put out the flames. Once the fire had been doused, the firefighter just pitched forward and lay very still on the ground. I clicked away as the senior officer frantically attempted cardiac massage, then felt for a pulse. My final shot was of the officer kneeling by the body, his face in his hands.

"Oh, God . . ." It was Anne. She was standing behind me, looking on in shock. "Is he . . ."

I nodded.

An officer approached us. "Time for you to go," he said. *"Now."*

We drove like bandits. Within ten minutes we were back on Route 200. "Guess that's the end of my cabin," Anne said. Her mobile phone rang. She answered it and was engaged in a rapid-fire conversation. "Yeah. . . . Color and black and white. . . . One dead so far. . . . We'll be there in an hour."

She turned to me. "That was the editor. He is thrilled we were almost charred alive and that you happened to be packing a camera

at the time. He is also holding the front page, so we have to hurry."
She cranked the MG up to ninety. "How many rolls you shoot?"

"Seven black and white, four color."

"Great. The color shots are going to be exceedingly marketable."

"To whom?"

"*Time, Newsweek.* Whoever pays the highest price."

"And who's going to sell them?"

"I am—in my capacity as photo editor of the paper."

"I didn't know I had agreed to *The Montanan* owning subsidiary
rights, Ms. Marketing."

She threw her eyes heavenward. "All right, let's get this over with.
How much for the first run of the pics in our paper?"

"Two grand."

"Be realistic. We're a small-town paper. Even a thousand dollars
would be excessive."

"Then I'll have to sell them elsewhere."

"Fifteen hundred. And a fifty-fifty split on everything we sell."

"Fifty-five forty-five."

"I hate you," she said.

I leaned over and kissed her hair. "Well, I love you," I said.

She turned suddenly and stared at me in shock.

"Keep your eyes on the road," I said.

She returned her gaze to the windshield. "What you just said
wasn't a negotiating tactic, was it?"

"Oh, you are a piece of work, Ms. Ames."

"Well," she finally said, "I guess I'll agree to your terms."

We made the paper in forty minutes. Anne's assistant, Jane, was
pacing the front lobby, waiting for us. "Now, honey," Anne said,
"rush Gary's film to the lab. I want contact sheets in an hour."

A middle-aged man in a tweed jacket came striding purposefully
toward us. "You must be Gary Summers," he said, and proffered
his hand. "Stuart Simmons."

"Our boss," Anne explained.

Stu turned to Anne. "I want you here until the pages are laid
out," he said, "but we'll need follow-up pictures for tomorrow. Gary,

you up for another stint at the front? Maybe get some night shots?"

It was hard to resist the battlefield analogy. I said yes.

"Great," Stu said. "But be very careful."

Anne handed me her mobile phone in case either of us needed to make contact. She touched my arm. "Don't get hurt," she said.

I was back at the fire in an hour. The scene on the main forest road had turned into a media circus. Four television crews. Two or three radio types. And Rudy Warren.

"What are you doing here?" I asked.

"Stu Simmons wants a commentary by eight tonight."

Rudy disappeared into the fray. Occasionally I grabbed sight of him scrutinizing the firefighters as they handled unwieldy water hoses and guarded each other's backs. From time to time he would pull out a notebook and jot something down. But basically, he just observed. Seeing him at work, I was reminded that writers were like scavengers—they foraged a scene for details that, when joined together, would beget the Big Picture. Photographers were always on the lookout for that one bold image that would define a story. But a writer knew that his craft was, in part, all about transfiguring small incidents into a compelling narrative. And it was a balancing act—a story without potent detail inevitably seemed bland. Yet one without a critical overview left you with the feeling that the writer hadn't grasped the larger implications of the events he'd observed.

Rudy Warren may have been one of Montana's major drunks, but when it came to writing, he understood this need to balance detail with an underlying theme. An hour after I arrived at the fire, he found me shooting a firefighter being treated for smoke inhalation.

"Lemme borrow your mobile phone," he said.

I turned it over to him. He called the paper, asked for a copy taker, and began to dictate his essay. Once or twice he referred to his notebook. But essentially it was a masterful, off-the-cuff performance. I listened, amazed by his use of revealing images.

"Firefighter Chuck Manning sat slumped by engine number two, wanting nothing more than a cold beer and a cigarette.

The beer wasn't forthcoming, but he did have a pack of Marl-
boros in his uniform. He fished one out, shoved it between his
blackened teeth. Slapping his pockets, he realized he didn't
have a light. Ten feet away a gush of flame suddenly incinerated
another corner of Montana's biggest forest preserve. He
blinked with shock in the face of this inferno. His cigarette
remained unlit."

When Rudy finished filing, he collared an officer passing by us.
"Sarge," he asked, "you figure out what caused it yet?"
"Probably some tourist tossing a cigarette out a car window."
I had a question for the sergeant. Did any of the lakefront cabins
survive the blaze?
"Believe it or not, the fire managed to skirt the entire shoreline.
No loss of property whatsoever."
"Anne'll be pleased to hear her cabin made it," Rudy said.
"How'd you know about her place up here?" I asked.
Rudy rolled his eyes. "You still haven't figured out this town."
The mobile phone rang. It was Anne. "You still in one piece?"
she asked.
"Yeah. And so's your cabin. Someone up there likes you."
"Someone down here likes you. Ever since we put your pics out
on the AP photo service—"
"You did *what?*"
"AP wanted visuals. I got ten of your best shots on the wire
immediately. They've been picked up everywhere."
I was flabbergasted. And nervous. "Oh," I said.
"Don't sound so happy," Anne said. "You got more film for me?"
"I do."
"Well, get it back here pronto." She hung up.
Rudy—the all-knowing—sniffed my unease and said, "You look
like a man who's not exactly coming to terms with success."
I followed Rudy's beat-up Bronco back to Mountain Falls. He
parked in front of Eddie's. I continued on to *The Montanan.* As I
walked in, the first edition was rolling off the presses. Anne came

running toward me, holding a freshly inked copy. The front-page headline read TWO KILLED AS FIRE RAVAGES STATE FOREST.

Beneath this was my black-and-white photo of the senior fire officer kneeling by the body of one of his fallen colleagues, his face hidden in his hands. Five more of my pictures adorned the inside pages. Stu Simmons joined us. "Amazing work, Gary."

Jane was seated at a nearby computer terminal. "Gary," she called out, "you've got to see this. It's *awesome.*"

We joined her at the terminal. She was scanning the Internet, calling up major newspapers around the country. One by one the front pages of *The New York Times,* the Washington *Post,* and *USA Today* flashed in front of us. All of them carried my photograph of the dead firefighter and his grieving boss. All of them also carried the credit: Photo by Gary Summers/*The Montanan.*

"Looks like you're famous," Jane said.

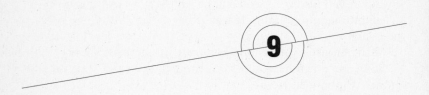

9

EVERYONE ran that photo. It was picked up by forty papers across the United States, according to Jane, who was assigned to track its placement.

By the end of the week I had come to understand one of the great truisms of American life: Once you are perceived to be hot, everyone wants you. The guy who's struggling is a despised figure in our culture. He's viewed as a loser who's desperately trying to convince a publisher, a magazine editor, a producer, a gallery owner that he could be a player—if only the right break came his way. But of course, no one wants to give him that break. Even if they think that he might have some talent, they're usually terrified of trusting their own judgment and backing an unknown quantity. So the no-body remains a nobody. Unless dumb luck intervenes. And the glow of professional good fortune envelops him. Suddenly he's the dude du jour. Everybody returns his phone calls now; everybody phones him. Because he's been anointed with the halo of success.

"Big news," Anne said one evening. "*Time* magazine called and asked us to send them fifty of your color transparencies. Their photo editor said they'd run a two-page color spread, accompanied by an essay."

That week Gary Summers became one of the anointed ones. It happened the day *Time* hit the streets. When I stared at the two magazine pages of pictures—my byline prominently displayed below the headline IN NATURE'S INFERNO—all I could think was, Everyone will see the pictures, everyone will see the name, and it will all start unraveling.

The next day the phone began to ring. Constantly. I let the answering machine deal with the calls.

The first was from Judy Wilmers. She was in a state of frantic mercantile fever. "What *can* I say? I saw it; I love it; you're a genius. And what this is going to do for Montana Faces I can't begin to tell you. Call me, genius. Call me."

The next call was from Jules Rossen, photo editor at *Destinations*. "Hey, Gary! Just got your phone number from Jane at *The Montanan*. . . ."

I'm going to kill her slowly, I thought.

"We need to do business, hombre," he said. "Ring me at . . ."

I certainly wasn't going to reply to Jules Rossen. He might won-der why Gary's voice had altered so dramatically since moving west. I needed a go-between. I picked up the phone and called Judy.

"Gary, *bello,* I was just on the verge of calling. How are you en-joying stardom?"

"It has its moments."

"Listen, you ever hear of Cloris Feldman? New York literary agent extraordinaire? You're her new client. For the book only, of course. I'm DHLing her the transparencies of the Montana Faces exhibition. She can think of at least five publishers who would vie for it."

"You are an operator, Judy," I said. "You wouldn't want to represent me for magazine work, would you?"

It took her a nanosecond to say yes. It took her two nanoseconds to assent to a commission of fifteen percent. And she also agreed to make a tape for my answering machine, informing anyone who called that all professional inquiries were being handled by Mr. Summers's agent and giving her phone number.

Within five days Judy had four offers. Two tempted me—a *National Geographic* proposal for an issue devoted entirely to Montana and a glossy *Vanity Fair* gig that would involve shooting portraits of big actor honchos who had bought ranches in the state. "They're calling the story 'Hollywood, Montana,'" Judy said. "You know what they want: Jane and Ted in denims and boots. You've gotta grab this one. You get established as a guy who can handle famous faces as well as gritty lowlifes, you can write your own ticket for the rest of your career."

I made reluctant noises about rubbing shoulders with the rich and fabulous. Until Judy mentioned the fee: $2500 a day for twelve days' work. And I could wait to start work on the assignment until after my exhibition opened in two weeks. This would give me enough time to knock off the *National Geographic* commission—a small portfolio on Montana roads.

"They've asked six photographers to concentrate on aspects of the state," Judy explained. "They thought you could be the highways guy. It's a terrific chance to strut your stuff as a 'Big Picture' photographer. Do the 'Lonesome Road' routine. Capture that two-lane blacktop disappearing into the sunset . . ."

"How much are they offering?"

"Four grand. And it'll get you out of town in the weeks running up to the exhibition. I don't care how cool a customer you are, a week before the opening you're going to get PET."

"What's that?"

"Pre-Exhibition Tension."

I laughed and accepted both commissions. Thirty-four thousand dollars for two assignments. The absurdity of success terrified me.

On the afternoon before I headed off in search of the perfect Montana road, a letter arrived from the Alternative Post Office in Berkeley. I recognized the graceful penmanship immediately.

Gary:

After I received your kiss-off letter in December, I vowed never to contact you again. Please don't think your spread in *Time* has suddenly made you a nice guy in my eyes. Your letter arrived just after the most appalling few weeks of my life.

Ben was killed in a boating accident on November 7. It was a desperate shock, and what made it even more unbearable was the fact that—as you well know—I had asked him for a divorce earlier that week. Though the official coroner's report was "death by misadventure," I can't help but wonder if he flipped while out there on the water and did something irrevocably self-destructive. The last time I saw him we had an awful scene over a bicycle he bought Adam. Two days later he was dead. The guilt I now feel is huge. I fear it will never go away.

Josh, of course, is too young to realize what's going on, but Adam has taken it very hard. For weeks after Ben's death he kept asking when Daddy would be coming home. When I finally told him his daddy had had an accident and would never be coming back, he was inconsolable. Months later he still is. He just can't accept it. And it's breaking my heart.

I stopped reading, tried to steady myself. I didn't succeed. I went to the bathroom, plunged my face into a sink of cold water. Then I picked up the letter again.

Your Dear John missive landed on my mat two weeks into this nightmare. Your timing was impeccable. Until recently I really considered myself a candidate for a nervous breakdown. Then I met Elliot Burden. You may have heard of him. Ex–big noise at Goldman Sachs who left Wall Street to open a gallery on Wooster Street. He's in his late fifties, divorced, with two grown-up kids. He may not be the love of my life, but he's affectionate and solid and solvent. And he's already begun to establish a rapport with Adam.

Elliot Burden. I conjured him up immediately. Probably looks like George Plimpton. A gentleman bohemian. Ralph Lauren blazer and Armani jeans. And now the surrogate father for my two sons. The man Adam will start calling Daddy before the year is out.

It was Elliot who convinced me to write. He felt that until I informed you about Ben, I wouldn't be able to achieve some sort of closure with you. I got your address from the New Croydon Post Office, but judging from what I read in *Time,* you're now based in Montana. Does this mean you also broke the heart of your Berkeley squeeze, or did she just get smart and throw you out? Anyway, Elliot happens to be a friend of Cloris Feldman. She showed us the transparencies of your forthcoming exhibition. Elliot loved the pictures. And though I'd rather not admit it, I was deeply impressed too. You've got it now. You're in the zone.

Beth

Closure. That inane '90s word. When you've killed someone and lost two sons, closure is impossible. Still, if Beth wanted a neat ending, I'd accommodate her. I opened the ThinkPad and began to type.

B: Your letter was waiting for me upon my return from Montana. I'm still maintaining a place in the Bay Area, though I seem to be spending a considerable amount of time in the redneck north these days. It sounds like you've been through the wringer. Still, this Elliot guy seems like good news—someone who will keep you in the style to which you are accustomed. Thanks for the thumbs-up about the pictures. It means a lot. Take care.

G.

I dispatched the letter to the Alternative Post Office, then drove over to *The Montanan.* Since I would be departing the next morning for the eastern extremities of the state, I'd promised to take Anne to dinner at Le Petit Place and had arranged to pick her up at the office. But as soon as I walked into the newsroom, I found myself dodging an airborne chair. It crashed to the left of my shoulder. Next a computer keyboard came thundering down near my feet.

"A little gift for the *Time* man of the year."

I gazed up just as Rudy Warren smashed his fist through the screen of his desktop Mac. Everyone in the newsroom looked on in horror as Rudy slumped down in his chair, his fist embedded inside the terminal. Blood began to dribble down the side of his desk. He stared at this circulatory leak with bemusement. That's when I knew he was drunk.

Anne came rushing out of her office, a first-aid kit in one hand. Her eyes grew wide as she saw the stream of blood now cascading down onto the floor. She looked up at her colleagues. "Well, don't just stand there," she said. "Somebody call an ambulance."

"Hey, sweetheart." Rudy flashed her a dipsomaniacal grin.

"Forget the sweetheart bit, Rudy. Shall we try to remove your hand from the computer?" She glanced up at me. "Meet you in the restaurant," she mouthed, then returned to the task at hand.

I was working on my second martini when Anne finally walked into Le Petit Place. "The suspense is killing me," I said after ordering her a drink. "Is his fist still in the Mac?"

"No. The removal operation was a success. He's currently being stitched up at Mountain Falls General. Hopefully, they'll chain him to a bed for the night. The guy had a gallon of J&B sluicing around in his veins." She laced her fingers through mine. "I'm going to miss you," she said. "A lot."

"It's only for ten days. Then I'm back."

"You sure you'll be coming back?"

"I'm sure."

"I wonder. Success is a dangerous drug. You'll grow to like it. People will soon tell you how important you are, and you'll start to think they're right. Just as you'll also start to think that your past can be discarded. It's how success works."

"Not in this case."

She shunned my gaze. "We'll see."

An awkward silence dominated the table. Anne kept staring into her drink, looking distracted.

I finally said, "It's only a week and a half, Anne."

"I know."

"And I'm only going to eastern Montana, not Iraq."

"I know."

"I'll call you every day. So don't worry."

"You really know nothing about loss, do you?"

I was on the verge of saying "That's not true," but I managed to stop myself.

"Loss makes you regard everything as tenuous, fragile," she said. "If a good thing comes into your life, you know it's only a matter of time before it will be taken from you."

"I won't be disappearing, Anne."

THE next morning, as I crossed the Continental Divide, I found myself thinking, Anne knows. She may not have figured it all out yet, but instinctively she suspects that I'm on the run from something. And she now fears what I fear—that success will lead to disclosure, forcing me to vanish from view.

But when I spoke to Anne that evening, after checking into a motel in a place called Lewistown, she was decidedly upbeat.

"Is the motel romantic?" she teased.

"Only if you're an Anthony Perkins fan."

"Speaking of psychotics, Rudy Warren has disappeared."

"No way."

"Checked himself out of the hospital last night, hasn't been heard from or seen since."

"Not a clue where he's gone?"

"His car is still parked outside the paper. No one saw him at the airport. My guess is he's hopped a bus. What's Lewistown like?"

"Total nowhere."

"I hate eastern Montana. Too flat. Too empty."

Anne was right. This quarter of Montana was a bleak, desolate terrain of scrubby vegetation and the occasional truck stop.

I wandered its byways for over a week. Passing through towns like Lustre and Antelope and Plentywood. Shooting roll after roll of film. I pulled into a motel every evening and made two calls to Mountain Falls. The first was the daily business update with Judy.

"Oh, by the way," she said one evening, "*National Geographic* wants a mug shot of you for their contributor's page."

"Inform them that I don't like being photographed."

"Very funny."

"I'm serious. The world doesn't need to see my face."

"Who the heck are you? Greta Garbo?"

"Just someone who doesn't want to play the promotion game. That's your job. Keep me out of it. And no pictures of me. Okay?"

"You're the boss. Unfortunately."

I think Judy bought my remote-artist routine. Anne, on the other hand, wanted me arraigned for haughtiness. A few days later our nightly phone call began with her question: "Did you really tell Judy you wouldn't let your mug appear anywhere?"

"I see the village drums have been beating again."

"You're dodging the question."

"Yeah. Those were my instructions."

"That's hilarious."

"I just don't want the attention. It will fuel the mystique."

"I heard an underlay of irony in that last statement, didn't I?"

"You did."

"That's a relief. Where are you tonight?"

"Mildred, Montana."

"Never heard of it," she said.

"You know who's living here now? Rudy Warren."

"Ha. Actually, he did finally phone Stu. Told him he was heading down to Tijuana and wanted six months' paid leave."

"Got to hand it to Rudy. He really understands chutzpah."

"Stu agreed to the leave. Unpaid, of course."

"What's old Rudy going to do in Mexico?"

"Kill his liver with cheap tequila—enlightened stuff like that."

"That's one of the disadvantages of eastern Montana. No cheap tequila. Don't suppose you'd want to join me out here?"

"In Mildred? Not a chance. But keep missing me."

"I will."

And indeed I did. But as I started to wend my way back west, I felt the onset of dread. Out here, in the great disconnected wilds, I felt safe. No one knew me. But back in Mountain Falls I was a face. And if Judy was doing her job properly, I might start being *a name.* Once I'd craved such consequence. Now I wanted to run from it. Because, inevitably, it would lead to exposure. And yet a voice within my head whispered, If you're careful, you can get away with it. You can achieve prominence as a photographer. You can have a life with Anne. You'll just have to withdraw from view.

On the morning of the exhibition opening, as I steeled myself for the final two-hundred-mile run back to Mountain Falls, the engine of the MG gave out. I was in Bozeman, and a local mechanic diagnosed severe internal combustion problems.

"We're talking a two-valve job here," he said. "And you ain't gonna see much change from a thousand bucks. The good news is, I've got a free day. You give me the go-ahead, I can have the car back to you by noon."

I tossed him the keys.

But the mechanic was overly optimistic. It was three o'clock when he finally turned the ignition key and announced, "You've bought yourself another hundred thousand miles of MG life. And all for the bargain price of nine hundred and eighty-four dollars and seventy-two cents."

I handed over Gary's Visa card. The mechanic made an imprint of it in his credit card machine and had me sign on the dotted line. He checked my signature and decided it was legitimate. "Going far?" he asked.

"Mountain Falls. And I have to be there by six."

"Two hundred miles on the Montana-bahn? You'll do that in two hours, no sweat. Happy trails."

He was right. On the no-speed-limit Montana highway it was possible to do one hundred miles per hour and not fear an encounter with a state trooper. Speed is the most intoxicating of drugs, and as I approached Mountain Falls, I was half tempted to bypass it altogether and roar on.

Anne was pacing outside the New West Gallery as I drove up. She was dressed for the opening, looking most fetching in an Annie Hall-ish man's suit with a tight vest.

"Where have you been?" she asked.

I started to explain the problem with the car.

"Shut up and kiss me," she said.

I complied. Judy came charging out of the gallery.

"You really know how to give a woman an ulcer," she said.

Still in mid-embrace, I raised a hand in greeting.

When I finally entered the gallery, I took a sharp intake of breath. There, on freshly whitewashed walls, were my forty portraits, beautifully framed, perfectly displayed, well lit. Judy and Anne looked on silently as I walked from photograph to photograph, trying to take it all in. I felt a curious detachment as I scrutinized my work. But I also felt that peculiar buzz of pleasure and terror that comes from knowing that at long last you have inched your way into the arena, that finally you can be taken seriously as a practitioner of your craft. For years I had fantasized about this moment. Now all I could think was, It's too bad Ben Bradford isn't around to enjoy it.

"Well . . . ?" Judy finally said.

"He might just have something as a photographer," I said.

"Yeah." Anne handed me a glass of wine. "He just might."

It was now 5:30. There was no time to go home and change, so I sat at a café table with Anne, nervously guzzling glass after glass of California chablis.

"Go easy," Anne said. "You'll fall on your face before seven."

"That's the idea," I said.

DAVE from Petrie Cameras and his wife, Beth, were among the first guests to arrive. I staggered up from the table and joined them.

A petite woman in her thirties, Beth was wearing granny glasses and denim overalls.

"This is the elusive Gary Summers," Dave said, introducing us.

"Are we ever going to get you over for dinner?" Beth asked.

I never got to answer that question, as Judy pulled me away to meet Robin Nickell, the owner of a big gallery in Seattle.

"Love the work," Robin said. "And I know we'll be able to get you fantastic publicity when we open the show in September."

"You've taken the exhibition?" I said, thrown by this news.

Judy chimed in, "We just did the deal last night."

"Gary Summers?"

I spun around and found myself facing a hefty, bearded man in a tweed jacket.

"I'm Gordon Craig, head of the fine-arts division over at the university. Wonderful show. Have you ever thought of doing some part-time lecturing?"

Anne saved me from answering that question, as she tapped my shoulder to make an introduction. "Nick Hawthorne," she said. "*Time*'s man in San Francisco."

"Was out here doing a story in Kalispell and thought I'd drive down for the opening," Nick said. "If you've got some time tomorrow, I'd like to meet and put a proposition to you. I'm working on a travel book about the New American West and am looking for a photographer to collaborate with. . . ."

Judy dragged me off to make small talk with some art dealer from Portland. I didn't catch her name, as the wine was finally deadening all cognitive faculties. There must have been over a hundred people now in the gallery. I was desperate for fresh air, but I kept being passed from guest to guest, nodding moronically as another person pumped my hand and tried to engage me in conversation.

Anne eventually caught up with me again. "You're drunk," she said. "Please switch to water. There's still an hour to go."

"Let's get out of here," I said.

"It's your party. You've got to stay. Anyway, Judy wants to introduce you to Elliot Burden."

I was suddenly sober again. "Who?"

"Elliot Burden. You know, the big Wall Street guy who gave it all up to run a gallery in SoHo?"

"He's here?"

"Just arrived. He's here with a former neighbor of yours in Connecticut. Beth something."

"Beth Bradford," I said, my voice barely a whisper.

"That's it," Anne said.

My eyes scanned the room. They were by the door, deep in conversation with Judy. Elliot Burden—tanned, lean, patrician in a blazer and flannels—was standing next to Beth. She looked wonderful, stylishly dressed in a short black dress. For a moment I couldn't move. But then Judy caught me staring their way, and I executed an immediate about-face.

"What's wrong?" Anne said. "You've gone white."

"Just need some air." I began pushing my way through the crowd, my vision fixed on a back door.

"Gary!" Anne shouted.

Suddenly I heard the voice of my wife. "Gary!" Beth said.

I froze, my back to her. Then I bolted for the door and dashed outside. I sprinted down a side street and ran for my apartment.

When I reached it, I tore up the stairs, burst through my door.

I hadn't been home for ten days and immediately knew something was wrong. There were empty beer bottles and brimming ashtrays and half-eaten tins of baked beans strewn across the floor. And there was the sound of running water from the bathroom. I kicked the door open and found myself staring at the naked body of Rudy Warren, standing under the shower.

"Hi, Gary," he said, turning off the taps and grinning broadly to reveal blackened gums devoid of dentures. "Have a good trip?"

"How'd you get in?"

"Had a key," he said, starting to towel himself off.

"You gave me back my key."

"Yeah, but I made a copy before—"

"You said you didn't make a copy."

"I lied."

"Aren't you supposed to be in Mexico?"

"Lied about that too. Needed some place to hole up, gather my thoughts. And since I knew you were going out of town—"

"Get out," I said, grabbing him by the arm.

He yanked himself out of my grip. "No need to play the heavy—"

He was interrupted by the ringing of the intercom. It had to be Anne. Rudy moved toward the buzzer that opened the downstairs door. "Don't answer that," I said.

"What's going on?"

"Just don't touch it."

We both stood still while the intercom buzzed continuously. After two minutes it stopped.

"You gonna tell me what's happening?" Rudy said.

"Eventually. Right now I need you to get dressed. Where are your teeth?"

"They took 'em when I checked into the hospital. And since I checked out without permission, the teeth didn't come with me."

"You've survived ten days without teeth?"

"Don't need chompers to eat cold baked beans."

"I need a favor."

"Depends," he said, pulling on the last of his clothes.

"On what?"

"How much you tell me."

"It's babe trouble, okay?"

"That's kind of vague, Gary."

"I can't say more."

"Then I don't think I can help you—"

"You want this place for another week or so?"

"It would be helpful."

"Then walk over to MacDougal Alley and bring me my car."

"That's dangerous. I'm supposed to be south of the border."

I held up the car keys. "Either get the car or get out."

He grabbed the keys, then opened the cabinet where I kept my booze and removed a pint bottle of J&B.

"You don't need whiskey," I said.

"Oh yes I do," Rudy said, taking a swig from the bottle. He flashed me a smile. "See you round the back in five." Slipping the pint of J&B into his jacket pocket, he headed out the door.

As I packed a bag, a plan fell into my head. I'd hole up in some motel for a few days. I'd call Anne tomorrow and explain that Beth was the married woman with whom I'd been entangled, and the sight of her, coupled with the anxiety of the opening, had sent me into gaga land. I'd tell Anne I'd be returning to Mountain Falls within a few days, when Beth and Elliot were safely back east. No doubt she'd be furious, but dealing with her anger was a more palatable alternative than an extended stint in a penitentiary.

I glanced out the kitchen window and saw the MG drive up into the alleyway behind Frontier Apartments. I left the apartment and took the fire stairs down to the rear door. But when I reached the car, Rudy wouldn't move from the driver's seat, saying, "I think I'll come along for the ride."

"No way." I grabbed the door handle and tried to yank it open, yelling, "Get out of the car, Rudy."

"Yell a little louder," Rudy said, "and you'll alert the entire town to your departure."

I ran around to the passenger door, climbed in. But as I attempted to pull the keys out of the ignition, Rudy gunned the engine and sped off down the alley. "So where to?" he asked.

"I should kill you," I said.

"You mean, like you killed Gary Summers?"

I went rigid. For a moment or two I stopped breathing.

Rudy flashed me a dark smile. "Thought that would shut you up. Now, where are we going?"

I couldn't speak.

"Cat got your tongue? How 'bout I take Route 200 east?"

I managed a nod.

"East it is, then." He reached into his pocket for the J&B, took a swig, then held the open bottle against the steering wheel. Half an hour went by before either of us spoke.

"How did you find out?" I finally said.

A low chuckle from Rudy Warren. "If only you had a television in your apartment, I'd never have known. Gimme a boob tube, I can veg in front of it all day. But as I was kind of confined to quarters and got fed up with your books, I started to snoop. One afternoon I opened up your computer and browsed through the files. Found those little love notes you wrote to B. Very touching, really. Snooped around some more and discovered that B.'s name was Beth Bradford. Then I stumbled on that kiss-off letter you wrote her in December, telling her you'd set up house with some babe in Berkeley. Only I remembered that around ten days before Christmas, I ran into Meg Greenwood. She told me how she'd just rented an apartment to a photographer from Connecticut, a real smoothy who talked her into a rent reduction by coming on as if he wanted to date her, but later fed her some jive about a girlfriend back east. If Meg rented you the apartment in the middle of December, there's no way you could have been in Berkeley around the same time. So I figured there was some very good reason why you didn't want this B. to know your whereabouts.

"But later on, while going through a pile of stuff in your darkroom, I found the letter B. wrote you just a few weeks ago, saying how her husband died in a boating accident in November. I couldn't help but note that your departure from Connecticut dovetailed rather neatly with the death of this Ben Bradford guy—whose wife you just happened to be sleeping with." He paused, took a long guzzle of J&B, and gave me another sardonic smile. "Like the story so far?"

I stared ahead at the black road and said nothing.

"Anyway, I thought it might be interesting to learn more about the late Ben Bradford. But as I wasn't supposed to be in Mountain Falls, I couldn't exactly hit the library and search through back copies of *The New York Times*. But I got lucky. Your IBM Think-Pad has a built-in modem and comes preloaded with America Online software. And the little cord that goes from the computer into the telephone jack was still in its carrying case. So I plugged it in, found your Visa number and the card expiration date in your

MONEYBIZ files—you really are very organized—and signed you up for the Internet. I surfed my way over to *The New York Times* and asked them to download everything they had on Ben Bradford. Sadly, there was no picture with his obit, so I surfed my way to a bunch of eastern newspapers—the Boston *Globe, The Wall Street Journal.* They all covered the story, but again, no pic. Finally I struck pay dirt. The Stamford *Advocate,* Ben's local newspaper. A huge page-three story about his death at sea. With a nice big photo of the late Mr. Bradford, who, despite your scuzzy beard and ponytail, was a dead ringer for you." Rudy raised the J&B bottle in mock salute, then gulped down another long shot. His words began to slur. "Game, set, and match, Ben. I can call you Ben now, I suppose."

My mind was racing. I gripped the door handle tightly.

"Pretty impressive detective work, don't you think?" Rudy said. "I mean, *I'm* impressed. Just as I'm also impressed with the way you set up your death and resurrection. I presume Gary's was the body on the boat, right?"

"Why didn't you go to the police?" I asked.

"And spoil a secret? The *bond* we now have between us?"

"What do you want, then?"

He upended the whiskey bottle again. "Well, as a lawyer, I'm sure you are familiar with the concept of quid pro quo?"

"Better known as blackmail."

"Or, in this case, the price of silence."

"How much?"

"Terms and conditions to be worked out. As you are about to come into some serious dough from your photos—and as I am in some serious debt—a significant sum will have to change hands. You and I are gonna hole up for a couple of days at Ms. Ames's cabin. Hammer out a settlement."

"Then let me drive. You're dangerous with that whiskey."

For a moment he took his eyes off the road to glower at me. "You ain't taking us nowhere. Anyway, I'm a pro when it comes to drunken—"

He never got to finish that sentence, as we were suddenly blinded by the glare of headlights. I yelled "Rudy!" as I realized that an oncoming truck was headed directly for us. Rudy spun the wheel wildly; we dodged the truck; the MG veered right and ran off the road, shooting down an embankment. I yanked open the passenger door and fell out just as the vehicle went airborne. My head slammed into the ground; a seismic jolt went through my right knee and elbow as I rolled down the hill. A large rock ended my slide. As I slammed against it, there was the sound of a crash, followed by an explosive whoosh. I peered over the rock and found myself staring into a deep valley, where the MG had landed and was now on fire. Within seconds the gas tank ignited with a roar. Flames engulfed the vehicle.

I tried to get up. It took some effort, but I made it to my feet, thinking I must get help. Every step was agony. But I kept moving for around a hundred yards, finding myself in a dense grove of trees. Then the world went black, and I pitched forward.

BIRDSONG. A whiff of morning dew. And in the distance the mechanized sound of a large vehicle. I opened an eye. Then the pain hit. My skull pulsated like an out-of-kilter metronome. There was a deep gash on my right knee. When I touched my face, my fingers turned crimson, smeared with blood.

I blinked with grogginess as the morning sun cleaved the night sky. The sound of clanging gears was distinct now. I managed to ease myself over onto my left side and watched as the MG was winched up from the valley. The car had been incinerated beyond recognition.

The world went dark again. And when I finally stirred, there was silence. I glanced at my watch. Eight forty-five in the morning. Using a tree as support, I stood upright. It took a moment to get my bearings. I was in a burned-out wood. Suddenly I remembered standing here several weeks earlier, snapping away as the fire raged. I was back at the scene of my professional triumph. Even in my battered state, the irony of it hit home. And though I was on the verge of struggling up to the main road and flagging down the first car I could find, I hesitated. Beth might still be in Mountain Falls. The cops would question me about the accident. No. It was best to retreat somewhere and consider my next move. But where?

That's when I remembered that Rudy and I had been en route to Anne's cabin. It was only a mile down the road. I found a stick, and using it as a cane, I began the slow, aching hike there. It took over two hours.

When I reached the cabin's front door, I fell inside and collapsed on the bed. Eventually I forced myself up, staggered over to the stove, and set it alight. When it was hot, I boiled four large pots of water, then dumped them all into the bath. I repeated the process twice and ended up with a half-filled tub of hot water. Stripping off my tattered clothes, I lowered myself into the bath, wincing. I sat in the tub until the water went cold.

In a chest of drawers I found a baggy pair of Anne's sweatpants and a large sweater that just about fit. I had no appetite—except for alcohol—so I uncorked a bottle of red wine and drained four glasses before finally turning on the radio. I got the three-o'clock news. Around five items in, the announcer said, "Police investigating the road death of Mountain Falls photographer Gary Summers . . ." I choked on the wine and was so stunned that I didn't catch the rest of the item. Frantically I scanned the airways for another news broadcast, but in the end, I had to wait until four o'clock to hear the item repeated.

"The driver of the truck said that Mr. Summers was traveling at considerable speed and ran off the road into Moose Lake Valley. That's a three-hundred-foot fall, and no one's going to walk away from a crash like that. The county medical examiner is performing an autopsy, but the body was so badly burned in the fire that even dental records won't help with the identification."

It took a moment or two to sink in. Thanks to Rudy's lack of teeth, his badly charred body had been mistaken for me. Then again, who else would have been in that MG but Gary Summers? The truck driver said he saw only one person in the car—he should get his eyes checked. And as for Rudy Warren, nobody would be

looking for him, because he was supposed to be south of the border.
I was dead again.

I had a hard time falling asleep that night. I kept thinking about the fact that I would never see Anne Ames again. And how my death would bring her to grief yet again. And how—along with Adam and Josh—I would mourn her every hour of every day.

Finally I fell deep into a black netherland and stayed there for hours. Until I heard a vehicle pull up outside the cabin and footsteps approach the front door. Stirring awake, I squinted at the clock. Twelve fifteen. I sat up in bed. And then I heard a scream.

A loud, piercing scream, followed by silence.

Anne was at the door, her mouth opened in shock. We stared at each other for a very long time. And then I started to talk.

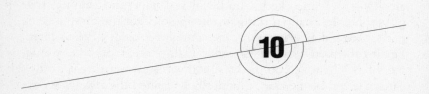

I TOLD her everything.

She remained standing while I talked, one foot in the door, as if ready to flee at any moment. When I got to the bit about killing Gary, I could actually feel her shudder, even though she was six feet from me.

After I told her about Rudy's blackmail threats, she finally spoke. "Did you kill him too?"

"No," I said. "The accident happened as reported. Only he was driving. And drunk. I managed to get out before—"

"Why should I believe that?" she said, her voice shaky. "Why should I believe any of this? Your whole life out here—*with me*—was a lie."

I didn't know what to say. So I said nothing.

"When I heard the news," she said, her voice barely audible, "I thought about killing myself. First Charlie, then you. You think you'll never survive the death of a baby. Finally you meet someone who makes you think there may be a way to live with the pain. And then—" She broke off and started to sob.

I was on my feet, approaching her. "No!" she said, putting two hands up to ward me off. I sat down on the bed again.

"The only reason I came up here today," she said, "was because it was here that I knew I loved . . ." She shook her head violently, as if trying to expunge that last sentence. "And now I wish I'd delayed a day. Because you would have been gone, wouldn't you? And I would never have known. You *are* going, aren't you?"

"I don't have much choice. The cops . . ."

"You're dead, remember? How will they know?"

"You." A long silence. I broke it. "You are going to tell them, aren't you?"

She stared at the floor. "I don't know."

Another silence. This time she ended it. "I have to go," she said. "I can't stay here."

"Will you be back?" I asked.

"I'm not sure," she said. "Will you go today?"

"I don't want to."

She shrugged. "Your call, Gar—" She cut herself off. "I don't even know what to call you anymore."

She left. And though I fully expected this to be my last day ever of freedom, I felt an eerie calm. I had confessed. The secret was no longer mine. I would always live with the guilt, the shame. But at least the burden of the lie had lifted.

At ten the next morning—a Saturday—I heard a car rumble down the dirt track. I sat on the bed awaiting the entrance of uniformed officers. But Anne walked in alone. "You didn't leave," she said.

"No."

"Why?" she asked.

"You."

"I see."

"You didn't go to the police," I said.

"No."

"Why?"

She shrugged. "You're being buried tomorrow," she said.

"Will you be going to the funeral?"

"Of course. So will Beth. She's still in town."

"Who's looking after the kids?" I instantly asked.

Anne let out a sigh. "Her sister, Lucy, is looking after them. Beth showed me a picture of them. They're beautiful boys."

"Yes," I said, "they are."

"Beth's very upset. First Ben, then Gary. We had a drink last night at her hotel after Elliot had gone to bed. She told me a little about her affair with Gary. And about her marriage to you. You know what I thought after she finished? I would never have gotten involved with that Gary, and I would never have married that Ben."

She shook her head, then looked me squarely in the eye. "I'm pregnant. And I'm keeping it."

I tried to reach for her—to gather her in my arms—but she pushed me away. "It doesn't mean I am also keeping you." She moved toward the door. "I'll be back in a few days. If you're still here, we'll talk again."

She returned on Tuesday evening with a pile of newspapers. There was half a page of funeral photos in *The Montanan*. *The New York Times* ran a story about Gary Summers in their National News section. So too did the L.A. *Times*.

"According to Judy, the phone hasn't stopped ringing at the gallery," Anne said. "Judy told me a staff writer at *The New Yorker* has been assigned to write a piece. And a bunch of Hollywood agents seem to think your life and tragic death would make a good movie. One of them called on behalf of Robert Redford."

I pushed the papers away. She knew what I was thinking.

"You never changed Gary's will, did you?" Anne asked.

"No," I said, "I didn't."

"And who will benefit from his famous death?"

"Bard College."

"They'll get everything?"

"Yeah, the works—except what's due in commission to Judy. She'll do very well out of this too."

"Great," Anne said. "Just great." She handed me a shopping bag. "I stopped at Kmart and picked you up some clothes."

"Thanks."

"Meg Greenwood asked if I'd help clean out your apartment tomorrow. I'm going to give everything to Goodwill. Okay?"

"Can you keep the laptop?"

"Don't see why not."

"When you get it home, wipe the hard disk. It contains . . ."

"Evidence?"

"Yes."

"You're asking me to be an accomplice."

"You can still go to the cops."

"Yes. I can. Anything else you want from the apartment?"

"Rudy's typewriter. I'm pretty sure he left it there."

"Why do you need it?"

"Rudy has to send a letter of resignation to Stu. From Mexico."

"I don't know if I want to be a part of all this," she said.

"Then don't be. Turn me in."

She was gone for four days. When she arrived on Saturday, she was carrying Rudy's old portable Olivetti. "The guy from *The New Yorker* has hit town and is interviewing everyone," she said.

"Will you talk to him?" I asked.

"No. I'm going to disappear for a while."

"Where to?"

"L.A. I have old friends there. I'll be gone a week, ten days. You have enough to see you through here?"

"I'll be fine."

"That is—if you're still here when I get back."

"I'll be here," I said.

"We'll see," she said.

On the morning before she left for L.A., she said, "I don't know how you live with it."

"Like you live with any grief," I said. "You just do. I didn't mean to kill Gary. I should have gone to the police. But I panicked."

"You thought you could get away with it. And you did."

"And I met you."

She frowned. "Big deal," she said.

Before she left, I handed her the letter I'd written to Stu Simmons on Rudy's typewriter—a rambling letter in which Rudy saw no reason why he should return to a newspaper where it was considered a capital offense to spit on the floor. Anne agreed to take a day trip to Tijuana and mail it from there.

She was gone eleven days. When she arrived back at the cabin, she said, "I've given notice at *The Montanan.*"

This took me aback. "Why?"

"Because my friends in L.A. introduced me to a guy who runs one of the biggest photo agencies in the country. He offered me a job—as his number two. Seventy-five grand a year. I accepted. You think you could live in L.A.?"

"You want me to come?"

"I'm not sure. But"—she touched her stomach—"this child will need someone to look after him while I'm at work. So . . ."

"That's the offer?"

"Yes," she said, "that's the offer."

I accepted it.

"We're going to have to find you a new name," she said.

I told her what to do. Within a week, after trawling through the death notices in the 1960 back editions of *The Montanan,* she found one for a four-year-old boy named Andrew Tarbell who drowned while on a family vacation in Mexico. After further checking, she discovered that back then death certificates of Montanans who died abroad were never lodged with the Montana Vital Records Office. Then she contacted the Alternative Post Office in Berkeley and said she was calling for Andrew Tarbell, who wanted to avail himself of their facilities. She also informed them that any mail they redirected should not contain his name on the envelope—only the number of the post office box she had recently rented in Mountain Falls.

Then I drafted a letter to the vital records office, saying I was Andrew Tarbell, giving my date and place of birth and requesting a replacement birth certificate. This letter was dispatched to those Alternative folk in Berkeley, who in turn mailed it back to Montana. In due course an official form arrived in Berkeley and was forwarded to Anne's post office box. The form required picture ID. I suggested that Anne make another call to Berkeley. "Sure, we do fake ID," the guy at the post office told her. Anne borrowed a Polaroid from the newspaper and bought a special film cartridge used for passport photos. She shot my portrait, then sent the two- by two-inch photo to Berkeley and wired them the $300 fee they demanded. (Fake identification doesn't come cheap.) Within a week a laminated picture ID arrived in Anne's post office box—an official-looking document from a place called Stockton Junior College. Beneath my mug shot were the words ANDREW TARBELL, FACULTY.

Anne made a photocopy of the ID card and, enclosing it with the completed application form, rerouted it via California back to the vital records office in Helena. Ten days later a replacement birth certificate for a thirty-nine-year-old white male named Andrew Tarbell ended up in my hands.

Anne made several trips to Los Angeles while I was awaiting the arrival of my new identity. She decided that as I needed to maintain a nonexistent profile, it was best if we didn't live anywhere too beau monde-ish like Santa Monica, so she rented a house in the San Fernando Valley—in Van Nuys. "I have to warn you," she said, "Van Nuys is a suburban wasteland. And the house is your standard three-bed ranch job. But you'll adjust."

And then one night Anne smuggled me out of Montana. It took us four days to reach Los Angeles.

She was right. Van Nuys was the ultimate suburban nightmare. And the house was Early Nothing. But we lived. She started her job. I spent my days stripping floorboards. Though I had to give a skeptical civil servant some story about being taken overseas by my parents as a teenager, I still managed to obtain a Social Security card. A driver's license followed. And after we got married that November, Anne got used to calling me Andy. She didn't take my name.

On February 2, 1996, our son, Jack, was born. For both of us it was love at first sight, though his presence accentuated my longing for Adam and Josh. Around the same time I read an announcement in *The New York Times* reporting the marriage of Elliot Burden and Beth Bradford. I lay awake for several nights wondering if Adam and Josh were now calling Elliot "Daddy."

When Anne returned to work, I assumed the duties of full-time househusband, looking after Jack all day and running the domestic business of the home.

And meanwhile, the late Gary Summers lurked everywhere. The rights to the story in *The New Yorker*—"Death of an Emerging Lensman"—were sold to Robert Redford's production company in an undisclosed six-figure deal. If a film does get made, I doubt I'll see it. My name is Andrew Tarbell now. Why should I be interested in some dead photographer named Gary Summers?

Still, later that year I did start taking pictures again. With her Christmas bonus Anne treated me to a spiffy new Nikon. And once we hired a baby-sitter to look after Jack in the afternoon, I began wandering the Valley, putting together a portfolio of suburban Angeleno portraits. Anne thought them technically more mature than my Montana work. But when I sent them out to the same photo editors who were chasing Gary, they all came back with rejection notes. Andrew Tarbell was a nobody.

Anne was even more upset than I was about the rejections. "You will get there again," she assured me. "You do have it. You'll always have it."

"I don't know anymore."

"It will work out," she said, stroking my hair. "Like we have."

I suppose our life together really has worked out. Marriage is all about rhythm, and we have a nice one going. We love our son. We enjoy each other's company. And though the Gary business is always there, hovering over us like a toxic cloud, so far we've managed to keep it at bay.

Of course, there are nights when I replay that split second in

Gary's basement and wonder where I would be now if I hadn't reached for that bottle. At least the old urge to run away—to flee domestic entrapment—has dissipated. When you've died twice and come back again, where can you run to anymore?

Still, urges never die; they simply lie dormant. And just last week, on the night Adam was somewhere in Connecticut or New York celebrating his birthday, I left the house around eight, telling Anne I was going to pick up a six-pack of beer at the 7-Eleven. But as soon as I edged out of our cul-de-sac, I was bound for the highway. Numbers, numbers. The 101 to the 10. The 10 to the 15. And before I had a chance to think about what I was doing, I was edging into the Mojave Desert, making a beeline for the Nevada border. I hit Vegas by two. With any luck I'd be in Salt Lake City by ten. And then? I kept asking myself that question. But I couldn't come up with an answer. Maybe because the only real destination on the road is home.

A fast exit off the eastbound 15. A fast entrance onto the westbound 15. Dawn over the Mojave. And I was back in Van Nuys as the sun reached full altitude. It was another perfect day in the Valley.

I pulled into our driveway. The front door opened. Anne stepped out into the sunshine, cradling Jack in her arms. She looked as if she hadn't slept. But she didn't say a word. She just gave me a tired shrug, as if to say, "I know, I know. . . . But this is it."

And then Jack looked my way and waved his arms.

"Daddy, Daddy."

I was being called. This is it.

Deborah
Smith

A
Place
to Call
Home

*R*oanie Sullivan has never had a home.

Claire Maloney has *always* had one —
a home rooted in the Georgia mountains,
nourished by a large and caring family.

Yet when Roanie's and Claire's paths
cross as children, their friendship is instant.
And the ties that bind them are strong
enough to last a lifetime.

It all has to do with a place called home.

"At once exciting and heartwarming."

— Booklist

PART ONE

Prologue

I PLANNED to be the kind of old southern lady who talked to her tomato plants and bought sweaters for her cats. I'd just turned thirty, but I was already sizing up where I'd been and where I was headed. So I knew that when I was old, I'd be deliberately peculiar. I'd wear bright red lipstick and tell embarrassing true stories about my family, and people would say, "I heard she was always a little funny, if you know what I mean."

They wouldn't understand why, and I didn't intend to tell them. I thought I'd sit in a rocking chair on the porch of some fake-antebellum nursing home for decrepit journalists, get drunk on bourbon and Coca-Cola, and cry over Roan Sullivan. I was only ten the last time I saw him, and he was fifteen, and twenty years had passed since then, but I'd never forgotten him and knew I never would.

"I'd like to believe life turned out well for Roanie," Mama said periodically, and Daddy nodded without meeting her eyes, and they dropped the subject. They felt guilty about the part they'd played in driving Roan away, and they knew I couldn't forgive them for it. He was one of the disappointments between them and me, which was saying a lot, since I'd felt like such a helpless failure when they brought me home from the hospital last spring.

My two oldest brothers, Josh and Brady, didn't speak about Roan at all. They were away at college during most of the Roan Sullivan era in our family. But my two other brothers remembered him each time they came back from a hunting trip with a prize buck. "It can't hold a candle to the one Roan Sullivan shot when we were kids," Evan always said to Hop. "Nope," Hop agreed with a mournful sigh. "That buck was a king." Evan and Hop measured regret in terms of antlers.

As for the rest of the family—Daddy's side, Mama's side, merged halves of a family tree so large and complex and deeply rooted it looked like an overgrown oak to strangers—Roan Sullivan was only a fading reflection in the mirror of their biases and regrets and sympathies. How they remembered him depended on how they saw themselves and our world back then, and most of them had turned that painful memory to the wall.

But he and I were a permanent fixture in local history, as vivid and tragic as anything could be in a small Georgia community isolated in the lap of the mountains, where people hoard sad stories as carefully as their great-grandmothers' china. My great-grandmother's glassware and china service, by the way, were packed in a crate in Mama and Daddy's attic. Mama had this wistful little hope that I'd use it someday, that her only girl among five children would magically and belatedly blossom into the kind of woman who set a table with china instead of plastic.

There was hope for that. But what happened to Roan Sullivan and me changed my life and changed my family. Because of him, we saw ourselves as we were, made of the kindness and cruelty that bond people together by blood, marriage, and time. I tried to save him, and he ended up saving me. He might have been dead for twenty years—I didn't know then—but I knew I'd come full circle because of him: I would always wait for him to come back, too.

The hardest memories are the pieces of what might have been.

One

IT STARTED the year I performed as a tap-dancing leprechaun at the St. Patrick's Day carnival and Roanie Sullivan threatened to cut my cousin Carlton's throat with a rusty pocketknife. That was also the year the Beatles broke up, and the National Guard killed four students at Kent State, and Josh, who was in Vietnam, wrote home to Brady, who was a senior at Dunderry High, "Don't even think about enlisting. There's nothing patriotic about this garbage."

But I was only five years old; my world was narrow, deep, self-satisfied, well off, very southern, securely bound to the land and to a huge family descended from Irish immigrants who had settled in Georgia over one hundred and thirty years ago. As far as I was concerned, life revolved in simple circles, with me at the center.

At the St. Patrick's Day carnival, held at the old arbor east of town, the Jaycees sold sandwiches, cookies, and punch at folding tables in a corner next to the arbor's wooden stage. The Down Mountain Boys played bluegrass music, and the beginners' tap class from my aunt Gloria's school of dance was decked out in leprechaun costumes and forced into a midyear minirecital.

Mama took snapshots of me in my involuntary servitude. I was not a born dancer. I was always out of step, and I disliked mastering anyone's routines but my own. I stood there on the stage, staring resolutely at the camera in my green-checkered bibbed dress with its ruffled skirt and a puffy white blouse, my hair parted in fat red braids tied with green ribbons.

I looked like an unhappy Irish Heidi.

My class shuffled through our last number, accompanied by a

tune from some Irish dance record. I looked down, and there he was, standing in the crowd at the lip of the stage, a tall, shabby ten-year-old boy with greasy black hair. Roan Sullivan. Roanie. Even in a small town the levels of society are a steep staircase. My family was at the top. Roan and his daddy were in the cellar.

He watched me seriously, as if I weren't making a fool of myself. I had already accidentally stomped on my cousin Violet's foot twice, and I'd elbowed my cousin Rebecca in her arm, so they'd given me a wide berth on either side.

I forgot about my humiliating arms and feet and concentrated on Roanie Sullivan, because it was the first close look I'd gotten at nasty, no-account Big Roan Sullivan's son from Sullivan's Hollow. We didn't associate with Big Roan, even though he and Roanie were our closest neighbors on Soap Falls Road, not two miles from our farm.

Everybody knew Roanie Sullivan was trash—came from it, looked like it, and smelled like it—so they steered clear of him in a crowd. Maybe that was one reason I couldn't take my eyes off him. We were both human islands stuck in the middle of a lonely, embarrassing sea of space.

My cousin Carlton lounged a couple of feet away, between Roanie and the Jaycees' table. There are some relatives you just tolerate, and Carlton Maloney was in that group. He was twelve, smug and well fed, and he was laughing at me. He was a weasel.

I saw him glance behind him—once, twice. Uncle Dwayne was in charge of the Jaycees' food table, and Aunt Rhonda was talking to him, so he was looking at her dutifully. He'd left a couple of dollar bills beside the shoe box he was using as a cash till.

Carlton eased one hand over, snatched the money, and stuck it in his trouser pocket.

I was stunned. He'd stolen from the Jaycees. He'd stolen from his own *uncle.* My brothers and I had been trained to such a strict code of honor that we wouldn't pilfer so much as a penny from the change cup on Daddy's dresser. Stealing was unthinkable.

Uncle Dwayne looked down at the table. He frowned. He hunted among the packages of cookies. He leaned toward Carlton and said something to him. From the stage I couldn't hear what he said, but I saw Carlton draw back dramatically, shaking his head. Then he turned and pointed at Roanie.

I was struck tapless. I simply couldn't move a foot. I stood there, rooted in place, and was dimly, painfully aware of people laughing at me. Daddy waved his big hands helpfully, as if I was a scared calf he could shoo into moving. But I wasn't scared. I was furious.

Uncle Dwayne, his jaw thrust out, pushed his way around the table and grabbed Roanie by one arm. I saw Uncle Dwayne speak forcefully to him. I saw Roanie's face turn to sullen anger.

His eyes darted to Carlton. He lunged at him. They went down in a heap, with Carlton on the bottom. People scattered, yelling. The whole Leprechaun Review came to a wobbly halt. I bolted down the stairs at the end of the stage and squirmed through the crowd.

Uncle Dwayne was trying to pull Roanie off Carlton, but Roanie had one hand wound in the collar of Carlton's sweater. He had the other at Carlton's throat, with the point of a rusty little penknife poised beneath Carlton's Adam's apple. "I didn't take no money!" Roanie yelled at him. "You liar!"

Daddy plowed into the action. He planted a knee in Roanie's back, wrenched the knife from him, and pulled him to his feet.

"Where's that money?" Uncle Dwayne thundered at Roanie.

"I didn't take no money." He mouthed words like a hillbilly. He had a crooked front tooth with jagged edges.

"Oh, yeah, you did," Carlton yelled. "I saw you! Everybody knows you steal stuff. Just like your daddy!"

"Roanie, hand over the money," Daddy said sternly.

"I ain't *got* it."

I was plastered to the sidelines but close enough to see the misery and defensiveness in Roanie's face. Oh, Lord. He was the kind of boy who caused trouble. He deserved trouble.

But he's not a thief.

Don't tattle on Carlton. Maloneys stick together.

But it's not fair.

"He didn't take it," I said loudly. "Carlton did! I *saw* him,

Daddy!" Everyone stared at me. I met Roanie Sullivan's wary, surprised eyes. He could burn a hole through me with those eyes.

Carlton's face turned crimson. Uncle Dwayne stuck a hand in Carlton's pocket and pulled out two wadded-up dollar bills.

And that was that. Uncle Dwayne hauled Carlton off to find Uncle Eugene and Aunt Arnetta, Carlton's folks. Daddy let go of Roanie Sullivan. "Go on. Get out of here."

"He pulled that knife, Holt," Uncle Pete said behind me.

Daddy scowled. "He couldn't cut his way out of a paper sack with a knife that little. Forget about it, Pete. Go on, everybody."

Roanie stared at me. There was this *gleam* in his eyes, made up of surprise and gratitude and suspicion, bearing on me like concentrated fire, and I felt singed. Daddy put a hand on Roanie's collar and dragged him away. I started to follow, but Mama had gotten through the crowd by then, and she snagged me. "Hold on, Claire Karleen Maloney. You've put on enough of a show."

Dazed, I looked up at her. Hop and Evan peered at me, and Violet and Rebecca watched me, openmouthed. A whole bunch of Maloneys scrutinized me. "Carlton's a weasel," I explained finally.

Mama nodded. "You told the truth. That's fine. You're done. I'm proud of you."

"Aren't you scared of Roanie Sullivan?" Rebecca blurted out.

"He didn't laugh at me when I was dancing. I think he's okay."

"You've got a strange way of sortin' things out," Evan said.

"She's one brick short of a load," Hop added.

So that was the year I realized Roanie was not just trashy, not just different, he was dangerous, and taking his side was a surefire way to seed my own reputation as a troublemaker and independent thinker.

I was fascinated by him from then on.

THE world in general didn't even know that Dunderry, Georgia, existed. We were barely findable on the creased, coffee-stained road map of Georgia that Mama and Daddy kept in the glove compartment of our station wagon. Atlanta rated a fat star, and Gainesville was marked with a circle. But Dunderry was only a black dot. We lived an inch to the left of Gainesville and an inch and a half above Atlanta. We had peace and quiet, a beautiful little courthouse square, treelined streets and handsome old homes, big farms tucked in broad, lush valleys, and cathedral-like mountains around it all to keep us safe.

Mama was a Delaney by birth and a Maloney by marriage; in other words, she stood proudly at the crossroads of the two oldest families in Dunderry. Her great-grandparents Glen and Fiona Delaney emigrated from Ireland in 1838, the same year as the Maloneys. But they were educated shopkeepers from Dublin, while the Maloneys were illiterate tenant farmers in the Irish backcountry. More important, the Delaneys were Protestant and my father's ancestors, the Maloneys, Catholic.

So pride, class, religion, and politics kept the Delaneys and Maloneys from intermarrying, even as they all gradually turned into prosperous Methodist Democrats. It took more than a hundred years until Mama and Daddy broke the stalemate.

Great-Grandfather Howard Maloney built the house I grew up in, on the foundation of a log cabin. It is where my grandpa Joseph Maloney and his five brothers were born and where Daddy and all six of his brothers and sisters were born.

Each generation added to it like a hope chest. By the time my brothers and I were born, the house had ten bedrooms, four bathrooms, and three chimneys, and its bottom-level additions sprawled from a two-story center inside wide porches, front and back. It sat in the center of the Estatoe Valley, with round green mountains rising on all sides. We were a kingdom of our own making.

Mama ran our household like a business. Spick and span, no room for messy customers. Beds made, fresh flowers in the vases, meals on time, clothes mended, silver polished, toilets sparkling, floors waxed. She marshaled doctors' appointments, school activities, and homework. The land was Daddy's, but the house was hers, and everything that went on in it was under her dominion.

When I was a girl, my British-born grandmother Delaney and my great-grandma Maloney lived with us. I learned the fine points of stubbornness and pride from the Old Grannies. Mama said anyone who lived in the house with her Mawmaw and Daddy's grandma could qualify as a saint. Or a lunatic.

Great-Grandma Maloney was a frisky eighty-eight, while Grandmother Delaney, as she reminded us often in her delicate English accent, was a very frail seventy. Frail like a cedar stump. Elizabeth Wallingford Delaney dyed her gray hair a flat nut-brown color and wore it pinned up with a hairpiece of coiled brown braids at the crown. She wore slender pale dresses, and if anyone failed to jump up fast enough when she asked for something, she hooked the offender with the brass goosehead handle of her mahogany cane.

She had been only seventeen, an orphan, when she met Grandpa Patrick Delaney in London during the First World War. She said he was a dashing American infantryman who regaled her with stories about his southern homeland. She married him and crossed the ocean with visions of antebellum plantations in her head.

She never quite forgave Grandpa Patrick after she discovered that her new home was a mountain town fed by dirt roads and that the big house was a drafty Victorian shared by Grandpa's parents.

Somehow Grandmother Elizabeth survived for the sake of four sons and four daughters. She actually thrived because the ladies in the county considered her an expert on matters of fashion and decorum, and after Grandpa Patrick became president of Dunderry Savings and Loan, her social dominance was cemented.

When I was four, Grandpa Patrick had a series of strokes that crippled him. They moved into our house, and for the next year I watched her care for him tenderly, her frailty forgotten. After he died, she channeled all her lonely energy toward aggravating Great-Grandma Maloney, who had the bedroom across the hall.

It was an old feud, birthed in their youth, nurtured in their prime, and still sizzling like banked coals in their old age.

Great-Gran's first name was Alice. Her husband, Howard Maloney, died of a heart attack twenty years before I was born. By then he and Great-Gran had turned the farm's management over to their son, my grandpa Joseph, but Great-Gran still ran the whole operation. By the time Grandpa Joseph retired and Daddy took charge, she still hadn't mellowed much.

Great-Gran's hair was a thin cap of blue-white spit curls above a thick face enormously wrinkled and weathered. She wore stern-looking brown dresses and thick-heeled flat shoes, was almost six feet tall, and weighed two hundred pounds.

She met Great-Grandpa Howard at a Sunday social sponsored by the young ladies academy where she was a teacher. She married him a month later and moved to Dunderry County to raise children and eyebrows: She wore overalls at home and marched for women's suffrage years before the female vote had any chance in Washington.

When Grandmother Elizabeth married Grandpa Patrick and came home with him from England, she immediately usurped Great-Gran's place as the most interesting woman in Dunderry and became the only permanent thorn in Great-Gran's side.

In 1950 Mama eloped with Daddy the night after her high school graduation ceremony. It was a scandal—Elizabeth Delaney's beautiful daughter Marybeth, who had just received her acceptance from a Methodist women's college, and Alice Maloney's favorite grandson, Holt, who rode a motorcycle and was working at the Maloney chicken houses. Elizabeth Delaney threatened to have Holt Maloney arrested for seducing a minor. Alice Maloney tried bitterly to have the marriage annulled. But Mama and Daddy were already expecting my brother Josh. So that was that. For better or worse the Delaneys and the Maloneys were shackled together by marriage. Grandmother Elizabeth and Great-Gran Alice remained dedicated to making each other miserable, and since both of them were living with us, they sometimes made us miserable, too.

Great-Grandma Alice's son Joseph and his wife, Dottie, lived in a small house a two-minute walk away. Dottie Maloney was still young at sixty, a hearty red-haired tower of feminine strength. A smart woman who knew about investments because her daddy was a banker, she tinkered successfully in the stock market and kept the farm's business accounts. I adored her, but Grandpa Joseph was my dearest mentor. He was a broad, strong old man, planted solidly on the ground. He moved like a bear, and he was completely bald except for a monk's fringe of white fur. He planted by the moon and astrology signs, and his stalks of corn grew at least twelve feet high.

Grandpa served in World War II, and when he came back home after V-J Day, the farm had just about sunk to nothing. He and Grandma were broke and would ultimately have seven children to raise. Holt—my daddy—was the oldest, and he was only sixteen.

The Latchakoochee Power Company hadn't gotten very far before the war; almost everybody in the mountains was still in the dark. Grandpa Joseph put together a crew that included Daddy and most of the men in the family. They went into the contracting business and installed power lines all over our part of the state. They made a small fortune. And Grandma Dottie began nurturing that fortune on the stock market.

Which was the main reason we had, as people said, more money than we knew what to do with. Around us were our fenced pastures, our broad fields, five large barns, and ten chicken houses, which produced fifty thousand fryers throughout the year.

So there we were—one great-grandmother, one old grandmother and one youngish grandmother, one beloved grandfather, Mama and Daddy, Hop and Evan, and Josh—after he came home from Vietnam—and Brady, visiting from college every month or so. Plus a hundred head of Hereford beef cattle, a dozen dogs, five cats, a housekeeper, ten hired hands and a foreman, tons of pumpkins, corn, and cabbages, and me.

Not to mention my thirteen aunts and uncles plus their spouses, my three dozen first cousins, and other assorted relatives, in-laws, and friends, who came and went as if our home were a train station at the center of the universe.

In the long run, Roanie Sullivan never had a chance. From the start he was only one against many.

HE AND his daddy lived in a trailer beside a gully filled with half-burned garbage. Big Roan had only one leg; the other was a metal contraption—so I'd heard, because I'd never gotten a peek at it.

Big Roan Sullivan, who was Irish but didn't have the luck, had rambled into town a year or two before the Korean War. He was an edgy hot-rodder who took a job at Murphy's Feed Mill. He got drafted and was immediately carted off to the front lines, where he'd lost his right leg when he stepped on a mine.

Daddy said he'd been surly before, but after the war he turned mean—a mean drunk, a condition that took some work, since the county was dry then. Because Big Roan was a war hero, Grandpa Joseph Maloney deeded him two acres in the hollow east of our farm. The V.F.W. bought him a used house trailer and an old truck. The Dunderry Ladies Association planted a lawn, and Mama set out a few rose shrubs. All five members of the Dunderry African Men's Association brought out a tractor and dug Big Roan a garden patch. Barker Murphy offered him his old job at the feed mill.

The salvation of Big Roan Sullivan was the biggest civic project since a tornado scattered the county courthouse to kingdom come, but unlike the courthouse, he couldn't be rebuilt. He let the lawn and the garden patch go to weeds. The roses shriveled, the trailer began to look like a garbage can, and Big Roan kept the truck working just well enough to drive down to Atlanta for liquor.

At least one part of Big Roan still worked, and it attracted a certain kind of girl. Word got around that Jenny Bolton was pregnant. Jenny, by all accounts, was a pretty little brunette, only about seventeen but beaten-looking already. When people figured out who'd knocked her up, they organized a righteous group that made Big Roan own up. In those days they called it a shotgun wedding.

Jenny moved to the Hollow with Big Roan, but when it came time for the baby to be born, he was passed out, drunk, behind their trailer. Mama felt sorry for Jenny and had been checking in on her nearly every day; she found her curled up and crying in the trailer's tiny, dirty bed. Daddy and Mama drove her to the hospital in Gainesville as quick as they could, but the doctors had to deliver the baby by cesarean—he was so large and Jenny was so small. When Mama asked her what she wanted to name him, she gasped, "Roan junior, please, ma'am," then fell asleep for the next twelve hours.

Everyone called the baby Roanie to distinguish him from Big
Roan. Five years later, right about the time I was born, Jenny caught
pneumonia and died. She had given all her willpower to Roanie, I
think. There was talk of taking him away from Big Roan, but people were squeamish—a man had an ordained right to his own seed.

And so, in the way even good people have of turning their backs
on messy problems, my family let Roanie grow up the way he did.

I figured his situation this way: I came into the world to take care
of him for his mama. No one else wanted to.

WHEN I started the first grade, Roanie was already in the sixth. I
watched him from a distance with horrified curiosity.

Roanie always looked dirty, and his jeans were too long one week
and too short the next. He was big for his age but wiry-thin, with
brown-black hair and huge gray eyes that looked out of a tight face.

Somebody was always messing with Roanie. *White trash. Smells
like a toilet.* He'd fight anything, anybody—older, taller, heavier—
and about half the time got the living daylights beat out of him. It
wasn't unusual to see Principal Rafferty dragging Roanie down the
hall to have the nurse stitch up or ice down some part of his face.

His fury and isolation and status as an outcast fascinated me because I was his opposite—the pampered darling of a prosperous
clan. But Roanie and I had one thing in common: My foibles, too,
were no secret. If I got into trouble for talking in class or for scrib-
bling knock-knock jokes on the wall of the girls' bathroom, the tres-
pass traveled the family grapevine faster than a monkey on pep pills.

I couldn't imagine someone who broadcast his notoriety without
benefit of three dozen cousins to transmit for him. *That* was power.
At the same time I felt sorrier for Roanie Sullivan than I'd ever felt
for another human being in my life.

Roanie didn't let people catch him standing beside the road at
the Hollow. I guess he knew how he looked, waiting for the school
bus by the lopsided mailbox in front of that awful sinkhole with its
junk and garbage-filled gully and rusty trailer.

But there was another reason, too: my older cousins Arlan and

Harold Delaney. They were already in high school, old enough to drive, and if they saw Roanie by the Hollow's mailbox, they'd take a whack at the mailbox with a baseball bat. When they could catch him, they took a whack at Roanie, too.

One morning in May, I was in a mood, an *ill* mood, because it was thundering and pouring rain outside, weather that made my curly dark red hair explode in fuzz. I knew I looked like cotton candy with a face. I sobbed and hid in my bathroom, so I missed the bus.

Grandpa was the only one who could stand me when I was being a brat, so he drove me, Hop, and Evan to school. We skimmed along Soap Falls Road, rain drenching everything. Rounding the curve at Sullivan's Hollow, we saw Arlan and Harold's truck speed off.

I shrieked, "They got Roanie again!"

Grandpa cursed under his breath.

Roanie was hanging on to the mailbox in that downpour. He had no raincoat, no umbrella, no *nothing* except a plastic garbage bag around his shoulders. His books were scattered in the weeds.

But as soon as he saw another car, he turned, staggered, fell, got up, and ran down the Hollow's mud-slicked driveway.

"Grandpa," I begged. "Grandpa, *please* stop."

Grandpa pulled off to one side.

"Aw, come on, Claire," Hop protested from the back seat.

"He'll smell up the car," Evan said.

Grandpa studied me, his head tilted. "Roanie's your fish, Claire. You'll have to get out in the rain and reel him in yourself."

I guess he was testing me to see what I was made of—vanity or valor. I pushed my door open and trudged down the muddy road. "Roanie!" I yelled. I slipped on the mud and sat down hard. "Roanie, we'll give you a ride to school! It's okay. I swear!"

Grandpa got out and stood beside me. "Come on, Roanie!"

Silence. Stillness. We called for ten minutes.

I knew Roanie was watching us from somewhere in the dripping green forest. I could feel his gaze. But he wasn't coming back.

"All right," Grandpa said wearily. "We can't get that cat out of his tree." He gently pulled me to my feet.

All my pent-up misery curled out in small choking sobs. I was muddy, I was soaked, and I was still better off than Roanie. "He thinks we're jinxed," I cried as Grandpa guided me back to the car. "Every time he has anything to do with us, something bad happens."

Grandpa patted me. "We're not jinxed. We just live on the opposite side of the fence. We're as strange to him as he is to us."

I turned toward the woods again. "You come over and see us!" I yelled. "I'm leaving a gate open for you!"

WHEN I was in the second grade, Neely Tipton made my life a constant hell. He was a year ahead of me, the third-grade bully, and he made a game of slipping up behind me, hissing "Bony Maloney," yanking my hair hard, then running before I could turn around.

Neely moved too fast for me to smack him. But he learned his lesson one day, and he never laid a hand on my hair again.

It started like every other Neely encounter. At recess I edged warily out a doorway to the playground. He was lurking behind the door, and the next thing I knew, my head jerked and I flew backward. I landed on my back and lay there, gasping for air.

"Bony Maloney, I gotcha," Neely yelled. Dazed, I propped myself up on my skinned elbows. Then I heard a whump and looked over to see Neely bounce off the brick wall and sit down hard.

Roanie towered over him. "You mess with her again," he told Neely calmly, "and I'll jerk your butthole through your mouth."

Roanie looked down at me with his eyes glittering. Maybe he expected me to insult him. "Thanks, Roanie," I said very carefully.

"I heard you, that time at the Hollow," he said. "You ain't like nobody else in the whole world." Then he just walked away.

That was the day I began to love Roanie Sullivan.

THE McClendon sisters lived in a cluster of shabby little houses and trailers in the woods north of town, on a dead-end dirt lane named Steckem Road. I'd done my share of snickering over Steckem Road's whispered nickname—Stick 'Em in Road.

I knew it involved men and women and their private parts. I also knew that if any of my brothers ever so much as set foot on Steckem Road, Mama and Daddy would skin them alive.

Mama would have skinned her brother Pete if she could. It was a well-known fact that Uncle Pete spent half his time with the McClendon sisters on Steckem Road. I had heard enough about his notorious habits to know he was the shame of the Delaneys.

There were four sisters—Daisy, Edna Fae, Lula, and Sally. Daisy was the oldest, about thirty-five when I was seven, though her bleached yellow hair and the hard lines around her mouth made her look older. She had a husband, but nobody had seen him in years. Daisy spent most of her time with Big Roan Sullivan. In some strange way I think she loved him.

Edna Fae and Lula had had a pack of husbands. "You could throw a handful of marbles at Edna Fae's and Lula's tribe of children and not hit two that have the same daddy," Grandpa said.

Sally McClendon was sixteen, the youngest of the sisters. She'd already dropped out of high school, and, worst of all, she had a baby. A son. I had heard that Sally was Uncle Pete's favorite.

The McClendon sisters survived on welfare checks and odd jobs, doing laundry and cleaning houses for people in town, supplemented by what they earned from the men who visited them. Uncle Pete, I decided, was just plain strange for wanting anything to do with them.

When I was older, I understood that the McClendon sisters were poor, uneducated, and abused. But at seven I only understood that they aroused both pity and disgust in my family. Polish those feelings with well-intentioned religion, and you get charity.

That's how Easter got tied in with the whole mess.

I'm ashamed to admit that I already thought of Easter in terms of goody baskets and egg hunts and frilly new dresses, not of solemn celebrations of Jesus ascending to heaven. I couldn't be solemn; I was the Easter princess. Mama bought me a pale pink dress with a skirt so ruffled it stood out from my waist like a shelf. I had white patent-leather shoes and a white straw hat with a pink ribbon.

The Saturday before Easter was egg-decorating day. We spent the whole day boiling eggs and dipping them in vinegar-scented pastel baths. We put some of the eggs in a dozen small Easter baskets, along with candy and Bible pamphlets. Those baskets were for the poor McClendon children of Steckem Road. Mama and other church ladies delivered the baskets to them every year.

I raced downstairs in my nightgown on Easter morning. And there, in the center of the library table in the living room, sat my personal huge pink Easter basket, exploding with pink cellophane and pink bows and a soft pink poodle doll. I tore a giant chocolate rabbit from his plastic wrapping and examined his molded perfection with my fingertips. I could already taste his richness.

Evan strode into the room dressed in his blue Easter suit and white silk tie, his white Bible in one hand. He was only twelve, but he was going through a holier-than-thou phase.

"This isn't what Easter is about," he announced. "I think we should wait."

"Evan's right," Mama allowed from the doorway. "Claire, don't eat that candy until after church."

I had the rabbit halfway to my mouth. Oh, temptation. Oh, interrupted greed. Oh, the sin of chocolate lust. "Oh, dammit," I blurted.

Doomed. Doomed that second. The Lord had not risen so that Claire Maloney could say "dammit" over a chocolate rabbit.

Which is why I had to sit out the Easter egg hunt and donate my beloved basket, chocolate rabbit and all, to the McClendon children of Steckem Road. And I had to go there, too, with Mama, my aunt Dockey, and the other ladies, to see why I should be humble.

THE McClendon place reminded me of Sullivan's Hollow, with paper trash littering a yard shared by a half circle of tiny dilapidated houses and rust-streaked trailers. Skinny dogs crept around, shy and standoffish, like the children. The porches sagged with junk.

We got out of Aunt Dockey's Cadillac, and the ladies made a fuss over the rag-tail boys and girls, who shuffled their feet and darted excited glances at me in my ruffled pink splendor and at my basket of Easter eggs that I lugged from the back seat.

Edna Fae and Lula and Sally strolled out to meet us. They were dressed in tight jeans and low-cut blouses, with lots of makeup on their faces. I was so busy staring, I nearly dropped my basket. "Well, ain't you pretty?" Sally said to me in a sly way. She grabbed a handful of my long hair and stroked the curls. "You look just like a strawberry shortcake with blue eyes. Them eyes. Bright as sapphires. You just take in the whole world with them eyes, don't you?"

Mama sidled over and got between us. Polite but cool, she didn't say a word. Sally backed off. Sally was scared of her.

Mama took her box of charity food from the trunk, then bent close to my ear and whispered fiercely, "You stay by the car. Hand out a few eggs if you want. We'll get the Easter baskets out of the trunk after the prayer meeting."

And then, unhappily, I was alone in the yard with a dozen grimy barefoot kids, all of them staring at my basket as if they'd like to knock me down and take it.

I sighed. "Y'all want some Easter eggs?" Quick nods.

I fished among the hard-boiled eggs and found the candy ones first. But the McClendon children didn't care. They snatched candy eggs and real eggs with the same fervor, then tore off the wrappings and peeled the colored shells with dirty fingernails, and ate slowly, relishing every bite.

I thought about Roanie, who was so proud, and how his daddy was so mean, nobody had ever dared go down to Sullivan's Hollow to bring *him* Easter eggs. I was glad that Roanie hadn't been turned into a charity exhibit like the McClendon kids.

I heard the rumble of a car coming down the dirt road, and lo and behold, as if he'd materialized from my thoughts, Roanie drove his daddy's beat-up truck into the yard.

My mouth fell open. He was only twelve years old! Yet he rolled that rattletrap into the yard and climbed out. Then he froze, staring at me with an almost painfully surprised expression.

"What are you doing here?" I demanded.

At that moment the front door of Daisy's house banged open. Daisy ran out, her gold-plated hair tangled around her face. One of her eyes was swollen shut. "You come git him, Roanie! You come get that s.o.b. outta my bed! I ain't puttin' up with him no more."

The kids scattered, while I stood rooted to the spot, fascinated and afraid. The door slapped open again, and Big Roan staggered out, lopsided on his metal leg, bare-chested. He was huge and black-haired. His bloodshot eyes settled on me, and I froze. "Don't you look at me, you little fluffball," he said loudly.

I backed against Aunt Dockey's car and gaped at him. He staggered down the steps toward me.

"Leave her be," Daisy ordered. "She's just a little girl."

"Shut up." He limped forward, swinging his arms. "See that young un over there?" Big Roan swung a hand toward a barefoot baby boy with light brown hair. Sally must have seen him from the other house, because she bolted outside and snatched the baby.

"Big Roan, he ain't yours!" she yelled. "Don't mess with him!"

He grunted at her. "I ain't got nothin' to mess with. Gov'ment sent me off to fight and left me poor." Big Roan swung toward me again. "Your daddy and his kind—gov'ment sent them where they'd be safe. I done their dirty work for 'em."

Roanie got between me and Big Roan. "Go on," Roanie shouted. "Get in the truck."

"Get out of my way, boy! When I want you to talk to me, I'll beat some talk out of you!"

My knees shook. They were all crazy. Big Roan jabbed his finger toward the baby boy in Sally's arms. "That young un—you know what he is? You ask your uncle Pete. That there's your fine uncle Pete Delaney's thrown-off bastard!"

My uncle Pete's?

Roanie made a sound like a wounded dog and shoved his daddy. Big Roan lost his balance and sprawled on the ground. "Git up," Roanie said between clenched teeth. "Git *up*."

Big Roan swept one thick arm out. He caught Roanie around the ankles and jerked his feet out from under him, and Roanie went flat on his back. Big Roan rolled onto him in a flash, pinning him by the throat. "Don'tcha gimme orders, boy!"

Roanie coughed and struggled. "Let him go!" Daisy shrieked.

I had a mean arm. A strong arm, honed by baseball-playing brothers, who'd taught me to throw. I didn't think; I didn't breathe; I was blind with rage and terror. I snatched a hard-boiled Easter egg from my basket and drew back like a major leaguer. I beaned Big Roan right between the eyes. They don't call them *hard*-boiled eggs for nothing.

Big Roan's eyes rolled up, and he slumped backward.

Roanie got up slowly. His face was tinged with blue, and the skin of his throat was dark red. He gasped for air, but he managed to keep his head up. He scrutinized me with his unwavering gray eyes.

"That's for Neely Tipton," I told him. "Now we're even."

He nodded weakly.

The battle had lasted only thirty seconds. By now Mama and everybody else had run out to us, and Edna Fae helped Roanie drag his father to the truck and hoist him into the back.

"Did I kill him?" I asked Mama tearfully.

"No," she said, putting one arm around me. "I'm afraid not."

"Mama, he said Sally got her little boy from Uncle Pete."

Mama's mouth flattened. "Some things we don't talk about."

Roanie climbed into the truck. Twelve years old and hauling his drunk daddy home on Easter Sunday, humiliation stretching every inch of his face. I couldn't let him go like that. I grabbed the giant chocolate rabbit from my basket.

I ran to the truck as Roanie cranked the engine. He stared at me warily as I thrust the rabbit into his lap. "You take this," I said, crying. "It's not 'cause it's Easter, and it's not for charity. It's because I *like* you. You take this rabbit, and you eat him!"

He swallowed hard. He shrugged. I struggled not to pull back from the stink of garbage and unwashed clothes.

After he drove away, I handed out Easter baskets to that pack of quiet, fearful McClendon kids. Sally ran into her house carrying her little boy. Uncle Pete's son. My cousin.

I was so ashamed of all of us.

From that day forward I vowed to save Roanie from the evil that pervaded our lives.

TWO

I DIDN'T get to see Roanie much for the next couple of years, especially after he entered Dunderry High, but I heard about him regularly.

"Roanie Sullivan showed up at school with a big knot on his forehead," Hop told us one night. "He caught Arlan and Harold knocking his mailbox again, and they took a swing at him."

"Roanie's bound to drop out of school pretty soon," Evan predicted. "Nobody could put up with the kind of nonsense he gets."

I was furious. At the next family get-together I told Arlan and Harold, "I hope you die and buzzards eat your guts."

But Roanie hung on as tenaciously as bitterweed in a cow pasture. He had no money for nice notebooks or pens or field trips down to Atlanta—things I and mine took for granted. He could never afford lunch in the cafeteria, and he never had money for the bare necessities to play a sport. He took as little as he could to get by.

He dropped out of high school only once, in the early spring when I was nine, after Big Roan robbed Uncle Pete's store.

The auto supply was in a low concrete building that Uncle Pete had erected on a backstreet in town. Big Roan, drunk as usual, drove his truck through the auto supply's big plate-glass window one March night, then loaded up with oil filters, radiator hoses, a CB radio, and a new set of tires. But Dot and Rigby Boyles, who lived next door, called Sheriff Vince O'Brien, one of Daddy's cousins, and Big Roan was in jail within thirty minutes. Uncle William Delaney sentenced him to two months. Roanie, who was only fourteen, hid in the deep forest above the Hollow. Daddy and Sheriff Vince tracked him for a few days without any luck.

"Roanie'll starve," I moaned to Grandpa Joseph.

He laid a finger to his lips. "No, he won't. I know where he is."

TEN Jumps Lake had belonged to Maloneys for as long as anyone could remember. It was nearly a mile off an old paved road that intersected Soap Falls above the farm. The lake was small and rimmed with high ridges, and the only way to get there was by a narrow trail that crawled around steep hillsides.

Grandpa said the lake was named for a Cherokee legend about a warrior who once crossed it in ten jumps, using the backs of giant turtles as stepping-stones. He had helped a great-uncle build a two-room hunting cabin there decades ago. The cabin was an odd creation made of timbers from an old yacht, with a chimney of smooth stones. One of the great-uncle's nieces had inherited the land and the cabin from him, but she lived in Minnesota, and we'd never met her.

Grandpa parked his truck behind a grove of thick green laurels, and we crept along the lake's edge. The cabin's broken-out windows and the black rectangle of its doorless doorway gaped at us.

"Is Roanie in there?" I whispered.

"Yep." Grandpa pointed. "He fishes for brim in the lake. I've seen him out a time or two, but I never let him know. This is our secret. Your grandma's the only other soul who knows. If he thinks we've found him, he might not come anymore."

I nodded. Then we went back to the truck, and Grandpa took out a cardboard box packed with food, and we left it on the lake bank in front of the laurels. Grandpa tore a sheet of paper from a notepad, and I wrote, "Roanie, it is okay to eat. My grandpa says don't worry. We won't tell. Your friend, Claire."

"If he trusts anybody, it's only you," Grandpa said.

When we went back the next day, the food was gone and the plastic serving containers were there, rinsed and stacked. I was so proud, I put long letters to Roanie in every box after that.

We left food every day for a month—Grandma Dottie's baked hams and roasted chickens, casseroles, and slabs of cakes and pies.

"Wherever the boy was hiding," Daddy mused after Big Roan

was released from jail and Roanie reappeared at school, "he looks like he lived off the land pretty well. I have to give him credit."

"You should, son. You should," Grandpa said.

CHRISTMAS in town was overwhelming and wildly uncoordinated and so bright it hurt my eyes, and I loved it. The ladies association ran the Christmas festival. On a Saturday night in December hundreds of people congregated in the square to listen to a church choir and watch a parade and the arrival of Santa and the lighting of the giant cedar tree beside the courthouse.

We Maloneys and Delaneys got there early and commandeered a whole street corner. I stood, warm in my wool coat in the crisp air, jostling excitedly against my brothers and cousins. I looked behind me for no particular reason and met Roanie's eyes. He was standing in the shadows under the tin awning of the dime store.

I was nine, short and plump. He was fourteen, tall and lanky. He looked ragged and grimy in faded jeans and a thin denim jacket. His shoulders were hunched against the night air.

I wormed my way unnoticed to the back of the crowd and leaned against an awning post. He studied me with a slight wariness in his mouth and silvery eyes. "Howdy, pardner," I drawled.

He could be the stillest human being, but it was the stillness of a cat watching a bird. I'm sure he weighed the consequences of speaking to a precocious little girl who had sadistic cousins and whose attention might get him in trouble with her overprotective parents and another two dozen righteous Maloneys.

"Funny little peep," he said eventually.

"So are you," I said back. "Funny *big* peep."

"Look like a red-haired elf."

My head barely reached the chest pocket on his jacket. "I'll grow."

He stared straight ahead. "Aw, you ain't too bad."

"You aren't either."

"Sure know how to scribble words."

I beamed at him.

The parade began. The big red fire truck crept by, with a dozen volunteer firemen sitting on top. They flung candy into the crowd. A bag of butterscotch drops bounced off my head, and Roanie caught it. He offered it to me. "Hit you first," he said.

"Huh? You caught it. It's yours. I don't like butterscotch." Which was a lie, but I wondered if that bag of candy was the only Christmas present he'd get. He shrugged, then carefully tucked the bag into his chest pocket.

"I can't see the parade," I said coyly. "Think I'll climb up on the windowsill."

"You'll fall off and bust something."

"Nah. I'll hold on to *you*." I grabbed his sleeve, and he stiffened. I clambered nimbly atop the wooden sill of the dime store's window. "Now don't move, and I won't fall."

"This ain't so funny. Get down and let go."

"It's okay. It's my idea."

At the front of the spectators I saw Mama search for me in the crowd. When she spotted me with Roanie, her eyes widened, and her mouth popped open, and she stared. She tapped Daddy on the shoulder, and he turned, too. I grinned at them. His red brows arched; then he rolled his eyes. Mama frowned hard. He took her by one arm, and they faced the parade again.

"See?" I chirped to Roanie. "Nobody minds."

After a moment he said darkly, "You don't know nothin'."

I thought I knew everything and started to tell him so, but the high school band marched by and drowned me out.

"You know what?" I said eventually, changing the subject. "You could cut some holly or mistletoe at the Hollow and bring it over to Mama, 'cause she uses it in her decorations, and she'd pay you with a box of homemade cookies."

"You don't know nothin'."

"You say that one more time, and I'll pull out all your hair!"

My threat was cut short by a collective gasp in the crowd. I heard someone yelp, "Oh, my gosh, somebody stop him."

Big Roan had joined the parade.

He limped up the middle of Main Street, apelike and huge in his plaid shirt and baggy overalls. His mouth was screwed down in sarcastic contempt. He staggered through the Girl Scout troop, waving a beer bottle. "Y'all want to see Santy Claus?" he bellowed. "I'll drop my pants, and y'all can kiss him on both cheeks!"

Then he threw the beer bottle. It hit a nervous horse on the rump. The horse bolted, the high school band split down the middle, and my cousin Aster toppled over with her tuba.

Daddy and some other men ran out into the street and grabbed Big Roan. He went down swinging and hit Daddy in the face.

I squealed with outrage and fear. Suddenly I realized that I was standing on the sidewalk, that Roanie had pulled me off the sill and set me there, and that I was by myself.

He'd melted into the shadows or evaporated from shame.

THE Atlanta newspapers and TV stations ran stories about the Dunderry Christmas parade. We were funny small-town mountain people. We were quaint. We were humiliated.

Daddy had a broken nose. Big Roan was sentenced to three months in jail. Cousin Vince, the sheriff, went after Roanie full-bore this time and caught him before he got to Ten Jumps. Uncle William signed the court order and sent him off to a state boys home. Aunt Bess told everyone it was a relief to know Roanie would be safe and well fed during Christmas. Some brands of kindness are hard to abide.

ROANIE came home finally, along with Big Roan. We heard Big Roan stayed down on Steckem Road with Daisy McClendon most of the time. That's why Aunt Dockey and Mama didn't go over there the next Easter. They sent Uncle Bert and Daddy to deliver the Easter baskets.

I don't know what kind of Easter Roanie had that spring. Hop and Evan saw him at school and said he was even more of a loner than before. I tried to talk Hop into giving him my Easter rabbit and a note, but Hop said he didn't want to be stuck in the family doghouse.

THAT SEPTEMBER I LEARNED that love is hard on a smile. It will knock your teeth right out.

Our whole clan went to almost every high school football game but especially to the first one of each autumn. That night was one of those delicious, barely past summer evenings when the warm air has spicy currents in it and the moon rises full and ripe over trees flecked with the first few hints of gold and red.

Along with related families—such as the O'Briens—Maloneys and Delaneys provided about half the team, plus a good portion of the cheerleading squad. The Dunderry High School stadium faced a football field ringed with a gray running track. Huge moths danced in the glow from the concession stand beyond the track's far turn.

It didn't take light to draw me down to the track. The lure of candy would do it. I was a moth after sugar. I flew with a small, flashy gang—we thought our wings were five feet wide and bright orange, but I'm sure to everyone else we were just giggling, nickel-size flutter-bys.

"I'm going to be a cheerleader when I get to high school," Rebecca announced as we sashayed along.

"Me, too," Violet chimed.

"Not me. I don't care," I said. Cheerleading was serious, regimented business. They would take away your pom-pom license if you improvised.

"I'm not gonna be a cheerleader." Tula Tobbler spoke up firmly. "I'm gonna be Alvin's manager. He's gonna be rich."

We all looked askance at Tula. Elfish, with skin the color of chocolate, she stared back at us from under a stiffly styled cap of black hair with bangs and curved-under ends.

A roar came up from the packed stadium behind us, and the band blared, and we all turned to watch an enormous, long-legged receiver spike the ball in the end zone.

Alvin Tobbler, Tula's brother, was the brightest football star, black or white, ever to carry a pigskin across green Dunderry grass. "See?" Tula said, grinning. "Alvin's gonna play for a big college, and then he's gonna play for the grown-up teams one day."

We all nodded solemnly and walked on. Next to the concession stand Tula and Alvin's grandpa worked at a small card table piled with apples—his way of cheering for Alvin.

Boss Tobbler was an apple man. His orchards stretched across stair-stepped hills outside town, and every Tobbler in the county worked for him in the autumn, harvesting and selling apples.

His first name really was Boss. He and Grandpa Joseph had hunted and fished together since they were boys. They both hated stupidity and meanness, and they were both as sweet as honey. Grandpa called him Boss T. Everybody else called him Mr. Tobbler.

A fantastic aroma rose from the apples and the melted caramel bubbling in a stewpot on a hot plate. A small crowd watched, awed, and as we sidled up to its edges, a familiar sense of awe settled on us, too.

Mr. Tobbler rolled the crank handle on an apple corer. Curlicues of red apple peel dropped to a mountain of apple peelings that climbed halfway up his pant legs. He popped the peeled apple from the corer's clamps, deftly sliced it into pieces with a sharp paring knife, spread the slices on a paper plate, and dribbled liquid caramel over them. Then he presented the plate to a waiting member of his audience, who tucked a dollar in a coffee can on the table.

"Granddaddy," Tula said, "will you fix us some candied apples?"

Mr. Tobbler nodded. "But I'm not gonna let y'all stand back like babies anymore." Hundreds of yellow jackets flitted around him, perching on his shirt and his hands. "Y'all know there's nothing to be afraid of. Fear is what stings. Come on. Come close."

Rebecca and Violet refused to budge, but I edged forward with Tula. Yellow jackets feathered our wrists; one sat on my forefinger. Though they never stung Mr. Tobbler, I expected to feel needle-hot stingers at any second.

"Now there, they know you got good hearts," Mr. Tobbler whispered as he handed us two filled plates. "They know you'll share with 'em." Victory! I sighed with relief as we backed away.

We said our thank-yous and dropped two dollars in the can because Mr. Tobbler donated the money to the booster club. And then we retreated. I popped a caramel-soaked slice of apple into my mouth and looked around to see who might be admiring me.

Roanie was standing on the hill above the concession stand.

I halted. Whether his gaze was admiring or not, I couldn't tell. At fourteen, he was as tall as a grown man and about as wide as a board. He was stuck with cast-off jeans and work shirts from the thrift shop; his enormous patched red flannel shirt looked like a tent.

"Why's he looking at you?" Rebecca whispered.

"He knows I'm not gonna sting him." Hypnotized, I climbed the hill toward him. Roanie straightened and frowned.

Rebecca called, "We better go tell your mama!" I glimpsed her and Violet and Tula take off toward the stadium.

"Get on back," Roanie called out, glancing around uncomfortably. His voice was deeper than I remembered from Christmas. "Git," he ordered firmly. "Little Peep, I don't want no trouble."

My heart broke. I stopped. "How come you're scared of me?"

"It ain't right, you chasin' after me," he said gruffly. "You're just a half-pint. You ain't got no idea how it looks. Go on."

"You're not so old!"

"Hey!" a voice called behind me. I turned. My cousin Carlton, a senior that year, big and fleshy, was glaring up the hill at us. A half dozen of his cronies were with him.

"Claire," Carlton yelled, "leave that white trash alone."

Nothing, no one, could have changed my mind then. I plowed uphill and planted myself beside Roanie.

Carlton raised his voice. "Leave that white *nigger* alone!"

Carlton uttered a word so petty and disreputable that it wasn't allowed in our house, not ever, for any reason.

"Get out of here, Claire." Roanie's voice was low, dangerous.

"But . . . but you *can't* let him call you names like that!"

What a little idiot I was, weighing my pride against his, not understanding what I added to his misery. Carlton suddenly strode up the hill. "I swear," he hissed at me, "at the rate you're going, you'll end up on Steckem Road with the McClendon whores."

He grabbed my arm, then shook it hard, just once.

Because then Roanie was on him, driving him down the hill. Carlton was falling, trying to punch back, yelling. If it had ended there and ended quickly, it would have been as brutally neat as a big dog snapping at a fly. But Carlton's slack-jawed friends joined in.

So there Roanie was, struggling inside a circle of swinging fists and knees, his head jerking back as a fist slammed into him. I couldn't wait for reinforcements. I launched myself down the hill, scrambled atop Carlton's bucking back, and sank my teeth into his neck. He squealed like a hog and shook me off.

I fell under the moving pistons of arms and legs, a hard shoe stepped on my hand, and then, as I tried to get up, Carlton drew back his fist and crashed it into my mouth.

I woke up with my head in Mama's lap, Mama yelling for Daddy to get ice, and blood streaming down my chin. I was dimly aware of a large crowd around us. Mama dabbed my lips with the hem of her skirt. I looked up into Grandma's calm blue eyes. "Marybeth," she said to my mother, "she's lost a couple of teeth."

Teeth? Something like hard pellets tickled the back of my throat. I retched onto Mama's lap, and two bloody specks fell out.

Grandma plucked my teeth up and wrapped them in a handkerchief. "They'll go back in," she promised Mama.

"Oh, her smile, her *smile!*" Mama cried. "When I get my hands on Roanie Sullivan—"

"Woanie!" That was the best pronunciation I could manage.

I saw him not far away, hunched on his knees, his arms braced on the ground in front of him. Grandpa and Mr. Tobbler squatted beside him, holding his shirttail to his mouth. Blood soaked it, falling in bright red splatters on his jeans. Inside the grimace of his lips I saw the dark gap where his snaggletooth had been.

"Your toof," I said sadly. Half fainting and hurting from the nose down, I opened my mouth and showed him my gap. "Woanie dida dah anythang wong," I announced loudly. "Carltoh dah it."

Mama wrapped her arms around me. "Hush, honey, hush."

Daddy ran up, dropped to his heels, and thrust a paper cup filled with ice into Mama's hands. His eyes flashed furiously.

"Dathy," I begged, "Carltoh started it. He knoffed me in tha mouf."

Daddy pivoted toward Roanie. "You tell me why you got my daughter into a brawl, or I'll break what's left of you."

"Son, back off," Grandpa ordered. "It wasn't Roanie's fault. It was Carlton's. Boss T saw the whole thing."

Daddy sat back. "That right, Mr. Tobbler?"

Mr. Tobbler barked out the truth. "That Carlton, he punched your little girl in the mouth. Did it deliberately, too. Holt Maloney, you want to break heads, go break your nephew's."

I felt Mama catch her breath. She and Daddy looked at Roanie. Daddy lifted a hand toward him. "I . . . I . . . Listen, boy, I—"

Roanie shrugged away, tried to get up, but sat down, clamping one hand across his ribs. "None of you got to worry about Claire when I'm around. I ain't gonna hurt her. I know what you been thinkin', but I wouldn't a-laid a hand on nobody, 'cept Carlton was hurtin' her. I . . . I won't let nothin' bad happen to her. Not ever."

He tried to get up again. He couldn't without help. Daddy took him by one arm, Grandpa by the other. Help was what he got, whether he wanted it or not.

That warm night Roanie began to be part of my family.

We were taken to my uncle Mallory Delaney's office—the doctor. Nothing wrong with me except busted teeth and some bruised fingers; nothing wrong with Roanie except a busted tooth and a cracked rib. Then, at Uncle Cully Maloney's office—the dentist—my two teeth were painfully cemented back in place, and Roanie's gap was measured for a permanent bridge.

Finally, we took Roanie under our own roof at the farm. Mama put him in a spare bedroom. Daddy tried to phone Big Roan but couldn't find him—he was off drinking somewhere.

There was a haunted, awestruck glimmer in Roanie's eyes that night. It wasn't easy for him to trust good luck or Maloneys. In the morning his window was open, and Roanie was gone.

I took a strong leap of faith myself and told Mama and Daddy about Ten Jumps. Daddy and Sheriff Vince caught him there.

"I'M SORRY," I HEARD SHERIFF Vince tell Mama and Daddy that night. "I caught him, and I've got a job to do as sheriff. He just can't run around loose anymore. Big Roan doesn't want to take responsibility for him, and there's nowhere for the boy to go."

"Bring him here," Daddy said. "We'll take him in."

Faith. It had worked. I was awestruck.

"Holt, I won't have that boy around Claire!" I heard Mama from my vantage point outside the living room's closed oak double doors. "We still don't know much about him. Claire has some kind of foolish crush on him. What if he's a pervert?"

"Then he'll be a *dead* pervert," Daddy answered firmly. There was a long silence punctuated by Mama's sniffling sounds. I peered through the crack between the doors and saw Daddy hugging her. Then he said, "If I thought there was anything sinister about the boy, Marybeth, I wouldn't let him set a foot on the place."

"What're we going to say to the family?"

"Don't visit the sins of the father on the son. That's what we'll say. Roanie can't help what he comes from. I feel bad for the boy."

They talked on, Daddy's voice low and serious, Mama's calm or resigned. Finally Mama said, "All right, Holt. But I'm going to figure out some way to clean the boy up. Start with the outside and work my way in."

I gasped. This was unbelievable. This was wonderful. This would split the responsibility for Roanie between me and Mama and Daddy, because what they'd offered would upset every Maloney and Delaney in the county.

"CLAIRE, Claire, what do you look so worried about?" Mama asked that night as she sat beside me on my pink-ruffled bed.

"Mama, Roanie isn't a pervert."

"Somebody," Mama said darkly, "was listening outside the living-room doors."

"I know he'll do fine. Big Roan can't take him back, can he?"

Mama looked at me sadly. "Big Roan said he doesn't care where Roanie lives as long as Roanie sends him some money."

A mixture of sorrow and relief burst from me in a long breath. "Big Roan never wanted him. But I do!"

"When Roanie gets here," Mama said slowly, eyeing me, "I expect you to treat him the same way you treat your brothers."

I whooped. Brother, my hind foot, I thought, but didn't say it. She looked at me with a troubled expression in her blue eyes, one hand stroking the tiny gray streak in the swath of hair splayed over the shoulder of her silk robe. She had Delaney hair, glossy brown, fine and straight, and she wore it pulled back with headbands or tiny barrettes. She was deceptively delicate-looking, like her mother, and loved delicate things. She always wore a pair of diamond-stud earrings Daddy had given her, even when she was dressed in jeans and an old T-shirt, digging in her flower beds or herb garden.

"Claire," she said finally, gently, "what is it you see in him?"

"He's my project. He's different. So am I."

"How are you different?"

"I gotta move all the time. I gotta think. Everybody else is like, 'Well, that's just the way things are.' But *why* are things one way and not the other? Why are there so many rules?"

"So decent people can live together in peace."

"Why? We've got lots of peace around here."

Mama sighed and smoothed the backs of her fingers down my cheek. "You're a very pretty little girl. You're a *perfect* little girl, and before long you'll be a perfect young lady. And I want you to grow up that way and go to college and get a perfect job and marry a perfect man and have perfect babies. Now that's a good row to hoe, and it's a straight row, and you can't look away from it for a minute."

"You think I wanta marry Roanie? Ugh! I don't want to marry anybody! I don't even want to *kiss* a boy!"

"Okay." She smiled. "That's fine with me."

"So don't worry about me liking Roanie *that* way. I just think we can hoe along together."

That set her back. She rubbed her jaw and sighed. Then she looked at me solemnly. "He's hoeing in a whole separate garden." She kissed me good night and turned out the light.

I dreamed fitfully. Hoes. Rows. Gardens. Roanie.
He was coming to live with us. That was all that mattered.

DADDY and Grandpa went up to town the next morning and got
Roanie out of jail. When I spotted Daddy's car from my writing
roost in the loft of the main barn, I nearly fell off the loft stairs hurrying to get down. Roanie eased out of the car and stood defensively
at the end of the dirt drive between the front fields.

I ran out of the barn as Mama strode from the house. Daddy and
Grandpa nudged Roanie forward, but he stopped under our oak
trees, looking grim and uncertain. I planted myself beside Daddy
and looked at Roanie squarely. But he refused to look at me.

"If you live in my house," Mama said, "you live by my rules."

Roanie cleared his throat. "Y'all paid for the doctor, paid for my
tooth. Now I gotta live here. But I ain't gonna take no charity."

"All right," Mama said. "How are you going to pay us back?"

"I . . . I'll work for you. Anything you want."

Daddy looked at Roanie. "You'll stay in school, you'll do chores
just like Claire and my boys, and you'll work like a field hand. And
I'll pay you a salary. You'll earn your keep."

I searched Roanie's face desperately. He looked stunned.

"Well?" Daddy said.

"Yeah. Yes, sir. You bet. Sure. Thanks."

I saw a smidgen of real satisfaction in Roanie's eyes. I waved him
toward our house. "I *knew* you'd be welcome," I bellowed.

The expression in his eyes was half tragic, half hopeful.

Mama gave him a bedroom downstairs, next to Hop's and Evan's
rooms. She told him he'd share the bathroom across the hall with
them. Clean up after himself, wash the tub, the same as them.

Before he set up housekeeping, I left a little wicker basket on his
bed, with a bottle of bubble bath in it and two of my personal
soaps, which were shaped and smelled like rosebuds. It was my last
chance to go into his room. I'd been forbidden to hang out there,
the same as if he were a brother.

When Roanie came to dinner, he was suddenly sparklingly clean.

He'd cut his hair, and his cheeks looked as if he'd scrubbed them nearly raw. He also had a rose scent.

He sat across from me at the dining-room table, stiff, quiet, his gray eyes alert and amazed. He handled the white stoneware dishes—which were just everyday china—as if breaking a piece would send him straight to hell.

I learned later that the water pipes to his daddy's trailer had frozen and burst one winter, years before, and Big Roan never fixed them. Instead he'd slapped together a wooden outhouse behind the trailer. Big Roan didn't have a washing machine, either, and he'd been barred from the Laundromat in town.

So I finally knew the reason for Roanie's shameful appearance and bad odor. That night I sat guiltily in my warm bubble bath in my personal boudoir, thinking about all he'd been through.

If cleanliness was next to godliness, Roanie wanted us to know he'd christened himself.

EVERY year I made the mistake of naming the newborn calves and making pets of them. I always picked a favorite, and the next year, without fail, we ate him. My bad luck was uncanny.

That fall the future contents of our meat freezer was a steer I called Herbert. Herbert the Hereford.

I knew, of course, that the cute red-and-white Hereford bull calves had one purpose—to grow up, grow fat, be castrated, and be killed before their meat turned tough. Either we ate them, or someone else would. If Daddy sold them, they were loaded into huge stock trucks and disappeared forever.

Herbert was like all of our castrated bovines—placid and unsuspecting, with dark, gentle eyes. When he was young, I'd fed him special formula from a bottle. I'd laugh and tell him, "Herbert, you're gonna taste good." Because I admitted that after Herbert was dead, I'd stop thinking of him as Herbert. He'd become a steak.

Then came Herbert's execution day. I was grief-stricken. I hid in the loft of the main barn and cried my eyes out.

Roanie found me up there, lying flat on my stomach between

pyramids of baled hay, my head buried in my arms. I sat up quickly, wiped my eyes, and looked at Roanie sadly. "Daddy's fixin' to shoot Herbert. I can't watch."

"I figured that. Grandpa Maloney told me that's why you went running out here. I told him I better keep you company."

"Thank you."

"I gotta go down in a minute. To help with the skinnin'."

"Yeah. Me, too."

"You, too?"

My mouth trembled, but I shrugged. "I'm not a sissy."

He nodded solemnly. "Yeah. I know."

I studied Roanie carefully. "You go hunting?"

"Yeah. I don't much like to."

"Then why do you?"

He didn't answer right away. Then, "Got used to it. It was better than eatin' cereal and bologna sandwiches all the time."

The distant pop of Daddy's pistol threw me down on the floor again. I pressed my hands to my ears. "Herbert," I moaned.

Roanie stroked my hair gently. "Herbert didn't feel no pain," he offered in a low voice. "So I'd say he had it pretty good."

Roanie had a low standard for happiness. All he asked was that things not hurt.

DADDY loaned him a deer rifle, and Roanie went hunting with Evan and Hop, and he shot a sixteen-point buck at dawn in the woods of Old Shanty Pass.

That buck made him a celebrity. To deer hunters, bagging a sixteen-point rack of antlers—which means there are eight prongs on either side—is like bringing home the crown jewels.

A parade of men and boys stopped by our farm to gaze longingly at the giant spread on the buck's glassy-eyed head, which sat in a place of honor on a workbench outside the barn. Uncle Cully arrived shortly, his expression mournful and awed as he examined the buck's head. Uncle Cully had twenty deer heads on the wall of the waiting room at his dental office. He loved deer heads even more than he loved teeth. "Oh, that's beautiful," he said to Roanie as he caressed the buck's antlers.

Roanie looked at Uncle Cully. "Will it pay the bill for my tooth?"

Uncle Cully's mouth fell open. "Your bill's been paid."

"I know. Will you give Mr. Maloney his money back?"

"You don't have to do that," Daddy said, frowning. "I said you could pay me out a little every week from your salary."

"This tooth thing'll take me forever. I want to get done with it."

Daddy studied him shrewdly. "Don't like to be in anybody's debt, hmmm? All right. I respect that. Cully, is it a deal?"

"Oh, Lord, *yes,*" Uncle Cully replied. Five minutes later he left with the buck's head in his trunk.

That prize rack of antlers had served its purpose.

"I give the boy credit," Mama said that night with no small amount of respect in her voice. "He knows what he wants."

I felt proud. Roanie was always smarter than anyone but me expected. He was the only person I've ever known who got Uncle Cully to fix a tooth for one buck.

Three

GRANDMOTHER Elizabeth and Great-Gran Alice weren't afraid of Roanie like some of my relatives were. They weren't afraid of anything except each other's opinion.

On a frosty Saturday not long before Thanksgiving, Roanie was thrust into the middle of the granny wars. It started at breakfast. Our family meals, even the most ordinary ones, were crowded events, and breakfast was eaten at the long oak table in the center of the kitchen, which was a kingdom of its own, big and sunny and cluttered, with squeaking wood floors and tall white cabinets. The basic group that morning included me, Roanie, Hop, Evan, Mama and Daddy, Grandpa and Grandma Maloney—who often walked over for meals—and, of course, Grandmother Elizabeth and Great-Gran Alice.

We were contentedly eating a huge country breakfast of sausage and fried eggs, biscuits, gravy, and slices of cantaloupe. I was sleepy, still wearing my pajamas and robe, as I sat between Grandmother Elizabeth and Great-Gran Alice. One of my duties was to pass platters of food between them so we could avoid their having to utter even a single word to each other.

"I'm going shopping today," Great-Gran announced suddenly. "I'm going to Atlanta. I'm going to Rich's."

This was not a request. It was a decision. Someone would be pressed into chauffeur service for the four-hour round-trip drive.

Grandmother Elizabeth piped up. "I believe I'll go as well."

Forks stopped moving. Coffee cups and juice glasses halted midway to lips. Roanie was the only one who didn't understand. But he stopped eating, too, and watched warily.

Great-Gran arched a white brow. "I didn't invite you, *Elizabeth.*"

"Mawmaw, I'll take you next week," Mama assured her mother.

Grandmother Elizabeth dabbed her eyes with a napkin. She could turn her tears on and off like a lawn sprinkler. "How will I do my Christmas shopping if everyone shuffles me aside until it suits their mood? I can't depend on my strength to hold out." A single tear trickled down her soft white cheek.

Great-Gran pursed her lips. "Quit sniffling."

Grandpa held up both hands. "Mother," he said to Great-Gran, "I'd rather cut off my own two paws than hear any more of this."

"*She* started it, Joseph."

Grandmother Elizabeth snapped to attention. "I most certainly *am* going shopping today. I'll take Claire to carry my packages."

I felt afraid to move.

"I'm taking Claire to carry *my* packages," Great-Gran said.

Grandmother shot back, "Since you're too ancient to drive us to Atlanta, *Alice,* I don't see how you can be in charge."

"It's *my* car. Carry your own damn packages."

"I don't wish to be cramped in your small uncomfortable car. It reeks of that vile tea-rose perfume you wear." Grandmother Elizabeth smiled around the table. "Now, who shall drive us?"

Excuses gushed out. Daddy and Grandpa had to go to Gainesville. Mama had to puree five bushels of apples for apple butter. But Grandma Dottie was caught without escape. She couldn't think fast enough. "I, well, I . . . hmmm," she began.

"You're not busy, daughter-in-law," Great-Gran proclaimed. "You can drive us. I'm so sorry Elizabeth butted in. If you can't stand her company, we can tie her to the luggage rack."

"I'm not the annoying old nanny goat in this family," Grandmother Elizabeth replied tartly. "We all know who that is."

"All right, all *right.* Hush, both of you," Grandma Dottie said in disgusted defeat. "I'll go. I'll drive. But hush!"

Grandpa tried to rescue her. "Well, y'all can't go to Atlanta today anyhow. I'm not gonna let y'all traipse off down there without me or Holt or one of the boys to go along. It's not safe anymore."

"There's our solution," Grandmother Elizabeth announced, gesturing toward Roanie. "Not a soul will bother poor, decrepit Alice with that brawny young knight by our sides. He can go."

Run, I mouthed to Roanie. He looked at me, puzzled.

But it was too late.

RICH'S department store in downtown Atlanta was a dream castle, a social touchstone for generations. You could furnish your whole house there. The grand, massive, dignified store was beginning to lose its luster when I was a girl, but it still had years to go before everyone agreed that no one shopped there anymore.

Grandma Dottie parked her big gas-guzzling station wagon and locked it. We were alone in the shadowy concrete womb of the store's parking decks, a vulnerable troop walking slowly, Grandmother Elizabeth tottering along with her cane and Great-Gran moving with the heavy-footed pace of sore knee joints.

A subtle but intense change had come over Roanie. I'm sure

Daddy and Grandpa Maloney had told him that his job was to protect the family's womankind. He scanned the dimly lit parking lanes and looked gracefully threatening, so quiet and controlled.

A shiver ran down my spine. I wasn't just scared of the parking deck, of muggers and rapists and all the other human monsters who lived in cities, according to every account I'd heard at home. No. I was a little scared of Roanie and strangely giddy inside—it was a confusing mixture, somehow involved with being female.

When we were finally inside the store, breathing in its scents, taking in its safe, nicely dressed people and beautiful merchandise, I still watched Roanie and felt, somehow, that trouble was brewing.

We were in men's accessories when it happened.

The Old Grannies settled into their standard shopping routine. Grandma Dottie convinced a salesman to drag a pair of chairs from a dressing room so that Great-Gran and Grandmother could sit while we presented merchandise to them for their appraisal.

Grandma Dottie smartly stationed them at opposite sides of the department; then, sighing, she escaped to the rest room for a few minutes, leaving Roanie and me on duty. Back and forth we went, ferrying neckties, driving gloves, pullover sweaters, and colognes.

There were only a few other shoppers in the department. The ones I noticed most were a well-dressed couple with a skittish blond boy who was maybe four years old. His daddy had a sharp, impatient look that set my teeth on edge. "Be careful!" he snapped at the woman as she helped him try on a tweed jacket. "You caught the lining on my watch." The woman smiled too quickly and apologized. I couldn't imagine Daddy speaking to Mama that way or her giving him a meek look if he had.

The harried salesman fawned over the man and followed the little boy around, straightening the clothes he dislodged. And when the salesman wasn't trying to baby-sit, he dogged Roanie's footsteps, frowning at him, even though Roanie wasn't doing a thing.

Roanie's expression grew darker every second. I couldn't figure out what was going on until Grandmother Elizabeth crooked a finger at the clerk. He went over and bent down, oozing attentive

charm, and I heard her whisper, "Dear young man, if you're worried about shoplifting, I advise you to stop following my helpers
and concentrate on that elderly lady across the way. She's quite
senile and has a habit of hiding merchandise in her coat pockets."

The salesman's jaw fell open. I was furious. So he thought Roanie
might steal something. He wandered toward Great-Gran. I stepped
in front of him and said angrily, "My grannies are crazy, but they
don't steal. And neither does my . . . my *boy*."

The clerk wiped his glistening forehead. "I should never have
quit bartending school," he said, and then he went over to the
cologne counter and shuffled invoices. I think he gave up.

Grandma Dottie returned. I filled her in on the situation—
Grandmother trying to cause trouble for Great-Gran, the salesman
making Roanie feel like a thief. She shut her eyes for a second, then
said, "Let's get done and go *home*. I have a headache."

What happened next happened so fast.

The little blond boy scooted past us. His mama called softly,
"Jimmy, honey, slow down," and then the daddy snared the little
boy by his shirt collar. "I told you to stay out of the way," the man
said loudly. And then he shook the boy, drew back one of his hands,
and slapped his son hard in the face.

The blow tumbled the little guy backward, and he fell. He curled
up, sobbing, on the carpeted floor.

I stared in unabashed shock. I'd never seen anything like this—
this sudden and untempered violence against a small child.

Grandma Dottie laid a hand on my shoulder. I could feel her
trembling, and when I looked up at her, she was staring at the man
with the compressed fury of a slow-burning firecracker.

The kid's mama gathered him up and glanced around, blushing,
avoiding our eyes. "Take him somewhere," the man told her.
"You're in charge of him. I can't shop with him underfoot."

"I'm sorry," his wife murmured. "He's just tired."

The man noticed us watching him. "You have nothing better to
look at?" he snapped.

"Nothing worse," Grandma Dottie answered stiffly.

He turned his back and flipped through a rack of dress shirts. His wife carried the little boy away. His whimpers faded slowly.

"I saw it," Great-Gran said behind us. "It was an abomination."

"I saw it first," Grandmother Elizabeth added. "Any man who treats his child that way should be horsewhipped."

They stood there alongside Grandma Dottie, muttering and slinging darts at the man's back with their gazes, but they didn't *do* anything, and I was locked in my own steaming, silent world of unanswerable questions. Why couldn't we do something? Shouldn't we say something? Tell somebody?

It happened so fast. Violence is easy; justice is hard. Roanie, accustomed to one but not the other, strode across the aisle and shoved the man on the shoulder. "You s.o.b.," he said.

"Hey," the man said, stepping back. "I don't have to take this."

"How'd you like it if somebody slapped you?"

"Don't threaten me, hillbilly."

Roanie hit him. Punched him right in the jaw. The man fell against a rack of pin-striped suits and sank between two of them.

"Hit him again, Roanie!" I yelled.

The salesman ran over, his mouth gaping. "Cool it, kid," he said, keeping his distance from Roanie. "I've called security!"

Oh, *no.* I switched from attack to retreat. Pushing Roanie was like pushing a brick wall. I plowed into his chest like a bulldozer, then looked up at him pleadingly.

"Don't you never hit your kid again," Roanie hurled over my head at the man. "It ain't right. It ain't fair."

"Assault," the man groaned. "I'll have you arrested."

A pair of security guards ran up. I latched my arms around Roanie's waist and held on to him. I wanted to cloak him, to make him invisible. *I know why he's like this. Big Roan hit him that way. When he was too little to hit back. And no one did anything to stop it.*

"Call the police," Grandmother Elizabeth piped up. "We'll just see who's arrested. I'll tell them exactly what happened."

"So will I," Great-Gran said loudly. "Let's get the law in on this. I saw a grown man knock a baby five feet across the floor."

"Oh, yes, I certainly saw that, too," said Grandmother Elizabeth. "We're in perfect agreement."

I think the world stopped turning.

TO MAKE a long story short, the man quit muttering about having Roanie arrested when the Old Grannies launched into the full story of why Roanie had hit him. The salesman confirmed their account. The store's security guards scowled and shifted their feet, obviously wishing we'd all just go away. Finally they let us.

And we got out of there. It wasn't dignified, it wasn't much of a victory, not with me sealed to Roanie's side and holding on to him like a vise, Grandma Dottie pushing us, and the Old Grannies bringing up the rear in slow tandem.

I couldn't change the future for a little blond boy any more than I could change the past for Roanie. All I had was the satisfaction of his long arm curled around me, our togetherness in trouble, and the righteous support of two very old grannies and one younger one.

Grandmother and Great-Gran discussed the fight with great relish all the way home. They sat in the back seat of the car close together. I sat in front between Grandma Dottie and Roanie. I had to know something. I whispered to him, "If some, uh, criminal tried to get me, what would you do to him?"

He didn't so much as bat an eyelash. "I'd try to kill him."

I wound my chubby, determined fingers through his and held on. His skin was sweaty and cold. I didn't realize it then, but he was scared sick that he'd get sent away for what he'd done.

Of course, that didn't happen. Daddy lectured him on the consequences of settling arguments with his fists, but it was a mild lecture. And then Mama sat him down at the kitchen table and wrapped the swollen knuckles of his right hand in a towel packed with ice and insisted he stay put while we set the table for dinner.

Hop and Evan came in—they wanted every detail of the Rich's fight. Roanie still looked as if he expected to be electrocuted.

"You're a hero," I blurted out. "Heroes have to get admired."

He drew back instinctively. "But I didn't *change* nothin'."

"You tried," Grandma Dottie said firmly. "Which is more than we had the gumption to do. And I want to apologize to you for not doing more sooner. About similar matters. All right?"

The world is spanned by small bridges between people. Roanie had crossed another one.

STILL, Roanie didn't know his place yet; he had been pulled up by the roots too many times. There was a lot of talk about place in my family. It was no small matter to know your place in the world. A place at the table. I mean a sense of belonging. A place in a family. A place on the land. A place in the heart.

Roanie had a place in our family, but he needed something else. I couldn't decide what it was until the day Grandpa took us up to Dunshinnog Mountain to gather mistletoe.

Dunshinnog towered over the eastern edge of our valley like the king of all mountains. Maloneys had owned it since the very first pioneer land-grant years. Dunshinnog wasn't valuable farmland, like the valley. You could only look at it and love it.

The mountaintop was wide and almost level, with a natural meadow at one end. We skirted patches of pine trees that stair-stepped down the easiest side, the west, where some long-dead Maloneys had once built terraced pastures for cattle. Otherwise the mountain was covered in old hardwood forest, and each spring we gazed up at its white clouds of dogwood blooms and then the pinkish clusters of laurel. In autumn it blazed with red and gold. In the early winter, when Roanie, Grandpa, and I went there, Dunshinnog was a spartan world of somber gray.

"Tell Roanie how the mountain was named," I said to Grandpa during the long hike.

Grandpa grinned. "The sidhe are in charge up there."

"Irish fairies," I explained to Roanie, who didn't dare laugh.

"The sidhe helped foxes slip down into the valley at night to steal Maloney hens," Grandpa went on with grand drama. "And the foxes were good at it, too, because the fairies put gloves on their paws so no people could hear 'em sneak in or out of the chicken coops." Grandpa raised his stubby hands and wiggled his fingers. "Every night the fairies would take the blooms off the flowers and put 'em on the foxes' paws, and when the foxes came home to the mountain every morning, the fairies put the blooms back on the stems, so a person could never catch on to the magic."

"Foxgloves," I interjected helpfully. "That's how come foxglove flowers are called foxgloves."

"My great-grandparents knew the only smart thing to do was honor the fairies and the foxes." Grandpa finished with a majestic nod: "So they named the mountain Dun-sionnach-sidh, which is Irish for the 'fortress of the foxes and fairies.' "

"But that big name was a mouthful," I told Roanie solemnly. "So it ended up being Dunshinnog. There. What d'ya think?"

Roanie mulled it all over. If he'd laughed, he'd have lost a lot of ground in Maloney territory. "Makes sense to me," he said.

THE green mistletoe hung in the tops of the tallest trees like remnants of forgotten summer. Grandpa pulled a sawed-off shotgun from his backpack, and he and Roanie took turns shooting into the branches. Clumps of mistletoe fell. We stuffed most of it into a sack, but I kept a sprig for myself.

I held up my personal commission in mistletoe. I had traditions, too. "I've got a smooch craving," I announced.

Grandpa laughed. He bent down, and I held the mistletoe over his head and kissed his cheek, and he kissed mine. Then I looked at Roanie. I just knew I had to kiss him, too. "Com'ere."

He shifted uncomfortably.

"Get it over with," Grandpa said, laughing harder. "It's something Claire has to do every year."

Roanie dropped to his heels. My hand shook. I held the mistletoe above his dark hair and quickly pecked his jaw. His skin was so warm. "Now you gotta do me," I ordered in a small reedy voice. He'd never kissed me before, and I wasn't certain he'd do it then.

He turned his face toward me. His winter-gray eyes met mine for an instant. Then he brushed his lips across my forehead.

I felt as if I were on fire and I could fly.

"Let's take in the view," Grandpa said. He led us through a meadow to a smooth shelf of silver-gray granite. The world as I knew it was spread out below us—the Maloney fields and pastures, our big house with its wide porches and triple chimneys, our barns and long, low chicken houses.

"This is a good place," Roanie said gruffly. "This is above everybody. Yeah. I can believe there's magic up here."

Grandpa performed the little ceremony his own grandpa had taught him. He took an Irish pennywhistle from the pocket of his shirt, fitted the tip in his mouth, and played "Amazing Grace."

The sweet, haunting song surrounded us and was picked up by the wind. Goosebumps crept up my arms. *I once was lost but now am found, was blind but now I see.* Roanie's eyes gleamed, his lips parted in absolute wonder.

He became, on that mountaintop, a boy who found magic and history, who joined a tradition that could fill empty places deep in his heart. Dunshinnog was our special place from then on.

I REACHED a new level of self-control that Christmas. I was always the first one up on Christmas morning, *always,* and my first act was to fly downstairs in my nightgown and robe and fuzzy pink slippers, when the house was filled with magical, expectant silence. I would open the double doors to the living room and slip inside alone.

But this time I hurried downstairs and tiptoed along the back hall to Roanie's door. I knocked softly until he finally opened it.

"What's wrong?" he asked in sleepy confusion.

"Nothing. It's *Christmas.* Come on!" I whispered urgently.

"Hold on. I gotta get dressed."

"No, no, no. Nobody gets dressed right away on Christmas." I peered through the opening at him, eager to see what kind of pajamas he slept in. I saw the frayed neck of a gray sweatshirt. Below it I saw bleach-stained gray sweatpants, a hole in one knee. "You look swell," I swore. "Come *on.* We don't have much time."

Frowning, he slipped down the hall behind me. I led him to the doors to the living room. "Now watch," I whispered. Holding my breath, I turned the long brass handles and eased the doors open.

It was like looking through a mirror into wonderland.

Glowing and winking with lights, the Christmas tree shimmered next to the fireplace, where a low fire crackled. The brightly wrapped presents stacked around the tree's base by mere mortals had mushroomed into a bonanza during the night. That whole corner of the room burst with packages. The soft voices of some Christmas choir purred from the stereo receiver.

I heard Roanie's quick intake of breath behind me. I looked up at him hopefully, and the expression on his face was open and easy.

"I never thought I'd see nothing like this. 'Cept on TV." He edged into the room with me.

"Oh, it's real," I said. "I get to open one present before everybody else 'cause I get up first. So you get to open one of yours, too."

He stared at me as if I were joking. "I got presents?"

"Of *course.*" I shuffled over to the tree and pushed the stacks aside, then popped up with a deep rectangular box wrapped in red foil paper and topped with a gold bow. "This is from me."

I held it out anxiously. He was absolutely still for a second; then he angled carefully behind the tree and dropped to his heels. When he stood, he held a tiny box wrapped in green paper.

"I got this for you," he said in an offhand way.

I felt as warm as a light on the Christmas tree. "Gimme."

We traded, then sat down side by side on the hearth. "Open yours first," I ordered.

He was so careful with the paper on his gift, not wanting to tear it, I guess. He opened the box and took out the blue pullover sweater I'd gotten him. He examined it tenderly, uncertainly drawing his fingers over the thick cable knit.

"No moth holes," he said. "Smells new. I like it."

He donned the sweater over his sweatshirt. He looked bulky but fine. "I was gonna get you something fun," I said. "Like a hunting knife or something. But Grandma Dottie said you'd like this." I sighed. "Clothes aren't much fun, though."

"It's the first *new* anything I ever got, Claire. It's great. Now open yours."

I ripped the paper and bow off the tiny box on my lap and flipped the top off. Inside lay an enameled green shamrock pendant about the size of a dime. It hung from a thin gold chain.

"Oh!" I loved jewelry the way squirrels love nuts. Mama limited my collection; otherwise I'd have decked myself out in every dime-store bauble my allowance could provide. "It's beautiful!"

I put the necklace on, then closed one hand over the shamrock. "It's the very *best* Christmas present I've ever gotten." I looked at Roanie, my heart racing. "I love you."

"Shh," he said, glancing around as if we weren't alone. "I know how you mean it, but nobody else would."

"Say it back to me anyhow. Say it."

"I don't think it's a good idea to say it."

"Just say it's forever."

He looked at me. "It's forever," he admitted softly.

THE day was a whirl of visitors. Roanie watched from the corners, absorbing it all with the quiet intensity of an animal that had been caged too long to step out quickly just because someone opened a door for him. Then, on New Year's Eve, I heard the deep voices of my brothers Josh and Brady in the hall. They were home from college for the holidays. Smelling intrigue like a mouse smells cheese, I went over to my door and cracked it open an inch, then listened.

"Did you see the look in his eyes? When Dad told him about talking to Aunt Bess and Uncle Billy? I was sure he was about to bolt before Dad explained why they were filing court papers."

"Well, the kid's tough."

"Mama says he'd fight tigers to protect Claire. She's right."

"Hey, listen to the way the Old Grannies talk about him. I think they've got a crush on him, too."

"Yeah. What a gas."

Roanie. They were discussing Roanie. I popped out of my room and stared at them. "What's going on?" I demanded.

Josh and Brady traded careful adult glances. I gave them a dirty look and ran downstairs, my heart in my throat.

Mama and Daddy were sitting at the kitchen table, their faces serious. I halted. "What's going on with Roanie?"

Daddy waved me over and curled an arm around me. "We made sure Roanie's never going back to the Hollow. It's permanent, sugar."

"You mean Roanie can live here forever?"

Daddy studied me. "That's what I mean, sweetie pie."

I ran outside. Roanie was out in a back pasture, sitting on a knoll. "You're permanent!" I said, flopping down beside him.

"Ain't that something," he said, his eyes glowing.

I touched his arm carefully. "I love you, boy."

"I love you, too," he said. "Don't tell nobody."

Four

THE Great Monopoly Game of February established what I'd suspected for a long time— when it came to land and money, Roanie was as flint-eyed as any Maloney or Delaney.

All of the Atlanta TV weathermen said it was too warm for an ice storm, but Grandpa Maloney knew better. "It'll be icier than an Eskimo's nose hairs," he warned as Daddy and Mama loaded Great-Gran Alice and Grandmother Elizabeth into the car that Saturday morning for a trip to Atlanta. The Old Grannies were determined to see Carol Channing in the road show of *Hello, Dolly!* They'd have crossed the Arctic in a dogsled to see Carol Channing.

"We'll be back before the roads close," Daddy said. "I'd rather risk frostbite than tell the Old Grannies Carol Channing's a no-go."

And off they went. Roanie and I stayed home with Grandpa and

Grandma Maloney, and just as Grandpa predicted, by four o'clock the farm was covered in a white crystalline layer of sleet, and the state patrol had closed all the roads. Daddy called and said that he, Mama, and the Old Grannies were stuck at a hotel for the night.

I couldn't have been happier. The electricity went out shortly after dark. We ate some sandwiches. Grandpa went to sleep in the recliner with a blanket wrapped around him. Grandma lit a pair of kerosene lamps on the library table, cracked her knuckles, and asked slyly, "Who's ready for a game of Monopoly?"

"Not me," I said. "She's a shark," I whispered to Roanie.

Roanie was great at Monopoly. He always won Hop's and Evan's money. "I'll play," he said with a wicked smile.

So Grandma and Roanie sat across from each other at the table, the Monopoly board spread out like a battlefield, the light of the fire and lamps flickering on their steely eyes. "She never loses," I murmured from a couch. Then I fell asleep.

When I woke up, shivering, it was early morning. The fire was out, the lamps were out, and Grandpa was snoring.

"One more game," I heard Grandma say hoarsely. "Best four out of five. You can't quit now. I deserve a rematch."

I blinked. Huddled at the table, bleary-eyed, Roanie looked at Grandma. "I'm so sleepy I can't even find Park Place anymore," he croaked. "Give it up, Miz Dottie. You can't beat me."

"You're a fair businessman, Roanie Sullivan. Don't begrudge me one more rematch. Here's my deal. If you keep playing, I'll explain high-yield bonds again."

His head bobbed. "Okay," he murmured.

Grandma made him drink two cups of coffee. They played Monopoly until Grandpa woke up and we had to go outside to feed the livestock. Then she made Roanie play some more.

When Mama and Daddy and the Old Grannies got home that afternoon, they found Roanie asleep on the floor and Grandma asleep on the couch. Both of them were clutching Monopoly money.

We all agreed: Anybody who shut out Grandma Maloney at Monopoly was destined for great things.

I WAS DESTINED FOR GREATNESS, too, I decided. I planned a great leap forward into the publishing world beyond my small fame as the 4-H Club correspondent for the Dunderry *Weekly Shamrock*.

WE WANT YOUR HOMETOWN STORIES, said the headline in one of Mama's magazines, the kind that told ladies how to make a perfect custard and have shapely thighs. The magazine offered fifty bucks. Fifty bucks! Why, I was full of stories.

I secretly tapped out five pages, single-spaced, on my typewriter. Using as many adjectives as I could find in the big leather-bound thesaurus in the living room, I related how Roanie shot a deer to pay Uncle Cully. I threw in asides about Grandpa shooting Japanese soldiers and Daddy shooting my beloved Herbert. My theme, I decided, was that people in my hometown felt sad every time they shot something. Therefore we were nice people.

The magazine's offices were in New York. I wrote the address in gold ink; then I furtively stuck the envelope in our mailbox.

And the answer came right back, a stern, flat letter:

> Dear Miss/Ms./Mrs. Maloney:
> Your writing lacks maturity and polish. The single-spaced format and numerous typing errors made your submission nearly unreadable. Most of all, as a person of Japanese descent, I found your analogy regarding Japanese soldiers and cows somewhat offensive. Best of luck with your future projects.
> Jane Takahashi, Editorial Assistant

I was flattened. I tore up my story and burned the pieces. Either Roanie smelled the smoke or sensed my misery. He found me huddled behind a chicken house, my face swollen from crying.

"What's the matter, Peep?" he asked anxiously.

"Nothing. Go away. I'm thinking."

He sat down regardless. "Why don't you think out loud?"

I let out one of those involuntary *huh-huh-huh* sounds of a stifled sob. And then, heartbroken, I poured out the whole tale.

"You wrote about me?" he asked.

I wiped my eyes. "Well, yeah, but I changed your name."

"What name did you give me?"

"Dirk DeBlane." His brows shot up. I cringed. It had sounded romantic at the time. "You hate it," I said sadly.

"Nah. I *like* it. Nobody ever wrote a story about me before." He mused over the name. "Why'd you write about me that way?"

"Because it's . . . romantic." My face burned. "I'm almost ten. Mama says I can start dating boys when I'm sixteen. So you only have to wait six years to go out on a date with me."

"Why, thanks," he said dryly.

"Well, you'll be busy anyhow. You'll go to college."

"Maybe. Haven't made up my mind about college."

"Of course you'll go. And then *I'll* go to college, and after I get out, we'll go off and see the world together."

"Whatever you say, Peep."

I ducked my head and scrutinized him from under my brows. "But I guess we'll have to get married then. So we can save money on hotel rooms."

"I plan to make a lot of money," he said, raising a determined gaze to me. But one corner of his lips crooked up. "We could afford two rooms. We wouldn't have to get married."

"I guess that's okay. As long as you don't marry anybody else."

"Don't plan to."

"So you don't need any girlfriends, right?" I said sternly.

"Cool off. I'm not gonna ask no girls out anytime soon."

"Look, I'm not stupid. I watch how you look at the girls who hang around Hop and Evan. I watch how they look back. They've got boobs, and I haven't. But I *will* get some. You just wait."

He scowled. "You ain't—you aren't—a girl. You're Claire."

"Why do you have to look at them?"

"They're fun to watch. But too much trouble."

"Yeah. I'm not any trouble. And I'm a lot of fun."

"It's not the same." His eyes narrowed. "Don't go around tellin' people I'm your boyfriend. It's not that way."

"What way is it?"

He studied me for a minute, very still, absorbing me. "You know what you are?" he said. "You're everything good I can imagine."

"What?" I leaned toward him, warm inside, distracted.

"You gave me a chance when nobody else would," he said softly. "People will listen to what you've got to say someday. You keep writin'. The rest of us don't have a voice unless you talk for us."

I nearly burst with fledgling, adoring hope. I burrowed my head on his shoulder and cried some more. He put his arm around me. "When you're old enough, I'll try to live up to ol' Dirk," he said.

ROANIE'S fifteenth birthday was on the last day of March. Nobody'd ever celebrated his birthday before. Fired with regrets and determination, Mama made a huge layer cake covered with white icing and blooming with blue sugar roses and fifteen blue candles.

I'd never seen a look on Roanie's face like the one I saw when I carried that birthday cake, candles blazing, out of the pantry and set it in front of him on the breakfast table. Not just surprise or gratitude, but the slow, dawning glow of understanding. This was what families were all about—a whole bunch of people who showed you they were glad you'd been born.

"Make a wish and blow out the candles, Roan," Mama said.

"Wish for an early spring," Grandpa said.

"Wish for extra rain this summer," Daddy added.

"She was special, wasn't she?" Roanie said suddenly.

Puzzled silence. "Who?" I asked in a hushed tone.

His somber gaze moved around the table, then stopped on Mama and Daddy. "My . . . my mama. I mean, she didn't hurt nobody— anybody. She would have been a real lady if she'd had a chance, wouldn't she?"

Mama blinked hard. Daddy and Grandpa got a funny look.

Mama cleared her throat. "Roan, she was a sweet girl, and she loved you dearly. She did the best she could. She *was* a lady. And I know she'd be proud of you."

After a moment of stillness, his solemn face dappled with the flickering light, he nodded and blew out the candles.

The spell of the sad mood was broken. Carried away on the

smoke. Relief. Movement. I galloped into the pantry and came back with my arms full of presents. He gaped at them.

Mama had orchestrated the gifts with practical matters in mind—a nice leather belt, new socks, a pair of cuff links, things like that. But I'd persuaded her to let me give him *good* stuff. He unwrapped my gift and examined it with a slight, pleased smile. It was one of those bulky red Swiss army knives. He pried each section open until it bristled with blades and bottle opener and corkscrew and scissors. It wasn't just a pocketknife to me; it was a symbol. We'd come a long way in five years since the time he'd threatened to cut Carlton's throat. He wouldn't poke a knife at anybody else, but at least if he did, it'd be a nice knife.

MY TENTH birthday, in May, was a milestone. Roanie left a dozen red carnations outside my door that morning, and I thought I'd die from happiness.

I can't quite describe what I must have been to him—innocence, loyalty, acceptance. A bossy girl he could tease and protect and talk with on some safe level. The difference in our ages and our dreams was invisible to me then, because I loved him from a child's viewpoint, without the influence of grim reality or raging hormones.

I didn't know it on my birthday, but we'd come just about as far as we were going to go.

Our magic stopped working on a steamy Saturday in early June. The air was as rich as soup. I remember that day in endless, painful detail, how it started and how it ended.

Mama and Grandma Dottie had taken Grandmother Elizabeth shopping in Atlanta. Daddy and Grandpa went to a luncheon in Gainesville. Hop and Evan went bass fishing. Josh and Brady weren't home from college yet. Roanie stayed home to tinker with the engine of an old Volkswagen that Grandpa had acquired.

As for me, I was assigned to go to the beauty parlor with Great-Gran Alice. She had turned ninety-three, after all. She didn't drive anywhere alone anymore. She shouldn't have been driving at all. She needed help getting out of her boxy blue Chevy, plus she needed a lookout to yell when she swerved too close to any object that couldn't run, like a tree.

So there we were, hurtling down the middle of Soap Falls Road into town like a bobsled down a chute. A huge chicken truck came around a bend. "*Watch out,*" I yelled.

Great-Gran said, "Wee, Laudy," and peeled off to the opposite side of the road. The Chevy's right headlight scraped half the real estate off a red clay bank, and we plowed to a stop.

The chicken truck and its driver disappeared around the next curve and didn't come back. For the next five minutes Great-Gran ranted about the near miss being all his fault. Then she took a nitroglycerin tablet from her purse and put it under her tongue and laid her head back on the seat. Her knobby, blue-veined hands trembled. I was shaking all over. "Great-Gran, you okay?"

"I just need to rest my heart," she said weakly.

"I'll get help!"

I leaped out. I looked back at the way we'd come. Home? Too far. I pivoted and stared at the curve ahead. The Hollow was close. *The Hollow. Big Roan.*

I couldn't waste time running home. I ran toward the Hollow.

My mind was blank except for whatever concentration moved my feet. When I reached the driveway, I plowed to a stop, sucking in deep breaths. I inched down the hill. I'd never been in Big Roan's yard before, never been inside the awful trailer. I swallowed hard.

Flies buzzed around me as I climbed the trailer stairs and knocked on a wooden door. I heard slamming sounds inside, and finally Big Roan flung the door open and glared down at me. His dark hair looked slimy, and there were wet stains down the front of his T-shirt. "Whatcha want?" he growled, swaying.

"Could I use your phone, please, sir?"

"What for?"

"Great-Gran had a car accident. I need to call for help."

Roanie. Roanie'll come get us.

"Huh." He rubbed his beard stubble. His eyes were bloodshot, and there were patches of broken veins on his cheeks.

He staggered to one side, and I edged past him. A table fan whirred in the nasty air. A baseball game was showing on a little black-and-white TV. Beer cans and liquor bottles lay everywhere.

"You scared of me?" Big Roan asked.

"No, sir." I bumped into the arm of a couch, and dust motes puffed out. He plopped down into a sagging green recliner, watching me. A black phone sat on a stack of magazines by his chair.

His slithery gaze stayed on me as I dialed the phone. I clamped the receiver in my hand. Ringing. Ringing.

"Hello?" Roanie answered.

"Come get us! We had a car accident! I'm at the Hollow! Great-Gran's sittin' in her car! I'm at the *Hollow!* Come get us!"

"Claire, go back to the road," he said immediately. "Go *right now*. I'll get Grandpa Maloney's car, and I'll be there in five minutes. Just hang the phone up and *walk back to the road*."

"I will. Hurry!"

I set the receiver back on its berth. "Thank you, Mr. Sullivan. I'll wait up at the road." I turned. Suddenly Big Roan raised his metal leg and propped it on the couch, trapping me.

"That was my boy on the phone, wasn't it?" he asked.

I stared at the way his pant leg hung on the metal limb. "You better put your leg down, Mr. Sullivan." I could barely breathe. "I don't want to climb over it. I mean, I might bend it."

He didn't budge. Neither did I. I heard the blood throbbing against my eardrums. Finally he leaned forward and whispered, "You turned my boy against me."

Ice in my veins. "No," I whispered. "Sir, I don't th-think so."

"What's so special about you?" He flung an arm out and plucked at the sleeve of my T-shirt. I flinched. "How'd you win him over, fluffy?" He fingered the hem of my sleeve between his thumb and forefinger. "You think you're a pretty little thing, don't you?"

My head reeled from the closeness, the stink, the terror. "You let go of my shirt. You put your leg down. *Right now*."

Big Roan's eyes gleamed. He raised his hand toward my hair.

I punched him in the face.

He bellowed in surprise and grabbed me with both hands. I screamed, kicking wildly, punching in every direction. Grunting and cursing, he dragged me across his thighs and slapped me hard on the side of my head. I couldn't see anything but stars for a second. I couldn't think. I didn't know where I was.

Then he had me by one arm, and I was face down on the cluttered floor, with him on top of me, mashing the breath out of my lungs. He twisted my right arm behind me, and something tore, something inside my shoulder, and the pain flooded me like a black wave. He jerked the straps of my overalls down my arms; he held me down; he pulled my overalls to my ankles. He grabbed me between the legs.

All I knew was that I had been snatched up in the jaws of a nightmare and that nothing in my entire life would ever be the same.

Then there were sounds. There was shouting—Roanie's voice, guttural and wild, like a dog's furious snarls. I don't know what happened exactly. Thudding noises, violence, chaos. I was free, pulled free of the weight, Big Roan yelling, cursing, Roanie's hands on me, dragging me across the dirty floor.

I heard Big Roan bellow, "You raise a hand against me, and I'll—"

And then the gunshot.

Moaning, crying, I rolled over and stared. Dear Lord.

I had never seen a person with his brains blown out before.

Roanie crawled to me on his hands and knees. I hurt all over. I passed out for a little while. When I came to, we were outside. Roanie was bending over me, crying. "Claire," he said. "*Claire.*"

That was the scene that God and Jesus and all the angels looked down on—a nearly grown boy and a half-grown girl with bloody faces, huddled together in the lowest, darkest place in the world.

Everything else was so quiet.

WHAT happened during the rest of that day was mostly vague and distant—the effect of shock, I suppose. I had never seen Mama in hysterics. I had never seen Daddy cry from sheer rage.

Roanie and I were taken to see Uncle Mallory. Our busted lips, my black eye, my sprained shoulder—I was numb to all the prodding and fixing until Mama and Grandma got me undressed and it sank in that Uncle Mallory wanted to look between my legs. Then I burst into sobs and had to lie on his table wearing nothing but a paper sheet while Mama cried and held my hand.

When I was dressed again, doped up on some kind of medicine, my right arm in a sling, Daddy carried me into the waiting room, and there was Roanie, his eyes haunted as he stared at me. All I could manage to do was paw my good hand at him, desperately trying to reach him, but when he raised a hand toward mine, Daddy turned away. "Is she all right?" Roanie asked hoarsely.

"Yeah," Daddy answered, but it was a tight word.

I was taken home and put to bed in Mama and Daddy's room. Great-Gran had already been put in her bed. Grandmother Elizabeth sat with her, and they drank peach brandy.

Every relative within reach came as soon as they heard. And Cousin Vince, the sheriff, showed up before long with his deputies, and they took Roanie into the living room and shut the doors.

I kept trying to ask about him, but my tongue wouldn't work. I sank into helpless, woozy, half-conscious sleep. "My little girl, my hurt little girl," I heard Mama sobbing.

"She's a trouper," Daddy answered. "At least she wasn't . . . Big Roan didn't . . ." Daddy's voice trailed off.

"He would have," Mama said. "Oh, my God."

"But Roanie saved me, and he didn't do anything wrong," I mumbled over and over to everyone, until finally Grandpa, realizing what terrified me, whispered, "Don't worry, sweet pea. Roanie's not going to jail. He did the right thing."

Okay. Then we would just forget Big Roan; we'd get well and go on. Of course. I fell asleep.

"WHERE'S Roanie?" That was what I wanted to know when I woke up. It was after dark.

"He's in his room," Mama told me, smoothing my hair.

"I want to go see him. I have to see him."

"Not right now. Vince wants to talk to you," Daddy said gruffly. "If you think you can do it. You don't have to."

"I don't mind. Why are you mad at Roanie?"

"I—I'm just mad in general, honey. Because you got hurt."

"But Roanie didn't do anything wrong! He came to help me."

"Oh, honey, don't worry about Roanie right now."

"When can I worry about him?" I was still fuzzy.

"Not ever again, if I can help it," said Mama.

MAMA helped me put on a nightgown and my pink terry-cloth robe. She gave me a pill. I didn't hurt at all. I felt quite happy, actually. Daddy carried me downstairs into the living room.

I knew things were bad when I saw Uncle Ralph on the couch. If Uncle Ralph had come from Atlanta, we needed lawyer advice.

Daddy held me on his lap. I clutched Mama's hand. Sheriff Vince sat across from us. He asked me to tell him exactly what had happened. I told him once. I told him again. He made notes.

"Now think hard," Vince said. "What did you hear Big Roan yell before you heard the pistol go off?"

I repeated, " 'You raise a hand against me, and I'll—' "

But it dawned on me what he was getting at and what I had to do for Roanie. I looked Vince straight in the eye. "Mr. Sullivan yelled, 'If you turn on me, I'll *kill* you.' "

Two words. That was all I had to make up. Vince looked relieved. "You sure about that last part, Claire?"

I nodded fervently. "I forgot before. But now I'm sure."

"There you go," Uncle Ralph announced. "That settles it. There's no question about the justification. Case closed."

"Roanie can't go to jail!" I yelled. "It wasn't his fault!"

"Whoa, whoa," Vince said. "He's not in trouble."

"Promise?" I looked at Mama and Daddy.

"He's not going to jail," Daddy said, looking away.

"Mama?"

"I promise," she said, covering her face with one hand.

"Okay. Then I'll go see him now."

"No," Mama said. "He needs to rest."

Something was peculiar. I just couldn't figure out what it was.

SULLIVAN'S Hollow burned that night. Big Roan's spattered blood and brains, his trailer, his garbage dump, his junk, his old truck, everything. Of course it wasn't an accident. Daddy and my brothers and our relatives did it, but nobody said so.

The next morning Daddy trailered the bulldozer over there and pushed every speck of Big Roan Sullivan's existence into the gully at the bottom of the Hollow and covered it over and planted some kudzu vines on top. He tore down the mailbox and wiped out the driveway. He erased the Sullivan from Sullivan's Hollow forever.

And he meant to erase Roanie, too.

But I didn't know about all that until later on.

"WHERE'S Roanie?" I asked the next morning when Daddy carried me downstairs. It was just him and Mama at the kitchen table. The house felt too quiet, eerily quiet.

"He and Grandpa went up on Dunshinnog," Daddy said. I watched the careful glances being exchanged.

"Why?"

Mama stood behind me, her hands cupped on my hair, stroking it. Daddy said gruffly, "Just to talk about things."

"For heaven's sake, Holt," Mama said. "I gave her some medicine when she woke up. Don't try to talk to her right now."

"She understands. She needs to know. Claire, we're trying to decide what's best for Roan to do."

"I'm going up to Dunshinnog," I whispered. "I have to go help him. 'Cause it's my fault he had to shoot Big Roan."

Mama started crying. I didn't get to go to Dunshinnog. I didn't get to help Roanie when he needed me. I had to go back to bed.

I hurt so bad for Roanie, I couldn't think at all.

Daisy McClendon showed up at the farm later. I heard her screaming in the yard, saying that it was all jealousy, jealousy over

Sally that made Roan kill Big Roan, that Big Roan wouldn't hurt a little girl, that we'd turned Roan against his own daddy.

Sally made the rumors worse by packing up her belongings and her baby son, Matthew, and disappearing in the middle of the night, not even telling Daisy or her other sisters where she was going. Word spread about Daisy's accusations. There was no stopping that gossip, just as there was no stopping the general belief that I was ruined, had nearly been raped, and would be scarred forever.

But I didn't hear all that, not then, because I was trapped in my sleepy, drifting dreamworld, nearly a prisoner in Mama and Daddy's bedroom, sheltered for my own good, they decided.

I heard the loud voices downstairs, and I crawled out of bed. I crept down the back stairs behind the kitchen, holding on to the rail with my good arm, the other in its sling.

Daddy's voice. "It's not a punishment. It's not a jail. It's a group home run by the Methodist church. They're good people. It's just temporary, until everything calms down." *What?*

"I'm not good enough for you." Roanie's voice, fierce and broken. "I won't ever be good enough. Even if I did what I had to do, and you know it, deep down you're thinkin', 'His old man was gonna do something terrible to Claire. We can't have that kind of evil in our house.' "

"Roan, there's nothing but suspicion toward you outside this house." Mama's voice. "Please try to understand."

"I trusted y'all. I worked as hard as I could. I did everything just the way you wanted it. You can't send me away. You can't."

Send him away?

I don't know what kind of sound I made. I staggered through the kitchen door, weaving, crying. "What are y'all doing to him?" There were Mama and Daddy, Josh and Brady, Grandpa and Grandma. And Roanie, standing all alone in the center of them.

He stared down at me. Oh, he looked awful. His face like stone, the expression in his eyes so devastated and lonely that I felt shattered. I ran to Roanie and threw my good arm around him. He sank to his knees and held on to me, his head against mine.

Everybody was crying then. "You can write to him, Claire," Mama said. "I promise."

"Don't send him away! We're his *family*. It's not fair!"

"It won't be forever," Daddy said hoarsely, squatting down beside us. "The church home—that's just for a few months. You've got my word on that, Roan."

"I'll die if you make him leave," I sobbed.

"It's going to be all right, honey. Believe me," Daddy said, taking me by my one good hand. "Come on now, let go."

But I wouldn't. I threw my head back and looked at Roanie. "I won't let anybody send you away. You tell 'em. You tell 'em you love me and we're gonna get married when we're grown up!"

I probably clinched it with that announcement. And when he bent close to me and whispered, with bitterness and misery and determination, "I won't never forget you, I won't never forget any of this," I knew he was going away, and I couldn't stop it.

I kissed him, my swollen mouth against the corner of his bruised one. He didn't kiss me back; he was like a blank rock.

That was what we did to him. We closed him up inside himself.

Daddy and my uncles took him away the next morning.

His room empty. His voice beyond my hearing. His smile beyond my horizons. I'd never felt such agony, such emptiness.

Mama gave me the address of the home. I had my plans. Roanie would be back home in a few months at the most. I had letters to write as soon as my arm worked again, and I sat staring out the windows, thinking about what I'd say: *Everybody's already forgetting what happened. They don't talk about it at all. When you come home, you and me don't have to talk about it either.*

A week later I started writing to him. A week passed, and he didn't write back. I could feel something terrible in our house, something secretive. "I'll just call him," I announced finally. "Okay?"

After stalling me for a few days, Mama and Daddy told me the truth—he'd run away from that home the day after they sent him there. And nobody was able to find him.

EVEN THEN I DIDN'T BELIEVE he was gone forever. I kept writing to him. I waited all summer. There was shame and regret in my family. I fed on my parents' good-hearted misery and believed that Roanie would sense it somehow, that he would know they'd make it all up to him if he would just come home.

They hired a private investigator recommended by Uncle Ralph. Sheriff Vince sent out notices to sheriffs and police chiefs in other states. They were searching for Sally McClendon and Uncle Pete's little boy, too. None of it did any good. Both Roanie and Sally had spent their lives learning how to hide from the good intentions of people they didn't trust.

Grandpa, who suddenly looked very old by autumn, finally took me up to Dunshinnog. I hadn't been out of the house in months. I huddled on the ledge, sobbing, and Grandpa stroked my hair.

"Look what I brought," he said gruffly, pulling a green wad of leaves and roots from a pocket of his trousers. "We'll start something up here, Claire Karleen. We'll fix a little place."

Foxgloves. The foxgloves had been in bloom when Roanie was sent away. "Magic," Grandpa was saying. He thought Roanie would come back someday if foxgloves were here to soften his step. I helped Grandpa plant them in the earth of the meadow.

But one morning not long after that, just before a cold, frosty dawn, I woke up after a bad dream, and I felt that Roanie must be freezing somewhere, that he would die somewhere, all alone, and I couldn't help him, and how would I ever know?

I went downstairs and got Mama's scissors from her sewing room and went back up to my bathroom, and I very carefully cut all my hair to small nubs, maybe an inch long.

Mama came up to get me for breakfast, took one look at my crew-cut head, rebellious eyes, sat down on the floor, and put her head in her hands. Daddy walked up soon and found us, her still sitting there, me staring at them both with a brand of stony anguish that was tearing my heart out of my chest. He squatted between us wearily. "We'll get over this. We'll keep looking."

It has been a long time since then.

PART TWO

Dear Claire,

I write you letters I won't ever mail. You probably don't need to hear from me. Or want to. You were so little and messed up because of me when your folks sent me off. I don't hate your family. Won't trust them again or expect anything again, but am not too bitter. I'm keeping the faith. Have to. Have to prove that I'm better than my old man.

Been keeping track of your stories for the college paper. You sure got a way with words. Easy to figure you're not a kid anymore. You or me. If you could see me, you might think I'm still pretty rough on the eyes, just bigger and filled out okay. Came out all right after some hard knocks. Got responsibilities. How to tell you? How crazy it turned out.

I had to get a look at you. Drove to Georgia like a fool. Hunted for you at school. I got no interest in college. But I *do* read. Promise you. Read, think, study, make money. Listen to smart people. You taught me. You know me. You always did.

So I just waited outside your dorm house. Watched you walk across the yard. Just wanted to see how you grew up. You walked so smooth. Gosh, your hair—it's pretty that way. Thought I'd never see that color red again. You looked so good. Nineteen. I couldn't dream you any better than you are.

One look, and I wanted to hold you. I wanted to kiss you. I wanted to do everything to you. Take you off with me and make love to you and hear you say my name and smile. Crazy. You grew up, and I have, too.

Sorry I came to take a look at you. It hurts. Bad.

But I'll be watching. Reading, anyway. And if you ever do need me, I'll know. I'll be there. Promise.

Roan

Five

LIFE turns in large cycles, too large to notice until they bring you back to some touchstone, to home, to fractured memories of a sanctuary you thought you'd never need again.

On a balmy northern Florida morning in March, 1995, I headed for lunch down a side street bordering the building of the Jacksonville *Herald-Courier.* The morning edition was still on display in banks of newspaper boxes along the curbs. Beside the lead story a promotional blurb blared:

TERRI CAULFIELD—FROM FEAR TO HOPE

Her story of marital abuse, courage, and triumph touched readers across the state last year. Terri Caulfield plans a bright future in an update by staff reporter Claire Maloney, whose award-winning series turned the young Jacksonville woman's struggles into a public crusade against domestic violence.

I walked on, pleased. Terri Caulfield hadn't had many opportunities to be noticed or fussed over. Abused by the uncle who raised her, beaten and stalked by the husband she'd divorced, Terri was only twenty-two, scared, depressed, and willing to talk.

I'd met her while researching an article on Jacksonville's battered-women programs. Six months and six articles later, I'd turned her into a minor celebrity throughout northern Florida. My series on her ran in syndication nationwide.

Hammered by public sympathy, a judge slapped her ex-husband with a heavy sentence on an arson charge after he set fire to her car. The ex had been in prison ever since.

The city rumbled and sang around me, the bright Florida sunshine glinting off parked cars. Thirty years old, I had lived and worked here on the Florida coast since college. I was only a day's drive from Dunderry, but I hadn't been home for a visit since Grandpa died a year ago. There was my troubled status in the family, of course.

I'd tried to make my life seamless with the uneasy glue of ambition and long hours at work. Loneliness got shoved under the clutter of my cubicle in the newsroom, my apartment. "You live on the edge of something," my cousin Violet had said not long ago when she and her preschool daughters spent a weekend with me. "Is it exciting? Everyone wonders. Your folks, Claire. They worry—"

"Life is short," I'd tossed back glibly. "Work hard, play fast, and never look back or down."

"He's always out there, isn't he?" she'd asked. "Roanie."

"He's probably dead. I try not to think about him."

Lies, lies, and damn lies. I nearly convinced myself.

I turned a corner past a taco stand, striding past my own image in store windows that cast me back in muted shades of blue skirt and gray blazer, fine bare legs stepping along in white mules, a mane of wavy red hair pushed back under a rolled white scarf.

I'd topped out at five feet nine—nothing voluptuous about the package but all the padding in perky order. Not a bad combination of sturdy Maloney bones and delicate Delaney proportions.

A taxi stopped at the end of the block ahead. A tall dark-haired man got out and strode into a nearby café. I ran up the street with my shoulder bag bouncing wildly against one hip.

I darted inside the café, took a deep breath, and halted behind the stranger. He turned. His face had nothing familiar about it. I walked out, one sweaty, shaking hand clamped around my bag.

I had done this kind of thing a thousand times over the past twenty years. I kept waiting, kept watching, stayed on alert. Years ago, when I was a university sophomore, I'd thought I glimpsed Roan in front of my dorm. I was walking across the lawn, and I could have sworn I saw him in a parked truck. But by the time I turned completely, the stranger was driving off.

I'd been running after ghosts too long. This self-humiliation had to stop. I was getting too old for fantasies.

A WEEK LATER SOME bureaucratic clerical error allowed Terri Caulfield's ex-husband a sudden and mistaken release on parole. He immediately left a strangled kitten in her mailbox with a note tied to its neck: "You are next."

That night, terrified, Terri sat on the couch in my living room, dressed in a pale yellow T-shirt and old jeans.

"You'll be fine here tonight," I promised. "Off to Miami tomorrow, living it up in a nice hotel. Drink margaritas, work on your tan." I was laying it on thick, praying my optimism was justified.

"Why are you doing all this for me?" she asked wistfully.

"You're my ticket to a Pulitzer nomination maybe. You sell newspapers. You're a good story," I said.

"Oh, come on, Claire. You're always writing about homeless bums and runaway kids and beat-up women. How come you care so much about strangers, but you don't have a husband and kids?"

"I'm too cranky to be a wife, too distracted to be a mother."

"I could use some distractions right now." She wandered around my apartment, studying an antique mahogany desk Grandpa had left to me. On it sat a stack of family photo albums.

Terri began gingerly picking through them and looked awed. "Are all of these people *relatives* of yours?" she asked.

"Those are my brothers," I told her as she pointed to one page. "And their wives. I've got eleven nieces and nephews. That's my oldest brother, Josh. His wife died when their daughter, Amanda, was born. She's about ten. She lives with my parents." I went on, telling her that Brady was a real estate developer, Hop and Evan were in the construction business together, and Josh was a state senator.

"Jeez," she said. "He looks important."

"Hmmm. He's also in the family poultry business. My father retired a few years ago, after he had a mild heart attack." I nodded toward a pair of stoneware vases on the coffee table. "My mother's a potter. It used to be a hobby. Now she sells her work."

"What a great family. You visit home a lot?"

"I moved out for college. Haven't been back much."

"Well . . . *why?*"

Twenty years of quiet estrangement couldn't be summed up easily. Or painlessly. "We had some disagreements," I said.

Suddenly we heard the slam of heavy footsteps climbing the stairs outside my second-story landing. Terri's face turned white. I laughed. "It's just the accountant who lives next door. Relax."

The footsteps grew louder, faster. "It's *him,*" Terri said frantically. I dutifully went to my kitchen and brought back the loaded pistol I kept in a drawer. The footsteps stopped. Someone pounded on my front door. "I know you're in there, you little bitch!"

Terri leaped up. "We've got to get out of here!"

She snatched my Jeep keys from the coffee table, then ran for the back door to the fire escape. I yelled for her to stop. An ear-splitting blast cut me off. Her ex-husband rammed a gun barrel through the ragged hole he'd shot in the middle of the front door.

I ran after her, hearing the final crash behind me as her ex burst through the door.

I should have shot him. Running was our worst mistake.

TERRI crouched on the Jeep's passenger side, wild-eyed, peering over the seat at the stream of headlights behind us on the old Florida highway. My pistol lay on the console between us. I threw my car phone in her lap. "Call the police," I repeated uselessly, because she continued to search the traffic behind us as I drove.

"There he is!" she screamed.

Suddenly an old sedan, dodging wildly, loomed beside me. I glanced over and recoiled. Driving with one hand and lifting the other, Terri's ex-husband pointed the shotgun at me. "Oh, Lord," Terri moaned. My half-raised window exploded. I threw up a hand instinctively as glass sprayed me.

Chaos. Tumbling. The world turned inside out. Silence. My right leg in a vise. The Jeep's steering wheel inches from my throat. I stared weirdly at the bent steel power pole that bit into the Jeep's mangled front end. We were tilted in a ditch.

Terri slumped in her seat, twitching, her blood spraying the dash. "I'm sorry," I whispered to the young woman I'd promised to protect. Pain swept over me in nauseating waves. I sank under, lost.

Death and failed intentions came back to Roan, to me, to us. I had brought them like a curse again.

"Who do you want us to call?" they asked me at the hospital. I was in a panicky stupor punctuated by blurred faces that appeared by my bed—doctors, nurses, cops, a fellow reporter.

"What about Terri?" I asked.

"Ms. Caulfield was shot. She didn't make it. I'm sorry."

I was told later that her ex-husband stood beside the Jeep, put the shotgun barrel in his mouth, and pulled the trigger.

Didn't make it. All my fault. What a dangerous fool I was.

"Who do you want us to call?" a surgical resident asked patiently.

Who was I? Who had I always been?

"Maloney," I said. I mouthed the family phone number in Georgia. "Tell them I'm okay. Don't scare them."

I was awake that night when Mama and Daddy arrived. My father gathered me in his arms, and my mother sobbed bitterly with her cheek pressed to mine. I wanted my family, desperately and without judgment, for the first time in twenty years.

———

Claire,

Writing this on a plane headed east tonight. Two hours ago I heard what happened to you from an investigator I hired in Florida. Hired him last year when you started the series on Terri Caulfield. Dangerous situation, I thought.

I let you down. Should have been there. All these years, trying to stay away, for good reasons—what difference does any of that make now? Nothing matters but seeing you again.

Please be all right when I get there. Please.

———

As I recovered after surgery—awake and fully alert for the first time in two days—irrational ideas moved through my mind.

"Torn ligaments, torn muscles," the surgeon was explaining to Grandma Dottie, who sat beside my bed. "A fracture of the femur . . . some nerve damage . . . recovery in about six months, though her leg won't be the same for a year at least."

"Was anyone here last night?" I asked after he left. Grandma Dottie was still sturdy, but white-haired and arthritic. "Was I alone?"

"We were all here, honey," she answered gently. "Not every minute, but we've been watching over you like hawks."

"No one saw anyone . . . strange?"

She peered at me through her bifocals, bewildered and alarmed. "You think somebody strange was here?" Grandma ventured.

"I . . . don't know."

Mama and Daddy came in, carrying flowers and fruit baskets.

"She thinks a stranger visited her room last night," I heard her whisper to Mama and Daddy. "I suspect she was dreaming while the anesthesia wore off." Mama took one look at me, saw that I was fully alert enough to talk, and began crying. So did I.

Because I thought I'd had a long conversation with Roan.

WHEN I was younger, I'd cultivated a fantasy that one day I'd look up and Roan would be standing there. He'd study me, and he'd say, "You're beautiful. I always knew you'd be beautiful."

I'd know, from the look on his face, that nothing about me disgusted or disappointed him, that he'd forgotten that battered little girl on the floor of Big Roan's trailer with her overalls down.

But what happened that night at the hospital had to be a drug-induced dream. I was floating in and out. I didn't remember parts of it later, and parts I remembered word for word.

I had heard footsteps on the room's hard, antiseptic floor—soft clicks, then the settling of a hand on rustling sheets. Fingertips brushed my hair from my forehead, then feathered over my cheek. I looked across the pillow. I saw silvery eyes glittering with tears inside a weathered face that had achingly familiar features, yet different— older, harder, hooded by ruffled dark hair. A handsomely rugged man in a pale leather jacket and an open-collared shirt.

My heart contracted.

"Claire," he said in a low, deep voice.

Time was confused. It had never passed us by. "They're not going to leave you at that boys home," I told him. "They know they were wrong. Don't worry. Oh, Roanie, I love you so much."

"I thought," he said as he bent close to my face and stroked my hair, "that you'd want to forget." His voice was hoarse.

"Roan," I murmured thickly, "I'm the reason Terri died. Like Big Roan. I'm sorry."

Those gray eyes shimmered in my dream, fierce and anguished. "It wasn't your fault. Not then. Not now."

And then he sat down and talked to me—for minutes, hours, or days. I couldn't be certain. Finally I said, "You don't need help with grammar anymore," and he bent his head in his hands. I talked to him while he sat there—about what, I couldn't be sure.

I felt serene because I hadn't completely failed him; he'd drawn on our memories to come back to me. "I still love you," I said.

He got up, carefully ran his hands over the cast that covered my right leg from hip to ankle, then kissed me. "I still love you, too," he said. "And when you see me again, I'll prove it."

I CAME home to the blue-green mountains, the family, the farm, the big, rambling house where generations of Maloneys had thrived. There I was, helpless, gawked at every time I crept out in a wheelchair. I was the only nonmoving part of a well-oiled machine.

I'd left for college when I was seventeen, vowing I'd never live in Dunderry again. My father had had his heart attack a year later, and I couldn't bear to stay away, so I returned for a summer. I came home when Josh's wife died after giving birth to Amanda. I came home when Grandpa died. But I made certain everyone understood that it took birth, death, and illness to force me back.

Mama put me in Roan's old bedroom because it was on the main floor and near the kitchen. Hop and Evan hung one of those trapezelike bars over the hospital bed Daddy had rented. I could ask for anything and be pampered without question.

As spring unfolded, I hid as well as I could on the veranda, pushing guilt and anger down under layers of familiarity.

I wanted to forget who I'd been before the accident. I wanted to stamp out the driven, ambitious, reckless woman who risked other people's lives. I wanted to subdue the Claire who'd treated newspaper work like a game of intrigue.

In short, I wanted to erase the Claire who hadn't always made the kindest, wisest choices. The Claire who was still so caught up in childhood fantasies that she had hallucinated a detailed conversation with a man who had been driven away because of her reckless efforts twenty years earlier. I kept trying—hopelessly—to remember everything Roan had said that night at the hospital.

As if he had been real.

Claire,

I try to stay busy and not worry about you. I arranged to get access to your medical records. I bought them from people who specialize in information. Sorry, but I need to know how you're doing. My information says you're not doing well. Could I make you feel worse by showing up now? Probably.

When you're better, I'll be there to help you. I'll take you anywhere you want to go, get you set up with your old job again or any kind of media job you want. Heck, I'll buy you a little newspaper to run if that's what you want. I won't let you sit there at the farm and forget everything you accomplished.

Don't give up. You never have before.

Six months and I'd be walking without crutches, the surgeons predicted. I was lucky; my leg showed every sign of a fast recovery. The reattached muscles twitched energetically. Rejuvenated nerve endings radiated needle-sharp pains. I took a lot of pain pills and could barely get out of bed.

This misery was the definition of a *good* recovery.

I began to let the yellow blooms of April daffodils hypnotize me. The smell of jasmine creeping over the veranda lattices was almost too beautiful. Dunshinnog rose in a natural cathedral of white dogwoods against a dark blue sky.

It belonged to me now. Grandpa had left me the mountain in his will. He'd walked up to the top last spring to see the foxgloves in bloom. When he hadn't returned, Daddy went after him. He'd found Grandpa sitting with his back against a tree, gazing across the valley where he'd been born, lived, and died. I missed him so much.

When I was about fourteen, both of the Old Grannies died in our house, in their beds, on the same night. After all the years they had spent feuding over who would outlast the other, neither had had the last word.

It was peaceful at the farm, and I looked out the windows at a spring palette of greens. I hurt constantly, ate badly, slept as much as possible, cried often when I was alone.

My niece Amanda, redheaded, freckled, tomboyish, and naturally charming, brought me fresh-baked cookies. She lived with my folks because Josh traveled so much. She became my constant companion. She was desperately lonely, motherless, idly neglected by Josh. And I loved her immediately because she needed me.

I didn't know what *I* needed yet.

AFTER the cast was removed, I staggered around on crutches. My right leg was strange—just *there,* swollen but pliable, as if it had been attached to me without my consent. I knew I was healing, that recovery was a matter of time and exercise, but I felt uninvolved.

So you quit your job. I have sources for this kind of information. I'm trying to analyze you, Claire. Are you running scared? That's not like you. I'll be back there soon—everything's almost taken care of—and I hope you'll explain it to me.

Watch the mountain at night. Jeez, I'm telling you as if you're reading this. I'll have a hard time face to face at first.

It's all I can think about. Seeing you again.

I HEARD loud voices in the living room. I struggled into my robe, hobbled in there on a pair of crutches, and found Mama and Daddy embroiled in a shocked conference with Hop and Evan.

"Wilma's daughter put Ten Jumps up for sale," Evan repeated for my sake. "And it looks like she's got a buyer. We don't know who, but we heard she's sold the property."

Wilma was the Minnesota relative who had inherited Ten Jumps. Her daughter had inherited it from her.

"Somebody has to take me out there." My voice sounded thin and distant. "Hop? Evan?"

"If you want to go," Evan answered slowly, eyeing me and stroking his beard. "I'll get my Land Rover."

We made it to the lake—Evan and I and Evan's unshakable wife, Luanne. The Land Rover's running boards dripped mud by the time we reached the lake cove where the cabin sat, surrounded by blackberry briers that grew in ten-foot-tall mounds.

We got out. Evan helped me perch on my crutches. "All right, sis, you're here. What's this all about?"

"I'll show you when we get inside. Let me look first."

I struggled through the briers as Evan and Luanne held them.

"Snug as a bug in a rug," Luanne said, surveying the cabin's musty, rain-weathered interior. She knocked on a wall. "Solid."

"Back there." I nodded toward a doorway. "The back room."

With Evan lighting the way with a flashlight, I thumped into the second room on my crutches. "There." The beam of light fell on a narrow opening with hanging shreds of some dank cloth.

"You came to see a *closet?*" Evan grunted.

I angled past him into the space and twisted. "Flashlight." Evan handed it to me. I raised the light to a plank just above my head. "This is what I want," I said.

Evan craned his neck and looked. "Good Lord, sis," he said.

Carved on a board, hidden in a place no one had bothered with for many years, was the simple inscription ROAN AND CLAIRE.

"Roan carved it," I explained. "I found it after he left."

I took the board home and put it in my dresser drawer.

"YOU'RE going to live here from now on, aren't you?" Amanda asked me during a Sunday gathering as we hid out on twin wicker lounges in the garden room. "Going to stay here forever?"

"I don't know. But I'll be here quite a while."

"So I can count on you to do stuff with me, huh? 'Cause Grandma's always busy with her pottery and Papa's gone all the time."

"You betcha. I'll always do stuff with you." I swept cupcake crumbs off my jeans. My fingers splayed over the deep scar hidden under the denim. "And when I die, you can have my money."

"Okay!" She grinned. "Papa says we gotta be patient with you. I heard him talkin' to Grandpa about it yesterday. Grandpa said we gotta make allowances for you. 'Cause a sad thing happened to you when you were little and you never got over it. How sad was it?"

I tightened all over and felt two decades burning in my chest like hot coals. "It was only sad because of the way it ended." I gauged my words carefully. "It was wonderful before that."

I told her about Roan. About the good Christmas we spent and the necklace he gave me. About Big Roan. About Sullivan's Hollow, which doesn't exist anymore. I didn't tell her Roan disappeared because my parents had shipped him off to a church home. Amanda wasn't old enough to understand how good-hearted people can commit terrible mistakes in the heat of the moment.

"Roan moved away," I told her. "And that was the last time we saw each other. When your grandpa says I never got over it, well, it's like what you tell me about your mother sometimes. How you dream that she's on the other side of a canyon and you can't quite jump far enough to reach her? That's what happens when somebody you love goes away. There's always a little part of you that's whispering 'Jump' even though you know it's too far."

Amanda stared at me. "Oh, Aunt Claire," she whispered. "Roan Sullivan *will* come back for you. I just *know* he will."

"No, sweetie," I said calmly. "Sometimes people change. They grow up and move further away from each other, until they forget how to jump. I'm not a jumper," I concluded. "I'm a sitter."

Her blue eyes flickered. She looked at me. "Sometimes I think you don't try very hard, Aunt Claire," she accused softly.

My throat closed up, and I couldn't say another word.

I JERKED AWAKE THAT NIGHT, not just crying but yelling, and beating the bedcovers with my fists. I hobbled to the closet and dug through a small wooden box I've had for years. I pulled my old faded shamrock pendant and its chain from a tiny cloth bag. I had worn the pendant for so many years, the green rubbed off and the chain turned the color of a tarnished nickel.

I had nearly forgotten the girl who had been tough enough to stand up for a boy no one else wanted.

I couldn't sleep. I sat in the dark by my bedroom window. Dunshinnog was encased in clouds that scudded across a full moon.

I saw a light. Small and flickering at the summit. There it was. Somebody was up there on my mountain, dammit. By the time I woke the household and marshaled their attention, the trespasser might have vanished.

I threw a windbreaker over my nightshirt, then crawled out the bedroom window. It was more painful than any physical therapy session, and I panted for air as I made my way around the house and into a battered old farm truck parked beyond the barns. I drove awkwardly, using my left foot on the pedals.

When I got to the top of Dunshinnog along an old, rutted logging road, the truck's headlights glanced off an unfamiliar car with a rental tag. Flames leaped from a small pyramid of brushwood and tree limbs on the stone ledge overlooking the valley.

Astonished, I struggled toward the fire, glancing around wildly. The moon had disappeared completely behind thick clouds laced with heat lightning. I smelled rain in the air.

"Who are you?" I yelled. "This is private property. *Private!*"

I tottered barefoot among the foxgloves, offspring of those Grandpa and I had planted years before. Watching, listening, swaying. I suddenly hated the foxgloves for surviving, for making promises they hadn't kept, for letting some stranger wander up here. I began smashing them with one crutch like some furious wooden-pronged animal. "Come out of the woods!" I screamed.

Rain began to fall—cold, a torrent that poured down on me. The fire coughed billows of white smoke. I slipped and fell down.

The next thing I knew, a pair of strong arms was lifting me.

I didn't know who had me or *what* had me. It was dark, and cold rainwater flooded my eyes, and I was dizzy from the fall.

"Claire," a deep voice said raggedly.

That was all it took. I swung my drenched head toward it, lightning snapped above the mountain, and I saw his face carved out against the night, his eyes boring straight into mine, holding me.

"Roan," I whispered in the middle of booming thunder that shook the air out of my lungs.

Roan.

I LIVED through that night as if I were drowning. The rain whipped us. Lightning split the torrent, and thunder reached across the valley in deep bellows of celebration as Roan carried me to his car. I didn't ask where we were going. I didn't care.

He drove, and I braced myself against the passenger door, studying his profile as best I could during the lightning flashes.

He's alive. He's come home. He didn't forget me.

"Are you kidnapping me?" I asked.

I saw the flash of his smile. "Hell, yes."

"Roan." It was both plea and thanks.

He jerked the car to a stop, then vaulted out into the rain and came to my side. In short order he lifted me in his arms again, then carried me through a thicket of some kind. Lightning flashed, and I glimpsed the old cabin. He'd brought me to Ten Jumps. I wound one hand in his shirt. His chest felt hard against my side.

He caddied me sideways through the doorway and put me down on an air mattress on the floor. There was a sizzling sound, then a flood of light from a camping lantern. An ice chest and a bulky duffel bag shared a dusty corner of the small bare room.

He dropped to his heels beside the mattress; in the eerie white light of the camping lantern he looked like weathered marble except for those gray eyes, as intense and quick as mercury. There was no point in talking; like wild animals, we gauged the dangerous situation with unblinking scrutiny.

Finally, after twenty years of unexplained absence, he said with more sorrow than sarcasm, "Home sweet home."

I looked into the face of the boy I remembered, now a grown man with dark hair slicked back from wide cheekbones and high forehead. "Yes," I said softly. "I still recognize you."

"I wouldn't be here if I thought you didn't want to see me."

Thunder shook the cabin. He jerked a blanket from beside his knees and swooped it around my shoulders. I finally realized I was shivering. But he moved too fast, with the unsettling grace of lean, male muscles. Maybe he saw the startled reaction in my face. He frowned, sat back on his heels, then glanced around my relative's cabin. "I bought this place," he said.

Silence again. I needed time to mull over the fact that somehow he'd made that much money, that he used it in secretive ways, and that his purpose had to do with me.

Rain beat on the roof. My leg had begun to ache. Suddenly I was exhausted and dizzy. "I have to rest," I admitted.

"Do you want me to take you back to the farm tonight?"

"No. I'm not going to let you out of my sight. I'm not even sure you're *real* yet."

He reached out carefully and laid his hand along my cheek for an instant. "As real as you are," he whispered.

Twenty years. I didn't have to say that out loud. His eyes darkened; he nodded. Keeping the blanket firmly around me, I lay down on my side as gracefully as possible, which wasn't too graceful. On an air mattress in a cabin with no amenities, in the woods, without another soul but him knowing where I'd gone.

He turned to the lantern, twisting a knob. Inky darkness enclosed us. For a split second I was disoriented. "Talk to me," I said quickly. "Tell me anything that matters to you. I want to hear your voice."

"I'm sitting beside the mattress," he replied, "listening to you breathe. This is the most peaceful moment I've had in years."

A contented fog began to slide over me in the wake of his voice—strange, because I knew that deep down I was bitterly angry with him. He had been watching me all these years and never let me know. "I dreamed you came to the hospital," I whispered finally. "I did."

EARLY morning sunshine whitewashed the cabin's spartan interior. My mood was a strange mixture of despair and excitement.
Roan.
Clutching the walls and the doorframe to steady myself, I half staggered onto the porch. My crutches lay propped against a broken section of porch rail. I hadn't realized that Roan had brought them with me the night before.

Roan stood in a small clearing fifty yards away with his back to me. Older, thicker. He seemed engrossed by the morning sky.
He's here. He's really home.
I pushed myself step by step. Roan's blanket slid down my arms. I shoved at briers, balancing wildly. I was wearing a nightshirt, a yellow windbreaker, and no shoes. Panting, I lurched into the clearing. Roan pivoted at the sounds and held out his hands.

He caught me as I started to fall forward. "Nice catch," I said.

"Glad to break your fall. I wish I'd been there for you two months ago."

"You were. Everything I've done for other people has been a substitute for what I couldn't do for you twenty years ago."

"Then we're alike. I've tried to live in a way that could make up for what happened."

All the unanswered questions, all the years. "I can't think straight right now," I offered. "I just need to look at you."

He had texture: rough khaki trousers, hiking boots with black laces, an old gray cotton shirt with rolled-up sleeves. And he had context: a heavy gold wristwatch, thick dark hair that was slightly longish, drying into unruliness. His hands looked callused.

"You're perfect," I said. Instantly aware of the pale thin leg with surgical scars, I pulled his blanket closer around me. His gaze slipped down to the hidden leg, then back to my stare.

"You're the most beautiful woman I've ever seen in my life," he said quietly. "Let's get that point settled right now."

"I was always afraid," I said slowly, "that one day I'd see you somewhere—in a shop, a restaurant. And I'd recognize you. I'd walk up to you, and you'd look at me without the slightest idea who I was. I'd have to explain. I'd try to tell you how much you meant to me when we were kids, but it wouldn't mean anything to you."

"The way I pictured it," he said slowly, "I'd walk up to you and say your name, and you'd step back. You'd ask me what on earth I wanted. And you'd look at me but see my old man."

I sagged a little. He pulled a folding chair from beside a camp stove, where a kettle bubbled over blue-gold flames. I sat down weakly. He poured me a mug of coffee.

"When I saw you at the hospital, when I knew you needed me, that was all I cared about," he said.

I leaned back. "How do you know so much about me?"

"I've read every article you've written. Not just from the *Herald-Courier,* but going back to when you were editor of the university paper. And before that. Issues of the Dunderry *Shamrock.*"

We were quiet for a long time. The lake shimmered; the season's first dragonflies darted above the surface.

I said slowly, "I developed some peculiar ideas over twenty years. Such as assuming that since I never heard a word from you, you'd either forgotten me, or you were dead. Who are you now? Where have you been? Do you hate the family so much you had to go to Dunshinnog first to prove you—"

"You asked me to do that."

When I gazed at him in disbelief, he said, "You don't remember. At the hospital. You told me I had to let the mountain know I'd come home. Something about foxgloves. I didn't understand it, but I promised you I'd go up there and build a fire."

"Did I also tell you to buy this property?" I asked fiercely.

"No." He squatted beside me. "I own a lot of property. Buy. Sell. It's natural for me to buy my way into a situation. And I wanted this place. It means something to me. I'll decide what to do with it later. In the meantime I intend to do the same thing for you that you tried to do for me when we were kids."

"And what is that?"

"You gave me something to believe in. I believed in you, and I never stopped believing."

The sunshine burned my eyes. I swept a blinded gaze at the scene around us. "You couldn't come back until you could buy this land? Make some statement about possession and control?"

He didn't comment on that. "I called home for you," he said abruptly. "From my car phone. I told your parents you were here and all right. The amazing thing, Claire, is that they haven't shown up here to intervene. I think they're in shock."

"You don't know how much they've wanted to find you all these years."

"That doesn't matter to me."

"It has to matter. I . . . need answers. There's something you're not telling me. I want to know everything about you."

He went very still, his eyes dark. He reached inside his shirt and brought out a wrinkled yellowed piece of paper, its creases as soft as old skin. "I wrote this to you the first summer," he said. "I have more letters you might like to read, but just read this one for now."

My hands shaking, I took the fragile paper:

You got words that come easy. I never had no words that come that easy. But I will practice writing to you the way you wrote to me that time I was so by myself at 10 Jumps, I wanted to die. Feel like I could die from being lonely right now.

Leaving this church home tonight. Running away. It hurts so much. What my old man done to you. What your folks done to me. Sorry. I will learn to be somebody new. I will be better than my old man. I will prove it some way.

If I ever get to see you again, I won't never hope for nothing but that you have forgot what my old man done to you. If I go away, maybe you will grow up okay and not be the girl Big Roan Sullivan hurt that way. Don't blame your folks. I had to go.

But I love you, Little Peep. And there is nothing nasty or sexy about it. It is the only easy thing I have done in my whole life.

I folded the letter and clutched it tightly. I was crying. "I want to read all of them," I said. "Every letter. Every one you wrote to me. I have to understand why you couldn't come back before."

He held out his hands. "Just for now, be a kid again. The one who didn't need answers before she'd take a chance on me."

My mind slid close to the edge of a razor. I glimpsed some hard exit, desolate but honest, in us both. I took his hands.

Six

HE RETURNED me to Dunshinnog to get the farm truck I'd deserted the night before, but the truck was gone. Daddy had probably sent one of the boys to retrieve it, not out of concern for the truck, but to make certain Roan had to deliver me to the house in person.

I stood, still barefoot and dressed in the nightshirt and windbreaker, balanced between my crutches in a sea of lavender foxgloves shimmering in fresh pink-tinted sunshine. They swayed heavily in small breezes. I told Roan why Grandpa and I had planted them. "He was right," I finished. "They brought you home."

Roan walked among the flowers, bell-shaped blooms brushing his hands. He halted in front of me, looking from me to the foxgloves around us and back to me. There was a tortured sweetness between us that no amount of unexplained misery could erase.

Twenty years. A grown man, a grown woman. No more little-girl innocence; no more big-brotherly resistance.

"Please, kiss me," he said.

I leaned forward and kissed one corner of his mouth. He bent his head. We shared a breath. Very slowly we came together. First it was gentle, but then it became a frantic welcome.

Suddenly we heard rustling noises in a thicket of laurel. Amanda burst out, her red hair tangled with twigs and leaves. She halted at the edge of the meadow a dozen yards from us. "Aunt Claire, he *did* come back! I *told* you he'd come back! Everyone's waiting to see him. Oh, he's just perfect!" Then she turned, darted back into the laurel, and disappeared from sight.

"You told your niece about me," Roan said softly. "Why?"

"Because she needs to believe in magic." So much for maintaining control. I turned away from the look in his eyes, desperately. "I think we've been ambushed by a fairy," I said.

ROAN made his face a mask as he guided the sleek gray rental sedan past the familiar mailbox with MALONEY FARM painted on it.

Mama and Daddy waited on the veranda. I hoped Roan saw them as I did—so much older, only human, not the icons of authority they had been in his boyhood. My father was turning into Grandpa, complete with the bald head and lumbering stance of an old bear; my mother was vulnerable in the graciously preserved aura of youth, slender in beige slacks, her shoulder-length hair tinted in expensive shades of brown and copper. Grandma Dottie sat royally ensconced in a white rocking chair, her eyes wide with hope.

I had no idea what to say or how to handle the reunion. My stomach was tight under my breastbone. Roan stopped the car and got out. I slung my door open before he could reach it and struggled to my feet, searching Mama's and Daddy's faces. They had the dumbstruck look of old grief and awkward concern.

Roan helped me get situated on my crutches, then stepped ahead of me and halted. He stood stiffly, not speaking, his head up.

Everyone studied him as if he'd emerged from a cloud of sulfurous smoke. And at me, in my nightshirt and barefoot, hair tangled madly, as if I'd been rolled in strange dough.

Daddy walked down the veranda steps to us. Mama followed him hurriedly. "Your mother and I can't tell you what to do," he said to me. "But we can tell you there's no reason for you to take sides. Roan's welcome in this house. You hear me, Roan?"

Roan inclined his head slightly, accepting and rejecting.

Mama's face was pale. "You think what you want, Roan. I don't blame you. If you're *half* as honorable as the boy we were stupid enough to send away, you don't need to explain a thing to anyone."

"I came here to do what I can for Claire. I'll help her any way she'll let me. I don't expect anything from anyone else."

"We have faith. I will say it and say it until you believe it. You're welcome here. You still have a home in this community."

"That's not important now." Roan turned to me. "I have work to do at Ten Jumps. Plans to make. So you know where I'll be."

"Don't leave like this. Come inside," I said frantically.

"Yes, *please* come in the house," Mama added urgently. "Talk to us. Tell us about yourself."

Roan straightened. "It's not that simple. This"—he swept my folks, the house, the valley, Dunshinnog, the whole farm with a burning look that settled finally on me—"was everything I cared about. I still care. But on different terms. My terms."

"This is how you're going to handle it?" I asked, stunned. "Don't set terms. People get ruined by setting inflexible terms."

As soon as I said it, he touched my face with the tips of his fingers, scalded me with a look that said I'd betrayed him by not understanding, then walked back to his car.

Blind with fury and confusion that rose up within me like a tidal wave, I stumbled after him. "You are still part of this family whether you like it or not! You have to be willing to forgive them!" The tips of my crutches caught, and I tumbled hard.

I heard Mama gasp, heard her and Daddy running to me.

Roan was beside me. "Easy, easy." He took me by the shoulders.

"Don't touch me. I don't need anyone to hold me up. Not even you. I won't be caught in the middle again."

Roan said, "Look at me."

I gave him a brutally honest stare. "I can't *chase* you," I said.

He lifted a devastatingly familiar hand, big-knuckled, with strong fingers, and gently brushed my tangled hair from my eyes. "You have to try," he said. "If I don't make you try, you'll keep sitting here like an invalid." He slowly slid his arms around me and pulled me to him. I stiffened more inside his embrace.

He bent his head next to mine. "How many times did you see me in trouble and filthy and hurt and alone?"

"It's not the same."

"Do you want to be helpless?"

"No."

"Then get up. You can do it."

I gripped his hands. I struggled. Sweating, breathing hard, my eyes never leaving his, I got one bare foot under me and swayed desperately. Roan's grip tightened on my hands. He pulled, and I shoved myself upward with every ounce of strength.

I stood. I *stood*. No crutches, wobbling, light-headed, my teeth gritted, but I stood. Some unspeakable devotion and challenge moved between us. "I want those letters you wrote to me," I said. "I want you to bring them here right now. All of them."

He arched a brow. "If you want the letters, you'll have to come to Ten Jumps." He wouldn't give an inch. "You can find me if you want to," he said.

"That's something new," I said. "Being able to find you."

Watching him drive away was one of the hardest things I'd ever done. Behind me, my parents looked shaken but resolute.

———————

Turned thirty this year, Claire, and put my first million in the bank. What would you think of that? I think you'd expect it. Money is power. I hope you'd be proud. Big business. Big parties. Money. Land. Opportunity. Women . . .

The women. I hope to tell you about them someday. Whatever you want to know. You'll tell me about the men. And then we won't talk about that part of our past again, either of us, because it was only loneliness and plain human need.

Strange stuff, these letters. I talk to you on paper and lock the letters up. Nobody who knows me now would believe I do anything this sentimental. But then, they don't really know me.

———————

I WAS BARELY ABLE TO MOVE for several days. The knee and ankle of my healing leg swelled, were hot to the touch; every muscle
in my body punished me for standing on the leg too much. Emotionally, I felt scared, excited, and holding on as hard as I could.

I wanted to make Roan come to me because I was furious and
hurt. For years he'd let me suffer and worry about him while he
watched me neatly from a distance. He owed me explanations.

I watched Dunshinnog for the lure of another light. There
wasn't any. I was almost relieved. He expected me to follow him
everywhere, just as I had when we were kids. Away from the family
this time, away from home, never resolving the betrayals and regrets
on either side. I was afraid he'd ask me to leave with him.

And that he already suspected that sooner or later I'd go.

ROAN brought in his own crew to renovate the cabin at Ten
Jumps. My uncle Eldon told us about it the day he sold the crew's
foreman a tractor-trailer load of lumber, plumbing, electrical supplies, concrete mix, and assorted other necessities.

The crew immediately cleared and graveled the dirt road that led
to the cabin, then built a pair of stone columns where the dirt road
ended at the public road and hung a stately set of black iron gates.
Everyone was flabbergasted. "I don't know what to think about that
gate," my father said to me angrily. "Roan's thumbing his nose at us.
What are you going to do about it?"

"What are you going to do about *him?*" Mama added more
specifically. "Because he's not coming here. That's obvious."

"If I go, I'm afraid I'll lose something," I said, shaking my head
at my own vagueness. "I'm afraid he'll make me choose sides. And
I don't know which side I'd pick."

My parents stared at me, unsettled by that honest information.

FOOD. Of course. Like the old days. I would send him food.

I enlisted Hop and Evan to take it to him. We put together boxes
and ice chests filled with enough food to feed him and an entire
army of construction workers for several days. Food is apology;

food is a sacrament. There is more generosity in pies and casseroles than in a thousand pious words.

I also went through some of the storage boxes from my apartment in Florida. I found the large paperbound road atlas. The major cities and towns of each state had black lines drawn through them.

I wrapped the atlas in tissue paper and enclosed a note:

> It took me a lot of years and who-knows-how-much money in phone bills, but every black line represents a place where I called information and asked for the telephone number of Roan Sullivan. I called each one. It was never you. Is it you now?

"WHAT did he say?" I asked after my brothers returned from delivering the food.

"He looked pleased, I guess," Hop said, frowning. "I told him he shouldn't have brought in outsiders, that me and Evan would have sent a crew, but he just shrugged. You ought to see what he's done with the place in a week's time."

"That's what Roan said," Evan interjected. " 'Tell her to come see for herself. I wanted a nice spot for us to get to know each other again. It's almost ready.' " He nodded fervently. "He gave me something to bring back, sis." Evan presented me with a large, bulky manila envelope.

I laid it on my lap, ripped the envelope quickly, and pulled out a half-inch-thick portfolio bound in leather. I hurriedly scanned the handsomely printed columns and lists on the pages inside the binder. I saw an address in Seattle. Why there? Hop and Evan peered blatantly over my shoulders.

Land. Houses. Apartments. Buying. Selling. Leasing. Several states, several cities. I was stunned by the enormity of it.

"Good Lord," Hop breathed. "This is some kind of prospectus on his property holdings and investments."

Evan exhaled loudly. "He's telling you what he's worth, baby sister. And he's worth a fortune."

Roan had also sent a note:

Here's a gift in return for the food. In return for the atlas. Now you owe me another gift. You see, I remember how traditions stick in the family.

I'm going to get you out of that house, out of your bed, Claire. And you're going to get over here and take care of your own situation. Nobody to blame but me now. I'm real now, not an unlisted phone number anymore.

I took out the piece of old wood he'd carved with our names. I wrapped it with a bow, and Hop delivered it to Roan with my note:

I don't want your résumé. I don't want to know how much damned money you have. I want to know everything that happened to the boy who cut his name and mine into this board. Until you *share that boy with me,* nothing else matters. *Come here and bring your letters.*

He didn't offer any answer at all in response.

I GOT up at dawn the next day, dressed in my robe and jogging shoes, went to the sunroom, and stepped slowly onto a treadmill. My brother Josh strode into the room; he'd arrived from Atlanta well past midnight. We brusquely exchanged good mornings. He sat in a wingback chair with his coffee cup perched on his knee. He told me he had a full week planned. He still used his old bedroom at home, but he was away three weeks out of four, traveling or in Atlanta. He was in the midst of a campaign for lieutenant governor.

"I've got no use for Roan if he's here to cause trouble," Josh said finally. "He's made money, but money's not the same as family. He can't buy family."

"Don't preach at me," I said. "Cut to the chase, big brother."

"It means so much to Mama and Daddy to have you back home. I don't want the family torn apart over you and Roan."

"I have no intention of tearing the family apart. Roan redefined this family," I panted. "Brought out the best and the worst in us. Now it's time to prove we've changed for the better."

"You think I'm a hypocrite."

"On the contrary, I think you're desperate to believe the world isn't completely screwed up. That's why you're afraid to get close to your own daughter. You're afraid to care too much."

"Don't change the subject. How will you deal with Roan?"

"I plan to do everything in my power to make him believe it's possible for him to still be part of the family."

Josh craned his head. "You talk as if you're planning a future with him. But he's a stranger, Claire."

"He's not a stranger to me. He never will be."

"You could let yourself get . . . *attached* to him and then make a choice that would hurt you for the rest of your life."

"That's not going to happen. I won't let it."

"Listen." Josh leaned forward. "When I was on duty one night in Saigon, I saw a lovesick bar girl pour alcohol over her head and strike a match. It happened so fast I couldn't stop her. She burned like a Christmas tree. Was it my fault? Hell, no. If I'd sat around for years asking myself what I could have done differently, I'd have ended up contemplating a bottle of booze and a box of matches myself."

I stumbled off the treadmill and took several breaths. "We all come home from our wars with scars we can't forget," I said softly. "Is that why you blame Amanda for being born? You lost a wife and got a daughter in return, and you can't forgive the trade?"

His head jerked up. "There's a lot you don't know about me, sis," he said. He fumbled with his tie, got to his feet, and walked out.

———————

Another woman just told me I was a lost cause. She said she catches me looking through her as if she's not there. She's right. Part of me isn't finished. Isn't there.

We won't have a future until the past is torn apart and settled between me and the family, Claire. Until you and I look at each other and decide how many people we're willing to hurt.

I won't get close to other people because I don't want to tell them about myself. I killed my own old man. That's not the kind of thing you tell other people. I'm always separate.

I want something good to remember, Claire. Something I can hold on to, something that erases what happened. I want you to talk to that kid I used to be and tell him it's okay to come home. That you still love him.

And I want you to tell my boy he can be proud of me.

AMANDA was furious with me. "I'm not speaking to you," she said one afternoon. "Why won't you go see Mr. Sullivan?"

"Sweetie, you don't understand. We have to get to know—"

"Grandpa and Nana told me. They told me they sent him away a long time ago, and it hurt your feelings, and it hurt his feelings, too, and they're sorry about it, and they're doin' their best to make it all right. But you gotta help."

"I'm trying to help, sweetie. But when you're older, you'll understand that grown men and women have to be very responsible about their friendship. They have to move slowly."

Her eyes filled. "You sound like Papa. He thinks about makin' rules and laws so much, he forgets I'm even around."

"Your papa's just busy. He loves you so much."

"No, he doesn't. He won't say so, so he must not love me. Just like you must not love Mr. Sullivan, 'cause you won't *tell* him."

"Sweetie, I love Mr. Sullivan in a certain way. But sometimes even when you love somebody, you don't know what to say to them. You almost wish they'd stay away until you do know."

"You kissed him! On the *mouth*. Right after he came home."

"People kiss for a lot of reasons—"

"I told him about you. I was at the Pick 'N Save yesterday, and he was *there*. I went up to him, and I said, 'My aunt Claire is pretty, isn't she?' And he said, 'She's the prettiest, smartest, strongest woman I've ever seen.' And so I said, 'Well, if you don't come to visit her, you're not ever gonna see her, 'cause she won't even go to town.' And he said, 'I bet I can make her go to town.'"

"You are *so* much like your papa," I said to her. "You're a little politician. When you get to be President, I'll come stay in the Lincoln bedroom and I'll steal the pillowcases."

"I *told* him how you said he was wonderful and you never forgot him. And I told him you've still got his shamrock necklace!"

I shut my eyes. "And I get to steal Lincoln's sheets, too."

THE small gold box was delivered by Roan's foreman, a burly middle-aged man. I stood on the veranda leaning on a cane I'd borrowed from Grandma Dottie. "Have you worked for Mr. Sullivan before?" I asked.

"Here and there over the years."

"What kind of projects?"

"Oh, this and that."

"I see. Here and there. This and that. You're a discreet man."

He smiled. "I'm a well-paid man, and I like working for Roan Sullivan. And I've heard that you used to be a newspaper reporter, so I suspect you're trying to charm information out of me."

"I'm rusty. I'll have to be more devious."

"You'll have to ask Mr. Sullivan for any details you want."

Standing next to me, Mama refused to budge while I frowned deeply and opened the gift package. Inside a long, slender jewelry case was a delicate gold chain and a small filigreed shamrock pendant dotted with shimmering stones. A shamrock to replace the cheap dime-store original. My breath caught in my throat.

"They're emeralds," Mama said with wonder. "And diamonds."

"Would you like for me to take a reply back to Mr. Sullivan?" the man asked.

I hesitated. Mama looked at me firmly. "If you go over to Ten Jumps and Roan gets you off-balance, just *promise* me you'll eventually come back home and make him come home, too."

I felt as if Mama and I had finally come home ourselves, back to the trust we'd had between us when I was a child. I nodded. "I promise." Then I turned toward the foreman. "Tell Mr. Sullivan," I said, "that I'll be over to see him in the morning at first light and I intend to trade this necklace for the letters he owes me."

Mama hugged me.

I exhaled as if I'd been holding my breath for years.

Seven

WHAT he and his crew had done to Ten Jumps in less than two weeks would become the stuff of local legend.

He had rebuilt the old cabin—a new roof, a new porch, doors, windows, wiring, plumbing; he'd added a kitchen at the back and a low, large deck that stairstepped down the slope toward the lake, narrowing to a stone walkway that led to a gazebo under the water oaks.

When I arrived in the early morning, I was dressed for a construction site, not a handsome scene. I eased from one of the farm trucks in my jeans and T-shirt and hiking boots and was confronted with an elegant little Eden filled with men who were installing squares of sodded grass along smoothly graded earth.

"It's perfect," I whispered just before Roan reached the truck and gave me a hard kiss on the mouth.

"It is now," he corrected.

The kiss happened so fast—the feel of him imprinted on my lips. I was dizzy, and the breath went out of me.

I cocked my head in the direction of the cane I leaned on. "Borrowed it from Grandma. No more crutches."

"And no more excuses?" Roan asked quietly.

"Who's dodging reality? Me or you?"

He arched a brow, then slid his arm through mine as cozily as an old pal set for a stroll, except for the fact that he brushed his forearm, deliberately, I thought, along the side of my breast. He was as handsome as I'd ever imagined him, and I felt soft inside and scared.

We sat in the gazebo at a picnic table covered in linen and decorated with a silver vase filled with red roses.

"Grandpa would be glad you bought the place."

"Are you glad?" Roan asked.

I looked at him. "You know I am," I said.

"I wish you'd worn the necklace."

"I want the letters you wrote me. They're mine."

He gestured calmly toward the cabin. "I told you all you had to do was come here and get them. But I'd appreciate it if you'd wait until the crew leaves at noon. The letters are private."

We traded polite nods of agreement. It was an excruciating deal.

"Tell me about your business. And tell me how you ended up on the West Coast," I said.

He turned his chair to face mine. "I find land in opportune places," he said carefully. "I slip in and buy it before it's worth much, hold on to it, then sell when it's worth a lot more."

"Buy low, sell high. Take what nobody suspects is worth having, prove it's special."

"It's all about looking closer than other people will and looking farther. I learned that from you."

The mood was tender and electric between us. Because there was no easier way to do it, I asked quietly, "Are you married?"

"Good Lord, no."

"Why aren't you married? You've never been married?"

"Never," he said, searching my face. "Why aren't you?"

"I've been around. I just never cared enough."

"Same here."

"There's a lot you still haven't told me."

He retrieved a manila folder from beneath the table and handed it to me. I opened it and skimmed more documents. Properties he owned on the West Coast. There was a business address under the name Racavan, Inc. I shut the folder and put it aside. "You still think this is what I'm most interested in? How much money you have?"

"I just wanted you to know that part first."

"You mean you wanted the family to know."

"All right, I wanted them to know." He filled two crystal glasses from a bottle of champagne he'd set to chill in a bucket. He handed me a glass and then clicked his to mine. "I don't drink very often, and when I do, it's for quality, not quantity," he said simply.

He's hard on himself because of Big Roan's drinking, I thought. "I haven't had a drink since before, well, before—" I began.

"The night of the accident. Just say it. Get past it."

"It was no accident. I don't know what to call it."

"It was as much an accident as everything else life throws at people." Roan leaned toward me intently. "The only part of my life that feels like destiny, not just plain dumb accident, is you."

I bent my head. I didn't want to cry in front of him.

"Go ahead and indulge," he whispered. "You're safe with me."

I drew back, swallowed my champagne. I sat there blinking helplessly. We were both desperate to get beyond the cautious formalities. "What does Racavan stand for?" I asked.

He took a pen from a dusty breast pocket of his work shirt, pulled the folder between us on the table, and wrote *Rathcabhain*. "Irish," he said somberly. "I boiled it down to Racavan."

"*Rath*. Fortress." I struggled to translate the rest.

"Hollow," he said. "The fortress of the hollow."

THE crew left just before noon. "You need lunch," Roan said when we were alone. He bounded to his feet and disappeared into the cabin. A few minutes later he carried a wicker hamper back and set out white china plates, heavy silverware, and white napkins. Then he produced ceramic bowls and, as neatly as a schooled waiter, dished out boiled shrimp and colorful salads and croissants. He finished with a flourish, pouring cold white wine.

I stared at the spread. "Is that hamper bottomless?"

He inclined his head. "You always brought food to me. Now I want to bring food to you."

"Then I'll just have to eat it," I said softly, singing inside.

WE TALKED all afternoon.

The day grew more peaceful, and the clean scent of water and woods combined with the wine and the emotions to make me suddenly turn to Roan, grasping his hands and looking at him tearfully.

I told him I was anchored and so was he; we came from the same people, even without a direct bloodline. My line of conversation clearly dampened the mood, although his large, strong fingers stroked my hands urgently.

He knew how it was with my family. The kindest things they say to one another are rarely said out loud: They bring food and personal support, gifts and photographs. I took a photo album from my purse and laid it open on the table. "There," I said, thumping the album. Parades, ceremonies, reunions. "You're part of all that."

"You don't see me in the pictures, do you?" he countered.

"If you hadn't run away from the church home, you'd have been brought back to the farm. If you'd only trusted me more."

"Trusted you? Peep, you're the only person I did trust."

Peep. Tears slid down my face. I brushed them aside angrily. "You *will* feel at home here soon," I insisted. I went on urgently, telling him that polite compromise can be a virtue.

He said very little, but something shifted and settled between us. "You don't really believe I've come back here to stay," he said. "This isn't permanent. I'm setting up housekeeping just long enough to persuade you to leave with me."

"You'll stay," I said. "And right now I can't stand to think about you being out here alone at night. Come to the house. You've been invited. Come on. Make the effort."

"You're a grown woman. Stay here. Keep me company."

"I'm living under my parents' roof. I can't upset them."

"Then how about this? We'll get in a plane, and I'll fly us over to the coast. We'll find a hotel right by the ocean."

"Are you trying to seduce a woman who only has one good leg to stand on?"

"If I seduce you, you won't have to stand on it."

The rush of sensation was addictive. To *feel* again—the memory of his mouth, the relaxation of the champagne, the May warmth. I got up, took my cane, and made my way along the lake's edge. He walked beside me. "I've got a lot on my mind," I said.

"All right," he said, offering me his arm. "I'll give you an arm, you loan me the rest of you, and I'll show you around the cabin."

I looked from him to the cabin, sitting beautifully in its new, pristine state. Renewal. Trust. Comfort. The lure of privacy between us.

An evening mist began to gather on the lake; a lone mourning dove flew into the forest, as if headed across the ridge that led to the Hollow.

The Hollow. Suddenly we were connected to the same earth as the Hollow. The terrible memories were too close by, and I saw them in Roan's eyes, felt them in my own. "Stop thinking about it," I said suddenly, as much to myself as to him. "You're not alone here now."

He looked at me gratefully. I slid my hand around the crook of his elbow, and we walked slowly up the slope.

I SAT with queenly luxury in an overstuffed armchair in the cabin's refurbished main room, next to the fireplace. Roan moved among the room's brass lamps, woven rugs, and dark furniture with a kind of charming masculine vagueness about the decor.

After a while I got to my feet, went to the bedroom door, and peered in at a large bedstead of thick posts in pale wood. The bed was covered in a voluptuous green comforter. Roan studied me, his hands on his hips. "I like green," he said. "But the first time I sat down on that comforter, I felt like a big rabbit in an Easter basket."

I laughed, then thought of Easter baskets, the McClendon sisters, and Big Roan, the violence that Easter at Steckem Road. I turned and went back to my chair, sank down in it unsteadily. Roan came over and placed my feet on an ottoman, then removed my hiking shoes and my socks. He curved his hands around the foot of my injured leg and pressed gently with his fingers, massaging. "I want to help," he said, "because you keep shifting your leg as if it's aching."

Scattered warnings moved through my thoughts, but they couldn't overcome the power of temptation. His hands felt so good. Roan molded them around my scarred ankle. The warmth spreading through my body became full, rich, and urgent.

I was letting him have his way with me, so to speak, poised on the chair with no willpower to stop him. "I don't know what to do about you," I whispered. "I'm just so glad you're alive."

He went still. He bowed his head slowly to my foot, then rested his cheek against the pink line of scar tissue. "I almost lost you forever. I don't want to let you out of my sight again. I don't care whether anyone understands how we can be this way with each other so fast. I want you."

I was shaking. I feathered my hand over his hair as he raised his face to my touch. He got up, bent over me, and we kissed in long, smooth sequences of exploration. I had my arms halfway up, to slip them around his shoulders, when I remembered how many years he'd let me agonize over him.

I pushed back from him. "This isn't fair, and you know it."

Roan gazed at me. "Has our situation ever been fair?"

"I love you," I yelled. "I know I do, whether it makes sense to love a man I haven't seen in two decades or not. And if you're using me to prove you can *own* me, I'll still love you, but I'll never touch you again. If you can't tell me why you disappeared for twenty years, then what we are to each other is a lie."

He turned and walked into the bedroom, then returned carrying a deep metal file box. He set it on the ottoman in front of me. "You may not want to touch me after you read these."

He opened the box and riffled through bulging file folders until he pulled out several wrinkled sheets of paper. "This is a letter you need to read first," he explained, laying it on my knees.

My hands shook. Haphazard handwriting filled the pages:

> He nearly died this week, and now I understand what I've got to do, Claire.
>
> It's been extra cold this winter, and I got a lot of work to do on a couple of rundown split-level ranches I bought last fall. I bring him with me to work every day after he gets out of school, and I give him some tools to learn with. He works hard, but he's not interested in property. He's crazy about animals.
>
> Anyhow, he got sick to his stomach the other afternoon and

started running a bad fever. I took him to the emergency room. It was his appendix. They had to take it out. I was so scared he might die. I couldn't stand to be that alone in the world again.

When he woke up after surgery, he held on to my hand like he did when he was a baby. He said he wasn't scared, because I was there. I rocked him and promised him I'd always be there.

That's when I knew how much I loved him and he loved me. I can't risk somebody taking him away from me. If I never do anything else good with my life, I have to raise him. I can be the kind of daddy I never had, and maybe that can make up for what my old man did to you.

But see, I know now that I can't tell you where I am. If I get in touch with you, the family would find out sooner or later. I can't have that happen, at least not until he's old enough to take care of himself. And so I'm missing you worse than usual tonight. I'm broken up inside. I'm going to raise this boy because I love him and because he's like a bridge to you.

You'd want me to do this, I think. Because if you knew what I know about him, you'd understand why your family's not ever going to want to know.

And you might wish I'd never come back.

I couldn't breathe. "You have a son?"

He hesitated. His eyes held my fixed gaze. "I adopted him."

"All right. Then you knew his mother? You must have loved her. Who was she?"

"I didn't love her," he said flatly. "I lived with her and the boy for a few years. The years right after I ran away. Then she died. The boy was only about seven then."

"Why couldn't you tell me? Why couldn't you risk having the family find out where you were and that you were raising a child?"

Roan put a hand over mine and gripped hard. "Claire, his name's Matthew. Sally McClendon was his mother."

I sat back, stunned. *"Matthew,"* I whispered.

My uncle Pete's son. Roan had raised Matthew Delaney.

THE MOON WAS HIGH, ITS white light cast down as shimmering silver on the lake's black mirror. Deceptive serenity.

I sat on the edge of the new porch of the cabin. Roan stood in the yard, his hands shoved in his trouser pockets. It was time to be still, to be quiet, sort through the labyrinth of emotion.

As a boy, Roan had listened to Sally talk about her daydreams. When she left, he had ideas about where she'd gone. He found her living in a small apartment and working at a strip club in a town he didn't name. She took him in for a few years.

Roan came over and sat down on the porch steps beside me. "I didn't sleep with her. Room and board. That's all it was."

I nodded, relieved. Sally got him a job in a back-alley chop shop, dismantling stolen cars. He was good at that and made money.

"What happened to Sally?"

"She was killed. She picked up the wrong guy one night, and he beat her to death in a motel room."

"How old were you then?"

"I was about nineteen, so I'd been with her and Matthew for maybe four years. I'd changed his diapers, fed him, read bedtime stories to him. I took care of him. I always did."

"You could have asked the family for help."

"Don't tell me that. Your folks wouldn't publicly admit Matthew was their own kin, much less take him in to raise. They'd have turned him over to foster care, just like they did me."

"You're wrong. They'd have welcomed you and him back."

"I'm not going to argue a useless point. It's done. I pretty much stole him after Sally died. Got him a fake birth certificate, changed his last name to Sullivan, and we headed west."

"Oh, Roan." When the family learned that he'd saved Matthew, he'd be showered with more love and admiration than he could imagine. And so would Matthew. "We have to tell them," I said.

"They don't want him."

"Oh, *Roan*. So much has changed. Uncle Pete was killed years ago in a hunting accident. Harold was killed on the stock-car track. Arlan's pretty much deserted the family."

"I know all about Pete and his boys," Roan said darkly.

I moved around in front of him on the steps, leaning into his chest with my hands around his face. "We can resolve this."

He covered my hands. "For twenty years I didn't know how we could deal with what I had to tell you, and I still don't know. But I do love you. Don't ever doubt that."

I put my arms around him. "I've never cared what other people said about us. All that matters is that I know *who* you are. Hello."

His eyes glittered. He laughed hoarsely and then kissed me, and we were frantic with relief, clinging to each other. He stroked my hair and face, the years fading and shifting.

He carried me inside and put me on that deep green new bed in the old cabin. Slowly he removed his clothes, and then, slowly, he helped me undress. "Well, here we are," he said quietly, looking at me in ways that brought goosebumps to my skin.

Breathless, I placed kisses down his body, and he did the same to mine. We lay together, our hands moving over each other. "We would have been like this years ago if we'd had the chance," he said softly. "Not a whole lot of grace, but plenty of love."

"A little grace and a lot of love is all I need," I told him.

He eased a pillow under my injured leg. It didn't hurt, I told him, and he swore he'd be careful, and I knew he would be. He put his arms under my shoulders, cradling my head, his mouth just above mine. "Help me go where I belong," he whispered.

And I did.

THERE was room for hope. I would coax Matthew McClendon Delaney Sullivan back home. All of Roan's mysteries would be explained, and anyone who had ever doubted him would be ashamed of themselves. I felt more serene and hopeful than I had in years.

"Thank you for calling last night to let us know you'd be home by morning," Mama said briskly when Roan and I returned to the farm at dawn. "We appreciate the courtesy."

"Roan and I had a lot to talk about," I answered, which at least proffered a dignified alibi.

All Daddy said was, "I'm sure y'all talked up a storm."

Roan stepped ahead of me, facing them. "I asked Claire to visit the West Coast with me for a few days," he said quietly. "Seattle."

Daddy thrust out his chin. "Seattle?" he barked. "Why?"

"It's all right," I said gently. "It's just a trip we need to make."

"You promised," Mama reminded me.

"We'll be back," I repeated. "And we'll bring you a gift."

By early afternoon we had flown more than halfway across the country. We spent the afternoon in a town just outside Seattle. The town reminded me of Dunderry when we were children: one main street, a lot of pickup trucks, a municipal park with benches.

Racavan, Inc., was based in a four-room suite in a small brick office building next to a coffeehouse. Roan introduced me to Bea, his assistant and the manager of the three-secretary staff. She bear-hugged me and said cheerfully, "R.S. warned me about you."

Roan said to me in a dry tone, "I told her you were probably the mysterious *businesswoman* who called last week pretending to look for commercial property. You can't hide your accent."

My face turned hot, but I shrugged. "I'm a journalist. I was just curious about your business. Nothing sinister about that."

"R.S. said you wouldn't be able to resist." Bea laughed.

"Do you know Roan's Matthew very well?" I asked abruptly.

Bea's brows shot up. "Of course. He and my grandsons are friends. They played basketball at school together. Matthew just graduated from the university this spring with honors. And he married the sweetest girl in the world. But you know all that."

"Of course. But thank you."

"He's married?" I said to Roan when we walked outside a minute later. "That wasn't worth mentioning to me?"

"I had to be at the wedding and the graduation this spring," Roan answered. "It's why I couldn't get back to you sooner. I don't like to talk about it, because it was hard to be torn two ways."

"You were right to be at his wedding and graduation," I said quietly. "You're his family. I understand."

"I know you do," Roan said, and put his arms around me.

ROAN'S HOUSE SAT ON A wooded back road a few minutes' drive from town. It was a handsome cedar two-story, with copper trim and fine stonework and a few acres of shady hilly land.

"It's a good, hearty house," I said appreciatively. "I like it."

"You might like living here," Roan said as we entered a hallway done in heavy woods and tapestry wall hangings.

"I'd enjoy staying here when we're visiting Seattle."

We looked at each other sadly, and the subject died.

But I picked up some good details about him that day. In his large closets there were fine suits and shoes, but also a row of unpolished western boots lovingly worn. Floor-to-ceiling shelves were filled with books, and in an alcove off the bedroom he had a computer, a printer, a fax machine, and a copier.

"Sleep. Work. Work. Sleep," I joked, pointing from the office alcove to the bedroom. It was late afternoon by then. I was exhausted; Roan looked tired, too. I took his hand. "We've got a long flight tomorrow. What would you rather do? Work or sleep?"

He picked me up. "You know what I'd rather do right now."

"Smart man," I said. We went to bed.

NEVER let it be said that I don't try to make calculated first impressions on people. Plain brown loafers for practicality, a calf-length black denim skirt to hide the funky leg, a delicate green sweater, and an ugly yellow rain slicker, which I purchased at the Seattle airport before we boarded our Alaska Air flight.

Roan, in creased khakis, a blue chambray shirt, hiking boots, and a brown leather aviator jacket, looked like a darkly rugged individualist who belonged in the Pacific Northwest. I looked like a rejected model for a Seattle Chamber of Commerce ad.

"I'm so nervous I feel sick," I said.

"You're perfect. Matthew will be impressed," Roan answered.

"I'm his cousin, Roan. We'll be okay with each other."

"You're a meddling stranger to him, Peep."

I chewed my tongue and looked at Roan pointedly. "Well, I'm obviously successful at meddling. I got you back, didn't I?"

THE ALASKAN MOUNTAINS WERE huge, wild, snowcapped monuments compared to the comfortable old blue-green ranges where we were born. Below the descending jet the ocean channels looked deep and far more frigid than any Georgia waters. I decided Alaska was a state of extremes. What had Roan taught my cousin Matthew? Independence, strength, confidence, a spirit of adventure? Or Roan's own isolation?

Roan held my hand as the small jet landed smoothly across the channel from Juneau, the state capital. A flight attendant carried the hand luggage down the stairway for us. I braced one hand on Roan's outstretched arm and clutched the staircase rail on my bad side, peering over him, searching the waiting area.

A tall, lanky young man with sandy hair strode purposefully across the tarmac. He was dressed in gray trousers, a plaid shirt, and hiking boots. Hurrying beside him was a short, plump, sweet-faced young woman in nearly identical clothes. Her dark blond hair flew back from her face like loose wheat straw. The pair looked wholesome and ruddy. The last of the fair-haired pioneers lived in Alaska.

Roan put an arm around me, and we faced the advancing pair. The young man walked up to us without hesitation, his green eyes shifting from me to Roan. He towered over me but was maybe an inch shorter than Roan. Then he smiled and thrust out a brawny hand. Beside him, his wife began to cry silently.

"I'm not going to shake your hand," I announced. "I'm not a stranger. I'm your cousin. You're part of my family." I gazed at the woman beside him. "And your wife is part of my family, too."

"I'm Mildred," she said. "But everyone calls me Tweet."

"Hello, Tweet. I'm Claire. Your cousin-in-law." Then to Matthew, who was gaping at me, I said, "I'm going to *hug* you if at all possible." I lurched at him, hugged him voraciously, and after a stunned moment he hugged me in return. Then Tweet and I hugged, and finally I turned toward Roan, who stood unmoving, his expression shuttered. I grasped his hand. See, I urged silently.

I thought the hardest part was behind us.

Eight

MY FIRST goal was to learn what had drawn Matthew to Alaska. Cold, gray, oceanfronted Juneau and wilderness backed the scenery; the city was secluded, to say the least. A summer honeymoon in Alaska had been one of Roan's wedding gifts to Matthew and Tweet.

Dr. Matthew Sullivan and Dr. Mildred "Tweet" Sullivan. Both of them were veterinarians, fresh from the state university in Washington. Smart and motivated, obviously. I couldn't see Uncle Pete's pugnacious face in Matthew's large-boned features. There was something Delaneyish about the bulldog set of his jaw maybe, but physically he was a troubling cipher.

As we drove home from the airport in Matthew's mud-spattered Bronco, Tweet kept turning to smile at me and wipe tears from her eyes. I reached between the front seats and tapped her shoulder. "I hear that you and Matthew are veterinarians."

She peered at me, nodding. "Brand-new doctors! This summer in Alaska is a working honeymoon. Wildlife rehab."

"Rescue work," Matthew added crisply. "Eagles who've swallowed fishhooks, wolves hit by cars—that kind of thing."

I glanced poignantly at Roan. He was very proud.

"I'll tell you the major reason we picked this place for the summer," Matthew said. "Roan said he'd probably have to tell your family about me, and I wanted to be someplace where it wouldn't be easy for them to find me unless I wanted them to."

"I see." I swallowed hard and nodded. "You deserve to make up your mind your way, Matthew. Just keep an *open* mind, please."

"I'll see what I can do," he agreed tightly.

Roan took one of my hands and cradled it in both of his. "I know what I want," he said. "I want Claire to have a little tour of town. Drive around for a few minutes, Matt."

Matthew whipped the Bronco along narrow streets that snaked up steep, crowded hills. "Tweet and I got the guest room ready for you, Bigger," Matthew said. "It's nothing fancy, Claire, but it has a private bathroom and a big . . ." His voice trailed off.

"Big what?" I mumbled. "Bigger what?"

Tweet pivoted in her seat, blushing. "A bed that's big enough for both of you," she finished. "And Bigger is Roan's nickname."

I glanced at Roan. "R.S., how many nicknames do you have?"

"When Matthew started school, he figured out that I wasn't old enough for him to call me his dad around the other kids," Roan explained with gruff exasperation. "And brother wasn't exactly right. So he decided to call me his Bigger. It just stuck."

"Bigger," I repeated. "It sounds funny, but it suits you."

"I didn't think it sounded funny when I was a kid who needed somebody to look up to," Matthew said with an edge in his voice.

Roan leaned forward. "Take it easy," he ordered quietly.

Matthew exhaled sharply. "I'm sorry, Claire. I just don't know what to say to you. You came here because you care, and I appreciate that, but Bigger and I've done pretty well on our own."

"You said hello to me," I replied softly. "You made me feel welcome. That's all I need right now and all I expect."

There was so much tension in the air. I took deep breaths to find oxygen. "Until a few weeks ago I was a basket case. Roan changed all that. I may not be Wonder Woman yet, but if you feed me dinner and give me a place to prop my feet up, I'll answer any questions you want to ask about our family, Matthew."

"Your family, not mine," Matthew countered. "They didn't want me. Roan's the only family I care about. Him and Tweet. I'm sorry, Claire. You're welcome here because Roan loves you. He told me all about you. But if you came here just for my sake, you came a long way for nothing."

"We'll see," I said. I watched Matthew tug at both earlobes, and

I thought with amazement, My brothers do that when they're wor-ried. So does Mama. So do I. It's obviously an inherited Delaney trait. I was certain then that I could coax him home to Dunderry. "But you know," I said suddenly, all charm and patience, "all I really want to do right now is hear all about the two of you."

"What a sweet thing to say!" Tweet exclaimed. "I'm so glad you're here. You're Matthew's cousin. We really do want to know about *you*, too. Matthew does. He really does!"

I glanced at Roan, watching me closely. He'd caught on. I was planning to sugar his boy, and he knew I'd made up my mind.

THEIR house was a wood-shingled bungalow perched up on a hillside. Matthew and Tweet had two dogs, shaggy mixed breeds who wagged and slobbered and flopped on the main room's braided rugs with their bellies exposed for me to scratch. A multi-level collection of perches sat in one corner of the living room. Two large green parrots, two cockatiels, and two parakeets fluttered on the perches, squawking with a cheerful bawdiness.

I knew I could pry more personal information about Matthew from Tweet. Reporters develop an instinct for the easy interviews, and she was one of the most openhearted people I'd ever met. While Matthew and Roan shared salmon-grilling duties on a back porch, I sat down with Tweet in the living room.

"Maybe I'm reaching here," I said as Tweet nuzzled each of her bird flock. "But I'd bet money that *your* nickname—"

"Yep." She grinned. "I love birds. This one"—she stroked one of the parrots—"was my first. My parents gave him to me."

"Where do your parents live?"

"They don't." She retrieved a glass of wine from a handsome oak table and sipped it. I sipped from my own glass. "They were killed in a boating accident when I was twelve. I was raised by friends of my parents. So I grew up like Matthew—adopted."

I found that very interesting. Tweet came over and sat down beside me. "Roan doesn't know this, but Matthew and I met in a support group for adoptees."

I inhaled sharply. "Why haven't y'all told Roan?"

"Because he doesn't understand how adopted people fantasize about their biological parents. Your family is a big mystery to Matthew, and he can't stop wondering about them."

I sat back, blinking in amazement. "I can't believe he's never *admitted* that to Roan. They're so close."

"Matthew doesn't want Roan to feel betrayed. Roan's always been dead set against Matthew contacting any relatives. When Roan suddenly told us he was going back to Georgia to see you, we were shocked. We thought Roan had *no* good memories about your family. That's one reason Matthew never pushed it."

I was stunned. "But Roan was mainly concerned about protecting Matthew when Matthew was underage. He thought my family might find him and interfere. He was wrong. They would have been good to Matthew and him, too, if he'd let us know where he was. And now Matthew's grown. There's nothing to worry about."

"Except that Matthew wants Roan's approval," Tweet whispered, glancing around. "He won't do anything that might make Roan feel discarded."

"Listen to me. If Matthew wants to meet the family, Roan will support his decision. You have to believe that."

"Don't get me wrong. Roan's been wonderful to Matthew. And to me. You should have seen our wedding this spring."

This spring. Roan had visited me in the hospital but couldn't stay. He had to be at Matthew and Tweet's graduation and at their wedding. Trying to do the right thing for me and for them.

"You look upset," Tweet said anxiously. "I'm sorry."

"No. Go on. Tell me about the wedding."

"Roan paid for the whole thing. Three hundred guests, an orchestra at the reception. It was magical." She dabbed her eyes. "Matthew asked Roan to serve as his best man. Roan was really pleased to be asked, I know. But he looked absolutely *miserable* during the ceremony. In fact, he was kind of strange during the whole spring, and now we understand why—he was going nuts over your circumstances, but he didn't tell us about you until after we were married."

"He didn't want to ruin your special moments," I told her. "You see, don't you? He did what was best for Matthew and for you."

Tweet leaned toward me. "Be honest with me." Her round sweet face became fierce; her voice shook with emotion. "I don't want Matthew to visit your family if they're going to reject him."

"Matthew's family," I corrected. "And they won't reject him."

"Matthew won't go if Roan doesn't agree."

"He will agree. You and Matthew," I said slowly, "don't know Roan the way I do. From childhood. He won't let you down."

"We know he was poor, of course."

"Do you know how my family treated Roan?" I asked carefully.

"He's always told Matthew they were good to him but that your parents finally decided he'd be better off in a foster home. That sounds pretty, hmmm, *cold* to me, Claire."

"My parents have never forgiven themselves for sending him away," I said, weighing every word. "What happened between him and my family wasn't his fault. And nobody wanted to lose track of Matthew either. I'm trying desperately to get everybody back together. I need some sense of redemption myself. Roan counted on me when we were kids, and he got hurt because of it."

Tweet frowned. "You sound so much like Roan. You're both really *into* guilt and responsibility. I'm missing something here."

I stared at her. "You know about me, of course, and what happened with Roan's father."

"Oh, yes." She nodded. "You were Roan's only friend. He was poor, you tried to help him, his mother died when he was little, Roan's father was kind of disreputable, and he died young."

Kind of *disreputable? Died* young? I studied her with growing dread. "Roan's father died . . . suddenly. But you know that."

"Of course Matthew and I know the important details about Roan's past." She gazed at me impatiently. "Roan's dad was a disabled Korean veteran. He drank too much. Roan pretty much raised himself. And then his dad died of a heart attack."

Oh, my Lord. Matthew and Tweet had no idea what a monster Big Roan had been or that Roan had *killed* him for my sake.

"Oh, come on, let's lighten up!" Tweet exclaimed suddenly. "I feel as if Matthew and I have known you forever. I'm so glad you're here!" She threw her arms around me and hugged me.

I sat there, frozen. I finally understood. If we brought Matthew home, Roan could no longer hide what he'd done to survive.

WE STAYED up late, talking to Matthew and Tweet. I made good on my plan to ask Matthew harmless questions about himself, and he warmed up to me, while Roan watched us with a wary smile.

It worked. When we said our good nights, Matthew hugged me. And so did Tweet again. I liked them together; they adored each other. Mama would melt with romantic approval.

I took Roan's arm, and we walked into the guest room. He shut the door. My façade crumbled, and I slumped on the bed. Roan sat down in a chair by the window without turning on a lamp.

"What do you want from me tonight, Peep?" he said quietly.

"You need to explain something to me."

He frowned but moved over and sat beside me on the bed.

"You've never told Matthew the truth about *how* your daddy died. And my part in how he died. Roan, you've got to tell him."

He shut his eyes for a moment. "I've tried to tell him a hundred times. But I couldn't stand to screw up a good thing."

"You wouldn't have ruined how he feels about you. I've only been around him a few hours, but I already see the tremendous love and respect he has for you. Tell him the truth now."

"I don't ever want him to feel sorry for me. Or embarrassed."

"Come on, Roan, he'll never reject you."

Roan turned toward me angrily. "After all these years, *now* I'm supposed to tell him, 'Oh, by the way, I blew my old man's brains out with a pistol after I caught him slapping Claire around.'"

"If you need to be that blunt about it, yes."

"And tell him how your family—*his* family—shipped me off because they couldn't stand the sight of a Sullivan anymore?"

"Yes." I was trembling. "Tell him exactly how it was, and we'll deal with it. You owe him the truth."

"I don't want him to see the Hollow. I don't want people to tell him about me—about white-trash Roanie Sullivan who smelled like garbage. He doesn't know what I was!"

"You were special. You were strong and decent and gentle. Anything ugly that he'll learn will only help him know how special you are because you overcame so much."

"There's nothing I can do about it if he doesn't want to go back. I keep telling you it's his decision."

"Roan, that's not true." I took his face between my hands and repeated everything Tweet had told me about Matthew's attitude and motivation. "He wants to go," I finished. "But he's loyal to you, and you have to let him know you agree."

Sorrow, shock, and finally resignation sank into Roan. "He's never even *hinted*," he murmured. "I didn't have a clue."

I put my arms around him. "He won't go unless you tell him you want him to go," I repeated. "I know you'll do it."

"I told you I wouldn't interfere when you tried to persuade him," Roan said. "But I never promised I'd help."

Amazed, I drew back. "What kind of life can we have together if you won't make peace with the past? You can't hide Matthew from my family. It'll all come out eventually." I paused. "Unless you and I go our separate ways and don't see each other."

He bent over me. "You know that's not an option."

"Then trust me."

"He doesn't belong in Dunderry," Roan said flatly. "He won't be accepted there. And neither will I. Stop counting on fairy tales." He got up, then walked out of the room and shut the door.

He came back an hour later, and I pretended to be asleep. He pretended to let me sleep until he brushed against me in bed, and then we made love to each other with tenderness and anger.

But we didn't talk.

MATTHEW and Tweet drove us to the ferry docks on the Juneau waterfront the next day, and the four of us boarded a small tourist ferry that Matthew and Tweet had hired for a private excursion.

"It'll take all afternoon, round-trip," Matthew explained politely. "You can sit, Claire. Take it easy, watch the world go by."

"I'd pay money to see her take it easy," Roan countered. I squinted at him, then feigned an innocent perusal of the box filled with photo albums I had brought from home. I set a half-dozen books on the table where the four of us sat drinking tea.

Matthew stared, bewildered, at the collection of books.

"Books about the Delaneys, the Maloneys, and the history of Dunderry," I explained.

Tweet blinked. "How many relatives does Matthew have?"

I counted Delaneys. "Twenty first cousins. Four aunts—including my mother—and three uncles. About forty second cousins."

"Good Lord."

I shuffled the books aside as a waiter began setting cups of fish chowder on the table. Matthew's expression grew agitated. He clamped a hand on top of the photo albums. "Claire, I don't think there's much use in showing me a bunch of family pictures." He jabbed a thumb at himself. "I won't find any baby pictures of yours truly." He glanced at Roan. "What do you think, Bigger?"

"I think you're right," Roan said. "There's no point in it."

"Claire, I don't care what these two say," Tweet muttered. "I'm going to look at the pictures."

"Thank you," I said with as much grace as I could. I watched Roan throughout the meal. He'd completely dissuade Matthew from ever meeting the family if he could. He wouldn't risk exposing his own history to Matthew. How could he be that heartless to Matthew? And how could he do it to me?

I snatched a stack of dog-eared snapshots from my tote bag. My hands trembled. Roan watched me grimly. "Matthew," I said softly, "are you a coward?" I shook the photographs at him. "These can't hurt you. They can't hurt Roan either."

Matthew frowned at Roan. "I *would* like to see if I can pick out Pete Delaney without you or Claire telling me who he is."

Roan's jaw worked. He appeared tortured. "Go ahead."

"I guess I need to know if I look like him." He flipped through the stack. I clenched my hands in my lap and glanced at Roan.

"This one," Matthew said. His voice shook as he planted his fore-finger on a snapshot.

Tweet gasped. "Oh, *yes,* honey. You look *exactly* like him."

In the old black-and-white picture the stalwart crew-cut young man gazing up at us seemed undeniable. He couldn't have resembled Matthew more. I finally understood what had puzzled me every time I looked at Matthew.

I felt as I had when Terri Caulfield's ex-husband shot at us and I lost control of my Jeep. Spinning, horrified, out of control. I pulled myself together and said, "No. That's my oldest brother—Josh."

I gazed hopelessly at Roan. His eyes were bleak but honest. I shoved another picture into Matthew's hands, then made myself say, "That's Pete. That's your father."

"Well," Matthew replied in a gruff voice after studying the photo for a long time, "it's no wonder nobody forced Pete Delaney to admit I was his. I didn't look remotely like him."

And then he tossed the picture in my lap and got up and went to Roan. "You were right," Matthew said gruffly. "It wasn't worth the trouble. I only care because—"

"You need to know where you came from," Roan said with slow agony. "Even if your old man was an s.o.b., you need to know. I see that. You're not going against my wishes. I know what you're feeling. I'm scared for you. Because it's hell when you want to love your old man, but he makes you hate him."

Matthew shook his head. "I don't think I'm a Delaney at all."

I was reduced to helpless rage. All the failures rose up in me at once: Roan killing Big Roan; Roan being taken away; being in the crumpled Jeep, lost in Terri Caulfield's bloody face; trapped on crutches and inside my own mistakes.

"You *are* one of us," I yelled at Matthew, and burst into sobs. Roan was beside me in an instant, wrapping his arms around me.

"Don't say any more. Not here, not right now," he whispered. "I'm sorry. Peep, believe me. I understand. Shh." He stroked my hair. I nodded against his shoulder and cried harder.

Now I knew the only secret that mattered, the secret that had always made a homecoming for him and Matthew impossible.

Matthew was my brother's son.

WHEN I was ten and Roan fifteen, during the spring when he lived at the farm, there was a huge work party one weekend to restore the Delaney covered bridge. Over the long Memorial Day weekend in May, dozens of Delaney kin descended on the site with tools and materials. The event quickly bloomed into a three-day festival complete with picnics and ad-lib entertainment.

Roan approached the weekend as part of his work chores for Daddy and, as always, kept to himself, while I circled from my cousins' orbit on regular swoops to bring him food and talk to him.

Josh came home from college for the weekend. I remembered him and Roan sitting astride the bridge's shabby peaked roof, ripping the frayed shingles. Uncle Pete chainsawed fresh timbers with a team of men that included Daddy and my uncles.

There was a general murmur of shock when Sally McClendon appeared at the edge of the picnic tables. She had Matthew in tow; he was about three years old then. She stood there, a beacon of shame and notoriety, clutching Matthew by the hand.

I glanced up from the immediate melodrama and saw Josh staring at Sally from the bridge's roof. Roan handed him a double-clawed crowbar, and Josh fumbled it. The bar fell between the exposed rafters, then fell through a hole into the river.

Josh never took his eyes off Sally and her son. Sally stared back at him. I'll never forget the look she gave him—accusing, mean, and helpless. She picked Matthew up and held him in the air toward my brother, like a proffered sacrifice. Then she flung him atop one hip and trudged off toward her ancient sedan.

Josh came down from the roof, jumped into the river, and hunted in the waist-high water beneath the bridge until he retrieved the crowbar. He never said a word to anyone.

The memory came back with terrible clarity now.

And finally made sense.

ROAN AND I WENT TO OUR room early that night, then sat on the edge of the bathtub with the faucet turned on. We were both a little paranoid about being overheard.

Roan spoke, his voice low. "I'm sorry I kept the truth from you, but I had to know if Matthew would pass for a Delaney. Now I know. He won't fool anyone."

"You're sure about Josh, aren't you?"

"Sally told me when I moved in with her. She wanted me to know why she left town. She thought Daisy was going to tell your folks the truth out of meanness after my old man—"

"What did she say about Josh? Tell me exactly."

"Josh would pick her up on the road north of Murphy's Feed Mill. Throw a couple of blankets in the back of one of the farm trucks, park in the woods. Use her, pay her, let her out."

"Oh, Lord."

"He only met her out there a few times. Then he stopped. She was scared to admit she'd ever been with him. She thought your family'd take the baby and chase her out of town. Believe it or not, she really did love Matthew. She wanted to keep him."

"Mama and Daddy could forgive Josh for fathering a child but not for being a coward who turned his back on his responsibility."

"All right, Peep. But here's the problem we've got to handle— you didn't have to look hard today to see the resemblance."

"Josh *knew* Matthew was his," I hissed. "He *knew*."

Roan hesitated. "That day at the Delaney bridge."

"You remember that, too!"

"I've thought about it over the years. Josh didn't want Matthew. It was obvious. That's why I never doubted that I was right to keep him. And I thought everybody in the family saw how strange Josh was around Sally and her baby that day. I thought other people saw the truth. It's what convinced me Matthew wouldn't get a fair shake if I brought him home."

I snatched my cane like a club. "I could kill Josh! How could he ignore his own *son?* He's the reason you had no choice."

"I still don't have many choices, Peep."

"I know. The family's going to find out about Matthew sooner or later. What we have to do is *manage* the process."

Roan uttered a dark sound of amusement. "Maloneys," he said.

I told Roan I thought I should speak to Josh first. Yell, scream, get it out of my system. Learn what he intended to do about Matthew. "This is something between Josh and me. Just us first."

Roan moved to sit in front of me on the bathroom floor, his expression harder than I'd ever seen it. "It's my business, too, Peep," he warned. "If your brother doesn't do the right thing by Matthew, I'll hurt him, Claire. I swear I'll make him pay."

That was chilling. "We can ease Matthew into it," I said. "Just get him there, get everybody warmed up to Matthew and Tweet and vice versa, and deal with Josh on the side, privately—talk to him, the two of us. It's *his* duty to confess to the family. And to Matthew."

"Matthew probably won't go to Dunderry anyway. He was disappointed and apathetic after he looked at those pictures."

I said nothing else and let Roan enjoy that small consolation for the rest of the night. Matthew would go home eventually. Like foxgloves, we always came back to where we started.

The next day Matthew and Tweet cornered us in the living room.

Matthew glanced from Roan to me, frowning. "Look, I need the truth from the Delaneys. I want to meet them."

Roan and I traded glances. Suddenly Matthew pushed a phone across the coffee table. "Speakerphone. Call your mother, Claire. Tell her about me. I want to hear her reaction." He smiled tentatively. "If I'm welcome to visit, I want to know it *now*."

"We're not going to do this," Roan said. "Not this way."

Matthew shook his head. "Bigger, you can't protect me anymore. I'm going to meet my father's family on my terms." He tugged on his ears firmly. "Either Claire places the call, or I'll do it myself."

I looked at Roan. We were trapped. Mama, don't fail me, I prayed silently as I reached for the phone.

"Claire!" Mama's voice sang out, melodic and southern and urgent. "Are you okay? Is Roan okay? Where are you?"

"We're fine, Mama. We're . . . in Alaska, Mama."

"What? Wait! Holt! Holt! Get on the other line. It's Claire. They're in *Alaska!* Just a second, sweetie. Daddy just came in from the barns."

"Hey," Daddy's deep voice grunted at us suddenly.

"Hi, Papa. Everything's fine. I just need to discuss something with y'all. Is this a good time?"

"Oh, for Lord's sake, *talk*," Mama said. "What's going on? You and Roan are coming home, aren't you? Tell me straight out."

"We're coming back," Roan interjected.

"Roan," Mama and Daddy said in unison.

"It's good to hear you," Daddy went on. "We'll take you at your word anytime."

"That's good to know," Roan replied evenly.

"What's in Alaska?" Daddy asked.

I hesitated. "It's not a what. It's a *who*."

Silence. Mama said quietly, "This who isn't a wife?"

"Not even a girlfriend," Roan answered in a strangled voice.

"Then you've got a child. Or children."

Silence. Roan looked at Matthew. "You could say that."

I took a deep breath. "He brought me here to meet *Matthew*. Uncle Pete's Matthew. Roan located Sally McClendon years ago. She died, and he adopted Matthew. That's why he's been so secretive. Matthew."

More silence. Matthew's expression went from hopeful to desperate. He stared at the phone. We all did.

Then came a wail of delight. "Is he there?" Mama shrieked.

Matthew's mouth opened and shut. "I'm here," he said.

Mama said, "Oh, thank you, Lord," at least a dozen times. "I don't care how this happened," she yelled tearfully, "but y'all bring Matthew *here*. You bring him *home* with you."

"Bring the boy home," Daddy said in a gravelly voice. "It's a miracle. Come home and worry about explaining it later."

Tweet started sobbing, and Matthew had tears on his face, and Roan and I sat there together on the couch, relieved by one small victory but too worried to relax. This was only a beginning.

Nine

I TOLD Mama and Daddy I'd call when we got to Ten Jumps. That we'd bring Matthew and Tweet to the farm for supper. We packed and caught a jet bound for Seattle the next afternoon and stayed at Roan's house overnight.

"I need a stiffer drink than this tonight," Roan complained in the shadows of the balcony outside his bedroom door. "And I don't say that often." He tossed the remnants of a beer away. I sat between his legs on the balcony's cedar floor.

"Here. You can have mine." I held my shot glass of bourbon to his lips. He took the rim between his teeth and tossed the bourbon into his throat. "No hands," I noted.

"I learned that trick when Matthew was still in diapers. Change enough dirty diapers, and you can learn to drink, eat, or sign your name without using your hands."

I tried to laugh, but I could imagine him all too well—a rough-looking, skinny teenage boy taking care of a child. "I love you," I said simply. "I love you more now than I did when we were kids, and more than I did when you came back a few weeks ago, and more than yesterday. And more than this morning."

He kissed me. "Are you a little bit drunk?" he teased gruffly.

"Maybe. But that only makes me clear on what I really feel. I need to make you believe we'll be okay back at home. Matthew will hear about Big Roan. About the past. But we'll be okay."

"I don't ask for guarantees. I'll tell you what I want. I want to laugh with you. Sit and look at you. Wake up with nothing to think about but how warm and smooth you feel against me. Make a life together. All of this has been worth it if we can have that."

"We can. I promise you. Sometimes it takes me a while to make good on my promises, but—"

"I'm not as good at waiting as I used to be," he said. "And I'm not looking forward to tomorrow."

"Me neither," I said.

SITTING stiffly beside Roan in the back seat of a limousine we'd hired at the Atlanta airport, I watched Matthew and Tweet, who sat across from us. They hadn't stopped gazing raptly out the window since our driver turned off the interstate. I tensed as the limousine lumbered down the narrow road leading to Ten Jumps. A hawk sailed along in front of the car at one point, and then a half-dozen fat wild-turkey hens ambled from a huckleberry thicket in front of us.

"Bigger, this place is incredible. I love it," Matthew said.

"Wait until you see the cabin and the lake," Roan said quietly. "I fixed up the cabin so you'd have something to call your own if you came here. If you like it, it's yours." Roan looked at me. I nodded, finally comprehending another reason he'd bought Ten Jumps. A person needed to own land to be taken seriously in Dunderry. He'd bought status for himself—and for Matthew.

Matthew reached out and affectionately shoved Roan on one arm. "This is your property, Bigger. You've always told me how you loved to explore here."

Hid here, tried not to starve here, I thought miserably. But Matthew didn't know that history either. "No. Dunshinnog is Roan's place," I said. "The mountain. That's our special place."

When we reached the cabin, Matthew and Tweet rushed from the car. They hurried down to the lake, gesturing at the scenery—a sanctuary of water, purple-and-gold sunset, and forest.

More had been done to the cabin since we left, and not by Roan's crew. The yard was a kaleidoscope of freshly planted shrubs and flowers. Four white rocking chairs sat on the porch.

"The family's been here." I nodded toward a late-model sedan in the yard. "Uncle Eugene sent a car from his dealership."

Roan said nothing as we went up the walkway. The door was unlocked, and when we stepped inside, we found an enormous vase of white daisies set on the fireplace hearth.

We went into the newly added kitchen, and I opened the refrigerator door. It was packed with food. I opened a cupboard. The shelves were stacked with handsome earthenware dishes colored in whirls of burgundy and gold. "Mama made these dishes last month. She wants you to have them. It's just one of the small ways they can show how they feel about you and what you did for Matthew."

He leaned against a countertop. "Your family may wish they'd burned the place down after they learn the truth about him."

I turned away. "I need to call Mama and Daddy."

We heard the sound of a car. "They're not waiting for a call," Roan said with a tired smile. "They probably had most of the family stationed near the main roads with binoculars."

I tried to laugh. "Probably. But it's good. They're enthusiastic."

We walked outside. Mama and Daddy had just stopped their car in the yard. "I was right," Roan said. "They couldn't wait until—"

His voice trailed off as Mama and Daddy got out of the car. They stared, emotionally riveted, at Matthew and Tweet.

And Josh walked down the slope to the lake, toward Matthew, who gazed back along with Tweet, smiling but obviously puzzled.

His father. *No.* Not here, now, like this.

Roan moved so quickly, he was striding down to intercept Josh before I realized I was stumbling forward, murmuring frantically, "Matthew doesn't know. He doesn't know," as if I could stop time. "Mama, what do y'all think you're *doing?*" I called out.

"Honey, it'll be all right," she called. "We couldn't keep Josh away after he heard about Matthew, but hon, you and Roan will understand why he's here after you learn the real story."

"You know?" I stared at her. "You already know about Josh?"

Mama's hand rose to her mouth. "Holt," she said urgently, "Roan and Claire *know* about Josh and Matthew."

"Oh, my Lord," Daddy said, and hurried down the slope.

"You deal with me," Roan said as he reached Josh and blocked his way. "Dammit, you talk to *me* first."

Josh halted, blinking. He looked dazed. Larger, older, heavier than Roan, he brushed at him with a benign shove of one hand.

Roan raised a fist, and I knew he would hit my brother. Daddy got there first and planted himself between them. Mama went to Matthew and Tweet, holding out her hands to them. "Please don't think we meant to ambush you. There's no easy way to do this."

Matthew gave her a blank look, then bolted to Roan. "Bigger, I don't know what's going on, but calm down." Roan pulled Matthew aside. Josh simply continued to gaze at Matthew.

I was the one who suddenly became unhinged. Twenty years Roan had sacrificed for Matthew, for the family, for Josh's cowardice. When I reached Josh, I grabbed his shirtfront. "How could you?" I demanded furiously. "Why? *Why?*"

Josh barely flinched. He shook his head slowly until Daddy thundered, "This is a helluva family reunion. Step back, or I'll start tossing you bulls into the lake. And you, too, daughter."

Some sense was restored. We all stepped back a few inches, breathing tensely. "Who are you?" Matthew asked Josh.

My brother struggled to speak. "Josh. Josh Maloney."

Slowly alarm dawned in Matthew's expression. His chin rose. "You're the one I picked out of an old photo Claire brought."

Painful surprise showed in Josh's eyes. "You did? Gosh! I was right. I can just look at you and know. And you recognized *me.*"

Roan spoke bitterly. "You don't owe him a thing, Matthew. Remember that. He has nothing to do with who you are."

Matthew held up both hands. "I don't understand what's happening here!" he yelled.

"I've tried to find you for years. You're not Pete Delaney's son," Josh said. "You're *my* son."

Beside me, Roan sucked in a breath. And in that shocked moment I saw the unexpected joy in Matthew's eyes.

Roan, dear Lord, saw it, too.

ROAN believed the family he'd created for himself was destroyed, almost by whimsy, in a bizarre turn of events we had never predicted. In a terrible way the best for Matthew was the worst for him.

Mama and Daddy celebrated Matthew, their firstborn grandson, in style. Relatives began arriving with food and guitars. Everyone thanked Roan, who had come full circle in their minds, sacrificing once again for the family, taking and bringing back.

A kind of break-your-heart generosity flowed. We sat in the living room—Roan and I with my parents, Mama perched beside Roan on the main couch. She clasped his hand in both of hers.

"I expect to be your father-in-law," Daddy told Roan. "As good, I hope, as the father you've been to Matthew."

"You couldn't be more dear to us, Roan," Mama said softly. "We're so sorry you thought we'd turn you and Matthew away."

"You might do it yet," Roan said.

"Stop it. Don't you ever say that again!"

"He's *my* family," Roan announced gruffly. "I never tried to make him hate anybody, but I told him the truth. The good as much as the bad. He doesn't hate any of you. He just doesn't know you."

"He'll be fine," Mama insisted. "And so will you, Roan."

And so a mostly unspoken understanding was settled between my parents and Roan.

Matthew responded to his homecoming welcome with blind fervor. Suddenly he and Tweet had more family than they'd ever imagined, and they were both drunk with pleasure. So was Josh.

Many people said Josh had suffered enough for denying Matthew years before—his guilt, his shame, his worry. But I didn't sympathize. Roan was the only reason we had Matthew back. Roan had suffered for his dedication. I had, too, in different ways. "When did you and Daddy first suspect?" I asked Mama that night.

She bowed her head. "You remember the time we had the big work party to restore the Delaney bridge and Sally showed up with Matthew? Your daddy and I watched her stare at Josh as if she wanted to scald him. And she held Matthew up toward Josh, and Josh was so upset he dropped the tool he was holding."

Mama and Daddy couldn't believe what they'd witnessed meant what they feared it meant. Then Sally disappeared in the aftermath of Big Roan's scandal, and Josh confided the truth. For years they'd quietly helped him search. They'd hired investigators, but no information had ever turned up. They had always looked for Sally and Matthew McClendon, of course, or Matthew Delaney. Never for Matthew Sullivan.

On the night we brought Matthew to the farm, cars filled the yard and dozens of Maloneys and Delaneys gathered on the porches, deep in conversation. Amanda was the only one missing— gone to summer camp for a week. The issue of how Josh should tell her about her half brother was thoroughly debated.

And how to thank Roan—that was debated, too.

"I know what brand of honor it took for you to come here and risk this," Daddy said to him. "Nobody's turning their backs on you this time. Not Matthew and not us."

"We kept Josh's secret because he grieved over it and wanted to make it right," Mama told him. "We're not washing our hands of his guilt. We know who did right when it counted."

Roan, who was quietly devastated, said, "I only want one promise from you. Don't tell him about my old man, the Hollow, what happened, nothing. I have to be the one to tell him."

Mama and Daddy promised.

In the meantime it was already clear that Matthew and Tweet could fit into the pattern of the family as tightly as a new seam. Every Maloney aunt and uncle came to the same conclusion that night—summed up out loud by Aunt Arnetta. "The boy couldn't have turned out any better if he'd been brought up here by his own people," she announced in front of Roan.

His own people. An embarrassed hush followed. Roan smiled thinly and walked away. "How could you?" I said to Aunt Arnetta.

I followed Roan. "Time to regroup," I ordered, snagging his hand. "We're going to the barn loft."

"Just like old times," he said.

He had to carry me up the staircase, but we made it. I sat on a bale of hay, while he stood leaning against the doorframe.

"You can't change their reaction to me," he said wearily. "I don't doubt I did the right thing by bringing Matthew here. They want him. And it's clear he's where *he* needs to be. He found out his old man didn't really desert him. That's powerful medicine."

"*You're* his old man."

"No. I never was. I forgot that fact sometimes."

We heard footsteps on the loft stairs. Josh made his way among the bales of hay and stopped by the door. "Roan, I believe you'd give me a fighting chance before you pushed me out this door," he said. "But I think sis would push me from behind and never shed a tear."

"You're damned right," I said slowly. "We're supposed to hug and smile because you had the guts to welcome your own son home after Roan took care of him for two decades?"

"I'm not asking for parenting awards. Roan, I'll never be able to do enough to thank you."

"I don't want any thanks from you. I want answers."

"At first I wasn't even certain he was mine. I'd been careful with Sally. I thought there was a good chance he was Pete's boy, like everyone assumed. And Sally had other . . . customers, too." Josh paused. "I told myself he could be Big Roan Sullivan's son."

"I wish he was," Roan replied flatly. "I'd have a blood tie to him. I wouldn't have had to hide him. I could have brought him back a long time ago. I could have told Claire, and Claire and I—"

Josh nodded. "I understand what you say, Roan."

I hunched forward. "You were *sure* about Matthew that day at the Delaney bridge."

"I was sure, sis. Yeah, I was sure. I spent too much time debating what the embarrassment would do to the folks. And to me, my plans. But I told 'em after everything went crazy around here that summer. Big Roan . . . Sally disappearing with Matthew."

"Lucky for you," I shot back.

He tossed both hands into the air and yelled, "There hasn't been a day since then that I haven't thought about him, sis. Wondered where he was, if he'd starved or been hurt, if he was dead."

"Good," I yelled back. "I spent twenty years torturing myself over Roan for the same kind of reasons. I'm glad you know how it felt."

Josh's arms sank limply by his sides. "I couldn't look at Amanda without thinking of Matthew."

"What are you going to tell her now?"

"That she's got a half brother. That he's terrific." Josh pivoted slowly toward Roan. "And we're going to do our best to convince him to stay in Dunderry."

Roan went absolutely still. "He's got friends on the West Coast," he said finally. "That's his home turf."

"I'd just appreciate it if you wouldn't try to influence him."

"Don't you dare," I said in a low, furious tone. "Don't you *dare* lecture Roan and dismiss him like a deliveryman."

"That's not what I meant, sis, and you know it. Hell, Roan, you're welcome around here. Ask Claire to marry you. Settle down. You'll be close to Matthew. Keep being what you've been to him. But understand that we'll have to come to terms about that. You've known since he was a kid that I was his father. Accept the new situation."

Roan swayed, his fists clenched by his sides.

"You knew." Matthew's voice came out of the shadows. My heart twisted. Matthew moved forward and halted before Roan. "You knew Pete Delaney wasn't my father, and you knew Josh Maloney *was*." His voice quivered. "How could you lie to me like that?"

Roan grabbed him by the shoulders. "Listen to me. I thought there was nothing worth coming back to here. I thought it was kinder to let you think your old man was dead. Safer."

"You lied to me. You let me think I had nobody but you."

"This family might have taken you away from me. I had no legal rights. Josh could have shipped you off to a foster home."

"You couldn't risk it? You couldn't risk simple contact with the Maloneys to find out for my sake? What did they ever do to you to deserve that kind of judgment? Nothing."

"You see them a different way than I do."

Roan still gripped Matthew's shoulders. Matthew shoved his hands away. "There's no excuse for what you did to me. You don't have the right to make choices for me anymore!"

"Make your own choices, then. Tell me what you intend to do."

Matthew inhaled sharply. He looked miserable. "Tweet and I are going to get to know the family. My grandparents. My little sister." He looked at Josh. "And my father." Matthew stared at Roan. "If you don't like that, you don't have to be a part of it."

Tell him, I begged Roan silently. Tell him why you lost faith in the family. Tell him what happened to you and me.

But Roan stood there, offering no excuses or apologies.

Ten

MATTHEW and Tweet settled into a big corner bedroom at the farm. Mama and Daddy pulled out all the stops to surround them with the Maloney clan. There were dinner parties with my brothers and their families, all done up in their prosperous best. Josh proudly introduced Matthew around Dunderry, wined and dined him constantly.

Roan and I stayed away.

Roan walked the woods obsessively. My leg wasn't strong enough for me to go along, and he didn't want me to, anyway, which hurt me. He didn't sleep well, and when we reached for each other in bed, we were wild, explosive together but miserably quiet afterward.

Every day he roamed from the lake to the Hollow and all the land he owned on either side.

"What are you looking for?" I asked gently, knowing that he was trying to make peace with what he'd been and done as a boy.

"Answers," he said.

He brought me wildflowers and turtle shells, birds' nests and interesting rocks, as if we were still kids. I cooked food we didn't eat and read box after box of his wonderful but emotionally exhausting letters to me, tears streaming down my face.

Josh brought Amanda home from summer camp and told her, during the drive back, about Matthew. When Josh introduced them, Matthew presented Amanda with a beautiful gold bracelet bearing a small round charm inscribed LOVE TO MY SISTER.

But Amanda shook her brother's hand and offered him nothing warmer than a crystalline blue-eyed stare. An hour later, when Josh and Mama checked on her in her bedroom, she was gone.

She left a note on her pillow:

> Dear Papa,
> You never show off for me like you do for Matthew. You never tell everybody how proud I make you. Now I understand why you don't love me. I'm not good enough. I'm not a boy.
>   Most sincerely,
>   Amanda Elizabeth Maloney

The entire family spent the next six hours frantically searching for her within a ten-mile radius.

Late that afternoon Roan and I returned to Ten Jumps. Amanda was sitting on the cabin's front porch.

Her face was swollen from crying. She was dirty and disheveled. When we reached her, she peered up at us with a flat, resolute mouth. "You won't tell anybody I'm here, will ya?" She focused on Roan. "Aunt Claire says this was always your safe hiding place."

"It'd be wrong to turn a needy girl out of Ten Jumps," Roan agreed solemnly. "You can stay here as long as you want."

I glanced at him reproachfully as he helped me sit down. I nudged her gently. "What did your papa tell you about Matthew?"

"Papa said he had a girlfriend a long time before he met my mama and they made Matthew together, but they weren't married, and she went away when Matthew was still a little boy. And then she died, and Roan took care of Matthew. And Papa's sorry he didn't take care of Matthew himself, and now he wants to."

"Then you understand why you have a brother?"

"Yeah. Half a brother. We've got the same papa. I get it. Papa's all excited about him. He doesn't need me anymore."

"Oh, honey," I said, "that's not true." I hugged her. "Everyone's looking for you. May I at least call and tell your papa you haven't been kidnapped by space aliens?"

"I don't want to go back. I'm going to live with Roan." She looked at me. "And you can be my mama. I won't be any trouble."

"All right, but maybe you should think about it and decide later. I have to call your papa. He loves you. I'm sure he wouldn't let anybody else in the world have you."

Amanda broke down in sobs, and I rocked her in my arms.

"Maybe Papa might want me to stay. He wants Matthew to."

"He wants both of you," Roan said. "Just the way I would if I were your papa."

She threw herself at him, and this man, who had raised a child and exuded more paternal sweetness than he'd admit to, carefully folded her in his arms and picked her up.

And we took her home.

OUR arrival brought Josh running from the house. "Here she is!" Daddy bellowed from the main barn. Mama ran out with a phone still clutched in her hand. Matthew and Tweet climbed out of a muddy truck, looking more lost than found themselves.

"Why did you leave home?" Josh growled to Amanda, dropping to one knee before her.

She stood at attention. "Roan and Claire said I could live with them. I could be Roan's little girl. But Aunt Claire said I oughta think about it some more."

Josh fired a furious look at Roan and me. "You scared me," Josh said to Amanda, taking her gently by the shoulders.

A tremor went through her. Her eyes widened. "I did? How?"

"I haven't been very nice to you, have I? I know it. I felt so worried about where Matthew was when he was growing up, because it was my fault he was lost. Now I have a chance to be a good daddy to you and Matthew. I'm going to try."

She wavered, then suddenly exploded with smiles. She put her arms around him, and he hugged her with a fierce affection.

"But"—Amanda turned a crumbling expression up toward Roan—"what's gonna happen to Roan? I promised him—"

"No, no," Roan said. "It's all right if you change your mind."

"Let's discuss this later," Mama said with alarm. She held out a hand to Amanda. "Come on, hon, let's go get your face washed."

Once she was safely inside, Josh said, "Roan, you stole one of my children for twenty years, and now you're trying to steal another?"

Roan punched him. It happened quickly—a recoil and release that slammed into Josh's mouth and knocked him on his back. "Claire's all I ever wanted from this damn family," Roan said.

"Easy, easy," I urged softly.

Daddy pushed Roan back carefully. "That needed to be done. Roan, you hear me? He had it coming. But it's done. Back off."

Josh nodded groggily. "Fair enough," he said.

Roan remained on guard until he noticed Matthew's humiliated stare. When Matthew dropped to one knee beside Josh and offered to help him up, Roan's fist unfurled in defeat.

ROAN and I went to Dunshinnog that night, gathered a small pile of tree limbs, and sat beside it, watching the fire burn to embers.

"Read this one," Roan said, handing me an old letter he pulled from his pants pocket. "He was ten years old when I wrote it."

Ever hit anybody? he asked me today. He's in trouble for popping a kid in the mouth at school. The kid knows Matthew's adopted. Teases him about it. Matthew had enough. So he knocked one of the kid's front teeth out.

He thought I'd be mad. I had to pretend I was. Did I ever hit anybody? Not since I grew up, I told him.

I told him there's only two good reasons to hit somebody. To protect another person from getting hit, or if you've got no other way to protect yourself. The people who don't hit—they're the people with real power. They're the smart people.

And I promised him if he'd never hit anybody without good reason, I'd never hit anybody again either. We shook on it.

I learned a lot from you, Claire. In a way your folks taught
me how to raise myself and how to raise Matthew. Funny. I
learned the most from the people who hurt me the worst. The
people I loved.

I put the letter down. "You didn't break a sacred vow today," I
said gently. "You didn't even break any teeth."

"I've worked all my life to be different from my old man.
Matthew was ashamed of me today. I saw the look on his face."

"You've got to talk to him, Roan. Tell him everything."

"This situation isn't going to work out. For anyone."

I drew back, the dread rising in my throat. "I know what you're
trying to avoid. But if you don't tell him the truth about Big Roan,
he'll hear it from other people. You have to trust him."

"I'll tell him soon. He'll never look at me the same way again. If
I stay here, I'll ruin everything for him. You and me—maybe we
could travel for a while, let things settle down."

We'll never come back, I thought desperately. "When we were
kids," I said, "there were times when I was ashamed *for* you, but
there was never a time when I was ashamed *of* you. You always
fought for me, and I fought for you. Matthew will feel that way
once he knows everything."

"If he doesn't—" Roan continued.

I pressed my fingertips to his mouth. "Have some faith," I said.

I WENT over to the farm to see Mama and Grandma Dottie. "Get
Tweet for me," I told them. "Just get her away from Josh and
Matthew for an afternoon. We're going to talk." Mama nodded.

When I met Tweet the next day, we hugged sadly. I drove her up
to the top of Dunshinnog. We sat on the rock ledge overlooking the
valley. Muggy June heat cloaked the afternoon.

"Matthew's not too happy about me visiting with you," she
admitted. "He thinks Roan's sent you to ask him to apologize."

"Roan's not waiting for an apology. But he doesn't owe Matthew
one either."

"You don't protect adopted people by hiding their identity from them! It's not fair! It causes more problems than it solves."

I quietly told Tweet how Roan grew up. About the Hollow. How Big Roan really died and why. And what the family did to Roan afterward. When I finished, she was pale and speechless.

I told her Matthew needed to see the Hollow. He needed to understand the place Roan had won and lost in our family.

"Oh, Claire," she murmured with sorrow and sympathy. "Now I understand Roan, but I understand you, too."

"There's nothing mysterious to understand about *me*."

"You won't really be home again yourself unless Roan stays," Tweet said. "You'll always feel you failed him if this isn't settled. If you can't keep him here, you'll go wherever he wants, even if it breaks your heart."

I felt the blood draining from my face. "He's not going anywhere," I said loudly.

JOSH took Matthew and Tweet on a tour of the local farms. They happened to be at Uncle Winston's when one of his Black Angus cows was struggling with a breech birth, and they delivered her twin calves. When Dr. Radcliff—Dunderry's aging veterinarian and a cousin of Mama's—arrived a few minutes later, he was very impressed. The event started discussions about the two of them interning at Dr. Radcliff's veterinary practice with an understanding that they'd buy the practice when he retired in a couple of years.

I heard this news and had to be the one to break it to Roan. I talked him into driving to the Delaney covered bridge. We sat on a blanket in the bridge's shade. Roan said, "You're tugging your ears. Whatever it is, just tell me."

I stalled. "Everybody who grew up in this town came here at least once when they were teenagers. It's the oldest make-out spot in the county. But you and I never got a chance."

He latched his arms around my back.

"It's not much of a notorious place in broad daylight," I began, losing the words when he kissed me.

"How's that for notorious?" he asked several minutes later. We sagged against each other, breathless. "Tell me," he repeated.

I did, and when I finished, with the river bubbling below us, Roan said quietly, "It's done, then. Matthew's staying. There's not a damn thing I can do about it. Except get out of his way."

WE WOKE the next morning at Ten Jumps with thunder rumbling in the distance and the air hot and oppressive. We dressed hurriedly in jeans and T-shirts. Roan knelt by the bed and slid my tennis shoes on my feet. "We have to talk about the future," he said.

"Let's just deal with the present. Check the weather."

We went to the porch. The sky to the east was turning an ominous purple-black. "I don't like this," I said.

Suddenly a wind sprang up, and leaves tore from the water oaks. "Roan," I said uneasily, "this feels like tornado weather."

He listened to the wind. "Let's go inside," he said.

The wind pushed at us, and we staggered inside the cabin. He carried me to the doorway between the bedroom and the kitchen, where we sat down, our arms curved protectively over our heads.

The wind began to howl. Then a limb slapped the bedroom window, and the panes shattered. There were thumps and thuds, but submerging every other sound was the wild bellow of the wind.

Rain whipped in through the broken window, but eventually the wind began to subside. The light grew brighter. I fumbled for the doorframe, pulling myself up. "Got to call home."

Roan vaulted up and ran to the front room. Shaking, I went after him. He already had the phone in his hand.

We stayed on the phone for almost an hour as Mama relayed information. Arnetta had lost the roof off her garage; Hop's bass boat and boat shed had been mangled. Josh, Daddy, Matthew, Tweet, and Amanda were fine.

Finally, exhausted, we walked outside. On the far side of the yard a swath had been cut through the forest, snapping the trees off halfway up. I felt Roan's hand gripping mine. The strange malevolent path disappeared in the direction of the Hollow.

ROAN SLOWED THE CAR AS WE rounded the curve, driving over small tree limbs scattered across the pavement.

My stomach lurched when I saw the twisted alley of destruction. The tornado had moved across the ridge from Ten Jumps to the Hollow and had pulled out the buried garbage and the deeply submerged ruins of Big Roan's trailer. I couldn't breathe, couldn't speak.

Roan's gaze was riveted to the exposed debris. He stopped the car, got out, and staggered down the rain-drenched slope. "Stay back," he called. "I don't want you down in this with me."

I struggled out of the car, grabbing my cane. "I've always been part of it. You keep me out now, you'll keep me out forever."

A car was coming. It was Matthew, driving one of the farm trucks. He parked on the shoulder and leaped out, frowning at Roan. "What are you doing down there?"

"Go get him!" I ordered. "Get him out of there!"

Matthew hesitated. "What is it? What's here?"

"Me," Roan said in a gutted tone. "What I was. What I'll always be to everyone who wants to forget."

"What?" Matthew stared at Roan. "Whatever this is about, just tell me." He clambered down the slope.

Roan lurched forward a step. "Both of you, stay up there!"

Matthew angrily pushed through the mud-spattered vines. "What are you going to do? Somebody gets in your face and the best you can do is knock him down? Go ahead. Show me who you really are."

Roan snatched him by the shirt and shook him. "This is where I grew up," Roan said to him. "In this garbage hole! Claire came here for help when we were kids, but instead of helping her, my old man tried to rape her. And when I got here—"

"Roan," I called brokenly.

Roan leveled an unapologetic stare at Matthew. "I killed him."

THE three of us sat on the soggy mat of weeds in the roadside by the Hollow. The past had been laid out in Roan's words and mine. The why, the how, Big Roan's unsalvageable violence and cruelty. Listening to Roan tell it made my skin crawl.

Matthew listened in incredulous silence. He seemed dazed.

Roan and I traded a helpless look. "I killed him," he repeated wearily. "And I'd do it again if I had to. What happened to me after that had as much to do with my lack of faith as the Maloneys' bad judgment. If I'd stuck it out at the foster home, I'd have had a chance to come back here and be part of the family again. But people make mistakes. I made one when I didn't tell you the truth about me and about who you are."

I bit my tongue, wanting to shake Matthew and make him see.

"I brought you home," Roan said. "You have a family now. You don't owe me anything. Now you know the truth about me. There's a lot more for you to be proud of as a Maloney than as a Sullivan."

Matthew moved in front of Roan and met his eyes. "You're not a murderer," Matthew said. He jerked his head toward the Hollow. "You don't belong here. You never did. And you don't have to deal with it by yourself. You think I'm ashamed of you?" His voice shook. "I'm still a Sullivan if you'll still have me."

There were a hundred images of Roan in my mind—the fierce accused boy at the carnival, the boy who knocked Neely Tipton down for me, the half-strangled boy carrying my chocolate Easter rabbit away from Steckem Road. And every time I had surprised him by loving him and fighting for him, and everything he had made of himself as a grown man, and for this young man, my nephew, whom he'd cared for and loved and raised as a tribute to what we meant to each other—all of that came together in him now.

"We're going to dig this place up," Roan said. "Clean it out. Get rid of it. Forget it was ever here. And then I'll *never* set foot in this hole again, and neither will anyone else I love."

Matthew draped an arm over his shoulder. And suddenly Roan put one arm around him and the other around me.

"I NEED chain saws," I said when I got to the farm. "Work gloves, bug repellent, and a watercooler." And then I explained why.

Tweet grabbed a pair of work gloves. "I'm going over there with you," she said. "Roan needs all of us."

It was hard work, and that was good, sweating out the poison. I moved around the perimeter of the Hollow clumsily, piling branches and small pine logs into heaps with my free hand, hating my cane. Roan and Matthew flung debris to the roadside, and Tweet tossed the pieces into the truck. Hot sun scalded us, and the damp air became a pine-scented sauna.

"It'll take *weeks*," Tweet murmured to me.

"Wait a minute," Matthew called. "Listen."

One of the farm's big hay trucks lumbered around the curve. Mama, with Amanda in her lap, and Grandma Dottie were packed into the front seat. They climbed down from the high cab.

Amanda, outfitted in pink sunglasses and a baseball cap, wandered to the edge of the road and looked around uneasily. "How come Papa isn't here yet, Uncle Roan?"

Uncle Roan. Roan's jaw worked. "We haven't talked to him, hon." He looked at Mama, bewildered.

"I can't speak for Josh," Mama said. "But the others are coming."

As if on cue, a fat yellow dump truck rolled between the steep, moist overhang of laurel and trees. Behind it came four more dump trucks, and then a tractor pulling a backhoe on a trailer, and another tractor, pulling a bulldozer on a trailer.

Hop and Evan waved from the lead dump truck. Brady, Uncle Winston, and several of my cousins climbed out of the others.

Roan inhaled sharply. "I don't know how to thank—"

"You've got no need to offer any thank-yous," Uncle Winston said. "We're here because we want to be."

A line of cars and trucks began to arrive. They came—aunts, uncles, cousins, in-laws—topping a hundred people by my count. More chain saws and shovels and axes; boxes of food, ice coolers, guitars, lawn chairs, and blankets.

Daddy climbed out of a car, the hot breeze picking at his shirt. He seemed to be sunk inside dark determination, the man who had buried the Hollow and sent Roan away unfairly.

Roan turned to me. "Did you ask them to do this?" he asked.

Crying a little, I shook my head. "They're here for *you*."

The Hollow was scalped of trees by late afternoon. The silence that followed hours of roaring chain saws felt heavy and portentous. Neat stacks of pine logs lined the clearing.

Roan walked over and squatted beside me. We gazed at a backhoe, manned by Hop. Roan fumbled for my hand and gripped it tightly. Matthew and Tweet stood nearby. "Now that push comes to dig," Matthew said, "this feels pretty gruesome."

It was tough. My skin crawled every time Hop dug the backhoe's claw scoop into the earth. Five feet down, the rusted-out hull of the pickup truck's roof appeared. Matthew grimaced, Roan raised a hand, and Hop stopped the backhoe. Roan walked over to the hole and stood looking down.

No one moved; no one breathed. A minute ticked by and then another one. The look in Roan's eyes tore me apart. I knew he was seeing Big Roan in that truck, seeing himself in that truck.

I slid my arms around him. "Let it go," I whispered.

"I can't. I can't stop seeing it."

"Wait." Josh, his expression resigned, stood at the road. We all turned in surprise.

My brother walked heavily through the raw clearing. Matthew watched him with troubled eyes. "Let me help," Josh said.

"Papa!" Amanda yelled, darting up the slope to him, then halting uncertainly. "I knew you'd come!"

That broke my brother's strained expression and curved his face into gratitude. He scooped her into a hug and lifted her up.

Tweet trotted to the truck's carcass, thumped one warped door that hung by a single hinge, then looked at Roan solemnly. "Looks like a fixer-upper to me."

There was relieved laughter. Roan and I looked at Josh, who held Amanda tighter. We hadn't brought him a son with no compromises, but we had given him a wholehearted daughter.

THE daylight was fading fast. Several dozen camping lanterns glowed with weird, festive charm. "There it is," Hop yelled as his scoop thudded on a metal wall. The trailer.

It took the backhoe and the bulldozer working together to wrestle that sunken hulk from the ground. Charred, collapsed, it lay there in the flickering lantern light, its closed, battered door dripping grotesque streams of muddy red water.

And then, through some obscene quirk of physics or fate, the closed, battered door slowly swung open.

There was a collective gasp as everyone except Roan and me backed away. We stared into that black rectangle. I was ten years old again and Roan was fifteen, and the old nightmare came at us.

Suddenly Roan's arms were around me, and I pulled his head close to mine and shielded his eyes with my hand.

I heard the door slam shut. Josh and Matthew stood there together, holding it closed.

The rotting trailer was then hauled away. The old truck, gone. The garbage, gone. The pit filled in.

We lingered in the darkness, in the lantern light, dozens of us.

That day, that night, Sullivan's Hollow was exhumed, prayed over, and pronounced dead of the most natural causes.

Hop said to Roan, "Evan and I'll take Matthew fishing this fall."

They funneled every social matter through a simple system—go into the woods, commune with nature via fishing rods and hunting rifles, and camaraderie would follow without discussion.

And Brady said, in his smooth, efficient way, "You'll need a stake here, Roan. Partnerships. Some plans. I have two words to say to you—outlet mall."

"Oh, I'll think about it," Roan promised solemnly.

We were giddy and carefree, so immersed in being together that we spent days at Ten Jumps without seeing a soul.

Roan and Matthew began planning to build a barn near the lake. The dogs and birds were shipped from Alaska.

All around us July began, the sun grew hotter, barbecue grills were scrubbed, colorful banners went up around the square, the Jaycees set up a stage for the Fourth of July speeches, and small children began to feel the prickly promise of public humiliation.

OUR LITTLE PEOPLE LOOKED like unhappy munchkins in an Irish version of *The Wizard of Oz*. About half of them were kin.

"Why do we have to do this?" Amanda whispered miserably to me, distracted by her fluffy green leprechaun dress.

We stood in the spare shade of an awning around the corner from Main Street, the parade staging area. "Because y'all need some embarrassing pictures to show your kids someday."

Josh walked up. He swept Amanda into his arms, beaming. "Papa," she said seriously, "I look like turnip greens with red hair."

"You're beautiful," he corrected. "I've never seen a prettier sight. I want to get some pictures of you with Matthew. Okay?"

"Sure. But Matthew has to wear something green, too."

Amanda smiled. Josh and I traded satisfied looks. Amanda waved at Roan, who had walked up the street from the Maloney viewing spot. He laughed as he stood there, large and handsome.

Several thousand people lined the town square. A Sousa march blared from speakers atop the fire department's hook-and-ladder rig, which began to creep forward to lead the parade.

There were dozens of Delaneys and Maloneys on either side of Roan, me, Matthew, and Tweet. Mama smiled at us over her sunglasses; Daddy fiddled with his camcorder. Roan put his arms around me from behind and latched his hands in mine.

The high school band marched past, playing "I'm Proud to Be an American." Fronting the leprechauns, a group of my more musical uncles, led by Uncle Dwayne, wandered along, playing a high-pitched Irish jig on fiddles and tin whistles.

I thought of us that day at the carnival, of Roanie Sullivan standing below the stage, both of us isolated and yet linked. And I thought about the Christmas parade, that year Big Roan ruined it, and the shame that made Roan nearly disappear into himself. Today we were together, and I could taste the happiness.

And then, suddenly, the parade skewed toward me.

Uncle Dwayne's group halted. They stopped playing. Amanda waved her green troops forward. A flock of little people gathered around the musicians, all of them staring and giggling at me.

I drew back against Roan, totally bewildered. "Either they think we're the secret parade judges," I whispered out of the corner of my mouth, "or they think we're hiding their pot of gold."

"Shh. Just wait," Roan whispered.

I turned my head and gaped up at him. Conspiracy gleamed in his eyes. I'd been had.

Uncle Dwayne began to play his fiddle, some old Irish ballad, lilting and sweet. Little people rearranged themselves into a line facing Roan and me. Small hands flashed out broad white cards, each one printed with a blocky green letter of the alphabet.

And there it was, printed out for the whole family, the whole town, the whole universe to see: CLAIRE, WILL YOU MARRY ME?

I looked up at Roan tearfully. His eyes glistened, too. There was such joy in him, such beauty. "Surprise," he murmured.

I unwound his arms, then limped into the street. I tapped shoulders, rearranged little people.

When I finished, I faced Roan, dimly aware of a cocoon of laughter and applause around us but riveted to his face as he read the rearranged cards: I WILL MARRY YOU.

He walked toward me and took my hands. We were part of the parade now. Part of it all.

I heard Mama's ecstatic voice. "And the bridesmaids' dresses will be gold and mauve and . . ."

Uncle Dwayne struck up "When Irish Eyes Are Smiling."

Matthew and Tweet grinned.

Roan and I gazed at each other without a shred of dignity.

Everything was absolutely perfect.

AUTUMN, and the old mountain drew us up to its brow with the murmur of its seasons, the patient circle of life that it anchors.

We climbed up the old hiking path to the top of Dunshinnog that fall, the day after we deeded Ten Jumps to Matthew and Tweet. They were clearly in love with the lake and the cabin.

My leg was strong, but the hike up Dunshinnog was a test I hadn't taken yet, and I had some doubts I could make it. Couldn't let Roan down, though, or myself. I had signed a contract to buy the Dunderry *Shamrock* from Mr. Cicero, the owner, who had decided to retire. I was nervous about the responsibility but excited.

"You can do it," Roan urged gently as I climbed the last, steepest knob on Dunshinnog. He held out a hand and helped me up on the granite overhang above the valley. I burst out laughing with victory. And he smiled broadly, at ease and pleased for us both.

We examined the small green rosettes of new foxgloves growing among their fading elders. "Best crop yet," I claimed. We found the spot we'd discussed; then Roan pulled a canvas knapsack off one shoulder, taking from it the old plank with our names carved on it. I held the plank on the side of an oak while he nailed it in place.

"The heart of the house. Right here," he said. "We'll sit here and look out at the sky. With the family. Friends. See for miles."

I took something from a pocket of my jeans. "This is for you. Grandpa would want you to have it. You remember when we came up here with him and he played 'Amazing Grace'?"

Roan took the old tin whistle between his fingertips. "I'll have to learn to play it, too," he said softly.

"You will. He always knew who to trust with the traditions."

Roan put his arm around me. There was no need to doubt the serenity in his eyes. He was happy. He'd come back to where we both belonged. He'd found his place. He touched a fingertip to my lips. An old kiss, from childhood. In the gathering dusk, the cool and ripe harvesttime of the year, we sat down on the ledge close together. The wind rose gently, a pure song. We shared the view across land and sky, remembering and looking beyond.

ROBIN
COOK

CHROM

SOME 6

Medical researcher Kevin Marshall
knows that what he has
created in his laboratory
is cutting-edge science.

He knows it can save lives.
It's what he doesn't know
that terrifies him.

IVEN a Ph.D. in molecular biology from M.I.T. that had been earned in close cooperation with the Massachusetts General Hospital, Kevin Marshall found his squeamishness regarding medical procedures a distinct embarrassment. Although he'd never admitted it to anyone, just having a blood test or a vaccination was an ordeal for him. Needles were his specific bête noire. Once, he'd even fainted in college after getting a measles shot.

At age thirty-four, after many years of postgraduate biomedical research, he'd expected to outgrow his phobia, but it hadn't happened. And it was for that reason he was not in Operating Room 1A or 1B at the moment. Instead he'd chosen to remain in the intervening scrub room, a vantage that allowed him to look through angled windows into both ORs—until he felt the need to avert his eyes.

The two patients had been in their respective rooms for about a quarter hour in preparation for their respective procedures. The two surgical teams were gowned and gloved and ready to commence. Watching as the patients were inducted under general anesthesia, Kevin did not experience the same sense of triumph he had enjoyed during three previous comparable procedures, when he'd exalted in the power of science and his own creativity. Instead he felt a mushrooming unease. His discomfort had started almost a week previously, but it was now, contemplating these patients, that he felt the disquietude with disturbing poignancy.

The door to OR 1A opened suddenly, startling Kevin. He was confronted by a figure whose pale blue eyes were framed by a hood and a face mask. Recognition was rapid: It was Candace Brickmann, one of the surgical nurses.

"The IVs are all started, and the patients are asleep," Candace said. "Are you sure you don't want to come in?"

"Thank you, but I'm fine right here," Kevin said.

"Suit yourself," Candace said.

The door swung shut behind her. Kevin watched her cross the room and say something to the surgeons, who turned and gave him a thumbs-up sign. Kevin self-consciously returned the gesture. The wordless communication magnified his sense of complicity. His unease was now tinged with fear. What had he done?

Spinning on his heels, Kevin fled from the scrub room and then from the OR area. He entered his gleaming futuristic laboratory.

On any other day merely walking into his domain would have filled him with anticipation. The rooms literally bristled with hi-tech equipment at his beck and call. Absently he ran his fingers lightly along the stainless steel cowlings, casually brushing the digital displays as he headed for his office. He touched the $150,000 DNA sequencer and the $500,000 globular nuclear magnetic resonance machine. It was an environment that had once filled him with hope and promise. But now each Eppendorf microcentrifuge tube and each tissue culture flask stood as a mute reminder of his foreboding.

Advancing to his desk, Kevin looked down at his gene map of the short arm of chromosome 6. His area of principal interest was outlined in red. It was the major histocompatibility complex. The problem was that it was only a small portion of the short arm of chromosome 6. There were large blank areas that represented hundreds of other genes. Kevin did not know what they did.

Kevin shuddered involuntarily. He raised his eyes to the large picture window above his desk. As usual, it was streaked with moisture from the tropical rain that swept across the view in undulating sheets. Roiling gunmetal-gray clouds filled the sky despite the fact that the dry season was supposed to have begun three weeks previously. Riotous dark green vegetation rose up along the edge of the town like a gigantic tidal wave.

Kevin's office was in the hospital-laboratory complex that was one of the few new structures in the previously deserted Spanish colonial town of Cogo in the little-known African country of Equatorial Guinea. The building was three stories tall. Kevin's office was on the top floor, facing southeast. From his window he could see a good portion of the town as it sprawled haphazardly toward the Estuario del Muni and its contributory rivers.

Some of the neighboring buildings had been renovated, but most had not been touched. A half-dozen previously handsome haciendas were enveloped by vines and vegetation that had gone wild.

In the immediate foreground Kevin could see beneath the arched arcade of the old town hall. In the shadows were the inevitable handful of Equatorial Guinean soldiers in combat fatigues with AK-47s haphazardly slung over their shoulders.

Finally, Kevin let his eyes wander beyond the town. Directly south he could just make out the forested shoreline of Gabon. Looking to the east, he followed the trail of islands that stretched toward the interior of the continent. On the horizon he could see the largest of the islands, Isla Francesca. In contrast to the other islands, it had a jungle-covered limestone escarpment that ran down its center like the backbone of a dinosaur.

Kevin's heart skipped a beat. Despite the rain, he could see what he'd feared he'd see. Just like a week ago, there was the unmistakable wisp of smoke lazily undulating toward the leaden sky.

Kevin slumped into his desk chair and cradled his head in his hands. He asked himself what he'd done. Having minored in the classics as an undergraduate, he knew about Greek myths. Now he questioned if he'd inadvertently made a Promethean mistake. Smoke meant fire, and he had to wonder if it was the proverbial fire stolen from the gods.

WHILE a cold March wind rattled the storm windows, Taylor Cabot reveled in the warmth of his walnut-paneled study in his sprawling Manchester-by-the-Sea home north of Boston, Massachusetts. On the arm of Taylor's chair balanced a glass of neat single-malt whisky. A fire crackled in the fireplace, and three built-in televisions were tuned respectively to a local news station, CNN, and ESPN.

Taylor was the picture of contentment. He'd spent a busy day at the world headquarters of GenSys, the biotechnology firm he'd started eight years previously. The company had constructed a new building along the Charles River in Boston to take advantage of the proximity of both Harvard and M.I.T. for recruitment purposes. Now he was reading the financial report scheduled to be released at the stockholders' meeting the following week. But he was also very much alert to the reporters' banter on the TVs. So when the name Carlo Franconi was mentioned, Taylor's head snapped up.

The first thing he did was lift the remote and turn up the sound on the local news. The anchor was talking about the killing of a New York Mafia figure associated with Boston crime families:

"A few days ago we reported that the ailing Franconi had disappeared after his indictment, and many had feared he'd jumped bail. But then he'd just reappeared yesterday with the news that he'd struck a deal with the New York City D.A.'s office to plea-bargain and enter the Witness Protection Program. However, this evening, while emerging from a favorite restaurant, the indicted racketeer was fatally shot."

Taylor was transfixed as he watched a video of an overweight man emerge from a restaurant accompanied by several people who looked like policemen. Just as he was bending to enter a limousine, Franconi's body jerked, and he staggered backward with his hand clasping the base of his neck. As he fell to his right, his body jerked again before hitting the ground. The men who'd accompanied him had drawn their guns and were frantically turning in all directions.

Taylor's eyes immediately switched to CNN, which was about to show the same video. He watched the sequence again. It made him wince. At the end of the tape CNN went live to a reporter outside the Office of the Chief Medical Examiner for the City of New York:

"The question now is whether there were one or two assailants. An autopsy is scheduled for tomorrow morning, and we assume that ballistics will answer that."

Taylor turned down the sound, then picked up his drink. Walking to the window, he gazed out at the angry dark sea. Franconi's death could mean trouble. He looked at his watch. It was almost midnight in West Africa. Snatching up the phone, he called the operator at GenSys and asked to speak with Kevin Marshall immediately.

Replacing the receiver, Taylor returned his gaze out the window. He'd never felt completely comfortable about this project, although financially it was very profitable. The phone interrupted his thoughts.

Taylor picked the receiver back up. After some static Kevin's sleepy voice crackled over the line. "Is this really Taylor Cabot?"

"Do you remember Carlo Franconi?" Taylor demanded, ignoring Kevin's question.

"Of course," Kevin said.

"He's been murdered this afternoon. There's an autopsy scheduled. Could that be a problem?"

There was a moment of silence. "Yes, it could be a problem."

"Someone could figure out everything from an autopsy?"

"It's possible," Kevin said. "I wouldn't say it's probable."

"I don't like possible." Taylor disconnected from Kevin and called the operator back at GenSys. Taylor said he wanted to speak immediately to Dr. Raymond Lyons in New York City. He emphasized that it was an emergency.

"EXCUSE me," the waiter whispered. He'd approached Dr. Lyons from the left side, having waited for a break in the conversation the doctor was engaged in with his young blond assistant and current lover, Darlene Polson. Between his gracefully graying hair and conservative apparel, the good doctor looked like the quintessential soap-opera physician—tall and tan, with patrician good looks.

"I'm sorry to intrude," the waiter continued. "But there is an emergency call for you. Can I offer you our cordless phone, or would you prefer to use the phone in the hall?"

Raymond's blue eyes darted back and forth between Darlene's affable but bland face and the considerate waiter. Raymond did not look happy. "I'll take the cordless," he said. He couldn't imagine who could be calling him on an emergency basis. He had not been practicing medicine since he'd lost his medical license after having been convicted of a major Medicare scam.

"Hello?" Raymond said with a degree of trepidation.

"This is Taylor Cabot. There's a problem." Taylor quickly summarized the Carlo Franconi situation and his call to Kevin Marshall. "This operation is your baby," he concluded irritably. "And let me warn you: If there is trouble, I'll scrap the entire enterprise. I don't want bad publicity, so handle it."

"But what can I do?" Raymond blurted out.

"I don't know," Taylor said. "But you'd better do it fast."

"Things couldn't be going any better from my end," Raymond interjected. "Just today I made positive contact with a physician in L.A. who is interested in setting up a branch in California."

"Maybe you didn't hear me," Taylor said. "There isn't going to be a branch anyplace if this Franconi problem isn't resolved. I'd say you have about twelve hours."

Raymond heard the phone disconnect.

"Trouble?" Darlene questioned.

It was more than trouble. It was potential disaster.

"What is it?" Darlene asked.

Raymond explained about the upcoming autopsy and repeated Taylor Cabot's threat to scrap the entire enterprise.

"Then tell them not to do the autopsy," Darlene said.

Raymond stared at his companion. He knew she meant well, and he'd never been attracted to her for her brainpower. "You think I can just call up the medical examiner's office and tell them not to do an autopsy on such a case?"

"But you know a lot of important people. Ask them to call."

"Please, dear . . ." Raymond said, but then he paused. He began to think that unwittingly Darlene had a point.

"What about Dr. Levitz?" Darlene said. "He was Mr. Franconi's doctor. Maybe he could help."

"I was just thinking the same thing," Raymond said. Dr. Daniel Levitz was a Park Avenue physician. He'd been easy to recruit, had brought in many clients, and as the personal physician of a number of New York crime families, he knew people who could do the impossible.

Raymond stood up. "Come on, we've got to make a house call."

JACK Stapleton bent over and put more muscle into pedaling his new mountain bike the last block along Thirtieth Street in Manhattan. About fifty yards from First Avenue he sat up and coasted no hands before beginning to brake. The upcoming traffic light was not in his favor, and even Jack wasn't crazy enough to sail out into the mix of cars, buses, and trucks racing uptown at seven twenty-five a.m.

The early March weather had warmed considerably, and the recent snow was gone save for a few dirty piles between parked cars.

Jack came to a stop at the corner to wait for the light, and as his foot touched down on the pavement, he surveyed the scene. Almost at once he became aware of a bevy of TV vans in front of his destination: the Office of the Chief Medical Examiner for the City of New York, or what some people called simply the morgue. Jack was an associate medical examiner. Usually such journalistic congestion meant there had been a death of someone at least momentarily famous.

With a green light Jack pedaled across First Avenue and entered the morgue through the receiving dock on Thirtieth Street. He parked his bike and took the elevator up to the first floor. The place was in a minor uproar. Several of the day secretaries were busily manning the phones in the communications room—they normally didn't arrive until eight. With curiosity mounting, he entered the ID room and headed for the coffeepot. Vinnie Amendola, one of the mortuary techs, was hiding behind his newspaper as usual. Generally Jack was the first pathologist to arrive, but the chief medical examiner, Dr. Harold Bingham, and Dr. Laurie Montgomery were already there, involved in a deep discussion with Detective Lieutenant Lou Soldano from homicide. Lou was a frequent visitor to the morgue, but certainly not at seven thirty in the morning. On top of that, he looked like he'd never been to bed—or if he had, he'd slept in his clothes.

Jack helped himself to coffee. No one acknowledged his arrival. Wandering over to the glass door to the lobby, he glanced out. The area was filled to overflowing with media people.

"Will someone clue me in to what's going on?" Jack asked.

Laurie was the first to respond. "You haven't heard?"

"Now, would I be asking if I'd heard?"

"It's been all over the TV," Bingham said.

"Jack doesn't own a TV," Laurie said. "His neighborhood won't allow it. He lives practically in Harlem."

"Enough, you guys," Jack said. "Fill me in."

"A Mafia don was gunned down late yesterday," Bingham said. "It's stirred up a hornet's nest of trouble, since he'd agreed to cooperate with the D.A.'s office and was under police protection."

"He was no Mafia don," Lou Soldano said. "He was nothing but a mid-level functionary of the Vaccarro crime family."

"Whatever," Bingham said with a wave of his hand. "The key point is that he was killed while literally boxed in by a number of New York's finest. The mayor, the district attorney, and the police commissioner are all under a lot of heat."

"Amen," Lou said. "Particularly the police commissioner. That's why I'm here. We've got to apprehend the perpetrators ASAP; otherwise heads are going to roll."

"I don't know, Laurie," Bingham said, getting back to the discussion they'd been having before Jack came in. "I appreciate you coming in early and offering to do this autopsy, but I might want to do it myself."

"But why?" Laurie complained. "Look, it's a straightforward case, and I've recently done a lot of gunshot wounds. Besides, you have to be at City Hall this morning. You can't be back here until almost noon. By then I can have the autopsy done and whatever information I come up with in the hands of the police."

Bingham looked at Lou. "Do you think five or six hours will make a difference with the investigation?"

"It could," Lou admitted.

Bingham sighed. "Okay. Laurie, the call is yours."

"Thanks, Dr. Bingham," Laurie said gleefully. She snatched up the folder from the table. "Is it okay if Lou observes?"

"By all means," Bingham said.

"Come on, Lou." Laurie started for the door.

Jack hesitated for a moment, then hurried after them.

Laurie stopped abruptly to lean into a forensic investigator's office and ask her to call CNN and get a copy of the video of Carlo Franconi's assassination. Then Laurie and Lou continued on their way.

"Hey, slow down, you two." Jack ran a couple of steps to catch up to them. "I don't mean to rain on your parade, but this is a politically sensitive case. No matter what you do or say, you'll be irritating someone. I think this one ought to be done by the chief."

"You're entitled to your opinion." Laurie hit the elevator button. "But I feel differently. With my work on the forensics of gunshot wounds, I'm fascinated to have a case where there is a video to corroborate my reconstruction of what happened. I was planning a paper on gunshot wounds, and this could be the crowning case."

"Oh, dear," Jack moaned, raising his eyes heavenward. "And her motivations were so noble."

The elevator arrived, and Laurie and Lou boarded. Jack hesitated, then squeezed through the doors before they closed.

"You are not going to talk me out of this," Laurie said. "So save your breath."

"Okay." Jack lifted his hands in mock surrender. "I promise— no more advice. Now I'm just interested in watching this story unfold. It's a paper day for me, so if you don't mind, I'll watch."

"If you want, you can help," Laurie said as the elevator jerked to a stop. The doors opened, and the three got off.

Laurie ducked into the mortuary office and came out waving a list. "Compartment one eleven."

She took off like a power walker. Jack and Lou had to hustle to catch up with her. She made a beeline for the proper refrigerator compartment and released the latch. In one smooth, practiced motion she swung open the door and slid out the tray on its ball bearings. Her brow furrowed. "That's odd," she remarked. The tray was empty save for a few bloodstains and hardened secretions.

Laurie slid the tray back in and closed the door. She rechecked the number. There'd been no mistake. It was compartment 111. Just to be sure there wasn't some stupid logistic error, she opened all the neighboring compartments one after the other. In those that contained bodies she checked the names and accession numbers. But it soon became obvious: Carlo Franconi was not among them.

"I don't believe this," she said. "The body is gone!"

KEVIN Marshall put down his pencil and looked out the window above his desk. In contrast to his inner turmoil, the sky outside was rather pleasant, with the first patches of blue he'd seen for months. Cogo's dry season had finally begun. Of course, it wasn't dry; it just didn't rain nearly as much as during the wet season. The downside was that the sun made the temperature soar. At the moment it hovered at one hundred and fifteen degrees Fahrenheit.

Kevin had not worked well that morning nor slept during the night. The anxiety he'd felt the previous day had gotten worse after the unexpected call from Taylor Cabot, the GenSys CEO.

Adding to Kevin's unease was seeing another wisp of smoke snaking its way up into the sky from Isla Francesca. He'd noticed it when he'd first arrived at the lab that morning. As near as he could tell, it was coming from the same location as the day before: the sheer side of the limestone escarpment.

Giving up on any attempt at further work, Kevin peeled off his white lab coat. He wasn't particularly hungry, but he knew his housekeeper, Esmeralda, would have made lunch, so he felt obliged to make an appearance.

He descended the stairs in a daze. Several co-workers passed him and said hello, but it was as if Kevin did not see them. He was too preoccupied. In the last twenty-four hours he'd come to realize that he would have to take action. The problem wasn't going to pass, as he'd hoped it would a week previously, when he'd first glimpsed the smoke.

Unfortunately, he knew he was no hero; in fact, over the years he'd come to think of himself as a coward of sorts. He hated confrontation and avoided it. As a boy, he had even shunned competition, except for chess. He'd grown up pretty much a loner.

Kevin paused at the glass door to the exterior. Across the square he could see the usual coterie of soldiers beneath the arches of the old town hall. Some were sitting in old rattan furniture playing cards; others were leaning up against the building arguing in strident voices. They were dressed in soiled jungle-camouflage fatigues with scuffed combat boots and red berets. All of them had automatic assault rifles either slung over their shoulders or within arm's reach.

From the moment of Kevin's arrival in Cogo, five years before, the soldiers had scared him. Cameron McIvers, head of security, who had shown him around, told him that GenSys hired a good portion of the Equatorial Guinean army for protection. Later Cameron had admitted that the army's so-called employment was in reality a payoff to the minister of defense. From Kevin's perspective the soldiers looked like a bunch of aimless teenagers itching to have an excuse to use their weapons.

Kevin pushed through the door and walked across the square. Some soldiers were watching him, and it made his skin crawl. Once out of sight, he relaxed a degree and slowed his pace.

Kevin's house was situated a little more than halfway between the hospital-lab complex and the waterfront, a distance of only three blocks. The town was small but had obviously been charming in its day. The buildings had been constructed primarily of brightly colored stucco with red tile roofs, colors now faded to pale pastels.

The streets had been paved with imported granite cobblestones that had served as sailing ships' ballast. In Spanish colonial times Cogo's wealth had come from cocoa and coffee production.

The town's history changed dramatically after 1968, the year of Equatorial Guinea's independence, when the popularly elected president quickly metamorphosed into the continent's worst sadistic dictator. After fifty thousand people were murdered, a third of the country's population fled. Cogo was completely abandoned. The jungle had begun to reclaim it by the time a representative of GenSys happened upon it seven years previously. This individual had recognized the town's isolation and its limitless surrounding rain forest as the perfect spot for GenSys's primate facility. Since the country was one of the poorest in Africa and its government was desperate for foreign exchange, negotiations proceeded apace.

Kevin rounded the last corner and approached his house, one of the more desirable houses in the town and a source of envy to a number of the other GenSys employees. Only Siegfried Spallek, manager of the Zone—the area occupied by the GenSys operation—and Bertram Edwards, chief veterinarian, had equivalent accommodations. The house had been built in the mid-nineteenth century by a successful importer-exporter in traditional Spanish style. The first floor was arched and arcaded like the town hall and had originally housed shops and storage facilities. The second floor was the main living floor and was surrounded by a veranda on all four sides.

Kevin entered and climbed a central stairway to the dining room, where the table had been laid for lunch. As if by magic, Esmeralda appeared. A pleasant woman of indeterminate age, she was dressed in a shift of brightly colored print fabric with a matching scarf wrapped tightly around her head.

Esmeralda lived in the maid's quarters Monday through Friday. On weekends she stayed with her family in a village that GenSys had constructed to house the local workers employed in the Zone.

"There is a phone message for you," Esmeralda said. "From Dr. Raymond Lyons in New York. He wants you to call back."

Kevin went to the living room and sat down at his desk. He nervously pondered what Dr. Lyons had called about and guessed it had something to do with the autopsy on Carlo Franconi.

Kevin had first met Raymond six years before. It was during a meeting in New York of the American Association for the Advancement of Science at which Kevin presented a paper. Kevin hated giving papers, but on this occasion he'd been forced to do so by the chief of his department at Harvard. His subject was the transposition of chromosomes—a process by which chromosomes exchange bits and pieces to enhance species adaptation and hence evolution. After this talk Raymond had approached him. The conversation resulted in Kevin's leaving Harvard and coming to work for GenSys.

With a shaky hand Kevin dialed the phone. Raymond answered on the first ring. "Good news," he said. "There's to be no autopsy."

Kevin didn't respond. His mind was a jumble.

"Aren't you relieved? I know Cabot called you last night."

"I'm relieved to an extent," Kevin said. "But autopsy or no autopsy, I'm having second thoughts about this whole operation."

Now it was Raymond's turn to be silent. No sooner had he solved one potential problem than another reared its head.

"Maybe we've made a mistake," Kevin said. "What I mean is, maybe I've made a mistake. My conscience is starting to bother me, and I'm getting a little scared. I'm really a basic science person. This applied science is not my thing."

"Oh, please," Raymond said irritably. "Don't complicate things. I mean, you've got that lab you've always wanted. I've beat my brains out getting you every piece of equipment you've asked for. And on top of that, things are going so well, especially with my recruiting. With all the stock options you're amassing, you'll be a rich man."

"I've never intended on being rich," Kevin said.

"Worse things could happen. Come on, Kevin. The system is nearly perfect. When it is and you've trained someone to take your place, you can come back stateside. With your money you'll be able to build the lab of your dreams."

"I've seen more smoke coming from the island."

"Forget the smoke," Raymond said. "You're letting your imagination run wild. Instead of working up a frenzy over nothing, start fantasizing about the lab you'll be building here."

Kevin nodded. Raymond had a point. Part of Kevin's concern was that if what he'd been involved with in Africa became common knowledge, he might never be able to go back to academia. But if he had his own lab, he wouldn't have to worry.

"Listen," Raymond said. "I'll be coming to pick up the last patient when he's ready, which should be soon. We'll talk then."

"All right," Kevin said reluctantly. He hung up the phone and tried to think of where he'd build his lab. There were strong arguments for Cambridge, Massachusetts, because of Harvard and M.I.T. But then again, maybe it would be better to be out in the countryside, like up in New Hampshire.

Lunch was a white fish that Kevin didn't recognize. He surprised himself by eating more than he'd expected. The conversation with Raymond had had a positive effect on his appetite.

CHAPTER 2

ELL, what do you want to do?" Franco Ponti looked at his boss, Vinnie Dominick, in the rearview mirror. They were in Vinnie's Lincoln Town Car with Angelo Facciolo. Vinnie was in the back seat, looking out at 126 East Sixty-fourth Street—a New York City brownstone built in a French rococo style with high-arched windows.

"Looks like pretty posh digs," Vinnie said. "The good doctor is doing okay for himself."

"Should I park?" Franco asked. The car was in the middle of the street, and a taxi behind them was honking insistently.

"Park!" Vinnie said.

Franco drove ahead until he came to a fire hydrant. He pulled to the curb, and Vinnie climbed out of the car. Franco and Angelo quickly followed. All three men were impeccably dressed in long gray Salvatore Ferragamo overcoats.

"Put the Police Benevolent Association Commendation on the dash," Vinnie said. "Might as well save fifty bucks."

They walked back to Number 126. Vinnie looked at the door intercom, pressed the button for Dr. Raymond Lyons, and waited.

"Hello?" a feminine voice inquired.

"I'm here to see the doctor. My name is Vinnie Dominick."

There was a pause. Vinnie played with a bottle cap with the tip of his Gucci loafer. Franco and Angelo watched the street.

The intercom crackled back to life. "Hello, this is Dr. Lyons. I'm not sure I know you. Could you tell me what this is in reference to?"

"It's in reference to a favor I did for you last night. Requested through a mutual acquaintance, Dr. Daniel Levitz."

There was a pause.

"I trust you are still there, Doctor," Vinnie said.

"Yes, of course," Raymond said. A raucous buzzing sounded. Vinnie pushed open the door and entered. His minions followed.

Raymond met his visitors as they exited the elevator. Obviously nervous, he shook hands with all three. He gestured for them to enter his duplex apartment and showed them into a small study.

"Coffee, anyone?" he asked.

"I wouldn't turn down an espresso if it's not too much trouble," Vinnie said. Franco and Angelo said they'd have the same.

Raymond used his desk phone to place the order.

Raymond's worst fears had materialized the moment he'd caught sight of his uninvited guests. From his perspective they looked like stereotypes from a B movie. Vinnie was darkly handsome, with slicked-back hair. He was obviously the boss. The other two men were both over six feet and gaunt. Their lips were thin and their eyes deeply set. They could have been brothers except that Angelo's skin, mostly scar tissue, looked like the far side of the moon.

"Can I take your coats?" Raymond asked.

"We don't intend on staying too long," Vinnie said.

"At least sit down," Raymond said.

Vinnie relaxed into a leather armchair. Franco and Angelo sat stiffly on a velvet-covered settee. Raymond sat behind his desk.

"What can I do for you gentlemen?" Raymond said.

"The favor we did for you was not easy to pull off," Vinnie said. "We thought you'd like to know how it was arranged."

Raymond let out a little mirthless laugh through a weak smile. "That's not necessary. I'm certain you—"

"We insist," Vinnie interrupted. "You see, getting a body out of the morgue is no easy task."

"I'd rather not be privy to the details," Raymond said.

"Be quiet, Dr. Lyons, and listen." Vinnie paused for a moment to organize his thoughts. "We were lucky because Angelo here knows a kid named Vinnie Amendola, who works in the morgue. This kid was beholden to a guy Angelo used to work for. Angelo, knowing what he knows, was able to convince the kid to tell us exactly where Mr. Franconi's remains were stored, and other information so we'd have some reason to be there in the middle of the night."

At that moment the espressos were brought in by Darlene, whom Raymond introduced as his assistant before she left the room.

"So we got the body out okay," Vinnie said. "And we disposed of it, so it is gone. But it was not a walk in the park."

"Well, if there is ever some favor I can do . . ." Raymond said.

"Thank you, Doctor." Vinnie polished off his espresso like he was drinking a shot. "You've said exactly what I was hoping you'd say, which brings me to why I'm here. Now, you probably know I'm a client like Franconi was, as is my eleven-year-old son, Vinnie junior. So we're facing two tuitions, as you people call it. What I'd like to propose is that I don't pay anything this year. What do you say? A favor for a favor."

Raymond cleared his throat. "I'll have to talk to the powers that be."

"Now, that's the first unfriendly thing you've said," Vinnie added.

"My information is that *you* are the so-called powers that be. So I find this foot-dragging insulting. I'll change my offer. I won't pay any tuition this year or next year. I hope you comprehend the direction this conversation is taking."

"I understand," Raymond said. "I'll take care of it."

"That's the spirit," Vinnie said.

IN HER apartment on Nineteenth Street, Laurie finished preparing the salad greens and put the lamb loin into a marinade she'd made earlier. It took only a moment to cut off the base of the artichokes and a few of the large, stringy leaves. Wiping her hands on the dish towel, she glanced at the clock. Familiar with Jack's schedule, she thought it was exactly the time to call.

She used the wall phone next to the sink. As the connection went through, she could imagine Jack coming up the cluttered stairwell in his dilapidated building. Laurie counted the rings. She got to ten, and was about to hang up when Jack answered.

"Yeah?" he said unceremoniously.

"You sound out of breath," Laurie said. "Does that mean you lost at basketball?"

"No. It means I ran up four flights of stairs to get the phone. What's happening?"

"Tonight's your lucky night. I picked up the makings of your favorite dinner on the way home. All you have to do is shower and get yourself down here. But no bike tonight. You have to come by cab."

"Taxis are more dangerous than my bike," Jack complained.

"No argument. Take it or leave it. When you slide under a bus and end up on a slab in the pit, I don't want to feel responsible."

"Okay," Jack said agreeably. "Shall I bring some wine?"

"That would be great." Laurie was pleased. She'd been unsure if Jack would accept the invitation. Over the previous year they had been seeing each other socially, and months ago she had admitted to herself that she'd fallen in love with him. But Jack seemed reluctant to allow the relationship to progress to the next level of commitment. When she tried to force the issue, he had distanced himself. Feeling rejected, Laurie had responded angrily. For weeks they only spoke on a professional basis.

Over the last month their relationship had slowly improved. They were seeing each other again casually. This time Laurie realized that she had to bide her time. The problem was that at age thirty-seven it was not easy. Laurie had always wanted to become a mother someday. She felt she was running out of time.

With the dinner essentially prepared, Laurie went around the small one-bedroom apartment straightening up. That meant putting odd books back on the shelves and emptying the litter box for Tom, her six-and-a-half-year-old tawny tabby. Next she took a quick shower, changed into a turtleneck and jeans, and put on a touch of makeup.

Jack arrived on schedule, and the dinner was a success. The food was perfect. The red wine was okay. Jack's excuse was that the liquor store near his apartment specialized in jug wine, not the better stuff.

During the course of the evening Laurie had to continually bite her tongue to keep the conversation away from sensitive areas. She didn't dare talk about their relationship. She sensed some of Jack's hesitancy stemmed from his personal tragedy. Six years before, his wife and two daughters had been killed in a commuter-plane crash. Jack refused to talk about it. Laurie sensed that this loss was the biggest stumbling block to their relationship.

Jack had no trouble keeping the conversation light. He'd had a good evening playing pickup basketball at his neighborhood playground. He'd been teamed up with Warren, an all-around impressive African American, the leader of the local gang and by far the best player. Their team didn't lose all evening.

"How is Warren?" Laurie asked. Jack and Laurie had frequently double-dated with Warren and his girlfriend, Natalie Adams. Laurie hadn't seen either of them since she and Jack had their falling-out.

"Warren's Warren." Jack shrugged. "He's got so much potential. I've tried my best to get him to take some college courses, but he says my value system isn't his, so I've given up."

"And Natalie?"

"Fine, I guess. I haven't seen her since we all went out."

"We should do it again," Laurie said. "I miss seeing them."

"That's an idea," Jack said evasively. He checked his watch. "Uh-oh. It's quarter to eleven, and bed is beckoning. I've got to find a cab for the ride home." He stood up and thanked Laurie for the meal.

Laurie got to her feet. "If you don't mind, I'd like to ride with you as far as the morgue."

"What?" Jack scrunched up his face in disbelief. "You're not going to work at this hour? I mean, you're not even on call."

"I just want to question the night mortuary tech and security," Laurie said as she went to the hall closet for their coats.

"What on earth for?" Jack asked.

"I want to figure out how Franconi's body disappeared." She handed Jack his bomber jacket. "I talked to the evening crew."

"And what did they tell you?"

"Not a whole bunch. The body came in around eight forty-five. Identification was made by the mother—a very emotional scene by all reports. At ten forty-five the body was placed in the fridge in compartment one eleven. So I think it's pretty clear the abduction occurred during the night shift, from eleven to seven."

"Why are you worrying yourself about this?" Jack asked. "This is the front office's problem."

Laurie pulled on her coat, and they exited into the hall. "Let's just say it irks me that these two-bit mobsters think laws are for other people. They think they can come into our morgue and walk off with the body of a man they just killed."

They emerged onto Nineteenth Street and walked to First Avenue. "What makes you think the mobsters are behind this?"

"You don't have to be a rocket scientist to assume as much." Laurie put up her hand as a cab approached, but it zoomed past. "Franconi was going to testify as part of a plea bargain. The higher-ups of the Vaccarro organization got angry or scared or both. Maybe they're afraid an autopsy would provide a clue to the killer's identity. Ultimately it doesn't matter why."

"I have a sense the 'why' might be important," Jack said. "I think by getting involved, you'll be skating on thin ice."

"Maybe so." Laurie shrugged. "I get caught up in things like this. I suppose part of the problem is that at the moment my main focus in life is my job."

"Here comes a cab," Jack said, deliberately avoiding having to respond to Laurie's last comment.

It was a short ride to First Avenue and Thirtieth Street. Laurie climbed out and was surprised when Jack did the same. "You don't have to come," she said.

"I know. But I am. You have me concerned."

Jack paid the cabdriver. They entered the morgue. "I thought you told me your bed was beckoning," Laurie said.

"It can wait."

The elderly night security man was sitting in his cubbyhole. It didn't take Laurie long to learn that he had little light to shed on Franconi's disappearance. He left his post twice during his shift to visit the men's room. On both occasions he'd informed the night mortuary tech, Mike Passano. Laurie thanked him and moved on.

They looked into the mortuary office and found Mike Passano busy with some receiving forms. Mike was in his early thirties and spoke with a strong Long Island accent.

"Did you docs come in to see the floater?" Mike asked.

"No," Jack said. "Is there a problem?"

"No problem. It's just in bad shape. The coast guard fished it out of the ocean."

"We've come to talk about last night," Laurie said.

"Dr. Bingham telephoned this morning and read me the riot act," Mike said with irritation. "But I didn't have anything to do with that body disappearing."

"The body disappeared during your shift," Laurie said. "That's not saying you are responsible."

"It sorta sounds that way," Mike said. "I mean, I'm the only one here besides security."

"Did anything happen out of the ordinary?" Laurie asked.

Mike shook his head. "It was a quiet night. We had two bodies come in and two go out."

"The bodies that arrived," Laurie asked, "did they come in with our people?"

"Yup, with our vans. Both bodies were from local hospitals."

"What about the two bodies that went out?" Laurie asked.

Mike grabbed the mortuary logbook from the corner of his desk and cracked it open. His index finger traced down the column. "Spoletto Funeral Home in Ozone Park and Dickson Funeral Home in Summit, New Jersey, picked them up."

"What were the names of the deceased?" Laurie asked.

Mike consulted the book. "Frank Gleason and Dorothy Kline, accession numbers 100385 and 101455. Anything else?"

"Were you expecting these funeral homes to come?"

"Yeah, of course. They'd called beforehand like always. I had the paperwork all done. They just had to sign off."

"And the bodies?" Laurie asked.

"They were in the walk-in cooler as usual," Mike said. "Right in the front on gurneys."

"Tell me, Mike," Laurie said. "If you had to guess, how do you think the body disappeared?"

"I don't have the foggiest idea. Unless he walked out of here." Mike laughed, then seemed embarrassed. "All I know is only two bodies went out last night, and they were the two I checked out."

KEVIN replaced the tissue culture flasks in the incubator and closed the door. It was now ten fifteen a.m., and he'd been working at the lab since before dawn. He'd awakened at four a.m. and had not been able to fall back to sleep.

What was troubling Kevin's sleep was his conscience. The nagging notion that he'd made a Promethean mistake had resurfaced with a vengeance. Lab of his dreams or no, he couldn't deny the horror he feared was evolving on Isla Francesca. He decided that the most rational course of action to find out if his fears were justified would be to approach someone close to the situation, such as chief veterinarian Bertram Edwards, whom he admired.

Kevin removed his lab coat and headed out of his office.

Descending to the first floor, he exited into the steamy heat of the parking area. He climbed into his Toyota Land Cruiser and turned right out of the hospital parking lot.

Traversing the north side of the town square, Kevin passed the recreational center, where GenSys showed movies. In the basement was a commissary serving American hamburgers. At the edge of town the cobblestoned street gave way to newly laid asphalt. After fifteen minutes of driving through a canyon of dark green vegetation, he could see the first buildings of the state-of-the-art animal complex.

The enormous main building looked more like an airport terminal than a primate housing facility. It was three stories tall and five hundred feet long. From the back of the structure projected multiple wings that literally disappeared into the canopy of vegetation. Two smaller buildings faced the main one. One housed the complex's contingent of Equatorial Guinean soldiers. The other was the headquarters of Moroccan mercenaries who were part of the presidential guard. The local president didn't trust his own army. These foreign special forces commandos dressed in ill-fitting dark suits, with obvious bulges from their shoulder holsters. Every one of them had piercing eyes and a heavy mustache. They were rarely seen, but their presence was felt like a sinister evil force. GenSys had sited the facility in equatorial Africa to sidestep the West's web of import-export restrictions associated with primates, as well as the disruptive influence of animal-rights zealots. The local government had even passed a law making interference with GenSys a capital offense.

Kevin parked next to a Jeep Cherokee he knew was Bertram Edwards's from the bumper sticker that said MAN IS AN APE. He pushed through the glass double doors. Edwards's secretary greeted him. "Dr. Edwards is in the chimpanzee wing," she said. "In the bonobo unit."

Kevin set off for the chimpanzee wing. He walked the length of the veterinary hospital. Another pair of double doors brought him into the part of the building that housed the primates. The air had a slightly feral odor. Intermittent shrieks and howls reverberated in the corridor. Through windows of wire-embedded glass he caught glimpses of large cages where monkeys were incarcerated. Outside the cages men in coveralls and rubber boots pulled hoses.

The chimpanzee wing was in one of the ells that extended from the back of the building into the forest. It too was three stories tall. Kevin found a stairwell and climbed to the second floor. He thought it was a coincidence that Dr. Edwards happened to be in the bonobo unit just when he was looking for him.

Six years before, Kevin had never heard of a bonobo. But that changed rapidly when bonobos were selected as the subjects for his GenSys project. He now knew they were cousins of chimpanzees, but in contrast to chimps, bonobo society was matriarchal, with less male aggression. Hence, the bonobos were able to live in large groups. Some people called them pygmy chimpanzees, but the name was a misnomer because some bonobos were actually larger than some chimpanzees and they were a distinct species.

Kevin found Dr. Edwards in front of a small acclimatization cage. He was reaching through the bars, making tentative contact with two adult females, and hooting softly in imitation of one of the many bonobo sounds of communication. He was a relatively tall man, a good three or four inches over Kevin's five feet ten. He had a shock of white hair, which contrasted with his black eyebrows.

"Excuse me, Dr. Edwards," Kevin began. The bonobos shrieked and fled to the back of the cage.

Dr. Edwards turned and smiled. "Kevin, please. I've told you a dozen times—Bertram. I mean, we've known each other five years."

"Of course," Kevin said.

"It's serendipitous you should come," Bertram said. "Meet our two newest breeding females." The two apes inched away from the back wall. Kevin had frightened them, but they were now curious.

Kevin gazed in at the dramatically anthropomorphic faces of the two primates. Bonobos' faces were less prognathous than chimpanzees' and hence considerably more human. Kevin always found looking into bonobos' eyes disconcerting.

"Healthy-appearing animals," Kevin said. "With our demand going up, they'll be put to good use."

"You'd better believe it," Bertram said. "These two are already spoken for. If they pass all the tests, we'll be over to your lab in the next couple of days. I want to watch again. I think you are a genius. And Melanie . . . I've never seen such hand-eye coordination."

Kevin blushed at the reference to himself. "Melanie is quite talented," he said to deflect the conversation. Melanie Becket was a reproductive technologist recruited mainly for Kevin's project.

"She's good," Bertram said. "But the few of us lucky enough to be associated with your project know that you are the hero. You know, through your project and its stock options, we're going to get rich. Just yesterday I heard from Melanie, who had spoken with Raymond Lyons, that we have two more clients from New York City. That will put us over one hundred."

Kevin looked back at the two females. They returned his stare with pleading expressions that melted his heart. He wished he could tell them they had nothing to fear. All that would happen to them was that they would become pregnant within the month and be treated to special nutritious diets. Then they'd rear their babies in the enormous bonobo outdoor enclosure.

"They sure are human-looking," Bertram said. "Sometimes you can't help but wonder what they are thinking."

"Or worry what their offspring are capable of," Kevin said.

Bertram glanced at Kevin, his black eyebrows arched more than usual. "I don't follow."

"I came over here specifically to talk to you about the project."

"How convenient," Bertram said. "I was going to call you today and have you come over to see the progress we've made. Come on."

Bertram pulled open the nearest door and set out across the veterinary hospital. Kevin followed.

"Progress?" Kevin questioned.

"You betcha!" Bertram said enthusiastically. "We solved the technical problems with the grid on the island. We can now locate any animal with the push of a button. It's just in time, I might add. With twelve square miles and almost a hundred individuals, it was becoming impossible with the handheld trackers. Part of the problem is that we didn't anticipate the creatures would split into two groups. We were counting on their being one big happy family."

"Bertram," Kevin said, marshaling his courage, "I wanted to talk to you because I've been anxious—" Before Kevin could go on, Bertram was stopped for a corridor consultation.

"Sorry," Bertram offered afterward; then he pushed through the last of the double doors. Kevin followed.

Passing his secretary, Bertram waved Kevin into his inner office and closed the door. "You're going to love this." He sat down in front of his computer and showed Kevin how to bring up a graphic of Isla Francesca. It was divided into a grid. "Now give me the number of whatever creature you want to locate."

"Mine," Kevin said. "Number one."

"Coming up." Bertram entered the information and clicked. Suddenly a blinking red light appeared on the map of the island. It was north of the limestone escarpment but south of the stream that had been humorously dubbed the Rio Diviso. The stream bisected the six- by two-mile island lengthwise. In the center of the island was a pond they'd called Lago Hippo, for obvious reasons.

"Pretty slick, huh?" Bertram said proudly.

Kevin was captivated. The red light was blinking exactly where he would have imagined the smoke was coming from.

Bertram got up and pulled open a file drawer. It was filled with small handheld electronic devices, like miniature notepads, with LCD screens and extendable antennas. "These portable locators work in a similar fashion." He handed one to Kevin.

Kevin played with the keyboard. With Bertram's help he soon had the island graphic with the blinking red light displayed. Bertram showed how to go to successive maps with smaller scales until the entire screen represented a fifty-foot square.

"How does this tracking system operate?" Kevin asked.

"It's a satellite system," Bertram said. "Each animal has a small microchip embedded just under the derma."

Kevin started to give the device back, but Bertram waved him away. "Keep it. We've got plenty of others."

"But I don't need it," Kevin protested.

"Come on, Kevin," Bertram chided. "Loosen up. You're much too serious. Now, what was it you wanted to discuss?"

"I—I'm concerned," Kevin stammered. "I've seen the smoke again."

"You mean like that wisp of smoke you mentioned last week?"

"Exactly. And from the same spot on the island."

"Ah, it's nothing," Bertram declared with a wave of his hand. "We've been having electrical storms just about every other night. Lightning starts fires; everybody knows that."

"Well, maybe. But even if it were to start a fire, would it last?"

"You're like a dog with a bone," Bertram commented. "Have you mentioned this crazy idea to anybody else?"

"Only to Raymond Lyons," Kevin said. "He called me yesterday about another problem."

"And what was his response?" Bertram asked.

"He told me not to let my imagination run wild."

"I'd say that was good advice. I second the motion."

"I don't know. Maybe we should go out to the island and check."

"No!" Bertram snapped, his blue eyes blazing. "I don't want to go there except for a retrieval. The animals are to remain isolated and undisturbed. The only person who goes to the island now is Alphonse Kimba, the Pygmy who pulls supplementary food across."

"I could go myself," Kevin said. "I wouldn't bother the animals."

"No," Bertram said. "There are to be no exceptions. Visits will provoke talk, and it could be dangerous. One of the Pygmy bearers was killed on the last retrieval. One of the bonobos threw a rock."

"Isn't that unusual?" Kevin asked.

Bertram shrugged. "Chimps are known to throw sticks when they are stressed. It was probably just a reflex gesture."

"But it's also aggressive. That's unusual for a bonobo, especially one of ours."

"All apes will defend their group when attacked." Bertram draped an arm over Kevin's shoulders. "Come on, Kevin. Relax. You've got to get out of your lab and do something to divert that overactive mind of yours. You're going stir-crazy, and you're obsessing. I mean, this fire stuff is ridiculous. What do you say?"

"I guess," Kevin said evasively.

FIVE minutes later Kevin climbed back into his vehicle, more confused than before. Maybe his imagination was working overtime, but short of visiting Isla Francesca, there was no way of knowing.

The ride back to the hospital was uneventful and quick. Kevin parked in his spot. Just with the short walk from the car, he could appreciate the intensity of the noontime sun. Once inside, he started up the cool, air-conditioned stairs.

"Dr. Marshall," a voice called.

Kevin looked behind him.

"Shame on you, Dr. Marshall." A woman was standing at the base of the stairs. Her voice had a lilting quality that suggested she was less than serious. She was clad in surgical scrubs.

"Excuse me?" Kevin said. The woman looked familiar.

"You haven't been to see the patient. With other cases you came each day."

"Well, that's true." Kevin recognized her. She was the nurse Candace Brickmann, part of the surgical team that flew in with the patient. This was her fourth trip to Cogo.

"You've hurt Mr. Winchester's feelings." Candace wagged her finger. She was a vivacious gamine in her late twenties with fine light blond hair done up in a French twist.

"I—I didn't think he'd notice," Kevin stammered.

Candace threw back her head and laughed. "I'm only teasing."

Kevin's face flushed. "Well, I meant to come and see how he was doing. I've just been too busy."

"You academic types crack me up," Candace said. "But teasing aside, I'm happy to report that Mr. Winchester is doing fine, and I understand from the surgeon that's largely thanks to you."

"I wouldn't go that far," Kevin said.

"Oh, modest too," Candace commented. "Smart, cute, and humble. That's a killing combination."

Kevin stuttered, but no words came out.

"Would it be out of bounds for me to invite you to join me for lunch?" Candace asked. "I thought I'd walk over and get a hamburger. I'm a little tired of hospital food. What do you say?"

Kevin's mind whirled.

"Cat got your tongue?" Candace lowered her head and flirtatiously peered at him beneath arched eyebrows.

Kevin gestured up toward his lab, then mumbled words to the effect that Esmeralda was expecting him.

"Can't you give her a call?"

"I guess. I suppose I could call from my lab."

Kevin had never met such a forward female—not that he had a lot of opportunity or experience.

Candace came up the stairs to stand next to Kevin. She was about five three in her Nikes. "Why don't I come up with you?"

"Okay," Kevin said.

Kevin's nervousness quickly abated. Usually what bothered him in social circumstances with females was the stress of trying to think of things to talk about. Candace maintained a running conversation going up the stairs, managing to bring up the weather, the town, and the hospital.

"This is my lab," Kevin said after opening the door.

"Fantastic!" Candace said. "You make your call. I'll look around."

After Kevin hung up, she commented, "This is some lab. I never would have expected to find it in the heart of tropical Africa. Tell me, what is it that you're doing with all this equipment?"

"At this stage I'm dealing with minor histocompatibility antigens— proteins that define you as a unique, separate individual."

"And what do you do with them?"

"Well, I locate their genes on the proper chromosome," Kevin said. "Then I search for the transponase so I can move the genes."

Candace let out a little laugh. "You've lost me already. Let's get some hamburgers before my blood sugar bottoms out."

Descending the stairs, Kevin felt a little giddy. He couldn't believe he was going to lunch with such an attractive, engaging female.

He had not been in the rec center since his initial orientation tour. He was surprised at how busy the commissary was. He and Candace had to stand in a long line before ordering. Then after they'd gotten their food, they had to search for a place to sit.

"There are some seats," Candace called out, pointing toward the rear of the room. Kevin followed as she squeezed between two tables. He put his tray down at an empty spot.

"Lively place," Candace said. "Do you come here often?"

Before Kevin could respond, someone called his name. He turned and recognized Melanie Becket, the reproductive technologist.

"Kevin Marshall!" Melanie exclaimed again. "I'm shocked. What are you doing here?"

Melanie was about the same age as Candace; she'd celebrated her thirtieth birthday the previous month. Where Candace was light, she was dark, with medium brown hair and coloration that seemed Mediterranean. Her dark brown eyes were nearly black.

"I'm Candace Brickmann." Candace reached out a hand. Melanie introduced herself and asked if she could join them.

"By all means," Candace said.

Melanie sat opposite Candace. "Are you responsible for our local genius's presence at the ptomaine palace?" she asked.

"I guess. Is this unusual for him?"

"That's the understatement of the year," Melanie said. "I've asked him to come here so many times to no avail that I finally gave up."

"Well," Candace said, "this must be my lucky day."

Melanie and Candace fell into easy conversation. Kevin listened but concentrated on his hamburger.

"So we're all three part of the same project," Melanie commented when she heard that Candace was the intensive care nurse of the surgical team from Pittsburgh. "Three peas in a pod."

"You're being generous," Candace said. "I'm just one of the low men on the totem pole. You're the ones that make it all possible. If you don't mind my asking, how on earth do you do it?"

"She's the hero." Kevin nodded toward Melanie.

"Come on, Kevin," Melanie said. "I didn't develop the techniques I use the way you did. It was your breakthrough that was key."

"No arguing, you two," Candace said. "Just tell me how it's done. I've been curious from day one, but everything's so hush-hush."

"Kevin gets a bone-marrow sample from a client," Melanie said. "From that he isolates a cell preparing to divide."

"I work with a transponase that I discovered almost seven years ago," Kevin said. "It catalyzes the homologous transposition—or crossing-over—of the short arms of chromosome six."

"What's the short arm of chromosome six?" Candace asked.

"Chromosomes have a centromere that divides them into two segments," Melanie explained. "Chromosome six has particularly unequal segments. The little ones are called the short arms."

"But I don't let the crossing-over go to completion," Kevin said. "I halt it with the two short arms detached from their respective chromosomes. Then I extract them."

"Wow!" Candace remarked. "You actually take these tiny, tiny strands out of the nucleus. What do you do with them?"

Kevin pointed to Melanie. "I wait for her to work her magic."

"It's not magic," Melanie said. "I'm just a technician. I apply in vitro fertilization techniques to the bonobos. Actually, Kevin and I have to coordinate our efforts because what he wants is a fertilized egg that has yet to divide. Timing is important."

"When Melanie delivers the zygote," Kevin said, "I repeat exactly the same procedure that I've just done with the client's cell. After removing the bonobo's short arms, I inject the client's short arms into the zygote. Thanks to the transponase, they hook right up exactly where they are supposed to be."

"And that's it?" Candace said.

"Well, no," Kevin admitted. "The short arm of chromosome six is a major segment that we're transferring, but we also transfer a relatively small part of chromosomes nine, twelve, and fourteen."

"Chromosome six contains the genes that make up the major histocompatibility complex," Candace said.

"Exactly," Kevin said. Not only was Candace socially adept, she was also smart. "There is no immunological reaction to worry about.

Histocompatibility-wise we're offering an immunological double, especially if I can incorporate a few more minor antigens."

"I don't know why you agonize over them," Melanie said. "In our first three transplants the clients haven't had any rejection reaction at all. Zilch."

"I want it perfect," Kevin said. "The reason the system works so well in bonobos is that their genomes and ours are so similar. In fact, they differ by only one and a half percent."

"That's all?" Candace was amazed. "They look so human. Doesn't it bother you guys when one of them has to be sacrificed?"

"This liver transplant with Mr. Winchester is only the second that required a sacrifice," Melanie said. "The other two were kidneys, and the animals are fine."

"Well, how did this case make you feel?" Candace asked. "Most of us on the surgical team were more upset this time."

"Yeah, it bothers me," Melanie said. "But we never expect to use many of them. They are like insurance in case the clients need them. We don't accept people who already need transplant organs unless they can wait the three-plus years it takes for their double to come of age. And we don't have the chance to form emotional bonds with these creatures. They live on an island by themselves."

Kevin swallowed with difficulty. In his mind's eye he could see the smoke. He could also imagine the stressed bonobo picking up a rock and throwing it with deadly accuracy.

"What's the term when animals have human genes incorporated into them?" Candace asked.

"Transgenic," Melanie said.

"Right," Candace said. "As much as I like the money and the GenSys stock, I'm not so sure I'm going to stick with the program. When we put that last transgenic bonobo under anesthesia, I could have sworn he was trying to communicate with us."

"Oh, come on!" Kevin snapped, suddenly furious.

Melanie's eyes opened wide. "What's gotten into you?"

Kevin instantly regretted his outburst. "Sorry," he said. He admitted he was upset.

"Can't you be more specific? What's bugging you?"

"I feel like I've made a monumental mistake by adding so much human DNA," Kevin said. "The short arm of chromosome six has millions of base pairs and hundreds of genes that have nothing to do with the major histocompatibility complex. I should have isolated the complex instead of taking the easy route."

"So the creatures have a few more human proteins," Melanie said. "Big deal."

"That's exactly how I felt at first," Kevin said. "At least until I found out there was a large segment of developmental genes on the short arm of chromosome six. Now I have no idea what I've created." Perspiration had appeared on his forehead. "And I'm terrified I've overstepped the bounds."

CHAPTER 3

ERTRAM pulled his Jeep Cherokee into the parking area behind the town hall. Taking the stairs behind the first-floor arcade to the veranda, he walked into the central office. By Siegfried Spallek's choice it had not been air-conditioned. A large ceiling fan rotated lazily, keeping the room's warm, moist air on the move.

Bertram had called ahead, so Siegfried's secretary, a broad-faced black man named Aurielo from the island of Bioko, was expecting him and waved him into the inner office.

"Sit down," Siegfried said without looking up. His voice had a harsh, guttural quality, with a slight Germanic accent. He was signing a stack of correspondence. "I'll be finished in a moment."

Bertram's eyes wandered around the cluttered office, which always made him uncomfortable. As a veterinarian, he did not appreciate the decor. Covering every available surface were the glassy-eyed stuffed heads of animals, many of which were endangered species—lions, leopards, cheetahs, and a bewildering variety of antelope. Several enormous rhino heads peered blankly down from the wall.

Even more bothersome to Bertram were the three skulls on Siegfried's desk. All three had their tops sawn off. They were used respectively for paper clips, as an ashtray, and to hold a large candle. Most visitors assumed they were from apes. Bertram knew otherwise. They were the skulls of people executed by the Equatorial Guinean soldiers after being convicted of poaching on the Zone land.

"There." Siegfried pushed the papers aside. "What's on your mind, Bertram? You don't have a problem with the new bonobos?"

"Not at all. The two breeding females are perfect," Bertram said. He eyed the Zone's site boss. His most obvious physical trait was a grotesque scar that ran from his left ear down across his cheek, pulling up the corner of his mouth in a perpetual sneer.

Siegfried had started his African career as a white hunter who, for a price, could get a client anything he wanted. West African game laws were not rigidly enforced. Things went well until some trackers failed Siegfried in a crucial situation, resulting in his being mauled by an enormous bull elephant and the client couple's being killed.

The episode ended his career. It also left him with his facial scar and a paralyzed right arm. Rage over the incident had made him a bitter and vindictive man. Still, GenSys had recognized his bush-based organizational skills and thought he was the perfect individual to run their multimillion-dollar African operation.

"There's another wrinkle with the bonobos," Bertram said.

"Is this new concern in addition to the weird worry of yours that the apes have divided into two groups?" Siegfried asked. "What do we care if they hang out in one group or ten?"

"Splitting up suggests they are not getting along," Bertram said. "That would not be typical bonobo behavior."

"I'll let you, the professional, worry about it."

"The new problem has to do with Kevin Marshall."

"What could that skinny simpleton do to get you to worry?"

"The nerd has worked himself up because he's seen smoke coming from the island," Bertram said. "He's come to me twice."

"What's the big deal about smoke?" Siegfried asked.

"He thinks the bonobos might be using fire."

"You mean like making a campfire?" Siegfried laughed.

"I know it's preposterous. The problem is, he wants to go out there."

"No one goes near the island," Siegfried growled. "Only the harvest team and Kimba the Pygmy, delivering the supplementary food. That's a directive from the home office."

"I told him the same thing."

"The little jerk," Siegfried said. "He's a thorn in my side."

"He told Raymond Lyons about the smoke," Bertram said.

Siegfried slapped the surface of his desk with his good hand loud enough to cause Bertram to jump. "What a meddling pain in the neck." Siegfried gritted his teeth. "What did Lyons say?"

"Nothing. He accused Kevin of letting his imagination run wild."

"I might have to have someone watch Kevin," Siegfried said. "I will not have anyone destroy this program."

Bertram stood up. "That's your department," he said.

THE combination of cheap red wine and little sleep slowed Jack's pace on his morning bicycle commute. His customary time of arrival in the ID room of the medical examiner's office was seven fifteen. But as he got off the elevator on the first floor, it was already seven twenty-five, and it bothered him. It wasn't as if he were late, it was just that he liked to keep to a schedule.

His first order of business was to pour himself a cup of coffee from the communal pot. He took his first sip and felt his mild hangover headache was already on the mend.

He stepped over to Vinnie Amendola, the mortuary tech whose day shift overlapped the night shift. As usual, his face was hidden behind his morning newspaper.

Jack pulled the edge of the paper down to expose Vinnie's Italianate features to the world. He was in his late twenties—in sorry physical shape, but handsome. His dark, thick hair was something Jack envied. Jack had been noticing a decided thinning of his gray-streaked brown hair on the crown of his head.

"Hey, Einstein, what's the paper say about the Franconi body incident?" Jack asked. He and Vinnie worked together frequently, both appreciating the other's quick wit and black humor.

"I don't know." Vinnie was embroiled in the Knicks stats from the previous night's basketball game.

Jack's forehead furrowed. Vinnie read the newspapers cover to cover every day. "There's nothing about it in the paper?"

"I didn't notice it," Vinnie said.

As Jack was about to turn away, he caught the headline MOB THUMBS NOSE AT AUTHORITY. The subhead read VACCARRO CRIME FAMILY KILLS ONE OF ITS OWN, THEN STEALS BODY FROM UNDER THE NOSES OF CITY OFFICIALS. Jack snatched the entire paper from Vinnie's grasp. "I thought you said the story wasn't in the paper," he said.

"I said I didn't see it."

"It's the headlines, you idiot," Jack said.

Vinnie lunged out to grab his paper. Jack pulled it away.

"Come on," Vinnie whined. "Get your own paper."

"As methodical as you are, you'd have read this front-page story on your subway ride into town. What's up, Vinnie?"

"Nothing," Vinnie said. "I just went to the sports page."

Jack slipped out the sports pages and handed them over. Then he went over to the scheduling desk and started the article. It cast equal aspersion on the police and the medical examiner's office and said the whole affair was another example of gross incompetence.

Laurie breezed into the room and removed her coat. She told Jack that she hoped he felt better than she.

"Probably not," Jack admitted.

"Good morning, Vinnie," Laurie said.

Vinnie stayed silent behind his sports pages.

"He's pouting because I violated his paper." Jack got up so Laurie could sit down at the scheduling desk. It was Laurie's week to divvy up the cases for autopsy. "The cover story is the Franconi incident."

"I wouldn't wonder. It was all over the news." Laurie started glancing through twenty or so folders. "Have you looked at today's cases?"

"I just got here myself," Jack admitted. He went back over to Vinnie and returned the paper. Vinnie took it without comment.

"Uh-oh," Laurie called out. "Here's that floater that Mike Passano mentioned last night. Who should I assign it to?"

"Give it to me," Jack said.

"You don't care?" Laurie hated floaters, especially those that had been in the water for a long time.

"Nah. Once you get past the smell, you got it licked."

"Please," Laurie murmured. "That's disgusting."

"I like them better than gunshot wounds," Jack said.

"This one is both," Laurie commented.

"How delightful! What's the victim's name?"

"No name," Laurie said. "In fact, that will be part of your challenge. The head and the hands are missing."

Laurie handed Jack the folder. He slid out the contents. There wasn't much information. The naked body had been discovered in the Atlantic way out off Coney Island by a coast guard cutter.

"Not a lot to go on," Jack said.

"All the more challenge," Laurie teased.

Jack headed for the elevator. "Come on, grouchy," he called to Vinnie. "Time's awasting." But at the door he literally bumped into Lou Soldano. Some of Jack's coffee had sloshed out onto the floor.

"Sorry," Lou sighed.

"Have you been partying all night again?" Jack said.

The detective lieutenant's face was stubbled with a heavy growth of whiskers. He had on a wrinkled shirt with tie askew.

"I wish," Lou grunted. "I've seen about three hours of sleep in the last two nights." He walked over, said hello to Laurie, and sat down heavily in a chair next to the scheduling desk.

"Any progress on the Franconi case?" Laurie asked.

"Nothing that pleases the captain, the area commander, or the police commissioner," Lou said dejectedly. "What a mess."

"So what's next?" Laurie asked.

"We're still following up leads," Lou said, "but mostly we're just keeping our fingers crossed for some sort of break. What about you guys? Any idea how the body walked out of here?"

"Not yet, but I'm looking into it personally," Laurie said. "I think it is important to find out how the body disappeared, for the sake of this office."

Jack threw up his hands. "I'm getting out of here." He tugged on Vinnie's shirt on the way out the door.

"Don't tell me we're doing a floater," Vinnie whined as he and Jack headed for the elevator.

"You sure do tune out when you read the sports," Jack said.

They boarded the elevator and went to the autopsy room. Vinnie went off to don his moon suit, lay out all the paraphernalia, and get the body onto the table. Jack went and found the X rays that had been taken when the body arrived. Then he put on his own moon suit and hooked himself up. He hated the suit in general, but to work on a decomposing floater he hated it less. As he'd teased with Laurie earlier, the smell was the worst part.

The first order of business was to look at the X rays, and Jack snapped them up on the viewer. He took a step back and gazed at the anteroposterior full-body shot. With no head and no hands, the image was like the X ray of some primitive nonhuman creature. The other abnormality was a bright, dense blob of shotgun pellets in the right upper quadrant. Jack's impression was that there had been multiple shotgun blasts.

"Whenever you're ready, maestro," Vinnie called out.

The floater was ghastly pale in the fluorescent light. The obese body was in sad shape, although it had obviously been in the water for only a short time. The shotgun blasts had damaged many of the internal organs. Not only were the head and the hands hacked off but there were deep gashes in the torso and thighs.

"Someone try to slice him up like a holiday turkey?" Vinnie asked.

Jack smiled at Vinnie's black humor. "Nah. I'd guess he'd been run over with a boat. They look like propeller injuries."

Jack began a careful exterior examination, working slowly and stopping frequently to photograph lesions. His meticulousness paid off. At the ragged base of the neck, just anterior to the collarbone, he found a small circular lesion. He found another, similar one on the left side below the rib cage.

"What are they?" Vinnie asked.

"I don't know," Jack said. "Puncture wounds of some sort."

A little later Jack said to Vinnie, "Enough of this external stuff. Let's move on to the internal part."

"It's about time," Vinnie complained. It was now after eight.

With all the obvious trauma, Jack had to vary the traditional autopsy technique, and that took concentration. But again his meticulousness paid off. Although the liver had essentially been obliterated by the shotgun blasts, he discovered the tiny remains of surgical sutures in the vena cava and in the ragged end of the hepatic artery.

"I think our chances of making an identification just went up a thousand percent," Jack said. "With sutures in the vena cava and the hepatic artery, my guess is that he had a liver transplant."

"HELLO!" Candace called out. "Anybody home?"

Kevin's hand flinched at the unexpected noise. It was five forty-five p.m. The lab techs had left for the day, and the laboratory had been silent save for the low hum of the refrigeration units.

"Over here!" Kevin yelled. He stood up.

"Am I coming at a bad time?" she asked.

"No. I was just finishing up."

"I've come to see if I can drag you over to meet Mr. Horace Winchester," Candace said. "He'd like to thank you in person for giving him a new lease on life."

Kevin struggled to think up a reason not to go and then was saved by another voice.

"Ah, my two buddies." Melanie came into the room wearing blue coveralls with ANIMAL CENTER on the breast pocket.

"I told Mr. Winchester about you guys," Candace said, "and he'd like to meet both of you. Kevin would be able to see the good side of what he's accomplished." She caught Melanie's eye.

Melanie understood Candace's motivation immediately. "Yeah," she said. "That should give us all a boost."

"I think it will make me feel worse," Kevin said.

Melanie put her hands on her hips. "Why?"

"Because seeing him will remind me of things I'm trying not to think about. Like what happened to the other patient."

"You mean his double, the bonobo?" Melanie asked. "You're taking this animal-rights issue seriously."

"I'm afraid it goes beyond animal rights," Kevin said.

"Okay, enough is enough." Melanie placed both hands on Kevin's shoulders and pushed him down onto his stool. "Friends talk to each other. They communicate. Do you know what I'm saying?"

"I think so," Kevin said.

As much as Kevin resisted expressing his fears, at the moment he didn't think he had much choice. Not knowing how to begin, he said, "I've seen smoke coming from Isla Francesca."

"What's Isla Francesca?" Candace asked.

"It's the island where the transgenic bonobos go once they reach age three," Melanie said. "So what's with the smoke?"

Kevin stood and walked over to his desk. He pointed out the window toward Isla Francesca. "I've seen the smoke three times. It's always just to the left of the limestone ridge."

"So big deal," Melanie commented. "A couple of little fires. With all the lightning around here, it's no wonder."

"But it can't be lightning," Kevin said. "Ever hear the expression lightning never strikes the same place twice?"

"Maybe some local fishermen visit," Candace suggested.

"All the locals know it is forbidden. It's a capital offense."

"Kevin!" Melanie exclaimed. "I'm beginning to get an idea what you're thinking. But let me tell you, it's preposterous."

"Will someone clue me in?" Candace asked.

"Let me show you something else." Kevin turned to his computer terminal and with a few keystrokes called up the graphic of the island. He explained the system to the women and, as a demonstration, brought up the location of Melanie's double. The little red light blinked just north of the escarpment.

"You have a double?" Candace asked. She was dumbfounded.

"Kevin and I were the guinea pigs," Melanie said. "Our doubles were the first. We had to prove the technology really works."

"Now that you know how the system operates," Kevin said, "let me show you what I did an hour ago. I'll have the computer locate all seventy-three doubles on the island sequentially. The creatures' numbers will occur in the corner, followed by the blinking light."

"Okay," Melanie said after a few minutes. "It's working just as you said. What's so disturbing?"

"Just hold on," Kevin said.

When the entire program ran its course, it indicated that seven of the bonobo doubles were unaccounted for.

"Is this what you found earlier?" Melanie asked.

Kevin nodded. "But when I tried it this morning, it wasn't seven missing, it was twelve."

"I don't understand," Melanie said. "How can that be?"

"When I toured that island, way back before all this started, I remember seeing caves in that limestone cliff. What I'm thinking is that our creations are going into the caves, maybe living in them. It's the only way I can explain why the grid would fail to pick them up."

Melanie brought up a hand to cover her mouth, horrified.

Candace saw Melanie's reaction. "Come on, guys," she pleaded. "What's wrong?"

Melanie lowered her hand. "What Kevin was referring to when he said he was terrified he'd overstepped the bounds," she explained, "was the fear that he'd created a human."

"You're not serious!" Candace exclaimed.

"I'm not suggesting a human being in the guise of an ape," Kevin said. "I'm suggesting that I've inadvertently created something akin to our distant ancestral forebears, who spontaneously appeared in nature from apelike animals four or five million years ago."

"You're talking about some early hominid-like creature, something like *Homo erectus,*" Melanie said. "It's true we noticed the infant transgenic bonobos tended to walk upright more than their mothers. We just thought it was cute."

"So to put it bluntly," Candace said, "we've got a bunch of cave-men out there."

"Something like that," Kevin said.

"What are we going to do?" Candace demanded. "I'm certainly not going to be involved with sacrificing any more. I was having a hard enough time when I thought the victim was an ape."

"Wait a sec," Melanie said. "We're jumping to conclusions. Everything we've been talking about is circumstantial at best."

"True, but there's more." Kevin instructed the computer to dis-play the locations of all the bonobos on the island simultaneously. Within seconds two red splotches began pulsating—one where Melanie's double had been; the other, north of the lake.

"There are two groups," Melanie said.

"It was the same earlier," Kevin said. "I think it's a real phenome-non. Bonobos should all be in one group. And Bertram told me one of the bonobos killed a Pygmy by throwing a rock. That kind of ag-gression is more associated with humans than with bonobos."

"But it's still circumstantial," Melanie said. "There is no proof."

"To prove it, somebody has to go to the island," Kevin said. "The trouble is, only Bertram Edwards or Siegfried Spallek can authorize a visit. I brought up the smoke with Bertram, but he made it very clear that no one was allowed near the island."

"Did you tell him what you are worried about?" Melanie asked.

"Not in so many words," Kevin said. "But he knew. I'm sure of it. He wasn't interested. The problem is that he and Siegfried are going to make sure nothing threatens their project bonuses."

"So that leaves it all up to us," Melanie said. "What do you say the three of us take a quick trip to Isla Francesca?"

"You're joking," Kevin said. "It's a capital offense."

"It's a capital offense for locals," Melanie said. "But what is Sieg-fried going to do, fire us? They can't do without you, Kevin. That's the reality."

"How do we get there?" Candace asked.

"There's a road that goes east along the coast," Kevin said. "It's paved to the native village; then it becomes a track. That's how I went before we started the program. The island and the mainland are only separated by a channel thirty feet wide. Back then, there was a wire suspension bridge stretched between two trees."

"Maybe we can view the animals without even going across," Candace said. "Let's do it."

"When do you want to do this?" Kevin questioned.

"I'd say now," Melanie replied. "There's no better time. Ninety percent of the town is either at the waterfront Chickee Hut Bar or in the pool."

Kevin drove. The sun was low in the west. On the east exit of the town, just beyond the soccer field, the vegetation closed in. Brightly colored birds flitted in and out of the deepening shadows.

They passed a number of Equatorial Guineans on their way home from work in Cogo. Most of the women carried jugs and parcels on top of their heads. The men were generally empty-handed.

"It's a strange culture," Melanie commented. "The women do the lion's share of the work."

"What do the men do?" Candace asked.

"Sit around and discuss metaphysics," Melanie said.

They reached the native village GenSys had built. The homes were circular, whitewashed mud brick with thatched roofs. The structures appeared traditional, but every one of them was new and spotless. They also had electricity and running water.

Past the busy general store the track became narrow, bumpy, and muddy. Branches stretched from one side to the other, slapping against the windshield and poking through the open windows.

"How far do we go on this cowpath?" Melanie asked.

"Only three or four miles," Kevin said.

Fifteen minutes later they entered a clearing, which marked the termination of the track. Kevin came to a halt, and they got out.

"There's a track over there to the water's edge." Kevin pointed.

Melanie glanced up at the sky. It was a pale lavender. "It's going to be dark pretty soon. Do you have a flashlight in the car?"

"I think so," Kevin said. "More important, I have some mosquito spray. We're going to get eaten alive unless we use it."

Kevin got the mosquito spray. While the women doused themselves, he found the flashlight in the glove compartment. As soon as they entered the path, he motioned for them to follow him. "Stay close. The crocodiles and hippos come out of the water at night."

"Is he joking?" Candace asked Melanie.

"I don't think so," Melanie said.

The closer they got to the water, the louder the monotonous night chorus of insects and frogs became. All of a sudden there was a crashing noise off to the left. Candace let out a muffled scream. "What was that?" she said when she found her voice.

"Probably a duiker," Kevin said. "A small antelope."

"Antelope or elephant," Candace said, "it scared me."

"It scared me too," Kevin said. "Maybe we should go back and return in the daytime."

"We're there," Melanie said. "I can hear the water."

For a moment no one moved. Sure enough, they could hear water lapping against the shore.

Melanie led the way as the path opened up into another clearing at the edge of the river. In the middle was a dark object almost the size of a garage. Kevin walked up to it. It wasn't hard to figure out what it was. "It's a bridge with a telescoping mechanism," he said.

Thirty feet across the water was Isla Francesca. In the fading light its dense vegetation appeared midnight blue. Directly across was a concrete support for the bridge when it was extended. Beyond that was an expansive clearing.

"Try extending the bridge," Melanie suggested.

Kevin found the control panel. "You need a key," he called.

Melanie and Candace had walked to the water's edge. Kevin joined them. "How can we get the bonobos to appear?" Candace asked.

"I doubt if we can," Kevin said. "By this time they're probably settling down for the night."

"What about the float Alphonse Kimba uses?" Melanie asked. "I've been told he pulls it across using a rope like a clothesline. If it makes noise, they might hear it. It would be like a dinner bell."

"Guess it's worth a try." Kevin shined the flashlight up and down the water's edge.

"Here it is." Melanie followed a path in the dense foliage to a pulley attached to a thick tree. A heavy rope hung around the pulley. One end disappeared into the water. The other end was tied to a four-foot-square float nestled against the shore. On the island a similar pulley was attached to a similar tree.

Kevin and Candace joined her. Kevin handed the flashlight to Melanie and grasped the rope that drooped into the water. When he pulled hand over hand, the pulleys complained bitterly with high-pitched squeaking noises. The float moved away from the shore.

Melanie swept the other shore with the flashlight beam.

When the float reached the other side, Kevin switched ropes and started pulling it back. "Ah, it's too late," he said. "This isn't going to work. The closest nesting area is over a mile away. We'll have to try this in the daytime."

No sooner had these words escaped from his mouth than the night was shattered by a number of fearsome screams. Then there was nothing but utter silence. All the night creatures had fallen silent.

"It's gotten too dark to see much even if they did appear," Melanie said. "And I'm spooked. Let's go!"

"You'll not get an argument from me." Kevin quickly hauled the float in. "It would be great to get a key for that bridge," he said as they hurried to the clearing, then entered the path leading to the car.

"And how do you propose to do that?" Melanie asked.

"Borrow Bertram's."

"But you told us he forbids anyone to go to the island," Melanie said. "He's certainly not going to lend the key."

"We'll have to borrow it without his knowledge," Kevin said.

"Oh, yeah, sure," Melanie said sarcastically. Then she stopped. "That's strange. The frogs and crickets haven't restarted their racket."

In the next instant all hell broke loose. A loud repetitive stuttering noise splintered the jungle stillness. Twigs and leaves rained down. Kevin recognized the noise and reacted by reflex. He literally tackled the women, so that all three fell to the moist earth.

Kevin had once inadvertently witnessed the soldiers practicing. The noise was the sound of a machine gun.

LAURIE looked at the label on the overnight package to find out the sender. It was CNN. What could CNN have sent her? She got her finger under the flap and pulled it open. Inside was a videotape labeled CARLO FRANCONI SHOOTING, MARCH 3, 1997.

After finishing her final autopsy that morning, Laurie had been ensconced in her office on the fifth floor, trying to complete some of her twenty-odd pending cases. She'd been reviewing microscope slides, laboratory results, and police reports, and for several hours had not thought of the Franconi business. The arrival of the tape brought it all back. Unfortunately, the video was meaningless without the body.

Laurie tossed the tape into her briefcase and tried to get back to work. But her mind kept toying with the baffling question of how the body had disappeared. One minute it was safely stored in compartment 111, and then poof, it was gone. There had to be an explanation, but she could not fathom it.

She turned off her microscope light and headed down to the basement to the mortuary office. The room was unoccupied. She went over to the log. Flipping the page, she found the entries Mike Passano had shown her the previous night. She took a sheet of paper and wrote down the names and accession numbers of the two bodies that had gone out during the night shift: Dorothy Kline, number 101455, and Frank Gleason, number 100385. She also wrote down the names of the two funeral homes: Spoletto in Ozone Park, New York, and the Dickson in Summit, New Jersey.

She was about to leave when her eye caught the large Rolodex on the corner of the desk. She decided to call each home. After identifying herself, she asked to speak to the managers. As she expected, both attested to the fact that the bodies had come into their respective homes and were at that time on view.

Feeling frustrated, Laurie drummed her pencil on the desk surface. She was sure she had to be missing something. Once again her eye caught the Rolodex, which was open to the Spoletto Funeral Home. Why was that name familiar? Then she remembered. A mobster had once been murdered in the Spoletto Funeral Home.

Laurie pocketed her memo and returned to the fifth floor. She walked directly to Jack's office. The door was ajar. She knocked on the jamb, and Jack looked up from his labors. "I had a thought," she said. She plopped down in a chair and told him about the Mob connection with the Spoletto Funeral Home.

"Good grief, Laurie," Jack complained. "Just because there is a Mob hit in the funeral home doesn't mean that it is Mob connected." He motioned toward his microscope. "Maybe I can channel your efforts into a more positive direction. Take a look at a frozen section. Tell me what you think."

Laurie got up from the chair and leaned over the microscope. "What is this, the shotgun entrance wound?" she asked.

"You're right on the money."

"I'd say the muzzle was within inches of the skin."

"My opinion exactly," Jack said. "Anything else?"

"My gosh, there's absolutely no extravasation of blood!" Laurie looked at Jack. "This had to have been a postmortem wound."

"Ah, the power of modern science. The shotgun wounds were definitely postmortem; so was the decapitation and removal of the hands. Of course, the propeller injuries were too."

"What was the cause of death?" Laurie asked.

"Two other gunshot wounds. One through the base of the neck, and another in the left side that shattered the tenth rib. The irony was that both slugs ended up in the mass of shotgun pellets in the abdomen and were difficult to see on the X ray."

"Now, that's a first. Bullets hidden by shotgun pellets."

"The best is yet to come. I think the shotgun blasts were an attempt to shield the victim's identity as much as the decapitation and removal of the hands."

"In what way?"

"I believe this patient had had a liver transplant not long ago," Jack said. "The killer must have understood that such a procedure jeopardized the chances of hiding the victim's identity."

"Was there much liver left?"

"Very little. But I found some tissue to corroborate the transplant. The clincher was the sutures in the vena cava and the hepatic artery."

"Well," Laurie said, "this should make identification rather easy."

"My thought exactly," Jack said. "I've already got Bart Arnold hot on the trail." Bart Arnold was the chief forensic investigator at the morgue. "He's been in contact with the United Network for Organ Sharing, UNOS. He's also calling all the centers actively doing liver transplants, especially here in the city."

"That's a small list," Laurie said. "Good job, Jack."

Jack's face reddened slightly, and Laurie was touched. She thought he was immune to such compliments.

DR. RAYMOND Lyons glanced at his watch as he entered his apartment on Sixty-fourth Street. It was after five and getting dark.

"You've had two calls from Africa," Darlene reported as he came through the door.

"Problems?" Raymond asked.

"There was good news and bad news," Darlene said. "The good news was from the surgeon. He said that Horace Winchester is doing miraculously and that you should start planning on coming to pick him and the surgical team up."

"What's the bad news?"

"The other call was from Siegfried Spallek. He said there was some trouble with Kevin Marshall."

"What kind of trouble?"

"He didn't elaborate."

Raymond wondered if it had something to do with that stupid smoke Kevin had seen. "Did Spallek want me to call back tonight?"

"It was eleven o'clock his time when he called," Darlene said. "He said he could talk to you tomorrow."

Raymond groaned inwardly. Now he'd have to spend the entire night worrying. He wondered when it was all going to end.

EVIN heard the heavy metal door open at the top of the stairs. Two seconds later the string of lightbulbs in the corridor went on. Through the bars of his cell he could see Melanie and Candace in their cells, squinting, as he was, in the sudden glare.

Heavy footfalls on the granite stairs preceded Siegfried Spallek's appearance. He was accompanied by security chief Cameron McIvers and Mustapha Aboud, chief of the Moroccan guards.

"It's about time, Mr. Spallek!" Melanie snapped. "I demand to be let out of here this instant, or you'll be in serious trouble."

Kevin winced. It was not the way to talk to Siegfried Spallek on any occasion, much less in their current circumstance.

Kevin, Melanie, and Candace had been huddling in utter blackness in separate cells in the hot, dank jail in the basement of the town hall. Each cell had a small, arched window, barred but without glass. The only comfort had been that they could easily talk to each other.

The first five minutes of the evening's ordeal had been the worst. As soon as the sound of the machine-gun fire died out, Kevin and the women were surrounded by jeering soldiers with AK-47s and by Moroccan guards. The guards had driven them in Kevin's car into town, where they'd been incarcerated in the old jail.

"This is outrageous treatment," Melanie persisted.

"On the contrary," Siegfried said. "I have been assured by Mustapha that you have been treated with all due respect."

"Respect!" Melanie sputtered. "To be shot at with machine guns! And kept in this hole in the dark! That's respect?"

"Those were merely warning shots directed over your heads," Siegfried corrected. "You had, after all, violated an important rule here in the Zone. Isla Francesca is off-limits. Everyone knows that."

Siegfried motioned to Cameron, who opened Candace's cell with a large antique key. "My apologies to you," Siegfried said to Candace. "I imagine you were led astray by our resident researchers."

Mustapha opened Melanie's cell and then Kevin's.

"I tried to call Dr. Raymond Lyons," Siegfried said, "to ask his opinion as to the best way to handle this situation. Since he was unavailable, I am releasing you on your own recognizance."

Mustapha extended Kevin's car keys to him. "Your vehicle is out back," he said with a heavy French accent.

"I will contact you individually sometime tomorrow," Siegfried said. "You may go."

Melanie started to speak again, but Kevin surprised himself by grabbing her arm and propelling her toward the stairs.

"I've had enough manhandling," she sputtered. She tried to pull her arm from Kevin's grasp.

"Let's just get into the car," Kevin whispered harshly through clenched teeth. He forced her to keep moving.

Outside, Candace climbed into Kevin's car, but not Melanie. She turned to Kevin, eyes blazing. "Give me the keys," she demanded.

Kevin handed her the car keys. Melanie immediately got in behind the wheel. Kevin climbed into the passenger seat. Melanie started the car, spun the tires, and drove out.

"I'm not going home just yet," she said. "But I'd be happy to take you guys home if you want."

"Where do you want to go?" Kevin asked. "It's almost midnight."

"I'm going out to the animal center," Melanie said. "I want the keys to that damned bridge."

"Maybe we should stop and talk about this," Kevin said.

Melanie jammed on the brakes, bringing them to a lurching stop. "I'm going to the animal center," she repeated.

"Why tonight?" Kevin asked.

"One, because I'm really ticked off," Melanie said. "And two, because they wouldn't suspect it. Obviously, they intend for us to go home and quake in our beds, but that's not my style."

"I think Melanie is right," Candace said from the back seat. "They were deliberately trying to scare us."

"And I think they did a good job," Kevin said. "Or am I the only sane one in the group?"

"Let's do it," Candace said.

"Oh, no," Kevin groaned. "How do you propose to get the keys? You don't even know where they'd be."

"I think it's pretty clear they'd be in Bertram's office," Melanie said. "You're the one who suggested he had them."

"Okay, they're in Bertram's office," Kevin said. "But what about security? Offices are locked."

Melanie pulled a magnetic card from the breast pocket of her coveralls. "You're forgetting that I'm part of the hierarchy. This card gets me in every door of the animal center twenty-four hours a day."

Kevin looked over the back of his seat at Candace. "If you're game, Candace, I guess I'm game."

"Let's go," Candace said.

The majority of the animal-center night staff worked in the veterinary hospital. Melanie took advantage of this fact by pulling up to one of the hospital doors. The car had lots of company.

"This place is huge." Candace leaned forward and gazed at the building. "For as many times as I've been to Cogo, I've never been out here. Is this part we're facing the hospital?"

"Yup, this whole wing," Melanie said as she alighted from the car. "Come on, the administration part of the building will be deserted. That's where Bertram's office is. Just to be sure we don't arouse suspicion, we'll head down to the locker room. I want you guys in animal-center coveralls, okay?"

"Sounds like a good idea to me," Candace said.

"ALL right," Bertram said into the phone. His eye caught the luminous dial of his bedside clock. It was a quarter past midnight. "I'll meet you at your office in five minutes."

When he got there, Siegfried was sitting at his desk with his feet propped up. In his good hand he gently swirled a brandy snifter. Cameron McIvers was sitting in a rattan chair with a similar glass. From the candle in the skull came a low, shimmering light, casting dark shadows on the stuffed animals.

"Thanks for coming out at such an ungodly hour," Siegfried said. "How about a splash of brandy?"

"Do I need it?" Bertram asked as he pulled up a rattan chair.

Siegfried laughed. "It can never hurt."

Cameron got the drink from a sideboard. He handed the snifter to Bertram and reclaimed his seat and his own drink.

"Usually when I'm called out in the middle of the night, it is a medical emergency with an animal," Bertram said. "Tonight I have the sense it is something else entirely."

"Indeed," Siegfried said. "First, I have to commend you. Your warning this afternoon about Kevin Marshall was timely. I asked Cameron to have him watched by the Moroccans, and sure enough this evening he, Melanie Becket, and one of the surgical nurses drove all the way out to the landing area for Isla Francesca."

"Damnation!" Bertram exclaimed. "Did they go on the island?"

"No," Siegfried said. "They merely played with the food float."

"Where are they now?" Bertram questioned.

"We let them go home. But not before putting the fear of God into them. I don't think they will be going near the island again, at least not for a while."

"This is not what I need," Bertram complained. "To have to worry about this on top of the bonobos splitting into two groups. Kevin Marshall must have said something to those women about the bonobos on the island using fire. If that gets out, we'll have animal-rights zealots coming out of the woodwork."

"What do you think we should do?" Siegfried asked.

"I think my idea of bringing them into the animal center should be reconsidered. I've got the cages out there."

"No!" Siegfried snapped. "The animals stay on the island. If they're brought in, you won't be able to keep it a secret. Even if they don't use fire, we know they're cunning from the problems we've had during retrievals. Handlers will start talking."

Bertram sighed and ran a nervous hand through his white hair.

"Tell me," Siegfried said, "if the animals are using fire, how do you think they got it? You still think it was lightning?"

"It could have been. But then again, they managed to steal a bunch of tools, rope, and other stuff when we had the crew out there constructing the bridge. They might have gotten matches. Of course, I have no idea how they could have figured out how to use them."

"You just gave me an idea. Why don't we tell Kevin and the women there's been a crew going out to the island to work? We can say they've been starting fires."

"Now, that's a good idea," Bertram said.

"Why didn't we think of it earlier? It's so obvious."

MELANIE led them to a position just outside Bertram's office.

"Now comes the acid test," Kevin said as Melanie tried her card. There was an immediate, reassuring click. The door opened.

They stepped inside. The only light was a meager glow that filtered through the open door into the inner office. "What now?" Kevin asked. "We're not going to find anything in the dark."

"I agree." Melanie switched on the light. For a moment they blinked at each other. "Whoa, seems awfully bright," she said.

"I hope it doesn't wake up those Moroccan guards across the street," Kevin said.

"Don't even joke about it." Melanie walked into the inner office. Kevin and Candace joined her. "I think we should be methodical about this," Melanie said. "I'll take the desk. Candace, you take the file cabinet. Kevin, why don't you take the outer office and, while you're at it, keep an eye on the hall? Give a yell if anybody appears."

A few minutes later Candace pulled a large folder from the file cabinet and called out, "This looks promising." In the upper-right-hand corner of the dark blue folder it said ISLA FRANCESCA.

Melanie pushed in the desk drawer she'd been searching and walked over. Kevin appeared from the outer office.

Candace slid the contents of the folder out onto a table. There were wiring diagrams of electronic equipment and numerous maps. There was also a large, lumpy manila envelope that had STEVENSON BRIDGE written across its top. "Now we're cooking." She reached into the envelope and pulled out a ring with five identical keys.

"Voilà." Melanie took the ring and removed a key.

Kevin had picked up a detailed contour map when he became aware of a flickering light—reflections of headlights. "Quick!" he said. "Get this all back into the file cabinet."

Melanie and Candace hastily crammed everything back into the folder, got the folder into the file cabinet, and closed the drawer. They heard the front door of the building open.

"This way," Melanie whispered frantically. She threw open the door to the hall, and they all raced toward the stairwell.

Melanie descended the stairs as fast as she could, with Kevin and Candace behind her. At the basement level, she groped for the door. She got it open none too soon. Above they heard the first-floor stairwell door open, followed by heavy footfalls on the metal stairs.

The basement was utterly black save for a dim rectangular outline of light in the distance—a fire door with light seeping around its periphery. Melanie opened it with her magnetic card. Beyond it was a brightly lit hallway. She pulled them to an abrupt halt halfway down the passageway and opened a door marked PATHOLOGY. "Inside," she barked. Wordlessly everyone complied.

They were in an anteroom for two autopsy theaters. There were scrub sinks and an insulated door leading to a refrigerated room.

"We have to hide," Kevin said.

"What about the refrigerator?" Candace offered.

With no time to argue, the three darted to the refrigerator, and Kevin got the door open. A cool mist flowed out to layer itself along the floor. Kevin pulled the door shut. Its hardware clicked soundly.

The room was twenty feet square, with stainless steel shelving from floor to ceiling that lined the periphery as well as forming a central island. The hulks of a number of dead primates lay on the shelves. The most impressive was the body of a huge silverback gorilla on the middle shelf of the central island.

Instinctively the three rushed around to the back of the central island and squatted down. Then they heard the unmistakable click of the refrigerator door's latch.

Kevin felt his heart skip a beat as the door was pulled open. He slowly raised his head to look over the bulk of the dead gorilla. It was two men in scrub suits carrying in the body of a chimpanzee. The men placed the body on a shelf to the right just inside the door and then left. Once the door was closed, Kevin looked at Melanie and sighed. "This has to have been the worst day of my life."

"It's not over yet. We still have to get out of here. But at least we got what we came for." Melanie opened her fist and held up the key. Light glinted off its chrome-colored surface.

Kevin looked at his own hand. Without realizing it, he was still clutching the detailed contour map of Isla Francesca.

"THIS is the damnedest thing." Jack was peering into his microscope at one particular slide and had been doing so intently for the previous half hour. His office mate Chet McGovern had tried to talk with him but had given up. When Jack was concentrating, it was impossible to get his attention.

"I'm glad you're enjoying yourself." Chet had just stood up in preparation to leave and was about to heft his briefcase.

Jack leaned back and shook his head. "Everything about this case is screwy." He looked up at Chet and motioned toward his microscope. "Come on, sport. Give me your golden opinion."

Chet peered into the eyepiece. "So you're still looking at this liver section." He played with the focus. "It looks like a granuloma." A granuloma is the cellular sign of chronic cell-mediated inflammation.

"That was my thought as well. Now, does this look like a liver that you'd expect to see in a relatively recent transplant?"

"No. I'd expect some acute inflammation but certainly not a granuloma."

"Thank you. I was beginning to question my judgment."

"Knock, knock!" a voice called out. Ted Lynch, the director of the morgue's DNA lab, was standing in the doorway. "I know you've been thinking you've got a liver transplant here, Jack," he said. "But the DQ alpha we did was a perfect match, suggesting it was the patient's own liver."

Jack threw up his hands. "I give up. I even called a surgeon friend to ask if there would be any other reason for sutures in the vena cava and the hepatic artery. He said no—it had to be a transplant."

"What can I say?" Ted commented.

Jack's phone jangled insistently. Jack motioned for Ted to stay while he picked up the receiver. "What?" he said rudely.

"I'm out of here." Chet pushed past Ted.

Jack listened intently. "Yeah, sure," he said into the phone. "If UNOS suggests we try Europe, give it a try."

Jack hung up. "That was Bart Arnold. I've had the forensics department searching for a missing recent liver transplant."

"Any luck?" Ted asked.

"Nope. It's baffling."

"Maybe it wasn't a transplant."

"I'm convinced it was a transplant," Jack said. "There's no rhyme or reason to take out a person's liver and then put it back."

"All right," Ted said. "I'll tell you what. I can run a polymarker, which compares areas on chromosomes four, six, seven, nine, eleven, and nineteen. A chance match will be in the billions to one. And I'll even sequence the DQ alpha on both the liver sample and the patient to try to figure out how they matched."

"I'll be appreciative whatever you can do," Jack said.

After Ted left, Jack switched off the light under his microscope and pushed back from his desk. He grabbed his jacket from the back of the door. He'd had as much sitting and thinking as he was capable of. He needed some mindless hard exercise, and his neighborhood basketball court was beckoning.

"WHAT are you doing here so late?" Lou Soldano asked. He sat down heavily in the chair next to Laurie's desk. He made no effort to take off his coat or hat, which was tipped way back on his head. "You know, you work too hard."

"You should talk," Laurie said. "Look at you. When was the last time you got any sleep?"

"Let's talk about more pleasant things," Lou suggested. "How about grabbing a bite to eat? I've got to run down to headquarters; then I'd love to go out for some pasta."

"Are you sure you're up for going out?" Laurie questioned. There were dark circles under Lou's eyes, and his stubble was more than a five-o'clock shadow.

"I gotta eat," Lou said. "Are you working much longer?"

"Maybe another half hour. Have you made any progress in the Franconi case?"

Lou let out an exasperated puff of air. "I wish. And with these Mob hits, if you don't score quickly, the trail cools mighty fast. How about you? Any idea how Franconi's body got out of here?"

"That trail is about equally as cool. I did have one thought. One of the funeral homes that picked up a body the night Franconi disappeared is called Spoletto. It's in Ozone Park. I remembered that the grisly murder of a young mobster took place there. Do you think that it's just a coincidence?"

"Yeah," Lou said. "And I'll tell you why. There is a loose connection by marriage with that funeral home and the New York crime establishment. But it's with the wrong family, not the Vaccarros."

"Oh, well. It was just a thought."

"So what about some dinner?" Lou said.

"How about just coming over to my apartment for spaghetti?" Laurie suggested. Lou and Laurie had become friends over the years. They made it a point to have dinner every couple of weeks.

"You wouldn't mind?" Lou asked. The idea of kicking back on Laurie's couch sounded like heaven.

"Not at all. In fact, I'd prefer it. I've got some sauce in the freezer and plenty of salad makings."

"Great! I'll grab some chianti on my way downtown. I'll give you a call when I'm leaving headquarters."

"Perfect," Laurie said.

After Lou left, Laurie sighed and gazed up at the ceiling. Every time she questioned how Franconi's body could have gotten out of the morgue, she agonized anew. Suddenly the idea of visiting the Spoletto Funeral Home seemed very appealing. She got up and got her coat, snapped shut her briefcase, and left her office. Outside, on Thirtieth Street, she hailed a cab.

"Where to, lady?" the driver asked.

"Ozone Park," Laurie said. "The Spoletto Funeral Home on Gold Road." She remembered the address from the mortuary Rolodex.

Laurie sat back with a contented feeling. Jack had been wrong. The home did have a Mob connection, and even though it was with the wrong family, the fact that it was associated at all was suspicious.

THE three-story white clapboard house had Greek-style columns. A glazed, internally lit sign in the middle of a postage stamp–size lawn read SPOLETTO FUNERAL HOME—A FAMILY BUSINESS. The establishment was in full operation. All the lights were on. People were visible through the ground-floor windows.

Laurie asked the driver to wait, then got out and started up the front walk. Soft organ music could be heard through the closed front door. It was unlocked, and she walked in.

Save for the music, there was little sound. The floors were heavily carpeted. To Laurie's left was a viewing room with people seated in folding chairs. A coffin rested on a bed of flowers.

A thin man with an ascetic face approached, dressed in black. "Are you here to pay respects to Jonathan Dibartolo?"

"No," Laurie said. "Frank Gleason."

"Excuse me?" the man inquired.

Laurie repeated the name. There was a pause.

"And your name is?" the man asked.

"Dr. Laurie Montgomery."

"Just one moment if you will," the man said as he ducked away. Laurie looked around at the mourners.

"Dr. Montgomery," an unctuous voice intoned, "I'm Anthony

Spoletto. I understand you are here to pay respects to Mr. Gleason."

"That's correct." Laurie turned to face a man also dressed in a black suit. He was obese and as oily as his voice. His forehead glistened in the soft incandescent light.

"I'm afraid that will be impossible," Mr. Spoletto said.

"I called this afternoon and was told he was on view."

"Yes, of course," Mr. Spoletto said. "But that was this afternoon. At the family's request the four p.m. viewing was the last."

"I see," Laurie said, nonplussed. "Well, would you know when the burial is planned?"

"Not at the moment," Mr. Spoletto said.

"Thank you," Laurie said.

"Not at all." Mr. Spoletto opened the door for Laurie.

Laurie walked out and got into the cab. She gave her address, and the taxi pulled away. It had been a wasted trip. Or had it? After talking with Mr. Spoletto, she'd realized that his forehead wasn't oily. The man had been perspiring despite the cool temperature inside the funeral parlor.

When the cab pulled up outside Laurie's building, she saw Lou Soldano slouched against the mailboxes in the foyer, clutching a bottle of wine. She paid the fare, then hurried inside. "I'm sorry. I thought you were going to call before you came over."

"I did," Lou said. "I got your answering machine."

Laurie glanced at her watch. She'd been gone for over an hour.

"I thought you were only going to work a half hour," Lou said.

"I wasn't working. I took a trip to the Spoletto Funeral Home."

Lou frowned.

"Now don't give me grief," Laurie said as they boarded the elevator. "The body I went to see was no longer on view. But the director acted a little suspicious. At least I think he did."

"How so?" Lou asked. The elevator opened. Laurie unlocked her door, and they entered her apartment.

She put her briefcase on the hall table. "He was perspiring while I was talking with him."

Lou paused with his coat half off. "Is that all? The man was perspiring?" He rolled his eyes. "Whoa! Another Sherlock Holmes incarnate. Maybe you should take over my job."

"All right, it was a wasted trip," Laurie said. "Let's get some food. I'm starved."

Lou switched the bottle of wine from one hand to the other, allowing him to swing his arm out of his coat. When he did, he clumsily knocked Laurie's briefcase to the floor. "What a klutz," he said. "I'm sorry." He bent down to retrieve the papers, pens, microscope slides, and other paraphernalia. After he'd gotten most of it back into the briefcase, he picked up the videotape. "What's this?" He read the label. "The Franconi shooting? CNN sent you this out of the blue?"

"No. I requested it."

"Mind if I look at it?"

"Of course not," Laurie said.

"MAN, this ain't your night," Warren teased Jack. "You must be getting too old."

Jack had decided when he'd gotten to the playground that he was going to win no matter whom he was teamed up with. But it didn't happen. In fact, Jack lost every game he played in because Warren and Spit had gotten on the same team and neither could miss.

Jack walked over to the sidelines on rubbery legs. He pulled a towel from where he'd jammed it into the chain-link fence and wiped his face. He could feel his heart pounding in his chest.

"Come on, man," Warren teased from the court. "One more run. We'll let you win this time."

"Yeah, sure," Jack called back. "I'm outa here."

Warren sauntered over. "What's up with your shortie?" he asked. "Natalie's been driving me up the wall asking questions about her, since we haven't seen you guys."

Jack looked at Warren. To add insult to injury, he wasn't even breathing heavily. "Laurie's fine," he said. "I was with her last night, and she was asking about you and Natalie."

Warren nodded. "You sure you're finished, or do you want to run one more?"

"I'm finished," Jack said.

"Take care, man," Warren said.

Jack pulled on his sweatshirt and started for home across 106th Street. The exercise had cleared his mind, and for the hour and a half he'd played, he hadn't thought about work.

He was rounding the third-floor landing of his refuse-strewn stairs when he heard the telltale sound of his phone. With some effort Jack encouraged his tired quadriceps to propel him up the final flight. Clumsily he fumbled with his keys at his door. He got to the phone and snatched it up. "Hello," he gasped.

"Don't tell me you're just coming in from your basketball," Laurie said. "It's going on nine o'clock. That's way off schedule."

"I didn't get home until after seven thirty," Jack explained.

"That means you haven't eaten yet. Lou is over here, and we have salad and spaghetti. Why don't you join us?"

"I wouldn't want to break up the party," Jack said.

"You won't be breaking up any party," Laurie assured him. "We have something to show you. Something that will surprise you."

"Okay," Jack said. "I'll shower and be there in forty minutes."

The shower revived Jack, and he decided to ride his bike.

He cruised south at a good clip. On Laurie's street, he secured his bike with a lock. Laurie met him at her apartment door with a grin on her face and gave him a hug. He could see Lou sitting on the sofa, with a smile that rivaled the Cheshire cat's.

Laurie took Jack's arm and pulled him into the living room. "Do you want the surprise first or do you want to eat first?"

"Let's have the surprise," Jack said.

Laurie guided him to the sofa. "Do you want a glass of wine?"

Jack nodded. Laurie disappeared into the kitchen but was soon back with his wine. Picking up the VCR remote, she joined Jack and Lou on the couch.

"What's this surprise?" Jack asked, sipping his wine.

"Just watch," Laurie said.

All of a sudden there was the CNN logo, followed by the image of a man coming out of a Manhattan restaurant surrounded by people.

When the sequence was over, Laurie and Lou had huge smiles. "Do you recognize what you've just seen?" she asked Jack.

"I'd say it was somebody getting shot," Jack said.

"It's Carlo Franconi," Laurie said. "Remind you of anything?" Jack shrugged.

"Let me run certain sections in slow motion." Laurie ran a sequence, then stopped it exactly at the moment Franconi was shot. She walked up to the screen and pointed at the base of the man's neck. "There's the entry point."

Then she advanced to the moment of the next impact, when the victim was falling to his right.

"Well, I'll be damned," Jack remarked with astonishment. "My floater might be Carlo Franconi."

"Exactly," Laurie said triumphantly. "Obviously, we haven't proved it yet, but with the entrance wounds and the paths of the bullets in the floater, I'd be willing to bet five dollars it is."

Over dinner the conversation turned to why no one even considered that the floater might be Franconi.

"I suppose when I realized the shotgun wound was postmortem," Jack said, "I was already engrossed in the issue about the liver. By the way, Lou, did Franconi have a liver transplant?"

"Not that I know of. He'd been sick for a number of years, but I never knew the diagnosis."

"If he didn't have a liver transplant, then the floater isn't Franconi," Jack said. "Even though the DNA lab is having a hard time confirming it, I'm convinced the floater has a donated liver."

"What else can you people do to confirm that the floater and Franconi are the same person?" Lou asked.

"We can request a blood sample from the mother," Laurie said. "Comparing the mitochondrial DNA, which all of us inherit from our mothers, we could tell right away if the floater is Franconi."

"X rays must have been taken when Franconi came in," Jack said. "That would do it. I suggest we make a little foray to the morgue."

As soon as they had finished eating, the three took a cab to the morgue. They went directly to the autopsy room.

"Okay, everybody," Jack said, walking over to the viewer. "The critical moment has arrived." First he slipped up Franconi's X rays and then the headless floater's.

"What do you know," he said after only a second's inspection. "I owe Laurie five dollars."

Laurie gave a cry of triumph as Jack gave her the money.

Lou said, "Now that we have a corpus delicti, we might make some headway in this case."

"And I'll be able to figure out what the hell's going on concerning this guy's liver," Jack said.

"And maybe I'll go on a shopping spree with my money," Laurie said. "But not until I figure out how and why this body left here in the first place."

UNABLE to sleep despite having taken two sleeping pills, Raymond slipped out of bed so as not to disturb Darlene. He noticed that it was three fifteen in the morning. At the Zone it was after nine, a good time to call Siegfried Spallek.

The connection was almost instantaneous.

"You are up early," Siegfried commented. "I was going to call you in four or five hours."

"I couldn't sleep," Raymond said. "What's going on over there? What's the problem with Kevin Marshall?"

"I believe the problem is over." Siegfried summarized what had happened and said that Kevin and his friends had been given such a scare that they wouldn't dare go near the island again.

"They didn't get onto the island, did they?" Raymond asked.

"No. They were only at the staging area."

"I don't even like people nosing around there," Raymond said.

"I understand. I don't think they'll go back. But just to be on the safe side, I'm leaving a contingent of soldiers out there for a few days."

"Fine," Raymond said. "As soon as the GenSys plane is available, I'll be over for the patient. It should be in a day or so."

"Let me know. I'll have a car waiting for you in Bata."

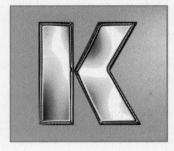

EVIN was totally unaware of the time when a knock interrupted the intense concentration he'd been directing toward his computer screen for several hours. He opened his laboratory door, and Melanie swooped into the room.

"Where are your techs?" she asked.

"I gave them the day off." Kevin sat at his computer screen again. "There was no way I was going to get any work done today."

"Have you seen Candace?"

"No," Kevin said. "Not since we dropped her off at the hospital this morning. She might be in her room in the Inn, since Mr. Winchester is doing so well." The Inn was the name given to the quarters for transient hospital personnel. It was part of the hospital-laboratory complex. "I came across something disturbing," he continued. "Let me show you." His fingers played over the computer keyboard. Soon the screen displayed the Isla Francesca graphic. "I programmed the computer to follow all seventy-three bonobos on the island for several hours. Then I condensed the data so I could watch it in fast-forward. Look what resulted." He started the sequence. The little red dots rapidly traced out weird geometric designs.

"Looks like a bunch of chicken scratches," Melanie said.

"Except for these two." Kevin indicated two pinpoints.

"They apparently didn't move much."

"Exactly. Creature number sixty and creature number sixty-seven." Kevin reached over and picked up the detailed contour map he'd taken from Bertram's office. "I located creature number sixty in a marshy clearing just south of Lago Hippo. Next I reduced the scale of the grid so that it represented that fifty- by fifty-foot portion of the island. Let me show you what happened."

Kevin keyed in the information and then clicked to start the sequence. Again the red light for creature number sixty was a pinpoint.

"He didn't move at all," Melanie said. "You think he's sleeping?"

Kevin shrugged. "I don't know. Maybe he died."

"I suppose that's a possibility. But I don't think it is very probable. Those are young, extraordinarily healthy animals. And they are in an environment without natural enemies."

"Whatever it is, it is disturbing." Kevin sighed. "And I pretty much confirmed my suspicion they're using the caves. Watch." He changed the coordinates of the grid to correspond to a portion of the limestone escarpment. He asked the computer to trace the activity of his double, creature number one.

Melanie watched as the red dot traced a geometric shape, then disappeared. It then reappeared at the identical spot and traced a second shape. A similar sequence repeated itself a third time. "I guess I'd have to agree," she said.

"If we go out there, we should make it a point to see our doubles," Kevin said. "They're the oldest of the creatures. If any bonobos are acting like protohumans, it should be them."

"Given the twelve-square-mile island, it will be extraordinarily difficult for us to find a specific creature."

"You're wrong. I've got the instrument they use for retrievals." Kevin showed Melanie the locator and explained its use, then asked, "Did Siegfried talk to you this morning?"

"No. Bertram did," Melanie said. "He said he was disappointed in me. I mean, is that supposed to break me up or what?"

"Did he give you any explanation about the smoke?"

"Oh, yeah. He went on at length how he'd just been told that Siegfried had a work crew out there burning trash."

"I thought so. Siegfried gave me the same story."

"Has your playing around with the computer this morning confirmed that the bonobos are in two groups?" Melanie asked.

Kevin nodded. "The first group stays around the caves. It includes most of the older bonobos, including your double and mine. The other group is in a forest north of the Rio Diviso."

"Very curious," Melanie said.

WITH a burst of speed Jack made the green light at the intersection of First Avenue and Thirtieth Street and sailed across. Angling his bike up the morgue's driveway, he didn't brake until the last minute. It was six forty-five a.m., and he was keyed up. After near conclusive identification of his floater as Carlo Franconi, he had gotten little sleep. He'd been on the phone with Janice Jaeger, the night forensic investigator, imploring her to get copies of Franconi's records from the Manhattan General Hospital. Her preliminary investigation had determined that Franconi had been hospitalized there.

Jack had also had her get the phone numbers of the European human organ distribution organizations from Bart Arnold's desk. Because of the time difference, Jack started calling after three a.m. No one he talked to had heard of Carlo Franconi. After a few hours of sleep he had decided to get to the morgue early.

"My word, you are eager," Janice commented as Jack came into her office.

"How'd you do at the hospital?" he asked.

"I got a lot of material. Mr. Franconi had multiple admissions over the years, mostly for hepatitis and cirrhosis. But no transplant." She handed Jack a large folder.

"Who is his doctor?"

"Dr. Daniel Levitz, on Park Avenue. His office number is on the outside of your folder."

"You are efficient." Jack smiled.

"I try to do my best," she said.

Jack whistled as he walked to the ID room. He could taste the coffee already. But when he arrived, he could see he was too early. Vinnie Amendola was just in the process of making it. "Hurry up with that coffee," Jack said. "It's an emergency this morning."

Vinnie didn't answer, but Jack's mind was already elsewhere. He'd seen the headline on Vinnie's paper: FRANCONI'S BODY FOUND. Beneath it in smaller print was CORPSE LANGUISHES IN MEDICAL EXAMINER'S OFFICE FOR TWENTY-FOUR HOURS BEFORE ID ESTABLISHED.

Jack sat down to read the article. As usual, it implied that the city's medical examiners were bunglers. He thought it was interesting that the journalist didn't appear to know that the body had been headless and handless. Nor did he mention the shotgun wound.

After finishing with the coffee preparation, Vinnie came over to stand next to the desk while Jack read. "Do you mind!" he said irritably. "I'd like to have my paper."

"You see this article?" Jack slapped the front page.

"Yeah, I seen it," Vinnie said.

"Did it surprise you? When we did the autopsy yesterday, did it cross your mind it might have been Franconi?"

"No. Why should it?"

"I'm not saying it should," Jack said. "I'm just asking if it did."

"No," Vinnie said. "Why don't you buy your own paper?"

Jack stood up and pushed Vinnie's paper toward him. "Maybe you need a vacation. You're becoming a grumpy old man."

"At least I'm not a cheapskate," Vinnie said.

Jack went to the coffeemaker and poured himself a cup. He took it over to the scheduling desk, opened the folder, and went through the summaries of Franconi's hospital admissions.

Laurie arrived next. Before she even had her coat off, she asked Jack if he'd heard the news. Jack told her he'd seen the *Post*.

"Was it your doing?" Laurie asked.

"The leak?" Jack gave a little laugh of disbelief. "I'm surprised you'd even ask. Why would I do such a thing?"

"I don't know, except you were so excited about it last night. But I didn't mean any offense." Changing the subject, she asked, "What cases do we have for today?"

"I didn't look," Jack admitted. "But the pile is small, and if possible, I'd like to have a paper day or really a research day."

Laurie counted the folders. "Only ten cases; no problem. I think I'll only do one myself. Now that Franconi's body is back, I'm even more interested to find out how it left here in the first place."

"I'm a little confused," Jack said. "Why does Franconi's return make you more interested in his disappearance?"

"Mainly because of what you found during the autopsy. At first I thought that whoever stole the body had done it out of spite, but now it seems the body was taken to destroy the liver. If I can figure out how the body disappeared, we might be able to find out who did it."

"I always thought the why was more important than the how," Jack said. "You're suggesting they are related."

"Exactly," Laurie said. "The how will lead to the who, and the who will explain the why."

AFTER his call to Siegfried, Raymond's brain had finally succumbed to the sleeping pills. The next thing he was aware of was Darlene opening the curtains. It was almost eight o'clock.

"Feel better, dear?" Darlene asked. She made Raymond sit forward so she could fluff up his pillow.

"I do," Raymond admitted.

"I made your favorite breakfast." Darlene went over to the bureau and lifted a wicker tray. She carried it to the bed. There was orange juice, two strips of bacon, an omelet, toast, and coffee. In a side pocket was the morning newspaper.

"Let me know when you want more coffee," Darlene said. Then she left the room.

With childlike pleasure Raymond sipped his orange juice. Taking a bite of bacon, he lifted the paper and glanced at the headlines.

He gasped, inadvertently inhaling some food. He coughed so hard, he bucked the wicker tray off the bed. It crashed upside down on the carpet.

Darlene came running into the room. Raymond went through a series of coughing jags that turned him tomato red. "Water!" he squeaked between fits.

Darlene dashed into the bathroom and returned with a glass. Raymond clutched it and managed to drink a small amount.

"Are you all right?" Darlene asked. "Should I call 911?"

"Did you see the paper?" Raymond croaked.

She shook her head, so he spread it out for her.

"Oh, my," she said.

"And you were wondering why I was still worried about Franconi!" Raymond forcibly crumpled the newspaper.

"What are you going to do?" Darlene asked.

"I suppose I have to go find Vinnie Dominick. He promised me the body was gone. Some job he did!"

The phone rang, and Darlene picked it up. After a moment she told Raymond it was Taylor Cabot, the GenSys CEO.

Raymond swallowed hard and took the receiver. "Hello, sir," he managed. His voice was still hoarse.

"I'm calling from my car phone," Taylor said. "So I won't be too specific. But I have just been informed of the reemergence of a problem I thought had been taken care of. What I said earlier about this issue still stands. I hope you understand."

"Of course, sir," Raymond squeaked. "I will—" He stopped speaking. He took the phone away from his ear and looked at it. Taylor had cut him off. "Just what I need," Raymond said. "Another threat from Cabot to close down the program."

By EIGHT a.m. Laurie and the others were down in the pit starting their autopsies. Jack had gone back to the forensics area to find the chief investigator, Bart Arnold.

"I suppose you've heard that my floater has been just about conclusively identified as Carlo Franconi," Jack said.

"So I've heard."

"That means I want you to go back to UNOS with the name. I spent most of the night on the phone with the organizations in Europe. I came up with zilch. Next I want someone to go visit Franconi's mother and talk her into giving a blood sample. Also to ask the woman if her son had a liver transplant."

Bart wrote Jack's requests down. "What else?" he asked.

"I think that's it for now. Franconi's doctor's name was Daniel Levitz. Is that anyone you have come in contact with?"

"If it's the Levitz on Park, then I've come in contact with him. He's a good internist who takes care of a lot of the crime families. Do you want me to go see him and get what I can on Franconi?"

"I think I'll do that myself," Jack said. "I have a sneaking suspicion that when talking with Franconi's doctor, what's unsaid is going to be more important than what is said."

JACK could rarely find an excuse to get out on his bike during the day, so it was with a good deal of pleasure that he pedaled up to Dr. Daniel Levitz's Park Avenue office. He had called ahead to make sure the doctor was in, but he'd specifically avoided making an appointment. A surprise visit might be more fruitful.

"Your name, please?" the silver-haired receptionist asked Jack.

He flashed open his medical examiner's badge. Its official appearance confused people into thinking it was a police badge.

"I must see the doctor," Jack said. "The sooner the better."

The receptionist disappeared into the depths of the office.

Jack's eyes roamed the waiting room. It was generous in size and lavishly decorated. Five well-dressed people all eyed him clandestinely as they continued to peruse their magazines.

The receptionist reappeared and guided Jack back to the doctor's private study. Dr. Levitz was dressed in his white coat, complete with pocket full of tongue depressors and assorted pens. A stethoscope hung from his neck. Compared with Jack's muscular six-foot frame, he was rather short and almost fragile in appearance. Jack immediately noticed the man's nervous tics, which involved slight twists and nods of his head.

Dr. Levitz shook hands stiffly, then retreated behind his desk.

"I'm very busy," he said as they sat down. "But of course, I always have time for the police."

"I'm not the police," Jack said. "I'm Dr. Jack Stapleton from the Office of the Chief Medical Examiner of New York."

Dr. Levitz's head twitched. "Oh," he commented.

"I wanted to talk about one of your patients."

"My patients' conditions are confidential," Dr. Levitz said.

"Of course. That is, until they have died and become a medical examiner's case. You see, I want to ask about Carlo Franconi."

Jack watched as Dr. Levitz went through a number of bizarre motions, making Jack glad the man had not gone into brain surgery. "I still respect my patients' confidentiality," he said.

"I can understand your position from an ethical point of view," Jack said. "But I should remind you that medical examiners in the state of New York have subpoena power. So why don't we just have a conversation? We might clear things up."

"What do you want to know?" Dr. Levitz asked.

"I learned from reading Mr. Franconi's hospital history that he'd had a long bout with liver problems leading to liver failure."

Dr. Levitz nodded.

"To come right to the point, the big question is whether or not Mr. Franconi had a liver transplant."

At first Levitz did not speak. He merely twitched. Then he said, "I don't know anything about a transplant."

"When did you see him last?" Jack asked.

Dr. Levitz picked up his phone and asked the receptionist to bring Carlo Franconi's record. "It will just be a moment," he said.

"In one of Mr. Franconi's hospital admissions about three years ago, you specifically wrote that it was your opinion that a transplant would be necessary. Do you remember writing that?"

"Not specifically," Dr. Levitz said. "But I was aware of a deteriorating condition, as well as his failure to stop drinking."

"But you never mentioned it again. I found that surprising when it was easy to see a gradual but relentless deterioration in his liver function tests over the next couple of years."

"A doctor can only do so much to influence a patient's behavior."

The door opened. The receptionist placed a fat folder on Dr. Levitz's desk and withdrew. He picked it up and, after a quick glance, said that he'd seen Carlo Franconi a month previously for an upper respiratory infection.

"Did you examine him?"

"Of course," Dr. Levitz said. "I always examine my patients."

"Had he had a liver transplant?"

"Well, I didn't do a complete physical," Dr. Levitz explained. "I examined him appropriately in reference to his complaint."

"You didn't even feel his liver, knowing his history?"

"I didn't write it down if I did," Dr. Levitz said.

"Did you do any blood work that would reflect liver function?"

"A bilirubin," Dr. Levitz said. "It was within normal limits."

"So, except for his respiratory infection, he was doing well."

"Yes. I suppose you could say that," Dr. Levitz said.

"Would you mind if I looked at his record?" Jack asked.

"Yes, I would mind," Dr. Levitz said. "If you want these records, you will have to subpoena them. I'm sorry."

Jack stood up. "I'll let the state's attorney's office know how you feel. There's something very strange about this case, and I intend to get to the bottom of it."

Out on Park Avenue, Jack smiled to himself as he undid the lock on his bike. It was so obvious that Dr. Levitz knew more than he was willing to say. Returning to the morgue, he stashed his bike in the usual location, then went to Bart Arnold's office.

"I've made a lot of calls," Bart said. "But you know the situation with voice mail. You get a lot of messages out there, waiting for call-backs. If it's any consolation, we did manage to get a blood sample from Franconi's mother. It's up in the DNA lab."

"Was she asked whether her son had a liver transplant?"

"Absolutely. She didn't know anything about a transplant. But she did admit that her son had been much healthier lately. She says he went away to a spa someplace and came back a new man."

"Did she happen to say where?" Jack questioned.

"She didn't know," Bart said. "At least that's what she said."

Jack nodded. "Figures."

"I'll keep you informed as I get callbacks," Bart said.

"Thanks."

Feeling frustrated, Jack walked to the ID room. He thought maybe some coffee would cheer him up. He was surprised to find Lou Soldano busily helping himself to a cup.

"Uh-oh," Lou said. "Caught red-handed."

Jack eyed the homicide detective. He looked better than he had in days. Not only was his tie in place, his hair was combed. "You look almost human today," Jack said.

"I feel that way. I got my first decent night's sleep in days. Where's Laurie?"

"In the pit, I presume."

"I gotta pat her on the back again for making that association with your floater. Already we've gotten a couple of good tips from our informers. It's stimulated a lot of talk in the streets."

"Laurie and I were surprised to see it in the papers this morning," Jack commented. "That was a lot faster than we expected. Any idea who was the source?"

"I was," Lou said innocently. "But I was careful not to give any details. Why, is there a problem?"

"Only that Laurie thought I was the culprit."

"Gosh, I'm sorry. I guess I should have run it by you. Well, I owe you."

"Forget it," Jack said, and poured himself some coffee.

"CALM down!" Raymond Lyons yelled into the phone.

"Don't tell me to calm down!" Daniel Levitz shouted back. "You've seen the papers. They have Franconi's body. And already a medical examiner by the name of Dr. Jack Stapleton has been in my office asking for Franconi's records."

"You didn't give them, did you?" Raymond asked.

"Of course not!" Daniel snapped. "But he reminded me he could subpoena them. I'm telling you, this guy suspects Franconi had a transplant. He asked me directly."

"Do your records have any information at all about it?"

"No. But it's going to look very strange if anybody looks at my records. I've been documenting Franconi's deteriorating status for years. Then all of a sudden his liver function studies are normal without any explanation. There'll be questions, and I don't know whether I can handle them."

"Let's not get carried away," Raymond said with a calmness he did not feel. "What about Vincent Dominick? He's helped us once. With his own child ill, he has a vested interest in our program's future."

Dr. Daniel Levitz stared at the phone. "Are you suggesting . . . ?"

Raymond didn't reply.

"This is where I draw the line," Daniel said.

"Then give me Dominick's phone number. I'll call him myself."

As soon as he could, Raymond got off the phone. Then he nervously dialed a number.

"Yeah, what is it?" a voice said on the other end of the line.

"I'd like to speak to Mr. Vincent Dominick," Raymond said with as much authority as he could muster. "It's Dr. Lyons calling."

The man said, "Hang on."

A few minutes later Vinnie Dominick's dulcet voice came over the line. "What can I do for you, Doctor?" he asked.

"Another problem has come up," Raymond croaked. He cleared his throat. "I'd like to see you to discuss it."

There was a long pause. "I'll meet you in the Neapolitan Restaurant on Corona Avenue in Queens in a half hour."

"I'll take a cab," Raymond said. "I'll leave immediately."

"See you there," Vinnie said before hanging up.

THE Neapolitan Restaurant was filled with the stale smell of a couple of hundred cigarettes. Vinnie Dominick was sitting in a booth, and his minions were lounging on stools at the bar. Raymond made a beeline for Vinnie's booth and slid in without invitation. He pushed the crumpled newspaper, which he'd painstakingly smoothed out, across the table.

Vinnie gazed down at the headlines nonchalantly.

"As you can see, there's a problem," Raymond said. "You promised me the body was gone. Obviously, you screwed up."

Vinnie picked up his cigarette, took a long drag, then blew the smoke at the ceiling. "Doc," he said, "I don't tolerate this kind of disrespect. Either you reword what you just said to me or get up and get yourself lost before I get really mad."

Raymond swallowed hard. "I'm sorry," he said meekly. "I'm not myself. I'm very upset. After I saw the headlines, I got a call from the CEO of GenSys, threatening the whole program. I also got a call from Dr. Levitz, who told me a medical examiner named Jack Stapleton dropped by his office wanting to see Franconi's records."

"Angelo," Vinnie called out. "Come over here."

Angelo ambled over to the booth. Vinnie asked him what he knew about a Dr. Jack Stapleton.

"Vinnie Amendola, our contact at the morgue, mentioned him when he called this morning," Angelo said. "He said Stapleton was all fired up about Franconi because Franconi is his case."

"You see, I've gotten a few calls myself," Vinnie said. "I also got a call from my wife's brother, who runs the Spoletto Funeral Home, the home that took the body out. He's all upset because a Dr. Laurie Montgomery paid a visit. And Angelo, tell Raymond what you learned today after we heard from the funeral home."

"Vinnie Amendola told me Dr. Laurie Montgomery at the morgue specifically said she'd make it her personal business to find out how Franconi's body disappeared. Needless to say, he's very concerned."

Vinnie said to Raymond, "See, we got a potential problem here just because we did you a favor. And the problem now seems to be focused on these two: Jack Stapleton and Laurie Montgomery."

Raymond raised his eyebrows expectantly.

"I'll tell you straight, Doc," Vinnie continued. "If it weren't for Vinnie junior and his bum kidneys, I wouldn't have gotten involved in all this. The fact that I've gotten my wife's brother into this situation compounds my problem. I can't leave him dangling. So I'll have Angelo and Franco pay a visit to these two doctors and take care of things. Would you mind that, Angelo?"

Angelo smiled. It wasn't much of a smile because of all the scar tissue, but it was a smile nonetheless.

Vinnie stubbed out his cigarette. "So, Doc, what do you think of Angelo and Franco convincing them to see things our way?"

Raymond let out a little laugh of relief. "I can't think of a better solution." He stood up. "Thank you, Mr. Dominick."

"Hold on, Doc," Vinnie said. "We haven't discussed compensation yet."

"I thought this would be covered under the rubric of our prior agreement." Raymond tried to sound businesslike. "After all, Franconi's body was not supposed to reappear."

"That's not the way I see it," Vinnie said. "This is an extra. Since you've already bargained away the tuition issue, I'm afraid we're now talking about recouping some of my initiation fee. What about twenty thousand? That's a nice round figure."

"It might take me time to get the money together," Raymond said.

"Fine, Doc," Vinnie said. "Just as long as we have an agreement."

Raymond was outraged. "Wonderful," he managed to say before leaving.

"When do we take care of those two?" Angelo asked Vinnie.

"The sooner the better. In fact, you'd better do it tonight."

"AT WHAT time did you expect your guests?" Esmeralda asked.

"Seven o'clock," Kevin said, happy for the distraction. He'd been sitting at his desk trying to fool himself into believing he was reading one of his molecular biology journals. In reality he was tortured by repeatedly running through the harrowing events of the previous night. He could still hear the sound of the machine-gun fire.

"The dinner is prepared," Esmeralda said. "I shall keep it warm."

Tossing aside his journal, Kevin got up and walked out onto the veranda. It was seven thirty, and he was beginning to worry about where Melanie and Candace could be.

Hearing laughter, he looked in the direction of the waterfront. A tropical downpour had ended fifteen minutes before. The cobblestones were steaming, since they were still hot from the sun. Into this lighted mist walked the two women, arm in arm, laughing merrily.

"Hey, Kevin!" Melanie shouted, spying Kevin on his balcony. "How come you didn't send a carriage?"

"What are you talking about?" Kevin asked.

"You didn't expect us to get soaked, did you?" Melanie joked.

"Come on up," Kevin said.

The women came up the stairs with great commotion. Kevin met them in the hall. Melanie insisted on giving Kevin a kiss on both cheeks. "Sorry we're late," she said. "But the rain forced us to take shelter at the Chickee Hut Bar."

"It's okay. But dinner is ready." Kevin motioned them into the dining room. Esmeralda had laid the table at one end, since it was large enough for twelve. There was a small tablecloth, just covering the area under the dishes, and candles burning in glass holders.

"How romantic," Candace commented.

"I hope we're having wine," Melanie said as she took a seat.

Candace went around and sat opposite Melanie. "White or red?" Kevin asked. As a member of the Zone's elite, Kevin was given a regular allotment of French wine, which he rarely drank. Consequently, he had an impressive cellar.

"Any color," Melanie said. Then she laughed.

"What are we eating?" Candace asked.

"It's a local fish," Kevin said.

"A fish! How appropriate," Melanie said, which caused both women to laugh to the point of tears.

"I don't get it." Kevin had the distinct feeling that when he was around these two women, he wasn't in control of anything and understood less than half the conversation.

"We'll explain later," Melanie managed. "Get the wine."

Kevin went into the kitchen and got the wine that he had earlier put into the refrigerator.

"Oh, my," Melanie said. "Montrachet! Aren't we lucky?"

The dinner was an unqualified success. As the dishes were being cleared, Melanie said, "You can't guess who was at the Chickee Hut. Our fearless leader, Siegfried."

Kevin choked on his wine. "You didn't talk to him, did you?"

"It would have been hard not to," Melanie said. "He graciously asked if he could join us and even bought us a round."

"He was actually quite charming," Candace said.

Kevin felt a chill descend his spine. "Did he mention anything more about what happened last night?"

"He apologized again," Candace said. "He assured us that there won't be any more shooting. If anybody wanders out there by the bridge, they will just be told that the area is off-limits."

"A likely story, as trigger-happy as those kids are," Kevin said.

"He did ask if we wanted to talk with some of the workers who'd been on the island burning underbrush," Candace said. "We told him it wasn't necessary. I mean, we don't want him to think we're still concerned about the smoke, and we definitely don't want him to think we're planning on visiting the island."

Kevin eyed the women while they smiled at each other conspiratorially. "Are we?"

"You wondered why we laughed when you told us we were having fish," Melanie said. "We laughed because we spent the afternoon talking to fishermen from Acalayong, about ten miles west of here."

"I know the town," Kevin said. It was the jumping-off place for people going from Equatorial Guinea to Cocobeach, Gabon. The route was served by pirogues, or dugout canoes, which had been motorized.

"We rented one of their boats," Melanie said proudly. "So we don't have to even go near the bridge. We can visit Isla Francesca by water. We've planned this carefully. Not only did we rent the large motorized canoe but we plan to tow a smaller, paddle version. Once we get to the island, we'll paddle up the Rio Diviso. Maybe we won't even have to go on land at all."

Kevin nodded.

"We already got food and drink from the commissary," Candace said. "And a portable cooler to pack it in."

"We'll stay far away from the bridge," Melanie said.

"I think it's going to be kind of fun," Candace added.

Kevin took a gulp of wine. "What time is this mission scheduled?"

"The sun comes up after six," Melanie said. "I'd like to be on our way by then. My plan is to head west, then swing way out into the estuary before going east. If anyone sees us getting into the boat, they'll think we are going off to Acalayong."

"What about work?" Kevin asked. "Won't you be missed?"

"Nope," Melanie said. "I told the lab I'd be at the animal center. Whereas I told the animal center . . ."

"I get the picture. What about you, Candace?"

"No problem. As long as Mr. Winchester keeps doing well, I'm essentially unemployed."

"I'll call my head tech," Kevin said. "I'll tell him I'm under the weather with an acute attack of insanity."

"Wait a second," Candace said. "I just thought of a problem."

Kevin sat bolt upright. "What?"

"I don't have any sunblock," Candace said. "I didn't bring any, because on my three previous visits I never saw the sun."

WITH all the tests on Franconi pending, Jack had forced himself to go to his office and try to concentrate on some of his other outstanding cases. To his surprise he'd made reasonable headway, until the phone rang at two thirty p.m. It was Ted Lynch, the director of the DNA lab.

"I think you'd better come up here," Ted said.

"I'm on my way."

Jack found Ted sitting at his desk, literally scratching his head. "If I didn't know better, I'd think you were trying to put one over on me," Ted said. "The results of the DNA polymarker test show that Franconi's DNA and the DNA of the liver tissue could not be any more different."

"Hey, that's good news. Then it was a transplant."

"I guess," Ted said without conviction. "But the sequence with the DQ alpha is identical, right down to the last nucleotide. The chances of that happening are so small, it's beyond belief."

"Well, the bottom line is that it was a transplant."

"If pressed, I'd have to agree. But how they found a donor with the identical DQ alpha is beyond me."

"I appreciate what you've done. Thanks!"

Jack was elated by Ted's results. Now that he'd documented that it had been a transplant, he was counting on Bart Arnold to come up with the answers to solve the rest of the mystery.

But Jack's elation was short-lived; it faded when he walked into Bart's office. The forensic investigator shook his head the moment he caught sight of Jack.

"No luck?" Jack asked.

"I'm afraid not," Bart said. "I really expected UNOS to come through, but they said that Carlo Franconi hadn't even been on their waiting list. I've heard from just about every center doing liver transplants, and no one takes credit."

"This is crazy." Jack told Bart that Ted's findings confirmed that Franconi had had a transplant. "If someone didn't get their transplant in North America or Europe, where could it have taken place?"

Bart shrugged. "There are a few other possibilities—Australia, South Africa, a couple of places in South America—but having talked to UNOS, I don't think any of them are likely."

"Nothing about this case is easy," Jack complained. He wandered out of the forensic area feeling mildly depressed. He had the uncomfortable sensation that he was missing some major fact. In the ID room, he got himself another cup of coffee. With cup in hand, he climbed the stairs to the lab.

"I ran your samples," the laboratory director said. "They were negative for both cyclosporin A and FK506."

Jack was astounded. "You must be joking. The patient had to be on immunosuppressants. He'd had a recent liver transplant. Is it possible you got a false negative?"

"We run controls as standard procedure," the director said.

Jack turned and made his way out of the lab. Now he was more depressed. Ted Lynch's DNA results and the drug assays were contradictory. If there'd been a transplant, Franconi had to be on either cyclosporin A or FK506. That was standard medical procedure.

He got off the elevator on the fifth floor and walked down to his office. Chet was getting his coat from behind the door.

"Hey, sport, how's it going?" Chet said.

"Not so good." Jack sat and turned on his microscope light.

"Problems with the Franconi case?"

Jack nodded. "It's like squeezing water from a rock."

"Listen," Chet said. "I have to duck out to get passport photos taken for my upcoming trip to India."

"Fine." Jack slipped the Franconi liver section onto his microscope's stage as Chet left. He was about to peer into the eyepiece when he paused. Chet's errand had started him thinking about international travel. If Franconi had gotten his transplant out of the country, there might be a way to find out where he'd been.

Jack picked up his phone and called Lou Soldano. "I have a question for you," he said when Lou answered. "Is there a way to find out if Franconi left the country recently, and if so, where did he go?"

"I have a friend in immigration," Lou said. "Want me to check?"

"I'd love it. This case is bugging me."

"My pleasure. As I said this morning, I owe you."

RAYMOND replaced the phone and raised his eyes to Darlene, who'd come into his study.

"Well?" Darlene asked.

Raymond leaned back in his desk chair and smiled. "Things seem to be working out. That was the GenSys operational officer up in Cambridge, Massachusetts. The plane will be available tomorrow evening, so I'll be on my way to Africa."

"Can I come?" Darlene asked hopefully.

"I'm afraid not, dear. With the patient and the surgical team, there'll be too many people on the plane on the return trip."

Darlene sighed and left the room. Raymond considered following her to console her, but a glance at his desk clock changed his mind. It was after three p.m. and therefore after nine p.m. in Cogo. If he wanted to talk to Siegfried, he felt he'd better try now.

Raymond called the manager's home. "Things still going okay?" he asked Siegfried expectantly.

"Perfectly," Siegfried said. "My last update on the patient's condition was fine. He couldn't be doing any better."

"That's reassuring. What about Kevin Marshall?"

"Everything is back to normal. I had an opportunity to have a drink with the two women this afternoon, and I have a feeling our nerdy researcher has something risqué going on."

"What are you talking about?" Raymond asked.

"You should have heard the women carrying on about their cute researcher. That's what they called him. And they were on their way to Kevin's for a dinner party. That's the first dinner party he's ever had as far as I know, and I live right across from him."

"I suppose we should be thankful."

"Envious is a better word."

"I've called to say that I'll be leaving here tomorrow evening," Raymond said. "I'll have the pilots radio ahead to tell you when we'll arrive in Bata."

"We'll be waiting for you," Siegfried said.

JACK scoured the liver section from one end to the other, staring vainly at a few curious flecks of basophilic material in the heart of the granuloma. He was about to take the slide over to the pathology department at New York University Hospital when Lou called.

"Bingo!" Lou said cheerfully. "I got some good news for you."

"I'm all ears," Jack said.

"Carlo Franconi entered the country exactly thirty-seven days ago on January twenty-ninth at Teterboro in New Jersey."

"I've never heard of Teterboro," Jack said.

"It's a private airport. There's lots of fancy corporate jets out there because of its proximity to the city."

"Was Carlo Franconi on a corporate jet?" Jack asked.

"I don't know. All I got is the plane's call numbers. Let's see, I got it right here. It was N69SU."

Jack wrote down the alphanumeric characters and the date. "Was there any indication where the plane had come from?"

"Oh, yeah," Lou said. "The plane came from Lyon, France."

"Nah. It couldn't have," Jack said.

"That's what's in the computer. Why don't you think it's correct?"

"I talked with the French organ allocation organization early this morning," Jack said. "They had no record of Franconi."

"The information that immigration has must correlate with the flight plan filed with both the FAA and the European equivalent," Lou said. "At least that's how I understand it."

"Do you think your friend in immigration has a contact in France?" Jack asked. "If Franconi was there, I'd like to find out when he arrived and any other information they have."

"Okay, let me see what I can do," Lou said.

"One other thing. How can we find out who owns N69SU?"

"That's easy. I've got a friend at the FAA. I'll call."

"I'll be much obliged," Jack said. "I'm leaving to run over to the university hospital. What if I call you in a half hour or so?"

"Perfect," Lou said before disconnecting.

After donning his jacket, Jack left his office for the hospital. It only took ten minutes by foot. Once there, he took the elevator up to the pathology department. He was hoping that Dr. Peter Malovar would be available. Even at the age of eighty-two he was one of the sharpest pathologists Jack had ever met.

Jack walked down to the aged frosted-glass door that led to what was known as Malovar's lair. Inside, he found Dr. Malovar bent over his microscope. The elderly man looked a little like Einstein, with wild gray hair and a full mustache. He greeted Jack cursorily while hungrily eyeing the slide in his hand. He loved people to bring him problematic cases.

Jack tried to give a little history of the case as he passed the slide to the professor, but Dr. Malovar lifted his hand to quiet him. Without a word he replaced his slide with Jack's and scanned it.

"Interesting," he said. "There's a small granuloma of the liver as well as some merozoites."

Jack nodded. He assumed that Dr. Malovar was referring to the tiny basophilic flecks.

"Definitely parasitic," the pathologist intoned. "But I don't recognize those merozoites. It's either a new species or a parasite not seen in humans." He looked at Jack. "Would you mind leaving this overnight? I'll have Dr. Hammersmith view it in the morning. He's a veterinary pathologist."

"Fine by me," Jack said.

After thanking him, Jack headed back to the morgue. He took the elevator to his office and called Lou at police headquarters.

"Hey, I think I'm getting some interesting stuff here," Lou said. "First of all, the plane is a Gulfstream 4, the Rolls-Royce of corporate jets, and it's owned by Alpha Aviation of Reno, Nevada. Must be a leasing organization. Also my friend from immigration called his French counterpart, and guess what?"

"I'm on pins and needles," Jack said.

"Franconi never visited France. Not unless he had a fake passport. There's no record of his entering or departing."

"So what's this about the plane coming from Lyon?"

"Saying the plane came from Lyon, France, doesn't mean anybody got out. It could have refueled."

"Good point. How can we find out?"

"I suppose I can call my friend back at the FAA."

"Great. I'm in my office. You want me to call you?"

"I'll call you."

When Lou called back, he said, "I've got some surprising information for you. This is one weird case."

"That's not telling me anything I didn't already know," Jack said. "What did you learn?"

Movement out of the corner of Jack's eye attracted his attention. Turning his head, he saw Laurie in the doorway. Her mouth was set in an angry grimace, and her skin was the color of ivory.

"Wait a sec," Jack said to Lou. "Laurie, what's the matter?"

"I have to talk with you," Laurie sputtered. "Now!"

"Okay, okay," Jack said. "Listen, Lou, Laurie just came in, and she's upset. Let me call you right back."

"Hold on!" Laurie snapped. "Ask Lou where he is."

Jack posed the question. "He's in his office," he told Laurie.

"Tell him we're coming down to see him," she replied.

"Did you hear that?" Jack asked Lou. Laurie then disappeared down the corridor toward her office.

"I did. What's going on?"

"Damned if I know. We'll be right there."

Jack hung up the phone and rushed out into the hall. Laurie was already struggling into her coat.

"What's happened?" Jack asked.

"I'm ninety-nine percent sure how Franconi's body was taken from here," Laurie said. "The Spoletto Funeral Home was involved, and the abduction was abetted by someone who works here."

"JEEZ, look at that traffic," Franco Ponti said to Angelo Facciolo. "I'm glad we're going *into* Manhattan instead of out."

Franco and Angelo were in Franco's black Cadillac, heading west on the Queensboro Bridge. It was the height of rush hour. Both men were dressed as if they were going to a ritzy dinner.

"What order do you want to do this in?" Franco asked.

Angelo shrugged. "Why don't we do a drive by Jack Stapleton's place? I'm a little surprised by this address. West 106th Street isn't where I'd expect a doctor to be living."

"I think a drive-by sounds smart," Franco said.

When they reached Manhattan, Franco continued west on Fifty-ninth Street, then headed north on Central Park West. Turning left onto 106th Street, they passed a basketball court on the right that was in full use. There were lots of people standing on the sidelines.

"It must be on the left," Franco said.

Angelo consulted a piece of paper with Jack's address. "It's coming up. It's the building with the fancy top." Unconsciously he moved his left arm so that he could feel the reassuring mass of his Walther TPH automatic pistol snuggled into its shoulder holster.

Franco slowed and then stopped to double-park a few buildings short of Jack's on the opposite side of the street.

"Why would a doctor live there?" Angelo said.

Franco shook his head. "Doesn't make any sense to me. The whole neighborhood is a dump."

"Amendola said he was a little strange," Angelo said. "Apparently, he rides a bike from here all the way down to the morgue at First Avenue and Thirtieth Street every day."

Franco's eyes scanned the area. "Maybe he's into drugs."

Angelo opened the car door and got out. "I want to make sure he lives in the fourth-floor-rear apartment. I'll be right back." He crossed the street and climbed to the stoop in front of Jack's building. He pushed open the outer door and glanced at the mailboxes. Many were broken. None had locks that worked.

Quickly Angelo sorted through the mail, finding a catalogue addressed to Jack Stapleton. He tried the inner door. It opened with ease. Stepping into the front hall, he eyed the trash on the stairs, the peeling paint, and the broken lightbulbs in the once elegant chandelier. He could hear the sounds of a domestic fight on the second floor. He smiled. Dealing with Jack Stapleton was going to be easy.

Returning outside, Angelo determined which sunken passageway led to the backyard. Then he walked its length. In the backyard, he looked up at the fire escape. On the fourth floor two windows had access. The windows were dark. The doctor wasn't at home.

Angelo returned and climbed back into the car.

"Well?" Franco asked.

"He lives there all right," Angelo said. "The place is not pretty, but for our purposes it's perfect. It'll be easy."

"That's what I like to hear. Should we still do the woman first?"

Angelo smiled. "Why not?"

Franco put the car in gear, and they headed south to Nineteenth Street. Angelo pointed out Laurie's building without difficulty. Franco found a convenient no-parking zone and parked.

"So, you think we should go up the back way?" Franco asked.

"For two reasons," Angelo said. "Amendola says she's on the fifth floor, but her windows face the back. Also her apartment has access to the back stairs."

"Let's do it," Franco said.

They got out of the car. Angelo opened up the back seat and lifted out his bag of lock-picking tools along with a Halligan bar, a tool firefighters use to get through doors.

The two men went through a passageway to the backyard, then carefully moved away from the building far enough to see up to the fifth floor. The windows were all dark.

"Looks like we have time to prepare a nice homecoming," Franco said.

Angelo took his lock-picking tools over to the metal fire door that led to the back stairs. The lock responded to his efforts, and the door opened.

Five floors up, Angelo didn't bother with the lock-picking tools. He used the Halligan bar. With a splintering sound it made short work of the door. Within twenty seconds they were inside.

AT POLICE headquarters, Laurie and Jack had to get ID badges and go through a metal detector before they were allowed to go up to Lou's floor. Lou was at the elevator to welcome them.

The first thing he did was ask Laurie what had happened.

"She's okay," Jack said. "She's back to her old rational self."

Laurie smiled. "Jack's right," she said. "I'm fine."

Lou breathed a sigh of relief. "Well, I'm happy to see both of you. Come on back to my palace." He led the way to his office.

Laurie took a chair, and Jack did likewise. "I think I figured out how Franconi's body was taken from the morgue," she began. "You teased me about suspecting the Spoletto Funeral Home, but now I think you're going to have to take that back."

Laurie then outlined what she thought had happened. She told Lou that she suspected someone from the morgue had given the Spoletto people the accession number of a relatively recent, unidentified body as well as the location of Franconi's remains.

"Often, when two drivers come to pick up a body for a funeral home, one goes into the walk-in cooler while the other handles the paperwork with the mortuary tech," Laurie explained. "The mortuary tech prepares the body for pickup by covering it with a sheet and positioning its gurney just inside the cooler door. In the Franconi situation, I believe the driver took the body whose accession number he had, removed its tag, stashed the body in one of the many unoccupied refrigerator compartments, replaced Franconi's tag with that one, then calmly appeared outside the mortuary office with Franconi's remains. All the tech did was check the accession number."

"That's quite a scenario," Lou said. "Do you have proof?"

"I found the body whose accession number Spoletto called in," Laurie said. "It was an unidentified corpse that had come into the morgue over two weeks ago. It was in a compartment that was supposed to be vacant. The name Frank Gleason was bogus."

"Ahhhh," Lou said. He leaned forward on his desk. "I'm beginning to like this very much. But I must insist on no more amateur sleuthing on your part. We take over from here. Do I have your word on that? These organized-crime people are dangerous."

"I'm happy to let you take over," Laurie said.

"I'm too preoccupied with my end of the mystery to interfere," Jack said. "What did you learn for me, Lou?"

"Plenty. My contact at the FAA was able to call an organization that doles out landing and takeoff times all over Europe. They also store flight plans. Franconi's private jet came to France from Equatorial Guinea."

"Where?" Jack's eyebrows collided in an expression of confusion.

"It's a little tiny country in western Africa between Cameroon and Gabon. The city that the plane flew out of is Bata."

"This doesn't make any sense whatsoever," Jack complained. "That's a fairly undeveloped part of Africa. Franconi couldn't have gotten a liver transplant there."

"That was my reaction too," Lou said. "But then I tracked Alpha Aviation in Nevada to its real owner. It's GenSys Corp. in Cambridge, Massachusetts."

"I've heard of GenSys," Laurie said. "It's a biotech firm that's big in vaccines and lymphokines. A girlfriend of mine who's a broker in Chicago recommended the stock. Is GenSys trying to hide the fact that they own an aircraft?"

"I doubt it. I was able to learn the connection too easily."

"A biotech company," Jack mused. "Hmmm. I don't know what a biotech firm would be doing in Equatorial Guinea. Laurie, how about giving this broker friend of yours a call and asking her if she knows? Lou, is it all right if Laurie uses your phone?"

"No problem," Lou said.

While Laurie was on the phone, Jack quizzed Lou in detail about how he had found out about Equatorial Guinea.

"I can't imagine what it's like in a place like that," Lou said.

"I can," Jack said. "It's hot, buggy, rainy, and wet."

"Sounds delightful," Lou quipped.

Laurie hung up the phone and twisted around in Lou's desk chair to face the others. "My friend was able to put her finger on her GenSys material in a flash. Apparently, the stock has tripled and then split. She said that one of the main reasons the company has been doing so well is that it established a huge primate farm. Other biotech companies and pharmaceutical firms have now outsourced their primate research to GenSys."

"And this primate farm is in Equatorial Guinea?" Jack asked.

"That's right."

"A primate farm," Jack repeated. "This is raising even more bizarre possibilities. Could we be dealing with a xenograft?"

"Don't start that doctor jargon on me," Lou complained. "What's a xenograft?"

"Impossible," Laurie said. "Xenografts cause hyperacute rejections. There was no evidence of inflammation in the liver section you showed me."

"True," Jack said. "And he wasn't on immunosuppressants."

"Come on, you guys," Lou pleaded. "Don't make me beg."

"A xenograft is when a transplant organ is taken from an animal of a different species," Laurie said.

"You mean like that Baby Fae baboon heart fiasco ten or twelve years ago?" Lou asked.

"Exactly. The new immunosuppressant drugs have brought xenografts back into the picture," Jack explained.

"Could Franconi have gotten a primate liver while he was in Africa?" Lou asked.

"I can't imagine," Jack said. "There was no evidence of any rejection. That's unheard-of even with a good human match, short of identical twins."

"But Franconi was apparently in Africa," Lou said.

"True, and his mother said he came home a new man," Jack said. He stood up. "It's a mystery." Laurie stood up as well.

"Are you guys leaving?" Lou asked. "How about we all head over to Little Italy for a quick dinner?"

"Not me," Jack said. "I'm exhausted, and I've got a bike ride ahead of me. At this point a meal would do me in."

"Nor I," Laurie said. "It's been two late nights in a row."

Laurie and Jack said good-bye and left police headquarters. In the shadow of City Hall, they caught a cab to take Laurie home and Jack to the morgue to pick up his bicycle.

"Feel better?" Jack asked Laurie as they headed north.

"Much," Laurie admitted. "I can't tell you how relieved I am to dump it all in Lou's lap. How are you bearing up? You're getting a lot of bizarre input on the case."

Jack sighed. "The next thing that's scheduled is for a veterinary pathologist to review the liver section. But I'm starting to think that my only option if I really want to solve it is a quick trip to Equatorial Guinea."

Laurie twisted around in the seat so she could look directly into Jack's face. "You're not serious. I mean, you're joking, right?"

"Well, there's no way I could phone GenSys or even go up to Cambridge and walk into their home office and say, 'Hi, folks. What's going on in Equatorial Guinea?'"

"But we're talking about Africa. Halfway around the world. Besides, if you don't think you'd learn anything going up to Cambridge, what makes you think you'd learn anything going there?"

"Maybe because they wouldn't expect it."

"Oh, this is insane," Laurie said, rolling her eyes.

"Hey, I didn't say I was going. I just said it was something I was beginning to think about."

The taxi pulled up in front of Laurie's building. She started to get some money out, but Jack put a hand on her arm. "My treat."

"Thanks." Laurie climbed out of the cab. "Good night, Jack," she said with a warm smile.

"Good night, Laurie," Jack said.

Laurie closed the taxi door and watched the cab until it disappeared around the corner on First Avenue.

As she rode up in her elevator, Laurie began to anticipate a shower. She vowed she'd turn in early. Slamming her apartment door behind her, she removed her coat and, in the darkness of the closet, groped for a hanger. It wasn't until she entered the living room that she flipped the wall switch and let out a muffled scream.

There were two men in the living room—one sitting in a chair, the other on the couch. The one on the couch was petting Tom, who was asleep on his lap. A large handgun was on the arm of the chair.

"Welcome home, Dr. Montgomery," Franco said. "Please come and sit down." He pointed to a chair in the middle of the room.

Laurie didn't move. She was incapable of it.

"Please!" Franco repeated with false politeness.

Angelo moved the cat aside and stood up. He took a step toward Laurie and backhanded her across the face. The blow propelled her against the wall, where she slumped to her hands and knees. A few drops of blood from her split upper lip splattered on the floor.

Angelo hoisted her to her feet, then powered her over to the chair and pushed her into a sitting position. He struck her again, half knocking her off the chair. Blood from her nose soaked the carpet.

"Okay, Angelo," Franco said. "Remember, we've got to talk with her." Angelo went back to the couch and sat down.

Laurie righted herself and pinched her nose to halt the bleeding.

"Listen, Dr. Montgomery," Franco said. "We're here to ask you nicely to leave the Franconi thing alone. Am I making myself clear?"

Laurie nodded. She was afraid not to.

"Good," Franco said. "Now, we'll consider this a favor on your part, and we're willing to do a favor in return. We happen to know who killed Mr. Franconi, and we're willing to pass that information on to you. You see, Mr. Franconi wasn't a nice man, so he was killed. End of story. Are you still with me?"

Laurie nodded again.

"The killer's name is Vido Delbario," Franco continued. "I've even taken the trouble to write the name down." He put a piece of paper on the coffee table and looked expectantly at Laurie. "So, a favor for a favor."

Laurie nodded for the third time.

"We're not asking much," Franco said. "I hope you will be sensible. In a city this size there's no way to protect yourself, and Angelo here would like no better than to have his way with you. Lucky for you, our boss is not heavy-handed. He's a negotiator. Understand?"

With difficulty Laurie managed to say she understood.

"Wonderful." Franco slapped his knees and stood up. "Doc, I was confident we could see eye to eye." He slipped his gun into his coat. "Come on, Angelo."

Angelo got up and followed Franco out the front door.

Laurie stood up on rubbery legs and heard the elevator descend. She rushed to the front door and relocked it. Then, realizing the intruders must have come in the back door, she raced there, only to find it wide-open and splintered. She closed it as best she could.

Back in the kitchen, she took the phone off the hook with trembling hands. Her first response was to call the police, but she hesitated, hearing Franco's voice warning her how vulnerable she was.

Fighting tears, Laurie replaced the receiver. She thought she'd call Jack, but she knew he wouldn't be home yet. So instead of calling anyone, she went into the bathroom to check out her wounds.

FOR most of Jack's bike ride home from the morgue he pondered about GenSys and Equatorial Guinea. He also thought about Ted Lynch. Before Jack left the morgue, he'd called him at home. Ted thought he'd be able to tell a xenograft by checking an area on the DNA that differed considerably from species to species. The information to make a species identification was available on a CD-ROM.

Jack turned onto his street. In the playground, he dismounted and leaned his bike against the fence. He didn't bother to lock it, though most people would have thought the neighborhood a risky place to leave a thousand-dollar bike. In reality the playground was the only place in New York where Jack felt he didn't have to lock up.

He walked over to the sidelines and nodded to Spit and Flash, who were waiting to play. The game in progress swept up and down the court, and, as usual, Warren was dominating the play.

Warren caught sight of Jack and strutted over. "Hey, man, you going to run or what?"

"I'm thinking about it. But I've got a couple of questions. First of all, how about you and Natalie getting together with Laurie and me this weekend?"

"Sure," Warren said. "Anything to shut my shortie up."

"Second, in this city of expatriates, do you know any brothers from a tiny African country called Equatorial Guinea?"

"Man, I never know what's going to come out of your mouth," Warren complained. "But to answer your question—yes, I do know a couple of people from there, and one dude in particular. His name is Esteban Ndeme. He lives two doors down from you."

"Do you know him well enough to introduce me?" Jack asked.

"Yeah, sure. Come down and run a few games; then I'll take you over and introduce you to Esteban."

"Fair enough." Jack went back and got his bike. Hurrying over to his building, he carried the bicycle up the stairs. He unlocked his door without even taking it off his shoulder. Once inside, he made a beeline for his basketball gear.

He was already on his way back out when his phone rang. It was Laurie, and she was beside herself.

JACK crammed bills through the Plexiglas partition in the taxi and jumped out in front of Laurie's apartment building. Laurie met him in the elevator foyer on her floor.

"My God!" Jack wailed. "Look at your lip." She started whimpering, and he put his arm around her to calm her.

"What happened?" he asked after getting her seated on the couch in her apartment.

"There were two of them," Laurie said. "In their words, I'm to 'leave the Franconi thing alone.' "

"I don't believe this," Jack said.

"Their warning was presented in the guise of a favor for a favor.

The favor was to tell me who killed Franconi. One of them wrote the name down." She handed the piece of paper to Jack.

" 'Vido Delbario,' " Jack read. He looked back at Laurie's battered face. Both her nose and lip were swollen, and she was developing a black eye. "I think you'd better tell me everything."

Laurie related the details from the moment she'd walked in. "What am I going to do?" she asked rhetorically.

"Let me look at the back door," Jack said.

Laurie led him through the kitchen and into the pantry.

"Whoa!" Jack said. The entire edge had split when the door was forced. "I'll tell you one thing, you're not staying here tonight. You're coming home with me. I'll sleep on the couch."

While Laurie packed, Jack paced her bedroom. "We're going to tell Lou about this," he said, "and give him Vido Delbario's name."

"I was thinking the same thing," Laurie said from the depths of her walk-in closet.

"We'll call him from my house."

Laurie came out of her closet with a hang-up bag.

"This episode makes the idea of going to Africa a lot more appealing," Jack said.

Laurie stopped short. "What on earth are you talking about?"

"I haven't had any personal experience, but I believe that if organized crime gets it in its mind to get rid of you, the police can't protect you unless they are guarding you twenty-four hours a day. Maybe it would be good for both of us to get out of town."

"I'd go too?" Laurie asked.

"We'd consider it a forced vacation. Of course, Equatorial Guinea might not be a prime destination, but it would be . . . different. Perhaps, in the process, we'll be able to figure out what GenSys is doing there and why Franconi made the trip."

"Hmmm," Laurie said. "I'm starting to warm to the idea."

In the cab en route to Jack's, Laurie reached over and gave his arm a squeeze. "I haven't thanked you yet for coming over. I really appreciated it, and I'm feeling much better."

"I'm glad," Jack said.

Once in his building, Jack carried Laurie's suitcase up the cluttered stairs to his door. He fumbled for his key, turned it in the cylinder, and preceded Laurie in to flip on the light. Laurie collided with him because he'd stopped suddenly.

"Go ahead, turn it on," a voice said.

Jack complied. Two men dressed in long, dark coats were seated on Jack's sofa, facing into the room.

"Oh, my God!" Laurie said. "It's them!"

Franco and Angelo had made themselves at home. They'd even helped themselves to beers. A handgun was on the coffee table. A straight-backed chair had been brought into the center of the room.

"I assume you are Dr. Jack Stapleton," Franco said.

Jack nodded.

"Don't do anything foolish," Franco admonished. "We won't stay long. If we'd known that Dr. Montgomery was going to be here, we'd have saved ourselves a trip to her place."

"What is it you people are afraid we might learn?" Jack asked.

Franco smiled at Angelo. "Can you believe this guy? He thinks we made all this effort to get in here to answer questions."

"No respect," Angelo said.

"Doc, how about another chair for the lady?" Franco said to Jack. "Then we can have our little talk, and we'll be on our way."

Before Jack could move, there was commotion behind him. Someone shouted, "Nobody move!"

Three African Americans had leaped into the room armed with machine pistols trained on Franco and Angelo. It was Flash, Spit, and David from the playground, still dressed in basketball gear.

Franco and Angelo were taken completely unawares. They sat there, eyes wide. Then Warren strutted in. "Man, Doc, you're dragging down the neighborhood, bringing in this kind of white trash."

Wordlessly Spit relieved Angelo of his Walther automatic pistol. After frisking Franco, he collected the gun from the coffee table.

Jack let out a breath. "Warren, old sport, I don't know how you managed to drop in on such a timely basis, but it's appreciated."

"These scumbags were seen casing this place," Warren explained.

"Laurie," Jack said, "I think it's time to give Lou a call. I'm sure he'd like nothing better than to talk with these gentlemen."

AN HOUR later Jack found himself comfortably ensconced in Esteban Ndeme's apartment, along with Laurie and Warren.

"Sure, I'll have another beer," Jack said in response to Esteban's offer. Jack was feeling progressively euphoric that the evening had worked out so auspiciously after such a bad start.

Lou had arrived at Jack's with several patrolmen less than twenty minutes after Laurie's call. He'd been ecstatic to take Angelo and Franco downtown. When Jack mentioned that he and Laurie were thinking of going out of town for a week or so, Lou was all for it.

At Jack's urging, Warren had taken him and Laurie to meet Esteban Ndeme. Esteban was an amiable and gracious man. He was close to Jack's age of forty-two, but where Jack was stocky, Esteban was slender. Even his facial features seemed delicate. His skin was a deep, rich brown, many shades darker than Warren's.

Jack sat back contentedly with a second beer. "Have you been back to Equatorial Guinea?"

"Several times," Esteban said. "I still have family there. My brother has a small hotel in a town called Bata."

"I've heard of Bata," Jack said. "I understand it has an airport." Then he asked, "Have you heard of a company called GenSys?"

"Most definitely."

"I've heard GenSys has a primate farm."

"In the south," Esteban said. "They built it in the jungle near an old Spanish town called Cogo."

"Do you know if GenSys built a hospital?"

"Yes, they did. They built a hospital and laboratory on the old town square facing the town hall."

"How do you know so much about it?" Jack asked.

"Because my cousin used to work there," Esteban said.

"If we were to go to Bata, could we visit Cogo?"

"I suppose. You'd have to hire a car. When are you planning to go? It's best to go in the dry season. That's now."

"Laurie and I are thinking of going tomorrow night," Jack said.

"What?" Warren said. "I thought me and Natalie were going out on the town with you guys this weekend."

"Ohhhh!" Jack commented. "I forgot about that. I have a better idea. Why don't you and Natalie come along with Laurie and me to Equatorial Guinea? It will be our treat."

Laurie blinked. She wasn't sure she'd heard correctly.

"Man, what are you talking about?" Warren said. "You're outa your mind. You're talking about Africa."

"Yeah, Africa," Jack said. "If Laurie and I have to go, we might as well make it as much fun as possible. In fact, Esteban, why don't you come too? We'll make it a party."

"Are you serious?" Esteban asked.

"Sure I'm serious," Jack said. "The best way to visit a country is to go with someone who used to live there."

"You're crazy, man," Warren said to Jack. "I knew it the first day you walked out on that basketball court. But you know something? I'm beginning to like it."

CHAPTER 6

AWN was breaking, and the pink-and-silver sky was clear overhead. As the faded red pirogue pulled away from the pier, Kevin, Melanie, and Candace looked back at Cogo to see if anyone was taking note of their departure. The only person was a man cleaning the Chickee Hut, and he didn't bother to look in their direction.

As they had planned, they motored west as if they were going to Acalayong. Kevin advanced the throttle to half open. The pirogue, which had a thatched roof over three quarters of its length, was thirty feet long and heavy, but it had very little draw. The small canoe they had in tow was riding easily in the water. To their right, the shoreline of Equatorial Guinea appeared as a solid mass of vegetation. Dotted about the wide estuary were other pirogues moving ghostlike through the mist on the water.

When Cogo had fallen significantly astern, Kevin steered the boat south. After traveling for ten minutes, he began a slow turn to the east. They were now at least a mile offshore, and when they passed Cogo, it was difficult to make out specific buildings.

When the sun did finally make its appearance, it was a huge ball of reddish gold. Its heat rapidly began to evaporate the mist. Melanie was the first to slip on her sunglasses. Candace and Kevin quickly did the same. A few minutes later everyone began to peel off layers of clothing they'd donned against the morning chill. Candace put on sunblock that Kevin had found in his medicine cabinet.

To their left was the string of islands that hugged the coast of Equatorial Guinea. Kevin had been steering north to complete the wide circle around Cogo. Now he pushed over the helm to point the bow directly toward Isla Francesca.

A welcome breeze stirred the water, and waves began to mar the hitherto glassy surface. The pirogue began to slap against the crests.

An hour and fifteen minutes after they had left the pier in Cogo, Kevin cut back on the throttle. A hundred feet ahead was the island's southern tip. "It looks sort of forbidding," Melanie said.

Kevin nodded. There was no beach. The entire shoreline appeared to be covered with dense mangroves. "We've got to find Rio Diviso's inlet." He pushed the helm to starboard and headed along the shore.

"What about where all those bulrushes are?" Candace called from the bow. She pointed ahead to an expansive marsh.

Kevin guided the boat in close to the shore. An opening appeared in the wall of reeds. He turned the boat toward it, turned the motor off, and tilted it up out of the water. The pirogue entered the reeds, then scraped to a halt. "Let's give it a try with the canoe," he said.

With difficulty they managed to get themselves into the unsteady, smaller boat along with their gear and Styrofoam food chest. Once in what they hoped was the channel, with Kevin paddling in the rear and Candace in the front, they were able to move at the pace of a slow walk. The six-foot-wide passage twisted and turned as it worked its way across the marsh.

"There seems to be some current," Kevin said, encouraged.

From her seat in the middle of the canoe Melanie was studying the contour map. "Why don't you try the locator?" Kevin said. "See if bonobo number sixty has moved."

Melanie entered the information and clicked. "He's still in the same spot in the marshy clearing."

"At least we can solve that mystery," Kevin said.

Ahead, they approached the high wall of jungle. As they rounded the final bend in the marsh, they could see the channel disappear into the riot of vegetation. Pushing branches aside, they silently slid into the perpetual darkness of the forest. It was like a muggy, claustrophobic hothouse. The thick canopy of tree limbs, twisted vines, and hanging mosses held in the heat like a heavy woolen blanket.

Almost from the moment the first branches snapped in place behind them, they were assaulted by swarms of mosquitoes and trigona bees. Melanie frantically located the insect repellent. After dousing herself, she passed it to the others. "It smells like a damn swamp," she complained.

"This is scary," Candace commented from her position in the bow. "I just saw a snake, and I hate snakes."

"All we have to worry about are the crocs and hippos," Kevin said. "When you see one, let me know."

"Oh, great," Candace complained nervously. "And just what do we do when we see one?"

"I didn't mean to worry you," Kevin said. "I don't think we'll see any until we come to the lake. And then they won't bother us. It's when they're caught on land that they can be aggressive."

Twenty minutes later the canoe glided out into the open water of Lago Hippo. The lake was not large. In fact, it was more like an elongated pond dotted with several lushly thicketed islands chockablock with white ibis. The wall of forest dropped away on both sides to form grassy fields, and above the forest rim the very top of the limestone escarpment was clear against the morning sky.

"Oh, no. I see hippos over to the left," Candace called out.

Kevin looked. Sure enough, the heads and small ears of a dozen of these huge mammals were just visible in the water. Standing on their crowns were a number of white birds.

"They're okay," Kevin assured Candace. "See how they are slowly moving away from us. They won't be any trouble."

"I've never been much of a nature lover," Candace admitted.

"You don't have to explain," Kevin said. He could remember clearly his unease about wildlife during his first year in Cogo.

"There should be a trail not too far away from the left bank," Melanie said, studying the contour map.

Kevin angled the canoe toward the left shore through a wall of reeds. Soon they bumped against dry land. After Melanie and Candace climbed out of the bow, he forced the canoe farther onshore.

Kevin got out of the boat with the gear bag over his shoulder, then pointed off to the right. "Bonobo number sixty should be no more than a hundred feet from here."

He struck off with the women following. About fifty feet from the pond they came across a well-used trail that ran parallel with the shoreline of the lake.

Candace sniffed the air. "I smell something putrid."

Hesitantly the others sniffed and agreed.

A few minutes later, with their fingers pinching their nostrils shut, the three stared down at a disgusting sight—the remains of bonobo number sixty. A wedge-shaped piece of limestone had struck the poor creature between the eyes. The rock was still in place.

"Ugh!" Melanie said. "This suggests that not only have the bonobos split into two groups but they're killing each other. I wonder if number sixty-seven is dead too."

Kevin kicked the rock out of the decomposing head. "That rock was shaped artificially." With the toe of his shoe he pointed to freshly made gouges in the side of the rock. "That suggests toolmaking."

Melanie grabbed Kevin's arm. With her finger pressed against her lips, she pointed to the south.

Kevin turned his gaze, then caught his breath. About fifty yards away was one of the bonobos, staring at them. The animal was standing ramrod straight and absolutely motionless. He was well over five feet tall, with an enormously muscular torso.

Being careful not to move too quickly, Kevin pulled the gear bag off his shoulder and got out the locator. He turned it on to scan. It began to quietly beep until he pointed it toward the bonobo. Kevin looked at the LCD screen and gasped.

"What's the matter?" Melanie whispered. She had seen Kevin's expression change.

"It's number one!" Kevin whispered back. "It's my double."

Kevin was struck by the coincidence that the first live bonobo they'd come across would be his double. Was he in some metamorphic way meeting himself five million years earlier? "This is too much," he whispered. "In some ways that's me standing there."

"He's certainly standing like a human," Candace remarked. "But he's hairier than any human I've ever been out with."

"Very funny," Melanie said without laughing.

"Melanie, use the locator to scan the area." Kevin handed her the unit. "Bonobos usually travel together. Maybe there are more around that we can't see. They could be hiding in the bushes."

"What's he got around his waist?" Candace asked.

"I can't make it out," Kevin said. "Unless it's just a vine that got caught on him when he came through the bushes."

"Look, Kevin." Melanie held up the locator. "You were right. There's a whole group of bonobos in the trees behind your double."

"Come on, let's see how close we can get," Candace said. "What do we have to lose?"

The three advanced carefully step by step. When they reached the midway mark, they stopped. Now they could see him much better. He had prominent eyebrows and a sloping forehead like a chimp's, but the lower half of his face was significantly less prognathous than that of a normal bonobo.

"Uh-oh. Can you guys see his thumb?" Kevin whispered. "It's not like a chimp's. His thumb juts out from the palm."

"You're right," Melanie whispered. "And that means he might be able to oppose his thumb with his fingers. Let's try moving closer."

"I don't know," Kevin said. "I think we're pushing our luck."

"I agree," Candace said.

"Well, I'm going closer," Melanie announced.

Kevin and Candace let Melanie get ten feet in front of them before they looked at each other, shrugged, and joined her. Moving slowly and deliberately, they came within twenty feet of the bonobo. Then they stopped again.

"This is incredible," Melanie whispered. The only way it was apparent the bonobo was alive was an occasional movement of his eyes and a flaring of his nostrils. "How do you think he got that scar?" A thick scar ran down the left side of his face.

Without the slightest warning the bonobo suddenly clapped his hands. "Atah!" he yelled.

Kevin, Melanie, and Candace leaped from fright, but then the bonobo reverted back to his stonelike state.

"What was that all about?" Melanie asked.

"Maybe we should just back away," Candace said.

"I agree," Kevin said uneasily. "Let's go slowly. Don't panic." He took a few steps backward, and the women did likewise.

The bonobo responded by reaching behind his back and grabbing a tool he had suspended by the vine around his waist. He held the tool aloft over his head and cried "Atah" again.

The three froze, wide-eyed with terror.

"What can 'atah' mean?" Melanie whispered after a few moments. "Can it be a word? Could he be talking?"

"I don't have any idea," Kevin sputtered.

"What is he holding?" Candace asked. "It looks like a hammer."

"It is," Kevin managed. "It's a carpenter's claw hammer. It must be one of the tools the bonobos stole when the bridge was built."

"We've got to get away from here!" Candace turned and started to run. But she only went a few steps before she let out a scream.

Kevin and Melanie turned in her direction and caught their breath. Twenty more bonobos had silently emerged from the forest and had arrayed themselves in an arc, blocking their exit.

Bonobo number one repeated his cry: "Atah!" Instantly the animals began to circle the humans. Candace backed up until she bumped into Melanie. The bonobos came closer, a step at a time. They stopped when they were an arm's length from the three friends.

"They seem mystified by us," Kevin said. "Maybe they think we are gods."

"How can we encourage that belief?" Melanie asked.

"I'll try to give them something." Kevin slipped the watch from his wrist and extended it to bonobo number one. The animal eyed the watch, then reached for it and slipped it onto his forearm.

"Good grief!" Kevin voiced. "My double is wearing my watch."

Bonobo number one brought his thumb and forefinger together to form a circle while saying, "Randa." One of the bonobos ran off into the forest. When he reappeared, he was carrying a rope.

"Rope?" Kevin said with trepidation. "Now what?"

The bonobo went to Kevin and looped the rope around his waist. The animal tied a crude knot tight against his abdomen.

"Don't struggle," Kevin said. "I think everything is going to be okay as long as we don't anger them or scare them."

The bonobo roped Melanie and Candace, then stepped back holding the end of the rope. Bonobo number one swept his hands away from his chest and said, "Arak."

Immediately the group started moving. Kevin, Melanie, and Candace were forced forward.

"It must mean 'move' or 'away,' " Kevin said. "They're speaking!"

They moved across the field until they came to the trail. While they walked, the bonobos remained silent but vigilant. The trail curved south and entered the jungle.

Kevin whispered, "We've only been on the island for an hour, but the question that brought us here has already been answered. We've seen totally upright posture, opposable thumbs, toolmaking, and even rudimentary speech."

"It's extraordinary," Melanie said. "These animals have gone through five million years of human evolution in a few years."

"Oh, shut up!" Candace cried. "We're prisoners of these beasts, and you two are having a scientific discussion."

The group passed a marshy area, then began a climb. Fifteen minutes later they were at the foot of the limestone escarpment.

Halfway up the steep face was the opening of a cave. At the lip of the cave a dozen female bonobos were striking their chests and yelling "Bada" over and over again. But at the sight of Kevin, Melanie, and Candace, the females fell silent.

"Why do I have the feeling the females aren't so happy to see us?" Melanie whispered.

"They hadn't expected company," Kevin whispered back.

Finally bonobo number one said, "Zit," and pointed up. The group surged forward, pulling Kevin, Melanie, and Candace along.

JACK'S lids blinked open, and he was instantly awake. Getting up off the couch, he wrapped himself in his blanket, went to the bedroom door, and cracked it. As he'd expected, Laurie was on her side under a mound of covers, breathing deeply.

As quietly as possible, he tiptoed across the bedroom and entered the bathroom. He quickly shaved and showered. When he reappeared, he was pleased to see that Laurie had not budged.

Getting fresh clothes from his closet and bureau, Jack carried them out into the living room and got dressed.

Laurie appeared a few minutes later clad in Jack's robe. All that was apparent from the previous night's run-in was a mild black eye. "Now that you've had a night's sleep to think about this trip, do you still feel the same?" she asked.

"Absolutely," Jack said. "I'm psyched."

"Are you really going to pay for everyone's ticket?"

"What else do I have to spend my money on?" Jack glanced around his apartment. "Certainly not my lifestyle."

"I can understand Esteban to some extent," Laurie said, "but Warren and Natalie?"

"I was serious about making it fun. I could see in Warren's eyes his interest to visit that part of Africa. And on the way back we'll spend a night or two in Paris."

"You don't have to convince me," Laurie said. "I'm excited."

"Now all we have to do is convince Bingham," Jack said. "Assuming that won't be a problem, let's divvy up the errands. I'll go get the tickets while you, Warren, and Natalie take care of the visas. Also we've got to arrange for some shots and start malaria prophylaxis. We really should have more time for immunizations, but we'll do the best we can, and we'll take a lot of insect repellent."

"Sounds good," Laurie said.

Together they cabbed down to the M.E.'s office. When they walked into the ID room, Vinnie lowered his newspaper and looked at them as if they were ghosts. "What are you guys doing here?"

"We work here, Vinnie. Have you forgotten?" Jack asked.

"I just didn't think you two were on call."

Jack and Laurie went to the coffee urn. Laurie glanced at Vinnie over her shoulder. He had gone back behind his newspaper. "That was a strange reaction," she whispered to Jack.

Their eyes met for a moment.

"Are you thinking what I'm thinking?" Laurie asked.

"Maybe," Jack said. "It kind of fits. He certainly has access."

As soon as the chief medical examiner arrived, Laurie and Jack went to his office. Dr. Harold Bingham regarded them curiously over the tops of his wire-rimmed glasses. "You want two weeks starting today? What's the rush? Is this some sort of an emergency?"

"We're planning an adventure-type trip," Jack said.

Bingham's watery eyes went back and forth between Laurie and Jack. "You two aren't planning on getting married, are you?"

"Not that adventuresome," Jack said.

"We're sorry not to have given more notice," Laurie said. "But last night both of us were threatened over the Franconi case."

"Does it have anything to do with that shiner you've got?"

"I'm afraid so," Laurie said. "Lou Soldano offered to fill you in on it and talk to you about a possible mole here in the office. We think we've figured out how Franconi's body was taken from here."

"I'm listening." Bingham leaned back in his chair.

Laurie explained, emphasizing that the Spoletto Funeral Home must have been given the accession number of the unidentified case.

"Did Detective Soldano think it wise for you two to leave town?" Bingham asked.

"Yes, he did," Laurie said.

"Fine. Then you're out of here. You people have a good trip and send me a postcard."

Laurie retired to her office while Jack left for New York University Hospital. Once there, he went directly up to Dr. Malovar's lab. As usual, he found the pathologist bent over his microscope.

"Ahhh, Dr. Stapleton," Dr. Malovar said, catching sight of Jack. "I'm glad you came. Now, where is that slide of yours?"

Dr. Malovar's lab was a dusty clutter of books, journals, and hundreds of slide trays. With surprising speed the professor located Jack's slide on top of a veterinary pathology book.

"Dr. Hammersmith identified the offending organism as *Hepatocystis*," Dr. Malovar said.

Jack had never heard of *Hepatocystis*. "Is it rare?" he asked.

"In the New York City morgue I'd have to say yes," Dr. Malovar said. "You see, it is only found in Old World primates, meaning primates in Africa and Southeast Asia. It's never been seen in humans."

"Never?" Jack questioned.

"Put it this way," Dr. Malovar said. "I've never seen it, and I've seen a lot of liver parasites."

"I appreciate your help," Jack said distractedly. This was a much stronger suggestion that Franconi had had a xenograft than the mere fact that he'd gone to Africa. Jack left the professor and took the elevator down to the ground floor.

Arriving back at the morgue, he went directly to the DNA lab. "Stapleton, where have you been!" Ted Lynch said. He handed Jack two sheets of film covered with hundreds of minute dark bands. "Hold them up to the light."

Jack did as he was told, and Ted pointed. "The first sheet is a study of the region of the DNA that codes for ribosomal protein of a human being. The other one is a study of Franconi's liver sample. Can you see how different it is?"

"That's the only thing I can see," Jack said.

Ted snatched away the human study and tossed it aside. Then he pointed at the film Jack was still holding. "I let the computer make a match of that pattern. It came back most consistent with a chimpanzee—well, kind of like a cousin of a chimpanzee."

"So from your perspective it was a xenograft."

Ted shrugged. "If you made me guess, I'd have to say yes. But taking the DQ alpha results, which show a perfect match for Franconi, into consideration, I don't know what to say. It's a weird case."

"Tell me about it," Jack said.

BERTRAM parked his Cherokee behind the town hall. He nodded to the soldiers lounging in the shade of the arcade. Taking the stairs by twos, he ignored Aurielo in his haste to get in to see Siegfried.

"We've got a problem," Bertram said upon entering Siegfried's office. "Melanie Becket didn't show up for a scheduled injection this afternoon, and Kevin Marshall is not in his lab."

"I'm not surprised," Siegfried said calmly. "They were both seen leaving Marshall's house before dawn this morning with the nurse. The ménage à trois seems to be blossoming."

"Where did they go?"

"I assume to Acalayong," Siegfried said. "They were seen leaving in a pirogue by a member of the janitorial staff."

"Then they've gone to the island by water."

"They were seen going west, not east."

"It could have been a ruse," Bertram said.

"It could have," Siegfried agreed. "But the only way to visit the island by water is to land at the staging area. The rest of the island is surrounded by a virtual wall of mangroves and marsh. And they couldn't have landed at the staging area because the soldiers are still out by the bridge itching to have an excuse to use their AK-47s."

"Maybe," Bertram said grudgingly. "But I'm still suspicious. I want to get into Kevin's office. I showed him how to tap into the software we've developed for locating the bonobos. I know he's accessed it on several occasions. I'd like to find out what he's been up to."

"I'd say that sounds reasonable." Siegfried called out to Aurielo to see to it that Bertram had a magnetic pass card for the lab, then said, "Let me know if you find anything interesting."

"Don't worry," Bertram said.

Armed with the card, he went to Kevin's lab. The first sign of trouble was a stack of computer paper—printouts of the island graphic. He examined each page, then went to Kevin's computer and searched his directories. For the next half hour he was transfixed. Kevin had devised a way to follow individual animals over time. He came across Kevin's stored information documenting the problem with bonobos number sixty and sixty-seven.

"Good Lord!" Bertram moaned. Snapping up the printed island graphics, he ran out of the lab. He raced across the square to the town hall and burst into Siegfried's office. "It's very bad news. Kevin Marshall figured out a way to follow the bonobos over time."

"So what?" Siegfried said.

"At least two of the bonobos haven't moved for more than twenty-four hours. There's only one explanation. They're dead. Those animals are killing each other."

"That's terrible news!" Siegfried exclaimed. "What can we do?"

"First, we tell no one," Bertram said. "If there is ever an order to harvest either number sixty or number sixty-seven, we'll deal with that problem then. Second, we must bring the animals in. The bonobos won't be killing each other if they're in separate cages."

Siegfried had to accept the white-haired veterinarian's advice. "When should we retrieve them?"

"As soon as possible. I can have a team of animal handlers ready by dawn tomorrow. Once we have all the animals caged, we'll move them at night to the animal center."

RAYMOND Lyons felt better than he had in days. Things seemed to have gone well from the moment he'd gotten up. Just after nine, a

Park Avenue doctor had called with two clients ready to plunk down their deposits. But what had pleased Raymond the most during the day was whom he didn't hear from. There were no calls from either Vinnie Dominick or Dr. Daniel Levitz. Raymond took this silence to mean that the Franconi business had finally been put to bed.

At three thirty the door buzzer went off. Darlene answered it and with a tearful voice told Raymond that his car was waiting.

Raymond took her in his arms and patted her on the back. "Next time maybe you can go," he said, and promised to call as soon as he arrived. He carried his bag downstairs, climbed into the waiting sedan, and luxuriously leaned back for the ride to Teterboro Airport.

When he got there, he positioned himself in the lounge, where he had a view of the runway, and ordered a Scotch. Just as he was being served, the sleek GenSys jet swooped down out of the clouds. It taxied over to a position directly in front of him.

A forward door opened. An impeccably dressed steward in dark blue livery descended the steps to the tarmac and entered the building. Once inside the lounge, he walked over to Raymond. "Is this the extent of your luggage, sir?" he asked, picking up Raymond's bag.

"That's it." Raymond followed the steward out into the gray, raw March afternoon. As he approached the private jet, Raymond hoped people were watching him. At times like this he felt as if he were living the life that was meant for him.

IT WAS like a party at the bar in the international departure lounge at JFK Airport. Even Lou was there, having a beer with Jack, Laurie, Warren, Natalie, and Esteban at a round table in the corner.

Natalie was a third-grade teacher at a public school in Harlem, but she didn't look like any teacher Jack could remember. Her features were reminiscent of the Egyptian sculptures in the Metropolitan Museum. She looked radiant in a dark purple jumpsuit.

Warren, sitting next to Natalie, was wearing a sports jacket over a black T-shirt. He looked happier than Jack had ever seen him.

Esteban too was smiling, even more broadly than Warren. And Laurie had her auburn hair braided and was wearing a loose-fitting velour top with leggings. She looked like she was in college.

"It's been a great day," Lou said to Jack and Laurie. "We picked up Vido Delbario, and he's singing to save his skin."

"What about Angelo Facciolo and Franco Ponti?" Jack asked.

"The judge set bail at two million each."

"How about Spoletto Funeral Home?" Laurie asked.

"That's going to be a gold mine," Lou said. "The owner is the brother of the wife of Vinnie Dominick of the Lucia organization."

"What about the mole in the M.E.'s office?" Laurie asked.

"Hey, we'll get to that," Lou said. "Don't worry."

"When you do, check out Vinnie Amendola," Laurie said.

"Any particular reason?" Lou asked.

"Just a suspicion," Laurie said.

"Consider it done."

A half hour later the group—minus Lou—merrily boarded the 747. No sooner had they gotten themselves situated than the huge plane lurched and was pulled from the gate.

"Africa, here we come!" Warren exclaimed.

CHAPTER 7

RE you asleep?" Candace whispered in the night.

"Are you kidding?" Melanie whispered back. "How am I supposed to sleep on rock with just a few branches strewn over it?"

"I can't sleep either," Candace admitted. "Especially with all this snoring going on. What about Kevin?"

"I'm awake," Kevin said.

They were in a small side cave jutting off the main chamber just behind the entrance. The darkness was almost absolute. The only light came from meager moonlight reflected from outside.

Kevin, Melanie, and Candace had been shuttled into this small cave immediately on their arrival. It measured about ten feet wide, with a downward-sloping ceiling that started at a height roughly equivalent to Kevin's five feet ten inches. There was no back wall; the chamber simply narrowed to a tunnel. Earlier in the evening Kevin had explored the tunnel with the flashlight in hopes of finding another way out, but the tunnel abruptly ended after thirty feet.

The bonobos apparently intended to keep them alive and well. They'd provided them with muddy water in gourds and a variety of food, unfortunately in the form of grubs and maggots.

The bonobos had made it clear that they were to stay in the cave. At all times at least two of the male bonobos remained in the vicinity. Each time Kevin or one of the women tried to venture forth, these guards would screech and bare their teeth.

"We're going to have to do something," Melanie said. "And we'll have to do it while they are all sleeping, like now."

Every bonobo in the cave, including the guards, was fast asleep on pallets of branches and leaves. Most were snoring.

"I don't think we should take the chance of angering them," Kevin said. "We're lucky they've treated us as well as they have."

"Being offered maggots to eat is not what I'd call being well treated," Melanie said. "Besides, they might turn on us."

"I prefer to wait," Kevin said. "We're undoubtedly missed back in town. It won't take Siegfried or Bertram long to come for us."

"Siegfried might take our disappearance as a godsend," Melanie said. "What do you think, Candace?"

"I don't know what to think. But one thing is for sure—I'm not going to be involved in any more harvests. Now that we know they're protohumans, I can't do it."

"I can't imagine any sensitive human being would feel differently," Kevin said. "But that's not the issue. The issue is that this new race exists, and if they're not to be used for transplants, what's to be done with them?"

There was a sudden bright flash of lightning, momentarily illuminating the cave, followed by a loud clap of thunder.

"That thunder was loud enough to wake the dead," Melanie said. "And not one of the bonobos so much as blinked."

"It's true," Candace said.

"At least one of us should try to get out of here and alert Bertram to rescue the others," Melanie said.

There were a few moments of silence. Finally Kevin broke it. "Wait a second. You guys are not suggesting that I go?"

"It was your suggestion to come out here," Melanie said.

"But I only said . . ." Kevin stopped. From where he was sitting, he could see a clear path of moonlight all the way to the entrance. Maybe he could do it. "All right. I'll try."

"If something goes wrong," Melanie said, "get back in a hurry."

Kevin began to pick his way along the path of moonlight toward the mouth of the cave. Every time his foot made the slightest noise, he froze in the darkness. All around him he could hear the stertorous breathing of the sleeping creatures. With additional light from the entrance, he began to feel a wave of relief.

Another clap of thunder was followed by a sudden tropical downpour. Kevin could see the black silhouette of the jungle below. He was worrying about how to make the steep descent to the ground when calamity struck. His heart leaped into his throat as something grabbed him around the ankle. Looking down in the half-light, the first thing he saw was his watch.

"Tada," shouted bonobo number one as he jumped to his feet, upending Kevin. The yell brought the other bonobos to their feet, and for a moment there was utter chaos. In an amazing demonstration of strength, bonobo number one picked Kevin up and held him off the ground. Then the bonobo marched into the cave and literally tossed Kevin into the smaller chamber. After a final angry word he went back to his pallet.

Kevin managed to push himself up to a sitting position. He'd landed on his hip, and it felt numb. He'd also sprained a wrist.

"Kevin, are you okay?" Candace whispered.

"As good as can be expected."

"We couldn't see what happened," Melanie said.

"My double scolded me," Kevin said. "At least that's what I think he was doing. Then he threw me back in here."

Melanie shuddered and then sighed. "It's hard to believe. We're prisoners of our own creations."

JACK realized he'd been clenching his teeth. The flight from Douala, Cameroon, had not been easy. The old commuter plane had constantly dodged thunderstorms, and the turbulence was fierce.

The flight from New York to Paris had been smooth and blissfully uneventful. Everyone had slept at least a few hours. Everyone slept even more on the Cameroon Airlines flight to Douala. But that final leg to Bata was a hair-raiser.

"We're landing," Laurie said to Jack.

Jack looked out the window. The landscape was uninterrupted green. As the tops of the trees came closer, he hoped there was a runway ahead. They touched down onto tarmac to his sigh of relief.

As the weary travelers climbed out of the plane, Jack looked across the ill-maintained runway and saw a strange sight—a resplendent white private jet, sitting all by itself.

In the airport arrival area they were met by Esteban's cousin Arturo, an enormously friendly individual with bright eyes and flashing teeth who was attired in colorful flowing robes and a pillbox hat.

They stepped out of the airport into the hot, humid air of equatorial Africa. The vistas seemed immense, since the land was relatively flat. Arturo had a rented van parked at curbside, and everyone climbed in.

Jack asked Arturo if they had far to go to the hotel.

"No. Ten minutes," Arturo said.

"I understand you worked for GenSys," Jack said.

"For three years, but no more. The manager is a bad person. I prefer to stay in Bata. I'm lucky to have work."

"We want to tour the GenSys facility," Jack said. "Do you think we'll have any trouble?"

"If they don't expect you, you may have trouble," Arturo replied. "The road to Cogo has a gate that is manned twenty-four hours a day by soldiers."

"I saw on a map that Cogo is on the water. What about arriving by boat?"

"I suppose," Arturo said. "You could rent a boat in Acalayong."

They were now passing through the center of Bata. The buildings were all low concrete structures. On the south side of town was the hotel, an unimposing two-story concrete building.

The proprietors—Esteban's brother and his wife—had prepared a huge feast. The main course was a local fish served with a turnip-like plant called malanga. An ample supply of ice-cold Cameroonian beer helped wash it all down.

The combination of plentiful food and beer took a toll on the exhausted travelers. With some effort they dragged themselves to their rooms, full of plans to rise early and head south.

BERTRAM climbed the stairs to Siegfried's office. He was exhausted. It was almost eight thirty at night, and he'd been up since five thirty that morning to accompany the animal handlers out to Isla Francesca to help get the mass retrieval under way.

Siegfried was by the window facing the square, a glass in his hand. The only light in the room was from the candle in the skull. Its flame flickered from the action of the overhead fan, sending shadows dancing across the stuffed animal trophies.

"Make yourself a drink," Siegfried said without turning around. He knew it was Bertram, since they'd made plans to meet.

Bertram poured himself a double Scotch and sipped the fiery fluid as he joined Siegfried at the window. The lights of the hospital-lab complex glowed warmly in the moist tropical night.

"What did you do with Raymond Lyons?" Bertram asked.

Siegfried gestured toward the hospital. "He's at the Inn."

"Has he asked about Kevin Marshall?"

"Of course," Siegfried said. "It was his first question."

"What did you say?"

"I told him Kevin had gone off with the reproductive technologist and the nurse and that I had no idea where he was."

"So they have not reappeared?"

"No. And not a word."

"What a mess," Bertram commented.

"How did you do on the island?" Siegfried asked.

"We did well, considering how fast we had to put the operation together."

"How many animals did you get to the staging area?"

"Twenty-one. We'll be able to finish up by tomorrow."

"I'm glad something is going right," Siegfried said.

"The animals we got today were part of the splinter group living north of the Rio Diviso. There was evidence of campfires."

"So it's good we're putting them in the cages," Siegfried said. "They won't be killing each other or playing with fire."

"That's one way to look at it," Bertram agreed.

"Any sign of Kevin and the women on the island?"

"Not in the slightest. But tomorrow we'll start retrievals near the limestone cliffs. I'll keep my eyes open for signs there."

"I doubt you'll find anything, but if they did go and they come back here, I'll turn them over to the minister of justice with the charge that they have severely compromised the GenSys operation. Of course, that means they'll be lined up in front of a firing squad before they know what hit them."

"Nothing like that could happen until Raymond and Mr. Winchester leave," Bertram said with alarm.

"Obviously," Siegfried said.

BEFORE dawn everyone met in the dining room. Jack reminded the others that going to Cogo wasn't a command performance. Those who preferred to stay in Bata should do so.

"You think you can make out on your own?" Esteban asked.

"Absolutely," Jack said. "I have a map."

"Then I'll stay," Esteban said. "I have more family to see."

By the time they were on the road in the rented van, with Warren in the front passenger seat and the two women in the middle seat, the eastern sky was just beginning to show a faint glow.

Two hours later they turned onto the road that led to Cogo. After passing through low, jungle-covered mountains, Warren consulted the map and said they were within twenty miles of their destination. Rounding another turn, they saw what looked like a white building in the middle of the road.

"I think it's the gate," Jack said. "Keep your fingers crossed."

Jack stopped the van about twenty feet from the fence. Out of the gatehouse stepped three soldiers carrying assault rifles.

"I don't like this," Warren said. "These guys look like kids."

"Stay cool." Jack rolled his window down. "Hi, guys."

The soldiers' blank expressions didn't change.

A fourth man stepped out into the sunlight, pulling on a black suit jacket over a white shirt and tie. The man looked like an Arab. "Can I help you?" he asked. His tone was not friendly.

"I hope so," Jack said. "We're here to visit Cogo."

The Arab asked Jack if he had a pass.

"No pass," Jack admitted. "We're just a couple of doctors interested in the work that's going on here."

"What is your name?" the Arab asked.

"Dr. Jack Stapleton. I've come from New York City."

"Just a minute." The Arab disappeared into the gatehouse.

"This doesn't look good," Jack said.

A few minutes later the Arab returned. "The manager says that he does not know you and that you are not welcome."

"Shucks," Jack said. With a sigh of resignation he did a three-point turn and headed back the way they'd come.

"Phew!" Laurie said. "I did not like that one bit."

"What now?" Warren asked.

Jack explained about his idea of approaching Cogo by boat. He had Warren look at the map to estimate how long it would take to get to Acalayong.

"I'd say three hours," Warren said.

Jack glanced at his watch. It was almost nine a.m. "I'd judge we could get from Acalayong to Cogo in an hour, even in the world's slowest boat. Say we stay in Cogo for a couple hours. I think we'd get back at a reasonable hour. What do you guys say?"

"Soldiers with assault rifles worry me," Laurie said, "but I think I'll be more worried if you go by yourself. Count me in."

"I'm cool," Warren said.

"Natalie?" Jack said. "Don't be influenced by these crazies."

"I'll go," Natalie said. "I'm finding it all interesting."

SIEGFRIED was mystified. The Cogo operation had been running for six years and never had they had someone come to the gatehouse and request entrance. This abnormal event was particularly unwelcome coming when there was a problem with the bonobos. Until that was taken care of, he didn't want any stray people around.

Aurielo poked his head in the door and said that Dr. Lyons wished to see him. Siegfried rolled his eyes. "Send him in."

Raymond came into the room, looking as tan and healthy as ever. "Have you located Kevin Marshall yet?" he demanded.

"No, we haven't," Siegfried said.

"I understand it's been forty-eight hours since he's been seen. I want him found!"

"Sit down, Doctor!" Siegfried said sharply.

Raymond hesitated.

"I said sit!"

Raymond sat.

"I do not take orders from you," Siegfried said. "When you are here as a guest, you take orders from me. Is that understood?"

Raymond opened his mouth to protest but thought better of it. "Of course. But please locate Kevin Marshall. I'm afraid he might have gone to the island."

"We don't think so. But even if he did, he would have been back by now. We'll continue to search."

Raymond sighed. "Worrying about him is driving me up the wall. It's just something else in a long string of problems going on back home that have made my life miserable."

Siegfried watched with satisfaction as the doctor turned meek. Then he remembered that Raymond was from New York. "Do you happen to know a doctor by the name of Jack Stapleton?"

The blood drained from Raymond's face.

"Just before you arrived, I got a call from our gatehouse," Siegfried said. "The Moroccan guard told me that there was a van full of people who wanted to tour the facility. The van was driven by Dr. Jack Stapleton of New York City."

Raymond wiped the perspiration that had appeared on his forehead. He kept telling himself that this couldn't be happening, since Vinnie Dominick was supposed to have taken care of Stapleton and Laurie Montgomery.

"You didn't let Stapleton and his friends in?" Raymond asked.

"No, of course not."

"Maybe you should have. Jack Stapleton is a very big danger to the program. I mean, is there a way here in the Zone to take care of such people?"

"There is," Siegfried said.

"Then if they come back, let them in."

"Perhaps you should tell me why," Siegfried said.

"Do you remember Carlo Franconi?" Raymond asked.

"Carlo Franconi the patient? Of course."

"Well, it started with him," Raymond said as he began the complicated story.

"YOU think it is safe?" Laurie was looking at a huge hollowed-out log canoe with a thatched canopy that was pulled halfway up the beach at Acalayong. On the back was a beat-up outboard motor.

"Reportedly it goes all the way to Gabon twice a day," Jack said. "That's further than Cogo. So let's get the show on the road. Unless you guys want to back out."

There was silence while the group eyed each other.

"I'm not a great swimmer," Warren admitted.

"We are not planning on going into the water," Jack said.

"All right," Warren said. "Let's go."

With the women seated in the stern, Jack and Warren pushed the heavy pirogue off the shore and jumped in. Everyone helped paddle out about fifty feet. To Jack's surprise the engine started after only two pulls. A moment later they were off, motoring almost due east. Crossing the two-mile-wide mouth of Rio Congue, they saw that the jungle-covered shorelines were hazy with mist—two thunderstorms had hit while they were in the van. After only twenty minutes they rounded a headland and saw Cogo's pier. Jack cut the engine as the town approached.

"Do you think that large building is the hospital?" Laurie asked.

Jack followed her gaze. "Yup, according to Arturo, and he should know. He was part of the initial building crew."

"I suppose that's our destination," Laurie said.

"Uh-oh. I see a soldier," Natalie said.

"I see him too." Jack's eyes had been searching the waterfront.

The soldier was aimlessly pacing a cobblestoned square at the base of the pier with an assault rifle slung over his shoulder.

"Obviously, he's where he is to interdict people coming off the pier," Jack said. "But look at that Chickee Hut on the beach. If we got in there, we'd be home free."

"He'd see if we ran the canoe onto the beach," Laurie said.

"Look how high that pier is," Jack said. "What if we were to slip underneath it, beach the canoe, and then walk to the Chickee Hut?"

"Sounds cool," Warren said.

Jack angled the boat so that the pier shielded them as much as possible from the line of sight from the square. He cut the engine just at the moment they glided under the pier. Grasping the timbers, they all guided the boat to shore. It scraped to a stop.

"So far so good," Jack said. He and Warren pulled the boat high on the beach. "Let's head for the Chickee Hut."

A few minutes later they were all in the deserted bar. Either the soldier hadn't seen them or he didn't care.

They headed out into the sunlight. After a short walk up a hot cobblestoned street they came to the treelined town square.

A group of soldiers lolled in front of the town hall across from where they were standing. "Whoa," Jack said. "No need to go over and announce ourselves. This is the hospital in front of us."

From the corner of the square the building appeared to take up most of the block. There was an entrance facing the square, but they went to the side entrance down the street to their left to avoid the lounging soldiers.

"What are you going to say if we're questioned?" Laurie asked.

"I'm going to improvise," Jack said.

After entering the building, everyone shivered with delight. Never had air-conditioning felt quite so good. The room they found themselves in appeared to be a lounge, complete with club chairs and couches. Behind sliding glass panels in the back wall, a black woman in a blue uniform was sitting at a desk.

Jack rapped softly on the glass. The woman slid it open. "Sorry," she said. "Are you checking in?"

"No," Jack said. "All my bodily functions are working fine."

"Excuse me?" the woman questioned.

"We're here to see the hospital, not use its services," Jack said. "We're doctors."

"This isn't the hospital," the woman said. "This is the Inn. You can either go out and come in the front of the building or follow the hall to your right. The hospital is beyond the double doors."

"Thank you," Jack said.

The woman watched as they disappeared, then picked up her phone.

Jack led the others through the double doors. Immediately the surroundings looked more familiar. The floors were vinyl, and the walls were hospital green. A faint antiseptic smell was detectable.

At a glass-fronted information cubbyhole, Jack again knocked on the glass. Another woman slid open the partition.

"We have a question," Jack said. "We're doctors, and we'd like to know if there are any transplant patients in the hospital."

"Yes, of course," the woman said, looking confused. "Horace Winchester. He's in three oh two, ready to be discharged."

"How convenient," Jack said. "What organ was transplanted?"

"His liver," she said. "Are you from the Pittsburgh group?"

"No. We're part of the New York group," Jack said.

He thanked the woman as he herded the others toward the elevators to the right. "Luck is finally going our way," he said excitedly. "Maybe all we have to do is drop in on Horace and get the low-down from the horse's mouth."

CAMERON McIvers was accustomed to false alarms. After all, most of the time he or the security office was called, it was a false alarm. Accordingly, as he entered the Inn, he was not concerned. But it was his job to check out all potential problems.

He tapped on the glass, and it was slid open. "Miss Williams," he said, touching the brim of his hat in a form of salute. Cameron wore a khaki uniform with an Aussie hat when on duty. There was also a holstered Beretta and a two-way radio at his side.

"They went that way," Corrina Williams said excitedly. She lifted herself out of her chair to point around the corner.

"Calm down," Cameron said. "Who are you talking about?"

"They didn't give any names. There were four of them. Only one spoke. He said he was a doctor. Two were black, and two were white. But I could tell from the way they were dressed they were American."

"I see," Cameron said. "Could I use your phone?"

"Of course." Corrina faced the phone out toward him.

Cameron called Siegfried and apprised him of the story. Siegfried's response was an angry tirade. Cameron was to get reinforcements over there immediately. Cameron handed the phone back, unsnapped the holster straps over his Beretta and his two-way radio, and made an emergency call to base.

ROOM 302 turned out to be empty, although there was plenty of evidence it was occupied. The television was on. The bed was disheveled. An open suitcase was poised on a luggage stand.

Laurie noticed the sounds of a shower behind the closed bathroom door. Jack knocked, but it wasn't until almost ten minutes later that Horace Winchester appeared.

The patient was in his mid-fifties and corpulent. But he looked happy and healthy. He padded over to a chair and sat down. "What's the occasion?" he asked, smiling at his guests. "This is more company than I've had the whole time I've been here."

"How are you feeling?" Jack grabbed a chair and sat down in front of Horace. Warren and Natalie, ill at ease, lurked just outside the door. Laurie went to the window. She was eager to make the visit short and get back to the boat.

"I'm feeling great," Horace said. "It's a miracle. I came here at death's door and as yellow as a canary. Now I'm ready for thirty-six holes of golf at one of my resorts. Hey, you people are invited to any of my places, and it will be on the house. Do you ski?"

"I do," Jack said. "But I'd rather talk about your case. You had a liver transplant here. I'd like to ask where the liver came from."

A half smile puckered Horace's face. "Is this some kind of test? Because if it is, it's not necessary. I'm not going to be telling anyone. I couldn't be more grateful. In fact, as soon as I can, I'm going to have another double made."

"Exactly what do you mean by a double?" Jack asked.

"Are you people part of the Pittsburgh team?"

"No. We're part of the New York team. And we're fascinated by your case. Why don't you start from the beginning?"

"You mean how I got sick?"

"No, how you arranged to have your transplant here in Africa," Jack said. "And I'd like to know what you mean by a double. Did you by any chance get a liver taken from some kind of ape?"

Horace gave a little nervous laugh. "What's going on here?"

"Uh-oh," Laurie suddenly voiced. "There's a bunch of soldiers running this way across the square."

Warren crossed the room and looked out. "They mean business."

Jack stood up and grasped Horace by the shoulders. He leaned his face close. "What kind of animal was it, a chimpanzee?"

"They're coming to the hospital," Warren yelled.

"Come on." Jack gave Horace a little shake. "Talk to me."

"It was a bonobo," Horace squeaked. He was terrified.

"We got to get out of here!" Warren was back at the door.

"And what did you mean by a double?" Jack asked.

Laurie grabbed Jack's arm. Reluctantly he let go of Horace and allowed himself to be dragged to the door.

Warren was waving frantically for them to follow him and Natalie. They ran all the way down through a set of doors, then skidded to a stop where the corridor formed a T. Warren looked left. At the far end was a fire alarm. Above it was an exit sign.

"Hold up," Jack said.

"What's the matter, man?" Warren questioned anxiously.

"This looks like a laboratory." Jack stepped over to a glazed door and looked inside. It was the most modern lab he'd ever seen.

"Come on!" Laurie snapped. "There's no time for curiosity."

"You guys go," Jack said distractedly. "We'll meet at the boat."

Warren, Laurie, and Natalie exchanged anxious glances.

The door was unlocked. Jack opened it and walked inside.

"You ladies go talk some sense into that man," Warren said. "I'm going to run down the hall and pull the fire alarm."

"What on earth for?" Laurie asked.

"It's an old trick I learned as a teenager," Warren said. "Whenever there's trouble, cause as much chaos as you can. It gives you a chance to slip away."

Laurie and Natalie entered the lab. They found Jack engaged in pleasant conversation with a technician wearing a white coat.

"Excuse me, Jack." Laurie struggled to keep her voice down.

"Laurie, meet Rolanda," Jack said. "She and her colleagues are working on the genes for minor histocompatibility antigens. They're moving them from a specific chromosome in one cell and sticking them into the same location in another cell."

Natalie, who'd walked to a large picture window overlooking the square, hastily turned back into the room. "It's getting worse. An entire carload of those Arabs in black suits are arriving."

At that moment the fire alarm in the building went off. It was followed by a disembodied voice: "Fire in the laboratory. Please proceed immediately to stairwells for evacuation."

Laurie grabbed Jack by both arms and shook him. "Jack, be reasonable. We have to get out of here."

"I've figured it out," Jack said with a wry smile.

"I don't give a damn," Laurie spat. "Come on."

They rushed out into the hall. Other people were appearing as well. Many were carrying their laptop computers. As they moved to the stairwell, Jack, Laurie, and Natalie met up with Warren.

"They have created some kind of chimera with these bonobos," Jack said. "No wonder the DNA tests were screwy."

"What's he carrying on about now?" Warren asked.

"Don't ask," Laurie said. "It will only encourage him."

The stairwell opened up into a parking lot. People were milling about, looking back at the building. A fire siren wailed.

"What should we do?" Laurie asked.

"Let's walk over to the street and turn left," Jack said. "We can circle around and get back to the waterfront."

They tried not to rush, to avoid attracting attention. No one even looked in their direction.

"So far so good," Jack said.

Warren was the first to reach the street. As he got a look around the corner, he stopped abruptly. "We're not going that way. They've got a roadblock at the end."

"Uh-oh," Laurie said. "Maybe they've sealed off the area."

"We've got to do something," Warren said. "The fire crew are already waving the people to come back in the building. We're going to be standing out here in this god-awful heat by ourselves."

"Let's cross the square before the soldiers return," Jack said.

Once again they tried to walk calmly. They got almost to the square, when they became aware of a commotion at the hospital door. They all turned to see Cameron and Siegfried come out. Cameron spotted the group and pointed. "That's them!" he yelled.

The soldiers immediately surrounded the trespassers. Every gun was pointed at them. Cameron and Siegfried walked over.

"We'd like to apologize for any inconvenience," Jack began.

"Shut up!" Siegfried snapped. "Search them."

Cameron quickly relieved Jack and the others of their passports, wallets, and car keys. Siegfried glowered at Jack. "I've been told you are a troublemaker."

"I'd rather think of myself as a tenacious competitor," Jack said.

"Ah, arrogant as well," Siegfried snarled. "I hope your tenacity comes in handy with the Equatorial Guinean military."

"Perhaps we can call the American embassy and resolve this," Jack said. "We are, after all, government employees."

Siegfried smiled, which only increased his scar-induced sneer. "American embassy? In Cogo? What a joke!" He turned to Cameron. "Put them in the jail."

CHAPTER 8

OMETHING very strange is going on," Kevin said.

"But what?" Melanie said. "Should we get our hopes up?"

"Where could all the other animals be?" Candace questioned.

Kevin and the women had been prisoners for over two days. They had not been allowed to leave the small cave the entire time. The tunnel now reeked like a mini-cesspool, and they were filthy from sleeping on the dirt floor.

Around ten o'clock that morning the animals had become agitated. Some had rushed out, only to return moments later making loud cries. Bonobo number one had gone out but had yet to return.

"Wait," Kevin said suddenly. "I thought I heard a voice."

"I just heard it," Melanie said. "It sounded like someone yelling 'Okay.' "

"Arthur heard it too," Kevin said. They'd named the bonobo

who often stood guard Arthur. Over the long hours they'd had what could be called a dialogue. They'd even been able to guess at some of the meanings of the bonobo words and gestures.

They were most sure of "arak," which meant "away," accompanied by the spreading of fingers and a sweeping arm motion. There was also "hana" for "quiet" and "zit" for "go." "Sta," accompanied by holding up one's hands with palms out, they thought might be "you."

Arthur stood up and loudly vocalized to the few bonobos remaining in the cave. They immediately disappeared out the front.

The next thing Kevin and the others heard were several reports from an air gun. A few minutes later two figures in animal-center coveralls appeared, silhouetted at the cave's entrance. One was carrying the gun; the other, a battery-powered lamp.

"Help!" Melanie shouted, waving frantically.

A loud thump echoed through the cave. Arthur let out a whimper. With a confused expression he looked at a red-tailed dart that protruded from his chest. Slowly he sagged to the floor.

Kevin, Melanie, and Candace emerged from their doorless cell.

"Are we glad to see you," Melanie said. "I'm Melanie Becket, and this is Kevin Marshall and Candace Brickmann."

"I know who you are," the man with the lamp said. "Let's get out of this hole."

Kevin and the women were happy to comply. Once out of the cave, the three friends had to squint in the hazy sunlight. Below the face of the cliff a half-dozen more animal handlers were rolling up tranquilized bonobos in reed mats and lifting them onto a trailer.

"There's one more up here," the man with the light yelled.

"I know you," Melanie said. "You're Dave Turner."

The man ignored Melanie. He pulled a two-way radio out of a holder at his waist. "Turner to base," he said into the instrument.

"I hear you loud and clear," Bertram said on the other end.

"We found Kevin Marshall and the two women in a cave."

"In what state?" Bertram asked.

"Filthy but otherwise apparently healthy. What do you want me to do with them?"

"Bring them in," Bertram said. "I'll inform Siegfried Spallek."

"Ten-four." Dave snapped off the radio.

"What's the meaning of this kind of treatment?" Melanie demanded. "We've been prisoners out here for two days."

Dave shrugged. "We just follow orders, ma'am. It seems you've riled up the front office big time."

"What on earth is happening to the bonobos?" Kevin asked.

"The bonobos' good life on the island is a thing of the past," Dave said. "They've been warring out here. So we're taking them all to the animal center. It'll be six-foot cells from now on."

Kevin's mouth fell open. In spite of his exhaustion, he felt a profound sadness for these unfortunate creatures who'd suddenly and arbitrarily been doomed to monotonous incarceration.

"All right, you three," Dave said. "Let's start back."

The climb down the rockface was the hardest part of the trip. Once on the flat, the walking was easy. Still, on the last mile to the staging area their legs felt like lead.

They emerged from the twilight of the jungle into the bustling staging area in the clearing. Another half-dozen blue-coveralled workers were unloading bonobos into individual cages before the animals revived. The cages were four-foot-square steel boxes, making it impossible for all but the youngest animals to stand up. Such small cages were supposed to be used only for transport, but a forklift was laboriously moving them into the shade of the jungle.

"I thought you said the bonobos were going to the animal center?" Kevin asked.

"Not today," Dave said. "Tomorrow or the next day."

The steel telescoping bridge had a hollow, drumlike sound as they trod across it. Parked alongside the bridge mechanism was Dave's pickup truck. "Hop in." He pointed into the truck's bed.

After the oppressiveness of the cave and the moist hothouse of the jungle, the breezy ride in the back of the truck was unexpectedly pleasant. The bed was filled with reed mats that had transported the animals, and they provided adequate cushioning.

Dave drove the truck to Kevin's house. Siegfried and Cameron were standing in front, along with four soldiers. Dave put down the tailgate. Kevin and Melanie climbed out. Candace followed.

"We had hoped you'd taken an unannounced holiday," Siegfried said scornfully. "Instead we find you have trespassed on Isla Francesca. You're all to be confined to quarters in this house."

Kevin was about to explain why they'd done what they had when Melanie pushed past him. "I'm not staying here, and that's final. In fact, I'll be leaving the Zone as soon as I can make arrangements."

Siegfried's upper lip hiked itself up. After a quick step forward, he backhanded Melanie viciously, knocking her down. Reflexively Candace dropped to one knee to aid her friend.

"Don't touch her," Siegfried shouted.

Candace ignored him and helped Melanie to her feet. A trickle of blood slowly ran down her cheek.

"You'll be leaving the Zone soon enough," Siegfried snarled at the sobbing Melanie. "But it will be in the company of the Equatorial Guinean authorities. You can try your insolence on them." He stepped back. "I've confiscated your passports. They will be given to the local authorities along with your persons. In the meantime, these soldiers have been ordered to shoot if you so much as take one step outside this house. Have I made myself clear?"

"I need some clothes," Melanie cried.

"I've had clothes brought from your quarters," Siegfried said.

"Okay, you've heard the manager," Cameron barked. "Upstairs, and no trouble, please."

As Kevin wearily climbed to the second floor, he saw Cameron organizing an area for the soldiers at the base of the stairs. Up in the front hall, he, Melanie, and Candace eyed each other.

Kevin breathed out. "This is not good news."

"They can't do this to us," Melanie whimpered.

Kevin sighed. "At least they didn't put us in the jail."

Outside they heard car engines start. Kevin went to the phone.

"Is there a dial tone?" Melanie asked.

"I'm afraid not." Kevin replaced the receiver.

"Let's take showers," Candace suggested.

"Good idea." Melanie made an effort to sound positive.

Kevin walked into the kitchen. The smell of roast chicken teased his nose. "Welcome, Mr. Marshall," Esmeralda said.

"Hello, Esmeralda," he said. "You didn't come out to greet us like you always do."

"I was afraid the manager was still here. He and the security man had come up earlier to say you were coming home and that you would not be able to leave the house."

"That's what they told me too."

"I've made food for you. Are you hungry?"

"Very much," Kevin said. "But there are two guests."

"I know," Esmeralda said. "The manager told me that as well." She hesitated. "There are many bad things happening in the town. Not only for you but also for strangers. My cousin who works at the hospital told me that four Americans from New York came and talked with the patient who got the liver from the bonobo."

"Oh?" Kevin questioned.

"They just walked in. They said they were doctors. The army came to take them away. They are in the jail."

"My word!" Kevin commented. New York reminded him of the surprising call he'd gotten a week previously about the patient Carlo Franconi, who'd been killed in New York.

"My cousin knows some of the soldiers," Esmeralda continued. "They said that the Americans will be killed."

Kevin felt a chill descend his spine. He knew such a fate was what Siegfried had in mind for him, Melanie, and Candace. But who were these Americans? Had they been involved with the autopsy on Carlo Franconi?

After a shave, shower, and clean clothes, Kevin felt revived. He found the two women equally refreshed. They settled in the dining room, and Esmeralda began serving the meal.

Melanie said, "A few hours ago we were living like Neanderthals. Now, presto, we're in the lap of luxury. It's like a time machine."

"If only we didn't have to worry about what tomorrow will bring," Candace said.

"Let's at least enjoy our last supper," Melanie said with her typical wry humor. "Besides, the more I think about it—"

"Excuse me," Kevin interrupted. "Esmeralda told me something curious." He told them about the New Yorkers in the town's jail.

"The world's getting smaller every day," Melanie said. "A couple people do an autopsy in New York, and they end up in Cogo."

"So you think these Americans came here following a trail that started with Franconi?" Kevin asked.

"What else could it be?" Melanie questioned. Twirling her empty wineglass, she looked at Kevin. "Where's some of that great wine of yours, bucko?"

"Gosh, I totally forgot," Kevin said. "Sorry." He pushed back from the table and went into the butler's pantry. As he was looking through the labels, he was suddenly struck by how much wine he had—more than three hundred bottles.

"My word," Kevin said. He grabbed an armload of bottles and pushed through the swinging door into the kitchen.

Esmeralda got up from her dinner. "I have a favor to ask," Kevin said. "Would you take these bottles of wine and a corkscrew down to the soldiers at the foot of the stairs?"

"So many?" she questioned.

"Yes, and I'd like you to take even more to the soldiers in the town hall. Tell them that I'm going away, and I wanted them to enjoy the wine, not the manager."

A smile spread across Esmeralda's face. "I think I understand." From a cupboard she got a canvas bag and loaded it with wine bottles. A moment later she headed for the front hall.

Kevin made several trips back and forth to the kitchen table. Soon he had several dozen bottles lined up. "What's going on?" Melanie inquired, sticking her head into the kitchen. Kevin handed her one of the bottles. "Oh, my, Château Latour," she said, ducking back into the dining room.

Esmeralda returned to say that the soldiers were very pleased. "But I thought I'd take them some bread," she added. "It will stimulate their thirst."

"Marvelous idea." Kevin filled the canvas bag with wine. "Let me know how many soldiers are at the town hall. We want to make sure there is plenty for everyone."

"There are usually four at night," Esmeralda said.

"Then ten bottles should be fine. At least for starters."

KEVIN rolled over and looked at the clock. It was just before midnight. He turned off the alarm, which had been set to go off at twelve p.m. He was too keyed up to sleep. There was also the problem of the drunken singing from the soldiers below.

Kevin dressed quickly in the dark, then knocked on Melanie's door. It was opened instantly.

"I've been waiting," Melanie whispered. "I couldn't sleep."

Together they went to Candace's room. She too was ready.

Out on the veranda, the sky was filled with puffy silver-blue clouds. A gibbous moon was high in the sky, and the jungle sounds were shockingly loud in the hot, moist air.

At the far corner of the veranda they secured one end of three sheets that had been tied together and dropped the other end over the side. They had no trouble making it down to the cobblestones.

In single file they inched along the back of the house in the shadow of its arcade. Each step took them closer to the central stairwell, where they could hear the soldiers. A cassette recorder playing African music had been added to the festivities.

They reached Kevin's Land Cruiser. He quietly opened the driver's-side door, released the emergency brake, and put the car in neutral. Returning to the women, he motioned to start pushing. They eased the car across the alley toward the hill down to the waterfront. Then Kevin dived in behind the wheel and jammed on the brakes.

The passenger-side door opened, and Melanie climbed in. Candace got into the back. Kevin eased up on the brake. The car gathered speed, and they rolled for two blocks until the hill flattened out. Only then did Kevin slip his key into the ignition, put the car in gear, and head for the town hall.

As they neared the town hall, Kevin doused the headlights. The room occupied by the army post was ablaze with light. As they got closer, they could hear the music. This group of soldiers also had a cassette player cranking out African music at full volume.

"That's the kind of party I was counting on." Kevin turned the car and backed up. He could just make out the window wells of the jail in the shadows of the arcade. He stopped within five feet of the building, and all three gazed into the room occupied by the soldiers. They couldn't see much—their line of sight was at an angle through the window. A number of empty wine bottles were on the sill.

"Well, it's now or never." Kevin climbed from the car and walked in under the nearest arch. The music was deafening. Looking down at the window well, he could see the barred opening. Beyond the bars was utter darkness. He lay on the stone floor with his face close to the bars. "Hello!" he called out. "Anybody in there?"

"Just us tourists," Jack said. "Are we invited to the party?"

"I understand you are Americans," Kevin said.

"Like apple pie and baseball," Jack said.

"Do you realize what a dangerous situation you've gotten into?"

"We thought this was how all visitors to Cogo were treated."

Kevin thought that whomever he was speaking with would certainly get along well with Melanie. "I'm going to try to pull these bars out," he said. "Are you all in the same cell?"

"No. We have two beautiful ladies in the cell to my left."

"Okay. Let's see what I can do." Kevin got up and went back for the Land Cruiser's tow chain. Returning to the window well, he hooked one end of the chain around one of the bars. Back at the Toyota, he secured the chain to the trailer hitch. He climbed into the vehicle and eased it forward to take the slack out of the chain.

"All right, here we go," he said to Melanie and Candace. He began to press on the accelerator. Suddenly the vehicle lurched forward. Hastily Kevin braked. Behind them they heard a terrible clanging. They looked back at the opening into the army post. To their relief no one appeared to check out the awful sound.

Kevin jumped out to see what had happened. He almost ran into an impressively muscled black man headed right for him.

"Good job, man. My name's Warren, and this is Jack." Jack had come up alongside Warren.

"I'm Kevin."

"Cool," Warren said. "You back these wheels up, and we'll see what we can do with the other opening."

Kevin climbed into the car and slowly backed up. He could see the two men had already detached the chain. A moment later they waved him forward. With the same amount of power there was the same sudden release and the same clanging noise.

Kevin detached the chain in time to see two women being extracted from the second window well. As soon as they were free, all four rushed for the car and climbed in. Jack and Warren squeezed into the jump seats in the back, while Laurie and Natalie joined Candace on the middle bench. Kevin put the car in gear and drove from the parking lot.

The escape had been a heady experience for everyone. After introductions the questions started. Everyone spoke at the same time.

"Wait a second," Kevin said. "We've got to talk about getting out of this town. How did you people plan on leaving?"

"By the same boat we came in on," Jack said.

"Where's the boat?" Kevin asked.

"We assume it's where we left it," Jack said. "Under the pier."

"Is it big enough for all of us?" Kevin asked.

"With room to spare," Jack said.

"Perfect," Kevin said. "Let's just pray it's not been found."

"We have a problem," Jack said. "We have no identification or money. Everything was taken from us."

"We have some money," Kevin said. "But our passports were confiscated when we were put under house arrest this afternoon. Did you people come here because of Carlo Franconi?"

"Whoa!" Jack said. "Such clairvoyance! How did you guess? What exactly is your role here in Cogo?"

"I'm a molecular biologist," Kevin explained with a sigh of regret. "One who overstepped his bounds. I stumbled on the way to move chromosome parts from one species to another."

"And what you were really doing," Jack said, "was custom-designing the perfect organ transplant source."

"Exactly. But I transferred too many human genes and accidentally created a race of protohumans intelligent enough to use fire, make tools, and even converse."

"Where are these creatures?" Laurie asked with alarm.

"They're on a nearby island," Kevin said, "where they have been living in comparative freedom. Unfortunately, that's about to change." He quickly related the creatures' fate of facing lifelong internment in tiny cells purely because they were too human.

"That's awful," Laurie commented.

"We're coming up on the pier," Kevin announced.

"Then stop," Jack said. "A soldier was there when we arrived."

Kevin pulled over to the side of the road. Jack and Warren got out, ran down to the corner, and disappeared. They reappeared in a surprisingly short time. Jack was holding a handgun, and Warren was carrying an assault rifle. They got into the back of the Toyota.

"Any problem?" Kevin asked.

"Nope," Jack said. "He was very accommodating. Of course, Warren can be very persuasive when he wants to be."

Kevin backed to an asphalt parking lot. Beyond the darkened Chickee Hut Bar the estuary shimmered in the moonlight.

"You all wait here," Warren said. "I'll check the boat." He climbed out with the rifle and disappeared around the bar.

"Gabon is about four miles straight across the water," Kevin said. "But we should try to get to Cocobeach, ten miles away. From there we can contact the American embassy in Libreville."

Warren reappeared. "We're cool," he said.

"Hooray," everybody replied in unison, piling out of the car.

It was dark beneath the pier, and Jack literally bumped into the pirogue. He pushed it out; then everyone climbed aboard. Reaching for the wood pilings, they pulled the boat silently along to the end of the pier. At that point they paddled out into open water.

Everyone looked back at peaceful-appearing Cogo, its white-washed buildings, shrouded in mist, glimmering in the silver moonlight. The surrounding jungle limned the town with midnight blue.

The night sounds of the jungle fell astern. Soon the only noise was the gurgle of the paddles passing through the water. For a time no one spoke. Racing hearts slowed, and there was time to think and even look around. The newcomers were captivated by the arresting beauty of the nocturnal African landscape.

After a while Jack dropped his paddle to the bottom of the boat. "Time to start the engine." He tilted the outboard into the water.

"Wait a second," Kevin said suddenly. "I have a request. Something I have no right to ask, but it is important."

"What's on your mind, sport?" Jack asked.

"See that island, the last one in the chain? That's where all the bonobos are. They're in cages at the foot of a bridge to the mainland. I'd like to go over there and release them."

"What would that accomplish?" Laurie asked.

"A lot if I could get them to cross the bridge."

"Wouldn't your Cogo friends round them up?" Jack asked.

"They'd never find them. From this part of Equatorial Guinea and stretching a thousand miles inland is virginal rain forest, parts of which are still unexplored."

"Just let them go by themselves?" Candace asked.

"That's exactly the point," Kevin said. "They'd have a chance, and I think they'd make it. They're resourceful."

Laurie looked at Jack. "I like the idea."

"We'd be going out of our way," Kevin admitted, "but not far."

"Hey, why not?" Jack said. "What does everybody else say?"

"Tell the truth, I'd like to see these animals," Warren said.

"Okay by me," Natalie said.

"I couldn't think of a better idea," Melanie said. "Let's do it."

Jack gave the engine cord a few pulls. The outboard roared to life. Pushing over the helm, Jack steered toward Isla Francesca.

SIEGFRIED woke up to the sound of loud West African rock music. He looked at the clock. It was close to two a.m. He got out of bed and stepped onto the veranda. To his surprise and dismay the music was coming from Kevin Marshall's. In fact, Siegfried could see who was responsible: It was the soldiers guarding the house.

Anger coursed through Siegfried's body like a bolt of electricity. He called Cameron McIvers, then pulled on his clothes and grabbed one of his old hunting carbines.

KEVIN motioned for Jack to slow down. Jack cut back on the throttle as the heavy pirogue entered the narrow channel between Isla Francesca and the mainland. The dense jungle on the right fell away as they reached the island's staging area.

"Oh, no," Kevin cried. "The bridge is not deployed."

"That shouldn't be a problem," Melanie said. "I still have the key. I had a feeling it would come in handy someday."

"Oh, Melanie!" Kevin gushed. "You're wonderful."

"A deployable bridge that needs a key?" Jack questioned. "That's mighty sophisticated for out here in the jungle."

"There's a dock to our right," Kevin said. "That's where we'll tie up." They quietly bumped against wood planking.

"Okay, everybody." Kevin took a breath. "Here's what I suggest. You all stay in the boat for now. I don't know how these animals are going to react to me, but I don't want to put any of you in jeopardy."

Melanie stood up and climbed onto the dock. "I'm helping whether you like it or not."

Kevin joined her. "We'll work quickly," he promised the others.

The first line of business was the bridge. As Kevin put in the key and pressed the button, he held his breath. Almost immediately he heard the whine of a battery-driven electric motor from the mainland side. Then in slow motion the telescoping bridge extended across the dark river to make contact with the concrete stanchion on the island.

Kevin climbed up on it to make sure it was solidly seated. Satisfied, he got down, and he and Melanie hiked in the direction of the forest. They couldn't see the cages, but they knew where they were. "Do you have any plan, or are we just going to let them all out en masse?" Melanie asked as they walked across the field.

"The only idea that came to my mind was to find my double,

bonobo number one," Kevin said. "Unlike me, he's a leader. If I can make him understand, maybe he'll take the others."

The cages were lined up in a row. As Kevin and Melanie walked along, Kevin shined the flashlight into each enclosure. The animals awoke immediately. Some backed against the rear wall; others stood their ground, their eyes flashing red.

"How are you going to recognize him?" Melanie asked.

"I wish I could count on seeing my watch," Kevin said. "I suppose it's up to recognizing that scar of his. My gosh, look!" The light illuminated bonobo number one's scarred face. He stared back defiantly.

"Bada." Kevin patted his chest as the bonobo females had done when he, Melanie, and Candace were first brought to the cave.

Bonobo number one tilted his head, and the skin between his eyes furrowed.

"Bada," Kevin repeated.

Slowly the bonobo raised his hand and patted his chest. Then he said "Bada" as clearly as Kevin had.

Kevin looked at Melanie. They were both shocked. Although they had tentatively conversed with Arthur, the bonobo guard at the cave, they'd never been sure they were actually communicating.

"Atah," Kevin said. It was a word they thought meant "come."

Bonobo number one didn't respond.

Kevin repeated the word. "I don't know what else to say."

"Let's go for it and open the door," Melanie said. "I mean, it is hard for him to come when he's locked up."

"Good point." With trepidation Kevin released the latch and opened the door. Bonobo number one emerged slowly and stood up to his full height. He looked at the two humans.

"Atah," Kevin said again, backing up. Bonobo number one started forward, and Kevin led him to the bridge.

Bonobo number one hesitantly climbed onto the stanchion. Kevin backed up until he was standing in the middle of the span. The bonobo came out onto the bridge warily, glancing from side to side.

"Sta zit arak." Kevin opened his fingers and swept his hand away from his chest. He hoped his sentence said, "You go away."

After repeating the phrase, Kevin pointed northeast in the direction of the limitless rain forest.

Bonobo number one rose up on the balls of his feet and looked over Kevin's shoulder. He then looked back in the direction of the cages. Spreading his arms, he vocalized a series of sounds.

"I think he's making reference to his people," Melanie said.

"Then let's let more of the animals out." Kevin left the bridge and set out for the cages. Bonobo number one immediately followed.

Kevin opened the door on the first cage while Melanie did the second. The animals emerged quickly and exchanged words with bonobo number one. Kevin and Melanie went to the next two cages. Within minutes a dozen animals milled about.

"It's working," Kevin said. "I'm sure of it. If they were just going to run into the forest here on the island, they would have already done so. I think they all know they have to leave."

"Maybe I should get Candace and our new friends," Melanie said. "They should witness this, and they can help speed things up." She ran off into the night.

By the time Kevin had released a half-dozen more animals, the humans arrived. At first they were intimidated by the creatures and didn't know how to act.

"They are so quiet," Laurie said. "It's spooky."

"They're depressed," Kevin said. "It could be from the tranquilizer or from having been imprisoned. But don't go too close."

"What can we do to help?" Candace asked.

"Just open the cage doors," Kevin said.

With seven people working, it took only a few minutes to get all the cages open. As soon as the last animal had emerged into the night, Kevin motioned for everyone to start toward the bridge.

Bonobo number one, who'd been shadowing Kevin, clapped his hands loudly, then vocalized raucously before starting after the humans. Immediately the rest of the bonobos followed.

The seven humans led the seventy-one transgenic bonobos in a procession across the clearing to the bridge of their freedom. Arriving at the span, the humans stepped aside.

"Sta zit arak," Kevin repeated as he spread his fingers and swept his hand away from his chest for the final time. Then he pointed toward the African interior.

Bonobo number one bowed his head momentarily. Looking out over his people, he vocalized for a final time before turning his back on Isla Francesca and crossing the bridge to the mainland. The mass of the bonobos silently followed. As if by magic, the animals melted into the dark jungle without a sound.

The humans didn't move or talk for a moment. Finally Kevin broke the silence. "They did it, and I'm pleased. Maybe now I can come to terms with what I did in creating them." He stepped up to the bridge and pressed the button. With a whine the bridge retracted. The group began to trudge back to the pirogue.

Halfway there, Melanie suddenly stopped and cried, "Oh, no! Look!" Everyone's eyes darted across the river in the direction she was pointing. Headlight beams could be intermittently seen through the foliage. Several vehicles were descending the track leading to the bridge.

"We can't get to the boat!" Warren blurted. "They'll see us."

"We can't stay here either," Jack said.

"Back to the cages!" Kevin cried.

They all turned and ran toward the jungle. The moment they ducked behind the cages, the headlight beams swept across the clearing. The vehicles stopped, but the headlights stayed on.

"It's a group of soldiers," Kevin said.

"And Siegfried," Melanie said. "I can recognize him anywhere. And that's Cameron McIvers's patrol car."

A searchlight played along the row of cages, then swept the riverbank. It quickly found the pirogue. A sudden burst of heavy gunfire shattered the night. An explosion rocked the air. "That must have been the gas tank," Kevin said. "So much for our transportation."

A few minutes later the searchlight went out. Then the first vehicle made a U-turn and disappeared back up the track. "What's happening?" Jack asked.

"My guess is Siegfried and Cameron are going back to town,"

Melanie said. "Knowing we're on the island, they probably feel pretty confident."

"Let's hope the soldiers are not planning on coming over here," Jack said.

"They won't come until dawn," Kevin said. "There's no way they'd come over here in the dark. Besides, there's no need."

"What are we going to do?" Laurie questioned despairingly.

"Listen," Kevin said. "The boat that Melanie, Candace, and I used to get here is most likely where we left it. It's going to require a little hike, but at least there's a freshly cleared trail."

"Sounds like a walk in the park," Jack said.

"We'd better start now," Kevin said.

The interior of the jungle was so dark, they didn't know whether their eyes were open or not. Kevin went first, making frequent wrong choices that required backtracking to find the trail.

When they finally deemed it safe to use flashlights, they made better progress. Still, by the time they reached the fields around Lago Hippo, the eastern horizon was beginning to lighten.

As the group neared the reeds where they hoped the small canoe was still hidden, they had to pass close by two particularly large hippos. The animals regarded them sleepily, until without warning they charged for the lake with a huge amount of commotion. For a moment everyone's heart fluttered in his chest.

The sky was now progressively brightening; they knew they had no time to lose. Kevin found the small canoe, but it was not big enough for seven people. After a difficult discussion it was decided that Jack and Warren would stay in the reeds and wait for Kevin to take the women to the motorized pirogue and bring the small canoe back.

Waiting was hell. Jack and Warren alternated between looking at each other and their watches while fighting off clouds of insatiable insects. Just when they were thinking that something terrible had happened, Kevin appeared like a mirage at the edge of the reeds.

"The powerboat's okay?" Jack asked anxiously.

"At least it was there," Kevin said. "We didn't try to start it."

Warren scrambled into the canoe, followed by Jack. They backed out of the reeds and started for the Rio Diviso. Unfortunately, there were lots of hippos and even a few crocodiles, forcing them to paddle twice the usual distance just to keep clear. Before they slipped into the foliage hiding the river, they caught a glimpse of soldiers entering the clearing in the distance.

"Do you think they saw us?" Jack asked from the bow.

"There's no way to know," Kevin said.

"We're getting out of here by the skin of our teeth," Jack said.

The waiting was as hard on the women as it had been on Jack and Warren. When the small canoe pulled alongside the pirogue, there were literal tears of relief. The final worry was the outboard motor. Jack pumped the gas, then with a little prayer, pulled the cord.

The engine sputtered and caught, loud in the morning stillness. Jack looked at Laurie. She smiled and gave him the thumbs-up sign.

Jack put the motor in gear, gave it a full throttle, and steered directly south, where they could see Gabon as a line of green along the horizon.

EPILOGUE

Lou Soldano flashed his police badge to get into customs and hoped he was not too late to greet the returning world travelers.

He made a half circuit of the Air France luggage carousel before seeing the group. He insinuated himself between other passengers and gave Laurie's arm a squeeze. She turned around indignantly, then gave him a hug so fierce, his face turned red.

"Okay, okay," Lou managed. He laughed. Laurie let him go so that he could give Jack and Warren a handshake. Lou gave Natalie a peck on the cheek.

"So, you guys have a good trip, or what?" Lou questioned.

"We had a fabulous trip," Laurie said. "The first part was a little harrowing, but we managed to survive that, and once we got to Gabon, we had a ball."

"Did you see any animals?" Lou asked.

"More than you could imagine," Laurie said.

The luggage came. They breezed through customs and passed through the terminal. Lou's unmarked car was at the curb. They put the luggage in the trunk and climbed in.

Lou drove out of the airport. "How about you?" Laurie asked. "Have you been making any headway back here?"

"Things have been going down like you wouldn't believe," Lou said. "It was that Spoletto Funeral Home that was the gold mine. Right now everybody is lining up to plea-bargain. I even got an indictment on Vinnie Dominick."

"What about the mole in the office?" Laurie asked.

"Solved. Vinnie Amendola has agreed to testify."

"So it *was* Vinnie."

"There was one unexpected twist," Lou said. "There was someone else mixed up in all this Franconi business who has taken us by surprise. He's apparently out of the country at the moment. His name is Dr. Raymond Lyons. Do either of you guys know him?"

"Never heard of him," Jack said.

"Nor I," Laurie said.

"Well, he had something to do with that organ transplant stuff you people were so interested in," Lou said. "But later for that. Right now I'd like to hear about the first part of your trip: the harrowing part."

"For that you'll have to buy us dinner," Laurie said. "It's kind of a long story."

ABOUT THE AUTHORS

BERNARD VIDAL

MARY HIGGINS CLARK

Mary Higgins Clark is often asked where she gets the ideas for her books. In the case of her latest novel she says, "I'd been thinking about doing something on the Witness Protection Program, but nothing had clicked yet." Then one evening at Rao's, a legendary New York City Italian bistro, one of the owners picked up a mike and began to sing an old Jerry Vale standard, "Pretend You Don't See Her." Clark said, "There's my next book! That's the title!" As for the singer, he won a heartfelt *"Grazie"* from the author.

DOUGLAS KENNEDY

SIGRID ESTRADA

Born and bred in New York City, Douglas Kennedy has been an expatriate since his 1976 graduation from Bowdoin College in Maine. Living first in Dublin and since 1988 in London, he's made a name for himself as a playwright, journalist, travel writer, and novelist. An inveterate adventurer, Kennedy favors journalistic assignments with exotic destinations—the Amazon, Cuba, and Tasmania being recent ports of call. *The Big Picture* is his first novel to be published in the United States.

DEBORAH SMITH

Deborah Smith describes herself as "a native Georgian from a long and colorful heritage"—not unlike her heroine in *A Place to Call Home.* In fact, she says, "I enjoy using that heritage for inspiration." The author of nearly two dozen books, Smith has won many awards, including the *Romantic Times*'s lifetime achievement award in 1988. A past president of the Georgia Romance Writers, Smith is married and lives in Dahlonega, in the hills of northern Georgia.

ROBIN COOK

Widely credited with inventing the medical thriller, eye surgeon Robin Cook gave up his private practice years ago to devote himself to writing. But he still keeps abreast of the latest scientific breakthroughs, which often turn up in his books. *Chromosome 6,* for example, grew out of up-to-the-minute experiments with cloning. Cook has written nineteen novels to date, many of which have appeared in Reader's Digest books. Many have also been adapted for the movies or television. Cook divides his time between Boston and Florida.

The volumes in this series are issued
every two to three months. A typical volume
contains four outstanding books in condensed
form. None of the selections in any volume has
appeared in *Reader's Digest* magazine. Any reader
may receive this service by writing to
The Reader's Digest Association (Canada) Ltd.,
215 Redfern Avenue, Westmount, Quebec H3Z 2V9
or by calling 1-888-459-5555.
You can also visit our Web site at
http://www.readersdigest.ca

Acknowledgments

Page 6: photo by Angelo Perrone.
Page 7: photo by Richard Hong.
Page 45: "Pretend You Don't See Her," words and music by Steve Allen. Copyright © 1957.
Revised 1966, 1985. Meadowlane Music, Inc. ASCAP.
Pages 146–147: Pete Turner/The Image Bank.
Pages 290–291: photo by William A. Bake; border design by Leo and Diane Dillon.
Pages 295, 312, 327, 339, 355, 372, 382, 394, 407, and 415:
chapter designs by Leo and Diane Dillon.